THE
CHAINS

Books by Gerald Green

Fiction

THE CHAINS
CACTUS PIE: TEN STORIES
THE HEALERS
HOLOCAUST
GIRL
AN AMERICAN PROPHET
THE HOSTAGE HEART
TOURIST
BLOCKBUSTER
FAKING IT
TO BROOKLYN WITH LOVE
THE LEGION OF NOBLE CHRISTIANS
THE HEARTLESS LIGHT
THE LOTUS EATERS
THE LAST ANGRY MAN
THE SWORD AND THE SUN

Nonfiction

MY SON THE JOCK
THE STONES OF ZION
THE ARTISTS OF TEREZIN
THE PORTOFINO PTA
HIS MAJESTY O'KEEFE
(with Lawrence Klingman)

THE
CHAINS

GERALD GREEN

Seaview Books
NEW YORK

Manufactured in the United States of America.

FIRST EDITION

Designed by Tere LoPrete

Library of Congress Cataloging in Publication Data

Green, Gerald.
    The chains.

    I. Title.
PZ3.G8227Ch   [PS3513.R4493]   813'.5'4   79-4885
ISBN 0-87223-567-X

For Marie,
wife, companion, and inspiration

THE
CHAINS

1960

Myron Malkin's Notebook

A smallish man, Mr. Martin B. Chain, but not at all dainty. About five-nine, hundred and forty pounds. Whippet-lean, muscular hands. He moves like a tricky backcourt man or a wide receiver. I can see him on the tennis or squash court—tireless, intense.

The face is dark and secretive. It gives you nothing. Long straight nose, high cheekbones, slightly slanted black eyes, long lashes, heavy eyebrows, thick straight black hair. And well tanned in November. A dark, foxy face.

The suit is Oxford gray and vested. Not the style you'd expect on a thirty-six-year-old who inherited a fortune. Made his multimillionaire father look like a cheapskate. Chain Industries. Chain Pharmaceuticals. Chain Distilleries.

Chunks of gold gleam on his trim figure. Cuff links that could be artifacts from a pharaoh's tomb. A Piaget watch as thin as a communion wafer. A wide wedding band. A class ring. Dartmouth? He's got his diplomas framed on the wall—Choate, Dartmouth, Harvard Business. An honorary degree from Brandeis.

"I'm quite busy, Malkin," he says. Low soft voice. Unlocatable accent. No need to shout. "The only reason I agreed to see you is, well, your uncle."

My late uncle, Dr. Samuel Abelman, delivered Mr. Martin B. Chain. And also his kid brother, Davey, and his sister, Iris. On Haven Place in Brownsville, Brooklyn. Quite a leap to a Park Avenue office. Before the family moved to their twenty-room mansion on Ocean Parkway. Long before young Martin moved to Fifth Avenue and Armonk with seasonal pads in Barbados and Klosters.

"I appreciate it, Mr. Chain. I know you have a lot on your mind."

No acknowledgment. He doesn't need a dingy reporter to remind him that he is very rich, very powerful, very social, and has a great deal on his mind. Our financial editor tells me that Martin inherited the empire, trebled its book value, turned it into one of the postwar industrial giants. And not just with whiskey.

The New York Times of Wednesday, May 18, 1960, is on his desk. The eight-column banner is about the collapse of the Eisenhower-Khrushchev meeting in Vienna:

SUMMIT CONFERENCE BREAKS UP IN DISPUTE; WEST BLAMES KHRUSHCHEV'S RIGID STAND; HE INSISTS ON EISENHOWER'S SPYING APOLOGY

"Quite a mess out there," I say. I'm a news junkie. I've already read the *News* and the *Times*. I'll read matchbox covers and box tops if there's nothing else. Martin stares at me over peaked fingers. Then I notice he—someone—has circled a smaller headline in red:

KENNEDY SWEEPS
MARYLAND'S VOTE

Gets 70% of Total in Routing
Morse for Sixth Straight
Primary Triumph

"That seems to have interested you, Mr. Chain."

"What?" Careful, careful. Not too close, Myron. We're about the same age. Born on the same street in Brooklyn. But that doesn't mean I can get comfy with him.

"Kennedy's primary win."

"He'll get the nomination and he'll be elected. No one seems to understand that his Irish Catholicism will win for him. It'll keep enough Democrats in line. People keep saying it's a drawback, but it's his biggest advantage over Nixon."

"The Chains are backing the senator?"

"Not a question of backing. We've given generous support to both men. They're both adequate. Kennedy is more conservative than people think, and Nixon is more liberal."

On reflection, I see he's right. Everyone drifts to some amorphous *center* sooner or later. And not just in politics.

"Why are you smiling, Malkin?"

"I was thinking of your late grandfather, Benny Otzenberger. The boss of Brownsville. If he didn't deliver at least ninety-eight percent of the vote for the Democrats, he cried. What would he say knowing his grandson was giving money to a Republican?"

"He'd understand."

I laugh weakly. Old Benny. Illiterate grocery wholesaler. Commissioner of weights and measures. A walrus-moustached blimp, one of my uncle

Doc's first patients. Fixer, job getter, rogue, personal friend of FDR. Otzenberger's daughter Hilda was Martin Chain's mother.

"Benny used to say it was Tammany Hall or no hall at all. He meant the union hall, I guess."

Martin Chain isn't buying my cozy recollections of Brownsville. "Malkin, you aren't here to discuss politics. I don't think you care about my grandfather."

"But I do. The other one. Jacob Chain."

He stiffens. The vulpine face pulls back a bit. I realize he's quite handsome in a dark, domineering way. "I see. Some tired old stuff about Crazy Jake? Sunday-supplement garbage? What was justice in this case?"

"I want the story on Crazy Jake Chain. The king of the *shtarkers.*"

"He's been dead a long time."

"Lincoln's been dead longer. They write about him."

Patiently, I explain it all again. I have already interviewed a flunky at his public-relations firm, his vice-president for PR, his secretary, and other people to whom he's shunted me.

Credentials again: I'm a reporter for World News Association. I freelance magazine articles. I'm fascinated with the Chain saga.

"Do you have a publisher?" Martin asks. He walks away and studies the Dow-Jones ticker. I'm reminded of a marvelous scene in *Citizen Kane.* Everett Sloane making the same move and saying to a reporter: *"It's not hard to make a lot of money—if that's all you want to do. . . ."*

No publisher yet. But I'm sure I can get it in print—as a magazine series or a book. The Chains are national names. I point to some photographs on the wall. Martin with Eisenhower. Martin's father, Mortimer, getting a plaque from Ben-Gurion. Martin and Mortimer, son and father, seated on a dais with Cardinal Spellman, John F. Kennedy, and Mayor Bill O'Dwyer.

"We won't cooperate," he says. There's iodine in his voice. No Brooklyn intonations. No dentalized *T*'s. Choate, Dartmouth, and Harvard have endowed him with a generalized Eastern Seaboard accent. He sounds a bit like a reformed rabbi in Scarsdale.

"I'd like to convince you it's in your interest to help me."

"Is that a threat? Forget it. My loyalty to Dr. Abelman for bringing me into the world has limits."

"Heck, no, Mr. Chain. This can be a fascinating book."

"When we want it written, we'll hire Allan Nevins."

Not bad, not bad. The official biographer of the big pirates. The Chains will go first-class.

"Mr. Chain, the *real* story is much better than the bland stuff you let out. I saw that article in *Town and Country.* Four pages of color photographs. Horses. Rare books. Vintage wines. Black-tie dinners at 1030 Fifth Avenue. Hunt-club breakfasts in Armonk."

"What are you trying to say?"

"The true story of the Chains is richer. From horses to horses in three generations."

There's a glint in his onyx eyes. It isn't friendly. "What does that mean?"

"Jake Chain was a seltzer-wagon driver. What Jews call a *balegolah*— a low type. My aunt and uncle remember him with his old horse. Before he became—ah, what shall I say? A union official?"

"It has its charm, Malkin. But we will *not* give you any help. In fact our lawyers will make it tough for you. You'll regret it. Stay with your job at World News—incidentally, I'm a squash partner of the chairman—and forget about this."

I'm getting it all. *Lawyers. Squash. Board chairman.* Even his twenty-dollar cologne is getting to me. I'm supposed to be intimidated. Screw him. I know the house where he was born. Puerto Ricans live there now. Forty of them in seven rooms.

"Let's not try to con each other, Martin," I say, astonished at my *chutzpah.* "Your grandfather was a strong-arm man. Crazy Jake, the one-man mob. It's nothing to hide. Americans love a tough cookie. That's the beautiful thing about this story. In 1910, 1911, 1912, your grandfather was beating up scabs and foremen. Torching pants factories. Today you endow research centers. If you can't see the drama in that—"

"You're warned. We'll stop you."

"I know something about the laws of libel and the rights of the press. You'd be surprised how thoroughly *The New York Times* covered your grandfather's career. Crazy Jake was great copy. Your father gave them more front-page stuff. The mysterious Mort Chain, baron of Rum Row, king of the Brooklyn bootleggers."

I start fumbling in my briefcase. I've made photostatic copies of some ripe articles from old newspapers. The New York Public Library, for modest fees, has duplicated dozens of columns about Crazy Jake for me. And even more newsprint about his son.

In my haste, clippings litter the two-inch blue velvet carpeting. I grab at a spread from *Vogue* I clipped recently. *Martin and DeeDee Chain, New York's dazzling young do-gooders and good-timers . . .* DeeDee Grau Chain. Emma Willard, Wellesley, Junior League, a Hoch-Deutsch princess of impeccable lineage. I doubt that among her department-store antecedents you'll find a fellow who set fires in lofts. Can't this stiff-ass see how funny it is?

As I'm gathering up the clippings (Chains Dedicate New Wing at Cancer Center; Chain Industries to Absorb Elm & Elm Factories; Justice Department Drops Suit Against Chains—Cites Lack of Witnesses), Martin is on the phone. He's talking to DeeDee. And glaring at me.

"Yes, dear. I'll try not to be late. I know it's an important dinner. You'll have to defend Jack Kennedy by yourself if I'm not there."

By the time I've gotten my papers together, he's buzzed for his secretary. She's a broad-beamed, white-haired woman who suggests an outside linebacker. "Miss Fleet, please show Mr. Malkin out."

I dig out a scrap of paper, a Xerox of a *Times* front page. "Care to hear about the price list, Mr. Chain?"

He's at the Dow-Jones machine with his back to me.

"This way, please," Miss Fleet says.

"Five dollars for a broken nose, ten dollars for a broken arm, twenty dollars for throwing a man down a flight of steps, fifteen dollars for a woman—"

"What are you babbling about?" Martin Chain asks. "Miss Fleet, if this man refuses to go, call Hayward."

I met Hayward on the way in. He guards the front desk. A uniformed Nubian.

"Funny you never knew about your grandfather's price list."

"This way, please," says Miss Fleet, the human enema.

"Is Eva Heilig alive, Mr. Chain? Do you know where I could reach her?"

"She's alive. I'm warning you, Malkin. If you keep after this, you'll regret it. Keep your nose clean. Maybe there'll be a job for you in our public-relations department."

He's a Chain. Charm, threat, bluff, promise, bribe. Uncle Doc always said that about them. And yet he liked them. Especially the old battler, Jake. I'm not so tolerant. Martin Chain may be worth over a hundred million dollars, but to me he's a spoiled, handsome punk. Or am I jealous?

PART I

1910

Chapter 1

On the fiftieth anniversary of the collapse of the Baum Building, a reporter for the *Daily Forward* recalled that, when it fell, the noise could be heard ten blocks away. For five seconds it was as if Niagara Falls had cascaded over Brownsville.

A rush, a roar. Then an eerie echo. Screams, sirens, shouts of people running to Van Dam Street, struggling to break through police lines.

A plume of dust (the writer remembered) rose a hundred feet into the crystalline blue summer sky, feathery dusty gray, suggesting death and mutilation and shame.

The building was a landmark in Brownsville. Four stories, red brick and granite. It housed the K & R Bathrobe and Kimono factory. The initials honored the brothers who owned it, Kalman and Reuven Baum, German Jews who lived on Riverside Drive and came to work every day in a chauffeured Oakland touring car.

The Baum brothers were equally famous for charitable activities and their refusal to deal with unions. They had, the old reporter reminisced, "fixed" every politician and police official in Brooklyn so that investigations of the disaster were derailed, frustrated, and ultimately abandoned. To this day (he wrote), no one knows the reason why twenty-seven immigrant girls were crushed to death in the avalanche of masonry, bricks, plaster, twisted metal, splintered wood.

Of course, it was never a secret that the floors were overloaded with heavy machinery. Isaac (Ike) Brunstein, president of the Bathrobe, Kimono, and House Dress Workers Union, Local 37, made the charge repeatedly. Cracks in the walls. Sagging floors. Weird creaking noises when the sixty machines were humming. As if the vibrations were aggravating strains in the old bricks.

Later it was proven that judges had been bought, witnesses bribed, state legislators persuaded that the accident was no one's fault.

"An act of God," intoned Francis Fagan Dullahan, state assemblyman and Brooklyn Democratic boss. " 'Tis a tragedy beyond doubt, and my heart grieves for those poor ladies and their dear ones, but there is no blame to be affixed, and 'tis best let alone."

"Even in the hour of our death," Eva Heilig had shouted at a hearing in Albany, "we girls were robbed of our dignity!"

She referred to the body searches by a woman foreman, a cousin of the Baums'. Seconds before the south wall slid away in a rush of dust, Mrs. Reich was peering into shirtwaists, skirts, corsets, and bloomers for stolen goods. Girls were herded in groups of four into the fetid ladies' room, forced to show that they were not stealing.

"Have they no shame?" Eva Heilig had cried out. "Have they no mercy? In seconds my fellow workers would be dead! And their feminine privacy was being violated for—*what?* A yard of flannel?"

On the steamy morning when the building collapsed, Jacob Chain had just unloaded a dozen cases of blue seltzer siphons at the Little Hungary restaurant.

Emerging from the restaurant, picking his teeth with a gold toothpick, was Benny Otzenberger, a whale in a white pongee suit. Otzenberger had just dined in imperial fashion, as befitted a rising political figure. He watched Jake Chain, in soiled undershirt and stained black trousers, heft the cases. The fat man admired the thick muscles on the driver's arms and back. What a brute! A regular Jeffries!

"Nu, Jake," Otzenberger teased. "You wouldn't want to be a prize-fighter? I'll manage. You'll train at Fein's gym. You could be another Joosh champeen."

"I ain't a fighter, Benny."

"Not from what I heard. Reds Mulqueen says he seen you lay out three wops with two punches. Look at them arms. Better than shlepping seltzer. You'll change your mind, talk to me. Joosh prizefighters are a good item."

A heavy-boned, flat-faced man in his twenties with smooth ruddy skin and a mop of straw-blond hair, Chain said no more. He hefted another case and started through the open cellar door. Then he stopped. A wild rushing noise roared through his ears. Benny Otzenberger was frozen, staring at the source of the thundering sound. A few blocks away, a column of dust rose above the tenement roofs.

Jake climbed aboard his wagon and hefted Benny to the seat. Then he slapped the reins on the mare's back. "Go, Kotchka, go!" he shouted.

People were running alongside the wagon, out of tenements, out of side streets. Jake saw Doc Abelman racing from the direction of Haven Place. He was coatless and carrying a black satchel, his legs pumping vigorously. Jake could remember him as a summertime gym teacher in the school-yards, before he hung out his shingle.

Callery, a policeman from the 71st, leaped onto the step of the wagon and shouted at Jake: "Baum's place! Explosion or something. Look at that smoke!"

Now they could hear shouts, shrieks, the sounds of—what? Rocks falling? A loud sliding sound.

"My wife works there," Jake said.

"*Oi vay,* your wife. And my son. Heshy, my heart." Otzenberger's son, Heshy, age twenty, was an assistant foreman.

A horse-drawn ambulance, with an intern standing on the wagon seat and clanging a bell, almost collided with Jake's mare. He drew the reins sharply. Kotchka reared, whickered, and pawed the air.

They were engulfed by the mob. Old Jews in yarmulkas, women in babushkas, barefoot street brats in torn caps, sweaty workmen, peddlers in the standard uniform—black derby, black vest, collarless white shirt, black trousers. Jake could see Dr. Abelman muscling his hard body through the mob.

It was impossible to go further with the wagon. Jake spotted **Sal Ferrante**, the fifteen-year-old kid who sold lemon ice and hokey-pokey from a cart. He was rushing toward the disaster. Abruptly Sal's cart was unable to move. Jake leaped down and handed the boy the reins. "Mind my wagon, Sal," Jake said. "I'll give you a penny."

Ferrante nodded. His older brother, Luigi, who had once boxed with Jake at the gym, ran past them. "The whole wall," Luigi shouted. "The whole *sfaccim'* wall fell down. Our sister's in there! Theresa's in there."

Patrolman Callery leaped from the wagon. Benny Otzenberger rolled off the other side; the pavement shuddered as his bulk hit the bricks. Jake helped him to his feet and raced off. With long hard arms, the legs of an athlete, he cut through the screaming mob. And gasped with his first look at the disaster.

It was like a doll's house, with the front removed, that he had once seen in a window on Pitkin Avenue. Open. Exposed. Sections of the upper two stories were standing—machines, benches.

Below, hidden in a cloud of dust, masonry, and dirt, was a pile of smoking rubble. How could anyone be alive under that mass of junk? The front wall of the building had tumbled entirely, a mountain of plaster and brick, twisted machines. He saw an arm waving feebly. The rest of the body was buried. A shoeless foot protruded from a mound of pulverized bricks.

Otzenberger (the police knew him well) was allowed past the line of officers. The fat man was bawling. Tears soaked his moustache. "My heart, my Heshy," he wailed. "Wait, wait, I'll fix those Baum bastards."

A hundred feet from the building one could see the wreckage more clearly. Wires and cables dangled like jungle vines from the upper stories. An entire bank of sewing machines, hanging from heavy tables, were tilted crazily on the top floor. Boards creaked and sagged. Blocks of plaster and random bricks fell from side walls. A cornice of granite shivered and broke away. People screamed and ran for cover. The chunk of stone exploded like a bomb on the pavement. A fragment broke the leg of an old man in vest, yarmulka, and *tsitsith*. He fell as if shot by a cossack's bullet.

In front of the collapsed wall, firemen in rubber coats were carrying out more bodies. Jake saw bloodied heads; arms and legs in positions not normal for anyone's arms or legs. Feet were pointing where they weren't meant to point. Heads were turned around. People gasped as half a torso —legs and groin—was removed. One girl had been stripped of her clothing. Shreds of petticoats clung to her dust-coated body. Her stockings and shoes had been stripped clean. A woman's body, so misshapen that it was impossible to imagine it had once lived, was wrenched free from a steel girder.

"Good God," Abelman gasped. "Hit them like a volcano." He ran into the schoolyard, following another ambulance and two interns in whites.

A fireman stumbled and picked up the body of a tiny woman whose face was crimson mush. Yet she was breathing. Calling for someone named Chayim.

In the schoolyard (where his son Mutteh played kickety-can and Chinese handball), Jake, numb, looked for his wife. Stethoscope in ears, Abelman joined the doctors from Saint Mary's. "Dead," Jake heard Abelman say. "No heartbeat. Didn't give them a chance. The bastards won't let you live."

Jake wandered amid the dying and the mutilated, their screams sailing the air.

Abelman dusted the plaster from a woman's face. Eyes opened in terror. "My arm hurts. It hurts, doctor." Jake saw Abelman stroke her forehead and reach into his bag for a syringe.

(*"Nightmares all my life,"* Abelman said years later. *"I never forgot the look on their faces. The living worse than the dead. . . ."*)

No sign of Sarah. Jake helped Abelman move a dead woman to another part of the schoolyard. Pink bubbles formed around her mouth. Her eyes were staring. The physician closed them and wiped her face. A doctor from Saint Mary's shouted at them to leave the bodies where they were.

"Dry up, sonny boy," Abelman said. "Dead on one side, those who have a chance on the other. Come on, Jake."

"My wife—my Sarah," Chain said. "You seen her?"

"No, Jake."

The police line sagged and broke. Relatives and survivors rushed to the building. A pall of dust covered the street. Chunks of plaster continued to topple from upper stories.

Against the wall of a grocery, Heshy Otzenberger was sobbing out the story of his miraculous escape.

"We heard it on the ground floor in Baum's office," Heshy bawled. Unlike his balloon of a father, he was stick-thin and round-shouldered, with a sallow sneaky face and a mop of dark brown Brillo rising over a low forehead.

"So you ran out, thanks God," Benny said.

"Me and the girls in the office and the Baum brothers. We heard it. Like cracking. Splitting. I seen this funny thing in the wall, like a line running up. So fast it happened."

Jake thought: Heshy and the Baums were safe. What about the girls locked in the workrooms? *Locked.* Bolts on the doors. Cloths over the clocks so they wouldn't waste time. Stairways blocked.

Luigi Ferrante, dark as a *shwarzer,* banana-nosed, ran to Jake. "Onna side, Jake, onna side of da building. I seen Theresa and ya wife."

Jake and Luigi ran around the corner. A section of the lower wall facing an alley had fallen away. The walls above did not look secure. Nothing seemed to be supporting them except a single steel beam.

Astonishingly, Theresa Ferrante was unhurt. Her clothing was filthy, her face smeared with plaster and blood, but she walked firmly, and flew to Luigi's arms. She was a dark girl, long-legged and graceful.

"Ya awright?" Luigi asked. "Bastards. I catch the *sfaccim'* what done this, they'll be sorry."

He put his arm around the girl and led her away.

Jake wondered: *What will you do, Luigi, you and Sal and your five brothers? Throw bricks at the Baums?*

He saw Sarah. Small, dark, weak. Jake vaulted over mounds of plaster. They had set Sarah on the pavement. No sheet. Nothing. A rush of guilt made him shiver. Six days in the factory. Five nights a week of work in the "outside place" for their landlord, Feigenbaum. What did Jake give her? Ten dollars a week from driving the wagon. The animals in the Prospect Park Zoo lived better.

Most of the dead and injured were in the schoolyard. More ambulances had arrived. Casualties were rushed to Saint Mary's or Brownsville Jewish. He could see Abelman helping girls onto stretchers, moving from one to another, taking pulses, listening to hearts.

"Sarah, it's Jake," he said. "Can you talk?"

Patrolman Mulqueen tugged at his shirt. "Jake, get outta here. The side wall is comin' down any minute."

Whistles shrilled. The crowd eddied, groaned. Mulqueen and Callery started clubbing people away from the alley.

"I can talk, Jake. But my legs. I can't walk."

"What else hurts?" He kissed her soiled forehead. Stared at her terrified eyes, her narrow face. A woman who never understood she was pretty. Black hair, piercing dark brown eyes. Too busy struggling to live. Others mocked her when she married Jacob Chain, a bum with no family, a man who could read neither Yiddish nor Hebrew nor English, a lummox good only for hauling boxes.

"I don't know—the legs, the knees—I tried to get out of the place—I fell—Jake, I'm dying."

Above him he heard a soft roar. *God in heaven, the upper wall.*

He lifted Sarah. She screamed. On a runner's legs he sprinted out of the passageway to Van Dam Place, battled his way through screaming women and howling men, a gauntlet of police billies. Soon he was in the sanctuary of the schoolyard.

"Doc, my wife, my Sarah!" Jake shouted. "Look at her!"

Abelman said something, but it was as if he had lost speech. His mouth moved. Jake heard nothing. They were stricken deaf by the roar. The side of the factory rumbled to earth, crushing everything in its path, creating a new mountain of junk, ruined machines, jungles of wires and tubing.

"Her legs," Jake screamed. "She can't walk."

"Easy," Abelman said. "On the stretcher. Don't touch her legs."

Sarah's knees were crazily angled. One pointing out, one in. Her shoeless feet, with torn stockings exposed, were flattened and shapeless.

"Something's sticking in my leg, Jake." She wept. "Something sharp in the left leg."

Abelman called for one of the interns. They gave Sarah morphine pills. She gagged and struggled to rise. Her eyes flooded. Spittle depended from her mouth. Jake knelt and held her forehead.

"She got to go to the hospital, Doc?"

"Looks that way, Jake. Give us a hand."

They lifted the stretcher. Another ambulance arrived. A smoky pall hovered over the yard. The fallen walls exhaled a miasma of filth and death. Gritty powder settled on weeping families, stricken girls, the dead.

Abelman and Chain guided the stretcher into the ambulance. Jake kissed Sarah's cheek.

"Does it hurt, little bird?" Jake asked. He smoothed her dusty hair.

"In my legs, dear husband. Like iron in them. Someone pushing it in. I can't move. I'm sorry I'm crying. I shouldn't make trouble for you."

She was born to apologize, to regret everything she did. *I am whole and strong,* Jake thought, *and she is broken and in pain, and yet she is sorry, she is unhappy that she is making me hurt. . . .*

The intern began to close the ambulance door. Jake embraced his wife, kissed her again. Within his iron chest, he prayed for forgiveness for his failure to do more for her and for Mutteh. *Bet ya five cents, Crazy Jake, ya can't lift anudda box, ya horse!*

"Twenny-two stiffs, forty hoit," he heard a cop telling a reporter. "And there's more they ain't found yet."

Jake shouted after the ambulance: "I'll come, Sarah, with our son."

People rushed by him. The mob was assaulting the Otzenbergers. Cunningly, the Baums had driven away to their apartment in New York. Let the assistant foreman and his father take the blows.

The punches were soft and ineffective. Hair pulled. Behinds kicked. The clawing and biting of people who did not know how to fight.

"Help, *police!*" shrieked Benny. He struggled like a gaffed whale until he and Heshy were hustled into a police van for their own protection.

A soft lavender sky settled over Brownsville. The mob broke through the flailing clubs and charged the police van. They hammered with weak fists at the side. Jake watched with contempt.

"You and me, Doc," he said in a cold voice. "If we wanted, we could turn it over. Scare Otzenberger and his kid. How come he's alive and the girls are dead?"

Arms flapping, Ike Brunstein came racing down the street. His pince-nez flew behind him. They were attached to his lapel with a black ribbon. Brunstein's mop of curly brown hair seemed a yard behind him.

"Outrage! *Outrage!*" Brunstein shouted. "Where is the police commissioner? The fire commissioner?"

Frustrated in its attempts to reach the Otzenbergers, the mob turned on the union president. Hands clutched him. Tearful faces howled for revenge, help, an explanation.

"You could have been here quicker, Brunstein," an old man wept. "My daughter—gone—my angel—my light . . ."

"Workers, we will not tolerate this!" Ike cried.

"Too late, Ike," Dr. Abelman said. "It's done." He wiped his hands on a bandage and sighed.

Brunstein flew at a sergeant. Would arrests be made? Would an inquiry be held? Were officials notified?

The cop shoved him away rudely. Ike, flustered, squinted at his badge number and began to write on a small pad.

The patrolman ripped the memo book from Ike's hand. The two began to wrestle for it. Raised from the sidewalk, Ike was shaken mercilessly. His pince-nez flew from his nose. His trousers sagged, ready to drop.

Another officer measured Ike's head with his club.

"Cossack," Ike wheezed. "Enemy of the workingman."

Jake Chain saw that Ike was about to be crowned. He ran between the club and the union man's head. As the club descended, Jake caught the officer's wrist and twisted it. The billy bounced to the sidewalk. The cocobolo wood clanked resonantly.

"Another smart kike," the cop said. He bent over for the club.

Jake grabbed his arm, spun him around, and held him at arm's length. The cop gasped. He recognized the huge flat-faced man. The hebe who once wrestled kegs for Mulqueen's father. His grip felt like the iron bands they put on kegs.

"Brunstein didn't do nothing," Jake said calmly. "He asked you a question."

The cop found his billy and raised it again. "You try askin' one, Izzy." The policeman moved forward a step.

Jake stood his ground. He had learned a long time ago, as a child on the piss-smelling immigrant boat, later in the Hebrew Orphan Asylum and on the streets of Brownsville, that a man never showed fear. Take a blow, give one. But never show fear.

"I didn't want you should hit a guy who can't fight," Jake said.

The policeman hesitated. The big man—Christ, he was a strong mocky —was standing with his arms apart, palms out.

"Smart kike, huh?"

"Lay off, buddy," Doc Abelman said, moving next to Jake. The unaccented English, the Indian face gave the officer pause. Why push it? Jews didn't fight. They didn't know their way around a saloon. They were mush, cowards, *shit*. Why start with a sheeny sawbones?

"That's a nice fella," Abelman said. The cop hung the club on his belt. He eyed Brunstein like a hawk cheated of a field mouse. Then he turned away.

Chain walked off. With his rotten luck, someone had probably stolen the horse and wagon.

Brunstein flew around the wrecked building looking for witnesses. It was no easy job. The survivors had left. The police patrolled Van Dam Place, the alley, the side street. No looting, Francis Fagan Dullahan had decreed by phone. The Baums' property was to be protected. Bad enough they'd lost a factory. (Dullahan was well greased by the Baums. The money came every month via Benny Otzenberger in a brown bag.)

Ike located a man from the *Brooklyn Daily Eagle* and another from the *Jewish Daily Forward*. They found two girls who had survived the disaster.

One of the women talking to reporters was Eva Heilig, the union secretary. Eva was twenty-four, small, shapely, with a cloud of curling blond hair rising over a carved white face. Stealing a pinch, Heshy Otzenberger would call her *Die Gibsoneh*—after Charles Dana Gibson's idealized beauties. But Eva was no lissome *shiksa*. A distant cousin of Jake Chain's, she was an activist, a street-corner orator. Now she had an audience and she was letting the reporters, and a group of girls and their relatives, hear her vibrant voice at its most outraged.

"No fire escape," Eva Heilig was saying. "The doors were bolted. God forbid a person wanted a breath of fresh air. Girls were inspected like cattle. They were warned if they didn't come in Sunday, they should stay away Monday. Cheating on paychecks. Charging us for needles, for machine oil, for any wasted cloth! A penny a day for lockers! You see how we are forced to live? And now this—this—"

"Twenty-two victims," Ike said as he came alongside her. "Blood on the hands of the Baums."

"A *Red*," the *Eagle* reporter said. He began to ask Ike and Eva about their association with the Jewish Trade Unions. Radical outfits? Bunch of foreigners? Guys with beards and accents?

Eva's pale green eyes widened. She was distractingly beautiful. The lustrous pile of golden hair, the fair skin (even though dirtied now with street grime), short nose, firm cleft chin, slender neck, ivory throat. The man from the *Eagle* had difficulty envisioning her as a Red. Brunstein was more like it. Dark suit, floppy tie, mop of hair, beard, pince-nez, built like a clothes tree. As if the long-legged goop were an actor trying to look like Trotsky.

"Quite a cookie, that Heilig," the *Eagle* reporter said when Eva and Ike had taken their leave. "What's she doing on a sewing machine? With that sweet ass, she could work at a lot of other things."

The man from the *Forward* (a socialist veteran) shook his head. A decent enough boy, his fellow journalist, but a *goy* in his heart. Women like Eva Heilig he would never understand.

When she and Brunstein had walked about a block, Eva saw her cousin Jake giving a coin to Sal the hokey-pokey vendor.

"Thanks, kid," Jake was saying. "Your sister okay?"

Sal Ferrante had a face as brown and as narrow as a piece of belting. He nodded. Theresa was cut and bruised. But she was okay. One dead lady, Angela Colucci, was an aunt or something. Lived with the Ferrantes. They didn't know much about her.

Eva listened. The unfathomable misery of the poor. And yet, Eva reflected, they had strength, resilience. Jews and Italians, poorest of the poor. They would not give up. What impelled them to struggle? The answer was evident. They worked or starved.

Eva watched Jake untethering his horse and climbing into the seat. The boor, the dumb ox of the family. Eva's parents and brothers treated Jake with indifferent contempt. But Eva had always nurtured sympathy for the crude man with his flattened face, his athletic grace, the stoic manner in which he accepted a brutish life. There was something to be admired in the man's affection for his birdlike wife and runty son.

"Jake," she called. "Sarah, is she all right?" She ran to the wagon.

Chain showed no emotion. "Both legs broke. They took her to the hospital."

"I'm sorry, Jake. Can we help? Ike, what can we do?"

"The union will raise a fund for the workers injured at K & R," Brunstein said. "Benefits will be small but they'll help. Burial expenses also."

Eva began to weep. She held a hand out to Jake. He took it clumsily, thinking, *Maybe I am too dumb to cry.* In his heart there was an ice pick. But the tears would not come. When had he last cried? Years ago. As a child in the orphanage when he learned that his father had betrayed him. Sent him off, and would never come to America for him, was unable to raise money for passage. The letter. He had saved it for years, burned it after he married Sarah Klebanow. His mother was long dead of typhus in the farmhouse in Glebocka.

"I'll bring supper for you and the boy," Eva said.

"It's all right. I have food. You were hurt?"

"I was lucky. I was in the office arguing with Heshy about the clocks. When the noise started, he dragged me out. I'll come with food."

As he snapped the reins and drove off, he prayed she would come. More beautiful than he could believe. Of his blood. How in the same family?

The blood relationship was frail (his mother was a second cousin of her mother) and the Heiligs had no interest in pursuing it. They were ambitious people, Eva and her two brothers. Eva went to night school and lectures. She was reading her way through the Watkins Avenue branch of the public library and attended Mrs. Abelman's poetry classes at the YWHA.

A plodding man, Chain knew one thing. Something he admitted to no one. Something he tried to stifle within his oak-hard chest: *He loved Eva Heilig.*

It was a sin, he was certain, thinking of her face, her body, what she would look like unclothed, when his wife was lying in a hospital with her legs smashed. A sin to think such things about a cousin.

Once he had had to punch Label Kuflik after the driver had read an article in the *Forward* about Eva. There was a photograph also—mass of blond hair, white face, wide eyes. The article was a tribute to the courageous working girls. Eva had earned a name among them: *Die Goldeneh Shtimmeh*—The Golden Voice.

At the end of the article, Kuflik sniggered: "But it don't say how she *shtups* for Brunstein."

A right fist had sent Kuflik sailing across Kolodny's stable into a pile of manure. Warning enough: Kuflik never mentioned Eva again.

I love her, Jake thought, *and it is hopeless.*

Jake drove into Kolodny's stable. He unharnessed the mare and went into the bottler's dusty office with the cash and receipts for the deliveries. Before his boss asked about Chain's wife, he scolded him for failing to get a receipt from the Little Hungary.

"I'll get it tomorrow. I had to drive away when we heard the building falling."

"No excuse, Chain," Kolodny said. "What do you got for brains? Horse piss? No wonder they call you Crazy Jake."

Kolodny was a hunchback. A bald-headed gnome. Squint-eyed, foul-tempered.

"I'll get the receipt on my way to the hospital. Mr. Kolodny, could you advance me a dollar? Who knows when my wife will be paid? And who knows if she can work again?"

"No advances. It says in the Talmud that the workman is like the ox in the field—"

"I'm too stupid to know if it's the truth or you made it up."

Kolodny's face twisted itself into a smile. He needed Jake Chain, a man who could handle horses, haul crates, work long hours, and, if necessary, give a competitor a *klop* on the mouth that could send him back to Chelm.

In the stable, Jake borrowed a half-dollar from Label Kuflik. Kuflik, a bulky man whose fleshy face was constructed around a swollen, pitted nose, had a heart of sorts. Jake thanked him.

There are people worse off than me, Jake thought. *But not many.*

Chapter 2

Old man Pasquale was playing the hurdy-gurdy as Jake approached. Children were holding hands in a circle and singing.

They formed a ring around the hand organ. Girls in wide skirts and high-button shoes, barefoot boys in loose-hanging knickers. Jake saw his son, Mutteh, a scrawny seven-year-old, pushing his way between two older girls. The children swung their arms in time with the ratchety music.

> *Who wants to come to the sisters' meeting?*
> *To the sisters' praying,*
> *Who wants to come, who wants to come?*
> *Who wants to come with me?*

The oldest girl, Kalotkin's daughter, formed the children into two lines and they began to "go in and out the window." Mutteh was the runt of the group.

Bernie Feigenbaum, the landlord's son, a fat, bespectacled kid, yanked Mutteh's cap off. Mutteh, a head shorter than Bernie, left the entwined arms and raced after his tormentor.

Bernie held the cap out of Mutteh's reach and taunted him. He fended wild swings with one chubby arm. "You be the nigger Johnson and I'll be Jeffries, okay?"

"Gimme my hat, fatso."

"Ya call me fatso, ya never get it. C'mon, you be Johnson."

"I ain't no nigger. You be Johnson."

"I'm Jeffries. A white guy can beat a nigger, 'cause niggers are yellow."

Mutteh grabbed the cap and jammed it on his head. The boys squared off boxer-style, jabbing and feinting. Mutteh was swift and lithe but so skinny he was barely visible when he turned sideways. Bernie's tits juggled under his shirt.

Jake did not interfere. He had a rule: Let Mutteh fight. He had taught him long ago. Fight fair. But if the other guy is dirty, use a stick, a stone, your teeth, your feet, your head.

Aaron Feigenbaum, landlord and sweatshop operator, leaned out the window. He crossed his woolly arms on the stone sill. He was walleyed and gray-bearded, a wraith of a man who mercilessly drove a family of eight and his part-time workers like Sarah Chain.

"*Nu*, Jake? Your wife's hurt?" Feigenbaum asked.

"Her legs are broke."

"A pity. A scandal and an outrage. How you'll pay the rent?"

"I'll work double shifts for Kolodny."

Feigenbaum demanded twelve to fifteen pairs of kneepants in a twelve-hour workday. The entire ground floor—dark, damp, floorboards piled with cuttings—rattled with the hum of sewing machines. Sarah worked as a "finisher"—buttons and buttonholes. No one was unionized in the "out-side" shop. Six dollars a week for a full-time worker. Three for Sarah, who sewed until ten at night after her work at Baums'.

Old Pasquale passed the hat. Pennies descended from the windows. Jake also tossed a penny.

Bernie threw a right at Mutteh's bobbing head. Mutteh ducked under it and drove a fist into "Jeffries's" paunch.

"Johnson's a nigger," Mutteh said. Bernie doubled over and hollered foul. "But Johnson won, right, papa?"

"Right, Mutteleh. He murdered Jeffries."

"Niggers fight dirty." Bernie gulped. He wiped tears from his eyes and looked around for a missile.

The children followed the hurdy-gurdy down the littered street. Jake could hear the sweet voices.

> *Nan-nan-nanny goat!*
> *Sew, sew sew,*
> *Sew my petticoat, no, no, no!*

"Ya got a penny for me, papa?" Mutteh asked. His bright eyes stared at his father's strong face. "A penny for a piece of candy?"

"Later, Mutteh. Son, mama is hurt. She got hurt in the building that fell down."

"She'll be better? She'll be all better?"

"Dr. Abelman said so. But you and me, Mutteh, we got to take care of the house. In September you'll go to school. So you'll not be dumb like your father."

"You ain't dumb, papa. Can I have a penny?"

Jake stroked his coarse black hair. It grew in stringy strands around his dark neck and ears. Sarah trimmed it once a month with a scissors. Jake had a terrible awareness of the boy's smallness. A crippled mother and a stupid father. What life for him?

"They told me mama was dead," Mutteh blurted out. He began to cry. "Bernie and some other kids. They said she was dead. They said her legs was cut off."

"Lies, Mutteleh."

Mutteh pressed his head against his father's sweaty shirt. Chain's chest was like a slab of concrete. Jake kissed the boy's head. It made him think of a bird's egg.

They walked to the corner. Streetlights blazed. Halos of night insects hummed around them.

"Hey, it's Aunt Eva," Mutteh said.

Jake saw his cousin approaching. She was carrying a blue enameled pot. As always, she was beautiful, graceful.

Mutteh ran from his father and buried his head in Eva's thigh. She gave the pot to Jake and kissed the boy's head. The boy sniffed her soapy sweet odor. He never understood why he liked it so much. A different smell from his mother. It excited him. Made him think funny things. Sometimes he thought he loved Eva more than he loved his mother.

Eva said to Jake, "We had more than enough to eat. Compliments of my parents."

Jake smiled. He knew Eva's mother didn't care for him. Eva's father, Avner Heilig, the eccentric "Uncle Sourmilk," had no feelings one way or another. A mathematician, he was preoccupied with proving the Triumph of Socialism Through Mathematics.

"Sour milk?" Jake asked.

"Mushroom-and-barley soup. I'll heat it for you."

She studied his blunted broad face. A handsome face. Wide cheekbones, strong chin, a nose slightly squashed from an old fight. His eyes were a clear staring blue. The shock of blond hair was a surprise.

They walked back to Feigenbaum's tenement. Bernie ran behind Mutteh, goosed him, then tripped over his own feet as he dodged Mutteh's swing.

Leaning on the windowsill, Mrs. Feigenbaum observed the visitor. That blondie, Eva Heilig. *That Red.* A shameless one who went to meetings with men, argued with men, hollered at girls to defy the bosses, and talked back to cops.

"Better you shouldn't come in," Jake said. "It's dirty inside. Your parents don't like when you visit."

"I do what I want. Go on, Jake. Mutteh, no more fighting." She wagged a finger at Bernie Feigenbaum. "You're twice his size. Let him alone."

"I c'n fight him, Aunt Eva," Mutteh said.

It was hot and malodorous in the basement. The stained walls shuddered with the rattling of Feigenbaum's sweatshop. There was a gas ring and a cracked sink. They used a toilet on the second floor. Once a week, Jake, Sarah, and Mutteh went to the public bathhouse. It was inconceivable to Eva (hardly a wealthy girl) how people could live so miserably. No one had earned such punishment.

With the soup, she had brought buttered rolls. Jake and Mutteh sat in the tiny room, eating noisily, saying little. He found it hard to thank her. Why did she do this? She owed him nothing.

Mutteh finished his dinner and flew from the room. The summer street beckoned—adventure, exploring empty lots, hitching rides on wagons, kickety-can, Johnny-on-the-pony.

"Jake, you have to look ahead," she said. "If Sarah can't work . . . Listen, you *must* learn to read and write."

"I'm fit only for a horse," Jake said. "Kolodny told me."

"Don't listen to a boss. They want to keep us stupid." She patted the back of his hand and felt the taut muscles. "Jake, you owe it to your son. Do something for yourself. I know you're angry. You've had a rotten life. Go to school. If you're embarrassed, I'll go with you the first day."

He laughed. "Like a mother taking a kid to class? The drivers would make fun of me. They'll say, Look, he can lift four crates on his back. He can lift a wagon. He's the guy who beat up three Italians. Why does an animal need to write?"

"Don't say that about yourself!"

He tried not to stare at her white shirtwaist with the dainty collar and muttonchop sleeves. Small mounds where her breasts showed. The tight-waisted pleated black skirt. High-button shoes and black stockings.

"You better not stay," he said. "Your father don't like it. That *yenta* Feigenbaum, she'll talk."

"Ridiculous. I'm your cousin." Eva smiled at him. Impoverished, un-learned, a strange Jew raised in back of a saloon, he had a stolid dignity.

He spoke her name, halted. Something more than his gratitude for the food was on his mind. His limpid blue eyes stared at her, suppressing emotion. She knew he loved her. He could not hide it. She did not want him to experience more pain than he was suffering at the moment.

She rose to leave, and he walked out to the street with her. The street teemed with people. Groups lounged on stoops, in front of pushcarts and stores. Many discussed the disaster at Baum's. A stout woman wept uncontrollably, rent her dress, tore at her hair. Two daughters dead, *dead*. On the corner, an orator—one of Brunstein's radicals—had drawn a crowd. Several police appeared.

"We welcome the police," the young radical cried. "We welcome our brother workers in uniform, for they, too, are exploited by cruel bosses. . . ."

Unmoved, the cops began to clear the street corner. "Okay, Moe, climb down," one said. "Enough revolution."

Eva shook Jake's iron hand. "The union will get Sarah a job. I promise you. And you promise *me* you'll go to school."

"I could become a professor. I'd be sixty years old before I'd be smart enough. Thanks for the soup." Jake held her hand, sensed the thrill of touching her flesh. He did it as naturally as breathing, walking. Some joke. A handshake. He squeezed the palm gently.

She looked at his street-hardened face. He deserved better of the world. Who knew if Sarah would survive? And what would become of the boy and of Jake himself? In her family, people studied, attacked books with a vengeance, availed themselves of every scrap of knowledge available in the new *Medineh*. For Jake Chain, it was all a cheat.

She kissed his cheek. She walked off. Jake watched her, full of cold pain. He had to go to the hospital; had to forget Eva.

In the hallway, Jake glanced into Feigenbaum's "outside" factory. All of the landlord's family, penniless greenhorns, and a few strays. Operator. Baster. Finisher. Presser. Girl for sewing buttons. Girl for sewing buttonholes. Bushelman. Fitter. Delivery boy.

A world of cloth, scissors, thread, weary fingers, bent backs, foul air. A hotbox in the summer, freezing in the winter. One filthy toilet. One sink. Four months of the year there was no work. Feigenbaum collected rents and waited for the next orders.

Maybe I'm better off with my strong back and arms, and the horse, he thought. At least I'm in the open, and I like the animal's stink, and the stable, and I am freer than they are. . . .

He dimly recalled a boyhood of deprivation and cruelty. Yet something sweet stuck in his memory. Meadows, a muddy barnyard. Chickens and geese. Fruit trees and a field of green vegetables. A carp pond. His father's place. Once men came with papers. There was an argument over who owned the land. His father, a big blond man like himself, was crying, then fighting with the Lithuanian policemen. His father's head was covered with blood. He was clutching at black boots. A man in a fur-collared coat gave orders.

Long ago. Later he was on a freezing train, tagged, a ticket in his pocket. A smoky, noisy city. Hamburg, someone said. And the hold of a ship, slippery with vomit, urine, crap. He had survived the passage—for what?

"She'll walk," Dr. Abelman said. "But she won't be the same."

The doctor was standing with Jake outside a ward in Brownsville Jewish Hospital. Outside, the dusk obscured the street, the maples and poplars.

"A cripple."

"Compound fractures of both legs. It'll take a long time, Jake. A wheelchair. Crutches later. She might never get off the crutches."

Jake folded his arms. A nurse walked by, wheeling a shriveled old woman. Sarah in ten years.

"No hope? An operation maybe?" Jake detested his ignorance. He felt guilty bothering Abelman. He did not charge for hospital visits; it was assumed this was part of his care. Office visits were a half-dollar. A house call cost one dollar.

"Jake, maybe it would be better if I died," Sarah said when she saw his face. "I won't be a bother to no one anymore. A woman with crippled legs. Maybe I'm better dead."

"Don't say it. You will live."

"A cripple. In a wheelchair. I know what Dr. Abelman said."

Abelman waved his right hand, smiled. "No, Sarah. You can walk again. You'll need help, but people use their legs again."

She wept apologetically, ashamed of adding to their misery.

Chapter 3

Jake approached Kolodny's bottling plant to load up his morning deliveries. It was a humid mid-September day, three weeks after the collapse of the Baum place. Trees beyond the soda-water factory were orange and red and purple. Colors Jake could not believe existed. He paused to look at them. Strange how people thought Brownsville was a slum. In 1910 it was also fields and meadows and farms.

Mutteh was in first grade. The smallest boy in P.S. 144. But he was enjoying the challenge of lessons and the daily fight. He came home with a blackened eye, a cut lip, never cried, did his homework. After school he hunted for soda bottles or tied old newspapers in bundles for Junkman John. The pennies he earned he kept.

The stable door was closed. An oak two-by-four was jammed into the wooden arms. Label Kuflik was standing in front of the door. His hairy arms were folded on his chest.

"So?" Jake asked. "It's a Jewish holiday?"

"Don't go in."

"Kolodny locked us out? That's all I need. With a sick wife and debts up to my belly button. Come on, open."

A scream emanated from the stable doors. Then another. The noise sickened Jake. He had been in enough fights. He knew the sound. Someone was being beaten.

"The boss," Kuflik said.

"He's hitting someone? That hunchback?"

"He's getting hit. You know Moishe Nigger?"

"The Horse Poisoner."

"He's inside with his boys. They killed two horses. Your Kotchka. Rafaelson's horse. By the time they're finished beating Kolodny, he won't have a hump on his back. It'll be in his throat."

Jake knew about the racketeers. Years ago when Benny Otzenberger had tried to make Jake a "prelim boy," he had met them at Fein's gym. Nifty dressers. White celluloid collars. Striped shirts. Box-toed shoes. Derbies. They extorted, terrorized, beat up storekeepers, threatened factory owners and organizers. They ran "hoo-er" houses and sold booze.

Kolodny howled again.

"I'm going in," Jake said.

"Don't be a shlemiel," Kuflik said. "Your horse is dead. You got no job. Bunchik, the Nigger's fella, gave me a dollar to watch the door. My horse they won't poison."

"Get out of my way, Kuflik."

"Wake up. In America a horse is worth more than a Jew."

"Kuflik, shove Bunchik's dollar up your nose. In a month you'll have a nose full of dollars and you'll be rich. Out of my way."

The driver backed off. "You'll be sorry, Chain. I got orders you shouldn't—"

Jake seized Kuflik by the shoulders and hurled him into the dirt. He lifted the beam and shoved the creaky doors apart. Shafts of morning light slanted into the stable. A horse whickered and stomped.

The hay and the horse odors smelled fresh and wild. Like the country-side of his lost youth in Lithuania. What was to fear? He had so little. Nothing to lose. Sick wife. No job. Anyone who stole bread from his mouth would have to be taught it was wrong.

A pale young man with a beaked nose and pimpled cheeks was guard-ing the side door that led to the bottling plant. He wore a white straw boater, a green-and-pink striped shirt, and bright green suspenders. As Jake entered, the youth, Bunchik by name, pointed an ax handle at him.

"*Out!* Kuflik, whaddya letting people in for?" he shouted.

Jake walked across the dung-strewn floor. Kotchka was lying on her side in the stall. The mare hadn't been much, but she'd been part of his life. A pile of manure rested under her tail. Even when they die they crap, Jake thought.

"Hey, jerk-off, get out," Bunchik called. "Moishe, a guy walked in."

A hoarse voice called from a stall: "Hit him in the head, Bunchik."

"He's too big."

In the last stall, Jake found Menasha Kolodny and his tormentors. Naked ass up, the bottler was doubled over a water trough. His pants and long underwear had been yanked down. He had a small wrinkled ass. It was covered with bloody welts.

A fat, broad-chested man, dark as a mulatto, dapper in a pearl-gray derby and striped orange shirt, was standing over Kolodny. He had a buggy whip in his hand. A second hoodlum, very short, in a checked beige-and-brown suit, was holding Kolodny's body down. The Nigger's assistant, Little Mendel, had a froglike face with a wide mouth and jellied green eyes.

The short man grinned at Jake. "*Putz,* get adda here. Beat it."

The man in the derby was Moishe "Nigger" Pearlberg. He shouted, "Bunchik, tell Kuflik if he lets anyone else in, he'll get his ass whipped also."

Moishe Nigger cracked the whip across Kolodny's buttocks. The owner screamed. Another red welt blossomed.

"Chain!" Kolodny screamed. "Go to the police! They killed two horses! They'll kill me! Get the cops! This is Moishe Nigger and his gang—"

Crack. Jake winced. Kolodny wailed like a starving baby.

Bunchik came back from the outer door and leaned against the stall.

"Who are you, Polack?" Moishe Nigger asked.

"I'm one of his drivers. Chain."

"Drive yourself out of here. Keep your mouth shut, or you'll get your ass whipped also."

"He looks like a toilet chain." Bunchik laughed.

Jake didn't move. "Me it won't help to whip, Mr. Nigger. I'm a poor man without ten cents. You could whip all day I couldn't give a penny."

"But you got a mouth," the froggy man squatting on Kolodny said. "You open your mouth you'll get worster. Right, Moishe?"

"Right."

Jake paused. He knew about Moishe Nigger.

"Look," Jake said softly. "All I understand is I lost my job. It isn't fair."

"This is fair," Moishe Nigger said. He cracked the whip against Kolodny. The bottler screamed. He wailed to be let up. He was ready to meet the Horse Poisoner's terms. They could discuss business in the office.

Bunchik jabbed Jake in the kidneys with the ax handle. "What do we do with the Polack, Moishe?"

"I ain't a Polack. I'm a Jew like you."

"You're too big for a Jew," Little Mendel said. "Your mother got it from a Polack policeman."

Jake let his arms hang limp. His fingers flexed, unflexed.

Blowing snot from his nose, Kolodny pulled up his suspenders and buttoned his fly. He walked gingerly.

"For ten dollars a week you needed this?" Moishe Nigger asked. He put a thick arm around Kolodny and patted the hump. "For good luck, Kolodny. Now we're partners."

"Please, don't talk. I'll pay."

Moishe's sallow face, bulbous nose, and low brow gleamed. "Kolodny, it's a good thing you're a Hungarian like me. If you was a Litvak or a Galitzianer I wouldn't be so kind."

"Mr. Kolodny," Jake said. "The horse—my deliveries—"

"I got no deliveries for you, Chain."

Bunchik and Little Mendel laughed and slapped their thighs.

The hunchback wept. "Chain, don't torture me. Tell Kuflik he ain't working neither. I don't know when you'll be back."

Moishe Nigger held the door open. He bowed to let his new client enter.

"What about this bum?" Bunchik had the ax handle pressed against Jake's kidneys.

"Let him shovel shit," the Horse Poisoner said, and followed Kolodny through the door.

"Pick up a shovel," Bunchik said. "You heard what Moishe said. Shovel drek." Bunchik dug the handle sharply into Jake's left kidney.

"No funny stuff," Mendel said. He walked away from the trough. A snub-nosed revolver was in his hand. He leveled it at Jake's midriff. "You got a hard belly, Chain. But it won't stop bullets."

"Where should I start?"

"Right here." Little Mendel, keeping the gun trained on Jake, threw a shovel at him. "Into the barrel. Maybe we'll ask you to climb in with it."

Jake walked to the stall where Kotchka lay on her side. Clouds of angry green flies buzzed around the dead horse.

"Start," Bunchik said. He sat on an upturned pail and lit a cigarette. As he did, he let the ax handle drop. Mendel kept the pistol pointed at Jake.

The flies nipped wickedly at Jake's arms. He worked slowly.

The gangsters smoked and chattered. When Jake moved to the next stall, they followed him.

"Listen, Chain," Bunchik said. "You see my shirt? Six dollars in Kossow's on Pitkin Avenue. *Silk.* The pants are from Jaffe's and the shoes from Siegel's. Only the best. I got silk drawers on. You got clothes like that?"

"No. I only got bad luck."

"Listen, Chain," Little Mendel said. "With those arms and hands, you could get a job with Moishe. He likes strong boys."

"Nah, nah," Bunchik sneered. "He's too dumb to be a *shtarker*. He'd hit the wrong guy. He'd hit his cock."

The flies swarmed around Jake. They were vicious and hungry. Like Moishe Nigger and his mob.

Bunchik tossed his Sweet Caporal away and stuck a fresh one in his mouth. He walked from behind Jake toward Mendel to borrow a match. Mendel reached in his back pocket.

"Tell us about your wife," Little Mendel said. "She's a Polack like you? A big blonde with tits like balloons?"

Jake watched from the corner of his eye. Bunchik struck the match on the sole of his box-toed shoe and lit up.

Chain moved around the dead horse. Suddenly he swung the shovel blade with all the power in his arms. Mendel tried to duck and caught half the force of the blow. The gun fell from his hand. He toppled senseless.

The wide arc of the shovel caught Bunchik in the face. The skinny man collapsed with a whoosh of air, as if a giant's palm had slammed him. The two fell, bloodied and unconscious.

He tossed the shovel aside. He enjoyed the summery quiet of the stable. A horse neighing and stomping. The buzzing of swarms of flies. Trickles of water from the tap. But there was no point in hanging around. No horse, no job. The bottler had surrendered to Moishe Nigger. And Jake had made an enemy of the liver-lipped thug.

More bad luck, Jake thought. A man with nothing to lose. That was why he had slammed the shovel against Mendel and Bunchik. They would come and look for him. It did not matter. Sarah was doomed. Mutteh would end up in the orphan asylum. And him? Maybe they'd shoot him in an alley some dark night.

When the King of the Horse Poisoners called for his lieutenants, he got no response. He waddled into the stable and found Mendel and Bunchik struggling to rise from the floor. Their faces were mashed and bloodied.

"The big guy," Moishe said. "You let him do this? You ain't worth the money I pay you. Who *was* that big bum?"

Chapter 4

"Socialism must triumph," Avner Heilig proclaimed (at regular intervals) to family, friends, and visitors. In proof he would produce stacks of dog-eared ledgers in which he had, through a series of involved computations, demonstrated that Marx was right.

Bundists, Social Democrats, Socialists, Anarchists, assorted left intellectuals came to visit Heilig. They studied his notebooks with the endless x's and y's and concluded he was a harmless nut.

Ike Brunstein, president of the Bathrobe, Kimono, and House Dress Workers Union, Local 37, thought Avner Heilig a fool. But Ike kept his opinions to himself. He pined for Avner's daughter, Eva. He hoped to marry her.

Visiting the Heiligs was always an exhilarating experience for Brunstein. A disciple of the legendary Barondess—orator, political figure, and union leader—Ike enjoyed status in Brownsville. Yet in the Heiligs' noisy apartment on Haven Place, three doors down from Dr. Abelman's house, he was not especially esteemed and often ignored. An ironist, Brunstein was amused. All the Heiligs were talkative, optimistic, and vigorous. They were a family bound together with love of one another and hatred of sour milk, the *Lactobacillus acidophilus* that Papa Heilig forced on his three children. Indeed (Ike noticed), sour milk was even urged on the scores of greenhorn "relatives" to whom the generous-hearted Matla Heilig, Eva's mother, offered a temporary haven.

At this moment, a young couple and a child, cousins so distantly removed as to make the tracing of bloodlines a job for Burke's Peerage, were seated in a dim corner of the kitchen drinking Uncle Sourmilk's cure-all. The man was shriveled and round-shouldered. He had Eva's green eyes and light brown curling hair. His wife was tiny. A black wig covered her shaved head. She cradled a howling infant in her arms. No sour milk for the child, she had evidently decided. But the two immigrants sipped it as if in payment for lodging in the Heilig ménage.

"New ones?" Ike asked Avner Heilig. Eva's father was making notations in a ledger.

"Yeah, yeah. From whose side of the family I'm not sure. I lose track, we have so many. They'll sleep in the living room until they find a job. Extra mouths we can always feed. Besides, with sour milk, other foods are unnecessary."

Avner's wife, Matla, a chirpy woman, as blond as her daughter and with Eva's clear green eyes, poked her head in from the kitchen. She and the younger Heilig son, Sol, were drying dishes. "So where is all *your* energy, Uncle Sourmilk? Who runs the candy store fourteen hours a day? Who shops, cleans, and cooks? Me! I *hate* sour milk. And you sit in a chair all day making fly tracks in a book."

"That also takes energy!" Avner Heilig shouted. "More energy! Recent studies in neurology bear me out. Every question in my analysis of the victory of socialism derives from mental gifts endowed by sour milk! Brunstein, don't smile."

No one took Avner Heilig seriously. He had not done a day's work in twelve years. Matla, a robust woman, ran the candy store with the help of her sons, Sol and Abe. When not assisting in the store, the boys worked at odd jobs—carpentry, electrical repairs, anything that would bring in a dollar.

Ike Brunstein admired the family. Not only were they his hoped-for in-laws, they were ambitious, undefeated, generous, full of good humor. The stew of his gloomy nature needed the spice of their laughter. Most of all he craved Eva. So lovely, so strong-willed, with her noble bearing and heavenly face.

She appeared in the door to the living room. Ike battled vertigo.

"I'm ready," she said. "Let's go, Ike. I don't want to get to the meeting too late."

Brunstein tried to keep his face from turning crimson, his hands from shaking. Eva had put on a tight blue skirt, a wide-brimmed blue hat. Her face, freshly scrubbed, was like a cultured flower. Her green eyes were shining.

Abe, a City College student, entered the room and tossed copies of the *Forward* (the socialist paper) and the *Wahrheit* (its anarchist rival) on the table. "There you go, pop. For once the two papers agree. Somebody's got to be punished for the *shonda* at Baum's." Abe kissed his mother, winked at Eva, waved at Ike. He was eighteen, intent on becoming a physician. He barely stopped, marched to the kitchen for a late dinner. Nobody moved slothfully or without purpose in the house except the head of the family.

Uncle Sourmilk leaped up and followed his daughter and Ike to the door. "Heed Maimonides," he said. " 'Anticipate charity by preventing poverty, assist the reduced fellowman, either by a considerable gift or a sum of money or by teaching him a trade or by putting him in a way of

business.' Like our *landsleit*. In helping them, we follow the Talmud and
Maimonides."

Ike said, "It isn't Maimonides we're dealing with, Uncle Sourmilk. It's
cheating employers, rotten politicians, and corrupt police."

"And our own frightened members," Eva added.

They had not walked a half a block when Ike proposed marriage (for the
fourth time that week) to Eva.

"United, we will be an even more potent force," Brunstein said. "Think
of it, Eva. A husband-and-wife team running the union. Who could prevail against us?"

Her beauty rendered him weak-kneed. It created quiverings in his gut,
caused him to speak breathlessly. Oh, he was not alone. Beauty and brains,
old Meyer Flugelman, the union theorist, said with a poignant leer, a
woman in a million. *And what courage!* Behind all the male admiration,
Ike knew, men craved her. The fine face, the glowing green eyes. And
what else . . . ? Beneath the layers of clothing . . . ?

Stop, stop, Brunstein! he had to tell himself. You are a beast, a monster
of sexual appetites!

"Eva, my darling," he pleaded. "I want to marry you. Don't you recipro-
cate my respect and admiration?" His voice shook. "And my love?"

"Respect and admiration, yes. I don't know what love is. It's a myth
invented by poets."

"I believe in the myth."

She laughed, cocked her head. "Oh, Ike. Go read poetry."

"Don't make fun."

"I've told you a hundred times, Ike. Emotions and the class struggle are
a bad mixture. You keep appealing to my social conscience to entice me
into marriage."

They approached the Jewish Fellowship Hall. It was a gray stone building plastered with handbills. Under insect-hazed streetlights, animated
groups had gathered. Survivors, relatives, union members, candidates. Boys
raced up and down the steps, slid down bronze banisters, flew in and out
the doors. Sal Ferrante peddled his hokey-pokey—shavings of unsanitary
ice doused with a choice of syrups that suggested Paris green, Prussian
blue, sulfurous yellow.

Bernie Feigenbaum bought a double scoop of the concoction. With a
lamprey's mouth, he sucked at the purple-stained ice. Mrs. Feigenbaum
shrieked, pounced on him, knocked the paper cup from his hand. She
yelled at Sal: "Gedda odda here, you poisoner! Those *fekokteh* syrups
they make from worms! You could die from such *chazerei!*"

"No it ain't," Sal said. "It's pure."

Susan Stofsky arrived in a wheelchair pushed by her brother. People
applauded and made way. Another girl came on crutches. Eva watched

with wrenching pity. Jake's wife, Sarah, would not be there. Her legs would
be in casts a long time.

As Eva and Ike entered, a pudgy man in a soiled black suit, soft shirt,
and black musician's tie jostled Brunstein. "So, Brunstein, more useless
gestures?" the man asked. He was in his sixties—frazzled, short-bearded,
gray, pouches the size and hue of small eggplants under popping eyes.

"Mosherman, please. Your anarchist manners are not in order tonight.
For a change, join us."

Across the street in a Chandler phaeton, Francis Fagan Dullahan, political
boss of Brooklyn, viewed his Hebrew constituents with keen Celtic satisfaction. Florid and fat, bald as a stone, Dullahan was an aging fox observing chickens.

With Dullahan was his Man in Brownsville, Benny Otzenberger. Two
hundred and eighty pounds in a gray linen suit with black velvet lapels,
Dullahan managed to make Benny look undernourished. A pair of ma-
rauding sea creatures they seemed—black whale, white whale. Benny was
spiffy in white linen, a white panama.

Dullahan gave Otzenberger a fistful of dark Coronas. "For the boys,
Benjamin. Too bad we have to do this, but Brunstein is a menace."

"Brunstein couldn't start a revolution in a men's room, Mr. D. He won't
even get a strike vote tonight."

Like an old turtle, Dullahan blinked his eyes and said nothing.

Heshy Otzenberger approached the phaeton. His father gave him the
cigars and a manila envelope. "Take care of them," Benny whispered.
"Tell the Nigger and his mob to do it fast and run."

"The cops?"

"They ain't gonna be around."

It took fifteen minutes for Ike to get the meeting organized. People drifted
in late. Bundists argued violently with Socialists. Mosherman the anarchist
detested everyone equally. An angry group of Labor Zionists got into the
debates. The old story, Ike told Eva—two Jews, three synagogues.

Ultimately it was Eva, with her assertive voice and her commanding
eyes, who restored order.

"Disgraceful!" she cried. "Stop this bickering, this fighting of Jew against
Jew! Take a lesson from our Italian sisters in the working-class movement
—they sit quietly, determined, mannerly, and wait for the meeting!"

A girl with her arm in a sling got to her feet. "It ain't easy, Eva. The
bosses find out you pay union dues, or go to a meeting like this . . ." She
looked around fearfully. "So you're the first one fired."

A few girls left. The Italians looked fretful. Lose a job? *Santa Maria,*
the end of their world!

"Yeah, yeah," Susan bawled from her wheelchair. "I got a union card. I pay dues. What did I get for it? Crippled. No chance for a husband or children."

A strange wailing arose from the audience. It was a moaning, undulant noise, begun by the parents of the dead.

"Our daughters, give us our daughters."

"God in Heaven, Lord of the Universe, give us our children, our daughters."

Brunstein flapped his arms. "It's hopeless. They can't be controlled. They won't listen. They wail."

Eva's eyes were angry. "I'll *make* them listen." She moved Ike away from the lectern. "All of you stop crying!" she shouted. "Sit down. Dry your eyes. Blow your noses. Act like proud human beings!"

Vibrant and clear, her voice silenced the stuffy hall. Girls snuffled quietly. Bereaved parents held hands.

"There is *one* answer," Eva said. "Listen to me. Susan Stofsky, stop crying at *once.*"

The girl in the wheelchair buried her face in a handkerchief.

"I say there is one answer," Eva said. "Strike! Strike! *Strike!*"

Two blocks from the Jewish Fellowship Hall, Heshy Otzenberger conferred with four men in the schoolyard of Public School 168. The men chewed on Dullahan's cigars, blew clouds of smoke.

Heshy was terrified of them. Especially Moishe "Nigger" Pearlberg in his gray derby and stiff collar. It was said he could bend a silver dollar in half between thumb and forefinger. Once he gouged a rival mobster's eyes from his head.

"My chest hoits, Nigger," Bunchik said. "I ever catch that bastard Chain, I'll mopolize him."

"Me too," Little Mendel whined. "You got to let us get that big bum, Nigger."

Heshy tried to suppress a smile. His pointed ears twitched. So. It was Crazy Jake who had done such a job on these animals. Mendel's face was a mass of red scabs, welts, and lumps. Bunchik looked lopsided. One eye was covered.

"Chain done this? That bum?" Heshy was grinning.

"Whaddya smiling for, *putz?*" Mendel asked. He took a pistol from his belt and jabbed it in Heshy's ribs. "Whaddya think, it's funny?"

Moishe counted the money in the envelope. "It ain't enough, Heshy. Twenny for me, ten for each boy?"

"My father says it's the first time you *shtarked* a union meeting," Heshy said. "Besides, it's almost all girls."

The fourth man, a youth with wide shoulders and a narrow waist, was dancing around the schoolyard, throwing combinations. He wore a heavy black sweater, black drainpipe trousers, and gym shoes.

"Who's he?" Heshy asked.

"Otzenberger, you never read the sports section?" Bunchik asked. "That's Duffy Plotkin, the next welterweight champeen."

Gevalt, Heshy thought. Why am I mixed up in this? A professional boxer to beat up factory girls?

A globelike figure, mincing on dagger-toed shoes, short arms pumping, porky face sweating, approached Moishe Nigger. "Ready, boss. The Saratoga Avenue Meal Ticket himself."

"Cops?" Moishe Nigger asked.

"Fixed," Heshy answered.

Little Mendel asked, "Could maybe an honest cop come by?"

"So what?" Heshy asked. "The judge takes his orders from Dullahan. You'll get medals for being patriotic Americans. Congratulations for *klopping* Reds."

Heshy peeked through a side window of the noisy hall. He knew the girls. Scared like mice. Afraid they'd be blacklisted. Now Eva Heilig had created an army of screaming warriors.

"Strike!" they shouted.

Eva shouted back: "Why wait? What do we fear? They have murdered our comrades! Twisted our sisters' backs, broken their legs, fractured their heads! We are persecuted, hated, exploited, and we—will—not—surrender!"

They were on their feet. Roaring, applauding.

Strike, strike, strike!

It was time to call Moishe Nigger.

Heshy whistled from the corner. Moishe led his troops. The Saratoga Meal Ticket walked delicately on small feet, twirling his cane, two paces ahead of Bunchik and Mendel. Each of the latter had brass knuckles in one hand, a bicycle chain in the other. Around them, ducking, bobbing, Duffy Plotkin threw punches. The Jewish Ketchell.

Fifty feet from the hall, the Nigger bought hokey-pokey for his boys from Sal—toxic-looking cherry, pineapple, raspberry, orange syrup poured over street-filthy ice.

"For you, you don't gotta pay, Mistah Pearlberg," Sal said. He smelled trouble.

Moishe let his gang suck at the flavored ice for a minute or so. The chanting of the girls surged out of the hall, wild and exhilarated.

The inside of the hall was bedlam. People stood on benches. They wept, embraced, shouted, laughed. Sal entered, found Theresa with two other Italian girls. He grabbed her arms. "Papa says you gotta come home." He dragged his sister to the door and raced down the steps, almost colliding with Plotkin.

Up the steps clattered Moishe Nigger's thugs. The Saratoga Avenue Meal Ticket, spinning on pointed feet, smashed his cane against an old man's astonished face. It turned crimson. His wife shrieked. They staggered down the steps. *Cossacks!*

Moishe Nigger led the charge into the hall, punching and kicking women, swinging a lead pipe. He dragged a fat woman by the hair from her seat, kicked an old man, spit in the face of an Italian girl.

Duffy Plotkin punched a man in the gut, grabbed another by the collar and threw him over a bench, hurled a third against a window and shattered it. A professional, he would hit only men. People screamed, hid, fled for the doors.

"Stop! *Stop!*" Eva shrieked. "We are your own people! What we do is for you also!"

"Oh, my God!" cried Brunstein. "They hired gangsters. Flugelman, somebody, call the police!"

Meyer Flugelman, veteran of a thousand discussions on Marx, Engels, Lassalle, and De Leon, his mind honed to an intellectual fineness that was the envy of every Socialist in Brownsville, shuffled to the rear door.

Bunchik, an apparition in bloodied bandages, cracked Flugelman across the kidneys with his bicycle chain. The theorizer howled.

"Stay there, ya bum," Bunchik said. "Ya holler copper, I'll beat ya brains out."

Eva hurled herself at Bunchik, clawing at what was left of his face, her arms beating at his chest. The hoodlum wriggled free and slapped her across the face. She came at him again. He hit her in the chest with his brass knuckles. She gasped. "Blondie bitch, stay away," he said. "We don't wanna hoit no one. Clear the hall."

"Reds, anarchists!" Moishe Nigger croaked. "Outta here! This here meeting is outta order." He grabbed two women by the hair and dragged them to the door. Mendel shoved them down the stairs, spun on an attacking brother, and hit him in the nose with a lead pipe.

Blood streamed down Eva's face. Her blouse was ripped. She ran back to the stage. "Workers! Do not be frightened! We have sent for the police! Don't let them scare you!"

The Meal Ticket pirouetted away from a girl who lay screaming on the floor, and grabbed Eva's skirt. He dragged her from the stage. She landed on him, swinging and scratching. The fat man grabbed her thighs, squeezed them until Eva shrieked with pain, lifted her, and threw her against Brunstein.

"Fight them!" Eva screamed. "Chairs, tables! Workers, don't give in!"

Seeing the Meal Ticket kicking an Italian girl, Eva pulled a pin from her hat, leaped from the stage, and jabbed it into his buttocks. He howled and straightened up. She stuck him again. He screamed, turned, and was confronted by her flaming eyes.

"I will kill you, murderer," Eva said. "I am not afraid."

The Meal Ticket's eyes glistened. Not a dame to muss up, but a dame to *shtup*. A piece of sweet candy.

"Stick me, huh?" the Meal Ticket asked. He bounced toward her. Ike leaped between them and struggled helplessly with the thug. Eva was pulled away by Bunchik. He pinned her arms behind her back.

"The skinny shmuck fighting with the Meal Ticket," Moishe said to Duffy. "He's the boss. Work him over and we'll go."

Brunstein was borne aloft by the Meal Ticket and the boxer Plotkin. A screaming Eva was restrained by Bunchik. Mendel and the Nigger chased stragglers from the wrecked hall. The Meal Ticket and the boxer carried Ike to the steps, one holding his legs, one holding his arms.

Tossed into space, Brunstein felt himself floating, airborne. He landed on a pile of sweepings.

"Meeting's over," Moishe Nigger yelled. "Duffy, stop. Bunchik, Mendel, Ticket. C'mon."

They did not look back.

Weeping, Eva sat on the steps of the wrecked hall. Blood trickled from her nose. One of the Marrotta sisters, her eye closed and purpling, sat with her and sobbed.

A police van pulled up. Sergeant Ahearn, Patrolman Mulqueen, and two other men walked out.

"Yez are all under arrest," Ahearn said. "Incitin' to riot."

"So," Eva said. "They bribed you. Someday you'll learn." Bone-weary, she got up. The blood dripping from her nose gave her strength. She licked at it with her tongue.

"I'm arrested also?" Angelina Marrotta asked. She was in shock. She had gone to the meeting in defiance of her parents.

Mulqueen and Ahearn shoved them into the Black Maria.

Eva, Ike, Flugelman, and Angie Marrotta were arrested, along with an old man selling knishes who was looking for his daughter.

Chapter 5

Three weeks after her discharge from the hospital, Sarah Chain hobbled on crutches. She had lost weight. To Jake, her body seemed to have shrunk. She was always a small woman, but now she was bent at her waist as if fearful of a blow. Her legs, with casts removed, were skeleton-thin. Her thighs had shriveled. Her breasts were two flaps. She needed help dressing and undressing. Mutteh had to be sent out of the basement when Jake assisted her.

But Sarah was pleased to see how clean the apartment was. Jake and Mutteh had swept and scrubbed in anticipation of her return. She was ashamed that she could not help them. It was a woman's job. People would laugh at Jake when they heard.

"Let them laugh," the big man said. "Only they shouldn't cheat me of money."

She needed medicine and food to build her up. Luckily, Kolodny kept Jake on the job. At first he was fearful that Jake's rude handling of Moishe Nigger's soldiers would make him a marked man. "Chain, I'm grateful what you did to those *mamzerim*," the hunchback said. "But suppose they blame it on me?"

"They know I did it. You pay protection money every week. That's all the Horse Poisoner wants."

Surprisingly, Moishe and his gang did not come looking for Jake. The Nigger was a shrewd businessman. He did not believe in pursuing vendettas that had no cash value.

Kolodny gave Jake an "inside" job, stacking, hauling, bossing the work crew inside the plant. Landlord Feigenbaum mercifully allowed Sarah to work a half-day for three dollars a week. She finished buttonholes on knee-pants. Mutteh was employed after school as a delivery boy. A wiry runt in tattered blue cap, baggy blue knickers, and high sox, he lugged piles of trousers taller than he was.

Dr. Abelman thought that Sarah would soon be able to walk without crutches. Two canes, maybe. But he gave no assurances. She needed exercise. But how? Half-days at the machines. One day a week off.

"It's wrong you should have to work," Jake said to her. They were in bed on a warm September night. Mutteh slept on the cot in the corner of the musty room.

"We have to eat. We have to send the child to school."

"But you're hurt. You should have time to go to the hospital and get exercise and get better."

There seemed no way out. She would hobble forever, Jake suspected.

Their sexual attachment was unraveling. Jake discovered she could not move her legs. The desire was in him. But although she functioned below the waist, the legs were immobile. The effort embarrassed both of them. She wept.

Once when Jake had succeeded in making love to her, she cried and pushed him away.

"I hurt you? I won't do it no more."

"No, Jake. It's wrong I should enjoy anything."

Nightmares, she sobbed to Jake. She would have nightmares for the rest of her life. In the midst of deep sleep, she could not catch her breath. She was suffocating. Her mouth and her nose were stuffed with plaster. Lucia, the girl who worked next to her, was screaming in her ear, but Sarah could not hear the screams. She saw Lucia's brown face with the red mouth open and no noise coming out. Then the two of them, covered by a gray cloud. A heavy cloud shoving them down. Something bursting their ears. She would awaken shivering, cold, unable to forget Lucia's face.

"I am no good to you," she said. "You can't do with me what husbands must do."

"I want you to feel better."

"It will make me cry again. My body is broken. Like a bird with broken wings. If you do with me what men do, what a husband should do, you'll become weak like me."

"It's not true." He put his arm around her. She trembled.

He could see Mutteh's eyes glinting at him from the floor. Jake stared at the boy. The eyes closed.

Sarah worried continually. She never smiled. The work for Feigenbaum was too much for her, hefting herself on crutches. ("One day I'll have to get rid of the *kolyaka,* the cripple," the landlord told his wife.) She worried about Mutteh. How could he stay in school? There was no one to give him a meal when he came home.

Her timid parents looked at her with dumb despair. What good was she to anyone? Her father, old Klebanow, a pushcart peddler, was in trouble again. Shakedowns from the cops. Unable to pay the five-dollar-a-month protection money. He could not help with their bills. He barely made enough for his rent. Speaking no English, Jake's father-in-law had not understood when the police ordered him, with flat smiles, to "come to Limerick." He learned soon enough after three arrests for loitering.

"We are no better than my papa," Sarah cried. She nestled in Jake's arms for protection. "Will Mutteh be better? Jake, what will happen to him?"

Ike and Eva got nowhere over the disaster at the Baum place and the attack on the meeting. The city received their appeals with the icy smile of officialdom. Even Jews in places of power had little patience. Troublemakers. Agitators. *Reds.*

Hauled into court for "illegal assembly," Eva, Ike, and a half-dozen girls were bailed out by Leo Glauberman, the union lawyer. Judge Younghusband, an austere Brooklyn Episcopalian, lectured the accused on "acts against God, society, and humanity."

"These people are fighting for their lives and livelihood, Your Honor," Glauberman argued. "Perhaps God and society are on their side. They should not be standing here on trumped-up charges. The gangsters who attacked them should. The police who failed to protect them. The owners who abused them—"

"That will be enough. I dismiss the case but I warn you against any further meetings or demonstrations that may incite violence."

Eva could not control her temper. "We incited nothing! We met peacefully to discuss rights! We were attacked. Look at the bruises on my arms! Hoodlums with chains and clubs—and we are the ones accused?"

Younghusband pounded his gavel. No further outburst would be permitted. Mr. Brunstein and Miss Heilig should consider themselves lucky.

Outside, Glauberman, a chunky man who looked like Teddy Roosevelt, told them that Benny Otzenberger's fat hand was at work in the dismissal. Benny knew he could not antagonize large segments of his constituency. Garment workers made up a large part of the Brownsville population.

"You'll still strike?" the lawyer asked. "Now that you've been freed?"

"The Strike Committee has voted for it," Eva said. "We will not be intimidated."

"They'll break the union," Glauberman said ominously.

Jake Chain, on his way to the bottling plant, saw Eva handing out "strike benefits." A dollar and a half a week, doled out from a metal box.

He did not greet her. Arms folded, shivering in the morning air, Jake watched his cousin, and felt a surge of love for her. Love. And all the other things.

Eva climbed to the hood of a Dodge car. It bore a sign on the side:

DEPARTMENT OF HEALTH. Cops watched with cold eyes. Jake heard one say, "Sheeny bitch. Do they screw like other women?"

A policeman started to drag Eva down from the car.

"Hands off me!" Eva shouted. "I want to talk to the girls!"

"City property, lady. Ya creatin' a distoibance."

The officer clutched at her. Eva would not move. There was a surge in the picket line.

Jake felt the old urge to *hit*. He looked at the cop—fat, puffy. He could lay him out, with or without the club. But there were seven policemen on duty. The patrols had increased. Prices had gone up for police protection, yet the owners paid willingly.

"Don't touch her!" Angie Marrotta screamed.

A tall woman in a black straw hat and a gray uniform got out of the car. She carried a black satchel. Jake moved closer and listened.

"It's all right, officer," the woman said. "I am Mildred Halstead of the Visiting Nurse Service. The mayor's office asked me to visit the picket line. I have no objection to this young woman standing on the car."

Jake looked at the nurse. Eyeglasses. Long straight nose. Plain hair. Very *goyisha*. He had to hand it to her. The police knew class when they saw it. They drew back. Eva continued her speech.

Miss Halstead joined Eva on the running board. She told the girls that if any were suffering bruises, cuts, headaches, or any other ailment, she would be glad to minister to them from the car, as soon as Miss—what is your name, dear?—finished her speech.

Angelina Marrotta, a minuscule girl, slumped into a dead faint. Miss Halstead helped Rachel Goldstein, the picket captain, carry Angie to the side of the building. Briskly the Visiting Nurse opened her bag, pulled the stopper from a green bottle, and waved it under her patient's nose.

Angie twitched, shook her head, and rubbed her eyes. The girls left the line and watched gratefully.

"Disgraceful," the nurse said. Her accent hinted at Bryn Mawr or Mount Holyoke. "This girl is undernourished. Look at her skin. Her wrists are like sticks."

Jake Chain watched. Life was a hard road. As Doc Abelman used to say in his tirades against city, employers, crooks, swindlers, and galoots, *The bastards won't let you live.* Jake tucked his lunch under his arm and walked away.

Kalman Baum shouted from the window: "Tell 'em to stop with this strike, lady! Then they won't starve! They want to starve, let them starve!"

The girls shouted back at the bathrobe king.

"Bloodsucker!"

"Thief!"

Mildred Halstead gave Eva a card. "Miss Heilig, I've read about you. If you ever need help, call me at my office. I'll drop by twice a week."

"You mean the politicians are *worried* about us?" Eva asked. She looked about nervously. Something distressed her. The police had vanished.

"You would be surprised, Miss Heilig, how many influential women admire you."

Eva's face manifested her gratitude. "I didn't know *anyone* was for us except our relatives. But why should you take time from your job to look after us? The judge said we were on strike against God."

Heshy Otzenberger, in a green-checked suit and orange shoes, was greeting the trolley car at the corner. It came to a clanging stop. Wild kids leaped off the back. From the door of the tram emerged four dark girls. Heshy led them toward the side entrance. He moved swiftly, prodding his new scabs in Yiddish and Italian. One was an older woman, slow-moving, in layers of black skirts and petticoats.

"Stop!" Eva shouted. *"Stop!* You are taking the food from our mouths! We are your sisters!"

"Per favore, non lavore qui!"

"Yiddishe maidlech, geh nicht arein!"

Eva led the charge around the factory to the side entrance. Pickets followed her.

"Please!" Eva cried, as the pickets surrounded Heshy's recruits. "We are your sisters in work! If you take our jobs today, you'll suffer tomorrow!"

The older woman tried to fight her way through the surrounding strikers. Her children were hungry, she wept.

Two girls tried to hold the stout woman back. They tore at her shawl, pulled at her arms. She stumbled and fell.

Panic overwhelmed scabs and strikers. Women shrieked, yanked at hair and clothing.

In Baum's office, four men waited. Kalman opened the door. "Go ahead, but don't hurt no one too bad," he said. "Chase those *kurvas* away."

Moishe Nigger tilted his derby and yanked at his suspenders. He led his gang across the factory floor to the side door. Bunchik picked up a two-by-four. The Saratoga Avenue Meal Ticket polished his brass knucks. Duffy Plotkin threw punches. Little Mendel had been left at home. His head bothered him. That gorilla Chain had fixed him for a long time.

Eva was trying to draw her girls away from the melee. She saw Moishe Nigger's grinning face as he charged from the door.

"Adda my way, adda my way," the King of the Horse Poisoners shouted. "Anybody gets in my way it's her own fault!"

He grabbed the sign from Angie, jammed the stick into her ribs, sent her sprawling. The Meal Ticket hit Rachel Goldstein in the teeth with his brass-covered right fist. Blood spurted from her mouth. She fell slowly. Girls screamed and ran.

Heshy shouted to his scabs: "Follow me, girls! Nothing to be afraid of!"

"Baum, you are responsible for this!" Eva shouted. She saw Bunchik raising the two-by-four to strike at Esther Levy. Eva flew at him and dug her nails into his face.

"You hoo-er," Bunchik said. "I'll loin ya." He swung the board again and hit Eva a grazing blow on the hip. She swayed, smothered the pain, righted herself. Bunchik was under attack from four girls. They ripped his raspberry-colored box coat, tore at his green drainpipe pants.

Moishe cracked a girl across the nape of the neck, punched another in the chest. Duffy Plotkin picked up Esther Levy and hurled her down the cellar steps.

Reuven Baum watched from the window. *"Oi, oi,"* he moaned. "Too much, Kalman. Broken bones, bloody heads. This I didn't want. Just to scare them a little."

Eva kicked the Meal Ticket's shins. He did a one-legged dance, spun like a ballerina, caught her left arm, jabbed a finger in her eye, spit in her face.

"You scum, you filth!" Eva shouted. "You are a Jew, Wesselberg. How dare you!"

"You should talk, hoo-er. Shaddap and get adda here."

A half-dozen girls were bloodied. Others had run off screaming for the police. Two lay where they had fallen. Miss Halstead, using her satchel as a shield, dragged them to the shade of a candy-store awning and ministered to them.

"Nigger, Nigger," Kalman cried from the window. "Enough."

Ten of Eva's pickets fled. Dresses ripped, stockings loose, some shoeless, others hatless, they scattered. Esther Levy stumbled up the cellar steps. She was hysterical and kept pointing to her left wrist. "Broke," she cried. "Broke. I can't move my hand."

Eva led her to the shelter of the awning. Miss Halstead peered over her rimless glasses. "Miss Heilig, go into that store and phone for an ambulance at once. Mention my name at Saint Mary's. They know me."

Esther groaned. "Eva, it's wrong we should have to stay on the picket line. We ain't protected."

Rachel nodded her dark head. Blood gushed from her lips. Teeth had been knocked loose from her jaw.

Enraged, Eva began to tremble. *Her* girls.

A siren wailed. A police van was approaching.

The nurse pressed a gauze bandage to Rachel's mouth. It turned crimson in a second. Angie became hysterical, shaking, banging her head against the brick wall.

Mildred Halstead shook her head. She watched the police park outside the factory. Moishe Nigger and his friends had disappeared as swiftly as they had attacked. The carnage had lasted less than three minutes.

Sergeant Ahearn jumped out of the van. Two policemen followed him. Miss Halstead got to her feet. She had been winding a bandage around Esther's wrist.

"Officers, these women were attacked," Mildred Halstead said. "I demand that your men look for the criminals who beat them."

Ahearn's eyes were cunning and secretive. He surveyed the beaten girls. The blond Heilig cookie, the Red.

"Yez are all under arrest," he said.

Chapter 6

Blaufox, a dapper lawyer in a cocoa-brown suit, represented the Baum brothers. Impeding legally hired workers. Obstructing the workings of a factory . . .

The city, with a sleepy assistant district attorney named Curtis presenting the case, was going to bring another suit. Violation of picketing regulations, inciting to riot.

Judge Younghusband yawned prodigiously. One slim girl in a torn shirtwaist, blond hair flying like a Medusa's, capable of all this? It was something to laugh at. But he owed people favors. Dullahan had nothing against working people—hell, he'd been a ditchdigger himself, a foundry worker. But this dame was a pain in the ass. Besides, the bathrobe makers had given him two thousand dollars to break the strike.

Eva had spent the previous night in a lockup. She was allowed no calls. Uncle Sourmilk and Abie came to the precinct and were turned away. Ike Brunstein could not get past the desk sergeant. Eva sent word out that she was all right. She was lecturing two prostitutes on Marx.

In the morning light, with Ike and lawyer Glauberman present, the judge listened dolefully as Eva protested.

"Your Honor, where are the gangsters who attacked us? Where are the hoodlums who broke Angie Marrotta's ribs, knocked the teeth from Rachel Goldstein's mouth, fractured Esther Levy's wrist?"

If not deaf and blind, justice was indifferent. Not a cruel man, Judge Younghusband nevertheless knew where the power rested. He said nothing.

Glauberman reviewed some points. They had a permit to picket. They had been peaceful. They were attacked.

Sergeant Ahearn disputed him. These women, led by the defendant, had obstructed the rights of other women to earn a living. The Heilig woman, using her picket sign as a weapon, had led the attack.

"But," Eva said, "you weren't *around* when it happened, if it happened at all. You and your policemen disappeared. You left us to the mercies of gangsters!"

The judge banged his gavel. "Silence, miss. Case seems clear to me. If you waive the right to trial, Miss Heilig, you will be fined a thousand dollars and released."

Eva whispered to Ike, "What do we do?"

"We haven't got four hundred dollars in the union treasury," he muttered.

"Your Honor," Eva said, "can't you see we are fighting for our lives?"

"You are guests in this country," he said. "Behave like good citizens. The police assure me that your pickets started the violence. A one-thousand-dollar fine to be paid now or a trial. The trial will go hard with you. I may ask the district attorney to open an investigation of this entire matter. I am sick and tired of violence in front of factories. Property owners have rights also."

Eva was allowed to have a conference with Ike and the lawyer. What could they do?

"We're doomed," Ike said.

"Ike, I'll be happy to go to jail. Why don't we refuse to pay and see what they'll do? The girls will be out on the lines again."

The judge summoned Glauberman to the bench. "Counselor?"

"My client is of a mind to ask for a trial."

"I will then set bail at *two* thousand dollars."

Eva winked at Ike. "I'm not afraid," she said.

Mildred Halstead, accompanied by a slender, bespectacled man in a severe black suit, entered the courtroom. She had come, unbidden, to testify in behalf of the girls. The man with her was her brother, a freelance journalist for the *Brooklyn Eagle*.

The Halsteads walked forward. No court attendant sought to stop them. They possessed command presence. The woman in dark gray uniform, the man in a black suit and high white collar, his light brown hair parted neatly in the middle, advertised their status: old-line New York Protestants.

"Your Honor, if I may," Mildred Halstead said. "I am with the Visiting Nurse Service. I was at the Baum factory when the fighting took place. Miss Heilig's version of the events is correct. She and her pickets were beaten by riffraff."

The man at her side nodded. He stared at Eva.

Brunstein and Glauberman turned to look at their new allies. Aliens, people from another planet.

Respectfully, Younghusband asked Mildred Halstead her name. She responded and identified herself as a city employee. "This gentleman is my brother, Mr. Garrison Halstead. He is employed by the *Brooklyn Daily Eagle*."

"You are related to Garrison Halstead, Senior?"

"He is our father," Mildred said.

"Your version of the events differs from that of the police," the judge said.

"The police were not present when the events occurred," Mildred said. "I saw a young woman beaten and thrown down stairs, other outrages. I should like, Your Honor, to locate the people who employed gangsters and confront *them* with the evidence."

Eva smiled at the Halsteads. The tall man with the lantern jaw and ruddy face smiled back. He seemed much more elegant than any reporter she had ever met—pressed suit, gleaming black shoes, a black leather briefcase under one arm.

"The fine must stand," Judge Younghusband said amicably. "I will drop the charge of incitement to riot and will not pursue any further investigation. But the union must pay the fine for obstructing other workers."

Brushing back his Teddy Roosevelt hair, Glauberman protested. "A thousand dollars? For getting beaten up?"

"Our treasury will be bankrupted," Ike said. "We have to feed hungry children, Your Honor."

"You should have thought of that when you disobeyed the law."

Mildred's brother stepped forward. "If it please the court, Your Honor, I'm also an attorney. I know this is irregular, but what law of society does Your Honor refer to?"

"Mr. Halstead," the judge said, "I wish to enter into no argument with you. I was speaking about the orderly processes of society. These strikes, this agitation by radicals, are threats to the fabric of our lives."

Halstead rubbed his jaw. He had pale gray eyes, Eva noticed, so pale as to almost make him appear eyeless.

"I have no desire to pursue philosophical arguments, Your Honor," Halstead said. "Can we not end this by my paying the fine? I am sure that the defendant's union will reimburse me."

Younghusband agreed at once. It solved everything. Keep the Halsteads on his side. Satisfy Baum and the manufacturers. And get that blond tigress off his back.

"That is acceptable," the judge said. "Give my regards to your father and your uncle. I had the pleasure of representing Halstead and Halstead on some matters when I was a young lawyer."

A clerk took Halstead aside and made the arrangements. No question about accepting a check from Mr. Garrison Halstead.

"All charges are dismissed?" Halstead asked.

"All," the judge said.

Ike sighed. Was this a way to advance the class struggle?

On the steps of the courthouse, introductions were hesitantly made. Eva, Ike, and Glauberman expressed their gratitude. Ike insisted on giving Garrison Halstead a written receipt for the thousand dollars. He would be paid when the union could afford it.

"Why did you do this for us?" Eva asked.

Halstead smiled. He had long white teeth. "My sister and I are interested in the trade union movement. You and these gentlemen must think it strange."

"Strange?" Glauberman asked. "No insult, Mr. Halstead, but, lawyer to lawyer, we didn't expect help from—from—"

"Bloated capitalists?"

The lawyer said, "Let's say the other side of the fence." Glauberman doffed his hat and excused himself. Ike departed with him. They had papers to file, appeals to make. The introduction of the gangsters was an increasingly frightening element in the strike.

"Why did you put up the money?" Eva asked Halstead when the other two had gone.

"In the interests of journalism."

"And justice," added Mildred. "Garrison and I are supporters of the unions. We worked with the cloakmakers last year. Garrison may do a book on the subject."

"I see," Eva said. "Observing us?"

"With a sympathetic eye and understanding heart, Miss Heilig," Halstead said.

Mildred left them. She had calls to make. Halstead invited Eva to dine with him. It was a bit early for dinner, but they could sit and chat in Gage & Tollner's.

Eva brushed her hair back. "I'm hardly in condition to be seen in a fancy restaurant, Mr. Halstead. My hair is a mess. My blouse is torn."

He took her arm. "Miss Heilig, you are one of the most attractive women I have ever seen. You need make no apologies for your appearance."

They walked down Fulton Street to the restaurant. Trolleys clanged by. Storekeepers lounged on the pavement, trying to "pull in" customers. Lawyers and courthouse flunkies stood on the curb and made deals. They discussed Mayor Gaynor critically and paid tribute to F. F. Dullahan.

As they walked, Halstead questioned her about the union. Eva told him of the difficulties organizing the girls. Especially the Italians. They trudged home after an exhausting day on the picket line and often suffered beatings from their fathers. *Not work? Talk back to the boss?* That was for troublesome Jews, not for good Italian girls who had to get married and have children!

"My goodness," said Halstead as he opened the restaurant door for her, "those men should be given a lecture on Garibaldi and Mazzini. They have a great revolutionary tradition and they must be made aware of it."

"The families need every penny the girls earn, Mr. Halstead."

"May I ask that you call me Garry? And may I call you Eva?"

She smiled. "Of course."

The caramel-colored headwaiter, in high apron and black jacket, studied her a moment—he knew Halstead well—and was offended by the tattered shirtwaist, the undone mass of blond hair. Garrison Halstead with a hooker? Impossible.

"A quiet table, Everett," Halstead said.

"Certainly, sir."

Halstead became uneasy when the headwaiter brought menus. "Goodness, I hope you don't observe dietary laws, Eva," he said. "I should have thought—"

"Don't worry. My family isn't observant. My father is a Socialist. We pay some respect to our origins. The intellectual and ethical traditions. But we never let a good meal be impeded by dietary laws."

Halstead asked her if she wanted a drink. She accepted a glass of red wine. He ordered whiskey.

"I have been told by some of my Jewish friends in the reform movement," Halstead said, "that they view socialism as secular Judaism. An interesting concept. How do you feel?"

"Mr. Hal—"

"Garry."

"I don't concern myself with theories. I am a working woman. I'm interested in improving the conditions under which people work. I don't want them to be afraid and uneducated. Whether it's socialism, or Judaism, or anything else doesn't bother me."

"You are a pragmatist."

"I don't know what that means."

Halstead sipped his whiskey. Eva tasted the wine. Not sweet and thick, like the wine they drank on holidays, but with a warming musty flavor.

"It means you are practical, that you do what is useful and productive."

"I suppose I am that way."

"You are also staggeringly beautiful. You must have a dozen beaus. I noticed the way Brunstein was studying you. I can't blame him. I envy him if he is indeed your lover."

"You are presumptuous, Mr. Halstead."

She had a slight accent, Halstead noted, a bit of ghetto singsong in her voice. And the word "presumptuous" amused him. A laboring girl?

He asked her, as the waiter served grilled lamb chops, potatoes au gratin, and crisp salad, about her family and her education. How did a working girl learn to speak so well?

With humor and verve, Eva told him about her head-in-the-clouds father. The renowned Uncle Sourmilk who swore by the life-prolonging power of *acidophilus*. A self-trained mathematician, he insisted on his sons attending college. Abe, her older brother, was already at CCNY. Sol, the younger, helped their mother in the store, but he, too, would be college educated.

"But you chose to do the meanest work available?" Halstead asked.

"I got involved in the union movement when I was young, and I did not want to desert my girls."

"*Your* girls?" Halstead realized she had a considerable ego.

"Ike says if we win the strike I'll work full-time for the union."

He marveled at her. Halstead, a socialist journalist (he was not fully employed by the *Eagle* but free-lanced for them), a nonpracticing graduate of Yale Law School, heir to the Halstead fortune, had never met a woman like Eva Heilig. His notion of a union official was some drab, unhappy man. She was exquisite and vivacious, an enchanting optimist.

"I'd like to see those galoots get theirs someday," she said. Eva ate with gusto, eager to try Gage & Tollner's blueberry pie on Halstead's recommendation.

"Galoots?"

"It's a word our family doctor uses. Those hoodlums who attacked us. It isn't fair. We know who hired them." She clenched her tiny fist. "Someday there'll be justice. You know something, Garry? Those brutes who beat our girls are Jews also."

"You are an innocent, Eva. There is a history of racketeers preying on their own people."

"On the East Side maybe. Not in Brownsville. We've tried to make it a better place."

He took her hand. "I'm sure you will, Eva."

"Please. We hardly know one another. I don't know what I'm doing here with you."

She changed the subject. Was he a journalist? Then let him write about the strike. The English-language press depicted them as Reds and criminals. Employers and police were never criticized. If he was truly interested in her, let him spend a day on the picket line or inspecting the worst of the factories.

"My education starts today. You may keep me after school any day, Miss Heilig."

"You mustn't be too forward with me. What do we have in common? I speak with an accent. My mother works fourteen hours a day in a candy store."

Outside, Halstead took her arm. The evening was soft and warm. This time she did not pull away. "You ask what we have in common, Eva. We believe in justice. I admire your people. Poor and despised, coming here with nothing more than hope. Am I being sentimental? They work and raise children, and like your brothers—who I am sure I would like—they strive to make a better life for themselves. I am astonished by Hebrews."

"You'll get tired of hanging around the poor. We can drive you crazy. Bickering, battling, bargaining, everyone against everyone else."

"That makes life exciting. Among my people, everyone is proper and in agreement on all matters. That's why my sister and I are considered eccentrics."

"Garry, I don't think so. Your sister is a marvelous woman."

"And her brother?"

She suppressed a teasing smile as she looked up at his sun-reddened face, the gold-rimmed glasses, the long jaw of the aristocratic, the light brown hair parted in the center. "I appreciate your sympathy for us. But you must assume nothing. Let's view each other as a journalist and his source of information."

"That is all I have in mind." He flashed his teeth. "For the time being." Halstead had parked his Oldsmobile a few blocks away. He had paid two boys a dime each to "watch" it.

Eva climbed in, trying to suppress her astonishment at its elegance. In glass vases, set in brass brackets, fresh flowers nested. The seats were covered with soft black leather.

The car created a sensation on Haven Place as Halstead wheeled it slowly toward the Heilig house. The only other car on the block was Dr. Abelman's Dodge. The Olds drew a crowd of admiring, staring children.

Halstead wanted to meet her parents. She told him she preferred that he not come out. Later, perhaps. No, she was not ashamed of her family. He assured her she had no need to be. He had already explained his admiration for Jews.

Eva could see her father sitting on the stoop, reading the *Forward*. Abie was visible in the ground-floor window, his eyes boring into a textbook. Resting against the cast-iron railing in front of the house were two of her battered picket captains, Rachel Goldstein and Angie Marrotta. They looked weary and miserable.

"Two of my front-line soldiers," Eva said. "Thank you for dinner, and for paying the fine, which will be returned. Goodbye."

Halstead wanted to kiss her. Impossible, of course, given the audience. Smudged white faces leered at him. Small Hebrews crowded on his running boards.

"Where can I reach you?" Halstead asked.

"On the picket line. Goodbye, Mr. Halstead."

Rachel and Angie had come to Eva's house to tell her there had been a riot at the union office where the milk and bread were being dispensed. They had run out of milk. Women had gone berserk, tearing apart the office, ripping Ike's coat, screaming that their children were hungry. *Union this! Union that!* They were ready to take anything the bosses offered.

"Where do we get the milk?" Eva asked.

Angie said it came from Greenbaum's dairy. He was selling it to them at a penny below his usual price. Still, Ike had been unable to pay the bills.

"And the bread?" Eva asked. "Karp's bakery?"

"They also ain't been paid," Rachel said. Her drooping dark eyes and melting nose were the essence of defeat.

"We will visit both those gentlemen *now*," Eva said. "They'll *have* to trust us a little longer. If they won't, no union member will buy their products when the strike is over. You two come with me."

Rachel looked at Angie. They got up and limped after Eva.

Chapter 7

Beyond Greenbaum's dairy and Kolodny's bottling plant, eruptions of industry on the bucolic outskirts of Brownsville, there was a meandering brook known as Amsterdam Creek. Some early Dutch settler gave it its name. No more than ten yards wide, it was fed by an underground stream and supplied water to farmers. On Rosh Hashanah, the Jewish New Year, it was the custom of Orthodox Jews to gather at the stream in the afternoon and perform the ceremony of *tashlik*.

A few days after Halstead's meeting with Eva, a half-dozen Orthodox Jews, prayer books under their arms, walked across the humming meadows to observe *tashlik*. Meyer Flugelman (himself a nonobserver) accompanied his ninety-year-old father, a white-bearded, straight-backed ancient, an honored holder of a seat on the eastern wall. In a trembling voice, the old man explained the prayers at the river's bank.

"According to midrashic interpretation of the holy books, when Abraham was on his way to sacrifice Isaac, Satan appeared to him as a river overflowing the sands of the desert."

"So why the prayers?"

"We discard our sins into the waters. On the New Year we ask the stream to take our sins."

Morris Kuflik, the father of the driver Label, agreed. "You're right, Flugelman, but there's more to it than that. There is an injunction in the Bible itself. The prophets tell us to pray by the waters."

Flugelman marveled: a learned old man with ignorant sons.

There were several groups of black-clad Jews standing alongside the stream. Sunlight sparkled on the winding waters, on bright stands of goldenrod. Strange, the way much of Brownsville was "country." No wonder Jews who remembered tiny villages and farms and open fields had been drawn there. Not all Jews were urban dwellers. Meyer Flugelman reflected that he might write an article for the *Forward* on "Early Days in Brownsville."

Old Asher Flugelman halted beside the waters. Yellow daisies and blue-bells bloomed along the banks. The black earth, nourished by Kolodny's horses and Greenbaum's cows, was rich and soft.

He opened his prayer book. "Micah Seven, verse nineteen, children," he said. "And then psalms thirty-three and one hundred and thirty."

On a knoll shaded by poplars and maples, some distance from the praying men, Jake Chain sat with his wife and son. Mutteh waded in the clean stream, picked flowers, and made mud pies. Sarah, now able to maneuver on crutches, was cheerful. They munched hard-boiled-egg sandwiches and watched Mutteh roll down the green hillside.

"Praying," Jake said. "The old men."

"We never pray," Sarah said. "If we could read . . ."

Jake laughed. "Hebrew, I had a few lessons in Glebocki. The teacher beat me with a stick and I ran away. That's all I remember."

"Mutteh will go to *cheder*," Sarah said.

"If we can afford. I suppose he should be a good Jew and go to shul."

He held her hand. She was seated on the grass, her back against a maple trunk. She smiled into the sun. She had combed her hair, tied it with a blue ribbon. She had patched and stitched her coat, polished her shoes.

Jake tried to suppress pity. Feeling sorry did not help. They did not sleep as man and wife. She could not accept his body. He was repelled by her dead limbs. She cried a great deal.

Yet they survived. Jake had a chance to become an assistant foreman at a new plant Kolodny was planning. The hunchback owed Jake a great deal. Moishe Nigger still collected blood money, but he did not raise the weekly tribute.

Jake put an arm around his wife. She drew close. "I am bad for you," she said. "I cannot be a wife any longer."

"It don't matter." He knew it did. His loins were burning. His manhood was starved. How change it? He was a vigorous man. Somehow he would have to be gratified. Whores? Behind the curtained windows of one of the gangsters' "beer halls" where the hoodlums kept *nafkas?* A joke! He could not even afford a visit!

Eva. He craved Eva. No good, no good. The man who married her, who knew her body, would win an unearthly reward. Brunstein was no man for her. Never. For all his revolutionary talk, he was the kind of radical who feared the sight of a cop, shrank from a blow, would not even cross the street against a red light.

Mutteh scrambled up the hillside. Jake realized with shame that he loved the boy more than he loved the broken woman sitting beside him. Mutteh gave his mother a bouquet of wildflowers. "Here, ma. I picked myself."

She kissed his head and held him close. He must, he *must,* she told herself, go to school, go to *cheder,* be a better American, a finer Jew, than they ever were. *It is no good to be poor, but it is the worst to be poor and stupid.*

"Mutteh, when you learn to read and write, you'll maybe teach your mother and father," she said.

"I hate school. I'll run away."

Jake grabbed him and tousled his head. *"Mozzik.* Imp. You'll learn."

Asher Flugelman started reading from his prayer book. The others joined in. ("Every man for himself," Doc Abelman used to joke. "It's not for each other's benefit. It's between them and God.")

Old Flugelman rested on his son's arm and savored the holy words:

He will turn again, he will have compassion upon us; he will subdue our iniquities; and thou wilt cast all their sins into the depths of the sea. . . .

At the edge of the stream, Mutteh watched, wondering why they talked so fast. He didn't understand the religion. But he knew it was a "sin" to tear a page in a Hebrew book and a "sin" to eat certain things or put on a light on Saturday.

Flugelman turned pages with a shivering hand. Others joined the worshipers. Three yeshiva students with curling earlocks and shaved heads appeared. They were shepherded by a frail redheaded teacher.

Rejoice in the Lord, O ye righteous, for praise is comely for the upright; Praise the Lord with harp; sing unto him with the psaltery and an instrument of ten strings. . . .

None of the praying men noticed four rough-looking youths drinking from pint bottles, stumbling along the edge of the brook fifty feet away. The newcomers halted and stared at the Jews.

. . . the eye of the Lord is upon them that fear him; upon them that hope in his mercy. To deliver their soul from death and to keep them alive in famine . . .

The first stone struck the carpenter Levine in the chest.

"Sheenies," one shouted. He was fat and freckled, no more than seventeen.

"Go away," Meyer Flugelman said. "We are praying."

"Pray on my ass, mocky," the young man shouted.

A weedy half-drunk boy of sixteen threw another rock. It struck the red-bearded Hebrew teacher.

Asher Flugelman behaved as if nothing had happened. He had survived cossacks, Lithuanian police, Okhrana agents, and was alive at age ninety. God would protect him on Rosh Hashanah.

Mutteh ran up the hill. He was terrified, his mind full of questions. Why did Jews let themselves be hit with stones?

"Ignore them," Asher Flugelman said. "Psalm one hundred and thirty."

The youths picked up sticks. A third stone sailed into the group and bounced off the curly head of Kalotkin the roofer. Kalotkin was no weakling. He folded his book and took off his coat.

"Papa," Mutteh called. "Those guys, they're picking on the people by the river."

Jake squinted across the meadow. He got to his feet and saw a hail of rocks descend on the Jews.

Out of the depths have I cried unto thee, O Lord. Lord, hear my voice, let thine ears be attentive to the voice of my supplication. . . .

But there is forgiveness with thee, that thou mayest be feared.
I wait for the Lord, my soul doth wait, and in his word do I hope . . .

They attacked Kalotkin first, four of them, shoving and punching the roofer. Kalotkin, dropping his prayer book, his new derby sailing off, landed in the muddy stream with a splash.

"Help, police, help!" screamed the yeshiva teacher. "Boys, run, run!"

The gang began pummeling Levine the carpenter. They ripped the book from his hand and threw it into the field. Then they lifted him up and hurled him into the creek. Water-choked, gasping, Levine and Kalotkin struggled to climb the slippery bank.

Flugelman kept praying. His son tried to drag him away.

My soul waiteth for the Lord more than they that watch for the morning; I say more than they that watch for the morning. . . .

Meyer Flugelman pleaded in terror: "Papa, they'll kill us."

"No, my son. I must finish *tashlik.*"

Let Israel hope in the Lord; for with the Lord there is mercy, and with him is plenteous redemption. . . .

The fat boy had a moonlike face awash with nickel-size freckles. He seemed an apparition as he picked up the teacher and began to pummel him.

"Help!" Meyer Flugelman howled. "Someone!"

Jake Chain was racing down the hill. *I'm dumb and I can't pray,* he thought, *but I can fight.*

Jake leaped down the incline and cocked his fists.

"Please, mister," Asher Flugelman said. He closed his book. Prayers had ended. Sins had been cast into the stream. "Please, mister," he said to Jake, "you shouldn't get them mad."

The attackers were pushing the teacher back and forth, tugging at his earlocks.

"Watcha got under the beard, Moe?"

They shoved him to the ground and kicked him. His students fled.

Blinded with mud, Kalotkin helped Levine out of the creek. Levine staggered away. Kalotkin could fight but he did not like the odds. Then he saw Chain.

"Chain, Chain, help!"

Jake said nothing. He charged for the fat boy who was yanking at Flugelman's beard.

"Ding-dong," the fat boy said. "Ding-dong, you old kike."

Jake grabbed the boy's collar and yanked him off his feet. A trick he had learned working for Mulqueen. When he dropped him, he slammed his left fist against the side of the youth's head, watched his eyes cross, heard the breath *whoosh* from his mouth, drove his right fist into the soft gut, an inch above the groin. The youth collapsed into the muddy bank. Jake kicked him into the stream.

The intruders stared at Jake. Who was he? Where did he come from? No beard. No black hat. No prayer book.

The thin boy brandished his stick. "C'mon, sheeny. Wanna fight?"

Kalotkin, rubbing mud from his eyes, lined up with Jake. "Chain," the roofer said. He peeled off his serge jacket. "I'm with you." Kalotkin raised his fists. He nodded at Jake.

The two sailed into the hoodlums, warding off blows with their arms and fists. One youth circled Jake, got his hands on his throat. Another started to punch at Jake's stomach. Jake reached behind and, with hands like an iron clamp, squeezed the strangler's balls. The boy screamed and let go. Jake grabbed the other, punched him twice on the nose, dropped him with a short blow of his palm against his gut.

Kalotkin pinned another youth and began to lecture him. "We are praying, understand? This is a holy place. What right do you have to do this? We don't do bad things to your church."

Stick to roofing, Jake thought.

"Let him up," Jake said. "They want to fight some more, I'll fight. Who is next? You? You?" Boxer-style, he held his fists up the way he had learned in the gym when he was sixteen. "Anyone?" Jake asked.

"Jewboy."

Sarah had struggled to her feet, picked up her crutches, and was limping down the hill. She screamed at Jake to stop.

Jake called to his awestruck son: "Mutteh, go to mama. Stop her. I'm all right."

Kalotkin got to his feet. He let his victim lie in the mud. "Enough?" the roofer asked, standing over the boy.

"Sheenies!"

Jake lifted the boy from the ground and held him over his head. The youth wriggled and spit curses.

"You won't pick on old people," Jake said. "You want to fight, fight me. You want to go in the river again, boy?"

Jake dropped him, yanked him close with one hand, and shook him a few times. Then he punched him in the throat. The boy doubled over and howled.

"Awright, Chain," Kalotkin said. "They learned a lesson."

Taking advantage of the fight—shades of Old Testament warriors, Meyer Flugelman thought—the worshipers halted at the path alongside the dairy. Flugelman watched in awe. Socialist, altruist, he was learning something. This Chain. This stupid man with no fear. None. Fists like cast iron. Was there a lesson? Something not in Marx or the Talmud?

The more Meyer Flugelman thought of it, the more the idea appealed to him. At a strategy meeting at the union office, he waited his chance to bring it up.

Eva, Ike, and the picket captains—Rachel Goldstein and the Marrotta sisters—were discussing the current situation. There had been two more attacks on picket lines. Moishe Nigger and his gang were so brazen that they now brought their girlfriends along.

"These dirty women, these *hoo-ers*," Rachel said. "They come in a taxi. They lean out the window and they cheer when those bums hit the girls."

Angelina looked at the floor. She remembered the whores laughing as she fell. Screaming as he twisted her ears and slammed a hand against her nose and made her weep. Women with piles of curls, red rouge, lipstick. One of them stuck a black-stockinged leg out the taxi door, pulled up her skirt, and showed a ruffled red garter to the pickets.

"We cannot," Ike said, with a glance at Eva, "count on socialites like Mr. Halstead raising bail or paying fines forever, Eva."

"Ike, stay on the subject," Eva said wearily.

He'd been furious when she told him that Halstead had taken her to dinner at Gage & Tollner's. A traitor to the cause and her class! Halstead was slumming. Looking for a story for the *Eagle*. He would use her, Ike said. His class always did.

Meyer Flugelman made a circle around the office, listening to the interminable arguments.

"Flugelman, stop the parade," Brunstein cried. "You want to help, sit down."

Meyer raised a hand. "There is a solution, if we have the courage."

They looked at him. To this point, he had been their resident philosopher.

Flugelman said that Jacob Chain might be a help. Did they know the big man?

"He is my *landsman*," Eva said.

"A *grub ying*—a stupid man," Ike said.

"I saw this fellow Chain destroy four bums who were tormenting Jews."

"So?" Brunstein asked.

"Why are we always meek? Why do we turn the cheek?" Flugelman asked. "I am talking about the time when I watched my aged father pelted with rocks. They pulled his beard. They threw Jews into the water on the observance of *tashlik*. But this ignoramus they call Crazy Jake came down like Joshua ben Nun—"

"Please, Flugelman," Ike interrupted. "Now, in the matter of benefits, I propose we—"

Eva got to her feet. "Meyer is right. Our own protection. Men who aren't afraid of Moishe Nigger."

Brunstein frowned. "Hmm. It's a bit irregular—"

"Brunstein!" Flugelman shouted, recalling his youthful days in the Beth Midrash. "Brunstein! Was Joshua irregular? The Maccabees? Simon Bar Kochba? Brunstein, Chain is a warrior!"

The union stalwarts were silent a moment; Flugelman had convinced them.

Chapter 8

Mutteh was sitting on the stoop of the Feigenbaum house doing his "hone-work." He had a ruled notebook on his lap. His teacher, Miss O'Neill, had neatly written his name and grade on the cover: MORTIMER CHAIN 1A3. In a neat hand, Mutteh was writing capital and lower-case letters. He did nine sets to a page, three-by-threes, licking his stub of a pencil, admiring his penmanship.

Eva kissed his head. "You like school, Mutteh?" she asked.

"Yeah. The kids pick on me 'cause I'm little. But I knocked two guys out yesterday."

Bernie Feigenbaum discharged a mouth fart from the window. But he was wary of the squirt. He had lost his last two fights with the newly christened Mortimer Chain.

"Papa's home?" Eva asked. She wanted to speak to Jake alone. Sarah would never permit him to take the job Eva intended to offer. Besides, the crippled woman made Eva nervous. Sarah had become a whiner, a woman drowning in ignorance.

"He went to the ice dock. They had a job for him."

Jake was picking up odd jobs. Working nights.

She thanked the boy, complimented him on his neat slanting *C*'s, and left.

Eva found Jake hauling blocks of ice from a wagon to the murky interior of the icehouse. He was barechested and bareheaded. An old burlap sack covered his back to keep the slabs of blue-white ice from bruising his skin. He carried the tongs as if they were tweezers.

She watched him a moment. *What strength!* A Negro on the truck slid the four-foot blocks toward Jake. Jake caught them with the tongs, spun them, set them against the tensed muscles on his back, and walked into the cold darkness.

Was she doing the right thing asking him to endanger himself? The union had been wary of doing what some of the East Side unions had done. They had fought fire with fire. She had read the names in the papers. Big Jack Zelig, Pinchy Paul, Joe the Greaser, Dopey Benny Fine. Horrid men.

Jake hauled the last of the ice from the truck and waved at the black man. He noticed Eva standing at the entrance to the icehouse. Ashamed of his nude chest, he put on a stained blue shirt. He tugged a frayed cap over his mop of yellow hair and approached her.

"You came to watch me haul ice?"

"You do it like an expert."

"Icehouse Sammy pays me a dollar two nights a week. It helps with Mutteh in school." He sounded proud of his son.

"I went to the house. He was doing homework. You should encourage him."

"We try. I'm ashamed Sarah has to work also. Tears all the time."

They walked down the darkening street. Peddlers, finishing a fifteen-hour day of hawking wares, pushed rickety carts. An old man wheeled a homemade cart with an oven inside. He was selling *haisa arbas*—hot chick-peas. Eva bought a bag for each of them.

"You shouldn't spend money on me," Jake said. "You haven't worked in six weeks. I heard the judge wanted to send you to prison."

"But I'm free. Jake, would you have rescued me from jail?"

"By myself." He knocked a fist against one palm.

They sat in a playground. It was deserted except for a drunk sleeping on a bench. Eva could remember as a child learning folk dancing and games with hoops and a basketball from Dr. Abelman when he was a medical student. Summers, Abelman had been the playground instructor.

She told him what the union had in mind—men to protect the pickets. They would be paid. They would see to it that the hoodlums would not terrorize the girls again.

Jake grinned. "You want me to be a *shtarker*."

"I hate that word. It sounds like a bad person."

"It's a bad business. But that's what you want. A *shtarker*, a strong one. Not like your friends who drink tea and talk about a revolution."

"All right, a *shtarker*."

"How do I live? What about my job?"

"What does Kolodny pay you?"

Jake was amused. A new side to his beloved cousin! She was always a goddess to him, lovely, bright, courageous. Now it seemed she had a head for business.

"Eleven dollars a week. I work inside now—load, stack, shlep. No more with the horse and wagon. Kolodny's cheating me. He fired an inside man and I do the work for two."

"The union will pay you fifteen dollars a week."

"What happens when the strike is over? When there's no more girls to protect?"

"We'll find work for you. I will insist that you learn to read and write."

"It's too late. I'm stupid."

"No!" She punched his shoulder. It was like hitting the poplar tree in front of Abelman's house. "If you're ashamed to go to night school, I'll get Abe to teach you. I don't want you hauling crates of soda forever. You've had a terrible life. I know how your father threw you away. No family. You ran away from the Hebrew Orphan Asylum and slept in back of Reds Mulqueen's bar. Hauling beer barrels when you were twelve."

"I learned to fight."

"But that can't be your whole life, Jake."

"How do I start?"

"I'll talk to the union."

Jake looked at her eyes. Clear green, with pinpoints of pale light. "I'll need other men," Jake said.

"Find them. We'll make you the subcontractor." Eva laughed. "Jake, you'll be a businessman."

He shook his head. He wanted to embrace her, inhale her sweet-soapy odor, crush her yellow hair with kisses. Never. It would never happen. He was a *bulvan,* a hardfisted tramp.

"What are you staring at, Jake?"

"You're so beautiful. I always—always—"

"No, no, that isn't what we're talking about. Beauty is nothing. An accident. It's what you *do,* how you *live,* that's important."

"Not when your wife isn't a wife anymore. And you are not a man."

"I'm sorry, Jake. Maybe we can get help for Sarah."

"Abelman says this is the best she can be." He got up, stretching.

He held Eva's elbow with a gentle touch as they crossed Sterling Place, and he was tempted to put an arm around her. He could not. If he touched her, he would want more. He knew himself. The streak of violence, the strength hidden by the solid exterior. Never, never. His love for her was like a high fever, making him dizzy, weak.

Garrison Halstead knocked at his sister's door and entered at the sound of her low voice.

Mildred was wearing a blue smock. She held a jar of poster paint in one hand and a brush in the other. Against her bed were four white cardboard rectangles. Halstead smiled as he read them.

NEW YORK WOMEN'S LEAGUE
SUPPORTS AND ENDORSES
THIS STRIKE

FELLOW WORKERS! DO NOT
CROSS THE LINE! IT IS YOUR
FIGHT AS WELL AS OURS!

He stroked his chin. *"Your* fight, Mildred? You and your friends haven't been treading the pavements for a ten-dollar week. I haven't heard of any of your Mount Holyoke friends being charged twenty-five cents for a locker or docked a week's pay for a broken machine."

"You're only mildly amusing, Garrison."

"You really intend to march on the picket line with the strikers?"

"I have organized a committee to support them."

She checked a notebook for names. Halstead was astonished. A Belmont, a Morgan, a Vanderbilt, other daughters of the ruling families. There were Quakers, Unitarians, and a defector from a rich Catholic family.

"You may get beaten and jailed for your efforts."

Mildred applied a final dab to a poster.

ORGANIZE! JOIN! WE ASK
ONLY A LIVING WAGE AND
HUMANE CONDITIONS!

"Why not? It will teach us about life. I would prefer, Garrison, that you not tell our parents of this enterprise. If you keep my secret, I'll keep yours."

"What's mine?"

"Your newest romantic interest. The Heilig girl."

"What makes you think I give a tinker's damn if they know? I suspect father is sympathetic to the strike. Mother will never budge from her conviction that they are in rebellion against God."

Mildred sat on the edge of the bed. She inspected a new pair of brown Coward's arch-supporting shoes. She would wear them when she and her friends joined the girls on the picket line. A grand joke there! Special uniforms for special pickets. She'd advised Dorothy Van Horn and Peggy DeWitt to do the same—flat heels, loose clothing, and a wide-brimmed hat in case of rain.

Garrison sat at her desk. In the light of the Tiffany lamp, he glanced at the *World.* "The free press is marvelous," he said. "It's always the strikers who start the violence. Never a word about the thugs who intimidate them. I may write a letter to the *Times* when I finish my piece for the *Eagle.*"

Mildred cocked her head. "If I know you, Garrison, neither will be finished. Your career as a free-lance journalist, now that you've decided law bores you, will be impeded by your bent for procrastination and moodiness."

"I listen to a different drummer."

Mildred had to agree. At Yale he had refused to join a club, failed to attend his graduation, angering his father and causing his mother to break into tears. Garrison had decided it was a farce. He had always been an outsider at Yale. Snob, intellectual, radical, contemptuous of athletes and aesthetes. What had saved him from *their* contempt was his wealth and his success as a Lothario. Riches had its own aura. The bearer of riches was permitted eccentricities, departures from the norm.

The lesson had not been lost on young Halstead or on his older sister. She had graduated from Mount Holyoke, worked at Bellevue, gotten her accreditation as a registered nurse, and gone to work for the city. He, leaving a Wall Street law firm, was determined to be a crusading journalist, to work with reformers, challenge the Tammany Tiger, cleanse the city of corruption.

"Tell me about Eva Heilig," Mildred said. "She's extremely pretty."

"A fascinating girl. In a torn shirtwaist and a soiled skirt, she was the most elegant person in the restaurant. She may have a Yiddish accent, but she has natural grace and dignity."

"And courage."

"Yes, that too."

"And how much of your interest in her is political and how much is personal?"

"I can't quantify my feelings."

Halstead lit a cigar, blew smoke toward the lofty ceiling. It was decorated with gold ormolu curlicues. They dined on Rosenthal china, ate with vermeil knives and forks. These hallmarks of great wealth reflected their mother's attitudes: Wealth demanded a certain seemly display within the confines of one's home. Their father was a different breed. He rode the elevated train to Wall Street, shined his own shoes, and owned three suits. Brooks Brothers affairs, durable and plain. He was a Quaker, a descendant of the Greenes of Rhode Island, and could trace a shadowy line to General Nathanael Greene.

"I can't dissemble with you, Mildred," Garrison said. "The woman fascinates me. She's without much more than a high-school education, but her native intelligence is high. She takes night courses at the Labor Lyceum. A Socialist, a pacifist, deeply involved in the union movement. And no despair in her, no solemnity."

"And she is beautiful."

"Quite beautiful. Don't misunderstand me. You know I am without prejudice. But she is not your typical heavy-featured Jewess. There's something Slavic or northern in her face. They tell me that, over the centuries, Jews frequently intermarried with Poles and Russians."

Halstead lifted one of Mildred's picket signs. "How do I look, Mildred? Do you think my Deborah of the streets will think better of me if I join?"

Mildred took the sign away. "It's a woman's job, Garrison. Don't get too intimate with the girl. Don't hurt her. You haven't hesitated in the past."

Halstead flicked ashes into a cloisonné tray, waved at the air to dissipate the smoke. Mildred was tolerant. Their mother forbade smoking downstairs. "She appears to me the kind who knows how to take care of herself," he said. "Neither police, nor hoodlums, nor crooked politicians seem to have gotten the best of her. Why should she fear a Yale man?"

Mildred shook her head. Garrison had long had the reputation of a rake. He had bedded down, Mildred knew, with chambermaids, nurses, and waitresses. "Why indeed, Garrison?"

"I'd like to be on hand when you and your sisters of the elite take your place on the picket line with Eva Heilig's Jewesses and Italians."

"Are you mocking us?"

"By no means. But no fair showing up just to get your names in the paper. You'll be expected to put in a full day of marching, chanting, and, if necessary, getting clubbed and bloodied."

"We are quite ready for that."

Garrison, before leaving for his evening chess game with his father, shook his finger at her. "Mildred, bear in mind that we are of the unarrestable class."

"There is no such word."

"There is such a word. I looked it up in Webster's. There is not only such a word, there is also such a condition of life, and we are exemplars of it."

Chapter 9

Kolodny was sorry to lose Jake. He told him he'd never get the job back. Business was lousy. He'd make do with a nigger. So what was Chain going to do? Who would hire such an ox? J. P. Morgan?

Jake shrugged. He knew enough to keep his mouth shut. Some new work, was all he said. By the way, he asked Kolodny, what had happened to Kuflik, the fat man with the potato nose?

Jake found Label Kuflik at the "Pig Market," the corner of Pitkin Avenue and Strauss Street where unemployed laborers gathered to pick up odd jobs as draymen or pick-and-shovel workers.

Kuflik's nose had gotten bigger and more misshapen since his unemployment. Jake seemed to see two Kufliks—the nose, and what was behind it, a burly man in a ragged jacket. With Kuflik was a man almost a head taller. He had a mashed, furrowed face. A kind of animal dumbness was etched in the low brow, the squashed nose.

"My cousin," Kuflik said. "Yussel Kuflik. I got to look after him. He ain't smart."

Look who's talking, Jake thought. "So? You got work?" Jake asked.

"A little here and there," Label said.

The giant Yussel nodded. "Yeah. Here and there."

"You want a job?" Eva had not specified how many men to hire. But he knew enough about street brawling. Five men should be sufficient.

"Chain, you're a boss now?"

The giant Yussel laughed, exposing a mouth of rotting teeth.

Jake explained in words that the Kufliks understood. They were to be *shtarkers*. They were to protect the girls on the picket lines. They would have to *klop* and get *klopped*.

"No thanks," Label said. "You see this nose? Who could resist hitting such a nose? How much it pays?"

"Fifteen a week, Kuflik. The same for this gorilla."

"Thanks, I accept," Kuflik said. "Him also. I know a little from this. We'll need lead pipes, bicycle chains, knives, and one pistol. Chain, you're the big shot. You can carry the pistol."

Jake shook his head. "Not until we need it."

Two more men.

He thought at once of the Ferrantes. Ever since he was a kid he had gotten along with Italians. With Irishers, the first words out of their mouths were always *sheeny, kike, hebe, mocky.* An Italian might call you that sometimes, but really didn't care one way or the other. Also, you never saw an Italian drunk in the gutter. And they kept secrets.

The Ferrantes seemed the logical place to start recruiting. Salvatore was only fifteen, but Luigi, he knew, was out of a job. He'd also met the eldest of the seven brothers, Frankie. He might be willing to join the "guardians," as Eva called them. With two Ferrantes and two Kufliks, he would have a good gang of *shtarkers.*

He found the Ferrante boys pitching pennies against the side of the tenement in which they lived on Pacific Street. The block was a Neapolitan enclave in Jewish Brownsville. Jewish boys and girls were warned to avoid the street; the *tolyinns* would pounce on them and steal their money. Jake had never had any trouble with them. Maybe because of his size.

"Eh, Crazy Jake," Luigi said. *"Come va?"*

Frankie, cross-eyed, pudgy, with oily black hair parted in the middle, looked suspiciously at Jake. "Whaddya want, seltzer man?"

"To talk."

Sal rested against the side of his hokey-pokey cart. He was sampling his own wares—a cup of shaved ice dripping with purple syrup. A drunken black stumbled by and bought a bottle of deadly green syrup. Makes his own at home, Jake figured. Salvatore screwed him on the change, Jake was certain.

"You talk, Chain?" Luigi asked. "Come on."

Theresa leaned on the windowsill. She was pretty—long-nosed, wide-eyed, with a cap of black curls. She had pouting crimson lips, broad cheeks splotched with blushes of red on the muddy skin. Next to her was a younger sister, Iolande. She was even prettier. Like an actress, Jake thought.

"Mistah Chain, wanna see my feet?" Theresa laughed.

"Feet?"

"Yeah. From walkin' the picket lines. Look."

Theresa lifted a long slender leg, displayed her right foot wrapped in a bloody bandage.

"Eh, put ya leg down," Frankie ordered. "You ain't no tramp." He squinted at Jake. "We don' want her to picket no more. She got sores on her feet."

Old man Ferrante, the patriarch, puffing a pipe he had bought to celebrate Garibaldi's entrance into Rome in 1870, said nothing. He was a sedate barber, who spent evenings in a cane-back chair on the sidewalk. Handlebar moustache, pompadour in the manner of King Umberto, a red-white-and-green medal on his breast pocket. His wife rarely appeared in the street. Bundled in black layers, she mourned lost children, a dead sister, a departed aunt.

"Come across the street, ya wanna talk," Luigi said. He preferred conspiracy, even though the only ones within hearing distance were his relatives. Frankie, belly overhanging his belt, joined them.

They sat on a bench in front of the Santa Lucia Mutual Association, a store with dusty green curtains in the window. Inside, old men played cards, smoked guinea-stinkers, drank red wine.

"I hear you guys ain't working," Jake said.

"I been laid off," Luigi said. He was chunky and resembled Frankie but was more muscular. It was rumored he had once choked a man to death in the Pig Market. The man, a drunken laborer, had made the fatal error of lifting Theresa's skirt.

Sal left the cart and joined them. He leaned against a lamppost, lithe, darker than his brothers. His goatlike face absorbed everything.

"I got work," Jake said.

From the Santa Lucia Mutual Association came the soupy sounds of a clarinet, the strumming of a mandolin. A few more Ferrantes, Vince and Baggie (Biagio), warming up. The brothers worked part-time as musicians.

"What kinda work?" Luigi asked.

"A buck more a week than you get pouring concrete or bricklaying."

K & R Robes, the Baum brothers' new factory, was chosen as a testing ground. Next to Finemaster's Fine Bathrobes, theirs was the biggest "inside" place. The Baums were in trouble. But they hung on grimly.

In a savage late October rain—it had turned cold and windy, and the poplars on Haven Place were denuding—Eva sent her pickets out early to prevent the entry of scabs. She had gotten a tip from a girl who remained "inside" and tolerated Heshy's pinches and kisses.

This morning, the girl said, Baum was bringing in a truckload of goods —bolts of flannel, cotton, and velvet. "The Nigger," Heshy said to Eva's spy. "The Nigger's gonna get it through the gate." Already the pickets had forced one truck to turn back.

On the picket line that morning, marching fore and aft of Theresa, were her brothers, Luigi and Frank Ferrante. Each had hidden a lead pipe in his belt.

Across the street, Sal lolled against his cart. He had a vat of hot water. A wood fire kept it boiling. In it floated ears of husked yellow corn. "Hotcorn," a penny apiece.

Jake and the Kufliks—Label and Yussel—waited in a rain-flooded doorway near the "hotcorn" cart. Sal complained that business was lousy. The rain kept putting out the charcoal fire.

Jake yanked his torn jacket around his neck. Maybe nothing would happen.

"*Nu?*" Label asked. "This is a way to spend a morning?"

Jake peered through the slanting rain. Gray street, gray factory. An old warehouse that the Baums had converted. They were two tough cookies. They were also running a secret factory in Jamaica, hidden in the meadows around the bay.

Jake could see Eva handing out raincoats to her girls. One girl began to cough. Eva led her to the shelter of a doorway. They often came to the picket lines with only a cup of tea sloshing in empty stomachs.

A Ford police van puttered by slowly. Maybe Baum was paying the police to escort the truck. It would mean that the gang probably would not show up. Jake understood the rules. He and his mob would not dare confront cops. Moishe Nigger's gang was a different matter.

The van slowed down. A cop jumped out, walked over to Eva, and asked to see her permit. Eva showed it to him. The cop nodded and climbed back into the van.

Another officer got out. He helped himself to four ears of corn from Sal Ferrante's boiling vat. He did not pay, laughed as he climbed back into the paddy wagon. Jake and the Kufliks retreated down the hallway, out of sight.

"Eh, ya lousy *polizia,*" Sal said to the rain.

"Here it comes!" Rachel Goldstein shouted. "Here it comes! Girls, form a line!"

The police van vanished and a truck rolled into view.

Jake understood. The cops were leaving the field to Moishe Nigger.

"A line, a *line!*" Eva cried.

The girls locked arms in front of the factory gates. Already the scabs had been spirited in—side doors, back doors. The pickets formed a ragged line. In the center stood a rain-soaked Theresa Ferrante. On either side of her were her brothers, Luigi and Frankie. The girls threw their signs down, locked arms and yelled at the driver to turn around.

Instead he inched the truck forward.

"Now?" Label asked Jake.

"Not yet. He hits anyone, we drag him outta the cab." Jake squinted through the pelting rain. He recognized the man at the wheel. It was the boxer, Duffy Plotkin.

"Get ready," Jake said.

"Don't move, don't move!" the girls chanted.

"No goods for the bosses!"

"Turn around!"

Plotkin inched the truck forward. Heshy came running from the front door. He stopped in the flooded courtyard and waved at Duffy to move ahead. A few scabbing men stood behind Heshy.

"Girls!" Eva shouted. "Comrades! Do as I do!"

Jake and the Kufliks watched in amazement. Eva had hiked up her skirt, yanked her hat down over her mass of hair, and had fallen onto the soaked pavement. She stretched her body in front of the truck, daring Plotkin to drive over her.

"Join me!" she screamed. "Join me!"

Rachel Goldstein and Esther Levy imitated her. They fell down, oblivious to rain and cold puddles, and lay alongside Eva. Theresa and Angie followed. Soon there was a row of drenched, shouting women in the courtyard.

"Bestids! Hoo-ers! *Nafkas!*" Kalman Baum was shoving Heshy forward. "Get rid of them! They got no right! They are taking bread from my children's mouths! Otzenberger, what do we pay your father for?"

"I can't," Heshy mumbled. His voice drowned in the downpour. "Too many . . . Plotkin . . . do something. . . ."

The boxer leaped out of the cab. But instead of attempting to drag the women away (he was deterred by the sight of the Ferrante brothers standing over the girls), he ran to the rear of the truck and undid a chain. The tailgate fell with an echoing clang.

Moishe Nigger jumped out of the rear. The Saratoga Avenue Meal Ticket, Bunchik, and Little Mendel followed. Each carried an ax handle.

"One side, one side, hoo-ers," Moishe Nigger growled. "Plotkin, ya shoulda runned them over."

A half-dozen screaming girls fled through the open gates. They yelled for police. There was not a cop within three blocks of the Baum factory.

The hoodlums began flailing at pickets, striking at legs, backs, breasts, and heads. The women shrieked, covered their drenched bodies.

"The ones in front!" Moishe Nigger yelled. "Beat the hell outta the ones trying to stop the truck. Get the blonde!"

Methodically the Meal Ticket and Mendel began to thwack the legs of the prostrate girls. Howls reverberated across the street, where Jake's crew awaited his signal. They could see Theresa being yanked to her feet. Plotkin punched her in the stomach twice. Luigi and Frank went for him.

Jake said, "I want the fat guy. Let's go."

Label Kuflik pulled the lead pipe from his belt. "What if they got guns?"

"We'll find out," Jake said.

A great calm had come over Jake Chain. Hitting and getting hit. It had been his life. It gave him a sense of relief. Bloodied lips and loose teeth and cut ears did not please him. But he had learned to accept them as part of his existence. There was always an exhilarating feeling of release. The satisfying thrill when you hit back.

Jake said, "I got the fat guy. Label, grab the prizefighter. Yussel, go for Moishe Nigger. Luigi and Frankie got the little guys."

Jake's gang raced across the flooded cobblestones.

The Meal Ticket was tearing at Eva's skirt, trying to yank it off. Her white petticoats were soaked and soiled. She kicked, struggled to rise, slammed at him with her picket sign. He kicked her ribs. "Hoo-er," the Meal Ticket said. Jake could see the agony on her wet face. But no tears.

Yellow shoes, Jake thought. Fancy as a pimp. What Doc Abelman would call a cake-eater. Chain rushed at the Meal Ticket with his long arms apart. He grabbed the velvet lapels with his left hand, slammed the lead pipe across the fat man's face with the other. Eyes, cheek, mouth slid softly to one side. The Meal Ticket had half a face. Blood spurted from the lips and the button nose. The Saratoga Avenue sport sat down in the wet. Like a buddha, he squatted in the rain, holding a hand to his mashed face, shaking his head. He was finished.

Luigi wrestled Mendel for his ax handle, twisted it out of his hands, cracked him across the chest with it. "Lay offa my sister," Luigi said.

Mendel yanked a knife from his belt and bent low. He had a reputation as a knife fighter. It was rumored he had cut off the tip of a prostitute's nose and made her chew it.

"Sfaccim'," Luigi said. With this tribute, Luigi, hard as the cement he poured, cracked the pipe against Mendel's knees. Mendel crumpled and joined the Meal Ticket.

Frankie tackled Bunchik. The latter and Duffy Plotkin were racing for the cab of the truck. The motor was running. The girls were on their feet. Some ran. Some clawed and scratched at their attackers, swarming around the Meal Ticket and Mendel.

Yussel lifted Moishe Nigger off the ground, threw him into the rear of the truck, slammed the tailgate, and hooked the sides. The Nigger knew when he was in a losing fight.

"Chain, you bastard," Moishe Nigger roared. "For this you'll die."

Frankie dragged Bunchik from the truck door and hit him in the teeth. He ran faster than any of the girls. Box-toed shoes and lollipop-stick shanks splashed through the street. He vanished. Memories of the way Crazy Jake had slammed a shovel against his head haunted him. And the big Polack was looking to kill someone.

The Kufliks tried to drag Duffy Plotkin from the cab. He was a tough nut—hard, fast, quick with his fists. He came out of the other side of the cab, with a wrench in his fist. Once he feinted, then he smashed it against Label's enormous nose. The nose turned purple and a waterfall of blood poured out. Tears clouded Label's eyes. Plotkin hit him across an ear. Label fell.

Plotkin feinted again with his left. With the wrench in his right hand, he cracked it against Yussel Kuflik's right wrist. A bone snapped. Yussel bent double. "Get him, get the bum!" he cried to Jake. Jake had just kicked the Meal Ticket in his mountainous ass as he tried to rise.

Kalman Baum was shrieking into a telephone for police. He shoved Heshy and his brother Reuven out of side doors. "Get the cops! Get them!"

Moishe Nigger crouched in back of the van, shouting to Duffy to drive off. Plotkin stood his ground, wielding the wrench, sneakered feet dancing on the paving stones.

Jake circled him. Girls fled. Eva pulled others away.

"Jake, Jake!" Eva shouted. "Tell him to go!"

"You heard her," Jake said. "Get in the truck and beat it."

"C'mon, ya bum," Duffy said. He had no nose. Forehead, nose, chin were in a perpendicular line. His brains were mashed, people said. Too many losing fights, too many blows to the head.

He swung at Jake with the wrench, ducked Jake's arms, swung again, caught Jake on the upper left forearm. The pain was like an electric shock, zigzagging up the muscle into shoulder and neck.

Jake got a right hand on the boxer's left elbow, tried to spin him, ducked again, caught the iron wrench on his right shoulder.

The Meal Ticket stumbled to his feet and tried to tackle Jake. Yussel clubbed the fat man with his pipe. The Meal Ticket collapsed again.

"Ya wanna fight, *fight*," Plotkin taunted. "Ya a boxer, Chain? Ya got a jab?"

Brains muddled, eyes crossed, Duffy hit Jake three more times with the wrench, twice on the arm, once on the hand.

Moishe Nigger crawled through the rear of the van, shoving aside the bolts of cloth. He wriggled into the cab.

"I'll kill ya, Polack," Duffy snorted.

Jake grabbed the right wrist. Plotkin struggled free and cracked the wrench again. Jake's arms were a mass of welts and bruises. *Next time I grab, he won't have time to hit,* Jake thought.

Moishe Nigger was pointing a black .38 out the window of the van. The hoodlums had never fired a shot in their assaults on pickets. It was an unspoken edict from employers. No shooting. No guns. Who needed guns against a bunch of girls?

"Jake!" Luigi shouted. "Watch out! The gun!"

Eva, shepherding girls across the street, also saw the gun. "In the truck, Jake!" she screamed.

The Nigger squeezed off a shot. It flew past Jake's tattered cap, richocheted off the side of the Baum factory, and fell harmlessly.

The King of the Horse Poisoners again aimed the stubby pistol. This time it jammed. He shook it as Jake and the boxer wrestled, cursed, grunted, and fell to the wet stones. Jake had torn the wrench from his hands.

Sal Ferrante knew about guns. They had four of them in the house. Italian Army relics.

Sal shoved his pushcart of "hotcorn" with its red-green-white umbrella across the street. He rammed it against the flank of the truck, opposite the bloody wrestling match between Duffy and Jake. Their bodies rolled in the water, thrashing, legs and arms locked. Duffy was trying to gouge Jake's eyes out.

Distantly a police siren wailed.

"We gotta beat it!" Luigi shouted to Jake. "Cops. Baum'll get us arrested. Me and Frankie are going. Let the stiff go."

Moishe Nigger unfouled his gun. Once more he leveled it at Jake. Plotkin had belted Jake on the cheek and opened a red gash. Chain tried to throttle the boxer, but Plotkin wriggled like a live carp in a fish tank.

The Nigger aimed the gun.

"The hot water," Sal said to his brothers.

Luigi understood. He and Sal lifted the vat of boiling water from the charcoal burner. The two of them counted to three, then leaped to the running board. As Moishe Nigger found his target and was ready to squeeze a shot, they hurled the scalding water at him. He screamed and dropped the gun. The derby protected his bushy head, but the hot water, richly scented with sweet corn, boiled his sallow face, his ears, his nose, his nigger-lips.

"*Oi, oi, murder, murder!*" he screamed. "Help! *Help!*"

The sirens were louder.

At the iron-barred window of his office, Baum was screaming for police.

Hearing Moishe's shrieks, Duffy turned. Jake hit him across the neck. Plotkin's head wobbled. He fell against the door of the cab and slid to the ground.

"*Basta,* Jake," Luigi said. "Let's go."

Jake looked at Eva and her girls. "You go also," he said. "Tell the girls to run."

Horrified by the bloody battle, the girls retrieved signs, gathered up hats and purses, and hurried away. The rain came down in drowning sheets. They could hear Moishe Nigger howling inside the truck.

Jake, Luigi, and Frankie raced down a side street. Sal did not run. All innocence, he hefted the kettle to the stove, picked up a few ears of corn, tossed them in, and pushed off. Every penny counted.

"*Hotcorn! Hotcorn!*"

Chapter 10

"It's wrong, it's wrong, it can only get us in trouble," Brunstein moaned. "Eva, don't you see where this will lead?"

"To victory. For once those scoundrels *ran*. For once we showed the bosses we wouldn't take their punishment."

It was a few days later. They were seated in the office of the attorney, Leo Glauberman, the toothy man with the spectacles and roached hair. Glauberman was a Socialist, but of his own design. He believed; he didn't believe.

The office was shabbily furnished and was located in a second story on the corner of Pitkin and Rockaway avenues. Below were the boarded-up ruins of the Jenkins Trust Company that had failed in 1907. Glauberman knew about bank failures. He had invested in three financial ventures and seen his money evaporate three times—Jenkins Bank, Union Bank, Allied Bank. A realist, he decided that union work was more stable. He listened with interest to the account of the battle royal.

"We are using armed hoodlums," Ike said. "We are no better than *they* are."

"Ike has a point," the lawyer said. "The fighting can't go on forever. But it's a warning to the bosses. You'll note, not a word in the newspapers. Baum and his friends were afraid to report it."

Glauberman's secretary went to the door in response to a buzzer. She opened it. Jake Chain walked in. He had his torn cap in his hand. The left side of his face was a swollen purple-crimson lump. He held his right arm close to his side, winced when he moved it.

"Our conquering hero," Brunstein said sarcastically.

Eva got up. The men remained seated, wary. Jake Chain was not their kind of Jew.

"Jake! Did you see Dr. Abelman? Are you better?"

"No doctor. It's just a few bruises."

Meeting Eva in front of these educated men reminded him of his low-liness.

"Jake, you know Ike, don't you? And this is Mr. Glauberman, our lawyer."

"Nice job, Chain," Glauberman said. "You were Hairbreadth Harry to the rescue. Got the girls off the railroad track before the train hit them."

Ike got up. "The less I know about this whole affair the better. God forbid it should get into the newspapers."

Jake sat uneasily on the edge of a chair, cap in his hands. He found himself staring at Eva. She winked at him, as if to say: *We won.*

"Wait till next time," Ike said as he walked to the door. "The papers were against us before this—this—development. When is there a good word written about us? That's all we need, hiring gangsters."

"Mr. Brunstein," Jake said gently, "I ain't a gangster."

"Hmmm? I guess not. Coming, Eva?"

Eva walked to the door. "A good job, Jake. It was fun seeing *them* catch it for a change. Mr. Glauberman wants to talk to you."

Jake stood up and nodded. Reds Mulqueen had taught him to stand up when a lady entered or left the room. But make sure she's a lady and not a hoo-er, Reds said. Eva was surely a lady.

When they had gone, Glauberman offered Jake a cigar, lit it, and took a bottle of Old Overholt from his rolltop desk. Glauberman said they should drink to further successes.

"You mean they want I should do this again?"

"That was the understanding."

His body ached from the blows from fists, from Plotkin's wrench. His right arm felt as if it would never be able to move properly. He had to grit his teeth as he crossed his legs.

"They gave you pretty good, Chain?"

"I gave them better."

Glauberman was appraising the big man the way a housewife studies a side of kosher beef. This was better than kosher, the glinting spectacles observed. This big bum was *glatt kosher,* a superior grade-A item. There was cash value in this hulking brute.

"Chain, listen to me. I am a lawyer and I understand the human mind. You follow me? Never mind, don't answer. You've spent most of your life smelling horse farts. There are opportunities for a man like you. I know about you from Mulqueen. There isn't anything you're afraid of. Any man who could take on the Nigger's gang is a man for me."

"For you or for the girls on strike?"

"You're not so dumb, Chain. Why did they call you Crazy Jake when you were a kid?"

Jake found the whiskey warming his insides, soothing his bloody bruises. The cigar smoke was pleasant, hazy, making him loose, more talkative.

"I was twelve years old. Three Italian guys tried to steal a keg of beer from Mulqueen. I beat up two of them, and ran after the third. He almost killed me with a lead pipe. Reds said anyone who'd pull such a thing had to be crazy."

Glauberman folded his hands on his vest. "There are easier ways to make a living than hanging around picket lines. Or fighting battles royal with Dago Johnny or the East Side bums they'll be bringing in. Chain, this is a life-and-death struggle."

The lawyer got up. His Teddy Roosevelt face looked out to Pitkin Avenue.

"Who needs fights in the street? Find the man who is giving us trouble and *klop* him a little," Glauberman said. "Make him worry."

"I should *klop* Baum? I should just grab Kalman Baum on the street and *klop* him?"

"Too big. Some pisher first. Maybe a scab from the Pig Market. Or you and your friends could get inside a factory and make a fire. Jewish lightning."

Jake gulped another shot of booze. He was giddy. He wished at times like these he were smarter. Why had Eva and Brunstein left him? Then he understood. Glauberman was handling the dirty end for them.

"All this for fifteen dollars a week?"

The grin sliced Glauberman's robust face in half laterally. "Let's take each job as it comes. Know the end of the trolley line by the brewery?"

"Yeah."

"Across from the brewery there's a small inside place. No sign. Gottlober's. The son of a bitch is going full blast with scabs. Too far for us to send pickets."

"So?"

"Supply him a little heating."

Jake hesitated. This was different from protecting Theresa Ferrante and Rachel Goldstein.

"For fifteen dollars? I should risk going to jail?"

Glauberman handed him an envelope. "From now on, we pay by the job. At fifteen a week you are a bargain. Take a look in there. Figure out how you'll pay off your employees."

There were ten ten-dollar bills in the envelope. Jake had only seen that much money when Mulqueen or Kolodny cleaned out the cashbox.

"Let me suggest ten for each of your friends and you keep the rest," Glauberman said.

He'd need only Yussel Kuflik, Luigi, and Frank. Thirty bucks. He'd keep seventy. *Seven weeks' work!* For a half-hour of dirty work.

Jake said, "Who is Gottlober? Why should I do this to him?"

"Don't worry about him. Here's a diagram of the place. You smash a window in back, reach in, and open the door."

"What happens if I get caught?"

"Do it fast and run. When you throw the match, keep in mind how your wife got crippled at Baums'."

Years later, when he was Jacob Chain, "labor consultant," Jake often thought of that job he pulled at Gottlober's factory. It was ridiculously easy. If you wanted to frighten a man, there were many easy ways to do it. It was, he told himself, the reason he rose so fast, made so much money, grabbed so much power.

Luigi borrowed a truck belonging to a contractor he worked for, a cement-caked Dodge. Yussel brought two cans of gasoline. Frankie Ferrante brought a supply of tools—crowbars, axes, sledges, wrenches.

Sarah complained when Jake left. He lied to her: an emergency at the bottling plant. But wasn't he quitting to work for the union? A last job for Kolodny, he said. She was afraid of being alone. He assured her she'd be all right. Mrs. Feigenbaum would come downstairs and give her "eat."

Leaving, he would see Mutteh's gleaming eyes fixed on him. Mutteh knew about what his father's gang had done to Moishe Nigger. It was becoming Brownsville legend.

Gottlober's two-story brick place went up in a cone of orange flame. The gasoline-soaked bolts of cloth burned like giant wicks. Jake's gang wrecked a dozen machines before they spilled the gas, and Yussel tossed matches. They raced through the rear door, climbed into Luigi's truck, and sped down Liberty Avenue to Brownsville.

In the garage, Jake paid them off.

"The big boss," Jake said, "says ten bucks for each of you, but I'm giving you fifteen, because it was the first job."

Fifteen bucks! A week's work of bricking or pouring cement! *More* than a week's work of shlepping cases of oranges! Jake doled out the bills. He would retain fifty-five dollars instead of seventy. But he would have the loyalty of the men.

The fire at Gottlober's created a sensation. Police interrogated Ike, Eva, Flugelman, and the picket captains. They knew nothing about it. But Ike and Eva knew where the orders had come from. They were paying fees to Glauberman. He had promised to end the strike, one way or another.

Benny Otzenberger invited Ike to lunch at the Little Hungary and pleaded with him not to let matters get out of hand. The Baum Battle was a bad sign. Gangsters, a bloodbath. And now Gottlober—ruined. Everyone knew it was Ike's local that did it. Better settle with the bathrobe manufacturers.

"And get rid of the whole damn shootin' match," Benny said, between mouthfuls of stuffed veal roast.

"Otzenberger, my workers had nothing to do with the fight at Baums', which was instigated by Moishe Nigger's gang." Brunstein sounded nervier than usual.

Benny belched loudly enough to be heard in Williamsburg. So much for Brunstein's professions of innocence.

"Just tell your new associate Mr. Chain to watch out," Otzenberger said. "One bullet is enough to stop even the biggest bull."

Jake could not lie to Sarah forever. He told her he had a new job. With the union. She was puzzled. He had no skills. He could not operate a machine or cut cloth, sew buttons. Odd jobs, he said. Eva asked him to help distribute milk and bread to the strikers, to "help" the pickets.

They were celebrating his new "job" with a roast chicken. It had unborn "chickie" eggs inside its golden carcass. Mutteh ate greedily. *Chicken in the middle of the week?*

Sarah, dragging herself about, had made dumplings, gravy, sweetened carrots. A feast for the Chains! Mrs. Feigenbaum sniffed unaccustomed aromas wafting up from the basement. She had her suspicions.

"So all this is from handing out food?" Sarah asked. "For watching that Esther and Rachel don't fall down?"

"I lay chiggy in case somebody is coming to make trouble," Jake said.

"Eva got you into this?"

"Eva?" He feigned innocence. "She and Brunstein and a few others."

"Eva. That blondie. They say she's like a man. She smokes cigarettes and drinks beer."

She is like no man, Jake thought. In deference to his wife's crippled legs (though she looked prettier lately), he said nothing.

"Papa," Mutteh said. "There's this kid in my class?"

"So?"

Mutteh swallowed a mouthful of white meat, gobbled the last of the "chickie" eggs. "This kid's name is Irving Bunchik?"

"He got tough with you?"

"Nah. Nobody gets tough with me. I sock 'em—pow, *pow!* Irving says guys are gonna kill you. He said you was all kinds of dirty things and his father was gonna break your arms and legs. He's lying, ain't he, papa?"

Jake lit a cigarette. The first decent meal they had had in months. God, what a difference a few dollars made! And more to come. *Much more.* Glauberman had plans for a man who was not afraid.

"What's he talking?" Sarah cried. "What is this, men will break your legs? It can't be true."

"It's not," Jake said. "You tell this boy your father ain't worried about anyone. You think these people scare me?"

"No, papa."

"Give a feel." Jake peeled back his shirt sleeve and flexed his right arm.

The biceps thickened and swelled. The cords on the forearm were like strips of harness leather. "Go on, feel, kid."

The muscles danced and writhed.

"Show-off," Sarah said. "You do this for Eva Heilig when you're watching the girls?"

"No," Jake said. "Only for my son."

Fascinated, Mutteh pinched the hard flesh of his father's arm. Let Bunchik's father try something. Nobody was as strong as his papa.

Sarah laughed. "Thank God you are strong for all of us. Even if I'm not sure what you're doing. Jake, don't tell me no more."

The envelope with the fresh hundred dollars felt comforting inside Jake's shirt pocket. He wore a heavy-knit dark blue sweater, like a boxer's pullover. He had bought it on Pitkin Avenue with money he had earned from Glauberman. The money always felt good, as if giving off heat, feeding his body.

He had talked to Sarah of looking for a new apartment. Maybe in a better neighborhood. Haven Place or St. Mark's Avenue. She protested: How could she get to work? As awful as the basement was, she had to climb but one flight of stairs to get to the shop. No more sweatshops, Jake said. Soon she would not have to work. She could look after Mutteh, cook, clean, be a good housewife.

Waiting in the early morning chill on a street near the Brooklyn Bridge, Jake felt a distinct joy in the job awaiting him. He had learned the lesson quickly: There was money, lots of money, to be made with fists and clubs. Eva assured him it was all for "a good cause."

There were rumors that the manufacturers were getting ready to make a deal. A fifty-hour week, a two-dollar wage increase. No more charges for needles, oil, lockers. But no recognition of the union, no closed shop. They were enraged and terrified. How dare the union resort to strong-arm men! It was a *shonda* and a *khoppa*—a scandal and an outrage. Intellectuals like Isaac Brunstein and Meyer Flugelman employing such monsters?

"Of course," Eva told Jake, as he pored over the alphabet with her brother Abe, who was teaching him to read, "of course we'll end this when we win the strike. I don't like what's happening any more than Ike does. We've left it to Glauberman."

Jake nodded, copied neat *M*'s and *N*'s in a notebook.

"Good work, Jake," Abe Heilig said. "I mean your letters."

Every morning at six, Glauberman said, a wagonload of scabs crossed the Brooklyn Bridge. Greenhorns from the East Side. Jake was to stop them.

"Women?" Jake asked. "I got to hit women?"

"*Scare* them," Glauberman said. "One look at you, they'll run. The wagon says Brumberg's Pickles."

Resting in the doorway of a closed grocery store on Adams Street, Jake yawned and wondered if he was doing the right thing. He was not a cruel man. Tough, crude, unthinking. But to hit women? Not a nice idea. Yet it made a difference when Glauberman counted out the bills. He could buy Mutteh a suit for Chanukah. A dress for Sarah. A pair of special shoes for cripples. Then they would move to a decent apartment.

The wagon was a flatbed with wooden rails on the side. It was open on top. A sign read:

BRUMBERG'S KOSHER PICKLES
QUALITY & TASTE

On the bed of the wagon stood a dozen barrels. The wagon was pulled by two spavined horses. In the icy morning air, their snorts formed clouds like the gusts from a pressing machine. There was a bearded driver wearing a black derby and a long black overcoat. Next to him was an enormous man in a leather jacket and leather cap. He carried four feet of two-by-four. A section had been chipped away to form a handle. The man seemed half-asleep. His lumpy red face suggested he was half-drunk.

"Where's the dames?" Luigi asked.

"In the barrels," Jake said.

Chain pondered their move. The street was deserted. He wanted to frighten the girls but not hurt them. A painful job. The battle at Baums' had been a pleasure. Even putting the torch to the Jamaica factory was fun. But to *klop* women?

"Yussel, grab the horses," Jake said. "I'll go for the guy with the club. Luigi and Frank, you hear me?"

They nodded. Unshaven, red-eyed, they evoked terror by their very appearance. "Yeah, Jake." Luigi yawned.

"Pull off the tops from the barrels. Roll a few off the back. Holler at them. They'll get scared and run. Don't hurt."

The wagon approached the corner. The horses stopped for a moment. One farted and dropped steaming road apples. The other bucked and whickered.

"Get them," Jake said.

Yussel lumbered in front of the horses and grabbed the bridles.

"Hey," the man in the derby said. "Beat it. Get away from the horses."

"Police," Yussel boomed. "Ya got no license to transport persons."

"This is pickles, *putz,* not persons."

Luigi and Frank climbed on the back of the wagon and yanked the lid off a barrel. Two terrified women in ragged coats and shawls crouched inside. Like canned cherry peppers, Luigi thought.

"Get out and beat it," Luigi shouted. "Against the law."

He grabbed a woman's arm. She screamed. Luigi and Frank pulled at her and kicked the barrel to one side. It knocked over the adjacent barrel, and the lid fell off. Two more women were exposed.

The giant next to the driver stood up, roaring and swinging his club. Jake dodged it. "Hey, fathead, it's me, Crazy Jake Chain. Ya heard of me? No scabs allowed in Brooklyn."

The fat man clambered into the rear of the wagon, swinging his club at the Ferrante brothers. The barrels toppled, rolled, and the women crawled out, screaming, falling from the flatbed.

"Stay, stay!" the driver shouted. "It's the lousy union. Get him, Yankele!"

Jake grabbed the driver by the coat and hurled him out of the seat. The horses reared and whinnied. Yussel held them firmly.

The guard, seeing he could not stop the unpackaging of his cargo—girls were screaming and falling from the wagon—swung his club at Jake, missed.

"Go home, go home!" Frankie yelled at the women. "Don't break no strike. G'wan, beat it."

The women needed no second warning. They scurried toward the bridge.

"Bestid," Yankele said. "I know from you." Jake was about to take the reins in the driver's seat when the man brained him. The club struck Jake at the base of his head. Only the thick collar of the knitted sweater, bunched at the neck, saved him from a fractured skull. The blow stunned him and knocked him out of the seat, onto the rearing horses.

Frankie and Luigi went for Yankele, twisted the club from his hands, ripped his jacket, and threw him off the wagon.

"Get Jake," Frankie shouted to Yussel.

The horses bolted, dragging Yussel, pulling an unconscious Jake, tangled in harnesses and braces. Dead to the world, his mind a black cloud, Jake's feet bounced against the cobblestones. A shoe came loose. Frankie Ferrante grabbed the reins and stopped the horses a block from Borough Hall.

A policeman came running up. "Trouble? What the hell you guys doing?"

"Deliverin' pickles, officer," Frankie said. "The horses bolted."

They hauled Jake aboard the flatbed. Brumberg's pickle wagon could serve as an ambulance. By the time Yankele and the derby-hatted driver had explained to the cop what had happened, the wagon was gone.

"Concussion," Doc Abelman said. He palpated the back of Jake's head with his hand. "I don't think there's a fracture. But, boy, what an egg somebody laid there."

Jake lay on the black leather examining table in Abelman's office. The physician had been awakened at seven in the morning. He was accustomed to emergencies.

"Fell off a wagon," Luigi said. "We was loading sacks, Doc, and Jake fell."

"On the back of his head? It looks to me like somebody tried to brain him."

Jake stirred as the doctor washed the area with iodine and looked for a break in the skin. Semiconscious, Jake struggled to get up.

"Take it easy, Jake. Who am I?"

"Dr. Abelman. It hurts."

"That's a good sign. You can feel pain. At least not everything is scrambled inside. You guys turn him around."

Luigi and Frankie—Yussel was reporting to Glauberman on the pickle-barrel affair—hefted Jake and sat him upright. Abelman held up three fingers. "How many?" he asked.

"Three. I ain't seeing so good. Like there's two of you?"

Doc shook his head. "Go home and rest." He scrawled a prescription. "Take two of these every four hours. A big galoot like you should get over a bump on the head. That's all I get lately. *Shtarkers*. You know a guy named Morris Pearlberg?"

The Ferrantes and Jake expressed ignorance. Silence. Never. Never heard of him.

"Hefty guy in a gray derby. They call him Nigger. Came in here with a pistol stuck in his belt."

"Maybe I seen him around, Doc," Frankie said innocently.

Abelman scratched his head. He looked from Chain to the dark brothers. Something going on here.

"This Pearlberg's face and arms were boiled pink. The guy looked like a lobster from Lundy's restaurant. I asked him what happened. He wouldn't say, but he said he was going to kill the bums who did it to him. Took his pistol out and counted off the shots. A bullet for every one of the guys who cooked him."

Jake was in bed three days with the concussion. Sarah wailed. She was certain he was involved in dirty business. She begged him to stop, to ask Mr. Kolodny to give him back his job.

She became a scold, weeping, limping around the basement on her cane, cursing their terrible life. Bad dreams troubled her. She saw monsters, demons, frightening animals that looked like people, or people that looked like animals, attacking her.

Jake silenced her with twenty-five dollars. She could not believe the money. When her brown eyes were as wide as they could get, he gave her twenty-five more.

She tucked the money into her corset top. *Fifty dollars!* And she had seen more. A roll from which he had peeled the bills. She limped upstairs to the sweatshop. She feared for Jake. She knew what he was doing. No secrets in Brownsville. Already he was becoming a hero to the working girls and the union people. Feigenbaum looked at him with wonder and fear. Sarah noticed that the sweatshop operator was more solicitous of her. Mrs. Feigenbaum offered her a glass of tea and a cookie every morning.

This is what comes of hitting, Sarah thought bitterly. Greeted by smiles from Boss Feigenbaum, she understood the power, the new money, the future that had to be better. She would quit the job and be a housewife the way Jake wanted. Her father could sell his pushcart and open a fruit-and-vegetable store.

Below, Jake moaned and took his pills. He dreamed of making love to Eva. All naked. The two of them. No shame. He would love her all over. He would make money on top of money, dress her in satins and furs, like the fancy New York women in the newspapers.

Chapter II

"No fire this time," Leo Glauberman said. "Just wreck the place."

"How much?" Jake asked.

The two were alone in "Teddy Rosenfelt's" second-floor office. On windy Pitkin Avenue, the Ferrante brothers waited in the truck with Yussel the Bear. They amused themselves whistling at women shoppers.

"Two hundred," Glauberman said. "Chain, a lot of this money I borrowed from the bank. It ain't the union's."

"Not enough. I want three hundred. Last time I got a terrible *klop* on the head, I could be dead."

Glauberman turned sideways and jiggled his pince-nez. A month ago, Jacob Chain had been a thickheaded horse.

"Take more than that to kill *you*, Jake."

"You ain't answered, Mr. Glauberman. Three hundred dollars to wreck a place? Whose?"

"Finemaster's."

"The price just went up to four hundred."

They haggled for ten minutes. Glauberman suffocated his Rooseveltian rage at this placid giant. They compromised on three hundred and fifty dollars, the highest fee to date.

Jake told the lawyer that his head was feeling better. He had come into the office with terrible aches and pains. It was a miracle how the lump went down when they agreed on three hundred and fifty.

It took Jake and his gang a half-hour to wreck Finemaster's factory.

The guard, an unarmed drunk, was tricked into approaching Sal Ferrante's "hotcorn" cart, hit on the head by Luigi, and lugged into the basement.

Yussel and Frankie clipped the lock on the front gate. Jake smashed a window. Jake, Yussel, Frank, Luigi, and little Sal smashed machines, threw acid on the cloth, broke the elevator cables, and tossed a stink bomb in the furnace.

"No cops," Jake said, as they rode off in the Ferrantes' truck.

"They been paid off," Sal said in his scratchy voice. "I heard Otzenberger hollerin'. He says the union is gettin' as smart as the bosses. They're also payin' the cops."

They stopped at Mulqueen's bar, where Jake gave each "soldier" twenty dollars. That left him with two hundred and seventy for himself.

They came out of Mulqueen's, Jake looming in their midst. The word had gotten around. Pimps, thugs, and shakedown artists stared at him. This was Crazy Jake Chain, chief *shtarker* for the union.

In beige tweed cap a size too big for him, Little Mendel came out of a car and shuffled toward Jake.

"Don't hit, Chain, don't hit," Mendel said. He had a white scar running across his forehead where the shovel had almost taken his head off.

"Who's hitting?" Jake asked. "And who's in the car?"

"Mr. Morris Pearlberg, who is in the same business you are in."

"What does he want?"

"To talk."

"I can't talk. Later, maybe."

Little Mendel shook his head. "It ain't my business, Chain, but you're making a mistake. What you done to Finemaster's, everyone knows. Better make a deal with Pearlberg so we can work together."

"I don't know from Finemaster." Jake looked at the Ferrante brothers and Yussel. "You?"

"Who the hell is Finemaster?" Luigi asked. "We been drinkin' beer all night."

Mendel crossed the street to the parked car. "You had your chance, Chain," he called. "You got a head could be broken, a heart could be stabbed. And a wife and a kid. And that blond bitch Heilig."

Jake started to cross the street. Blood pumped in his head. He'd kill them. On the street. Luigi and Yussel grabbed his arms. Frankie and Sal clung to his legs. He struggled in rage, finding no words, spitting at the car as it pulled away.

Moishe Nigger pointed a pistol at them. The gun clicked harmlessly a few times.

Yussel took Jake to a *weisbierstube* on Belmont Avenue. The owner was a one-eyed woman named Tante Bella Botkin. Yussel said it was a safe place. Moishe Nigger never went there—Aunt Bella was too tough. She was protected by another mob, the Belmont Bulldogs. Her son, Bulldog Botkin, was the boss.

"So what happens here?" Jake asked. He rarely drank. He did not play *shtuss* or poker; his mind could not follow the action. What he craved was knowledge, deciphering letters and numbers. He felt he was getting rich. Money on top of money. Tomorrow he would open an account in the East New York Savings Bank. Glauberman was a good fairy, a wizard.

He nursed a beer at Aunt Bella's and watched Yussel get into a *shtuss* game. In a half-hour the Bear lost the twenty Jake gave him.

"Want some fun, Chain?" Yussel asked.

"A woman?"

"It's all right. No one'll know except you and the hoo-er, and me and Tante Bella."

Jake felt his neck turn scarlet. He had always been hesitant with women. Strange, sweet, soft creatures. Vague memories of his mother—a soft breast, hands that stroked him. Long ago. Carried in her arms. So young he could not walk. The farm, the trees. A field of yellow flowers.

Sarah had been beautiful once. Lithe, dark, like a forest bird. And Eva. More beauty than he could envision. He could never stop imagining her naked, glowing, waiting for him.

"Come on, Chain," Yussel said. "Bella knows you're a big shot. She saved the best for you. For two dollars, what can you lose?"

He would have asked God to forgive him, if he believed. If he could pray. If it mattered. Sarah would not know. What harm?

Over the saloon were three small rooms. In each were a cot, a shaded lamp, a table, a basin, and a pitcher of water.

Yussel, with a throaty roar, blundered into the first room and greeted a woman. He spoke Russian.

The girl in the next room was fat but pretty. She had a small beaked nose, painted red lips, a mass of curling black hair. Her cheeks were round, rouged, and puffy, and her eyes were black and slanted, suggesting a strain of Hungarian.

"Hello, Jake Chain. My name is Minnie Fassbender."

"You know me?"

"You're famous. I used to make fun for Moishe Nigger at another place. The girls who work there told me you boiled him like a chicken. So what are you staring?"

She had taken off her green satin kimono. Jake gawked, intrigued with the round flesh. She bulged the laced corset, the ruffled blue silk drawers, red garters, black stockings. His hands trembled. His throat turned to sandpaper. If Moishe Nigger and the mob caught him now, he'd be dead in a minute. Helpless on his belly. He would not have the strength to lift a fist.

"Whaddya lookin' at, Crazy Jake? Ya like me?" She snapped a garter, turned, and showed him her blooming cheeks.

"I love you." His voice drowned.

"Oh, sure. C'mon. Don't stand there shaking. Let's see if you can love as good as you fight."

He fell to his knees and embraced the silken hips. He could not stop his hands from shaking.

When it was over, he was as drained as any empty seltzer siphon. He did not feel shame. He felt elated, rewarded. He gave her five dollars instead of her usual two.

"Come back, Jakie," she said. She wiggled fingers in his ears, kissed his thick hair, ran her tongue over his face. "Ask for Minnie."

Aroused again, he craved her. They made love again. He gave her five more dollars.

He watched her pulling on the stockings, tying the strings on her underpants, standing in front of a cracked mirror and painting her lips. She combed her hair. A plain girl. *Tsatski'd* up with makeup, perfume.

He grabbed her from behind, cupped her breasts, and bit her neck with his lips.

"Enough. Twice is enough."

"I'll be back."

"I'll be here."

Reaching between her legs from the rear, grasping her lower parts in one hand, he was gentle and possessive. This, too, came with money, fame, and the terror he was learning he could arouse in people. He had been faithful to Sarah for one reason: poverty.

Chapter 12

A week before Chanukah, the bosses were ready to settle.

Moishe Nigger's mob was no match for Jake Chain's *shtarkers,* although the parboiled Nigger counterattacked. Frankie Ferrante was ambushed and beaten up by Duffy Plotkin and Bunchik. They clipped off a third of his left ear and smashed his nose. Undeterred, Jake, Luigi, and Yussel intercepted a wagonload of scabs on Fulton Street, unhitched the horses, and drubbed the driver.

The Baum brothers and Finemaster contacted Brunstein. Enough was enough.

"Not enough scabs, gentlemen?" Ike asked loftily. "You have learned something of proletariat solidarity. Not a worker in Brownsville will scab for you."

They sat in the Little Hungary restaurant—Kalman Baum, Finemaster, Ike, and Flugelman. The union men sniffed victory with the beef goulash and stuffed cabbage.

Kalman, who had lost ten pounds, sipped bitter seltzer. "Solidarity my ass, Brunstein. It's the gangsters."

"Gangsters? How dare you!"

"Never mind," Baum said. "The Heilig woman, that Red. Some citizen you turned out to be, Isaac Brunstein. Your father was a Hebrew teacher and look at you. Not only a Socialist but hiring criminal scum."

Finemaster's voice trembled. "Eight thousand dollars' equipment wrecked in my place. The insurance companies hear Brownsville and they run. You did it to us, gentlemen."

Outside they could hear chanting. All four men, napkins tucked in shirt collars, went to the window. A waiter complained. So what was new? The unions again.

A strange procession. First, two mounted policemen. Then a butcher's wagon. A policeman rode on its rear platform. What was he guarding? Then two more mounted police. Behind them a funeral procession. There were at least forty people, most of them girls on strike. They carried black candles. Rachel Goldstein and Esther Levy bore a sign: RIGHTEOUS-NESS SAVES FROM DEATH. Eva Heilig was leading the parade.

"They're crazy," Baum muttered. "All of them."

"Not so crazy," Ike said. "Inside that butcher truck are twenty scabs for your factory. But they'll never get there. We shamed them into refusing to work and they are being escorted back to Manhattan."

Flugelman nodded. "You'll notice, gentlemen, police protection. A change in attitude in City Hall. Mr. Otzenberger understands where votes come from."

Baum gritted his teeth. *Damn that bastard Chain!* Flugelman, Brunstein, the Heilig woman, they could yap forever about union solidarity. But when it got down to cases, it was Jake Chain who had ruined them.

From his second-story window, Glauberman watched the "funeral cortege." His idea. Escort the handful of remaining scabs back to the bridge. And police yet! Otzenberger was seeing the light.

Jake stood next to him. He wore a heavy blue serge suit, a stiff white collar, a dark blue tie. He had been barbered, shaved, and powdered. His enormous freckled hands hung clumsily from the starched snowy cuffs.

"It's over, Jake," Glauberman said. "By tonight the bosses will settle. Fifty-hour week. Ten-percent wage increase. Time off for the toilet, lunch, sick leave. Shop stewards to mediate infractions. Jake, you don't seem interested."

It was lost on him. What the hell was an infraction? He had twelve hundred dollars in the East New York Savings Bank. Sarah was going that night—in a taxi!—to buy a fur coat. In a few days, they would say goodbye to the basement. Jake had rented the lower floor of a house on Haven Place—three big rooms, a kitchen, a spotless bathroom.

Jake could see Eva leaving the procession. She was talking to a man in a fur-collared greatcoat and a black homburg. A young-looking man. Something *goyish* about him.

Jake edged closer to the window. Snow was swirling, an early dusting on a dark December day. He could see Eva's round fur hat, the long heavy coat. Shamed, he thought of his visits to the "hoo-er." Did it matter? He went there to fill a need. Sarah could not supply it. And he would not dare think of Eva sleeping with him. When he went to the noisy, crowded, overheated Heilig house for his lessons and sat at the kitchen table with Abie, spelling words, he could not stop staring at her. She was always in motion, always talking. The Heiligs had had a telephone installed. She was on it forever. Picket captains. City Hall. Ike. Support from the Jewish Trade Council. An article in the *Forward*.

"Now the strike's over, what do you need me for?" Jake asked. He wondered about the new apartment on Haven Place. Mutteh was asking when they could buy an automobile.

"Strikes or no strikes," Glauberman said, "you'll be needed. I am getting into the union myself. Not just as their attorney but in a more direct way. You can help, Jake."

"How?" He was wary of something cunning, secret, in Glauberman. The lawyer had changed in the past few months.

"The labor movement is going to need help. Chain, there are wet-wash workers, butchers, kneepants makers, cloakmakers, bakers, carpenters, all kinds of working people who need help. It's good you're learning to read and write. You could be an executive."

To celebrate the end of the strike, Garrison Halstead invited Eva to dinner at Luchow's. It was a snowy, crisp evening, a few days before Christmas.

Eva was no longer a mere worker. Ike, Flugelman, and the others had decided that the union would pay her as full-time "vice-president for organizing." She was a find. A natural. Old Socialists swallowed their chauvinism. When she spoke, workers listened. Her tiny figure, the mass of blond hair, the intense green eyes, the assertive chin, disarmed (and sometimes frightened) employers.

Halstead congratulated her on her new job. He lifted his glass of Rhine wine. She smiled and did likewise. A gypsy orchestra played Strauss waltzes. The restaurant, with its penumbral walls, stuffed stag heads, obese waiters bearing trays of golden beer and gargantuan portions of veal Holstein and hasenpfeffer, filled her with a vague dread. It was not only terribly Christian. It was barbaric, savage, something out of northern forests. She looked in vain for a Jewish face, listened for a snatch of Yiddish. Nothing. But plenty of *Deutsch.*

"To your new eminence," Garrison said.

"Don't make fun of me. This wine is too *sour.*"

"It's called *dry,* Eva."

"You see my ignorance? How can you be interested in me?"

She looked around the smoky, tumultuous restaurant. The gypsies had retired in favor of a German *oompah* band in leather pants, embroidered suspenders, and green hats with feathers. Jew-killing after the roast goose, she thought. Or roast Jew?

"You're the most beautiful and intriguing woman here," Halstead said. "My sister tells me that even on the picket line when you're screaming at the girls, you're beautiful."

Eva blushed. His sister Mildred was too generous. Eva had told Halstead to thank her for the support Mildred had gotten from her friends. They had raised money, marched with the girls, allowed themselves to be arrested in a show of unity.

"Look around you," Garrison said. "These are women of wealth, actresses, some *horizontales.*"

"What?"

"Fancy prostitutes. Don't look shocked. You're a Socialist and a realist.
You know how the rich arrange things. Eva, there is more beauty in your
freshly soaped face than in all of these lazy pampered women. See that
man staring at you? The bald one? My father's associate in real-estate dealings. Mr. Ten Eyck. He knows quality when he sees it. His Dutch brain is
wondering right now: Who are you? What am I doing with you? How in
God's name did I find someone so beautiful?"

"The wine is sweeter every second."

"If those Tyrolean nincompoops would stop blaring, I'd tell you I love
you."

His voice was drowned out by a thumping, bleating chorus of "Watch
on the Rhine." She was unable to read his lips.

"What did you say?" Eva shouted. She held her ears.

"I'll repeat it outside. I want us to be alone when I tell you."

She confessed she was enjoying a taste of the high life. Quite a change
from Brownsville. But the barbaric "Christianness" (as she put it) of the
restaurant frightened her. The soaring Christmas tree was like a glittering
green monster.

The wine made her light-headed, happily giddy. She realized she was
beautiful. It gratified her. Men stared. Women whispered. Hardly like
meetings in drafty factories, in Ike's grim headquarters—interminable
arguments over tactics, procedures, dues, benefits.

"This is fun," Eva said. "But why do I feel strange? The wine? Because
Christmas isn't my holiday?"

"Now, my dear," Halstead said, taking her hand. "We are both Socialists, correct?"

"Yes."

"And atheists?"

"Yes."

"So none of this means anything to us, except having a good time. There
could be a crucified Christ on the wall of the restaurant in place of that
stag's head, or a Virgin Mary in place of the evergreen, and it would mean
nothing to either of us. Statuary. Neither fear in you nor respect from me.
Isn't it heartening that we can feel the same way?"

"I guess so." She hiccuped. The fried veal, covered with bread crumbs
and a shiny egg, was more than she could manage. The egg stared at her
her—the eye of a troll. The sweet-and-sour red cabbage clogged her nose.
She drank more wine. "But you have a head start. You can make fun of
Christmas because you were raised with it. I am a child of the ghetto.
Christianity means what? Hating. Killing Jews. The fear is natural, even
though my father says there'd be no anti-Semitism if everyone studied
algebra."

"A wise man, your father. I look forward to meeting him."

The *oompah* band paraded around the restaurant. Christmas carols boomed in the smoky air. A bespectacled man in a tuxedo came by to whisper in Halstead's ear. It bothered Eva. Garry did not introduce her, although the man stared at her with an impertinent smile.

"You see?" she said when the man left. "You can't overcome your class, Garry. No introduction?"

"You're too good for him. Horace Vermont. Formerly Grunberg. Spoiled, rich, haughty, ashamed of his Jewish origins. He asked who you were."

"What did you say?" The wine made her giggle.

"I told him you were a dangerous anarchist. I knew him at Yale. A bad lot. No one is meaner about Jews than a rich Jew who tries to hide it."

When the music subsided, Halstead tried to coax her to taste a vast apple pancake, big enough, Eva thought, to feed half the Hebrew Orphan Asylum. As she pecked at it, he asked her about the strike settlement. The pretext for the dinner had been his need for a story for the *Eagle*. The editor was aware that the burgeoning Jewish population in Brownsville was educating itself, learning English, becoming politically active. Why not try to win them as readers?

As they sipped coffee, Halstead confessed his ignorance of labor matters despite his avowed socialism. It was astonishing the way the employers had acceded after such a bitter battle. They had used all their resources—thugs, politicians, police, courts, scabs.

Eva said, "We have much work ahead of us. We will not stop until they recognize the union as bargaining agent and give us the union shop."

Halstead laughed. His pince-nez jiggled, his reddish face turned a shade darker. *What teeth he had!* she marveled. Each one a snow-white work of art. The rich had superb teeth. And ruddy complexions, and neat hands, and graceful feet, and, very often, long narrow jaws.

"Why do you laugh?" she asked.

"Eva, when you are declaiming your dedication to the cause—and I mean no offense—you're even more beautiful. It is as if a Botticelli angel were to start quoting from *Das Kapital*. I love you for it."

She tried to stop his praise. It embarrassed her. She did not know how to respond. So she asked that he interview her on how the strike was won. In responding to his questions, she said not a word about Jake Chain.

Halstead was no fool. The police at headquarters had told him of a mob of gangsters the union employed. (A police captain found it amusing. "Sheeny against sheeny, Mr. Halstead." Captain O'Connor laughed. "The kike bosses started it, and the kike strikers copied them. Hired some big hebe to scare them out of their skullcaps. I bet a few beards got pulled.")

Later they strolled along Fifth Avenue. They walked past the brownstone mansions. They paused in front of the First Presbyterian Church.

Garrison asked if she wished to go in; the stained glass was stunning and there were enchanting Christmas decorations.

"I think not," Eva said.

"My atheist? Why not look at it as art with no religious connotation?"

"I can't help it. We don't go to synagogue and we regard all these things as distractions—"

"So do I."

"It just makes me nervous."

"I didn't think anything did."

"Garrison, I'm brave enough on the picket line or at a meeting or facing a boss. My voice scares them. But—I'm afraid."

"Of me?"

"No."

Christmas worshipers in furs, muffs, high hats, and greatcoats emerged from the Gothic church. Halstead nodded at a few. It was not his family's church. They were Episcopalians.

They walked uptown on Fifth Avenue. He took her arm.

"I guess it's the old ghetto fear," Eva said. "It doesn't leave you. Always waiting for the next blow. That's why my father retreated to mathematics. My brothers are intelligent. Much more so than I. They'll escape. And I fight my way through the labor movement." She stopped and cocked her head. He adored her at that moment, snow flecking her mass of hair. "They call me the leader of our 'burning Jewish maidens.'"

Halstead smiled and tapped his cane in the snow. "Really? How delightful. How does it sound in Yiddish?"

"Unsere verbrente Yiddishe Maidlech."

"My burning Jewish maiden," he said. Halstead embraced her. He kissed her gently on the lips, the cheeks, the closed eyes. "My beloved Eva. I intend to marry you."

She shoved him away with firm gloved hands. No one had ever kissed her in that manner. "No, Garrison. That is nonsense. Your father does not want in-laws who run a candy store. We are poor Jews."

"I shall marry you. In fact, we are going to make love before the wedding. You and I, Eva, are free souls."

"Maybe *you* are. You're rich and you can do what you want. I can't. You must remember. All my Jewish radicalism is based on a code of ethics. I can't abandon it overnight. I'm sorry, but that is how it is, Garry."

"I have an apartment on Gramercy Park. Let's stay there awhile. We'll sit by the fire."

"No, Garry. I know I sound ridiculous. A liberated woman who will not let her passions be liberated. I am fond of you. But the more we get involved with each other, the worse it will be someday."

"Nonsense. We need never see my family again if they reject you."

"It's not that. *You'll* reject me at some point. My accent. My Jewishness."

"I only know that you are the bravest, loveliest, most desirable woman in the world. You've taught me of the potential in women. Not just beauty and grace, but courage, sense, dedication. Please come with me, Eva. I do love you."

She shook her head, then rested it against the thick beaver collar. "No. No. I won't."

Halstead kissed her forehead. "Thy cheeks are comely with rows of gold," he whispered. "Thy neck with chains of gold."

"Garry, don't try to make me give in by quoting my ancestors' love songs. I'm a long way from the queen of Sheba."

The snowflakes on her hair and face, he thought, are like the rows of gold. A natural beauty, this descendant of desert wanderers and warriors.

"A bundle of myrrh is my well-beloved to me," Halstead said. "He shall lie all night between my breasts."

"*I* am supposed to say that, but I won't. Good night, dear friend."

"You will sleep with me, Eva. I will marry you."

"Garry, don't speak about things that can't happen."

He summoned a cab for her and kissed her again as he helped her in. "They will happen, if your parents think I'm good enough for you. Your lineage is more distinguished than mine, Eva."

Watching the horse-drawn carriage depart, thinking of her small figure snug in the cab, the blankets drawn over her, he shivered with desire. She would be his wife.

"I don't understand," Sarah Chain said. "This work for the union. It's over now that the strike is settled. How will you live? How can I quit my job?"

"You'll quit. There's plenty work for me."

Snow whirled in light gusts, spreading a cleansing dry powder over Haven Place. Jake helped Sarah out of Glauberman's Oakland. He had learned to drive. The lawyer had lent him the car for the day. On the last day of 1910 they would move into the house on Haven Place—the entire ground floor for themselves. A living room, a kitchen with a gas stove, a separate bedroom for Mutteh, a larger room at the rear for Jake and Sarah.

She refused to believe their good fortune, refused to believe it could continue. Frightened, subdued, she was wary of reaching too far.

"Jake, I'm afraid," she said. She limped on her cane around the large empty rooms. They would need furniture, rugs, curtains. Mutteh raced from room to room, sliding on the waxed parquet floors.

The landlord, who kept the flat immaculate, lived upstairs. He was named Aaron Rimkoff. An Orthodox Jew, an elder with a seat on the eastern wall of the synagogue, he owned a prosperous dairy store in the indoor market on Haven Place. He employed only Orthodox Jews. Rimkoff and his colleagues deplored his younger son, a scrappy lightweight and pool shark named Bobby Rimkoff.

Jake had signed a year's lease and paid three months' rent in advance. He didn't care. The money was sitting in the bank. There would be more to come.

"Work, work," Sarah said sadly. "I know what you're doing."

They were in the middle room. The house was attached to identical houses on either side. The interior rooms and hallway were dark.

"You *know*," he said with annoyance. "Don't talk about it."

"You are a *shtarker*. You hit people. You burned a place. You wrecked Finemaster. Everyone knows."

He took her in his arms. She was still pretty. She set her hair and used perfume now. "Don't be afraid. No one can hurt Jake Chain."

"The people at Feigenbaum's say the bosses will get you. They'll pay Moishe Nigger to kill you. They won't let you do what you do." She began to weep.

"Never. Glauberman says I'm a labor consultant. You hear, Sarah? A consultant, your husband."

She hobbled away from him into the rear room. This was nicer. A big room with two windows and a door to the kitchen. There was a view of a backyard. Earth, trees, open ground. Maybe in the spring Mrs. Rimkoff would let her plant vegetables and flowers. Window boxes with yellow daisies. No more basements, no more damp floors, toilets on the second floor. They would live in light, with fresh air, dry walls, a stove that worked, beds fit for human beings. It was wrong for her to *kvetch* at Jake.

"Wow, a yard!" Mutteh shouted. He was dancing in front of the rear window. "Look, Papa—trees! I can build a snowman!"

Jake joined his wife and son at the window. Maybe he was moving up too fast.

Chapter 13

"Say hello to Mr. Harris Tsipkin," Glauberman said, grinning. "Mr. Tsipkin, the famous Jacob Chain."

"Famous I don't know. Others things I know."

Harris Tsipkin was not quite five feet tall. His feet barely touched the floor as he sat in a cane-back chair. He kept his long *kaputa* buttoned. Only the lower half of his face peeked from a derby a size too big. Orthodox, he refused a shnapps, explaining to Glauberman that it wasn't the refreshment he feared but the unclean glass.

"So we'll get you a paper cup," Glauberman said.

"No thanks. A man never knows how they manufacture such *chazerei* in *America Gonif,* where all kinds magic things can happen."

Jake remained silent. He wore a dark gray vested suit, a stiff collar, a striped blue tie. But the massive hands gave him away: the hands of the *shtarker*.

"Let me explain Mr. Tsipkin's problem. He is the acting president of the Jewish Painters Guild—or as Mr. Tsipkin would say, *paintners.*"

Glauberman went on. Tsipkin and his colleagues were craftsmen, he told Jake. There was a building boom in Brownsville. Houses springing up all the way to the Queens county line. Yet they were having difficulty getting work. When they did, it was always below the union wage. Why? Because the crafts unions—painters, carpenters, electricians, bricklayers, masons, and plumbers—were controlled by gentiles.

"They won't give you a card?" Jake asked. His flat eyes were expressionless.

Tsipkin said, "For a hundred dollars, a hundred fifty, they'll give a temporary card. But next comes a test in English words. Who understands it? My members know to mix paint, to put on sizing, to scrape, to clean, to patch a hole with plaster, to put up wallpaper. But examinations? So the unions take the hundred dollars and goodbye job."

Glauberman gave Jake a slip of paper. "Here is the address of the

United Painters Guild of Brooklyn, Local Seventy-two. The president of this guild is Mr. Otto Lentz. You should arrange to have his office redone. After the redecorating job, I will call him on Mr. Tsipkin's behalf."

"I ain't sure I like this," the painter said. "No one should get hurt."

"What's to like or not like?" Glauberman asked. "It's how things get done."

Tsipkin scratched his short beard. "I have a wife and seven children to feed. I have union brothers who ain't working. Mr. Glauberman, whatever this man Chain does, keep it secret."

"Silence is our watchword. Mr. Tsipkin, you will give us a three-hundred-dollar deposit. When the work is done, another three hundred."

With a paint-stained hand, Harris Tsipkin obliged.

The wrecking of the United Painters Guild office on Bushwick Avenue would have gone more smoothly had not Mr. Otto Lentz and his secretary chosen to stay late.

Jake, Luigi, and Frank entered on rubber-soled shoes. They were masked. They surprised Mr. Lentz with his pants off, on top of Miss Margaret Mulhouser, on the office couch. She was a stout, big-boned woman. Even in the semidarkness of the December dusk, Jake and the Ferrantes could see that Mr. Lentz had to work extremely hard. In the flickering light of a coal stove, Jake could see a rose-colored petticoat on the frayed rug. Otto Lentz labored like Hercules atop her. He barely saw or heard the invaders.

She screamed as the men entered. But she followed orders, retrieved her underclothing, and allowed herself to be locked, sobbing, in the ladies' room. Mr. Lentz was bound and gagged, tied to his swivel chair. Jake, Frank, and Luigi methodically destroyed files, records, furniture, typewriters.

Halfway through their work, the union president tried to stumble toward the door. Jake hit him once with the flat of the hand. "It ain't personal," Jake said. "It's only my job. You'll get further instructions."

After a talk with Leo Glauberman, Otto Lentz decided that certain qualified craftsmen could be accepted as new brother unionists. Jobs opened for them at once. Harris Tsipkin forked over another three hundred, and each newly employed "paintner" now paid Leo Glauberman five dollars a month.

Before entering Reds Mulqueen's saloon (a place where normally he would not set foot), Ike Brunstein saw the Ferrantes' Dodge truck rumble by.

Jake Chain, like a stone monument, was standing in it, with one of the Ferrante boys. They were holding together a pyramid of furniture. The lummox was moving to Haven Place, five doors down from the Heiligs, six from Dr. Abelman. The street with Abelman's beautiful trees. Two-story houses. Respectability. Ike shuddered. In wondrous ways did the revolution advance. He hated himself for letting Eva, Flugelman, and others convince him that Chain was needed.

Inside Mulqueen's, Benny Otzenberger, in a raccoon-lined coat and a plug hat (he was on his way to the mayor's New Year's party at City Hall), was drinking beer on the house. Ike, in his black cloak and flowing tie, felt like a mouse in a cage of snakes. Otzenberger was one of the few Jews who frequented Mulqueen's. It reeked of beer, cigar smoke, heavy farts. Sawdust floor, posters of busty actresses. *Where Jake Chain had grown up,* Ike reflected. *While I was disowning my faith for Marx. Which of us was more of an apostate?*

Benny wished Ike a Happy New Year. "You win, Brunstein. Who said I ain't for the workingman? Heshy tells me everything is hunky-dory now that the *tsatske* Heilig quit her job and is doing union business."

"You will kindly not refer to Eva Heilig as a *tsatske.*"

"No offense. Beer, Brunstein? Whiskey?"

"A glass of red wine will do, thank you."

Mulqueen looked the union president over with a gummy gray eye. Bomb thrower. Red. But scared of his own shadow.

"So what did you wish to tell me, Mr. Otzenberger?" asked Ike.

"Your friend Chain."

"What about him?"

"He's making it bad for everyone in Brownsville. He's in with Glauberman. Between the two of them, nobody'll be able to make honest graft anymore. Brunstein, the world has to go on. Unions, bosses, manufacturers, they all have to live, give, take."

In his haughtiest manner, Ike reminded the politico that Chain was not his responsibility. The big man had merely supplied protection for the harassed girls. A one-shot affair. Ike had no connection with Chain.

"No, but the *tsatske*—excuse me—Miss Heilig does. She's his cousin. It's no secret he's in love with her. He's got a thing in his pants the size of a salami for her and he'll listen to any—"

"You disgust me, Otzenberger."

"Forget any personal remarks. I'm warning you. Since they did a job on the painters' union, I ain't heard the end of it. Me, they blame. I'm supposed to keep Jews quiet."

"We got rid of Chain as soon as we won the strike."

Otzenberger shifted his elephantine ass and blew foam from his stein. "He's building a mob, Brunstein. Those greaseballs the Ferrantes. There's so many wop brothers, even the father, the barber, don't know. He's afraid to smack a kid in the street because it might be his. I see what's coming and I don't like it. Brownsville is respectable. So far I've run things pretty good."

"Mr. Otzenberger, it is no secret you sided with the bosses in every single strike until our girls stood up to you. Your son was the most notorious contractor for scabs in Brooklyn."

"I warned you, Brunstein. Wait, it'll come the turn of the tuxedo makers, the cloakmakers, the building trades, the bakers, the kosher butchers. Brunstein, talk to your fellow unionniks. You asked a puppy into your house to be a watchdog, right? It can grow up into a wolf and eat you."

Brunstein finished his glass of wine. He put his wide-brimmed black trilby on. "You seem to be in favor of hoodlums, so long as they work for the bosses. When we defend ourselves, it's un-American. Your son hired bullies to beat up women. Why the double standard?"

Otzenberger's piggy eyes were half-shut. He did not respond. He knew Ike spoke the truth. And he was on the spot. How to jump? Each side had its mobsters. All were dangerous. And there were votes from the workers who were swiftly becoming citizens.

"Tell Miss Heilig to warn her cousin Chain. He's looking to get himself in a cement mixer."

The Ferrante truck lurched up to 1667 Haven Place, came to a clanking halt. It was bitter cold. He and Luigi wrestled a new purple brocade-covered sofa off the back of the truck. Jake had covered it with brown paper. Sarah loved the new furniture. Especially the dining-room table. Solid oak. Carved legs. Yes, Jake thought as he and Luigi hefted the sofa up the stone steps, it would be nice if they could have a real sabbath on Friday nights. Lights, *chalah,* wine. Like others in Brownsville. Mutteh—now Mortimer—could go to Hebrew school and learn to pray.

Frankie of the clipped ear followed. He bore two ornate brass lamps with green parchment shades. Jake had gotten a "special-for-you" price from the owner of the big furniture store on Rockaway Avenue. The Chain reputation had spread. It was amazing the way people wanted to do favors for him.

Jake rested his end of the sofa on the cast-iron balustrade. He searched his pocket for the key to the front door.

The landlord, Rimkoff, peered out the upstairs window watching his new tenant move in. Fancy furniture. More stuff piled on the Ferrante truck—overstuffed chairs, cabinets, dismantled beds. Rimkoff nodded sagely. So that's what came from being a *shtarker,* a man unafraid to use his fists. The landlord couldn't complain. Chain had paid up, flashed a thick roll, showed him his passbook from the East New York Savings Bank.

His hands freezing, Jake inserted the key and opened the front door. There was an enclosed vestibule between the street door and the door to the foyer. Stairs to the left led up to the Rimkoff apartment. Often Jake could hear Bobby Rimkoff, the future "champeen," doing laps or skipping rope when his father was not at home.

A second key opened the inner door. Luigi held the outside door open with a foot, allowing Frankie, the lampbearer, to enter. Outside, smoking a cigarette, Sal lounged against the truck, watching the rest of Jake's possessions. Snow settled on his dark, wraithlike figure.

"Wait, wait," Jake said. "The light on the wall. I paid rent already. Rimkoff should have the electric on."

He fumbled for the switch, found it, flicked on the yellow-gray hall light. The walls were newly painted—cream and chocolate brown. He pointed to the right, the front room, through which they could carry the couch.

Jake leading and the Ferrantes following, they maneuvered the sofa around the sharp corner into the barren room.

"Through the sliding doors," Jake said. "I'll open them. Put the couch down. Slow. Sarah will get sore if it gets scratched."

Luigi and Frank waited in the gloom. Business must be good for Jake, Luigi was thinking. Not bad for them either. They worked part-time for him now. The rest of the time they laid brick, poured cement.

"Door's stuck," Jake said. He lit a match. The lighting fixtures were missing in the front room. Something had wedged the door. He crouched, trying to pry the sliding doors apart with his hands.

The doors creaked open on dry runners.

Later he remembered only the first few shots. But the guns started shooting immediately when his huge figure was visible to the shadowy men in the center room.

Jake saw the orange-yellow flashes. Bursts of flame in the wintry dark. The noises were not as loud as he had expected, popping sounds, like firecrackers. His scalp was hot and wet; his legs rubber.

Behind him, he heard one of the Ferrante brothers screaming. The other shouted and ran.

Bullets ravaged Jake's head, his arms, his chest. He stumbled forward. "Bastards, fight," he said. "Throw away the guns."

No one was in back of him. Frankie Ferrante would no longer be ashamed of his clipped ear and bent nose. He was dead. A .38 slug had passed through his left eye. Luigi, winged on the left arm, holding a broken bone, raced to the street screaming for help, police, shouting at Sal.

Blood streaming from his scalp, his cheek, his hands, Jake plodded forward. He saw the two figures—derby, short coat on one; the other a fat man in a checked coat, a big cap. A fat man who moved on little feet, making gestures with little hands emptying his revolver.

> *Hit him again.*
> *No use, I emptied both guns, the bastard's still coming.*
> *He gotta be dead. He gotta.*
> *I think we got one of the wops.*

Doors slammed. Hard heels clattered on the parquet floor. There was a rush of icy air from the rear door. Sounds of huffing, a door closing, then silence.

Jake brushed blood from his eyes. He tasted blood, choked on blood, felt himself drowning in it. Wet and warm. A funny taste. Like iron. He hit the floor, thinking that it was one hell of a way to spend the first day in his new home.

Chapter 14

"He's made of iron," Dr. Abelman said to the young intern. "Twelve bullets."

Jake lay in Brownsville Jewish Hospital. He was covered with bandages. They had counted twelve holes in him. Scalp, cheek, jaw, both arms, chest, groin, legs. And not one of them fatal—unless hemorrhaging started or he developed an infection. Abelman and the resident had found eight of the lead pellets.

The ward held six patients, one of them dying noisily with gasps, moans, and delirious curses.

Abelman, brushing back his shock of Indian-black hair, shook his head in wonder as he looked at Jake's morphine-dulled body. Incredible. Apart from considerable loss of blood, a possible jaw fracture, and the new orifices opened in him, Chain was going to survive. The worst of the wounds, in the groin, had passed through, missing vital organs. Creased scalp, a hole in his cheek, a somewhat askew jaw, assorted other wounds—and alive.

"Your patient?" the intern asked.

"Yeah. Strong as an ox."

"Somebody really wanted to get rid of him."

Bandaged, splinted, covered with splotches of iodine and bloody stains, Jake slept soundlessly. His huge chest rose and fell. A rock, Abelman thought, indestructible. He knew Jake Chain was involved in dirty business. He'd heard stories of some not-so-nice things Chain and his buddies had done. But he had always liked the man—plain, honest, paying his bills on time.

At the entrance to the overheated ward, two detectives appeared. Sergeant Flannery approached the bed. "This Jacob Chain?"

Dr. Abelman nodded. The intern left.

"Can he talk?" Sergeant Pope asked.

"Usually," Abelman said. "But not with twelve holes in him and enough morphine to put a whale to sleep."

Flannery clucked admiringly. "Big bastard. Look at them arms and legs." He squinted at Abelman. "Some dago with him was shot dead. Guy named Frank Ferrante. Another guinea got clipped, his brother Luigi. Know any of them?"

"I only know Chain. He won't be in condition to talk for another twenty-four hours. Loss of blood. Shock."

"Whaddya know about him?" Flannery asked.

"He's learning to read and write. Maybe he'll write you a letter when he learns the alphabet."

"Muscleman," Flannery said to his partner after Dr. Abelman had left. "His partner is Glauberman, the shyster. They teamed up a few weeks ago. Union rackets."

"I never heard of him."

"You will. If he lives much longer."

A bawling and shivering Sarah came to see Jake. She left Mutteh in the care of the Feigenbaums. It would terrify the child, she thought, to see his father all bloody. The incident had scarred her mind, filled her with fears, tremors, a desire to run, hide.

Incredibly, Jake was sitting up in bed. His jaw had been wired and he could barely speak. He took nourishment through a glass tube. Liquids would be all he could manage for a while. He was hungry and angry.

"Jake, everyone in Brownsville knows. Gangsters tried to kill you. Because you are a gangster too."

"Nah, nah," he mumbled. "I'm in business. Don't worry." Mashed, distorted, he sounded like a retarded child.

"I'm afraid. We paid for the furniture. The rent on the apartment. New clothes. Now what? You won't be able to work. You, my husband, you are almost dead."

Wailing, she tried to embrace him, but he cautioned her. Full of holes. Some of them still open. If she needed money, Leo Glauberman would take care of her. They had an agreement. In fact he wanted her to make sure the lawyer paid for Frank Ferrante's funeral.

Sarah told him she was afraid to go to the new apartment. The police had taken her there and asked questions. The floor was covered with blood, pools of it, where he had fallen in the center room, full of hot lead and holes.

"The furniture is okay?" he mumbled. "They didn't ruin the couch or the lamps?"

"Who cares about couches and lamps?" Sarah sobbed.

"I do." He tried to smile. He thought his jaw would come apart. Wincing, he asked for her hand. "We'll move in, dear wife. Our new place."

"They'll try to kill you again."

In the night he bled copiously from the wound in his groin, developed a fever, became delirious. He thrashed in the narrow bed—too short for his giant frame—and stained the sheets crimson. The nurses took turns quieting him, changing bandages. But he did not appear weaker to them. To their amazement, running a fever of 103°, bleeding, in pain, he tried to climb out of bed.

"I got to get them," he said. "Nobody kills Jake."

It took two nurses and an intern to subdue him.

Awakening, he saw Eva standing at his bedside with a tall woman in a gray uniform and a straw hat. The city nurse who took care of the pickets at Baum's.

Eva had brought him hothouse flowers and a box of chocolates (which his wired jaw could not tolerate and he gave to the nurses) and fifty dollars in an envelope. This had been Meyer Flugelman's idea.

Ike had objected to giving money so blatantly to Chain. The newspapers were full of the story. The hoodlum Ferrante dead. The boss mobster Chain filled with bullets. A scandal. A disgrace. Rabbis and other respected members of the Brownsville community denounced the affair. *The union's fault! Bringing hoodlums into labor dealings! Using scoundrels like Crazy Jake Chain!*

The woman in the gray straw hat was Mildred Halstead, Sarah told Jake. Mildred was making sure that he got the best of attention. The Halsteads carried a great deal of weight in city hospitals.

"Thanks, lady," Jake said, through semilocked teeth.

"Twelve bullets," Eva said. "Jake, how awful. We were afraid we'd never see you again. We'll get those men. Rimkoff gave a description of the two who ran into the backyard."

"I know who they are. I'll take care of them myself."

He told Eva that until he got out, he wanted protection for Sarah and his son. They were to be moved into the new apartment.

"The police also say you know who shot you," Eva said. "But they said you aren't cooperative."

"What does that mean?"

"You won't tell them anything." Eva looked at his smashed, discolored face. A crude and hard man. But he had a primitive sense of justice.

"The cops can ask me a hundred times. I won't tell them."

Mildred Halstead cocked her head. What a strange man! (Really, she thought, what a strange *Jew*.) He was huge, muscled, fair. A Viking warrior recovering from wounds of pike and sword.

"Why won't you tell them?" Eva asked.

Through the miasma of alcohol, iodoform, disinfectant soap, he smelled Eva's sweet scent. He would love her all his life. "Because, Cousin Eva, it's my fight. I'll get them."

If you are not killed, she thought.

Garrison Halstead appeared in the doorway. Halstead had talked to other reporters. Gang warfare. The respectable Jewish community shaken by gunfire, a murder, dreadful acts of vengeance. And here was the cause of it all—Crazy Jake, cousin of his beloved.

Halstead did not enter the ward. Jake saw him. A tall man in a fur-collared black coat, eyeglasses on a black string. The long jaw and white teeth. He knew about him. This man also loved Eva. Jake had heard stories. The two of them at fancy restaurants, the Broadway theater.

Eva kissed Jake's bruised forehead. As soon as he was stronger, Dr. Abelman said, they'd start pulling the rest of the bullets out of his body.

That night, under morphine, Jake dreamed of making love to Eva. Bleeding, suppurating, his mind muddled, he had to battle the surge of sexual desire that elevated his fever, inflamed his wounded groin.

Eva questioned Bobby Rimkoff about what he had seen that night. The Ferrante brothers—Luigi, Sal, Vince, Baggie, and the others—had no interest in her investigation. They would "take care" of the men who killed their brother in their own way. Besides, she was a woman, and it was none of her business.

Rimkoff was a slow-talking youth, forever shadowboxing, snorting through a mashed nose, unable to string sentences together with much sense. Some thought him retarded. But he told her (as his Orthodox parents wrung their hands and threatened to have Sarah evicted) that he had seen two men climbing the rear fence after the shooting.

"I seen 'em," Bobby said. "One was a fat guy, I 'member, 'cause he couldn't climb the fence. He got his pants tore. The guy in a derby pulled him over."

Moishe Nigger and the Meal Ticket.

Armed with this knowledge, Eva walked into the 71st precinct and demanded to see Captain Hanratty. In front of the red-haired officer, she made Bobby repeat his eyewitness testimony. The young pugilist did so. If a bit awed by the captain, promptings by a determined Eva jogged his memory.

Hanratty winked at a sergeant. Freckles scattered as he grinned.

"What does that mean, captain?" Eva asked. "What's so funny?"

"Miss Heilig, it sounds like you've coached your friend. Besides, he isn't exactly a witness. Punchy. Cuckoo. How long you been in school, Rimkoff?"

"I finished fourth grade. I ain't neither punchy."

"That has no bearing on his testimony. Captain, a man was murdered on Haven Place. Mr. Chain took twelve bullets in his body and might have been killed."

"Let's be honest, Miss Heilig. It was scum versus scum. I can't go arresting people on the testimony of this half-wit."

Captain Hanratty whispered something in the sergeant's ear. The latter retired to a rear room and phoned Francis Fagan Dullahan. Both officers knew who had killed Frank Ferrante and made a clay pigeon of Chain.

Dullahan gave the word to the cops: *Lay off*. Morris Pearlberg and Herman Wesselberg were a pair of ticking bombs. If ever *they* opened their traps, the political structure would be in trouble. The sergeant was given his orders: Soft-soap the Heilig bitch, warn Rimkoff to shut up.

Captain Hanratty got the word in whispers. He turned on a charming smile and used his softest Sligo accents. "Well, then, we'll look into it. A man in a derby? A fat man? That should narrow our suspects down to about a million, Miss Heilig. A grand challenge it is."

Eva's eyes burned. "You know who they are. The same men who attacked our pickets."

"There's no evidence, Miss Heilig. If I were you, I'd forget it. You too, pinhead."

Not unexpectedly the executive board of the bathrobe makers union was of the same opinion. Let well enough alone. Too bad the Italian—what was his name?—died. Be grateful Chain was alive, but he was an embarrassment any way you looked at it. *Shtarkers* had been used as a desperate measure. Now that things were settling down, why start up?

"Life means little to a bum like Chain," intoned elegant Boris Chachkes of the Jewish Trades Council. "We have no obligation to seek justice. That is the civil authorities' job. Such members of the *lumpenproletariat* can be discarded when they outlive their usefulness."

Eva raged at him: "You ingrate! You arrogant know-it-all! Chain saved your necks! He put the fear of God into the bosses! Now that he's dying, you won't help find the people who tried to kill him?"

Chachkes blew white smoke to the ceiling, played with his ivory cigarette holder. The less said about Crazy Jake the better. No union officer should *in any way* hint at a relationship between the labor movement and savages like Chain.

"Mr. Chachkes is right," Ike said. "It's the only way." He was less eager to placate Eva these days. He knew he had lost her to Halstead.

"You are cowards, hypocrites, and mealy-mouthed schemers," Eva said. "And you will not stop me from what I intend to do."

Several days later, an interview with Eva under Garrison Halstead's by-line appeared in the *Eagle*. In it Eva charged that Frank Ferrante and Jacob Chain had been attacked by Morris Pearlberg and Herman Wesselberg of the notorious "Moishe Nigger Gang." The headline read:

BATHROBE UNION OFFICIAL CHARGES
NEW YORK HOODLUMS KILLED FERRANTE

****

Enemies of "Crazy Jake" Chain
Named by Eva Heilig as Gunmen
Who Shot Him Twelve Times

Leo Glauberman also gave Halstead a statement. The lawyer's intuition told him to remain silent, but he admitted to Halstead that there had been bloody threats from Moishe Nigger ever since he had been parboiled. It was no secret that Pearlberg hated and feared Crazy Jake.

"I know," Glauberman told Halstead after Eva had convinced him to speak out, "that Chain is no angel. But that hardly justifies murder. Justice must prevail, or the labor movement will become an arena for fraternal carnage."

The *Eagle* article was like an explosion from one of Jake's gasoline bombs. Phones buzzed. New York papers called Eva. Old police reporters with underworld connections found Moishe Nigger in his *shtuss* house on the Lower East Side. Pearlberg denied it. He was out of town that day. The Meal Ticket was visiting his mother in Hartford the night Ferrante and Chain were shot. Chain was crazy, a liar, a killer.

F. F. Dullahan and Benny Otzenberger, disturbed by Eva's interview, held a meeting in the boss's red brick mansion in Brooklyn Heights.

"Tell Hanratty to move his ass," Dullahan said. "Get the New York cops to haul those tramps in, question them, confirm their alibis, and turn them loose. Benny, they are grand fellows, the Nigger and the Meal Ticket. But we must make sure they keep their mouths shut."

Pearlberg and his fat aide were taken in and questioned for an afternoon by the police. They were turned loose for lack of evidence two hours later.

Again, Garrison Halstead wrote a long article on the Chain-Ferrante affair, and again Eva was quoted.

"These killers have no right to roam the streets," the Golden Voice said. "The police and the politicians are protecting them. I will not be silent until they are brought to justice."

Chapter 15

January's icy wind howled through the Abelman house. A hell of a way to start 1911, the doctor thought.

Unable to sleep, he nevertheless muttered his usual litany of curses when the doorbell buzzed at one in the morning.

"Bastards won't let you live," Abelman said. He got out of bed, his feet searching for the scuffed slippers. It was frigid in the house; the basement coal fire had been banked.

"I'll go, Sam," his wife said.

"Nah, nah. It's my job." He was young, strong, undeterred by night calls. In a snowstorm two days ago he had rented a horse and sleigh and toured Brownsville like a grim Santa Claus.

Abelman walked through the darkened house to the front window and threw it open. January air rushed at him and made him catch his breath.

The buzzing had not stopped. He stuck his head out, holding the pajama collar around his throat.

In the half-light of the snow-covered street he saw a woman standing on his top step, face upturned. She was crying.

"Dr. Abelman—please—help—"

"I'll be right down."

The physician hurried down the stairs, went through the foyer into the vestibule (the house was a replica of the Chains' and the Heiligs'), turned the lock and opened the bolt.

Eva Heilig, her face bloodied and bruised, collapsed in his arms. "Doctor—please—take me inside. They did this—hurt me. . . ."

(Years later, Abelman would recall that even battered and half-conscious, Eva Heilig had shown little fear. He marveled at her. Iron in the girl. She was a woman he would never forget, long after she had left Brownsville.)

Mrs. Abelman—a dignified woman who taught poetry at the Lyceum—came down to help.

Eva gasped out the story. Two men had grabbed her when she left the Utica Avenue subway station and was walking down Park Place. They had dragged her into a hallway and stuffed cloth in her mouth, punched her repeatedly.

"You didn't shout for help?" Abelman asked. He lifted her eyelids. No sign of internal bleeding. But she had an enormous purpling welt under each eye. The upper lid of the left eye was twice its size.

"They said they knew me," she said. "That they wanted to talk to me—" Eva covered her face and sobbed.

Abelman said to his wife: "Make some hot tea. With a shot of brandy."

Eva talked. The doctor wiped the blood from her face and she winced. She was coming home from a lecture she'd given at the Young Socialist League. A lot of talk, plans, theorizing. (She was getting a reputation. She was in demand as a speaker. The beautiful girl who had won the bathrobe strike.) She could find no cab. Tired of waiting for the St. John's Place trolley car, she began to walk. Arctic air invigorated her.

"You knew these galoots?" Abelman asked.

She shook her head. Strikebreakers, thugs. She had tangled with them before. She covered her face and sobbed in great convulsive heaves. Abelman patted her head like a father.

Eva took off her dress. The physician looked for fractures, internal bleeding. There was a severe bruise on her upper back, across the shoulder blades. The skin was scraped as if she had fallen heavily.

"They threw me against a radiator in the hall," she said, wiping her nose. "Hit my back on it, punched my eyes."

"The bastards should have their hands cut off. Anything special hurts?"

"This wrist. I fought with them. One of them twisted it."

Mrs. Abelman returned with the brandy-laced tea, kissed Eva, and left. Did she want to call her parents?

"No, please. Not yet."

"The police?" asked the doctor.

Eva shook her head. "They know me from the other side of the law," she said. "The Red, the agitator. Oh, that hurt when you touched my wrist. I twisted it again trying to get away."

"The wrist may be broken, Eva," Abelman said. "I'll put a cast on it. We can have it X-rayed tomorrow. Lie down and tell me anything you want."

He began to soak plaster-caked strips of cloth in warm water. She cried softly and he gave her something for the pain.

"Dr. Abelman—they did to me—they . . ."

"What? What did the galoots do?"

"They tried to rape me."

Abelman breathed deeply. "I'll have to examine you. You know what I mean."

"It's all right."

Abelman locked the door. Gently, he conducted the examination, trying to be detached, to suppress the anger in him that said: *Go out and kill the villains who did this.*

He found bleeding but no sign of penetration. He did not have the heart to ask her anything further. She would weep, sniffle, wipe her face, and then, with a courage that astonished him, would stop. Analytically, detached, she began to question him. Was it—could she have children? Would a husband know . . . ?

"You're all right," he said. No rupture of tissue. "You must have fought like hell."

She sat up and buttoned her chemise. "I scratched one of them so he'll have marks on his face a long time."

"They didn't do what they wanted to, Eva," the doctor said. "You're what you were. I know it isn't easy to accept, and it's easy for me to make speeches. But you aren't hurt that badly. It's the broken wrist we have to fix."

The doctor wrapped layers of plastered gauze around her wrist, reducing the fracture by manipulating and extending her arm.

She began to sob again, racking, gulping noises, as if she could not suck enough air into her lungs. She rested her aching head against the doctor's chest and would not stop bawling. They must have hit her fifty times, he thought. But she had fought back. He wondered why they had let her go before finishing their dirty work. The noise may have awakened people. Someone entering the building. Miraculously, she had walked two long blocks.

When she was dressed, he let her rest and finish the tea. He wrote a prescription for her pain. He had some morphine pills in his medicine cabinet, ointment for the bruises. These would tide her over, help her sleep.

At the door she made him promise to tell no one about the attempted rape. And until she decided what she wanted to do, she would not name the men who attacked her.

"I will use it for political advantage, for the *cause*," she said. The Heilig chin thrust forward. The eyes were dry, eager for a fight. "I don't mean a thing, Dr. Abelman. But what I'm fighting for does. I'll use this to destroy our enemies. What happened to me is our secret."

"I'll walk you home if you wait a minute."

"You're in your bathrobe, and it's cold and dark outside."

The physician laughed. "I'm tough, Eva. Remember when I ran the summer playground and taught you gymnastics?"

She smiled. The doctor put on overshoes and a heavy coat. He called to his wife that he'd be gone a minute, and escorted Eva to her house. Brave girl, he thought. Too brave.

* * *

Her parents reacted with hysteria, Brunstein and Flugelman with fear, Halstead with Protestant indignation.

Avner and Matla Heilig and her brothers Abe and Sol were all for a full report to the police, a demand that the ruffians be apprehended. Eva, her broken wrist in a bright red sling, her bruised eye closed, dissuaded them. Abe and Sol swore vengeance, but only halfheartedly. They were scholars, not brawlers. She lied that she did not know her attackers. Two strange men.

Brunstein and Flugelman wrung hands, feared for themselves, worried about her: She talked too much, talked back, challenged people unnecessarily.

"But the union is not recognized!" she said. "We don't have a union shop!"

Ike said he would bear more of the burden.

"Eva, you must not be on the barricades," Flugelman said protectively. "You must be careful. You are a woman."

"It had nothing to do with my union work, Meyer. It was a robbery by criminals."

Halstead proposed an article for the *Eagle,* kissed her battered face and her immobilized wrist, suggested that his father's political connections—more awesome than Dullahan's—be utilized. Obviously the bosses' thugs had done this. Revenge. The Chain business. They feared him. Having failed to kill Chain, they were warning Jake to lay off. If they could not murder him with twelve slugs, Halstead said, they would go after an unprotected woman.

"I am not weak and I do not feel unprotected," Eva said. "I will walk the streets at night. I will make speeches and I will challenge the oppressors."

"My darling, lower the red flag. You're too good to be shedding blood for it. You should be Mrs. Halstead."

She mocked him. "We could have the wedding reception in my mother's candy store."

He kissed her. They were in his apartment on Gramercy Park. She would not let him make love to her. She feared that she had been damaged. She suspected Abelman may have lied to comfort her. But she did not *feel* different. When they had spread her legs, punched her, tried to force their way into her, her struggles had been so intense that now she barely remembered what happened.

"Let me love you," he said. "I've never loved anyone. Anyone. Eva, my exotic Oriental."

"Stop, Garry. I'll laugh at you. And don't kiss my wrist again. It hurts."

On a warm February day Jake Chain learned the truth about the attack on Eva Heilig, from the "hoo-er," Minnie Fassbender.

He was dressing, moving slowly—the wounds had healed, but his muscles and bones were sore—when Minnie began to prattle about a visit she'd had recently with Moishe Nigger.

"Pearlberg?" Jake asked, buttoning his fly. He winced. The bullet had passed through his groin, missing vital parts, but the stitching and repair work—"the plumbing," as Abelman called it—left him with pains, the itching and strain of the healing process.

"Yeah, him. The one you boiled."

"I thought he was out of Brooklyn."

"I went to his place in New York. A big party on Washington's Birthday for the Morris Pearlberg Benevolent Association. He wanted extra girls. He ain't as good as you, Jake."

"So what did Pearlberg say?"

"Wouldn't *you* like to know." Minnie stuck her tongue out at him. She wrapped a kimono around her fat body. Nowadays, when he was finished with her Jake always felt a mild disgust. He came to her once a week; each visit satisfied him briefly, but left him empty and frustrated. Yet he needed the release. He and Sarah were strangers at night. He had bought twin beds, spent nights away from home, playing cards, visiting prostitutes, sometimes eating at the Ferrantes', where there was always a dinner setting for their *goombah* Jake.

"Tell me."

"When I told him how good he was, he give me an extra twenty dollars. And he said . . ." She stopped talking, walked to the mirror, and in the rose-colored light began painting her face.

Jake studied her overstuffed behind. "Hey," he said. "What did Moishe Nigger tell you?"

"Nothing, Jake. Nothing."

He twisted her arm behind her back. The green kimono opened, revealing her pink thighs, the gartered black stockings. She cried.

"The Nigger said he and the fat guy screwed Eva Heilig," Minnie said. "Jake, don't say I told you."

"He said this?"

"They got her in a house on Park Place. When she got beat up? I seen her with her arm in a sling. I wondered what happened."

"What else did he say?"

"He said they beat her up good so she wouldn't hire people like you no more and then they . . ."

"What else?" His voice was distant, an echo.

"He said if they couldn't kill a horse like you, they would kill *her* someday."

His blood was thundering. The old street anger. Different from the time he fought the men who tried to steal the keg of beer. Different from all the times he had thrown foremen down steps, battled Moishe's gang on the picket lines, scattered wagonloads of scabs.

This was something else. Now he understood why Eva was so secretive about the "robbery." Why only a halfhearted report to the police had been made.

"I don't like how you look, Jake," Minnie whimpered.

He jammed his cap on his head, paid her, and walked stiffly to the door. He did not hear her appeals.

"Jake, please, don't let them find out I told you. They'll kill me!"

In the street, he gasped for air, watched kids playing stickball under the streetlights, tried to control the rage in his chest. They could not kill him. So they had turned to an easier victim. They would pay.

Chapter 16

Jake told only one person, Luigi Ferrante. And he told him little. "Just find out for me," Jake said, "where the Nigger lives, where he goes, what he does at night."

A few days later, Luigi and Baggie scouted Moishe Nigger's territory. They learned he was separated from his wife and lived in a walk-up on Rivington Street. Usually he spent evenings at his *shtuss* house and came home late with his bodyguard, Duffy Plotkin. One or two o'clock. He drank little, carried a gun, talked about killing Crazy Jake Chain someday.

Jake and Luigi visited the street where the Nigger lived. A lively place—tenements, pushcarts. Less so in the winter. Late at night it would be deserted. Laboring Jews, peddlers, housewives, and students went to bed early and rose early. Some of them journeyed halfway across the city to jobs. Only people like Moishe stayed up late, gambling and whoring.

"The chicken market," Jake said to Luigi. "Down from where he lives?"

"Three stores down."

"Pick the lock for me the night I go."

"I want to work on him also."

Jake shook his head. "It's personal. Just break the lock."

Jake heard at Dannenfelser's poolroom that Plotkin was fighting in Boston on Saturday night. Good chance the Nigger would not go. Duffy was washed up, a bum who took tank jobs. Bobby Rimkoff had knocked him out in two rounds.

Sarah asked where he was going so late at night.

"Business meeting," Jake said.

"Eleven o'clock? Jake, you're starting again. Full of holes, almost dead . . . Don't go."

"It's nothing. Night shift in a hat factory in Queens. The workers need advice."

"Where? What Queens? You never went there."

"Glauberman asked me to go." He kissed her cold forehead. She was always cold, even in the overheated apartment. "If anyone asks, I was home all night. *All night,* you understand, dear wife?"

"Jake, come to me. We'll try again. Like a man and a woman who are married."

"Maybe some other time. I'll be back late."

Luigi drove him to the East Side and dropped him two blocks from Moishe Nigger's home. If necessary, Jake was prepared to come back night after night to find him.

He waited in the alley next to the chicken market. Luigi broke the lock on the side door and vanished. Jake fingered the open latch and stuck his head in once. No lights. No watchman. It stank of chicken shit and chicken blood. The doomed birds huddled in the cane cages. Some life, Jake thought. Not much different from the way people were treated. Food, crapping, a slit throat.

He hid in the angle that the poultry mart formed with the street and watched two cops walk by. A drunken Irish laborer rolled into the gutter. With surprising vigor, he came alive and started to punch when the cops tried to drag him off. They clubbed him mercilessly. He spat at them, cursed, fell, was dragged to his feet again. They clubbed him all the way to the corner.

Sorry, buddy, Jake thought. The busier cops were with drunks, the better for him.

Two weary prostitutes ambled by, handbags slung over their shoulders after a hard night's labor. A peddler shoving an empty cart—where was he going at such an hour?—creaked by.

Close to one o'clock, when he was bone-chilled, half-paralyzed, suffering pain from the healing wounds, he saw Moishe Nigger.

The Horse Poisoner was alone. No bodyguard. But armed, Jake was sure. After all, Pearlberg was extorting money from a hundred East Side businessmen. Anything from pushcart peddlers to factory owners. He looked fatter and huskier. He seemed sober, whistling between his teeth, jaunty. Pearl-gray derby, beaver-collared gray coat, gleaming black shoes. He was puffing a Havana. Near the market he stopped, tossed the butt in the gutter. Then he opened his fly and urinated against a garbage can.

Like a dog, Jake thought. And he'll die like a dog.

Jake came out of the alley and walked behind the Nigger. He grabbed him by the throat with his right arm while he cranked the Nigger's arm behind his back.

The victim writhed. Gurgling noises issued from his throat. Once he tried to reach behind him—Jake's old trick—and grab Chain's crotch.

Jake almost broke his hand. There was less and less strength in Moishe's arms.

"Ch—Chee . . ."

Pearlberg was trying to say Jake's name. Chain's right forearm pressed tighter against Nigger's neck. No words issued from the mobster's mouth. Pearlberg lurched, kicked, strained his muscles. Their legs entangled and they rolled in the gutter. Jake would not release him. He could feel the heavy body going limp. But he did not want him to die in the street.

With an effort that made him gasp, caused the wounds to scream, Jake dragged Pearlberg to his feet. He hit him in the neck with the edge of his right hand. The Nigger wheezed, coughed, lumbered toward Jake. He pulled a pistol from his belt. Chain grabbed his right arm. The gun fell from his fingers. Jake kicked him twice and pulled him into the alley.

"Chain, don't be crazy," the Nigger croaked. "You and me, we can work."

"You tried to kill me."

Something had happened to the Nigger's voice, something had been crushed and deformed in his throat. "My guys will get you. A hundred bullets this time."

At the door to the chicken market, Pearlberg tried to reach for a second revolver, but it had slipped inside his belt and was resting on his left buttock. Jake saw the floundering right hand and smashed it. He yanked the pistol from the Nigger's belt, stuck it in a side pocket.

"Heeelp!" the Nigger screamed. "Murder! Heeelp!"

Spinning Pearlberg around, Jake brought his forearm and fist to the hoodlum's throat, squeezed it until Moishe made gargling sounds. Like my old horse dying, Jake thought.

Jake kicked the door of the chicken market open and shoved Moishe Nigger inside. His gray derby had fallen off. The pomade on his kinky black hair clotted Jake's nostrils. Did Eva, he wondered, sniff the fancy goo when the Nigger and the Meal Ticket forced her legs apart?

"Lay off, Chain, lay off—we'll make a deal—"

"Tell me about the deal you made with Eva Heilig, Nigger. It felt good when you raped her?"

"I didn't—it was Meal Tick—"

"It was you, you bastard. For that you have to die, Nigger."

There were no more appeals from the mobster. He lived in violence; he would spit defiance.

"Can't keep her mouth shut. I shoved it in her. Me and the Meal Ticket —took turns—good. You shmuck, Chain, you'll never even see it. You like what I'm saying?"

Jake braced a knee in Moishe's back and shoved him toward the center of the chicken market. Mashed odors clogged his nostrils—chicken shit, chicken feed, chicken blood, street dirt.

A steel drum stood amid the cages of clucking, jittery birds. The drainings from the slashed necks of hens finished off by the ritual slaughterer, the *shochet*. In bloodstained smock, with sharp steel knife, he dispatched them. Jake had often heard the screams, seen the knife flash.

"This is how a dog like you has to die, Nigger," Chain said.

"I screwed her," Nigger wheezed hoarsely. "You never will, you dumb bastard."

"But I'm alive and you're dead."

With his left fist, he punched Pearlberg at the base of the skull. Then he lifted the heavy body and dumped it head-down into the drum. He listened awhile to the gurgling, bubbling noises. One iron hand kept the frizzy hair and dark face immersed in blood. Jake watched bubbles rise to the surface and burst. The bubbles got smaller and smaller. Then they stopped.

Moishe Nigger's ass and legs dangled over the side of the drum. A big hen. A fat chicken for some East Side housewife.

In the alley Jake found the gray derby. He dusted it carefully, the way he had often seen Moishe Nigger do it, and returned to the market. He sailed the derby into the drum of blood.

The nifty hat floated on the surface like a child's boat.

1960

Myron Malkin's Notebook

She's sitting half in shadow, half in sunlight on the glassed-in porch. The edges of her face glow with gold but the fine features are shadowy. In profile, with summer brightness filtered through the green glass, she looks astonishingly young and beautiful. One of the most beautiful women I have ever seen. By my computation she is now seventy-four years old.

We're alone on the porch. Outside, the steely blue Atlantic beats at the lifeless gray sands of Long Beach, New York. A handful of bathers on the beach. Sun too hot, air too humid. But inside the Star of Zion Nursing Home it's frigid. Mechanical iciness. I wonder whether it's good for the old bones and sagging bodies of the frail residents.

The chill doesn't seem to bother Eva Heilig Halstead. Although she is crippled and anchored to a wheelchair, she's alert and talkative, smiles at my jokes and flashes healthy teeth. There's sparkle—damned near flirtation—in her green eyes. I understand now why men fell in love with her. Why the immigrant girls braved the picket lines at the urging of "The Golden Voice."

"Of course I know you," she says. She turns her face to accept the glow of the sun. Her skin is a bit wrinkled, but it has a healthy sheen. No makeup. Mass of snowy hair piled high. As raffish as a Gibson girl's. "You are Dr. Abelman's son."

"Nephew, Mrs. Halstead."

"I don't use my married name. I'm Eva Heilig again. For a few years it was important to be Eva Halstead—when I wrote, when I lectured. But it was really fake. Married, yes. But a Halstead? Never."

"I looked up the old newspapers. It was quite a shocker. Jewish girl from Brownsville marrying rich New York WASP."

"Oh, yes. Quite an event."

I show the old woman a clipping. *"New York Times.* June 4, 1912. Want to read it? About the minister. And the way your family and your union sisters mingled with the Four Hundred in Sag Harbor."

"Yes, yes. You know, young man—what's your name?—it ended rather early, all that storybook romance."

I know, I tell her.

She's a legend. Not too well known anymore. She's been ill and out of action a long time. Paget's disease, a weakness and softening of her bones. Her legs are extended in metal braces. Her spine is askew. But the softening has not affected her face. The lines are firm, the forehead and cheekbones elegantly formed, the chin as determined as it was when she rallied the working girls.

"*Die Goldeneh Shtimmeh,*" I say. "The Golden Voice. You're in the books about the American labor movement."

"Am I? I've lost interest. Tell me, how is Dr. Abelman and your aunt, that lovely woman who taught poetry."

"Uncle Doc died five years ago. A heart attack. My aunt is fine."

"A wonderful man. He was the Heilig family doctor. My brother Abe swore by him, my brother Sol, all of us. A temper and a bad tongue, but he cared about people. Abe became a doctor because of him. You know Abe?"

I do. A. M. Heilig, M.D., is chief of surgery at a New York hospital.

She keeps derailing me with questions about Uncle Doc and about Brownsville. How is it today? she asks. Black, I tell her. The poplars on Haven Place that my uncle planted? Dead. Stripped bare by wild *shwarzers.* They come and go, the poorest, the dispossessed.

Abelman, Heilig, Chain. We lived on the same street.

"The Chain family, Miss Heilig. Can I ask about them?"

"Dr. Abelman's nephew can call me Eva. What about the Chains?"

I explain my notion. A magazine piece. Maybe a book. An American story. From a founding father who was a street hoodlum to a grandson who endows a medical school.

She laughs. "Myron, what a nice idea. The irony of it. Have you spoken to Martin?"

Yes, I think to myself, I've met that sleek, smart, dark young man. He wants no part of my article. *Town and Country* is fine. Black-tie evenings. Charity balls. Presidential commissions. Forget about the way it started. How a talent for busting heads grew into one of the hugest fortunes in America.

"Martin is a good boy," Eva says. "Oh, his wife, DeeDee, gives him fancy ideas. But they're happy. And so rich. They take care of me. I'm penniless, you know. I never asked Garrison Halstead for a nickel. I never earned much with my lectures and writing. An old broken-down Socialist."

Memories muddle my mind. The two-story attached homes of Haven Place. Old Brownsville. I recall Morty Chain, Crazy Jake's son, driving up to my uncle Doc's office in a black LaSalle. He'd moved his family from Haven Place to Ocean Parkway. A red brick mansion with a Spanish-tile roof and green-shuttered windows. My aunt said there were twenty rooms in the house, including a servants' wing. And an armed bodyguard, a big black, on duty. The second-generation Chain was getting shot at like his father. It ran in the family, this talent for becoming a moving target.

But nobody shoots at Mr. Martin Chain.

The old lady seems to be reading my mind. She asks me again about Martin—industrialist, real-estate king, adviser to governors.

"He was polite but not helpful. He says if he wants anything written about the Chain empire, he'll hire a professor to do it."

"And how can I help you?"

The loose green housecoat disguises the cruel curving of her spine. Now, shifting her slender body in the wheelchair and fixing those luminous eyes on me, I see the warmth and the spirit that made men love her. Garrison Halstead had not hesitated to leap across centuries of tradition to marry her.

"You're part of the Chain saga."

"Am I really? My daughter ended up fighting them."

"But you were related."

"Distantly. *Landsleit.* Does it matter anymore?"

"People say Jake Chain was in love with you."

"I suppose he was. That poor ox. I know, the newspapers called him a hoodlum, a gangster, a murderer. But . . ."

"What about the early days? How did Jake become your *shtarker?* The tough guy who'd protect your girls?"

She tells me an involved story that I can't quite follow. Something about Jews praying at a stream on Rosh Hashanah. A gang of toughs attacking them. Jake scattering the hoodlums.

"And Jake never went to shul, he couldn't pray." She laughs. "He learned to read and write when he was twenty-five! My brothers taught him. Did you know that?"

"Sol? The prosecutor?"

"Sol and Abe both. I can see so clearly the parlor in our house on Haven Place. Jake, so huge, with arms like a Greek statue's. Ashamed because he thought he was stupid. Sol used to go over his spelling.

"The Chains. They were a force of nature, Myron. The ambition was in their blood. *America Gonif,* where miracles occur, was invented for them. I liked Jake. A crippled wife. No education. An orphan. But there was tenderness and honesty in him."

"But, Eva, he was a *killer.* It's no secret. He did away with people. He was never convicted, but from what I've read there's little doubt that he—"

"I don't condone it. He lived violently. But we helped create him. He was our *golem.*"

"And his son?"

"Mortimer? Mutteleh? Oh, he was a *chuchem,* a *kluger.* You know what that means?"

"Clever."

"I'm sure you have plenty of clippings from the papers. Bootlegging was not my business. I was a Socialist. Birth control, pacifism, abortion, women's rights, rights for black people. Name a cause, I was part of it. Who cared about bootlegging?"

"And Martin?"

"How can I dislike him? He supports me. A thousand dollars a month to keep me in this kosher jail? Surrounded by ghosts, people I can't talk to? Who in this place knows about dialectical materialism? Anyway, I'm grateful. I've had Paget's disease for six years. A bad way to die, Myron. But I should not complain. Martin is—well, he's *Martin*. His younger brother, Davey, lives in Israel. He writes once a year. Iris, the sister, is in Hollywood. Martin got all of Mortimer's money. Believe me, Myron, it was *money*. Tens of millions, more. So much they never know."

"I admire him for helping you out."

"I'm nothing to him. If he doesn't come to see me, neither does my own daughter."

I consult my notebook. *Lillian Halstead, lawyer, Department of Justice, Washington, D.C.* I ask about her.

"Lillian? She was closer to me than she was to Mr. Halstead. I think he loved me so much he could not love our child. Do I sound conceited?"

She's crying. A film of tears on her exquisite eyes.

"I'm sorry," I say. "I didn't mean to revive so many memories."

"Oh, I'm enjoying it. So few visitors. No one to shmooze with. You know what it is to shmooze?"

"In the garment district. They stand in the street and talk on the lunch break. Politics, the union, business, sports."

"I was a good talker, Myron."

"And a marvelous woman. You still are."

"I wish Dr. Abelman were alive. I'd tell him what a nice nephew he has. I hope you write the book."

"But the Chains . . ."

She looks as puzzled as I do.

"What made them go?" I ask. "Where did they get the nerve, the ambition, the energy, the brains? Jake was a hoodlum. But he was rich when he died. He had the unions scared out of their wits. Look at Mortimer. Eva, he was so powerful during Prohibition, even the Italians and Irish, with all their murderers, couldn't touch him. They'd try, and *they'd* end up dead. And Martin. He's on the society or business page three times a week. How?"

"It was there for the taking, Myron. Some old Bolshevik once said Lenin found power lying in the street and picked it up."

"And the Chain family?"

"Something like that. The money was there. Ways to make money. Ways to grab power. They grabbed it."

I kiss her goodbye. Nearby, the Atlantic beats against the bleached sand. Eva Heilig smells sweet, clean, and young. I would have fallen in love with her myself fifty years ago.

I turn for a last look at her. She is nodding faintly as if reminding herself of her tenuous hold on life. The late-afternoon sun forms another edging of gold on her profile. The white hair is touched with glory.

I wish Uncle Doc were alive. I'd ask him about Paget's disease. He knew everything. He might have told me what kind of course it runs. What her prospects are. And surely he would have visited her.

But I have the feeling she doesn't want to see people. She was holding back. Unwilling to talk too much about her past or about her rogue relatives the Chains.

PART II

1922

Chapter 17

"A little shnapps, gentlemen?"

Leo Glauberman removed a fifth of Mount Vernon from his desk, found three shot glasses, turned the bottle of booze so the sunlight sparkled on the brown glass.

"The real thing. You see what the practice of law does for a man, Mr. Wallowitz?"

Jake Chain was seated in a corner of the law office. He was rubbing the long white scar in his awry jaw, watching the byplay. Glauberman was warming up a new client. Ike Brunstein, seated next to the client, maintained a hands-off attitude. Ike was prematurely gray. His scruffy moustache drooped, his slouch was more pronounced, and he looked shrunken inside his sleeveless cloak of black alpaca. Once a theorist and visionary, he had abandoned much of his idealism in favor of bread-and-butter issues—wages, hours, working conditions, pensions. Although he regarded Jake Chain as a criminal and Leo Glauberman as worse, his success in staying afloat in union waters was due in no small part to his access to them. Slightly ashamed of the tactics of Glauberman & Chain, Labor Consultants, he had nevertheless brought Mr. Wallowitz to the Pitkin Avenue office for help.

Hyman Wallowitz was a new fish. Walking delegate of the Wet Wash Laundry Workers Union, a struggling, underpaid group, he had come to Ike in desperation. Wallowitz was a cadaverous man suggesting a ruined Lincoln—long limbs, hands boiled out of shape by hot water. He was sunken-cheeked, tufted-browed, and hollow-eyed. He sat on the edge of his chair and listened. During the last strike he had been drubbed by Duffy Plotkin, who punched three teeth out of Mr. Wallowitz's mouth. The gaps in his jaw muffled his speech.

"Prohibition, my *tuchas,*" Glauberman said. "So they passed the amendment two years ago. All those dumb Baptists. *Goyim* who feel up women in the church pews, ministers who screw the ladies in the choir. But God forbid a human being should desire a shot. Enjoy, Wallowitz. You too, Ike."

"Good booze, Mr. Wallowitz?" Jake asked gently.

"You'll excuse me," the ravaged Lincoln said, "but normally whiskey I don't take. Maybe a little for my heart now and then."

"So your pickets have been beaten up?" Jake asked, prodding him.

"Three times. Look at my teeth."

"The owners won't talk?" Glauberman asked.

"Only to tell us we'll get *worse*. They got nonunion Italian ladies. In laundry hampers. They bribed a shop steward. A lousy five-dollar raise and he quits the union and he's bringing in scabs for Metzinger's Wet Wash."

"The gentleman's name?" Glauberman asked. Teddy Roosevelt was in action, scribbling notes on a yellow pad.

"Who?"

"Who is sneaking in scabs?"

"Shikey Frummer. But, please, don't start with him. He got a brother, Futka, a gangster, a murderer."

In anguish, Brunstein stared at the ceiling. Ideals! *Ideals!*

"Who's doing anything?" Jake asked. He got up, huge and broad-shouldered in a vested gray tweed suit, and put a hand like a canoe paddle on Wallowitz's shoulders. "You ain't a client yet. Nothing happens until you sign up."

The gaunt man looked at Brunstein. "So? You brought me here."

"Wallowitz, I don't like this any better than you do. But sometimes harsh choices must be made. If the union treasury can afford it . . ."

Wallowitz blinked. "The cops arrested a picket line yesterday. Twenty men. My wife was threatened on the street by a fat man in a checked suit."

Jake laughed. "Wesselberg is back, Mr. G."

"Tell him about your services." Ike sighed.

Jake picked up a leather folder with a celluloid envelope within. It resembled a menu holder. Inside the transparency was a typed list. Jake read haltingly. He was no longer the illiterate workhorse of twelve years ago. At the age of thirty-seven he was a man of substance.

"For me and Mr. Glauberman, thirty dollars a day each," Jake said. "A bargain. That's basic expenses, whether we work or not, or whether a job is done or not. For each man we have on duty, seven and a half dollars a day. That's cheap. It ain't easy to hire *shtarkers.*"

Ike covered his eyes. He was mortified.

"Why is that?" Wallowitz asked. "Business should be good."

"There's better jobs in booze." Jake raised his shot glass. "We got to compete on the labor market. Not like wet wash, where there's always cheap labor."

"Seven-fifty a day to have a man standing around?"

"Wallowitz," Glauberman said, "if our associates don't stand around, you'll have pickets with bloody heads and in jail." Glauberman leveled his specs at the gaunt man. "So a Shikey Frummer arranges for scabs. Futka brings them in. Next time they may stink-bomb your office. Or beat up your little boy on the way home from school."

"I got no boy. Only three girls, God bless them."

"Worse. What people like the Frummers do to girls I can't mention."

Jake resumed reading from his folder. "Wrecking a small factory or laundry or storeroom, two hundred dollars. The price can go as high as seven hundred and fifty, depending on the size of the place. Metzinger's is pretty big. You want a full job on it, dyes in the vats, acid in the pipes, stink bombs, the electric burned out, it might go as high as a thousand."

"A down payment of fifty dollars is required," Glauberman said.

"It's usual," Ike said.

The wet-wash delegate unfolded five creased ten-dollar bills. Hard-earned dues from his members. He put them on Glauberman's oak desk. "Why?"

"Expenses. Remember, Mr. Wallowitz." Glauberman leveled the pince-nez at him. "Any of our employees gets jailed, you must put up bond for him."

"And tell the whole world we're in with you?"

"The money can be given to this office," the lawyer said. "There is one final thing."

"In enough trouble I am. What else can happen?"

"Leo Glauberman, yours truly, will be elected executive vice-president of the union."

"Impossible," Wallowitz said. "Brunstein, tell them—"

"That's how it works," Ike mumbled. "You want to win the strike? The bosses started it with Pinkertons and gangsters. I don't care for this any more than you do."

For the wet-wash job, Crazy Jake imported four anonymous *shtarkers* from Jersey City. They were dock workers, Italians, recruited by Luigi Ferrante. Luigi and his brothers Baggie and Vince were the nucleus of the new mob. Sal sometimes helped out. Yussel Kuflik, the Bear, did odd jobs, specializing in arson and stink bombs. Label Kuflik had been shot to death in a poolroom brawl over a bet on the Willard-Johnson fight.

Jake's free lancers started by dropping Metzinger's foreman down an elevator shaft. He suffered a broken leg, a broken arm, and pangs of conscience. He found it difficult, from a hospital bed, to truck scabs to Brownsville. Metzinger's office was wrecked with a grenade. Two of his trucks were overturned and the drivers beaten.

In two weeks' time, the Wet Wash Association had settled with Wallowitz's union. Glauberman was installed as executive vice-president.

A week after the contract was signed, Jacob Chain, in new blue serge suit, white straw boater, and stiff collar, visited four other laundries. He was accompanied by Luigi Ferrante. A stubby .38 peeked from Luigi's belt.

With barely audible protest, the owners agreed that it was a splendid idea to pay Glauberman & Chain fifty dollars a week to ensure that no more violence was unloosed on their laundries and that workers remained uncomplaining.

Chapter 18

Eva could see Garry coming down the gravel path from the main house. He carried tennis rackets and a reticule filled with new balls. He walked like all the Halsteads—an odd short-gaited, knock-kneed walk, as if the legs were a bit underdeveloped. Inbreeding? she wondered. Mildred walked that way. So did Mr. Halstead, Sr. As if their slender limbs and narrow feet avoided maximum contact with the common clay of this world.

I can understand it in my father-in-law, she mused. But Garry and Mildred have touched earth many times and I love them for it. So why can't they plant their feet *firmly* on it?

She jotted down her speculation in her *Book of Personal Thoughts*. She was seated in the gazebo of the Halstead summer mansion in Sag Harbor on Gardiner's Bay. Sailboats skimmed by. Screeching gulls wheeled and dipped. Terns chased schools of bait fish. Above the slow rise of golf-green lawn bordered with formal hedges—azaleas, yews, ilex, forsythia—rose the clapboard "cottage." She laughed when Garrison first took her there before their marriage ten years ago. Some cottage! Twenty-seven rooms, stables (converted to a five-car garage), outbuildings, a greenhouse, vegetable gardens, a tennis court, and a landing dock.

Eva liked the gazebo best. She had a writing table installed there by Harms, the Halsteads' mulatto groundskeeper (there were six in help), and she often worked on her articles and lectures in the white latticework structure. Cardinals and yellow warblers twittered about the feeders Harms kept filled. A tiger swallow-tail butterfly settled with tremulous wings on lavender phlox.

Mr. Garrison Halstead's Brownsville Butterfly is a delicate and lovely creature rising from the fetid slums of Brooklyn. She did not seem at all fazed by the luxury surrounding her. . . .

She cherished the newspaper reports of the wedding. The social sensation of the year. A Halstead marrying a Jewish immigrant girl. The papers had started reporting their romance with a mocking tone. *Two Socialists? Worlds apart but finding love in their dedication to reform?* After the reporters attended the wedding—the service performed by the groom's uncle, the Reverend Isaac Yates of Saint Matthew's—they stopped sniggering.

Mrs. Halstead wore a gown of white lace tulle and a corsage of pink orchids attached with a bright red ribbon. She also wore a white lace headdress edged with bright red. When asked why she had chosen the scarlet accoutrements, the Cleopatra of the tenements smiled and said: "To remind all here that the revolution is yet to be won."

They had been married in 1912. It was two years after Halstead had first seen her in magistrates court, a woman accused of violent acts and disobeying a police order. She had to laugh. She recalled Garry putting up her bail. Her gray champion, as in the Hawthorne story. Only Garry had no gray hair, then or now. But her champion.

She had taken her notebooks and scrapbooks with her that morning. *Liberty* was interested in an article about their married life. A storybook romance, the editor said to her. After ten years, the well-nigh unbelievable Heilig-Halstead union was functioning, stronger than ever. No children, to be sure, but a happy marriage. Why not publicize it?

"You aren't going to indulge that fool of an editor?" Halstead asked. He had entered the gazebo on sneakered feet, kissed her neck, glanced at the clippings on the table. She was more fragrant than the meadows and flowers that surrounded her.

"I thought I might try it a different way, Garry. Forget all the society nonsense, forget my ghetto origins, and do a story about two people working for good causes."

"It won't satisfy them. They want to know if you use the right fork at formal dinners."

"We hardly ever go to any."

"They'll assume you do. They want to hear that the Brownsville beauty drinks from the finger bowl."

Eva laughed. "But I did once. On our honeymoon at that place in Bar Harbor. I was *thirsty.* You people drink so *much.* Liquor, wine, beer. I'm sorry if I was raised on sour milk."

Eva had rejected Uncle Sourmilk's panacea when she was twenty. "Poor papa," she mused. "Bloating himself with sour milk and dying at age fifty-five of influenza."

"It's possible the bacillus was contraindicated for influenza."

He looked at his wife's notes. Another lecture. He could not decipher her scribbles on the yellow pad. She had taken a course in shorthand and typing when she began to work as a union organizer.

"We Jews have that problem," Eva said. "Wrong bacilli, wrong choices, wrong politics. I don't believe our friends in Russia are backing the right people. A day of reckoning will come."

"Trust Lenin, my love."

Eva laughed so hard she had to cover her mouth. "Oh, my precious husband! In your tennis outfit from Abercrombie and Fitch! With your racket and tennis balls! On your Long Island estate, you tell me—*me!*—to trust Lenin!"

She almost fell from the wicker chair. Halstead caught her, kissed her open mouth. He stroked her breasts. It was astonishing. The longer they were married, the more he craved her. In bed he was tender, possessive, insatiable. *Stop, Garry, stop, you are wearing me out, I'm weary, I can't again. . . .*

Often distant and walled-in, Halstead conceived of himself as the weaker member of the marriage. Except in the dark privacy of the bedroom. There, his male needs, his gentile sword, conquered the Semite daughter, descendant of prophets and priests. Sometimes, he whispered to her, he felt like a soldier of the Tenth Roman Legion, taking his reward for the burning of the temple. Or perhaps a crusading knight with Godefroy de Bouillon raping a Jewess in the slums of Acre.

Reserved, at times unresponsive, she knew she was a disappointing sexual partner. Her radicalism preoccupied her. In demand as a lecturer, a writer, the voice of New American Women, she was a well-known name. Eva Heilig Halstead, organizer, labor executive, Socialist. More than once Garry had been referred to as "Mr. Heilig." At the Yale Club they joked behind his back about his Hebrew whore. The story came back to him and he resigned with an angry letter to the president.

"Who are you playing with today?" Eva asked.

He mentioned the names of neighbors—a broker, a banker. She could not tell them apart. They all appeared a great mass of pink healthy faces, strong white teeth, lean muscles. She refused to learn to play tennis, yet envied the women who did. They accepted her but did not understand her. *Garrison's little Jewess.* Most of them understood that if her origins were humble, her ambition was great. She wrote. She was published. She spoke to cheering crowds on pacifism, disarmament, equal rights for women, race prejudice, child labor. And now a new crusade—against the ravages of union racketeers.

"Work in progress?" Halstead asked. He got up from the bench that lined the interior of the gazebo.

"Gangsters in the unions."

"Ah, back to Brownsville."

"I promised the Labor Lyceum three speeches a year. They are one group that will never have to pay to hear me. Besides, I haven't seen my family in a long time."

"I'll go with you. What's all this about mobsters in unions? I thought all of that ended."

She showed him a *New York Times* article. One Herman Wesselberg had just been elected chief executive officer of the Bottlers and Soda-Water Wagon Drivers. A notorious criminal, tried for murder and acquitted. Twelve arrests. Her old enemy, the Saratoga Avenue Meal Ticket.

"Mr. Wesselberg and his kind were known to me when I was in charge of pickets," Eva said. "He's back, stronger than ever. Listen to this. 'Other notorious hoodlums, most of whom began their careers working for legitimate unions or employers, are moving in on positions of power in the labor movement. Captain Eric Stutz of the Seventy-first Precinct in Brooklyn reports that six unions in Brooklyn are currently dominated by underworld elements. He named the Wet Wash Workers, the Dairymen, the Furriers, and the Water Bagel Bakers. "Once they're in the house," Captain Stutz said, "it's hard to get these lice out. They frighten the workers as well as the bosses and extort money from both." ' "

"Would that include your cousin Mr. Chain?"

Halstead had heard stories about Crazy Jake and his mob. How they forced the bosses to give in by paying them back in kind. She had lost touch with Jake the past few years.

"Jake would not be a part of that," Eva said. "He's no angel, but he worked only when we needed him, and only for us."

He kissed her again.

Eva looked forward to the visit to Brooklyn and her family. She missed them. Her indefatigable mother, Matla, ran a prospering stationery store on Sutter Avenue. Abe had hung out his shingle on Pennsylvania Avenue and was on staff at Beth-Moses Hospital. During the dread influenza epidemic of 1919, when Uncle Sourmilk died, Abe and Sam Abelman had climbed hundreds of tenement stairs, leaped across roofs, worked a twenty-hour day trying to save lives. They had become good friends.

Her younger brother, Sol, was practicing law with two friends from Brooklyn Law School in a modest office on Court Street. Sol was in politics. There was talk that he might run for the state assembly. A strange fish, Sol, a *Republican,* coming out of Brownsville, where Socialists and Democrats prevailed.

There would be dinner at her mother's on Haven Place, then the ride in Abe's new Oakland, with Abe's sniffish wife Leah (daughter of the medical pioneer Aaron Lemkau), to the Lyceum. Garrison mingled with her old friends and family without discomfort. In his books *New Ghetto* and *Jewish Pioneers* and in articles, he had written about these energetic, talkative, intelligent hardworking people. It was, he noted, as if they were so in love with their adopted country that they were working overtime to pay off a debt. When they said *America Gonif,* it was uttered not as an insult but as a subtle term of approbation. Turn on an electric light? *America Gonif!* Admire a new Ford? *America Gonif!* They would be part of America, make no mistake, he wrote. And the nation would be better for their presence.

Garrison kissed her again now and went off to his game. Soon she could hear the distant *thwack-thwack* of tennis balls. There was no denying the beauty of the place. Still, she preferred their townhouse on Tenth Street. There they had only a maid, a cook, and a man-of-all-work, and they had been taught to keep their distance from the woman of the house. Eva wanted to hear nothing about menus, broken lamps, window cleaners. She wanted to immerse herself in her work.

"Married in a church?" Sarah Chain, walking with a cane, had asked when Jake had haltingly read the account of the wedding in the *News.*

Jake had read the description of the ceremony, the bridesmaids, the procession of cars and carriages from the white church in Sag Harbor to the estate.

A hoo-er, a *nafka,* that Heilig woman. Sarah and her neighbors on Haven Place (except for the dignified Mrs. Abelman) agreed as they haggled over the price of chicken in the open market.

Now that Jake was a "labor consultant," Sarah had her hair bobbed and slicked down. She wore bright stylish dresses from Loehmann's and purchased orthopedic shoes that minimized her limp. She smoked cigarettes incessantly. But she could not read. She learned to play cards and was an avid participant in penny-ante poker games.

Whenever Eva's name came up, memories of the daughter of Uncle Sourmilk, there were exchanges of narrow glances and arch comments over the ladies' poker table. Sadie Levinson and Molly Bauer and Rose Cohen knew. Jake Chain had been in love with his cousin. And maybe he still was. Who could blame him with a crippled wife who had developed a sharp tongue?

Chapter 19

"No fat," Minnie said. "If you were a chicken, I wouldn't buy you. But in a man. Oh, boy."

The prostitute ran her fingertips over Jake's naked body. He was like leather. Tough, resilient, scarred with the bullets that had cut him down in 1910. "Can I count them, Jake?" she asked.

Minnie had not aged. The first time Jake had made love to her she was eighteen—pudgy, round, cherry-lipped. There were old men in Brownsville, in fur-trimmed hats and long coats, who refused to believe that Jewish girls could be whores. Jake knew otherwise.

Her soft hands fluttered over his iron body. She excited him, but he did not kid himself. She was a substitute for his lost Sarah, for Eva. A man was like a machine. He had to be oiled and fueled. Minnie, with the soft, sluggish body of a girl who ate too much and hated work, was no real substitute.

Entering her, discharging his passion, he was filled with images of Eva. A stolid, uncomplaining man, who wasted no time on lost causes, on what could not be, he could not eradicate Eva's face, her voice, from his mind. Feared, hated, a power on the fringes of the Brownsville underworld, he had a reputation. People wanted to do favors for him. But the favor he craved, Eva's love, was one that no one could grant him. And he did not delude himself. No one ever could.

Twelve healed wounds. Twelve bullets from Moishe Nigger and the Meal Ticket. Wesselberg was still around, a big man in union rackets. When the Nigger drowned in chicken blood, when the Ferrantes made a torch of Little Mendel in Canarsie, the fat man inherited their illegal trade.

"On your jaw," Minnie said. "The long white mark. And a little mark on your head, where the blond hair grows over it. Thank God, Jake, *this* one didn't hurt you, or I'd be sad." Minnie stroked his crotch, probing the indentation to the left of his member. The bullet had ripped through hip and thigh. The two slugs that had bitten into his right leg bothered him more. Two others remained in him, one lodged against a bone.

"The man they couldn't kill," Minnie said. She stroked him to rigidity and played with him as if he were a gearshift. "Everyone's a-scared of you, Jake."

"Why? I'm a puppy dog."

Minnie maneuvered. "Neutral. First. Second. Third. Reverse is all the way over here. You didn't know I could drive? When I get outta here and don't have to work for Bella, I'll get a car. Jake, if you married me, I could have a car. A house in Crown Heights. I wouldn't have to be a hoo-er."

"I'm married."

"Some marriage. That *yenta*. I'm sorry, I'm sorry. Don't hit. You're a big man, Jake. You'll be rich someday. I could dress fancy, learn in night school, be a good wife. Then people wouldn't call me a hoo-er. It's no fun. Ten years with men I hate. You're the only one I love."

"Sorry, kid. I got Sarah and the boy. Maybe I don't sleep with my wife but I owe her plenty."

"What? A barrel of guilt? Like a keg of herrings in the appetizing store?"

"When we didn't have what to eat, she worked. She made buttonholes. She dressed Mutteh for school. I'm sorry, Minnie."

With an athlete's grace, he turned, naked as a carp, and entered her.

"Good," she said. "Only for you I do it for real."

He dressed quickly. A cut rate from Bella the madam. She knew a friend when she saw one. If Jake Chain was your friend, it was unlikely that Futka Frummer or his brother Shikey would come around for "protection." They avoided Crazy Jake's friends. The underworld knew what had happened to Moishe Nigger.

On the corner near the Lyceum, where Eva was to speak, Jake saw his son Mutt standing with Benny Otzenberger's daughter Hilda.

The boy was no longer Mutteh, or Mutteleh, but plain dumb-sounding *Mutt*. Miss Condon, his first-grade teacher, had decided that his name was Mortimer. And so it was entered in the school records. But to his friends he was *Mutt*. At eighteen, he bore both names proudly. He signed himself Mortimer J. (for nothing) Chain. But to the young toughs, the hustlers, the smart kids around Dannenfelser's poolroom, the up-and-coming boxers, he was Mutt Chain, Crazy Jake's son.

Mutt was lean and stringy, three inches shorter than Jake. He had a sharp dark face, pointed ears, solemn brown eyes, a nose like a blade, and a taut mouth. A fox's face. Sarah's face. Sarah's dark skin and near-black hair, parted slickly in the middle. He did not smile often, but when he did, the effect was disarming. A handsome kid, intelligent. He had dropped out of Thomas Jefferson High School in his last year. It bored him. Besides, Kolodny the hunchback (now mixing bootleg hooch) had offered him a job as a "salesman," handing out cards to speakeasies, private customers, restaurants.

"*Nu,* Mutt?" Jake said. "Hello, Hilda."

Mortimer J. Chain sized the old man up. Just had his piece of ass. He knew. The kid knew everything. He knew his parents never made love. Jake slept in the front room on a sofa. Under the purple brocade slip-covers were three bullet holes from the shooting. It was as if Jake, a giant of the streets, renewed his strength on the wounded couch. Sarah slept alone in the middle room.

"Mama says don't come home too late," Mutt said. He smiled slyly. "She says she worries when you're late."

"You told her where I was going? To the Lyceum to hear the talk?"

"She didn't believe me. Until I said Cousin Eva was speaking."

Hilda Otzenberger, the most delectable of local beauties, was a moon-faced, raven-haired girl with a wide mouth, a snub-nose, and darting black eyes. She took Mutt's hand and pressed her warm thigh against his. She laughed softly.

How an ox like Benny Otzenberger could produce such a beautiful daughter eluded all of Brownsville. People expected a small whale, a fat shapeless girl. Hilda was exotic and lush, suggesting harems, biblical temptresses.

"Your cousin Eva is *famous,*" Hilda said to Jake. "Honest, Mr. Chain. All the time in the newspapers. Once we even heard her on the radio."

Jake surveyed Hilda's inflated bosom, the luxuriant ass. Good for Mutt, he thought. And not a bad marriage, if it developed. Political connections would help now that he and Glauberman were expanding. Not that they didn't have Benny's blessing already.

"Papa, you haven't been to the Labor Lyceum in how long?" Mutt asked. He was taunting the old man.

"I don't listen to speeches," Jake said.

He watched the chattering crowd enter. Eva always drew them. They remembered The Golden Voice, even if she deserted Brownsville for a swanky *goy* husband.

Jake saw his father-in-law Klebanow and his wife entering. Klebanow was no longer the ragged peddler of twelve years ago. Using his mount-ing earnings as a "labor consultant," Jake had bought him a fruit-and-vegetable store on Prospect Place. Klebanow had prospered, almost seemed to have grown an inch or two. It was amazing what a little money did for people.

"There's grampa and grandma," Mutt said. "Since when do they go to lectures?"

"To hear Eva Heilig, everyone goes."

Mutt told him about Kolodny's plans. Bootlegging, the hunchback said, was the best racket. People wanted booze. It didn't matter what kind or how you got it. Maybe his father wanted to talk about it?

Jake smiled. No, the labor business was fine. Let Mutt be careful. He should always look around in dark places, never turn his back on an enemy.

"So far all I do is hand out cards."

Hilda Otzenberger listened, suspicious. What was all this talk? Speakeasies, bootlegging, merchandise from Canada. What did it mean? And who cared?

Mutt showed his father an embossed card.

HAPPY TIMES SPIRITS
PRESIDENT 4-4889 CALL ANYTIME, 10 AM–MIDNIGHT
FULL STOCK, FAIR PRICES, DELIVERIES

SCOTCH—RYE—GIN—BRANDY—CORDIALS—WINES

"Kolodny built a new place, papa," Mutt said. "Next to the old bottling plant. Bricks, cement, a big garage for trucks. And a separate part for the booze. He isn't so dumb."

For this my son dropped out of Thomas Jefferson High School? Jake wondered. He failed to understand his own role in shaping Mutt's life.

Chapter 20

"But there seems to be a mistake, Mr. Chain," Simon Baum said. "I've already signed a contract with the Glaziers Union."

Simon was the son of Kalman Baum, the old bathrobe tycoon. Simon was in his late twenties. Sleek raven hair parted at the side, pale oval face, piercing brown eyes, a waxed black moustache. He was one of Brownsville's leading builders, and his lavish office testified to his success. His current project was an enclosed market in East New York.

"I know you signed," Jake said. "But because I was just elected vice-president of the Glaziers, they want me to review the contract."

Simon Baum looked at his father's old enemy. Hoodlum. Bum. Seltzer-wagon driver. The bastard who had broken the bosses' united front, ruined factories, forced employers to give in. Nothing had been the same since. Young Baum found it convenient to forget that it was his father and his uncle who had unleashed hoodlums on women strikers in the first place. To Simon, Crazy Jake was no avenging angel of the unions but a ruffian, an extortionist, a liar, and probably a murderer.

There were stories. Chain had been interrogated and released twelve years ago after the murder of Moishe "Nigger" Pearlberg. Probably guilty as hell, Baum thought. And those reptiles, the Ferrante brothers. One of them, Luigi, stood at the door, trimming his nails.

"Elected, Mr. Chain? Or did you and Glauberman force the Glaziers Union to accept you? What is your experience in collective bargaining?"

Jake tilted his chair back and hooked thumbs in his vest. He was wearing his spiffy straw boater in the office. It was pushed forward on his flat face. Baum studied the hard cheekbones, the blunted nose, the scar on the jaw. The Nigger should have killed him.

"How many windows you got installed in the East New York market?" Jake asked.

"Ninety."

"Call up your foreman on the job, Baum. He'll tell you you got only fifty windows. Half of them got broke while we were talking."

Baum hunched his shoulders. *Bastard, bum, hoodlum.*

"Very nice, Mr. Chain."

"The union says that the price for replacing the windows is double." Jake's half-shut eyes never left Baum's face. Let him suffer. The collapsed factory. Sarah crippled for life.

"That's a violation of the contract," Baum said.

Luigi Ferrante pared his nails with a four-inch blade. He wore a brown box-backed jacket, beige slacks. His yellow cap fell over the side of his head like an artist's beret.

"Maybe, maybe not," Jake said. "Unless you and me can come to an agreement, there'll be ninety busted windows in the market."

Baum picked up the phone and said to his secretary, "Tell Mr. Heilig to come in."

Sol Heilig entered, chubby, rumpled, smiling. He had Eva's fair coloring but none of her grace. He was a political comer, everyone said.

"Hi, Jake," Sol said. "Hi, Vinnie."

"Luigi," Luigi mumbled.

"Of course. Vinnie's got an ear missing."

"That's Frankie and he's dead." Luigi was hurt.

"Sorry. Anyway, I know Sal. He catered the booze for our New Year's party. Poison from Kolodny's warehouse."

Baum was getting impatient. "Can't we get down to cases? Mr. Heilig is my lawyer. He knows you are threatening me. He knows you are in violation of my contract with the glaziers."

"What violation?" Jake asked. "I'm acting as vice-president. They want an extra five dollars per window. Hazardous work."

"My, my, Jake, *hazardous,*" Sol said.

Jake doffed his straw hat to Sol. "A credit to you, Solly. Remember when you and Abe learned me English?"

"Jake, we *taught* you, not *learned*. Anyway, what do you want?"

Jake twirled the straw hat on one finger. "Mr. Baum needs protection."

The phone rang. Baum took the receiver off the hook, listened, grunted as if he'd been kicked in the stomach. He hung up. "Ten more windows smashed. Your friend, counselor Heilig? Your relative?"

Jake yawned. "I have no idea who done such a thing."

"Did such a thing, Jake," Sol corrected.

"God in heavens, they're destroying me, and my lawyer is giving grammar lessons."

"How much do you want, Jake?" Sol asked.

"Fifty dollars a week. We'll make sure not a single window gets broke. No extra charge from the glaziers for fixing busted windows."

Heilig lowered his head. The *golem* was devouring everyone.

"I'm ashamed of you, Jake. You shake down Mr. Baum for protection, which means your people won't destroy his buildings. Then you cheat your own union members. You make both pay off."

"I won't stand for it," Baum said.

"Take thirty dollars a week," Sol Heilig said to Jake.

"Forty," Jake said.

"Thirty-five."

"A deal. First payment right now."

Baum shook his head. Where would it end? Tomorrow, next week, Jake Chain and his mob could ask for fifty, then a hundred.

"Jake, get out of it," Sol said solemnly. "This is no good for you."

Jake pocketed the bills. Luigi frowned. Hardly worth the threats. But he knew why the boss had gone easy on Baum. After all these years, Crazy Jake still had hot pants for the Heilig dame. He'd murdered the Nigger because of her.

"Listen, Mr. Baum," Jake said, "you got a bargain. Futka Frummer would charge seventy-five."

Chapter 21

Canada.

It sounded mysterious to Mutt. He drove his Chandler taxicab expertly, shifting gears on hills, handling the clutch, the wheel, the brake like a professional. Sal Ferrante, in the taxi ahead of him, warned him with brake lights when to slow down, used his left arm to signal turns. Sal drove an Essex. It was his own cab. He had purchased it with the profits from his fleet of hokey-pokey carts.

At twenty-seven, the youngest Ferrante was an entrepreneur. The kids who pushed the carts sold shaved ice for a penny or two cents and paid tribute to Sal. He disdained his brothers' careers as masons and strong-arm men for Chain. Sal was determined to be in business for himself. The wheezing Essex taxi was a common sight in Brownsville. It was rumored that a few of Chain's enemies, in need of education, had taken unwilling rides in the back seat. Like a neat housewife, Sal always washed away the stains.

But he did not care for the work, even if it meant a five-dollar tip from Jake. The day Prohibition went into effect and Reds Mulqueen's bar closed, Sal sighted a bigger pot of gold than *shtarking*. Booze.

His new career started in a lunatic way. Cruising downtown Brooklyn, he was flagged by a white-haired drunk in a pale blue suit and a floppy white panama. The gentleman staggering out of the Original Joe's was named Brian O'Toole, a political lieutenant of Francis Fagan Dullahan.

"Lousy rotgut, drugstore alky," Mr. O'Toole blubbered at Sal. "Take me to Canada, kid. Need some real stuff."

"How far?" Sal never wasted words. He had achieved much by listening, waiting.

"Goddamn near four hunnert miles. Turn off the meter and I'll give you fifty bucks."

After inspecting Mr. O'Toole's roll of bills, Sal helped him into the back seat. In a good week he was lucky to clear forty dollars with the taxi. It sounded like a profitable deal.

Arriving in Montreal, under Mr. O'Toole's guidance, Sal purchased a case of Canadian whisky for ten dollars. Mr. O'Toole bought four cases. *Thirsty.* He was always thirsty, he explained. Border guards were no problem. They waved the cab in and waved it out.

Back in Brooklyn, Sal sold his case of bonded Canadian rye to a speakeasy owner on Fulton Street for a hundred dollars. He did not need anyone to tell him that he had cleared *ninety dollars' profit* at the cost of a couple of tankfuls of gasoline.

A week after that first trip to Canada, Sal approached eighteen-year-old Mutt Chain and asked him to join him on a second trip.

"It's easy," Sal whispered. He hissed through his teeth. His eyes had developed a strange habit of looking into corners, past the person to whom he was talking. Arrested five times for vending without a license, three times for carrying a weapon, twice for breaking and entering, he had never been convicted. People did not like to give evidence against a Ferrante. And they were made queasy by his dancing eyes.

"Easy?" Mutt asked. He was working out with barbells in Futcher's Garage while his own taxi was getting a grease job. Futcher owned a dozen cabs. Mutt drove for him, ran errands in the cab for his father, for Otzenberger, for Mulqueen, for Kolodny.

Jake had wanted Mutt to go to college like the Heilig brothers. But Mutt was street-wise, tough, impatient. A wild hair up his ass, Otzenberger said. Lean like his mother, he had his father's strength. His hands seemed to belong to a man twice his size. And his temper was far worse than that of lethargic Jake. He had a glib, quick tongue.

"Get the cab from Futcher for a couple days," Sal said. "We drive up to Montreal, load up, and come back."

"What if we get caught? A Jew and a guinea? They'll hang us."

"Never. The guards let you in and out without lookin' at what you got."

"Even in a taxi?"

"Especially. Taxis go in and out alla time."

Sal told him of his trip to Montreal with O'Toole. Nothing to it. He lied about the profits. A ten-dollar case of booze could be sold for sixty, Sal said. He'd handle the sale in Brooklyn. Okay?

Mutt rubbed his chin. "If it's such a good thing, why just a case in the trunk? Why don't we take along a lot of valises, bags, crap that people on vacation carry? We can buy a real load."

Sal liked the idea. But it disturbed him a little that this punk had wised up so fast.

It took little to convince Mr. Futcher to lend Mutt the Chandler. *A pleasure, Mortimer.* Jake Chain provided "protection" for Futcher's Garage. He saw to it that Futcher's cabs got the best stations at the Utica Avenue and Sutter Avenue stops of the IRT. He made it easy with the hack bureau when licenses ran out. If Mr. Futcher got caught with phony meters that registered hastily, Jake Chain knew how to fix it.

It then occurred to the inventive Mutt that if they were lugging all those valises and trunks to Canada, a "passenger" would help.

Mutt had the answer. Ripe Hilda Otzenberger, two years older than Mutt, his steady girl, could play the part. Of course Benny would take some convincing. Luckily, Hilda was one of the few people in the world—perhaps the only one—to whom he could not say no.

"Ah, come on, pa." Hilda pouted. "Morty is a nice kid. Sal is just on the trip to show the way."

"And tell me, Hilda dollink," Benny asked, "for what is this shlep to Canada?"

"To see Niagara Falls."

"That's the other end of Canada. That much I know even if I can't read. Montreal is the other direction, where people talk French."

"Mort says we'll see Niagara Falls on the way back."

"A long trip. You'll sleep in different rooms, please."

Benny knew what you could get in Canada. *Real booze.* Friends of his were already looking into prospects. Leave it to that ginzo Salvatore. And now Jake Chain's son was in with those Ferrantes.

Now Hilda sat in the front seat of Mutt's rattling Chandler, dodging his exploring hand, slapping, teasing, letting him know just how far he could go.

"Lemme see your garters," Mutt said. They had left Albany and were headed north on the state road.

"Fresh."

"One garter."

"Okay, but that's all."

She raised her black serge skirt, revealed black stockings, a heavy alabaster thigh. A frilly pink garter pinched the soft flesh. Mutt reached across the gearshift to snap the elastic. She cracked his hand. "I said *no.* And we ain't sleeping in the same room. You can sleep with that wop."

"But I love you. You're the most beautiful girl on the block."

"Block? Boy, what a compliment. Hands off. I mean it."

Leaving Saratoga, he reached around her shoulder and began to massage one cushiony breast. She was wearing a hard corset. It made contact difficult, but elevated her bosom endearingly. Hilda got bored with his hand and pinched it.

"When I say no, it's *no.* Drive."

The road was bumpy and endless. At Glens Falls the scenery became more interesting. Pine forests. Lakes. Mountains. Mutt could recall going to a *kuch-alein*—a bungalow in the Catskills where his mother cooked in a tiny kitchen. It was after Jake had been beaten up by the Frummer brothers, the heirs of Moishe Nigger's gang. It was a warning. *Lay off.* His father was *shtarking* for the Carpenters Union, beating up scabs, wrecking nonunion shops.

They had broken Jake's nose, fractured his left arm, covered him with welts and bruises that would have sent any other man to a hospital for weeks. The next day Crazy Jake was back on his feet, guarding pickets. Three days later he was escorting wife and child to the mountains.

Doc Abelman had suggested he get away. It was wartime. Doughboys, parades, Liberty bonds. Bobby Rimkoff, the landlord's son, had enlisted in the Rainbow Division. He was not only divisional lightweight "champeen," but a hero of the battle of Saint Mihiel. There was talk of naming a street for him (a short one, to be sure, as befitted a lightweight) in East New York.

In Brownsville, a heavy demand for uniforms had the shops working overtime. Unions were in battle not only with bosses but with each other. The Bolshevik Revolution had split labor leaders eighteen different ways.

Mutt nurtured memories of bond rallies, a parade on Eastern Parkway. Rimkoff coming home a hero, challenging any welterweight around. (They'd start him with old stumblebums like Duffy Plotkin and Negro shoeshine boys before getting him a bout in the Garden.)

There was excitement in the air. He was sorry his father had not been part of the AEF. Jake would have made a natural first sergeant, people said. But he was so full of bullets, so scarred and bruised, that he would never be allowed to shoulder a rifle. Plenty of Brownsville boys enlisted or were drafted. Mutt envied them "over there."

It was over as soon as it began, it seemed to Mutt. He was fourteen, a kid in corduroy knickers and a "beanie" cap made from Jake's old brown fedora, when he stood on Eastern Parkway and watched the victorious army parade.

The war over, his father's "business" grew into a big-time operation. Everything was booming—building, needle trades, food processing, trucking. Glauberman & Chain, Labor Consultants, grew with the times. For a long time Mutt was not certain what Jake did. But he understood that his father was feared. People deferred to him. They wanted to do favors for him. The way Futcher had donated the taxi for the ride to Canada.

"I got to pee," Hilda said.

"You were supposed to go at the gas station in Saratoga."

"I can't help it. All that orange soda I drank for lunch. Listen, I'm your passenger. I'm the rich girl going to visit her family in Montreal, right? I need two cabs to get me there, I'm so rich. So you gotta do what I say."

He honked three times, a prearranged signal to Sal, who drove like a madman, turning corners on two wheels, passing double lines, running lights. It surprised Mutt. Sal had a cautious manner—forever scheming and figuring. Mutt filed the knowledge. It was always good to know these things about people.

For identification at the border, Hilda had a copy of her birth certificate. Mutt and Sal showed registration papers from the New York hack bureau.

The Customs and Immigration guards at Rouse's Point could not have cared less about the concocted story. Miss Otzenberger was en route to Montreal to visit her family. They looked at the trunks and valises filling the cabs and assumed she was a rich lady who always traveled with luggage.

"I tol' you," Sal said when they stopped for lunch. "Nobody knows what's going on here. They act like it's nothin' for a guy to ride a taxi in and outta Canada."

The lessons were not being lost on Mutt. Lie. Bluff. The law was blind, dumb, and uncaring.

It took them an entire day to load up with liquor. They were able to pack eight cases each of scotch and gin into the cabs, using the trunks, the seats, and even the roof of the Essex, on which they improvised a rack. The scotch had gone up slightly in price, eleven dollars for a case of twenty-four bottles. The gin was ten dollars the case. All told, they spent one hundred and sixty-eight dollars, saving just enough for gasoline and food for the return trip.

They stopped at a garage run by a friendly Breton. In French-accented English the mechanic said, "Plenty Americans come here with cab, right? Good booze, good business. You need partner?"

No, not a partner, Sal said. But a friend in Montreal wouldn't hurt. The garage owner's name was Louis Lamotte. He gave Sal a card. Glad to oblige an American. Business would be booming.

Later, Sal and Mutt settled accounts. Sal had laid out the cash for each purchase. Now, he told Mutt he was a "third" partner and thus owed him fifty-six dollars.

"Whatddya mean a *third*."

"A third, a third. It was my idea." Sal's eyes flitted left, right.

"Bullshit."

"That's right," Hilda seconded. "Bullshit."

The three were seated in a shabby truckers' diner a mile north of the border crossing. People were speaking French. Sal and Mutt had parked their taxis where they could keep wary eyes on the liquid treasure. They sipped coffee and ate cheese sandwiches. Mutt had done some fast mental arithmetic. The alcohol in the cabs was worth almost a thousand dollars.

"A third is all you get," Sal said. He looked creepy. Creepier than Mutt had ever seen him. He was slumped in his seat as if he had a flexible spine.

"He's cheatin' you, Mutt," Hilda said in a singsong. She took Mutt's hand. Suddenly she was afraid of Sal. She could remember him when she was a little girl. Sal the hokey-pokey man. Never smiling, rattling pennies in his soiled apron. Always something scary about him.

"Take it or leave it," Sal said. His eyes jumped—ceiling, counter, window.

"The way I figure," Mutt said, "is *I* should get two-thirds and you only a third."

"Eh, Mutt, don't be a *stroonz*." Sal did not smile.

"*Stroonz* yer ass," Mutt said. He spoke softly. "I brought Hilda and her valises and trunks. We're a team—two of us, *one* of you. I brought a cab of my own. So we should get two-thirds."

Mutt held Hilda's chubby hand. Nervy girl. One you could love. Benny would scream bloody murder if Jake Chain's son, a cabbie, asked for his daughter as a wife. Some son-in-law! Benny and his wife wanted doctors and lawyers, not a squirt like Mutt Chain.

"Hilda, go to the toilet," Mutt said. "Sal and I got business to talk."

"No. I wanna hear. I'm part of this deal. Anyway, what am I getting out of it besides my father will holler on me for running off? He woulda hit me if he could run faster."

"Go on, sweetie," Mutt said.

They watched her ample figure swivel to the ladies' room. The behind was big, the hips full, the legs nicely shaped. The cook also stared at Hilda's behind. It was of a shape and lilt that would attract stares when she was in her fifties; not just big, but wonderfully constructed.

"Ya get into her pants yet?" Sal asked.

"None of your business."

"Dry runs and jerk-offs?"

"I'm warning you, Sal, lay off. This is business. I want half the profits of everything. I'm giving you a break."

"Whaddya gonna do if I say no?"

"Beat the shit out of you. I'm not afraid of your gun."

Sal, for the first time, smiled. His beady eyes looked at the parked cabs. Big business beckoned: *trucks*. It was easy. So easy. All you needed was nerve, contacts, dependable partners. To be tied in with Crazy Jake and Benny Otzenberger had advantages.

"Okay, halfies," Sal said. His voice was dead.

"And no double-crossing. I'll go around with you when you sell the stuff."

The john door opened and Hilda emerged, crinkling her nose against the reek and smoothing her skirt.

"You big shots got it all settled?" she asked.

"You bet," Mutt said. "Finish your coffee."

At the border crossing they ran into trouble.

Cars and trucks were backed up fifty yards on the asphalt highway. It was a hot spring day. Engines were overheating. Cars were pulled off the road with their hoods up. Cursing men in shirt sleeves were repairing blowouts and steaming radiators.

Ever cautious, Sal stopped the Essex before he got to the waiting cars. He got out and stood on the running board.

Mutt braked the Chandler. It groaned and creaked under its load.

"What's wrong?" Hilda asked.

Sal gestured to Mutt to follow him to the roadside. The backup was a bad sign. Usually autos were whisked in and out.

A rangy man with a mop of Brillolike red hair saw the taxis parking and approached Sal. He was a thick-shouldered, unshaven rube with a checked green cap pulled to one side of his head. Although his blue work shirt and trousers were soiled, he wore a green satin bow tie.

"Runnin' booze?" he asked Sal.

"No. This lady is coming back from a week with her family in Montreal. She hired us to carry her stuff."

The redhead winked. He stuck his head in the window of Sal's cab. "You got an awful big load, mister. It ain't the Canadians stopping cars. It's the American Customs. They got tough a couple or three days ago. That's the holdup. Making people open trunks."

Mutt got out of the Chandler and walked to Sal's cab. The redheaded man was pointing west.

"Got fifty bucks? I'll get you out of here on a logging road. It's rough, but you'll end up near Malone, which is New York State. If your axles is strong, you'll make it."

"Fifty bucks?" Sal asked. "Just to show the way?"

"Or else you get searched." The redhead pointed to the queue of cars. It had gotten longer. Men were cursing and mopping their faces. Small boys urinated at the side of the road. A woman held an infant girl over the grassy shoulder to let the child pee.

"I'll give you twenny," Sal said.

"Make it thirty."

"Okay."

"Glad to help a couple of Yanks. Name's Bradford. I'm no lousy Canuck. You can depend on Emmett Bradford. I've hunted every acre around here. I know the roads."

"Get in," Sal said. "I have to talk to my partner."

Sal and Mutt walked to Mutt's cab. Sal opened the door and told Mutt to get in. He pulled a .38 from his pocket and gave it to Mutt. "I don't trust that redheaded guy," Sal said. "You know how to use this?"

"Sure."

"Now we got two. I always carry an extra."

Hilda gulped. "I don't wanna go along. Let me cross over on foot and I'll meet you somewhere." She was sweating. Her ripe body gave off a perfumy odor. It seemed to come out of her loins, her breasts.

"Nothing'll happen," Mutt said. He had his father's pride in getting jobs done, a cold view of the world. *Them or us.*

Sal returned to his car. Following Bradford's instructions, he made a U-turn and headed south. A mile down the road they turned left through an open wooden gate and clattered onto a red dirt road. It led through stands of giant pine and fir. There was no sign of habitation. Not a house, not a farm.

"Lumber company land," Bradford said. "I used to work it. Know the logging roads. How much you boys carrying? Big load? My God, I never knowed Americans were so thirsty. How much?"

"Enough."

They rode for ten minutes. Sal maneuvered the bone-rattling cab over pits and rocks, stopping now and then to move a fallen tree. The road was single-lane and followed the natural contours of the terrain.

In the car behind, Hilda bounced on the hard leather seat. Bruises blossomed on her tender buttocks. She grabbed the meter for dear life. With the other hand she braced herself against the door, ready to throw it open if they fell off a cliff or into a marshy pond.

The forest thickened, vast stands of commercial trees. They jounced past eerie bogs and dismal swamps peopled with dead stumps.

"I hate this place and I hate this ride," she wailed. "Morty, what's this all about?"

"We got to save the booze. The guy said the American Customs are inspecting cars."

"I hate your lousy booze and I hate this trip."

He assured her that after a few more trips he'd be rich enough to marry her. Benny might settle for having a successful bootlegger in the family. Mutt saw great possibilities. A great future for an eighteen-year-old who'd dropped out of Thomas Jefferson High.

The winding road was like a rust-colored scar in the green forest. Once they forded a shallow stream. Hilda blubbered as the Chandler sunk to its hubcaps in water. The engine coughed and died. It took a great deal of coaxing to get it started again. Mutt had to shout to Sal to wait. Then he got out and, knee-deep in water, hand-cranked the motor.

A half-mile beyond the stream, Bradford cut a wire fence, pulling apart the strands. It looked to Mutt as if he had done it many times. He did not trust the big man with the orange hair and green bow tie. He was glad he had Sal on his side and that both were armed. A certain exhilaration suffused his chest. He was his father's son.

Don't act yellow, his father told him, *don't move back, and when you're in a corner, keep swinging. And don't show the gun or the shiv unless the other guy does.*

The woodlands thinned. Mutt could see through the hazed green cover a distant lake—cool, clear. Nice to take a swim, relax, to admire Hilda's "built" in a bathing suit. But they had goods to deliver. A lot of money was waiting for them in Brooklyn.

Sal signaled Mutt to slow down. His Essex was turning right, following the red dirt track. Mutt could see a faded gray house with a broken porch.

A rusted wreck of a Ford stood in the front yard, surrounded by oil drums and piles of firewood.

The Essex stopped. Bradford got out. Three men in rough clothing were waiting for him. They were pitching horseshoes, but halted when they saw the taxis. One of them, a full-bearded man with a vast paunch, shaded his eyes and peered into the rear of Sal's cab.

Sal did not get out. Bradford was talking to the other two men. They kept their horseshoes in their hands. One, a starved, chinless man, picked up an ax. They kept their backs to Sal.

Mutt stopped the Chandler. He smelled trouble. His Chain blood told him when things weren't kosher. Too many times Jake had been shot at, beaten, ambushed. *Always watch yourself,* his father warned him. *When there's money involved, a shakedown, a swindle, a bribe, watch out.*

"I don't like those guys," Hilda said. "I'm scared." Her voice quavered.

"They just want a cut for getting us through."

Bradford picked up a two-by-four. He left his friends and was talking to Sal.

"New York State's right ahead, son." He turned and smiled at the bearded man. "Got us a couple of smart city boys here with a load of bonded. Not just in the car trunks. But all them big valises."

"Open the trunk," the bearded man said to Sal. He had a weary voice.

"It's stuck."

"You a smart Jewboy? Or a wop? Come on, skinny, open it." He slammed a horseshoe against the lock.

"You'll bust it worse," Sal said sadly. "Mutt? Pull up, huh?"

Mutt shifted into low gear and aimed the nose of the Chandler at the fat man's ass.

On the slanted porch a gaunt woman in a stained dress puffed a cigarette.

"Thirty bucks, you said, for getting us here," Sal said sorrowfully. "And here it is, Mr. Bradford. A deal's a deal."

Mutt could see Sal handing bills to the redheaded man through the window.

"That's okay for me," Bradford said, "but my family here, they tell me it ain't nearly enough for helping two cars past Customs."

"I guess you're right," Sal said. "Can I ask my partner?"

Bradford grinned. "Sure."

"Mutt? Can we pay a few dollars more?" Sal called.

Mutt nodded his agreement. His car was a few yards behind Sal's. He drew the .38 from his belt. Hilda gagged, slid toward the door. Mutt grabbed her wrist. "Duck down when we go. Don't be scared. Put a hand-kerchief over your mouth."

"Whaddya want?" Sal asked stupidly.

The bearded man had opened the rear door and was inspecting valises. Luckily, the two bags stacked on the seat were extremely heavy and were wedged against the seat. He yanked at one and could not budge it. He shouted at the chinless man to help him.

"Half the load, son," Bradford said. "If it's real good stuff, maybe two-thirds."

"That ain't fair," Sal said. "You said thirty bucks to get us across. I'll give you fifty. Please, sir."

Bradford laughed and slapped his thigh. The bearded man and the chinless one began to tug at a wicker trunk. They grunted, worried the handles, trying to yank it through the narrow door.

Bradford lifted the two-by-four and aimed it, as if batting, at Sal's face. "Don't move, youngster. I'll ram this through your nose."

Sal turned and, with his darting eyes, signaled to Mutt—a wink, a flicker of the lids. The woman was trudging through the mud toward the Chandler. She carried a crowbar.

Mutt gave Hilda the .38. "It's cocked. Just point it and pull the trigger. I got to handle the wheel."

"I c-can't. I'm scared."

"You'll be dead if you don't."

"Gimme the keys to the trunk, son," Bradford said. "I know it's full of booze. Turn that engine off before you get a mouthful of pine splinters. Ever eat a two-by-four?"

Bradford was yawning, displaying rotten teeth, when Sal squeezed a single shot from his .38. The flame scorched Bradford's astonished mouth. The bullet entered between his tongue and upper teeth. Bradford's eyes popped, offended and outraged, and he walked backward, blood and brains spouting in a pink cloud from the back of his head. Then he sank slowly. He appeared to be praying before he fell on his face in the mud.

The woman shrieked. The bearded man grabbed one door, the chinless man another.

Sal gunned the engine, picked up speed, and dragged them along. Mutt followed him, bouncing over holes, ruts, rocks. The woman smashed the rear windshield of the Chandler with her crowbar. Glass splattered inside the taxi. Hilda screamed and ducked. But she was no coward. Otzenberger's daughter had *gedarim*—guts. She fired twice through the broken glass. Both shots missed, but the pursuit stopped. The woman howled and ran to Bradford's body. She embraced him in the mud, screamed at him to wake up.

The bearded man had gotten both feet on the running board of the Essex. He was clinging to the half-opened door. Sal turned and fired again. But the man was hunched low, protecting himself. Sal's .38 missed.

Mutt could see the man clearly—patched blue coveralls, flowing whiskers, a belly like a basketball. He was taking a wrench from his rear pocket.

Both cabs burst onto a tarred dirt road. They had left the logging road. A sign read: PLATTSBURGH.

New York State. Past the Customs. And a corpse left behind, a dead crook. Hilda was oyster gray, hysterical. She put the gun on the seat and began to have an attack of asthma.

"For chrissake," Mutt said. "Put the gun on safety. One jolt and it'll go off." He knew about guns. Jake kept a few in the house.

She was too shaken to obey him. He reached across her lap and put the safety on. Jesus, his first rum-running and a man was dead. What if those hicks had taken the plate numbers? Mutt realized his immediate problem was the bum clinging to Sal's running board.

"Hang on," Mutt said. "I'm gonna bump that fat guy."

"No more shooting," she bawled. "Mutt, no more!"

"Just a shot in the keester."

He honked loudly at Sal. Sal waved him on. The road curved and rose between pine forests. Not a car in sight, not a house. Least of all a cop.

It was funny (Mutt thought later) the way he and Sal had understood each other. Hated each other's guts sometimes, never trusted each other. They could guess the other guy's mind. Maybe because they were alike in many ways.

Sal understood. He slowed down and moved to the center of the road so Mutt could get a clear shot at the man hanging on to the running board, swinging the wrench every few seconds, then ducking to avoid the pistol.

Too late, potbelly saw what was coming. With raging eyes he turned his bushy head, trying to make up his mind whether to hang on and keep trying to kill the driver or save his own life.

Mutt rammed him broadside with the bumper and radiator of the Chandler. The fat man roared curses. His insides turned to mush. Bones cracked and splintered in his legs. He unloosed his grip and rolled into the dirt, tried to stand, and walked on his knees several yards before collapsing.

Sal stopped the Essex. He shifted into reverse and backed up. Then he aimed the car at the crawling monster. He was going to run over him.

"Jesus, no, Sal, no!" Mutt shouted. "He can't do no harm."

The fat man flopped like a beached codfish, spattered the dirt with blood.

"Screw him, he's through," Sal agreed. "But you shoulda killed him."

The taxicabs sped toward Plattsburgh with their alcoholic loads. Hilda stopped crying and nestled against Mutt. She worried: What if they were found out? *What if . . . ?*

Chapter 22

Mrs. Wallowitz was gaunt and shabbily dressed. A poor woman, she was nonetheless mannerly and not without a certain dignity.

She was leaving Dr. Abelman's office on Haven Place when she spotted Jake Chain getting out of his shiny black Hupmobile. A tall woman with a haggard face, she lurched toward him.

Sarah Chain, sporting a tightly curled permanent and wearing a smart royal-blue dress from Loehmann's, sat on a cane chair on the stoop, gossiping with Mrs. Rimkoff. They were discussing Bobby Rimkoff's rising career as "The Brownsville Belter." He was ready to fight the number-one challenger. Mrs. Rimkoff didn't like the idea, although her Orthodox husband said he would let Bobby keep fighting "until he lost." Apparently, there was a talmudic precedent.

Jake paused under the poplar tree and looked at the kids in loose knickers and beanies playing stickball. Years ago he could belt a rubber ball two and a half "sewers." But he'd never had much time to play. He'd always had to work to keep bread in his stomach.

"Mr. Chain, please," Mrs. Wallowitz said.

"Yeah?"

Sarah and Mrs. Rimkoff watched. Sarah pouted. This one was obviously not one of his "hoo-ers." The woman was plain and poor. Mrs. Rimkoff had similar thoughts but said nothing. Everyone knew the pain Sarah Chain suffered. But at least she had money, a car, nice clothes, and new furniture. So her husband had *nafkas*. What else did anyone expect from a gangster?

"I'm the wife of Hyman Wallowitz."

"So?"

"This morning on the way to work they broke his legs."

Jake had spent the day in Queens, checking a local of the Glaziers Union. He had succeeded in getting boss and workers to agree to a "sweetheart" contract neither of them liked. It included a fee for Glauberman &

Chain. It had gotten so that the very presence of labor consultant Jacob Chain produced cooperative feelings on the part of adversaries.

"You are supposed to protect him," she said. "I was by Dr. Abelman just now. My husband is in Brownsville Jewish. Maybe he'll be crippled." Mrs. Wallowitz glanced at Sarah as if to say *like your wife.*

"I don't know nothing about it," Jake said.

"My husband is an honest workingman. All his spare time he gave to the union. Then you and Mr. Glauberman came in and you got a contract. But ever since then . . ."

She began to bawl. Her shoulders heaved. Rocks had been thrown through their windows, she said. Her daughter found a dead cat in the airshaft of their apartment. And now this! Two men, Italians, breaking his knees with baseball bats! What kind of protection was that?

"I'll find out," Jake said. "Don't cry, don't cry."

When she left, he walked up the steps and kissed Sarah. He tried to dismiss the Wallowitz incident. He had bought a new Zenith radio, a huge mahogany set, complete with earphones. It was the envy of the neighborhood. A little music after dinner. But the attack on Wallowitz gnawed at him. Disturbed, he left his house and drove to Glauberman's.

Leo Glauberman lived in a yellow brick mansion on President Street, as befitted a successful attorney and union official. He had escaped Brownsville for the luxury of Crown Heights.

"What about Wallowitz?" Jake asked his partner.

"What about him?"

They were in Glauberman's study, a walnut-paneled room with a high carved ceiling and a view of a greenhouse. The curtains were dark green velvet. The lamps on Glauberman's desk were also dark green. They gave his Teddy Roosevelt face a sinister greenish tint. The pince-nez had no eyes (it seemed to Jake), just two glasses glinting green.

"Who broke his knees?" asked Jake.

"Guess."

"Not my people. I learned about it from his wife."

Glauberman blew air from puffed cheeks through his cupped hands. In a nearby room Jake could hear a scratchy Victrola.

> *Yes, we have no bananas,*
> *We have no bananas today!*

"Wallowitz was a troublemaker. He made a deal with us but he was welshing."

"How?"

"Listening to grievances from his people. Some of them didn't like the settlement we got for them. So he began to complain also."

"Maybe they got a right to complain. It was a sweetheart job."

"Jake, forget your noble past. There are no more Eva Heiligs. These are just a bunch of ungrateful crybabies."

"Working people."

Glauberman got up. He drew the blinds so the view of the greenhouse was obliterated. "It's business. We took over the local. We also get paid by the owners. Metzinger is giving us a hundred bucks a week to keep things quiet. Wallowitz refuses to be quiet. Because the *putz* looks like Abraham Lincoln, he thinks he's freeing slaves."

"You didn't have to break his knees. Who did it?"

"Futka's mob."

Jake spoke slowly. "The deal was that we get rid of Shikey and Futka Frummer. We promised the wet-wash workers we'd protect them."

Something was bothering Jake. Some old loyalty, some sense of who was right, who was wrong. It had been simpler twelve years ago when he was beating up hoodlums. He understood things better then.

"Right! When we hit Wallowitz, we were protecting him from his own foolishness."

Jake shook his head. His starched collar felt too tight. The checkered vest bothered him. He wasn't meant for fancy clothes. "Who decided Wallowitz had to get beat up?"

"The court."

"What court?"

"Five of us meet every few weeks. People with contacts with the police and politicians. We figured you might not like the idea of hitting Wallowitz, so we asked Futka to handle it."

"Brownsville is my territory, not the Frummers'. Leo, you done me a lousy trick."

"Jake, the big money is working *both* ends. We *are* the unions. So what are we doing different than Brunstein or Flugelman, those socialist farts? We get the workers a living wage. We keep the bosses happy. Don't become a Red on me."

"I ain't no Red, Leo. At least we should do something for Wallowitz," Jake said. "The hospital bills, benefits. We should make out like we didn't have nothing to do with it."

"Fine, take care of it." The TR head leaned back. Sightless eyes, gleaming teeth, brush cut tinged with green. "Don't get sentimental, Jake."

Mrs. Glauberman, a busty blonde in a black silk dress and pearls, smoking an oval cigarette, knocked on the door. Oh, it was Mr. Chain? Would he like to stay for tea? Mr. Otzenberger was dropping by. And Judge Nitkin and Assemblyman Franzese . . .

Jake thanked her and refused. Too fancy company for him.

* * *

From his hospital bed, Wallowitz told Jake that he did not recognize the men who had waylaid him on Ralph Avenue. They had dragged him into a car and smashed his knees.

"The pain, the *pain,*" he muttered. "Mr. Chain, what did I do? You and Mr. Glauberman are supposed to protect us."

"What did they look like?"

"Who knows? It was night. One was fat, round. The other I don't remember."

The Meal Ticket? Jake wondered. Herman Wesselberg, meet Hyman Wallowitz.

Troubled, Jake left the hospital. Why had Glauberman gone to East Side mobsters? The answer was clear. Jake Chain, soft of heart, an old hero to workers, could not be trusted to *klop* a union man. For that they needed a real son of a bitch, a *paskudnyak* like Futka. It was a different game. He had been too dumb and too greedy to realize it.

Jake drove across the Brooklyn Bridge, past pushcarts and delivery vans, and parked in front of the Cayuga Social Club on East Houston Street. He had been there before. It was the Frummers' headquarters. Jake could recall a meeting there a year ago when they had agreed to divide up the city.

A dingy tan curtain masked the window. Kids played stoopball next door. Others wrestled on the dirty pavement.

"Ya fadder's ass!"

"Ya mudder's twat!"

Jake found two of the biggest boys and gave each a nickel. "Watch the car," he said. "A nickel more for each of you when I come out."

Inside the clubhouse he found Shikey and Futka Frummer playing *shtuss* with two of their associates.

"Chain, pull up a chair," Futka Frummer said. He was short, round-headed, and jug-eared, a natty dresser. The late Moishe Nigger's aides had joined his gang.

Shikey was a respectable "front man"—labor negotiator, contractor. Younger than Futka, he was also small, with soft shiny skin. He was freshly barbered and powdered. Black hair, slicked down. Shikey had a spiked moustache and wore three rings. Futka was tougher, meaner, a loan shark and policy banker.

"So, Chain?" Futka asked. "All the way to Houston Street?"

"What about Wallowitz?"

The game stopped. Men in striped shirts, suspenders, and straw hats leaned back and stared at Jake. He was really *crazy.* The madman from Brownsville. The giant who boiled Moishe Nigger and survived twelve pieces of hot lead. (And, rumor had it, drowned the Nigger in chicken blood.)

"The scar on your chin, Jake," Shikey said. "It's getting bigger. Maybe it needs one on the other side?"

"I asked about Wallowitz." Jake sat down. He knew that he was safe. So long as he had Glauberman, and Glauberman owned judges and politicians, the brothers would not dare work him over.

"Ask Mr. Glauberman."

"So it's true. You broke his knees."

"Chain, you were one of the first to do this. A man breaks his word, what else can we do? Who cares if he was a union officer or a nigger who cleans toilets? Don't look so innocent. You started this with your price list."

"What did you get?"

"Fifty for each knee."

"The Meal Ticket around?" Jake asked. "I hear he *shtarks* for you sometimes."

"He had to visit his aunt in Jersey," Shikey said. He ordered one of the punks to deal. "Chain, don't become a boy scout in your old age. A lot of *shtarkers* don't trust you. Your trouble is you think only the jerks on the picket line deserve a break. Wrong. Whoever pays gets service."

Jake declined the offer of a drink. Real booze that Shikey was running in from the Bahamas. He walked into the noisy street. The kids were waiting for him. As he was about to enter the car, he saw Herman Wesselberg rolling toward the clubhouse. The Meal Ticket had gotten rounder and fleshier. But he was still light on his feet. He wore a high-crowned fawn homburg, beige tie, a chocolate box-backed suit, two-toned brown shoes. *You got off easy,* Jake thought. *I owe you.*

There was an alley crammed with garbage cans to the right of the clubhouse. Jake pulled his straw hat over his face and left the car. With a swift move, one that almost made it appear he was summoning a friend, he grasped Wesselberg's lapels and spun him into the alley. No one noticed. The kids were matching baseball cards.

"Christy Mathewson!"

"Walter Johnson!"

"Joe Dugan!"

The Meal Ticket gasped and sailed off his pointy feet like a rising balloon. Jake pinned him against a brick wall on which was scrawled in chalk: HOUSTON STREET TIGERS.

"Chain. Whaddya want, jerk? Whaddya doin' in Manhattan? This ain't your place."

"Brownsville ain't yours, Wesselberg."

"Leggo. I'll holler. Futka'll finish what we done to you twelve years ago. Bullet number thirteen."

"Meal Ticket. This is for Wallowitz. One for each knee." And, he wanted to add, for Eva.

Jake's arms worked like pistons. Two blows to the soft gut. A right, a left, below the navel, digging deep into the soft belly. The Meal Ticket's eyes crossed. Breath whooshed from his mouth in a long airy wheeze. He slid to the soiled pavement. "Don't hit, Chain. Don't hit no more."

Sometime after midnight, while a floor nurse dozed and a resident was summoned to emergency, a man sneaked into Brownsville Jewish Hospital and put a bullet through Wallowitz's forehead.

The gunman left no trace. Mr. Wallowitz died in his sleep, deep in morphine. He was mourned by his wife, his four children, and the members of the wet-wash workers local.

Chapter 23

For weeks Hilda Otzenberger had nightmares of the trip to Canada. She'd shrieked all the way to Plattsburgh, babbled, fainted once, clutched at Mutt. *That bastard Sal. That crazy wop.* Now the cops would be after them.

She kept calling Mutt when her parents weren't home. What if the cops came after them? Couldn't those farmers have written down license plates? Two New York cabs? Would they be so hard to find? *And, oh, God, God in heaven,* Hilda wept, *the way the blood and all that white stuff came out of the back of his head . . .*

Mutt told her to shut up. Say nothing. Those men were crooks, stealing whiskey from honest American bootleggers. They weren't the kind who went to cops. It could ruin their own business. They didn't give a shit if one of their gang lived or died. Bradford was dead, maybe the bearded man. Nobody would care.

But he was frightened himself. Already he was planning ahead. He'd get an airtight alibi from his boss Futcher. Sal would get one also. Benny Otzenberger had friends in Albany. Mutt calmed Hilda and made plans for another trip with Sal.

They had sold their sixteen cases for sixteen hundred dollars, more than Sal's phony estimate. With deductions for gasoline and minor repairs to the cabs, they each came out with a clear profit of almost seven hundred dollars. As Mutt had insisted, the deal was fifty-fifty. He knew Sal had lied about the sale price, but did not call him on it. Why louse up their future? Mutt reasoned.

"We need trucks," Sal said as they divided the cash inside his cab. "Cabs are too small. Maybe some drivers we can trust."

They had sold the booze to Reds Mulqueen's brother Babe. Babe ran an elegant speakeasy on Fulton Street, near the courthouse and Borough Hall. He had a blond chorus girl mistress and drove a Cadillac. His place was a well-known watering spot for thirsty politicians. Babe was grateful for, and a bit stunned by, the good stuff that two young punks in greasy caps had brought him.

"See this?" Babe Mulqueen asked. He showed them an empty green bottle with a fancy black-and-gold label. The label read: OLD McCUL-LOCH SCOTCH WHISKY, *Distilled and Blended in Glen Glarney, Scotland, U.K.*

"Who got ya that?" Sal asked. He spurned the "green" beer Babe offered him.

Babe arched tufted eyebrows. Silent, absorbing everything, Mutt stared at the bottle and at Babe's cunning eyes. He knew Babe trusted him. He was Jake Chain's son. Reds Mulqueen vouched for all of the Chains. When Reds's bar closed in 1920, Jake got him a job as foreman at Kolodny's.

"What's the empty bottle for?" Sal asked.

Babe Mulqueen picked up the corked and sealed bottle of eighty-six-proof scotch that the boys had taxied in from Canada. "See this stuff you sold me?" he asked. He appeared regretful. "One-third goes into the Old McCulloch bottle. Plus one-third water from the Brooklyn Water Company. Plus one-third grain alcohol neutral spirits. Presto, change-o! We get three times as much scotch as what you brought me. Same with the gin. For that I got a fancier bottle."

Mulqueen reached under the counter of the walnut bar and showed them another empty. A clear glass bottle with a flat shape and a red-and-blue label: UNION JACK GIN, *Distilled and Bottled in Wolverhampton, England, U.K.*

"Pretty neat," Mutt said. "You get three bottles for every one we sell you. How much is each worth when you sell shots to your customers?"

"A fortune, lads, a fortune. Now that I shown yez the tricks, don't get smart on me. I know all the Canadian brands and I want sealed bottles in unopened cases. You kids got a good customer in me, so don't screw me up. Understood?"

"Big Irish donkey," Sal muttered as they walked to their cabs. "Cheated us."

"No he didn't," Mutt said. "We learned something. Next time it'll be a hundred and *sixty* bucks a case. If he doesn't like it, there's lots of other speaks'll buy from us. Or maybe we can cut it ourselves."

That afternoon they made down payments on two used trucks. Luigi, an ace mechanic, tested the motors and found them sound. One was a Reo, the other a White. They came with slatted sides and canvas "tarpolions." Sal and Mutt invested in old mattresses and quilts, and several hundred yards of rope. They were ready to go into business in a big way—bribes, secret roads, protection.

Two days after the Wallowitz murder, Jake was picked up for questioning. He and Sarah had just come back from the movies at Loew's Palace. They had seen Milton Sills in *The Sea Wolf*, three short comedies, an "Out-of-the-Inkwell" cartoon, a newsreel, and a "serial."

As they approached the Hupmobile, two city detectives halted him. Would Mr. Chain mind joining them for a talk? At first Jake objected. What had he done? The Wallowitz case, one of the cops said.

Wallowitz's murder had been front-page stuff in the papers. Sarah had asked him about it. Wasn't Mrs. Wallowitz the skinny *yenta* who was bothering him last week?

"What did my husband do?" Sarah asked.

"A half-hour is all," the detective said. "At the Brooklyn D.A.'s office. You don't mind, do you, Mr. Chain?"

"My wife is crippled. I got to drive her home first. What do you want from me? Wallowitz was my friend."

"Then maybe you can help."

Sarah started to tremble. The cops agreed to follow Jake back to Haven Place in their car and give him a few minutes at home.

At the house he told her not to worry. She wept. She knew what he was doing. What he was up to. Why? *Why?* Did he kill Wallowitz?

Lean and sweaty in an undershirt, Mutt was sitting in the kitchen adding up figures. In one trip they could handle a hundred cases. Fifty to a truck. A hundred cases could bring in as much as *twelve grand!* Babe Mulqueen or some other speakeasy owner would welcome them with a pile of hundred-dollar bills. More money would mean more trucks and more drivers.

"What's the matter, papa?" Mutt asked. He looked up from his blue notebook.

"Nothing, Mutt. Tell your mother to stop crying. The cops want to talk with me about Wallowitz."

Mutt had no idea what his father had to do with it. But he did not fear for him. There was something bred in the Chains that obliterated fear.

The assistant D.A. was a smooth-cheeked baldish young man named Wayne Ordell. He wore a striped suit and a black tie and fussed with a briefcase a great deal. The detectives stayed in the room. One took notes while the other guarded the door and answered phone calls.

Jake knew the man guarding the door—a rock-fisted dick named Vorstadt. During the war, Jake had him on the payroll. Ten bucks a week to look the other way while Jake and the Ferrantes "settled" a strike at a pants factory with stink bombs. Vorstadt had showed up during scuffling on the picket line. Jake had lost no time lining him up.

Chain had learned the wisdom of the underworld adage "The store is open." Translated, it meant the cops and courts and politicians were fixed and the swindle or scam or roughhouse could start.

Assistant D.A. Ordell did not look like a man whose store could be opened.

"Jake, about the Wallowitz murder," Ordell said. "Did you know him?"

"Of course. I was an officer of the union."

Ordell looked at papers on his desk, studied mug shots. He held up a fuzzy profile and full-face of the Meal Ticket. "Know this man?"

"Sure. Herman Wesselberg. The Saratoga Avenue Meal Ticket."

Vorstadt stood in back of Jake. He cracked the flat of his hand against Jake's neck. It was like hitting an iron post. Coloring crimson, Jake barely moved.

"Talk, Jewboy," Vorstadt said. "You started *shtarking* in 1910. We got such a file on you, you couldn't read if you had ten years of Jew holidays."

Jake rubbed his neck. It stung a little. A hide like one of his horses, Kolodny used to say.

"That's enough of that, Vorstadt," Ordell said. "Mr. Chain will be truthful with us. How many times have you been arrested since 1910, Jake?"

"Twice, three times maybe."

"Your record shows eleven arrests in twelve years, Jake," the assistant D.A. said. "Charges dismissed every time. Carrying a concealed weapon three times. Assault and battery twice. Breaking and entering twice. Extortion twice. Bribery once. Burglary once."

"All frame-ups," Jake said. "Not one stuck. Mr. Ordell, I'm no criminal. I'm in a rough business."

"But who killed Wallowitz?"

"I don't know. But if I catch them, you won't get a chance to give them a third degree. I'll handle them myself."

Ordell reviewed the facts. Wallowitz had agreed to a new contract drawn up by the firm of Glauberman & Chain. Further, he had invited them to be "officers" of his local. But wasn't it true Wallowitz's workers didn't like the deal? Was it not true that an East Side hoodlum named Shikey Frummer had broken the man's knees? Why?

Jake's face revealed nothing. Glauberman had let the Frummers do the dirty work. Get rid of Wallowitz. And Glauberman's hands would be clean.

Or was it *his* fault? He had gone to Futka and warned him to lay off his fellow officers. In a rage he had beaten the Meal Ticket. Craving revenge, the Meal Ticket had then murdered Wallowitz. A helpless cripple in a hospital bed.

Glauberman would do nothing, for he had made a deal with Shikey and Futka, Jake knew.

"So, Jake?" Ordell asked. "Is it true you visited the Frummer boys' club and had words with them?"

"A social visit."

"But you hate their guts," Ordell said. "You kicked Shikey out of Brownsville, the way you—let's see . . ." Ordell consulted notes.

A file on me like a *megillah,* Jake thought. They know a lot, but they had never made a charge stick. There was always Otzenberger to bail him out.

"... just the way you tangled with a gang led by Morris Pearlberg ..."

"Moishe Nigger," Jake said.

"... and forced him out of Brownsville years ago. Sent him back to the East Side. A year later someone drowned him in chicken blood."

Vorstadt said, "Crazy Jake Chain, Mr. Ordell. The man they couldn't kill. How many slugs did you take, Jake?"

"Twelve. Four still in me. On rainy days they hurt."

Vorstadt circled the chair and put a hand on Jake's shoulder, thinking, the big bastard is made of *cement*. "Something'll hurt you worse if you don't talk to Mr. Ordell. You and Glauberman know who killed Wallowitz. What are you guys doing? Double-crossing your own union members?"

"I never did nothing that was against a worker. Look at my record. So I'm no angel. So I did some rotten things. But only for poor people."

Ordell was summoned by a secretary. When he was gone, Vorstadt taunted Jake with his .38. He ran the barrel across Jake's neck, over his forehead. Jake did not move. Vorstadt didn't scare him. A man you could buy was a man who had no balls.

Ordell returned. "You're to be released, Jake," he said. "Somebody from the mayor's office called. You can go."

A few days later, a Prohibition agent came to Benny Otzenberger's clubhouse and queried the district leader about a trip his daughter had made to Canada with two young men.

Benny now spent virtually all his time in the clubhouse office or touring Brownsville in a chauffeur-driven air-cooled Franklin. He had turned his wholesale grocery business over to his nervous son Heshy. Heshy was a skilled factory foreman, but things were getting rough in the garment trades, what with Jake Chain and his gang extorting money from unions *and* bosses. That rat Glauberman (Benny knew) was the power behind it, but what could he do? Glauberman took care of him to the tune of a thousand dollars a month to keep judges and cops happy.

Otzenberger could neither read nor write, but he always carried a *New York Times*. In the olive-green Franklin, strolling down Pitkin Avenue, seated in his thronelike chair in his clubhouse, the paper was always under his chunky arm or spread in his lap. Evidence that he was a learned man! Often he could be observed, thick glasses on his nose, "reading" the *Times* upside down. He would stroke his thick moustache, like a talmudic scholar pondering marginalia. ("Benny's problem," Dr. Abelman said, "is he can't tell the white from the black. He isn't sure which part he's supposed to read.")

It was thus that the snooper found him. Benny's beady brown eyes were studying a front-page story about President Harding's grief over the suicide of his pal, Jess Smith, the head of the Veterans Administration. *Some pal!* A bunch of crooks, with their oil leases, their payoffs. *Thanks God,* Benny thought, *all Republicans.* (Benny could not read, but one of his young clubhouse lawyers always circled the important stories and gave him a verbal précis.)

"Canada? Why my daughter should go to Canada?" Benny asked the snooper. "She's a girl who stays close to home. And with two men? What two men?"

When the snooper persisted, Benny calmly offered him fifty dollars wrapped around a bottle of "real stuff"—eighty-six-proof McCulloch Glen Scotch. It was part of the last shipment that Mutt Chain and Sal Ferrante had trucked in from Canada. This time they had gone without Hilda.

The snooper was deeply grateful.

"Forget it, Mr. Hutchins," Benny said. "This is from a personal friend. My daughter Hilda is pure as the snow, a daughter in a million, a sweetheart. For what would she want to take rides to Canada?"

Hutchins, a retired fireman from Queens, hired in the mad rush to enlist agents, knew when he had a good thing. He had heard about Otzenberger's power. And he didn't care too much about the daughter. It was two smart kids he was after. Jake Chain's son and one of those guinea Ferrantes. Italians were running alky cookers in their homes and garages all over Brooklyn. You could smell the mash stewing and vaporizing over half of Pacific Street. One of the Ferrante brothers was into something big, he'd been told. A company had been formed—F & C Cereals. Buying trucks. Paying off local cops.

"Your word is good with me, Mr. O," the snooper said. He pocketed the fifty and put the bottle in his briefcase. If he ever caught up with those two wise kids, it would cost them more than fifty bills.

Chapter 24

Mutt decided, after they had made their first run with the trucks and unloaded the cases of gin and scotch to Babe Mulqueen for a profit of eleven thousand dollars, that they were selling themselves cheap.

Sal had similar thoughts. Babe had paid them well for the truckloads, but he would make a fast *hundred grand* before he was finished serving it watered down in shot glasses to his parched customers.

As Mulqueen counted out the money in the back of his speakeasy, he'd bragged about the manner in which he would rebottle the booze, cutting the liquor with water and grain alcohol.

"And a little caramel coloring, lads, and a touch of fusel oil for flavor, so's the customers don't wise up," the speakeasy owner said. "Jesus, it's a grand game. Glycerin helps to give the booze a 'bead.' Remember who your friend is. And don't get shot by a snooper or some big crook. Melvin Schonkeit likes to think the Canadian run is his. Look out for his fellows."

Melvin Schonkeit was a shadowy gambler, fixer, and money man. He was a king bootlegger and loan shark. He stayed out of sight, out of the newspapers. It was rumored he could fix anything. He was a department store of crime, a genius known as the Paymaster.

"Screw Melvin Schonkeit," Mutt said.

"Fongool Schonkeit," Sal added.

"Listen to them," Babe said. His eyes vanished in a piggy grin. "Crazy Jake Chain's son, right? Afraid of nothin', Mortimer? Isn't that the square handle, Mortimer J. Chain? Or is it Morris or Morton or Myron?"

"Mortimer, Mulqueen. And you're right. Chains aren't afraid of nothing."

After Mutt had deposited his share in the Dime Savings Bank—under the eyes of a stunned vice-president—he met Sal and Hilda in an Italian restaurant on Atlantic Avenue. They munched pizza and sipped cream soda. Sal objected to her presence. It was supposed to be a business meeting.

"She's in on it," Mutt said. "She made the first trip with us. Besides, we're getting married."

"Since when?" Hilda asked. "Honest, Morty."

Sal's eyes found the ceiling. "Ya supposed to leave dames out of it."

"You know, you can be a real creep?" Hilda said to Sal. "Why don't you look someone in the eye for once in your life?"

Sal said nothing. He disliked the girl. But she, like his partner Mutt, was part of the scheme of things. They needed Benny Otzenberger. They would need him even more now.

"We're *rich*," Mutt said to Hilda. "We're getting married. Sal can be best man."

"Hah! They wouldn't let him in the synagogue. My father would *plotz* if he showed up."

Mutt snapped her garter, nuzzled her neck. Let Sal stew. His sneaky partner never seemed interested in women. His brothers were all married, turning out mobs of small Ferrantes. Sal remained single and secretive.

"Some way to propose." Hilda pouted. "In a Nitalian restaurant over a lousy pizza. With Smiley here as a witness. Honest, Morty, even if I wanted to marry you—"

"You'll marry me, kid. I love you. Right, Sal? Didn't I always say I loved her? When we went to Canada?"

"Yeah, yeah," Sal said. Hilda was a stiff pain in the butt to him. She'd get in the way, and he and Mort had big plans. They had decided to screw Mulqueen. But they weren't sure how to go about it.

Over coffee and cigarettes, the youthful partners decided to buy Kolodny's bottling plant. He was a small-timer. And he was sick, coughing his guts out. A little convincing from Jake Chain's son would help in the negotiations.

"Whaddya gonna do?" Hilda asked. "Go back to peddling seltzer, like your old man?"

Mutt ignored her. They needed a warehouse. A place they could lock at night, a secure plant to mix and rebottle their own booze. A place to park trucks. To hell with Mulqueen and the other chiselers. Why should they make all the profit? Already Mutt was planning on buying two more trucks. But instead of selling the good whiskey to middlemen, they would rebottle it themselves. Mutt was going to see a printer in New York who specialized in labels. The guy designed them himself—reds, golds, and blacks, anything you wanted. Invent a fancy English or Scotch name, print as many as you needed. Also government tax stamps.

"Bottles also," Sal said. "Corks. Maybe bottles you can't fill again so no wise guy can use our old ones."

"I get it," Hilda said. "Oh, I get it."

"Keep ya mouth shut," Sal said. "Ya never heard us."

"Creep."

Hilda entered the conversation with gusto. She was full of ideas. She had taken a two-year course in stenography and bookkeeping at Pace Institute. Why didn't she go to work for them? She could be the office manager for F & C Cereals, Inc.

Sal frowned. In his family women were kept ignorant of business dealings. Cook, clean, have babies.

Mutt thought it was a great idea. "Hey, yeah. We put Hilda on the payroll. Office manager, bookkeeper. A nice-looking dame to talk to customers."

The deal was looking better and better. Kolodny's warehouse and bottling plant. A supply of phony bottles and fake labels. Four or five trucks running booze in from Canada, past Customs guards and Prohibition agents. Payoffs to whoever needed paying off—cops, judges, feds. Benny would help.

"All we need is the alcohol," Mutt said. "Lots of it. We got to get a steady supply. It ain't easy."

"Government warehouses are full of it," Sal said. "But try to get it out. Guys get killed going after it."

"You scared?" Mutt asked.

"I ain't a-scared of nothin'."

"Wanna pull a heist? There's a government warehouse out in Ozone Park."

"No," Hilda said. She grabbed Mutt's hand. "No. No funny business, Morty. I'm in the company now. You two *shmendricks* think you're hot stuff. I know what Mulqueen told you. Look out you don't get Schonkeit sore at you. Five trucks, six trucks, so what? You're just kids. He'll kill you both."

Mutt smiled at her. He kissed her nose. Sal cringed, looked at the door, the waiters, the menu stained with tomato paste. He wished they'd do their smooching somewhere else. Not in front of him. The notion of a woman, a twenty-year-old dame, knowing about their operations rankled him. Deep in his Neapolitan soul, he knew women were the devil, *sfaccim'*, bad luck. He grabbed his balls to ward off the evil eye.

"I need a haircut," Sal said. "I'm gonna see my old man."

The three of them left together. On Pacific Street they paused outside old man Ferrante's barbershop.

In the window was a row of hair-tonic bottles. Lucky Tiger. Westphalia. Attar of Roses. Vitalis. Something clicked in Mutt's mind. He was always full of new ideas, angles.

"Hair tonic," Mutt said.

"Whah?" asked Sal. Sometimes he couldn't figure Mutt out.

"Hair tonic. It's fifty percent alcohol. Some guy on Belmont Avenue went blind drinking it. But the alcohol is okay. Or you can make it okay."

Sal blinked. "Whaddya wanna do? Strain them bottles through white bread like the niggers do?"

Mutt squinted, thinking. "No. But maybe your old man sets himself up in business. Ferrante's Hair Tonic. Or some fancy name—Pacific Breeze Hair Tonic. Get it? Then we could get alcohol from the warehouse."

Sal shook his head. The Ozone Park warehouse? Impossible. It was guarded. No windows. Steel doors. Armed guards.

"Ever hear of a Permit of Withdrawal?" Mutt asked.

"What the hell is that?"

Hilda listened, stunned by Mutt's knowledge. He was eighteen!

"The government gives them out if you got a legitimate business," Mutt said. "Also if you got a friend or someone to bribe." He looked at Hilda. "Your old man must know someone."

"What legitimate business?" Sal asked. "We gonna tell them we need their grain alky to cut booze? Oh, boy. You're a *chooch,* Mutt."

"We set up the Pacific Breeze Hair Tonic Company. Your old man is president. He gets stationery, bills of sale, a card. He needs alcohol, right? To make hair tonic. Let's talk to him. C'mon, I need a haircut also. Hilda, I'll see ya tonight."

Hilda sighed, swiveled her hips, walked away. She decided she was in love with Mutt. But she wished people would call him something else. Mortimer wasn't much of an improvement. Mort. *Morty.* If they got married, she told herself, he would be her Morty, and she would demand that everyone else call him Morty.

Old man Ferrante, veteran of Garibaldi's campaigns, wasn't quite sure what his son Salvatore and Chain's son had in mind. But he agreed. His own hair tonic! *Pacific Breeze.* He'd need coloring agents, essential oils, a preservative, and, of course, alcohol. Mutt would supply bottles and labels. They'd sell the hair tonic in the store and peddle it to barbershops all over Brooklyn. Luigi could be a traveling salesman.

The barber, with his roached white hair and Umberto moustache, his drooping face, listened. Then he said, "Salvatore, no fool the old man. You want alcohol to make booze. Okay, I am partner. But also got to make hair tonic, so if cops ask question, we got hair tonic in bottle to sell. *Capisci?"*

A week later, Mortimer J. Chain and Salvatore Ferrante paid Benny Otzenberger a thousand dollars to get them a dozen Permits of Withdrawal. These testified that Papa Ferrante, barber and manufacturer, of Pacific Street, Brooklyn, was the sole owner and operator of Pacific Breeze Hair Tonic Products. That same week they bought out Kolodny and installed fireproof steel windows and doors.

On a summer afternoon, Sal and his father, with Mutt riding on the truck bed, backed the Reo up to the loading dock at the bonded government warehouse. There, Sal paid fifteen hundred dollars for two thousand gallons of neutral grain spirits. Clear liquid treasure in government bottles, crated and insulated with straw.

The custodian of the government warehouse, Mr. Phil O'Connor, was paid off with five hundred dollars. He did not seem to mind. "Dumb donkey," Sal sneered. "He coulda got a grand if he had any brains."

The alcohol was stored under twenty-four-hour guard in Kolodny's warehouse. Two small signs were nailed to the metal doors that had replaced the old wooden door to the stable:

PACIFIC BREEZE HAIR TONIC PRODUCTS

F & C CEREALS, INC.

No one (the police least of all) was curious as to why a hair tonic company and a cereal firm shared a former bottling plant. No one asked. A week after the first shipment of alcohol arrived, Mutt saw to it that twelve patrolmen, two sergeants, and a captain went on a monthly payroll. His father's old adversary, Sergeant Pope, was appointed bagman.

Mutt learned from his father that "the store had to be open." A price list. A firm schedule of payments, Jake said. Ten bucks for flatfoots, twenty for sergeants, fifty for the captain. Plus extras at Christmas.

"You got any trouble," Jake told his son, "ask me." He was delighted by Mutt's enterprise.

An unemployed pharmacist named Charlie Goldsturm was hired to do the "mixing," set up an assembly line, supervise cutting, flavoring, and bottling.

Mortimer J. (for nothing) Chain and Salvatore Ferrante studied their first bottle of Highland Cream Scotch. The label assured the buyer that it was bottled in bond by master distillers in the Scottish highlands. It had won two gold medals! Eighty-six-proof blended whisky. Actually it contained a third of the scotch trucked in from Canada, a third Brooklyn tap water, and a third of the "purified" alcohol destined for old Ferrante's hair tonic.

The "factory" produced six cases of real hair tonic a week. One bottle was displayed in the office that Mutt and Sal used, and a case was kept handy for the police to observe in the "showroom." Mutt had an artist get up an elaborate display card, a Rudolph Valentino type dousing his head with Pacific Breeze.

Hilda was put on payroll as receptionist, bookkeeper, and secretary. She took orders on the phone, handled the accounts, and flirted with customers. Mutt decided that for sales to *individuals,* one case was the limit—at two hundred dollars the case. Big buyers like Mulqueen and the downtown speakeasies got a twenty percent discount.

Goldsturm proved to be a genius. He put in a store of burnt sugar, prune juice, oils of bourbon, scotch, and rye, juniper flavoring, glycerin, fusel oil, creosote, iodine, and several barrels of charred wood chips, for "aging."

So long as they could keep the Canada run operating, and get "Permits of Withdrawal" via Benny's friends, they were in business. Luigi and Baggie quit their construction jobs and were hired as drivers and handlers.

But F & C Cereals, Inc., and Pacific Breeze Hair Tonic remained wholly owned by the young corporate visionaries who had founded the firms, Salvatore Ferrante and Mortimer Chain. Each owned fifty percent.

So busy were the partners, collecting vast sums of cash, watching bank accounts inflate, contacting new customers, supervising the Canada trips that autumn, that Mutt found he was neglecting Hilda.

It was still his intention to marry her. He loved watching her in the office. Somehow, the simple dark skirts and severe white blouses, the plain pumps, the pencil stuck in her luxuriant hair made her even sexier.

One evening, when "Professor" Goldsturm, as Mutt had nicknamed him, had closed up shop after "purifying" a batch of denatured alcohol and cutting it into a hundred gallons of drinkable spirits, Mutt found himself alone in the bottling plant with Hilda. She was rolling her stockings, straightening the seams, smoothing her skirt in front of the mirror, when Mutt, redolent of the foul bourbon and scotch "essences" that permeated the plant, seized her from behind.

"I waited long enough," he said. "I'm nuts about you."

"No, Morty. No. After we're married." She was as cool as an icehouse. "What's the difference?"

For all of Mutt's shrewdness and brashness, he had treated Hilda like a princess. Benny's daughter was no one to mess with. And he was a mobster's son, two years her junior. On the trip to Canada, a few feels, strokes, tweaks were all he attempted. And all, he knew, she would permit. Now, he embraced her, hugged her soft body, let his young rod press against her abdomen. His hands cupped her breasts. Handfuls! She sighed and surrendered. Her father would kill her, she said. Her mother would throw her out of the house.

Protesting as Mutt sought her mouth, kissed her lips, glued his tongue to hers, she let herself be wrestled to the abraded leather couch, a relic of Kolodny's day.

"It's the first for me," she said breathlessly.

Never, never, never was it so good, Mutt decided. And never would it be so good again. He told Hilda afterward, as they lay panting in the gloom, in the silent, fruity-smelling office, that he loved her forever, as no man could love her.

He watched her go to the bathroom and return. She wore a pink lacy slip that could not hide (indeed emphasized) her billowing breasts and delicious hips. Again she nestled close to him.

Once more they made love. Mutt understood at once. He would never be able to love a woman as he loved Hilda. Others would come to him, to seek out the king bootlegger, to be impressed by his power and wealth. But Hilda would be supreme. His first, his best.

"You used something?" she asked.

"No. I was too excited." The rusting tin of Peacock Lubricated Reservoir Ends had remained unopened in his trousers.

"Oh, God. Oh, God." She began to whimper. "What if you gave me a baby? My God, Morty. You're a kid, eighteen. What if you, you know . . . ?"

"It doesn't matter. We're getting married. You won't get no baby."

He held her close, joined to the soft, loving body. Something comical about it, he couldn't help feeling. His pants on the floor. Her clothes all over the place. But the best thing in the world. In the midst of a third round of love—neither seemed capable of tiring—he felt a profound pity for his father. Tied to a crippled, bitter wife. He knew they never slept together. All that strength in the old man, that power, going nowhere— except to hoo-ers.

"Again, again, again," Hilda moaned. "Oh, Morty. I'll love you my whole life."

Chapter 25

"It has gotten out of hand," Ike Brunstein said angrily to Eva Halstead. "It is a curse, a crime. Eva, we need help."

"Tell me. I want to help."

They were seated in the sunny parlor of Eva's brownstone on West Tenth Street. Prematurely gray, his moustache drooping, Ike sat opposite his lost love. Eva sat at her desk. Her mass of yellow hair was bright with afternoon sunlight. Two pencils were jammed into the thick curls around her tiny ear. She wore a short-skirted green silk dress. Her crossed legs were shod in dark Parisian silk. On her delicate feet were expensive black pumps, with heels a bit higher than Ike ever recalled her wearing.

Her desk was an antique rolltop, piled helter-skelter with books, clippings, magazines and photographs. A huge new Woodstock typewriter squatted on a wheeled table. Telephones rang incessantly. Finally, in deference to Ike, she took them off the hook. One was for private calls, she explained, the other for business.

He could see a blackboard above the desk, with a list of her engagements.

Sept. 7—Cleveland—Women's Rights, etc.
Sept. 10—Cincinnati—Birth Control
Sept. 12—Pittsburgh—Disarmament, For'n Affairs

On the wall around the blackboard were photographs of the late Uncle Sourmilk, of Dr. Abraham M. Heilig, his wife and children, and her younger brother Sol, the lawyer whom Ike often worked with on union matters. There was an old family photo, faded sepia, in a gold frame: her parents, young and smiling, and the three handsome children. Eva must have been five. Golden, minuscule, dainty in a pale ruffled dress. A heart-breaker, exquisite and desirable, even as a little girl. Sorrow withered Ike's heart.

"I wish Garry were here," Eva said. "It sounds like something for the police and he has good contacts. Not all judges are corrupt, Ike."

"I am beginning to wonder."

The labor movement needed her, Ike said. Things were falling apart. Yes, he had joined the Communist party. They seemed to him more effective, more disciplined.

"Then you don't need me. I sympathize, Ike, but I'm afraid I'm old hat to the labor movement. The Golden Voice has been stilled as far as the rank and file is concerned."

She was right, he supposed. She was a lecturer and writer. In the newspapers every week. The marriage to Halstead had elevated her from an obscure radical to an object of curiosity, a valuable by-line.

She agreed that the situation in Brownsville was a disgrace. All New York was being plagued by the gorillas who were terrorizing unions, brazenly taking them over, extorting money from members, selling workers out.

"The Communists won't stand for it," Ike said.

"What will you do?"

"Hire our own *shtarkers*. It's the only answer."

"What an answer! More force? More terror? Really, Ike."

"We aren't afraid to use force. Revolutions aren't made by gentle people. I had enough theorizing when I was a Socialist. Look at Debs. Jail, convictions. An idiot like Harding had to save his neck. No more accommodation with capitalists. We'll make a new world like they're making in the Soviet Union."

Laughing, Eva covered her mouth. She leaned back in the swivel chair. Ike was mortified. Her joyous face was a mockery and a goad. *Oh, to have her naked and at his mercy!* But he never would. Breasts like rosebuds. The tiny waist. Cheeks like lilies. The rest, the secret golden filaments . . . He gagged slightly.

"Ike, if you Communists are so tough, why do you have to hire hoodlums? You should have lots of brave young men who'll drive the gangsters out."

He tried to strangle the desire to grab her, tear the green dress from her. When she moved, he got a glimpse of a green lace slip. He wanted to bury his face in her, enter some kingdom of delight known by few mortals. But he was grubby Brunstein, a starveling radical.

"You know as well as I do," Ike said. "What are we? Ghetto intellectuals sitting in dingy rooms arguing about Marx. There's not a knife or a gun in a crowd of fifty of us. Eva, our Communists are the most law-abiding people in the world. Dogs scare us. And we're starting a revolution? In the privacy of my misery I laugh at myself."

"So you're going to find your Jake Chain."

"You did. You didn't have to look far."

She leaned on one hand and smiled at her old comrade. "Ike, you complain that the gangsters are taking over, and what are you going to do? Hire your own mob to make a revolution!"

"We're talking to Melvin Schonkeit."

"Worse than Jake Chain. Much worse. You'll regret it, Ike."

"No choice, Eva."

Without knocking, Halstead entered the room, greeted Ike, and kissed Eva's cheek. Tall and straight, with his lantern-jawed face, finely tailored suit, and stiff collar, he seemed terribly alien to Ike. Brunstein studied him with envy and awe. The thought of this *langeh lukshen,* this quintessential *goy,* caressing, kissing, and entering his beloved dismayed him. Religious and racial backgrounds, Ike always felt, meant little. Brotherhood of Man. Jew, gentile, poor, rich. Character was what mattered. But it was no assurance to him as he watched Halstead talk casually with Eva, exchanging bits of household talk, discussions of their work. He was chairing a committee to force the British to free Gandhi.

"Nonviolence, noncooperation?" Ike asked. "He'll never succeed. The British will shoot his workers down."

"I'm afraid I disagree, Ike," Halstead said. "Gandhi is the model for future revolutions."

"Not in America," Ike said bleakly. "Try nonviolence in the garment district and see how far it will get you."

After mentioning a brief trip he was taking for *Scribner's* to do a piece on the Ku Klux Klan, Halstead left. Another gentle kiss planted on Eva's serene forehead, a loose handshake for Ike.

"How come you have no children?" Ike asked when he'd gone. "After ten years married?"

"I have my career. I like children, but they'd be a burden." She appeared irritated by his nosiness.

"I'm no one to talk. I'm not even married. I only loved you. I still do."

Ike pursued the point of his visit. He wanted Eva to talk to Jake, to plead with him to stop playing the double game, to stop sucking the blood of the unions, to stop double-crossing workers, terrorizing poor people. Jake had served a function once. But he was a parasite now. He and Glauberman and the Ferrantes, the criminal scum of Brooklyn, were monsters who had run amok.

"I see," Eva said. "But it's all right for you to hire Schonkeit's mob to achieve the revolution?"

He looked miserable, his head drooping, his figure slumped. Never a Trotsky. Not even close. He could never organize the Red Army from a military train. He needed Schonkeit's sinister power to battle the bourgeoisie. Eva was right. It was scandalous.

"I'll talk to Jake. But he won't listen. He's becoming a rich man."

"He'll listen to you, Eva. The way all of us do."

Listening to Ike Brunstein, the party leaders decided that fire would be fought with fire. The Communists were no mean force. They had members, money, contacts with segments of the Yiddish press. It was unfortunate that the social awareness of the proletariat was not "mature" enough to comprehend the need for revolution. Not at this point, anyway.

Thus, in Melvin Schonkeit's twelve-room duplex on Central Park West, a humble Brunstein and his comrades met with the great fixer. For ten years Schonkeit had spread his web over every form of criminal activity—narcotics, bootlegging, loan sharking, numbers, and, increasingly, union affairs. In the early days, reputable labor leaders had come to him for help against the bosses, as they had come to Jake Chain. A man to be trusted, Melvin Schonkeit. He came from a prosperous family. His father was considered a saint; he was a reader of the Talmud, a supporter of charities. The son, slender and handsome, married to a redheaded Follies girl, was a different plate of borsht.

"The key to the problem is this fellow Chain," Schonkeit told the Marxist delegation.

"Well," Ike said. "Chain and others."

"He is unpredictable," Schonkeit said. "That makes him dangerous."

Schonkeit's wife passed among them. Lissome and redolent of French perfume, she served "the real thing," scotch imported from the Bahamas on one of the host's rum-running boats. She twitched her shapely silken ass, dispensing eroticism with the whisky.

Ike sipped it warily. Dreadful taste. What did *goyim* see in such poison? Why all the fuss to kill, bribe, fight, cheat, to drink such mouth-searing *drek?*

"The price for getting rid of Jacob Chain," Schonkeit said carefully, "will be three hundred thousand dollars."

Brunstein gulped. He looked goggle-eyed at his aides, an old Marxist named Caplow and a young firebrand named Yodelman.

"We don't have it," Ike said.

"You'll raise it. Assess your membership. You control seven unions, Mr. Brunstein. You want to get rid of Jake Chain? You want to dominate the labor movement? These things cost money."

"There'll still be Glauberman," Yodelman said. "He's the brains. And those bloody Italians, Chain's pals."

Schonkeit stared at the ceiling. Jake had never seen such a ceiling. Gold curlicues in the corners, a painting of Greek gods in the middle. Everything in Schonkeit's living room was heavy and dark, full of texture, smelling of money. The Paymaster lived well. A wonder at age thirty-five.

"So who will protect us? Who'll be on our side during the next negotiations, the next strike?" Ike asked.

"My people."

"Who? *Who,* Mr. Schonkeit?"

"What's the difference, Brunstein? So long as we get rid of Chain. If you must know, the Frummer group. Shikey, Futka, Wesselberg."

Ike looked again at his comrades. Help! *Help!* Was this a way to make a revolution?

"This Herman Wesselberg," Ike said. "They call him the Meal Ticket? Mr. Schonkeit, twelve years ago when I led the strikes in the needle trades, this man was the vilest, rottenest strikebreaker. Chain was an angel alongside such a monster. And he'll be our protector now?"

"Times change, Brunstein."

"Can we—can we—keep all of this secret?" Ike asked.

"That is the way we operate."

"There's Glauberman," Yodelman persisted. "You get rid of Chain, please don't tell me how, Mr. Schonkeit, but Glauberman has power. . . ."

Schonkeit tinkled a copper bell. His leggy wife opened a sliding door, winked at someone in the study. Into the carpeted room walked Leo Glauberman.

"Gentlemen, meet my new partner," Schonkeit said. "Mr. Glauberman is in accord regarding our plans for Jacob Chain."

Wrong, wrong, wrong, Ike felt. Betrayal. Blood on his hands. Chain was a thug, yes. But was Ike now delivering his hardworking members, the *revolution itself,* to people far worse? Yodelman drained his scotch and gagged. Caplow shook his bushy head. He would say no more. He wished he had not come.

"Ends justify means, gentlemen," Glauberman said. He grinned his Teddy Roosevelt grin.

Chapter 26

Jake parked his Hupmobile on lower Fifth Avenue. He got out and stretched in the early September sunlight. Washington Square Park looked lovely, inviting. He wondered why he never went to the city anymore. More and more he seemed locked into Brooklyn—Brownsville, Williamsburg, Gravesend, Flatbush. He had a yearning for his youth, when he and Sarah and little Mutteh took trolley rides to parks, meadows, the zoo. No more.

He was ashamed of his dullness, his slavery to a life of violence. A movie once a week. The radio. Hanging around Glauberman's office. Out in the street, in factories, speakeasies, restaurants, making deals with union officials, bosses, politicians. Usually he would sit silently, a big strong man, staring at his watch, flexing his massive hands. Glauberman or Otzenberger did the talking. Jake's presence was a warning. A show of strength. People understood his power.

Under the green-yellow dappled leaves, near the stone arch, Eva was waiting for him on a slatted bench. She wore a maroon silk dress falling loosely around her slender form. A string of amber beads, a tortoiseshell comb in her hair. She had taken to wearing it piled high, tucked behind her ivory ears. Small pearl earrings, a pearl brooch.

She was feeding pigeons. They flocked to her, as if aware of her beauty, Jake sensed. *Bushwah,* he reflected. They get fed, they come. They would as soon flock to the drunken Mary Sugar-Bum who staggered from bench to bench begging for pennies if the hag fed them.

Kids played hopscotch in the leafy park. Small boys in beanie caps flipped baseball cards. Others played "war" with checkers on a chalk battlefield drawn on the paving stones. Two kids chased each other on homemade scooters—orange crates nailed to a board, old roller skates bolted to the bottom. Jake recalled making one for Mutteh when the boy was ten.

"Hello, Jake," Eva said.

"Eva, how are you?"

"Tired."

"It's not a long walk. You live—what? Two blocks away?"

He had never been invited to the brownstone on West Tenth Street. Even now she preferred to meet him in the park. Very few of the old Haven Place crowd visited her there. The word was she had become snooty, famous, rich. Eva Heilig and her *shagitz,* with his banker father. Some friend of the working girl!

"I love to walk. But I've been working hard. I lectured last night at CCNY. We're starting an inquiry into the murder of the pickets in Rhode Island."

He had no idea what she was talking about. She explained. Strikers shot down by police in Pawtucket. Private police outside a struck mill fired without provocation. The state and the owners were covering up, bribing witnesses, refusing to prosecute. She and Garrison were heading a committee to investigate the outrage.

"Sounds like they need Crazy Jake," he said.

He sat close to her. Her face was a bit lined, with smudges under her eyes from too much reading. But the eyes were as clear and dazzlingly green as ever. Her perfume dizzied him. The maturity, the lines at the corner of her mouth, gave her a new serenity, a gentleness.

"The old Jake. The defender of the pickets."

"I'm still around."

"So I'm told. Ike Brunstein visited me."

"He's with the Communists, right?"

"I was annoyed with him, and I told him so."

Jake stretched his legs. Who cared about these political shmucks? In the long run, all of them depended on the same things—the fist, the club, the gun. And the bribe, the fix.

Eva asked about Sarah and Mutt. What was he called now? Mortimer? Morty?

Jake shrugged. Not much change with Sarah. She limped, needed a cane. She refused to go to night school, but he had taught her a little, enough to struggle through the *Daily News.* They both laughed—not at poor Sarah, but at the way the Heilig boys' educational efforts with Jake had trickled down to Sarah.

And Mutt? Morty? she asked.

"What a kid," Jake said. "Eighteen years old. He could have been anything he's so smart. An accountant, a lawyer, gone into business. But he quit high school. He's driving a truck."

"That's a pity," Eva said. "I always thought he was intelligent. Send him to see me. Maybe I can convince him to do something better."

"Mutt is his own boss. He's happy. He and one of the Ferrante kids—you remember them—they got a trucking business, a warehouse."

He knew damned well what they had. He had visited Kolodny's old place, walled with cinder block, steel-doored, guarded. A cereal storehouse? Hair tonic? *Hah!* Every flatfoot in Brooklyn knew what was going on inside. Professor Goldsturm's magic. But why tell Eva? Why upset her? Every problem in the world seemed to be hers, Jake reflected. No wonder she and Halstead had no children.

She came quickly to why she had asked him to meet her. Ike was distressed. So were other union officials. Decent workingmen, honest union officials were at the mercy of hoodlums who claimed to be benefiting them but sold them out to the bosses. Those who did not accept gangster rule were eliminated. What did Jake know about a man named Hyman Wallowitz?

"They shot him dead in the hospital."

"Who?"

Jake professed ignorance. Wallowitz was his client. A good guy, not a Red, not a crook. Maybe it was a personal grudge.

Eva said Ike had told her otherwise. Chain & Glauberman had represented the man and his workers. But the rank and file charged they were sold out. They complained to Wallowitz, and he in turn had asked that negotiations be reopened. Did Jake know about that?

From anyone else in the world Jake could have accepted the challenge. Played dumb. A film of innocence over his flattened Slavic face. Nothing. Not his doing. And in a sense it wasn't. He had not killed Wallowitz. He knew who had. The Meal Ticket on the Frummers' orders. A warning to Jake Chain not to get too big. And, Jake suspected, done with Glauberman's connivance. He'd heard rumors. Paymaster Schonkeit was running things from his Central Park West apartment. The gangsters would, as the kids playing marbles said, "divvy up" the unions.

"What do you want from me, Eva?"

"Get out. Stop what you're doing, Jake. I am ashamed of you."

"Were you ashamed when I boiled Moishe Nigger? When I wrecked factories for you? When I beat up scabs so you could get a contract?"

She lowered her head. Sunlight gleamed on the piled golden hair. He loved her so painfully he thought he would faint. Or grab her, there in the crowded, noisy, sunny park, and crush her to him.

"I accepted you and what you did."

"You asked me to do it. I did it. Why? Not for the money, not for the glory. What was glory in clipping a *mamzer's* ear off? Eva, I did it because I—" Hesitant, he grasped her hand. "Because I loved you. I still love you. For you, Eva, there is nothing Jake Chain won't do. I knocked over wagons, beat up foremen, set fires. A bum, a mobster. Another Pinchy Paul, a Jack Zelig. I was the scum, the filth of the Jewish community. A scandal to decent people. Rabbis called me names. But you won the strikes."

"Yes, we won." She studied his pale eyes, the ruddy skin, the nose beaten flat in a hundred fights, the lopsided scarred jaw. There was a Grand Canyon, a continent, separating this crude hard man from Garrison Halstead—let alone an Ike Brunstein. And she had to respect him. When they'd needed strength, when the downtrodden had needed a defender, he was there.

"I shouldn't tell you this," he said. Passion inflamed him, rose like a fire from his groin, engulfing his gut and his chest, infusing his face with a scarlet glow. She could almost feel the heat.

"What is it?"

"What those guys did to you, I know."

She shuddered and closed her eyes. "Nothing. I was beaten up, robbed."

"No, I know the truth. I found out."

Eva's eyes, rimmed with tears, looked at his peasant face—fair, fearless. On the surface, a man lacking in emotions. Clod, horse, wagon driver. Hauler of ice, crates, beer kegs.

"The men who did it. I took care of one of them."

"I don't want to hear."

Why was he telling her this? Having opened the subject, he was now uncertain. He was saying in his fumbling way, This is the way Jake Chain operates. This was how I avenged you. And now you come to me, to give up my livelihood? New suits from Jaffe's, a new car, fine furniture, a fat bank account. People wanted to be Jake Chain's friend.

He was telling her that his fists and his courage and his anger had punished the monsters who had hurt her. *Know it, Eva, understand it.* It is not easy for a lout to change. And were he less of a *shtarker,* a man who could hurt, who could *kill,* they might strike back. Shut her golden mouth forever.

"You, Jake. I suspected. Oh, how awful."

"Pearlberg. He won't hurt women no more. Not with his fists or . . ." Gagging, he forced the words out: ". . . or anything else, God curse his rotten soul. Yes, Pearlberg. With my hands."

"I heard he died drunk, an accident."

Jake held up his massive hands. "Drunk, yeah. With these. Maybe he was practicing to be a kosher butcher. He got too close to where they kill the chickens and fell in. Someday I'll finish the fat guy. I know, Eva. In Brownsville I know everything."

Horrified, she touched her lips, drew away from him. "It was wrong. Yes, they hurt me, but not as bad as you think. Look at me, I'm alive, strong, happy. You shouldn't—God, Jake . . ."

"I did it because I love you. No man can do that to you. I killed Moishe Nigger, you hear?"

"Stop. I won't listen."

A rubber ball bounced between them. Jake fielded it, flipped it to a kid in kneepants. "For you, Eva. So no man could hurt you. Someday, the other one also. He'll find out what it is to hurt Jake Chain's—Jake's—"

"Don't say it."

"—the woman I always loved. I never talk like this to no one. Oh, *they* talk. *Yentas.* Bums in the poolroom. But they don't know how I feel.

In my heart. When Sarah was hurt, I remember you came with food for me and the boy. In your long skirt and shirtwaist. Covered with plaster and dirt from the building. Your hair all messed. I can see you. As if you're walking across this park. Small, angry. Your friends were dead. But dinner for me and Mutteh. Why?"

"I felt sorry for you. You are of my blood. My family always felt an obligation to you. Abe and Sol always ask about you." She smiled. "When they read in the papers how you've been picked up for questioning again."

"Tell them Jake Chain is all right. The police never got me. I don't need help anymore. I didn't want help from your family. I wanted you."

"No, Jake. I can't bear to hear this."

"It's true. I'll love you until I die. People look at me—Chain, the bum, the killer. They don't know I started in the roughhouse business because you asked me. And if you asked again I'd do it. For you, Eva, anything."

He shut his eyes, ashamed of his confession. Not the kind of words that Jake Chain uttered. Pigeons skittered, pouted, waddled around their feet. A squirrel chased them, claimed prior rights to the corn kernels Eva had thrown about. The way people chase each other for a dollar, Jake thought.

"Then do what I ask. Get out of the rotten business."

"You think it will make a difference? There'll still be gangsters."

She squeezed his hand. Iron, hardwood. "You could cooperate with the district attorney. Tell what you know. Garrison can arrange it."

"Eva, you don't know me. Chain a squealer? When I was in the hospital with twelve holes in my body, I wouldn't tell. So why now, when nobody's got anything on me? Besides, I'd have to tell how you hired me. I won't talk."

"Jake, we're in different worlds."

"No, Eva. The same world. Like a man and a woman. What you do, all the good things you want for people, I'm not sure I understand. People want—what? Money, power, an easy life. That's all I understand. And I want you more than any of that, but I know it's useless."

"Jake, stop what you're doing. Leave Glauberman. Talk to the district attorney. You can do it secretly. Tell them what you know about the way gangsters are taking over the movement. Give them names."

Jake's eyes were half-shut. He stroked her arm. The thrill unnerved him and loosened his tongue.

"Ask Brunstein, Eva. He knows. I heard he's gone to Schonkeit for *shtarkers*. Good luck."

"How did you know that?"

"It's our business to know."

"All the more reason for you to get out. To find other work. I'm afraid for you."

And staring at him, long-bodied, the power evident in the arms and legs that seemed to burst the tan linen suit, the corded neck and impassive face, she realized she truly cared for him. She could never love him. To her family he had been an oddity, a freak, a matter for minor shame. Like the half-witted relative who, every Friday night, showed up for dinner at the Abelmans' house, was fed, thanked no one, and vanished. . . .

"Don't worry about Crazy Jake," he said.

"I worry about you all the time." She hesitated. "And I feel guilty. Ike and I started your career."

"Don't be sorry. It made me a rich man. Better than living in a base- ment and driving a wagon. Sarah's going to have another operation. The doctors say she could walk without a cane. You should see how fancy my wife is. A fur coat. Dresses from Loehmann's. Thanks to you and your unionniks."

"And you're never afraid? All that violence? And what they may try to do to you?"

"Afraid? Who'd touch Jake Chain? Glauberman and Chain are friends with every precinct captain, every judge in the city. They're on our pay- roll."

Halstead, with his knock-kneed walk, came across Washington Square Park. He seemed daintier to Jake. The pince-nez jiggled on his long nose. Funny thing about these *goyim,* Jake thought. They float, they're on air.

"Hello, Jake," Halstead said. He extended a soft hand.

Jake got up. His powerful body seemed to uncoil. He was four inches taller than Eva's husband. "Mr. Halstead, how are you?"

"Please. Garry. You're family. What does Eva say? *Machutonim?*"

"*Machutonim.*" Jake laughed. "In-laws. I'm not one you're proud of, I guess."

"Eva is worried about you. We hear disturbing things. The governor can't permit it. Your Jewish civic groups are furious. I have access to the Seligmans and the Schiffs and the Loebs and other important people in the Hebrew community. They are distressed."

"Give my regards to Mr. Schiff and Mr. Loeb." Jake's eyes were merry, sly. "I'm a Litvak. We don't talk to German Jews."

Halstead looked puzzled.

"Garry, Jake is pulling your leg."

"What? Oh. Oh, I see. Of course. The Schiffs and the . . . Yes, you wouldn't really . . ."

They were dining with the Roosevelts that night, Halstead reminded his wife. They had to dress, arrive early for cocktails.

"Hmmm. Same as Brownsville. Everyone has booze."

Jake walked a brief distance with them.

Halstead said, "Prohibition can't last. The country can't tolerate these killings and gang wars and violations. I agree with the wets. Repeal the damned thing."

"Not too fast," Jake said, enjoying his role as rogue. "Give my son a chance to make his fortune. He's got a good business going."

Eva pecked Jake's cheek. Halstead patted his back warmly. He regarded

Chain as a source of comical stories, a troglodyte from some netherworld.

Jake watched Eva and Halstead leave under the arch and start uptown on Fifth Avenue. Two beautiful, graceful people. One could think her a fair Protestant daughter of wealth, graduate of a fancy college. She had lost her accent, eradicated the singsong cadences in her speech. Her legs were elegant and silk-shod, and her figure as lean and shapely as it had been when she was a girl on the picket lines.

The hunger gnawed at his insides, filled him with lost hopes, passions that would never be satisfied. He and Brunstein, he decided, should start a club. No one—Halstead, Ike, no man—could ever have loved her with body and spirit the way he could have.

Hungry for Eva, driven by visions of her body, the limbs and breasts, belly and hips he would never have, Jake went to Bella's in late afternoon. He telephoned Sarah. Business. A late meeting with Glauberman. Sarah sulked. There was a Clara Bow movie at the Palace. Could they go later? Maybe, he said. She tried to keep him on the phone. She was worried about Mutteh, all that business with the trucks in Canada . . .

"He's a big boy," Jake said, calling from a phone booth in Pomerantz's drugstore.

"Oh, sure. Eighteen years old. Jake, what is he doing? New suits, new shoes. Where he gets such money?"

"The trucking business is good. I'll be home in time for the movies. But I won't eat. I ain't hungry."

Brooding, silent to the prostitute Minnie's pleas for a gift—she needed a watch—he emptied his passion into her. Drained, he sensed that it had given him only marginal relief. It was no substitute for Eva. Only in the heights of passion, the speedy climax, the loud exhalation of breath, the release of desire, was he relieved. Five minutes later the hunger was in him. But not for Minnie Fassbender.

He gave her twenty dollars. A sport, Jake Chain. A few seconds after he had put on his jacket and left, she ran to the telephone.

Hanging up, Minnie began to sob. She could see his huge figure getting into the Hupmobile. "Oh, God. Oh, God in Heaven, I'm sorry for what I do. They forced me, they made me do it. . . ."

He'd be late getting home. Cold dinner, sullen wife. Maybe they'd have time to catch the movie. Always, after emptying himself into his "hoo-er," he felt a surge of guilty loyalty to Sarah. Not a bad woman.

An unsubtle man, he understood that what a man's body needed and what his spirit yearned for were quite different. The surge of power in his loins, the craving for flesh, was at times unbearable. Hence, Minnie. But shreds of love and pity, a sense of partnership, were what he felt toward

Sarah. Eva was his only love. Unattainable, distant. Fading, fading further from him with each year of his life. He wondered, as he parked the car and entered Fishman's Bakery on Belmont Avenue, if he had been educated, rich, respectable, and dignified, a man of the world, would Eva have accepted him?

The bakery was crowded with early evening shoppers, workers coming from the shops, peddlers, housewives, students in yarmulkes, Hebrew books tucked under their arms. Jake towered over them—blond, rugged, an alien presence. Some knew him. Two women whispered: *the gangster.*

Hirsh Fishman, the owner, flour dotting nose and neck, hairy and muscular in white undershirt and white apron, a spotless paper cap on his head, heard Jake's voice and came out of the oven room. Jake ordered a whole corn bread, bialys, onion rolls, a pound of aromatic *mohn* cake, Sarah's favorite. And for Mutt, the businessman, danish with nuts and raisins for breakfast.

Fishman came out from behind the counter, entangling himself in the string that unwound from the overhead spindle. He cursed, spread a trail of flour, intercepted Jake as he was about to pay the girl. "For you, Mr. Chain, a present. Forget it."

"Why? My money's good."

The baker pulled Jake's hand away and steered him to a corner of the store. "Listen, I know it's good. A man in business needs friends. You, I trust. I respect you. Enough? I can't talk too loud. Some young tramps are asking protection for my window. But if they know I'm a friend of Jacob Chain, maybe they won't suck my blood."

"I understand, Fishman. You get trouble, come see me. But I got to pay you." He was getting tired of people fawning on him. For what? For his fists and his power?

"All right, all right. You're a *mensh,* Mr. Chain. But at least take an extra from me for your wife. A fresh pumpernickel, the best. Like Russian health bread. Delicious." The baker tossed the huge loaf into a brown bag and forced it on Jake. He now had two large bags to carry to his car, which was double-parked across the street and surrounded by pushcarts. "Remember, Mr. Chain, anything special your wife wants—a birthday cake, catering—drop by. For you, special prices."

"Thanks, Fishman."

Jake crossed the garbage-littered street to where his car was double-parked. Remnants of wooden crates, cardboard boxes, rotting vegetables, newspapers. He liked the bustle and noise of the place. It was alive, bursting with good food, talk, money changing hands. His father-in-law's prospering fruit-and-vegetable store was just a block away. Business had never been better. Around the corner, Eva's mother, the diligent Matla Heilig, always in her green smock, puffing Fatima cigarettes, ran the best stationery store in Brownsville.

Disturbed, he saw himself as apart, isolated. When Rabbi Piltz denounced gangsters and parasites from the pulpit in Talmud Torah Tiphereth Hagro last Passover, without mentioning names, Jake knew whom he was talking about. But how could he explain to the rabbi that he had begun innocently twelve years ago, protecting young girls?

A cartload of bananas approached Jake's Hupmobile. Piled high with bunches of green-yellow fruit, it was pushed by a squat Italian in a ragged coat. Behind the pushcart, a Dodge sedan honked angrily.

"Move, ginzo," someone called from the car.

"He blocka me," the vendor said, pointing to Jake's parked car. "Pleez, mist'."

"Hold your water, banana man," Jake said.

Balancing the two bags of bread, Jake tried to open the door of his car. Always alert, gifted with a sense of danger, he realized he was too late. For one thing, he never carried a gun. Assistant D.A. Ordell had warned him: We catch you on a violation, Chain, we'll throw away the key.

No gun. Arms loaded with bags of bread.

The stumpy wop had stopped pushing the bananas. He opened his old coat—it looked like army issue—and was leveling a revolver at Jake's head.

Pops of orange fire, a cracking, small noise amid the shouts of vendors, the cries of *I gotta apple, pear, grapes* . . .

Jake ducked his head behind the bags. Some old instinct prevented him from dropping Fishman's oven-warm bread and cakes. It saved his life.

Six shots were fired. The Dodge sedan backed away to the center of the street. Pushcarts scattered. Jake fell. Hit? Missed? He could not tell. So close was the gunman that he could smell burning powder. Women were shrieking. Peddlers and shoppers were flying toward the stores, falling into doorways. Oranges fell from a cart, bounced and rolled.

The gunman stumbled to the sedan. Hands dragged him in. Honking, knocking over carts, the car sped down Belmont Avenue. A hand emerged from a rear window firing a second fusillade at Jake.

Old gutter fighter, the animal who smelled death, Jake rolled under the Hupmobile, slithering on rotten tomatoes and wilted lettuce. *A salad,* he thought. *With my blood for dressing.*

Fishman was screaming to call a cop. He had seen it all. With floury eyes he watched Jake Chain crawl on hands and knees from the garbage, still clutching his bags of bread.

"Cops, an ambulance, help!" the baker screamed. "They tried to kill Chain! I seen it!"

Jake was on his feet. His head was soaked in blood. Eyes unseeing. People shrank from him. The peddlers flanking his car fled their carts and hid in an appetizing store. He was known to the merchants. The sinister giant. The man they couldn't kill.

Chapter 27

His head had been creased. The first shot, Doc Abelman said, had cut a path through his mop of blond hair, leaving a bloody path on the scalp, splitting the skin. Blood had poured down his face and his shirt and blinded him. Relieved, Jake realized it was the only bullet that had found a mark.

Sergeant Vorstadt and a plainclothesman had taken over Abelman's waiting room, chasing an elderly couple out, warning Mrs. Chain and Morty to wait until the doctor was finished treating Jake.

"He's my father," Mort protested.

On the doctor's waiting-room table, next to his tray of calling cards, Vorstadt had emptied the brown bags from Fishman's Bakery. "Hold your water, Chain," the detective said. "Be glad your old man is alive."

"Beats me." The other cop stared at the mangled loaves. "Saved his goddamn life. He used them as a shield."

Mr. Fishman's iron crusts and thick doughs had absorbed the impact of four slugs. One had missed completely. Two misshapen chunks of bullets nestled in the corn bread like iron raisins. Two more had made their journey through the giant pumpernickel, battered harmlessly against Jake's left arm, and left bloody welts.

"He's got more luck than he has brains," Vorstadt said. "Saved by two loaves of Jew bread."

Abelman opened the green-shaded office doors. Jake came out. He wore a blood-stained bandage around the upper half of his head. He was unsteady on his feet.

"Had to shave his head," the physician said. "Fourteen stitches, but only the scalp was split. I always said pumpernickel was made with a little cement."

Sarah flung herself at Jake, limping with her cane, weeping in convulsive gasps. She had dolled herself up for the movies—a permanent, makeup, a new short-skirted blue dress. He felt guilty. Whorehouses, lying.

He put an arm around her. He felt wobbly from loss of blood and sat in one of Abelman's oak-and-leather chairs. Sarah fell to her knees, rested her head in his lap.

"You okay, pop?" Mort asked. He lifted his mother to her feet.

"Terrific. Ask Doc."

Abelman nodded his head. "Nothing like last time. Maybe he should carry a few pumpernickels around with him. Better than a bulletproof vest."

Mort looked at his bawling mother and his stoic father. A strange pair. But she wasn't as weak as she appeared. Now she was dabbing at her eyes, pleading with Jake to tell the police what he knew.

"How about it, Jake?" Vorstadt asked. "Who was it?"

"Some wop selling bananas."

The detective shook his head. They had witnesses. A Dodge car. The gunman had been hauled into it. Someone fired at Jake after he fell. Who? Did he recognize anyone?

"Strangers. Why would anyone want to knock me off?"

Vorstadt blew air out of his cheeks. Tough cookie, Chain. No emotions. A slab of muscle. But how smart was he, getting shot at all the time? The word was out in the underworld—he was *marked*.

At the breakfast table with her husband, Eva adjusted her eyeglasses and read the front-page account of the attempt to murder Jake. She read aloud, distressed, and did not appreciate Halstead's mocking smile.

UNION MOBSTER SHOT AT AGAIN
GUNMEN FAIL TO KILL CHAIN

Jacob Chain, 37, notorious labor racketeer, was gunned down today by rival hoodlums in the Belmont Avenue pushcart market in Brooklyn. He survived with a severe scalp wound.

Chain, a so-called labor consultant and a well-known "shtarker" or enforcer, has been the target of several murder attempts, earning him the sobriquet among New York police of "The Clay Pigeon."

Witnesses said that as Chain emerged from Fishman's Bakery, a gunman posing as a banana peddler opened fire. Miraculously, only one bullet found its target. The others missed, or were stopped by loaves of bread the victim was carrying.

Police said the would-be assassin fled in a black sedan from which additional shots were fired. No clues were found on the banana cart.

Chain would say nothing, observing an underworld vow of silence.

A much-feared figure in the Brownsville section of Brooklyn,

Chain got his start wrecking factories in 1910. He has, in interviews, claimed to be "for the workingman." But police sources said that he now sells his services to the highest bidder. . . .

Eva read on. Hints at disaffection in Chain's mob. More important and more powerful people out to get him. A series of charges being drawn up by the district attorney.

Halstead laughed. "For what? Endangering life and property by showing himself in public? My God, the man draws fire the way honey draws flies. Why are you so concerned about him?"

"He helped me once."

"His time has passed. He's an anachronism, an abysmal brute, as Jack London would say. Honestly, were it not for your blood relationship, I'd think—"

"What?"

"Perhaps you had a girlhood crush on him. Stupid and brutal as he is, he *is* a handsome man."

"Nonsense. I feel guilty, Garry. We used him. We encouraged him. He'll be killed someday. Blasted to bits by people far worse than he is. And who'll be to blame?"

"Not you, Eva. Chain is a product of his time. Forget about him."

She adjusted her glasses and tried to shut Jake from her mind by reading the rest of the front page. Gandhi was in jail again. More scandals in Harding's White House. Investigations into oil swindles. Off Montauk, the captain of a rum-running vessel had shot and killed a bootlegger.

The newspaper, propped amid the gleaming silver and imported china in the sunny breakfast room, dismayed her. What a gulf between the real world and hers. Did she deserve all this? For being beautiful, aggressive, someone who had caught a rich man's eye?

Halstead got up. He kissed her neck, cupped her breasts.

She sighed. "I don't give you all you need. I lack something."

"Never, my lover. The sight of you gratifies me."

When he had left to visit an editor and discuss a book on the future of American socialism, she telephoned Jake's house. Sarah was cool and unfriendly. Jake was sleeping. He had pain. The doctor had given him pills to sleep.

"Can I come to see him?" Eva asked.

There was a pause. "Listen, Mrs. Halstead, better you should stay with your friends in New York."

She could not blame Sarah Chain for her bitterness. She surely knew how Jake felt about Eva, the temptress who first inveigled him into using his fists to make a living.

"I understand, Sarah. Please tell him I called. And if I can help in any way, you know I want to."

"You, Mrs. Halstead, you can't help him anymore."

In her study Eva tried to finish a speech against child labor she was to make at Cooper Union that night. She had trouble focusing her mind. Someday, she sensed with a tremor, Jake Chain would not be so lucky. Why, she wondered, did he not give up his brutal life? And she knew the answer. It was all he knew.

Chapter 28

"Meet Professor Goldsturm," Mutt Chain said. "Charlie Goldsturm, this is my father."

The bald, pint-sized pharmacist, in starched white smock, flowing black tie, gold-rimmed glasses, let his tiny hand be swallowed by Jake's mitt. "Ah, the famous Jacob Chain." Goldsturm's eyes twinkled behind the fancy cheaters. "Years ago, Mr. Chain, when they called you Crazy Jake—"

"They still do."

"Yes, the old-timers. Anyway, years ago—mind you, I don't hold it against you—some of your boychicks threw a brick through my drugstore window because I wouldn't cough up five dollars a week."

"Impossible," Jake said. "Breaking a window I never did for less than ten bucks."

"Anyway, it's a pleasure. Imagine, now I'm working for your son and Mr. Ferrante. It's better than filling prescriptions."

Mutt had brought his father to the old Kolodny place, now the warehouse and "cutting plant" for the Pacific Breeze Hair Tonic Company and its mysterious associate, the F & C Cereal Co. Inc. The gloomy plant had expanded, added a great deal of stock, varied its line.

Recovered from the stitching in his scalp—he still had a few attacks of dizziness and double vision—Jake decided he wanted to see what his eighteen-year-old son had been up to. Jake wore a rakish brown plaid cap to cover his shaved skull.

He was impressed. Kolodny's office had been enlarged. There were two girls on the phones, keeping books, sweet-talking customers, handling contacts with buyers and suppliers. One was steamy Hilda Otzenberger, whom Mutt had already told his father he intended to marry. The other was Sal's older sister, Theresa, dark, low-voiced, quite beautiful, with her long Arabic nose, cap of black curls, Greek olive eyes.

Some years ago Theresa had taken a course in shorthand and typing, determined never to go back to a sewing machine. Jake could remember Mutt's telling him how her father and her older brothers had threatened her with a beating if she dared to improve herself, dared to go to a commercial school. She was to get married, have kids, cook, and wear black for the dead Frankie.

Young Sal, however, had visions, big ideas. He would need a front-office girl someday. Who better than his sister? Sal prevailed over family objections. Theresa looked spiffy, Jake thought. A tight lavender blouse bulged by her big bazooms. She wore a short black skirt. He could see the edge of her rolled stockings. Long, thin legs.

Jake could hear Hilda's nasal voice on the phone. "That's right, Mr. Hochstadt. Scotch is up to a hundred and ninety dollars a case. Listen, it's a bargain. We got bigger expenses. What? A dozen cases? Which, Highland Cream Special or Old MacDougald?"

Mutt was getting rich. The kid had never told him much. But he knew about the bank accounts. Sarah knew. As a minor, Mutt had to have someone cosign for him when he opened the accounts. Jake, rarely at home, checking on factories, meeting with union officials and bosses, had become a stranger to the boy. Then, while convalescing from the shooting at the bakery, Mutt had casually shown Jake a passbook from the Dime Savings Bank. Mortimer J. Chain had squirreled away a cool forty grand—*just in that one account.*

There was a rotting fruity odor in the "factory." It permeated everything, emanated from Professor Goldsturm's white-smocked figure. Beneath the smock, Goldsturm wore a tweed vest and trousers. A chain with a fancy gold insignia dangled over his tiny paunch. From time to time, the professor consulted a railroad man's watch attached to the chain. Jake liked him. Class. Brains. Even if he smelled of cheap booze.

"The big vats are for the mixing," the professor explained.

There were six giant copper kettles in the middle of the sawdust-covered floor. The walls had been plastered to double their original thickness. Racks and shelves had been extended. Jake noticed the steel doors. He had a memory of the day Kuflik tried to keep him out of the stable, and how he had damn near killed Bunchik and Little Mendel with a shovel. The old stalls, where the Horse Poisoner had done his dirty work, had been bricked up. Steel beams and steel lolly poles supported the roof. Two trucks were parked in what had been the stalls. From one, Stroonz Rizzo (a Ferrante cousin) and a fat black man named Buster Twine were unloading cardboard crates.

Jake shook his head in wonderment.

"Fresh stuff," Mutt said. "From the Canadian run. The new big truck holds about a hundred and eighty cases. Ten or eleven bucks a case in Canada, but that doesn't count gasoline, repairs, and payoffs."

Rizzo squinted at Mutt and his father and hefted a case of eighty-six-proof Bellows into the cutting plant. "And gettin' shot at," Rizzo whined. "Mutt, next time I wanna partner with a shotgun. Maybe Bobby Rimkoff can go with me."

"They got shot at?" Jake asked.

"He's exaggerating."

Mutt explained that two other trucks were headed north right now, to make purchases in Canada. He and Sal had a contact there, a liquor dealer to whom they paid an extra fee to keep them supplied, help them through Canadian Customs, and guide them over back roads. But the competition was getting tough. Schonkeit was financing his own mob of bootleggers. They were probably the ones who had taken potshots at Stroonz and Buster.

"Gentlemen, please," Goldsturm said. He motioned them from the doorway leading from the cutting plant to the garage. The chemist was intensely proud of his work. People praised his cut booze. *The real thing.* The alky from Pacific Breeze Hair Tonic, barkeeps and customers agreed was terrific. A real *bead.* A wallop. Good taste. You could feel it in your toes. It conquered thirst. O'Toole, O'Connor, Casey, all the regulars from the Brooklyn courthouse crowd, had become devotees of Highland Cream and other decoctions sold by Mortimer Chain and Sal Ferrante.

"The cider is for applejack," Goldsturm said, "but we don't get much call for that. Some of the hicks out in Queens, a few *shwarzers.* On the racks behind you, Mr. Chain, empty bottles, made special to order, all with our own labels. Notice the fancy one for our top-line scotch. It says blended and bottled under His Majesty's Government supervision. And it won the gold medal at the St. Louis Fair. Who can prove it didn't?"

On a long messy slate table, to one side of the malodorous vats, were Goldsturm's magical ingredients. He showed them off to Jake with professional enthusiasm.

"Creosote for scotch flavor. Distilled from the best wood tar. Go ahead, Mr. Chain, *shmeck.* Almost like scotch, no? It can't hurt. But don't try it straight. It'll take the enamel off your teeth."

Jake smiled.

"Iodine is also good for scotch," the professor went on, "but you got to be careful. Too much gives it a stink. It's good coloring for any brown booze. Prune juice is better. See? From the finest prunes. In the big jugs on top. I also got oil of juniper, oil of bourbon, oil of rye. And fusel oil for a clear color."

Jake sniffed the opened neck of a slender dark brown bottle. He got dizzy at once, slightly nauseated. There were hundreds like it on the shelves, labeled, neatly arranged. The odor was appalling. Like rotting garbage. *This was bourbon?* The "oil of rye" was worse. Like the vilest laxative or cough syrup.

Goldsturm showed off the rest of his equipment. Barrels filled with charred wood chips for "aging." Drums of pure ethyl alcohol drawn from the government warehouse with fake "Permits of Withdrawal." Drums of denatured alky, which the professor "purified" as needed.

Jake nodded. "I thought you used only pure alky. Didn't you say so, Mutt?"

"Both, papa. We get the denatured stuff legally. We don't even pay a tax. But we also got an arrangement with the storekeepers and gaugers. The poor shmucks get paid four bucks a day. So for a grand a month they give us an equal amount of *pure* ethyl alcohol."

"Like this," said Goldsturm. The chemist held up a jug of clear fluid. "Finest ethyl. For use only in hospitals and pharmacies. This is beautiful stuff. Just mix with water, whiskey, and a little coloring and fusel oil. Out comes our top product. Old Highland gets only pure ethyl. For the lower-priced brands we use the *drek*. I get most of the crap out of it, but it isn't easy, Mr. Chain. The government is full of tricks. Would you believe the wise guys have eighty different ways of poisoning good alcohol which people could otherwise enjoy? Pyridine, benzene, sulfuric ether, ammonium iodide! People less honorable than your son sell that *chazerei,* and customers die, go blind, go lame, go crazy. Your son will not countenance such disgusting practices."

Inspired by his own oratory, Goldsturm pulled a dark green bottle of Highland Cream from a case. Proudly he displayed the fake Canadian seals, the fake government stamps, the phony label. He held the bottle high to the overhead light and rotated it.

"The *bead,"* he said. "Look at the bead. The way it shines, clear, brilliant. No poisons. We have a certain competitor who when his scotch drips on the floor it eats a hole in the rug. In the kitchen it dissolves the enamel from the sink. I am not joking."

Mutt showed his father stacks of filled orders, paid for in cash. Goldsturm waddled off to supervise the cutting of a shipment of gin. Juniper oil, water, ethyl alcohol, plus thirty percent English gin purchased in Canada.

Jake was feeling prouder of his son every minute. The old dreams he and Sarah had entertained—a lawyer, an accountant—seemed trivial.

"We're also working on reconsignments," Mutt said. "I got a connection with a dispatcher at the Long Island Railroad in Jamaica. We pay off the railroad guy to reroute the stuff to us. Then we pay off the paint or varnish people who bought the alky. They don't care. They make more dough selling us ethyl alcohol than they can manufacturing paint. We'll unload at the East New York station."

"You had any trouble from competition?" Jake asked.

"Some. Your name helps."

"I thought it would. They know who your old man is."

Winking, Mutt led his father past the shelves stacked ceiling-high with cartons ready for shipment. "Some guineas came around. They make their own stuff on alky cookers in their homes. Sal and I only buy from his brothers. But these other wops distill it from anything—garbage, potato peelings, rotten vegetables. The only reason I buy from the Ferrantes is they're old friends, and they work for us. Besides, the old man is an officer of the hair-tonic company. That's how we got our first alcohol."

They paused outside the office, where Theresa and Hilda, ripe dark fruits of the Mediterranean, labored. Theresa was making entries in the books. Three sets of books. One for Pacific Breeze; one for F & C Cereals; a third secret set.

"Wine?" Hilda shouted to Mutt. "We handle wine?"

"Not yet," Mutt called back. "Who wants it?"

"Friend of Hochstadt's. He needs six cases of red wine."

"Tell him to call back in an hour. I'll think of something."

Jake was getting an education. He looked into the factory. Professor Goldsturm was supervising Stroonz and the black man, Buster, in an odd maneuver. They were immersing cases of cut scotch in a metal vat.

"What's that?"

"Seawater," Mutt explained. "We let it stain the cases. It stinks from sea salt. The suckers are convinced it's the real stuff from Long Island. A guy complains it's cut, we say to him, smell the seawater on the label."

The steel garage door groaned on its rollers. Sal and Stroonz were pushing it open. One of the trucks from Canada was inching in.

In broad daylight, Jake marveled. They had to be paying everyone off. It was surely easier than *shtarking.* No worry about Communists, union officials, Wallowitzes—people Jake did not want to harm. Mutt, Sal, and the professor supplied a *need.* Everyone cooperated. Everyone took a cut.

"How'd it go?" Mutt asked the driver. It was Baggie Ferrante.

Baggie pointed to four round gouges on the metal door of the cab. "Shot at us again," he said. "Me and Vin were lucky to make it."

"Schonkeit's mob, or the hicks in Canada?"

"Feds guarding the lumber road. I think maybe we busted a couple cases."

"Gentlemen," Goldsturm said, approaching Mutt and Jake with a bottle. "To mark Mr. Chain's recovery. Newly mixed, fresh from the vat, my deluxe line for the new label. Aberdeen Dew. Go on, have a snort."

He passed the bottle to Mutt, who declined and gave it to his father. Even good whiskey nauseated him. Mortimer J. Chain was a cream-soda and celery-tonic man.

Jake took a swig. His eyes popped, his throat constricted. He felt as if the wound on his scalp would be blown apart. Staggering backward, he shoved the bottle of "Aberdeen Dew" at its creator.

"A little strong, Mr. Chain?"

"It tastes like horse piss, professor."

"We can't make enough of it." Mutt laughed.

In the office Jake could hear Hilda taking another order. *Ten cases of Highland Cream, six cases of Parliament Gin, six cases of Kentucky Meadow Bourbon . . .*

Goldsturm let his lips touch the mouth of his new creation, blinked a few times, exhaled. "I'll soften it with ethyl. The stuff we get from the backyard stills has too much potato peel. It gives it a stink."

Jake looked at his pocket watch. He had a meeting with Glauberman. His first since the banana man tried to kill him. A lot of things were bothering him. The lawyer was trying to run the whole labor show—Communists, right-wingers, Jewish unions. Cut the unions, cut the bosses, make everyone pay. Jake wondered about the attack on him.

"Pop," Mutt said, at the door. "Join the business. Enough with *shtarking*. This is better."

Jake shook his son's hand. "Only if I can help, Mutteh. No free ride for Jacob Chain."

Mutt smiled. The dark foxy face was full of intelligence, a face that understood the power his father radiated, the respect his name evoked. It would mean dividing the profits. But Mutt saw that the business was growing faster than they could control it. Extra hands, extra brains, extra courage would be needed.

The following Saturday night, Sarah's parents, the fruit vendor Shimen Klebanow and his minuscule wife, Leah, came to the Chain house for dinner. Mutt was not there. Saturday nights were his to court Hilda. They were off to a vaudeville show at the RKO Albee and a trip to Coney Island. A power in his own right in Brownsville, Mutt, finished with the menial work of cabdriving, had access—in exchange for a bottle of "real stuff"—to the unlimited use of Futcher's yellow cabs. Hilda complained about being hacked around Brooklyn in a taxi. Mutt assured her that he was eyeing new cars. A Buick or a Chandler.

Shimen Klebanow was Orthodox. Now that he was a prosperous merchant, thanks to Jake's generosity, he was afforded a better seat in the synagogue. He made contributions to the building fund, toward the purchase of a new Torah, to the Hebrew school. A shy man with a full gray beard and curling earlocks, who wore a black homburg and a black "alpaca" coat on the sabbath, he regretted his daughter's ignorance and his son-in-law's shadowy pursuits. But he rarely expressed an opinion.

His wife, Leah, withered at fifty-five, looked to be seventy. Yet she worked a twelve-hour day, running the cash register and keeping the books. Their store was famous for the quality of its fresh melons, excellent vegetables, and luscious fruits.

The sabbath having just ended with an evening service which the Klebanows had attended, the four settled down to a meal of brisket of beef, cholent, carrots and prunes from the Klebanow store, and a noodle pudding laced with raisins and cinnamon.

Jake ate sparingly. His head ached. He had been told by Doc Abelman that he might have sustained a concussion. Rest, get away, no exertion, the doctor said. Abelman had arched his eyebrows as if to say, "And no more *shtarking.*"

Jake admitted to himself he was in trouble. Glauberman was proving a pain. He was always busy or in New York, or downtown at the courthouse. Jake didn't like getting the runaround. About all he had to cheer him up, apart from his son's booming business, had been a phone call from Eva. The fluty voice made him shiver. He told her not to worry about him. It was nothing. The *gonovim* who were after him were such cowards they had to hire a dago with a banana cart. Better he should have tried to hit him with bananas than fire bullets. Lousy twenty-twos, at that, Jake said as Eva gasped. They couldn't kill him with a thirty-eight years ago. . . .

Eva began to cry on the phone. *"Get out, get out,"* she pleaded. The D.A. knew her husband. He had warned Halstead that the day of labor racketeers was ending. The governor would not tolerate it. . . .

When she hung up, Jake sensed the old hunger for her. Worse than ever. He would die craving her.

Dinner did little to relieve his gloom, except for one aspect that amused him, and then intrigued him. Klebanow had brought a bottle of legitimate kosher wine from a New York State distillery.

"Pop, where did you get this?" Jake asked. He sipped it. Sweet. Pure. Not like the poison Professor Goldsturm had forced on him.

"Rabbi Piltz made me a present."

"Where does he get it?"

"For rabbis they got a special arrangement." The fruit vendor spoke a Romanian-Yiddish. Jake had trouble following the explanation. But he absorbed enough of it, ignoring Sarah's interruptions.

Since wine was obligatory in synagogue services and in the sacraments performed in the home, rabbis and priests were given a monthly allotment of wine drawn from government warehouses. The wine was sold to members of the congregation at cost—a gallon of wine a year for each adult member of the family, up to a total of five gallons.

Jake was fascinated. A new one on him. Something called a "Permit of Withdrawal" allowed the rabbi to procure the wine. The rabbi would present a list of his congregation and an estimate of their needs. No questions were asked.

"Just like that?" Jake asked.

"Just like that."

Sarah and her mother, bored with the talk about wine, cleared the table and went into the kitchen to clean up. Sarah had promised her mother an evening of listening to the new radio. Beautiful music, she said, a treat.

"Listen, papa," Jake said. "I got an idea. You want to help me and my son?"

Klebanow shifted uneasily in the dining-room chair. He knew all about his son-in-law. A gangster. A man who killed. Hardly an admirable Jew.

Rabbi Piltz, a revered Vilna scholar, would never mention Jacob Chain's name in or out of his shul. He tolerated Shimen Klebanow as an honest man, a *gelernter* and a donator. But his son-in-law! A scandal and an outrage!

"Papa, get me from the rabbi's office some sheets of his stationery. What he writes his letters on."

"Why?"

"I'll explain later. When he ain't looking, grab a bunch of papers."

Klebanow feared his son-in-law. But what was S. Klebanow before Jake had set him up in a store? A peddler shoving a pushcart through Brownsville. Getting up at four in the morning to shlep the cursed cart to the wholesale market, haggling over carrots and potatoes and onions with heartless merchants. Now they came to *him,* delivering fresh-from-the-farm tomatoes and soup greens and asparagus. Klebanow's Fancy Fruits and Vegetables was no cheap operation. And he had Jake to thank for it. Rabbi Piltz would not miss his stationery.

"One other thing, papa," Jake said.

"Please, I can't steal the rabbi's prayer books."

"Meet me by the Kolodny place on Monday morning with three of your friends, and the stationery."

"What kind friends?"

"The older the better. Beards, black hats, long coats, *tsitsith*. Like rabbis."

Chapter 29

The show at the Albee was terrific, Mutt and Hilda agreed. Eight vaudeville acts! Plus a Charlie Chaplin short, a newsreel, an episode of *Tarzan,* and a western movie. On the stage a man juggled bread knives, a "tramp band" had them in hysterics, and a woman in a green velvet evening gown sang arias from Italian operas, while two stooges smoked through her act.

In the balcony, Mortimer Chain, bursting with desire, slipped one hand under Hilda's skirt and inside her green silk bloomers. She locked her thighs and trapped him. With the other hand he massaged her left breast. She protested, wriggled away from him, punished him with ineffectual slaps on his hand. They seemed to him more like invitations than protests.

Later, they parked on Surf Avenue near Pallini's restaurant. Hilda staggered from the taxi. Mutt had taken her on a wild careening ride through Brooklyn. She had tried to make him slow down. They'd get a ticket, for sure, she shouted, they'd be stopped by cops. And she knew that he always carried a "sample case" in the trunk of the taxi.

"Morty, you're crazy," she had cried. "Right through a red light! On Ocean Parkway!"

"It was changing."

"You'll see, wise guy. A cop'll stop you. He'll look for the booze. It still smells in here from a broken bottle."

"I'll hand him a sawbuck and a bottle of Highland Cream and he'll let me go. C'mon, sit closer. I wanna touch you."

The construction of Mr. Futcher's Yellow Cab presented problems for traveling lovers. There was no seat next to the driver, just a dusty grease-stained black pit, for change box, rags, tools. Mutt had improvised a seat of sorts—a cane-back chair with cut-off legs and a soft kapok-filled cushion. On this unsteady throne, Hilda had sat, clinging for dear life to the meter, her body jolted black and blue as the rattling Checker bounced toward Coney Island.

"Hands off," Hilda said. "Honest, I never saw anyone with such hot pants."

"Because I love you. I mean it."

Hilda believed him. A kid, a *shnook*. Two years her junior. But already the "Boy Wonder" of booze. Her astute father was awed by the aggressiveness and ambition of Mortimer J. Chain. He was making his old man Jake look like a tinhorn.

In the middle of the spaghetti with red clam sauce (Hilda shied away at first because she had never eaten a clam), Mutt decided to contract business. He left her dipping crusty bread in the clam sauce, lugged his sample case from the trunk of the cab, and went into the kitchen to talk to Dominic Pallini. Dom was an old associate of the Ferrantes'. Who was the leading retailer in the Coney Island area? Mutt asked him. Did Dom sell booze? What about speakeasies? Coney Island had to be loaded with them.

"You kiddin'?" the pot-bellied man in an undershirt and sauce-stained apron asked. "You can buy booze in any store onna block. The drugstore. The barbershop. The candy store. *My* jernt. Any other restaurant. Any candy store. There's an undertaker around the corner sells wine in the back room. Some days the stink from hooch is so bad you can't smell the ocean."

Mutt absorbed this. He took out a sealed bottle of his chemist's latest achievement—Aberdeen Dew, guaranteed eighty-six-proof, Distilled and Blended in the Scottish Highlands under the Supervision of His Majesty's Government. The handsome black-and-gold label displayed two medallions—First Prize, St. Louis Exposition; First Prize, Paris World's Fair.

"Try this, Dom. We also got gin off the boat from the islands, real Kentucky bourbon, anything you want."

The restaurant owner stirred a frypan full of sizzling veal, peppers, and mushrooms, added a bit of garlic, then opened the foil cap, tore away the "revenue stamps," and yanked the cork out with his teeth. He wiped his mouth—"Get the garlic taste out, or it'll ruin the scotch," Mutt advised—and took a long draft of Goldsturm's elixir.

Dom Pallini was an experienced taster, a retailer who knew his booze. And although he had a generous capacity for alcohol, he was never drunk. Aberdeen Dew watered his eyes, turned his cheeks as red as his tomato sauce, and left him gasping. He reeled backward.

"Jesus. Jesus, it's got a kick like a *sfaccim'* Mack truck. I'll take a case."

"We don't sell less than six cases, Dom. Ten-percent discount for twelve cases. A bargain. A hundred and eighty bucks a case. The real item, right from Canada. You can see the original seals yourself. Just the way they bottled it in Scotland."

"Let's try it again."

Pallini took a second swig from the bottle. He was seized with a fit of coughing that almost blew out the gas jets under the simmering veal. He bent double, grabbed his diaphragm, straightened up, and said, "Boy, that's *prima* stuff, kid. It got to be from the other side. Whadda kick! My customers been complainin' the scotch I get is too watery, you know? I'll take the twelve."

Pallini was turning pea green. Sweat issued from his swarthy face and dripped into the veal cacciatore.

"Good stuff, kid. Kicks like a *chooch*."

"Sale?" Mutt asked.

"You got it."

Mortimer Chain smiled. This *proved* it was real stuff.

Returning to the table, Mutt found Hilda pouting. "What were you doing in there so long? Honest, Mutt. Business, business, business."

"I made a big sale. A new customer."

"Is that all you ever think of?"

"One other thing. I love you, babe. Let's get married soon, huh?"

"You're eighteen."

"But I'm a man, right? What about all those guys who wanted to marry you? The lawyer, and the accountant, and the guy with the drygoods store. I'm better than any of them."

"Well, you're *nicer*." She tossed her hair, looked out at the surf and the gray beach. "My father doesn't care for your family, Morty. He says I'm asking for trouble. He doesn't even like that I work for you and Sal."

Mutt lit a cigarette and passed one to Hilda. "Your old man is scared I'll get shot at. Is that it? Or blown up? Never. My father's coming into the business. A partner. Nobody messes with Crazy Jake. Tell that to Mr. Otzenberger."

"Oh, my God," Hilda moaned. "Worse and worse. Papa'll never let me marry you. He says your father is on a *list*. They'll get him someday."

Mutt paid the bill, helped Hilda up, and guided her into her topcoat. It was mid-October, cool near the ocean. "Nobody gets the best of the Chains, Hilda. Tell your old man. Know why? 'Cause we ain't afraid of anyone."

They turned a breezy corner. The sea wind swirled Hilda's dark green skirt. She giggled and held it down. Mutt drew her close. They walked toward the boardwalk. The concessions were boarded up; a lone sign for "Skee-Ball" rattled in the wind.

"Morty, I'm scared," Hilda said.

"What are you scared of?"

"I know what happens. I went to Canada the first time with you. When that creep Sal—when he— Morty, I still have nightmares about that redheaded guy. Someday the Canadian cops, or his family . . ."

"Nobody messes with the Chains."

"And the trucks that come back with bullet holes. I hear what you and the Ferrantes talk about. Schonkeit. And the Customs guards, with guns. Morty, I love you, even though your hands are all over me. I don't want you to get hurt."

His hands were, indeed, caressing, kneading, stroking her back, her waist. Soft and full. She wore no corset. The feel of her flesh, even beneath layers of clothing, inflamed him.

"We're getting rich," he said. "Nobody can hurt us. We're getting married."

They heard the beating of the surf. A mysterious sound. Mutt could recall his father telling him about the first time he saw the ocean. From the rail of a ship leaving Hamburg. So much water, so much to fear. Jake was alone, in patched clothing, carrying a sack of torn underwear and darned socks. A passport was sewn into his ragged coat. A tag with the name Yankele Schoen was tied around his starved neck. He had been given a paper bag of hard bread, sausage, and rocklike cheese to last him for fifteen days at sea. That and water had kept him alive. For ten days he remained unclaimed at Ellis Island, until the Hebrew Orphan Asylum took him.

"I'm freezing," Hilda said. "Let's go back to the car. I don't know what's worse, freezing here or getting bounced around in that taxi."

"I'll make you warm."

Mutt spread his jacket on the sand. He pulled her down with strong hands and fell on top of her.

"Ouch. Ouch. Don't hurt."

His moves were so swift, so expert, so coordinated that she barely gasped when he entered her.

"Oh, Morty. We're one person again."

"Forever, kid."

The following Monday, Hilda was still finding sand in her shoes, her skirt, her coat—indeed, in the most personal parts of her body.

Mutt teased her. "Hey, Sandy," he said. "That's your new nickname. Like the dog in 'Little Orphan Annie.' Say 'arf,' kid."

"That isn't funny. And not so *loud.*"

Theresa Ferrante entered the office. The girls got to work early. Both complained to their bosses. There was more work than they could handle. They needed a third girl to help with phone orders.

Mutt tickled Hilda's neck and kissed her ear.

"You two better stop necking in here," Theresa said. "I'll snitch to someone."

"To who, Theresa?" Mutt asked. "Hey, Theresa, we're getting married. First thing next year. You're invited. You and all your brothers."

"It's true," Hilda said.

"So where's your ring?" asked Theresa. "Or at least a watch?" The rule was strict among Italians. Watch first, when the engagement was announced. Ring when the wedding date was announced. And a schedule for shopping for bridal clothing, furniture . . . Mutt and Hilda were different. Maybe because Hilda had no mother, Theresa thought. Besides, with her politician father and Mutt's money—*the fortune that punk was making!*—they would have no problems.

Sergeant Pope of the 71st Precinct appeared with his monthly checklist. Grumbling and rubbing his eyes, Sal joined Mutt. They did business with the bagman on the hood of one of the new White trucks. The list was checked carefully. Sal gave the officer a thousand dollars in twenties in a tan envelope.

"We're getting two more trucks," Sal said. His eyes never met Pope's. "In a few weeks we're knockin' a wall down and adding garage space for two more trucks. We'll get permits. We just don't want no trouble from cops when the work starts."

"*Eight* trucks?" asked Pope. "That may mean a little extra."

The Reo pulled into a bay and began unloading home-cooked alcohol in glass jugs labeled "Adirondack Mineral Water." Sal had bought a supply of jugs and labels and distributed them to the cottage cookers.

The home distiller, a squat Italian with a handlebar moustache, was helping Buster unload. Sal walked up to him and in a menacing voice began berating him in Italian.

"What's one wop saying to the other wop?" Pope asked Mutt.

Mutt had picked up some Italian. "Cockroaches," he said. He smiled at the officer.

"Hunh?"

"Cockroaches. Those dumb guineas use anything to cook alky. Bugs get into the mash. We had complaints about Juniper Tree gin. It's the cheap line, so what's a few dead bugs?"

Sergeant Pope gagged. He'd been drinking Juniper Tree since last month's payoff. "I'll take Aberdeen Dew this time."

The cutting plant and the loading bay were always busy on Mondays. Several Ferrante brothers were on hand, as well as Professor Goldsturm, Buster, Stroonz, and the girls.

Officer Pope, carrying a three-pack of scotch sewn into a "burlock," walked out of the steel door. He bumped into Jake Chain as he stepped onto the pavement.

"Well," Pope said. "If it ain't the proud daddy of a grand businessman. No wonder nobody hijacks them. They know who they'd have to fight."

Jake did not smile. "Me? I scare people? That's funny, officer. I ain't *klopped* no one in years. *Years.* Give my regards to the people at the Seventy-first. I remember them from the old days on the picket lines. How come you were never around when Moishe Nigger hit girls?"

"I remember the time we picked you up after the Nigger went under for the third time."

"A pity. He thought the chicken blood was the Betsy Head Park pool. Imagine. Swimming in the middle of the night."

Politely, Jake held the door of the prowl car open. "And a good day to you, sir." He doffed his checked cap as the car pulled away. "Lousy donkey," Jake said softly. "You'll be on somebody's payroll all your life."

He waited in the autumn sunlight, enjoying the mild day. He hadn't yet seen Glauberman to tell him of his decision to quit. By now he was convinced the banana peddler had been hired by Schonkeit, maybe with Glauberman's consent. But since he was alive, he'd give Leo another chance. They would part amicably.

Shimen Klebanow, accompanied by an older and tinier man, came shuffling down the street. Both wore black alpaca coats and undented homburgs. The little man had a beard twice as long as Jake's father-in-law's. It was creamy white, tinged with a becoming yellow around the edges. His eyes glinted with old intelligence.

"Good morning, papa," Jake said respectfully to Klebanow. "Your friend? Only *one*? I could use two or three."

"Mr. Gelb. Retired. A cutter for the furriers, sixty-two years."

Ancient Gelb grabbed Jake's hand. "You I remember. Jake Chain. In 1912 you stuck up for us against the bosses. I was on strike twenty-eight days."

"Let's see," Jake said. "At Koppelman's Furs? Blake Avenue?"

"That was me. I was a kid sixty-five years old, a first-class cutter. The bosses tried to bring in scabs. Mr. Chain, you turned over a truck and started a fire. We all cheered. I'm right?"

Jake grinned. "You're right, Mr. Gelb."

Klebanow fidgeted. If Mr. Gelb knew what his son-in-law was up to (the fruit vendor himself wasn't certain), he might not be so overjoyed at the reunion. *Oi, those Chains.*

"Come in, gentlemen," Jake said. "Take a seat in the office and we'll get to work."

The oldsters followed Jake into the warehouse, past Professor Goldsturm's aromatic vats and stained tables, past the shelves of cases and bottles. Klebanow had been there before. He was used to the odor. Old Gelb sniffed and licked his cracked lips. "I could use it at night a little drink myself sometimes. For my heart."

You'll get a drink and more, zayde, Jake thought.

In the office Mutt joined them. "Hey, grampa, whaddya doing here? Grandma's by herself in the store?"

"Monday is slow," the old man said.

"You got the rabbi's stationery?" Jake asked.

Klebanow handed him a manila envelope. Jake extracted a half-dozen large white sheets. At the top was the name of the synagogue, its address, and in smaller letters, in Yiddish and English characters: *Rabbi Leb Benjamin Piltz, Graduate of the Vilna Yeshiva.*

"Pop, what's going on?" Mutt asked.

"I heard you needed wine. Watch how your father knows a few things.

First, we'll need a lot more copies of this. I can't keep sending grampa into the rabbi's study to borrow stationery."

"I got a printer can make all we need," Mutt said.

"Hilda, you ready?" Jake asked.

"Sure."

"Type me two letters. How do you say it? To the person in charge? To the warehouse? What?"

"To whom it may concern."

"Nice. Then say, 'The bearer of this letter is my associate, Rabbi Shimen Klebanow—' "

"I'm no rabbi."

"Me neither," said Mr. Gelb.

"It wouldn't hurt to say you are. You're so religious, you're *almost* rabbis."

"Hilda? You listening?" Jake asked. She nodded, taking shorthand notes. "Rabbi Shimen Klebanow, who is my associate, presents to you a list of his congregation, and their needs for sacramental wine. Then say something nice, like he thanks them for their consideration, whatever you say polite at the end of the letter. Then another letter to introduce Rabbi— what's your first name, *zayde?*"

"Schmul."

"Rabbi Schmul Gelb, an associate who presents a list of his congregation and their needs for wine."

Mutt was laughing. "Pop, you think this'll work?"

"Watch me, sonny. Now we need lists. Theresa, go through the Brooklyn telephone book. Make two separate lists. Only Jewish names from Brownsville and East New York. Mix it up, like every other one gets two gallons, then a few with three gallons, and some for four and five."

"Just names outta the book?" Theresa's eyes were as round as the glass dishes in which Goldsturm mixed fusel oil.

"Sometimes two in the family, anything up to five. Each person gets a gallon, but five is the most."

Mutt said, "Pop, you'll need the Permits of Withdrawal. We fill in everything except the amount. Better be ready to grease the guy. All this trouble for a hundred cases of kosher wine?"

Jake winked. "You could give them to your professor, and it could come out *three* hundred cases, right?"

Jake shepherded his bearded friends into his Hupmobile. Buster Twine, the black workman, was to follow him in the Reo truck. Two hours later the Reo was groaning and rattling under the weight of one hundred and eighteen gallons of genuine Concord grape wine.

The scheme had worked like a new Ford motor, humming, purring, all the parts in order, Jake reflected as he returned to his son's warehouse.

The storekeeper, a rat-faced clerk named Curtis, had surveyed the two "rabbis" with mean eyes. Jake slipped a fifty-dollar bill in with the papers.

"Pair of beavers," the man said to Jake. "Them old hebes really guzzle sweet wine."

"For religious purposes only."

Curtis assumed that all old Jews in black coats and long beards *had* to be rabbis. The lists were nothing new. He'd seen dozens of them. Assured he was dealing with honest men, he did not bother to check the congregations. It was lucky, Jake thought, that he hadn't. Theresa, prodded by Jake to hurry up, had included several Italians, a few Irish, and a Methodist minister from Ridgewood.

After Buster and Jake loaded the trucks—he could still put in a day's work—Jake returned to Curtis.

"I was wonderin'," Curtis said. "Who are *you?* How come the old guys didn't come by themselves?"

"I'm in charge of the Hebrew school. Helping out because my English is better, Mr. Curtis."

Curtis eyed the muscular man in the expensive tweed suit and the gray checked cap. "You look familiar. I seen you around? At Otzenberger's clubhouse?"

"Possible. You'll excuse me, I got a class this afternoon."

O'Connor, the warehouse superintendent, came out of his office. He caught a glimpse of Jake ushering his "rabbis" into the Hupmobile.

"Who'd that horse say he was?" O'Connor asked. He was a ruddy curly-headed man, pale as bleached dog turds.

"Hebrew teacher."

"The hell he is. That's Crazy Jake Chain. One of them kike gangsters."

As far as Mutt was concerned, Jake had proved himself. There was no question that he had imagination, the guts to go along with his awesome reputation. He was a born bootlegger.

Jake gave Glauberman the news a few days after he had brought in a third truckload of kosher wine. He was finished with *shtarking.* He didn't like the way it was going. Goodbye, Glauberman & Chain, Labor Consultants.

The lawyer's face sliced itself into two sections with a toothy grin. The moustache bristled, the roached hair rose like the ridge on a dog's back.

"Getting soft, Jacob?"

"Never, Leo."

"The banana man? I don't blame you."

"Maybe I blame *you,* Leo."

Glauberman's square face turned sideways. He licked his moustache. Had to be careful with his partner. Illiterate, thick-headed bum. He had been the club, the gun in Glauberman's hand. Now that the firm had a half-dozen unions in its pocket, and was getting juicy fees from others, he didn't want trouble. But orders had come down from Schonkeit: *Get rid of Chain.*

Leo realized he had made the mistake of depending too much on Jake, on the terror he inspired, on his reputation as a defender of workingmen. There was an ample supply of strong-arm men available—unemployed kids out of the army looking for work, uneducated stiffs.

Schonkeit, knowing about Jake through his police contacts, understood as soon as he entered the unions rackets that Chain was a menace. The man had a strain of noble hero in him; he believed the crap about protecting the poor. Such a man was useless to the crime empire the Paymaster was building.

Glauberman, also, had grander notions. With Schonkeit's backing and the Frummer mob, he was now specializing in "strike insurance," exorbitant initiation fees, and illegal "work permits." Schonkeit had taught him to work on a fixed eight-percent graft on all contracts, all salaries, all fees. Ike Brunstein, trying to install Communists in positions of power, had learned the lesson soon enough, Schonkeit said. His frightened Lenins of the sewing machines were soon siphoning off union funds to the Paymaster's hoodlums. Glauberman would be Schonkeit's man in Brooklyn.

"Okay with me, Jake," Glauberman said now, ignoring Jake's pointed remark. "Whatever I owe you, you'll get. I think we're even."

"Even, yeah. Except for five grand for the job we did last month for the restaurant owners' association."

"I'll have the girl send you a check."

"Cash. Before I leave."

"Impossible. I don't keep that kind of cash around."

Jake got up from the leather chair. He walked to the mahogany desk and lifted the lawyer out of his swivel chair by the lapels. Glauberman was a heavy man. Jake handled him as if he were a child. He slammed Glauberman against the semicircular window with the gold lettering: GLAUBERMAN & CHAIN.

"Easy, Jake." The lawyer's voice shivered.

"Five grand and we're even. I know you're playing ball with Schonkeit, that pig who wants to eat everything in the city. His bums tried to kill me. The guinea with the pushcart and the guys in the Dodge. You finger me for them?"

"I don't buy in Fishman's Bakery."

"But you know I go to Bella's place."

"Nonsense." He squirmed. Jake held him in an iron grip. His hands were anchored to the blue serge lapels. He nailed Glauberman to the window.

"If you didn't finger me, you gave the okay. Schonkeit wouldn't try to knock me off without telling you. He knows you got Otzenberger's ear. Connections with judges."

"Jake, let go of me. You've been listening to idiots like Sol Heilig and his reform crowd. And his sister. Your old sweetie—"

The back of Jake's right hand, like a sheet of steel, cracked across Glauberman's cheek. The pince-nez flew from his nose and smashed against the window.

"Shut up, shyster. Don't talk about Eva Heilig. Five thousand and I'm out of the business. I'm going into bootlegging with my kid. You can have all the union *drek*. It's where you belong. I won't suck blood from workers anymore."

"Take your hands off. I could have you—"

"What? Assault and battery? With what I could spill to the D.A. about you? What I know about us?"

"You'll get put away before I will, Jake."

Jake slammed him against the wall, but did not go after him again.

The lawyer retrieved his fragmented pince-nez. He walked to the safe in the corner of the office. He had a lot more than five thousand dollars in it. Payoffs in cash were part of his daily transactions.

"Good luck running booze, Jake," he said as he counted bills. "The labor business isn't for you anymore."

Glauberman tried to be fatherly. But he was shaking. His insides had turned to jelly. God help the bootleggers once Crazy Jake was turned loose.

"Listen to your former partner, Jake," Glauberman said at the door. "Nobody's safe anymore. Nobody's honest anymore. Your friend Brunstein, he's with Schonkeit. We all need the Paymaster. Ike is like the fella in the Hasidic story. The devil talked him into giving him a finger. Then a hand. Now the devil has Brunstein's arm, and he's getting ready to eat him."

"I ain't Brunstein. I ain't got the brains to go with Schonkeit. I'm a horse, remember? Chain, the *bulvan.*"

"You got guts, Jake. I enjoyed working with you. There aren't many around could do a job like you could."

"So long, Leo. If anything happens to me, the Ferrante brothers will know where it came from."

He jammed the checked cap on his head and left Glauberman's office for the last time.

Glauberman at once phoned Melvin Schonkeit. The union rackets had seen the end of Jacob Chain. A blessing, the lawyer thought, an end to a dangerous nuisance.

Chapter 30

"Sherry," Goldsturm said to Jake. "Next time you go with the rabbis to make the pickup, ask for a few cases sherry."

"That ain't kosher wine. Even those idiots at the warehouse, Curtis and O'Connor, know that."

"Tell them it's for a reform congregation. Get a young fella in a frock-coat and plug hat like a rabbi from a rich temple in Crown Heights. They'll believe."

"They'll believe if I give them a hundred bucks apiece. Why sherry?"

"The fusel oil is bad quality. Sherry gives a nice color for scotch and rye."

Mutt and Sal came out of the office. They were so backed up on orders that they had rented a truck to make the Canada run. The Brooklyn Democratic Club was having its annual beefsteak dinner. Benny Otzenberger had arranged for F & C Cereals, Inc., to be sole purveyors of liquid refreshments.

"Nobody drinks like Democratic regulars," Mutt said. "But if we fill the order, it'll clean us out for a week. We got to get an inventory."

Goldsturm began to complain to the partners. The last batch of counterfeit government stamps was awful. The cross-hatching was blurred. Any agent could spot them as phonies. The customers didn't care, but a snooper might. Could Mortimer please see about getting a new printer or telling the current one to hire a better engraver?

Jake listened, smiling. *This was business!* Better than union rackets. It supplied a need. Everyone cooperated. The public admired an honest boot-legger. A man had status and respect when he could furnish unlimited cases of Highland Cream, Aberdeen Dew, Juniper Tree gin, Kentucky Sweetwater.

"The stuff from the alky cookers stinks," the chemist whined. "Sal's relatives got to replace the copper coils. They're patched with tin and the alcohol comes out gray. Then it turns black after I mix it. Nobody'll drink black booze. And for God's sake, they should spray their places with Flit. Cockroaches, bedbugs, spiders!"

"Get on their ass, Sal," Mutt said.

Ferrante nodded.

Jake watched them. Clearly his kid was taking over. The partners split profits, but Mutt came up with the new ideas. Mutt had connections. Moreover, he was a born salesman. Sincere, well spoken, polite. People liked and trusted young Mortimer J. Chain.

Sal was shaking his head. "Schonkeit hijacked the Reo last week, that's why we're short. I tol' our guys not to shoot back. He's too big for us. We're gonna have to get more alky out of the warehouses and get more from my *goombahs.*"

Mutt looked solemn. He stroked his long nose, craned his neck to catch a glimpse of Hilda crossing her legs. A flash of thigh. Ah, tonight. In back of the new Chandler.

"We gotta have more real stuff to make the fake," Mutt said. "But I don't like fighting with Schonkeit either."

Recently a truck from F & C, loaded with Montreal scotch, had run into trouble. Buster Twine had been driving, with Baggie Ferrante riding shotgun, and they had done all the right things. Bribes to the Canadians. Bribes to the Customs guards.

But outside a diner in Plattsburgh, in broad daylight, two dagos had shoved a .38 into Baggie's left nostril while Buster was checking a tire. Buster fielded a sap with the back of his head and was left for dead. (It proved to be a mild concussion.) Then Schonkeit's hoodlums drove off with the truck and its load. The state police found it in downtown Albany, empty.

"How'd you know it was his guys?" Jake asked.

"They bragged about it," Mutt said. "The Paymaster wants it all. He picks on guys like us because he thinks we ain't tough."

"You got *me.* Maybe I can help. When's the rented truck going up?"

"In an hour. Buster says he's okay. He'll drive. Baggie's sick. Vince'll ride up front."

"And me."

"You, pop?"

Sal's eyes vanished. Nothing scared old man Chain. Baggie had come back from the hijacking in Plattsburgh shaking like a woman. He'd turned yellow. Luigi said maybe Baggie was finished with the truck run. You needed guts. Maybe they could find a safe job for him in the cutting plant.

"Jake, there's only room for two guys inna cab," Sal said.

"On the way up Vinnie can ride in the back," Jake said slowly. "On the way back, leave out a few cases. I'll ride there."

"It's a rough ride, pop," Mutt cautioned.

"I got an iron *tuchas.*"

Jake drove home in the October sunlight, past kids playing "salugi." The poplars on Haven Place sparkled green and gold. Doc Abelman was on his stoop, talking to Rabbi Piltz.

Poor old Piltz. He never suspected that his stationery had gotten the Chains into the wine business. The rabbi was a stiff-backed man with a full black beard. Jake was wary of him. Piltz denounced "gangsters, *gonovim,* and Jewish *tromboniks*" regularly, and once even mentioned Jake by name. Jake had been hurt. Someday, Jake thought, F & C would make a contribution to the synagogue.

Sarah was in the kitchen preparing a roast. She sulked when he told her he was going on a trip. Just upstate, to make a few sales, collect money for Mortimer. He'd be away overnight.

"Jake, I don't like what he's doing, or what you're doing. You shouldn't encourage him."

He kissed her cheek, patted her shrunken hips. Guilt and shame ate at him. They had not slept together in years. Yet, oddly, she did not object. Her legs were atrophied, but she managed nicely with a cane. It was as if the expensive clothes, the well-supplied kitchen, the radio, the car, made up for the lack of sex. Poor, hungry, lonely as a child, she relished their prosperity.

"I'll be back tomorrow, *ketzeleh,*" he said.

"I worry."

"Never. I'm finished with *shtarking.* I quit Glauberman."

"But what you're doing is maybe worse?"

"Safe, safe. Everybody gets paid off. Everybody is part of it. The people need it."

In the bedroom he found a blue-black police .38, a gift from the Ferrante brothers on his thirty-fourth birthday. Jake loaded it and took a box of cartridges. The patch pockets on his gray jacket accommodated gun and bullets.

He walked upstairs and buzzed the Rimkoffs' apartment. Bobby, feinting and ducking punches, came to the door. Nose busted five times, ridges like leather over his eyes. *He'll be a contender when he is forty,* Jake thought.

"Bobby, boychick," he said. "That stuff you brought back from the army? The bayonet, the helmet? In the trunk?"

"Yeah. Watcha want?"

"Just to look."

Bobby ducked, belted the air with a right cross. "I'm fightin' Paco Gomez next week. I'll kill him."

"Good luck, kid. You'll be a champ someday."

In the bedroom were two photographs of the boxer. They were half lifesize, fuzzy black-and-whites, tinted with watercolors. One was Bobby at age eighteen. Crouched, fists up, a tiger in Everlast trunks and BenLee shoes. The tough Jewboy who destroyed Irish Danny Regan in one round. The other was Bobby in the uniform of the Rainbow Division—Private Robert Rimkoff, U.S.A., AEF.

The boxer dragged a khaki-colored metal box from under the bed. "That's my footlocker. Tell me watcha wanna see. My medals? The Joiman helmet? The bayonet?"

Bobby lifted the lid. Jake kneeled. He'd heard Bobby bragging about the stuff he'd smuggled home in a duffel bag.

Jake saw what he wanted.

That afternoon the rented Mack headed north for Canada. Buster started the driving. Vinnie slept in back on the quilted padding with which all of F & C Cereal's trucks were equipped. Jake rode up front with the black man.

In Kingston they switched. Jake took over the wheel, Buster slept in back, Vinnie moved up front. They took turns. Only once Buster expressed his fears. "Them Schonkeit people stop us again, I hope leastwise they don't hit my head."

"This time, maybe they'll be nice."

Buster looked sideways at the big man. He knew about him. He'd heard the stories. Clay pigeon. Shooting gallery. So full of lead, wise guys said, he'd sink if he took a swim at Coney Island.

"What you got in that box in the back?" Buster asked.

Jake had placed a wooden cheese box, the kind in which the schoolkids grew flowers, under the quilting.

"Lunch."

"How come it ain't here where you can eat it?"

"I ain't hungry."

Lamotte, the Canadian mechanic-turned-supplier, loaded the truck and accepted a cash payment from Jake. No receipts were given. Checks were never used. The business was always cash and a handshake. The Mack took less than the usual hundred and eighty cases. Jake told the loaders to leave a space big enough for him to sit.

"Here, Frenchy," Jake said. "I'll pay for the full hundred and eighty cases, twenny bucks a case, right?" He peeled off three thousand and six hundred dollars. "Ten cases you'll hold for the next shipment, okay?" Lamotte counted the bills in his office. Jake had learned that the goodwill of suppliers was always worth a few dollars. "Anything we can bring you from the States, Lamotte?"

"No, but I think of something, I ask." The supplier smiled. He liked this big *type*. The kid's father. Jake Chain, *formidable*. Tall, husky, with long arms and hands, *sacrebleu*, like a lumberjack. And the flat face, from *le box* perhaps.

"You know the new road?" Lamotte asked Buster. "Go west far as you can on the logging road. *Compris?* The guards let you through for a hundred bucks."

Buster knew. He'd be damned if he'd take the direct route to Plattsburgh. They'd stop for no lunches. They'd eat sandwiches and pray.

The loaded truck, with Jake squatting behind a flapping tarp atop cases of scotch, headed south. The French Canadian shook his head. Too bad he hadn't had the guts to tell him that Schonkeit's gangsters were patrolling every road on the New York side. Two days ago some *salaud* driving a load of gin had his head blown off. He'd tried to run a log barricade. *C'est la vie,* Lamotte thought.

Jake told Buster to stop a few hundred yards before the border. The Customs station was a popular one with the bootleggers. The guards were friendly; they were determined that their children would have better lives. Each man took home close to a thousand dollars a week in "donations." The most popular mode of payment was to drop a matchbook with a fifty-dollar bill folded into it.

"Listen," Jake had told them before they drove off, "if we get stopped— I don't mean by agents or Feds—I'll give a signal. I'll yell 'Union.' "

"Union?" Vinnie asked. "What does that mean?"

"It don't mean anything," Jake said. "It's a signal. When I yell 'Union,' fall down and cover yourself. Roll under the truck or get behind a tree."

"You know what you're doing, Jake?" Vinnie was slim and nervous. He was regarded as dim-witted by the other brothers.

"I ain't sure I like this," Buster said. "You gonna pull some of that Crazy Jake stuff you pull when you with the union? Mr. Chain, your son tell us never shoot, never fight back."

"That's my son. I'm me. Remember, when I holler 'Union,' fall down."

Buster shook his ebony head. *Crazy Jake.* Why did he get mixed up with this man? A man with no fear in him was worse than a coward. His head began to ache again. Frowning, Vinnie climbed into the passenger seat and waited for Jake's signal to move off.

Jake settled into a niche amid the crates of booze. On his lap he held the cream-cheese box. Suddenly he remembered Mutteh sniffling because they could not afford to buy seeds. Marigolds. Zinnias. Lily-of-the-valley. Bernie Feigenbaum had three cream-cheese boxes sprouting flowers. Mutt had wept when Jake told him he didn't have the money for seeds.

*   *   *

The guards were their usual accommodating selves. Jake sat behind the tarp, holding the cheese box. He heard Buster and Vinnie talking, first to the Canadians, and then to the American inspectors. Mutt had given his crew standing orders—a hundred bucks a man if necessary.

The matchbox must have been dropped, Jake thought. He could hear the Mack's tired motor rumbling, Buster shifting gears. They were back in New York State.

The old thrill was warming Jake's blood. He could not explain it. He feared death. He feared mutilation. But the anticipation of violence, of someone threatening him, the prospect of striking back, never failed to fill him with a wild joy. Was it because he had had so little as a boy, as a young man? That his fists and his strength and his lack of fear made up for bad food, miserable rooms, harsh work, being despised and unwanted?

He was glad Mutt was smarter. Finished high school—almost. Clever kid. The boy had inherited one trait from Jake that would be invaluable— *courage*. He had observed Mutt since he was a squirt—never flinching, never running away. It helped. It helped even more if you were smart.

Lulled by the bouncing of the Mack, Jake rested against the wall of booze. It was not quite clear in his mind what he would do if the hijackers drove off with the truck with him in it. He might be spotted. Maybe it would be better if he were fully hidden.

He decided to rearrange a few cases. Working slowly, maneuvering his huge frame, he built a wall five cases high and crouched behind it. They wouldn't see him. The imminent violence was damned near as good as sex, Jake thought. Maybe because sex was so bad in his life. A fat whore, a cold wife, a woman he loved and could never have. Getting shot at, shooting back, using his fists, made up for it. Almost.

He must have been dozing. The voices awakened him in his prison of scotch.

"Pull it over, Rastus."

"Both of yez, hands over your heads. Up, dago. Drop the shotgun. Denny, pick it up. Watcha got in there?"

Neither Buster nor Vinnie was responding. They knew enough to be silent. They had been fingered. Schonkeit's hijackers usually knew who was carrying what. Sometimes the Customs guards worked with them.

The truck made loud crunching noises as Buster pulled it off the asphalt to the dirt shoulder. It kept moving, heading into the pine forest. Jake could hear a second motor. A vehicle was following them. He moved a crate and parted the tarpaulin. A huge White truck rumbled no more than fifteen feet to their rear. Dimly he could see a driver and a second man. A third man was riding up front of the Chain truck, either jammed into the cab with Buster and Vinnie or on the running board. Jake could hear a strange voice.

"Over there, nigger. By the stone fence. Stop when I tell you."

"Yassuh, boss."

"You, you wop, sit still or I'll give you a shot in the head. Want an earful of hot lead?"

"I ain't doin' nothin'," Vinnie said.

Heart pounding, Jake wondered when to make his move. If he did it now, with the trucks moving, he might miss. If he waited until they began to unload, the hijackers would be in a better position to hit back. With two men locked inside the cab of the White, they were sitting ducks.

Carefully, he moved two more crates and edged closer to the tailgate. He loosened his right arm, flexed the muscles, braced himself against the cases. He opened the cheese box. Inside a nest of absorbent cotton were two gray-green hand grenades from Bobby Rimkoff's war souvenirs. Bobby had explained how they worked. Yank the small pin, hold it like a baseball, lob it with the whole arm. "Don't snap ya wrist like a baseball or ya'll sprain your wrist and it won't go far. Use the whole arm. Get height on it. With *your* arm you could throw it into Joisey."

"Here, nigger. Stop! Dumb coon."

Through the crack in the tarp, the sun glinting in his eyes and impeding his vision, Jake saw the pursuing truck stop. Buster's Mack rolled a few feet, then jolted to a halt.

Hit them now, Jake thought. While they were in the cab, unarmed, unsuspecting. Then he'd worry about the *mamzer* up front. He hoped he'd get a chance to get his hands on him before he hurt Buster and Vinnie.

"*Union!*" Jake shouted. He parted the tarp. "*Union!*" he shouted again. "*Union!*"

Jake pulled the pin from the pineapple, drew his arm back, and, with all his strength, lobbed Rimkoff's souvenir in a perfect arc. It crashed against the windshield of the pursuing truck.

The explosion, no more than five yards from the rear of his own truck, shattered bottles around Jake and soaked him with expensive hooch. Goldsturm would never forgive him.

The hijackers' truck blossomed into a fireball, roaring, exploding, as the engine blew apart and the gasoline ignited. Blinded and bloodied, the men staggered from the doors and rolled in the dirt. One stopped rolling. A chunk of glass a foot long was stuck in his throat. His neck spurted a crimson fountain.

Jake leaped over the tailgate. He had the second grenade in his pocket. In his right hand he held his .38. Running low to the ground, he came around the side of the Mack, saw the man on the running board, leveled the .38, and shot him twice in the legs. It was almost funny, the dumb bastard, a fuzzy-haired thickset man in a red plaid lumberjacket, frozen, wondering who in the hell was yelling *Union,* staring at his exploding truck.

The man dragged himself on his hands and elbows, looking for his shattered eyeglasses. His gun, an army regulation .45, was in the dirt, a few feet away. But without his specs he couldn't see it. Jake picked up the gun, then crunched the eyeglasses with his shoe.

"Ya big bum," the man said.

Jake smashed the butt of the .38 against his ear. He stopped crawling.

"You guys okay? Buster? Vinnie?" He leaped to the running board. Both men were crouched below window level, arms clamped over their heads like a pair of war prisoners. "He hit you? You guys get hurt?"

"I'm okay, boss," Buster said. "I think Vinnie got part of his head blowed off. It landed on me."

Jake pulled Vinnie's arms back. The side of his head was a mass of blood, bits of bone, brain. Jake felt sick; he was bad luck for the Ferrante brothers.

"He dead, Mr. Chain?"

"Looks like it. Anyway, the guy who did it won't be able to brag about it."

Jake fired a shot into the neck of the man on the ground. Might as well, he felt. He'd be no good to Schonkeit anymore with busted legs. No good to anyone. If they wanted a hijacking war, Crazy Jake would be happy to oblige them.

"I can't drive with Vinnie up here. I got me a nervous stomach."

"Gimme a hand, Buster. We'll stick him under the quilts."

Buster got out. He was shivering. Darkness was enshrouding the looming pines. He wanted to be home with his woman and his sons and his pint of gin. Friends had warned him about that wild man Jake Chain. A prudent, churchgoing black, Buster Twine wondered why the young Mr. Chain, so nice and sensible, would let his crazy father do this.

They tucked Vinnie's corpse under the quilting and stacked cases around it. Buster, gagging, cleaned the front seat with a rag. The White truck behind them exploded again. The fire soared higher, threatened the stands of pine trees. Jake ran to the two men on the ground. He lifted the one with the shard of glass in his throat and threw him into the blazing wreck.

As he went for the other, he heard a siren. No way of knowing if it was for them. The roads were full of troopers and Prohibition agents. He looked at the darkening sky. The smoke from the blazing truck was boiling and churning wildly into the sky above the treetops. A forest ranger's station would surely spot it and send someone out to investigate.

"Let's beat it, Buster. You drive." He took a last look at the other man. The burned, peeling face looked familiar. Who?

They backed up the Mack, made a wide circle past the wreckage of the burning truck. Buster covered his mouth and nose and coughed. "Don't like that smell. A man burnin' in there."

"Buster, that kind of *paskudnyak* don't mind getting burned. He was born for that. Come on, step on it. When you hit the main road, don't stop."

Outside Glens Falls the Mack broke down. Jake had to pay a hundred dollars to a mechanic who was getting ready to close down. On the bumpy back roads, a ricocheting stone had cracked the gasoline pump. Jake telephoned Mutt from a pay station. There'd been a "little trouble." But they were all right. They had the load.

"You alone, Mutt?" Outside he could see Buster and the mechanic bending into the engine. The man was working with a huge wrench, struggling to dislodge the broken gas pump.

"Yeah."

"Vinnie's dead. They took his head off. Don't say nothing to the family till I'm back."

Mutt lowered his voice. He glanced at Theresa. She was checking the seams in her stockings, getting ready to leave. *Another brother shot to hell.* First Frankie. Now Vinnie. Mutt wondered how Sal would react. Maybe he would get sick of supplying corpses for the Chains. "Okay, pop. I'll wait for you here."

"We won't make it till the morning. The guy has to send out for a new pump."

"I'll be here."

Jesus, Mutt thought, *Vinnie dead. I send the old man on his first run to the border and I lose a good man.* But what else was Jake to do? Schonkeit was determined to eat them up, the way he was eating up other bootleggers on the Canada run. He could not blame his father. But he should have guessed that sending Jake north was bound to end in violence and death. He wondered what the old man had done to *them.*

Mutt sweet-talked Hilda into staying after Theresa had left. He sent out for corned-beef sandwiches and cream soda. They discussed their wedding plans. Then Mutt made leisurely love to her on the leather couch.

In the darkness, locked between her naked thighs, he felt confident, buoyed. His father's call had shaken him, filled him with sudden dread. *Vinnie dead.* And God knew what his father *hadn't* told him. Talking to Jake, he had gulped, paled, turned his head away so the girls could not see his face, the tremor in his lips. Now, deep in Hilda's warmth, he sensed a rightness, a fulfillment. It was no longer a joining, a conquest, a release. It was as if her plump body told him that life was full of rewards. It gratified him that she would be his for a long time, always there to embrace and enfold him, to comfort him when he was frightened.

"I love you, baby," Mutt whispered. "I always will. I need you. Maybe I'll do some rotten things. But I'll try not to."

"I love you too, Morty. Oh, my God, so good, so good. We're not supposed to love it so much."

"Who says so?"

When he came, he cried for joy.

* * *

In the half-light of dawn, Sal looked at Vinnie's bloodied corpse. Dumb Vinnie. The jerk of the family. Frankie and Sal had been the smart ones. But Sal did not weep. He made the sign of the cross, glanced for a last time at Vinnie's shattered, blood-matted head, and telephoned Locatelli, the funeral director.

Then he called his father, the old barber. They were not to leave the house, he said, papa or his black-layered wife. Sal would come home to talk to them. And the brothers—Baggie, Dom, Luigi, Petey—were all to be present. And Theresa and Iolande.

Locatelli came with his hearse. He and Buster loaded Vinnie into a canvas bag.

"I want an open coffin," Sal said. "Fix his face. And the biggest cross and the biggest rosary you can buy for his hands."

Troubled, Mutt got up from his rolltop desk in the office. Jake was sitting on the couch, legs crossed, cap pushed back on his head. He was weary. Too much for him. He was sorry about Vinnie.

"Mr. Locatelli," Mutt said, "the biggest floral display you can get, from the Chains. A big heart. A big cross. Send me the bills for the whole funeral. They can have any kinda coffin they want. The most expensive. And a nice stone, with angels."

As he spoke, Mutt made mental notes: Benny would have to fix the cops, the coroner, everyone. Better no one knew how Vinnie cashed in. A fake death certificate—heart failure.

Locatelli departed with Vinnie's earthly remains. Sal remained in the doorway of the office. Once he wiped at his eyes. Nothing more. *Cry, damn you, cry,* Mutt wanted to say.

Sal nodded at Jake. "You. You done it to him."

"Me? I killed him? You're crazy. Ask Buster." The black man, exhausted, was outside unloading the rescued shipment.

"Ya *got* him killed. They call you crazy, you're crazy all right. But someone else gets it alla time. What'd you do? Pick a fight?"

Patiently Jake explained what had happened. The other truck, the three men, the grenade. It was tough for Vinnie. But they'd taught Schonkeit's mob a lesson. Three of them dead. A truck blown to hell. Nobody would start with F & C again, Jake said. When you were in a tough business, you took risks. He wished he could bring Vinnie back, Jake said.

Sal sighed and folded his arms. He looked as if he had no spine. He began to bite the nails of his left hand, refused to meet Jake's eyes or Mutt's sorrowing face.

A *creep,* Hilda had called him. *Creepy Sal.* The kid selling hokey-pokey ices from a two-wheeled cart. With a red, green, and white umbrella. The soiled gray apron for change, the torn sneakers, a cap two sizes too large. Darting eyes. *Little punk,* Hilda sneered. Never looked anyone in the eye in his life.

"I started the business," Sal said. "Me and the taxi." The eyes flew to the corner of the office, settled on the electric fan, flitted to the calendar with Clara Bow's face.

"So?" Mutt rested his head on one palm.

"Maybe you guys should realize that."

"Hold it," Mutt said. "We went to Canada partners the second time. And we split the dough. I helped pay for the trucks."

"It ain't *you*." His reptilian head bobbed toward Jake. "Him. Your old man. He'll get us all killed."

"My old man stays."

"Who says so?"

"I do. You're upset because Vinnie cashed in. We're sorry. It was an accident. Look what my father did. They won't futz around with our trucks again."

"Mutt is right, sonny boy," Jake said slowly. "I can't spend my life riding with trucks. When there are Schonkeits in the world, there's only one way to handle them. Don't be so cute. You once blew a Canuck's head off."

"You wasn't supposed to know." Sal's head sagged beneath his shoulders. These goddamn Chains. They came in. They took over. "Just the two of us from now on," he said hoarsely. "Me and Mutt. When I get enough, I'll buy Mutt out. Just me. No Chains."

Father and son looked at one another. They understood. Jake eased his body forward. He let his hands dangle between his legs. He was a little shaken. And he felt genuinely sorry for Vinnie. With Frankie, he owed nobody apologies. Frankie caught a stray chunk of lead. With Vinnie it was different. If Jake had surrendered to the hijackers, showed a yellow streak, maybe Vinnie would be alive. But that was not Jake's way.

"Salvatore, listen to your uncle Jake—"

"You ain't no uncle. You're trouble. Luigi warned me. Baggie warned me."

"Listen, *walyo*. I like you. I like your family. But you won't get rid of the Chains."

"No?"

"Mutt built the business with you. I'm in it now because I can help. We'll make you a millionaire if you stay calm. Know why?"

Sal did not answer.

"I'll tell you why, *walyo*. You know that girl who sits in the office with your sister, the girl Mutteleh is going to marry, Miss Hilda Otzenberger?"

"Pop, leave Hilda out of this."

Jake ignored his son. "Salvatore, her father is Mr. Benny Otzenberger, and he's the key to every fix we have. Every cop, every Fed, every judge, every D.A. You can't run an operation like we have without fixing. The store has to be open. Mr. Otzenberger is our fixer. Right? If you decide we're out, Mr. Otzenberger will fix for us, but for people like you there'll be shit."

"You guys always got an angle."

"It's not an angle, Sal," Mutt said placatingly. "It's good for all of us."

Sal picked his nose thoughtfully. "Your old man goes on payroll. No split."

"Sorry, Sal," Mutt said. "We cut everything three ways. A third to you, a third to me, and a third to my father."

Mutt was surprised: His voice did not shake and his hands were steady. He leaned back in the swivel chair and picked up the ringing phone. An early morning order, even before the girls were in. A rich guy in Lawrence, Long Island, throwing a wedding party. He'd heard from Mr. Dullahan, the politico, that F & C handled a high-class line of imported booze.

All politeness, Mutt took the order. Jake put an arm around Sal. They walked out of the office. As they did, Theresa entered from the exterior steel door. She'd heard: Vinnie was dead. She had disobeyed her father and come to work. Her screams and howls slammed and reverberated around the cutting plant. A few seconds later she fainted. Jake and Sal carried her into the office and placed her on the couch.

She revived after Professor Goldsturm arrived, learned of the tragedy, and forced her to drink some of his "French Cognac." Her howls became weird strangling noises. She began to give Jake a headache. He gestured to Sal to follow him to the street.

"I'm sorry about this, Sal. But don't try to screw us. Stay with the Chains."

"What choice I got?"

"None, *walyo*. I like you. I like your family. They'll forgive me."

Chapter 31

"So. Pregnant at age what? I lose track. Or maybe it isn't polite to ask."
Dr. Abraham Heilig smiled at his sister. "You look the same. The same
way you looked when you were a *pisherkeh* on the picket line. *Oi,* that
voice."

"You know how old I am, Abe. I'm thirty-six."

"A little late for a kid, but it should be all right."

"You're sure it's in there?"

"The tests don't lie, Eva. I'm sorry papa isn't alive. Proof of the power
of sour milk! His daughter conceives in her mid-thirties. You should have
had kids sooner. It's easier. What am I giving you advice for? You never
took it anyway."

"It won't be any burden for me. I'll never nurse a child. I'll never change
a diaper. I'm rich, Abe."

"Don't sound so bitter. It should happen to all of us."

Eva laughed. He looked very much at home in his green-shaded, oak-
paneled consulting room. An up-and-coming surgeon, he had a red
brick house and office on President Street, a few doors down from Glauberman the lawyer. The houses were completely detached on plots of manicured grass. Through the rear window, Eva could see a garden, with
maples and oaks flaunting autumnal colors.

"Sol sent me this," Abe said. "Our eminent brother was in Albany for
a committee meeting and this turned up in the local newspaper."

Eva put on her rimless eyeglasses. She had taken to wearing them
more frequently. My God, Dr. Heilig thought, the way she's used those
green eyes. Even with glasses, they were something. Reading, writing,
hypnotizing people with them. But she seemed tired. He wondered if the
pregnancy was a good idea. Evidently she and Halstead had agreed that
their lives needed more than causes. *A child.* Abe, a keen psychologist,
thought to himself: *Perhaps a child to save the marriage.* She rarely volun-

teered a word about Garrison or about their friends. Eva, once so open and frank, had become secretive where her personal life was concerned.

Eva read the short newspaper story:

TWO DEAD IN MYSTERY EXPLOSION
NEAR PLATTSBURGH, THIRD INJURED

Two men were found dead, one in and one near the burning remains of a truck in a clearing off U.S. Route 9, ten miles south of Plattsburgh, state police reported today. A third man was found alongside the wreckage, seriously burned.

State Trooper Sgt. William Hernley said that the surviving man has been identified as Philip (Futka) Frummer, a New York City bootlegger, age 33. The dead men are as yet unidentified.

The truck is believed to be one used on bootlegging runs from Canada, since it contained quilted pads used for transporting liquor. The wounded man and one of the deceased were trapped in an explosion that destroyed the truck and set it on fire. The other unidentified victim was shot three times. His body was thirty feet from the truck.

Police said they have no suspects. Shootings and ambushes have become commonplace in the frontier area because of "wars" between rival gangs.

"So?" Eva asked. "Why show it to me?"

"Sol had the same idea I did. It might involve our esteemed cousin."

"Jake?"

"Don't look surprised, Evitchka. Ordinarily I'd say so what? Gangsters killing each other, good riddance. But it so happens, on the day after this was reported in Albany, they buried one of Jake's partners. One of the Ferrante brothers, Vincent. Could be Jake's trying the Canadian air."

"It proves nothing."

"Just thought you'd like to see it. You always were a sort of heroine to that rogue. I must say, he isn't stupid. When Solly and I gave him lessons, he learned fast. He's still learning. Maybe *giving* lessons now."

"I don't see any connection. . . ."

Dr. Abe didn't press the point. He didn't care that much about Jake Chain one way or the other. But surely Eva knew that Jake's son was up to his *pupik* in bootleg booze. He had heard from patients about Mutt's booming business. One of the fastest-growing industries in Brooklyn. His "calling cards" turned up everywhere—price lists, special offers, catering.

"To heck with the Chains and the Ferrantes," Dr. Heilig said. "Someday Crazy Jake'll catch the right bullet. The one with his name on it."

"Don't say that."

"Why did he stop *shtarking?*"

Eva winked and pointed at her chest. "Your big sister. I had a talk with Jake."

"*Hoohah!* You can think that if you want to! The word I get is that Mutt convinced him there was more money in booze and that it was safer."

They chatted about the old neighborhood. All three Heilig children had outgrown it. Eva, in her elevated position as the wife of a socialite, Abe in his medical practice on President Street, lawyer Sol with an office on Court Street and a house on Carroll Street in Crown Heights. Sol was in line for an appointment as a deputy attorney general, a special post to investigate rackets. Sol would never be rich, but he'd be happy, they agreed.

Dr. Heilig stroked his brown moustache and stared for a moment at his bookcases and the framed photographs of Dr. William Osler and Dr. William Welch on his wall. He mentioned to Eva that someday, *someday,* Sol might find himself trying to send Jake and Mutt Chain to jail. Or maybe even the electric chair.

"Abe, please. That's ridiculous."

"I'm kidding. But face it, Eva, there's something destructive about the Chains, *père et fils.* I won't say that they are genetically criminal, or even that they're basically antisocial. But they can't resist anything crooked."

"That doesn't make them much different from our big corporations. Or our esteemed President Harding and the criminals around him. I'm not so sure the Chains are out of step with society. Labor violence was inevitable. Bootlegging? I can't get exercised over it. The Volstead Act was the real crime. All those holier-than-thou Methodists and Baptists forcing their fanaticism on the people. So now we have gang wars and murders and people dying of wood-alcohol poisoning."

"Don't tell me. I see them. Blind, lame, ruined from drinking anything in a bottle." Abe sighed. "Anyway, Doc Abelman tells me that Mutt sells only nontoxic beverages. Their poison might give you a bad headache and the runs, but it doesn't kill."

Eva laughed. "Oh, goodness! How does Abelman know?"

"He's still the Chain family physician. He patched Jake up after the famous banana attack. Sam tells me Sarah is doing quite well. Gets around the house without the cane, wears spiffy clothes. She gets her hair done twice a week and plays poker."

Eva shuddered. *Limited aims, limited ambitions.* Her heart went out to Sarah Klebanow Chain, that maimed woman. But dammit, why couldn't she take courses at the Hebrew Educational Society? Or be something other than a drone? She repressed a bit of guilt: Sarah might have been more of a woman if Jake had not abandoned her to nurture a hopeless love for Eva.

"Enough on the Chains," Abe said. "How are you, sister?"

"Fine. See for yourself."

"I see a new short haircut, very attractive, maybe from a Fifth Avenue salon. I see an expensive blue velvet dress with a skirt maybe a little short for your age, but you have the legs to justify it. I see black crocodile shoes with a matching bag. Clear skin, beautiful eyes, the ivory chin. That's all on the outside. Inside?"

"Pregnant. Full of life."

"I mean the things that don't show in a laboratory test. How are you and Garry getting along?"

"Why do you ask? You know we're compatible."

Abe sighed. "We don't see you that often. Leah is a little put off. So's Solly and his wife."

"I'm busy. I'm not a snob. You know that. Maybe that's one of my problems."

"Problems?"

"We just don't socialize. With anyone."

"Snotty little remarks about his Jewess?"

"We try not to let it bother us. Garry's above all that. People think twice before insulting a Halstead to his face. I suspect he has his moments of—"

"Regret?"

"Not at all. He's as kind and good to me as ever. There's no other woman."

She could not bring herself to tell Abe that her passion had never equaled Halstead's. Jewish women, so the rumor went, were supposed to be mother lodes of passion. Levantine Liliths bursting with erotic desires, like the ripe persimmons of the Holy Land. *What nonsense!* But she could never tell Abe or anyone—*he is too hot and I am listless.*

"Are you happy, Eva?"

"What is happiness?"

"Come on, *ketzeleh,* this is your brother Abe."

"Of course I am. Look at all I have. My career. A rich husband. A reputation. I'm thrilled when the garment workers cheer me, when I get a scrawled letter from some girl in the shops."

"But with Garry, everything's all right?"

"Do you think we'd be having a child if it were not the case?"

Abe bit on the templepiece of his spectacles. "I was wondering. After ten years and no kids? Maybe the pregnancy was a way to patch things up. Don't be ashamed. Others have done it. It often works. Motherhood, fatherhood. It makes a difference. Leah and I had a few tough moments before Sidney was born. What a blessing that little *shmendrick* was! I come home from the hospital, tired, angry, maybe I lost a patient, maybe I screwed up a case—for your ears only, Eva—and I see that *mozzik* with his yellow hair and his green eyes and the way he grins at me, and I know the world is a better place. You'll see, Eva. Wait till you have your own."

Eva wondered. Leah Lemkau Heilig was a doctor's daughter, a "Mrs. Yifnif." Furs, jewels, vacations at Schroon Lake. A Crown Heights family, claiming to be German although Eva suspected they had twisted geography a little.

"I'm glad you and Leah are happy."

"You say it as if *you're* not."

"I'm happy in my work. Garry and I are busy, independent people. Maybe we subordinate our emotions to our work, but that's the way we want it."

She's lying, Dr. Heilig thought.

Shikey Frummer entered the Polo Pony Club on East Fifty-fifth Street and worked his way through tobacco fumes, past tables filled with early evening drinkers sipping their cut scotch, rye, and gin at a dollar a shot. A patent-leather-hair dude with a waxed moustache, he found his way to Melvin Schonkeit's private table at the rear. As usual, the Paymaster, comfortable in his own speakeasy, one of twenty-two he owned, was drinking milk.

"So?" Schonkeit asked.

"It was Chain."

"Which one?"

"Crazy Jake. Futka wrote it on a piece of paper. He can't talk. His mouth and tongue are burned up. Maybe he ain't gonna live, Mr. Schonkeit."

Melvin Schonkeit ignored Shikey Frummer's tear-rimmed dark eyes. There was little sentiment in the Paymaster. And Shikey expected no expression of sympathy. With Schonkeit, it was *tuchas af'm tisch*—ass on the table, *get down to facts*. His brother Futka lay dying of third-degree burns and internal hemorrhaging, and from their employer not a word of sympathy.

"Let's see," Schonkeit said.

Shikey, slicking back his gleaming hair, handed the Paymaster the bit of paper. In a quivering faint hand was written the single word: CRAZY.

"Crazy? That proves it?"

Shikey nodded. "It's Jake Chain. We didn't know he was working with his kid. When I think what that bastard done. Two guys dead. Them I don't care about. But my brother maybe ain't gonna live."

Schonkeit signaled for another glass of milk. He did not offer Frummer anything. The man had failed him. A patron at the next table was advised by the Paymaster to extinguish his cigar or get out of the Polo Pony Club. The rule at the speak was that no one within *two tables* of Mr. Schonkeit smoked. He himself never touched tobacco. He wore high starched white collars, bankers' maroon ties, somber dark blue suits. Clear-eyed, smooth of skin, soft-spoken, he might have been a successful obstetrician or surgical dentist. Schonkeit detested violence and physical effort.

"You're to blame," Schonkeit said. He smiled with his mouth. The rest of his face was impassive.

"Me, Mr. Schonkeit?"

"You and your stupid brother. You should have known that Chain was riding the convoys."

"After we tried to kill him with the banana cart, who'd think he'd have the guts to start again? Me and Futka said how many times we got to shoot this bum to kill him?"

"Did your brother say anything else?"

Shikey wept. His waxed moustache wilted. Schonkeit turned his head away in disgust. Bullies, cowards, fools. No wonder he had amassed an empire so quickly. It required brains, confidence, vision, an ability to gauge weaknesses, to dominate animals like the Frummers.

"Well?" Schonkeit asked.

"Mr. Schonkeit, he can't talk. Big black blisters all over like he was roasted. But it was Chain. God knows how he blew up the truck. Anyway, we killed that dago Ferrante. That'll learn him."

"You're a bigger fool than I thought. Frummer, we buy and sell and kill people like that for a case of bad scotch. We lose a truck and three men, and they lose a Ferrante."

"Mr. Schonkeit, gimme another chance. I'll put the Meal Ticket on it. He owes Chain. He'll shoot the bastard in the back some night. He'll stick him so full of holes with an ice pick he'll be a Swiss cheese. He'll blow him up with TNT."

"No. You're all stupid. You're stupid and maybe yellow."

"That ain't fair, Mr. Sch—"

"Shut up, Frummer. Beat it."

Dabbing at his eyes, Shikey left. Suddenly he hated the high rollers, the society people and the newspapermen, who patronized Schonkeit's elegant speak. The Polo Pony Club was the prize of his collection. And what did Shikey have? A dying brother, and not much of a future. He'd kill Jake Chain someday. And as he thought of it, fear twisted his guts. He knew he wasn't man enough to do it.

When Frummer had left, Schonkeit telephoned Leo Glauberman and told him about the bungled hijacking, the unexpected appearance of Crazy Jake Chain and the dire consequences. Both men found the incident grimly amusing.

"Melvin," Glauberman said, "take my advice and let the Chains alone. Brooklyn isn't your bailiwick. I'm glad he's out of the labor business. We have enough problems with Reds these days."

"Leo, he's a bigger problem. And I have the feeling his son will be an even bigger one someday. I agree, let's stop trying to—ah—eliminate him. But maybe we can put him out of business politically. Why be violent when you can do things other ways?"

"You mean get to his rabbi? Knock off his connections?" Glauberman chuckled. "Fat chance, Melvin. The Chains and Benny Otzenberger are on the same team. The Chain kid is going to marry Benny's daughter."

"Otzenberger is a small-time ward heeler."

"Not quite, Melvin," Glauberman said firmly. "Not *quite*." He felt impelled to defend Brownsville and Benny. The attorney had used Otzenberger, been used by him, fought him at times. But he knew that the fat man had power. He paid off.

"Melvin, Otzenberger has Dullahan's ear. There isn't a cop or a judge or a prosecutor that can't be bought out of Dullahan's office. So don't tell me we can short-circuit Mort Chain and his father."

The two agreed: For the time being, the Chains would enjoy special privileges on the Canada run. It amused Schonkeit. It tickled his sense of the romantic. A coward who never carried a gun and ran from fights when he was a little rich kid in blue velvet knickers, a sissy who went to dancing school and had a German nanny, he admired the coarse strength of a Jake Chain. He'd seen the man once. Slavic-faced, with a mop of dark blond hair, something of the Viking about him.

Chapter 32

By Thanksgiving, Jake was working full-time with Mutt. Sal reluctantly accepted him. The money was pouring in in such staggering quantities that it barely mattered whether it was split two ways or three. No papers of partnership were drawn up. All transactions were in cash, including salaries to the girls (a third had been hired), drivers, warehousemen, and Professor Goldsturm. Buster, for loyal service on the Canada run, was given a raise.

The old Kolodny plant was becoming cramped. They had to use one of the truck bays for the storage of raw alcohol. Mutt did not like leaving the trucks on the street at night. He began to look for a bigger place, something secure, isolated, with more office space and maybe a reception room for clients.

Sal, a loner who lived with his parents, while all the surviving brothers were married and raising new broods of Ferrantes, remained their "outside" man. He organized trips to Canada, dispatched trucks, provided protection, bribed "dry" agents, handled the purchases of alcohol, real booze, flavoring agents, barrels, bottles, and labels. Mutt wondered if he was a secret fairy or if he couldn't get it up. Girls made him stammer.

Crazy Jake proved a decided asset to F & C Cereals and its affiliate, Pacific Breeze Hair Tonic. His presence alone would have justified his third of the profits. The word spread quickly in the underworld. *Crazy Jake Chain was in bootlegging.* The muscleman they couldn't kill was back in business. Politicians and rich sports who did business with F & C, and heard that Jake Chain was a partner, expressed a desire to meet him and shake his hand. The newspapers made a quasi-celebrity of him: the colorful scoundrel who once boasted to a reporter about his price list for *shtarking*—a hundred bucks to wreck a small factory, up to six hundred for a big place. He was always good for a story.

Mr. Jacob Chain [a reporter for the *World* wrote] has turned his talents to greener pastures. Interviewed at his pleasant home in

Brownsville, with his attractive wife, Sarah, listening, he explained he is an executive of a cereal company and a hair-tonic firm. Bootlegging? Ridiculous, Mr. Chain said. He would not indulge in anything that circumvented the law. He expressed sympathy with the temperance movement and efforts to enforce the Volstead Act.

At thirty-seven, Mr. Chain is powerful and muscular, a forbidding presence with a flattened nose, high cheekbones, and calm blue eyes that tell the visitor very little indeed. He is almost handsome.

"One thing I don't like," Jacob Chain said, "is this Crazy Jake business. I'm not crazy. I never was. I had little education. I was an orphan. I didn't learn to read or write until I was twenty-five. Does that make me crazy? I wish you people would cut it out. It doesn't look nice for my wife and my son to see that in the papers."

In their living room—Sarah had just bought a new white mohair couch —Jake read the article to her. She smiled. She had come to look more favorably on Jake's career. They had a lot of money in the bank. Morty would soon be married to a lovely girl. Socially, it would be a step up. Benny Otzenberger was moving to a three-story brownstone on Montgomery Street. Brownsville was getting a little dingy—more Italians, more Polacks, even a *shwarzer* family here and there.

She looked at Jake, sipping his tea, reading the paper slowly, missing nothing. She had never imagined he was so smart, so interested in reading. Sadly, she felt unequal to him. She had remained mired in her ignorance. Yet she was a pretty woman. Face, hair, figure had all improved as she aged. Away from the rattling sewing machines, concerned now with her elegant apartment, her husband and son, she looked very much the prosperous housewife.

"Jake . . . maybe we could go together again?"

"Where? The movies?" He regretted the words as soon as he uttered them. He knew what she meant. His heart yearning for Eva Heilig all these years. Sarah knew. A lot of people knew. He had used his wife's deformity as a cheap excuse, gone to hoo-ers.

"I got a new nightgown. You'll like it. Lace, pink silk. A present to myself before Chanukah. Do you want me to wear it?"

He walked from the table to the couch, sat down alongside her, and lifted her bent legs. One had all but healed. The lower bones on the left leg remained thin and shortened. The surgeons had done all they could.

"Sarah, *ketzeleh,* I love you. I do. It's hard for me to be romantic, like Valentino. I'm a *bulvan.* I don't know fancy words."

"Then you could kiss me sometimes. Hold me. Do what we used to do."

He kissed her cheek, her forehead, her lips. She shoved her tongue between his teeth. "Please, Jake. Be a man with me."

"I can't."

He wondered: How can guilt grow in a man like weeds until it chokes out everything else? It was like a child being bad. Mutteh had been like that. If he lied or stole from the candy store and was punished, it only made him lie again and steal again. As if to prove to Jake and Sarah that he was right and they were wrong. So now did he nourish his own guilt; repelled by his wife, he refused to change.

"What did I do to hurt you?" She wept. "I am young. I have a body. You were so good to me after the accident, in the hospital. You give me everything now. Nobody has what I have—furs, jewels, nice clothes. So give me something else."

"I can't."

"You have another woman."

"You are my only woman. You worked when we were poor. You worked harder than I did. You suffered. You were a good mother. Who else could I love?"

"Then come to the bed with me. I'll wear the new nightgown. We'll be like young people. I need you, Jake."

He smiled. "You have me."

"Only like a boarder. A greenhorn off the boat who lives here. I feed, I make his bed, I wait till he gets a job and moves. You are no greenhorn." She cried, burying her face in his shoulder. "You are my husband."

He stroked her back, ran his hand down her thigh, sniffed the expensive perfume. Women envied her and whispered about her. *Yentas* gossiped about snooty Sarah Chain who couldn't read or write. What else from a gangster's wife? A disgrace for Haven Place!

He carried her to the bedroom, kissed her face and her naked arms. But he could not love her.

Later, alone in the living room, listening to the radio—a rum runner had been killed off Montauk, Henry Ford was fighting the Interstate Commerce Commission, the League of Nations wanted to cut European armies in half—he picked up the newspaper again. Boy, that Dempsey. *There* was a man!

On an inner page he saw a small item: MRS. HALSTEAD DENOUNCES PROHIBITION, CALLS IT CRIME. Again Eva. She managed to make the papers about once every two weeks. Last time what was it? Handing out birth-control pamphlets? Chuckling, he shook his head. They couldn't stop her. Now she was forming something called the Woman's League to Repeal.

"I do not drink myself, and I deplore the ravages of alcohol," she was quoted as saying. "But this monstrous legislation is making us a nation of criminals. The government is party to this fraud, an act passed by bigots and hypocrites. Let the people have access to pure, unpoisoned liquor, and the gangsters will wither away. In the Congress of the United States, in the halls of the Senate, the reek of illegal liquor is pervasive. Legalize!"

And put me out of business, Jake thought. Funny, he could never be in harmony with her. Or understand her. The Heilig children were a different race. The surgeon Abe, a man of talent and wealth. Sol, the lawyer, who had been named to investigate the rackets. And Eva, so bright, so full of ideas. How could he be of the same blood?

The radio crackled and whistled. He switched stations. Another newscast filtered through. Again, the dead rum runner. The report was more detailed. Off Montauk and the south shore of Long Island, the announcer said, vast fleets were assembling, selling booze in unimaginable quantities. It was like an armada. Rowboats to huge oceangoing craft. Buyers and sellers did business past the three-mile limit under the noses of the coast guard.

Jake had never been on anything more dangerous than the Staten Island ferry. Of boats he knew nothing. But about whiskey he was learning a great deal. He would have to do some investigating. As a partner, some contribution was expected from him. If Canada was getting crowded, there was apparently lots of space in the ocean.

The next day, Jake asked Professor Goldsturm for a bottle of their best scotch. *"Uncut,"* Jake emphasized. "Not that horse piss you bottle for our customers."

"Of course, of course, Mr. Chain," Goldsturm said. He emerged from toxic vapors with a sealed bottle of Glenlivet. The professor turned it in the harsh light. Jake inspected the revenue label. No fakery, no counterfeit stamps. As of last week Mutt had ordered the chemist to start cutting the booze by a *fourth*—one-quarter real liquor, the remainder water and questionable alcohol.

Jake told Mutt he'd be gone for the day. Personal errands. Mutt nodded. Things had calmed down up north, thanks to Jake's appearance. Schonkeit's mob was laying off since the grenade incident. Futka Frummer had died three days ago in a Plattsburgh hospital. That made three Jake had dispatched. His reputation was becoming legend up north, just as it had been magnified in Brownsville. Big operators along the border were honored to learn that Crazy Jake was in their ranks. It was as if an exclusive golf club had landed a Vanderbilt or a Whitney.

Jake put the bottle of scotch in a paper bag and drove through gray November streets to Sheepshead Bay. He knew the waterfront area slightly, having taken Sarah and Mutt there on the trolley years ago. It was picturesque, pleasant—the bracing sea air, the pungent odor of fish and clams, the resturants, boats slapping gently against the wooden piers in the autumnal wind.

He drove by Lundy's restaurant. Maybe he'd have dinner there. Maybe invite some person who could help the business. He had discovered that his bold, big appearance, or even the mere mention of his name, often evoked a friendly reaction. He marveled at how his reputation had grown since the years of the strikes. It was one thing to be a stupid wagoneer, and another to be celebrated as a "labor consultant." And now he was a businessman.

He parked on Emmons Avenue. With the bottle in the pocket of his blue cheviot topcoat, he strolled along the waterfront. Flapping wooden signs advertised fishing boats. It was off-season. Most of the berths were filled with idle craft. The boats looked wide, sluggish, and sturdy. They were designed to hold up to a hundred fishermen packed against the iron railing that circled the deck. There was usually a small cabin for gear, and a high bridge for the skipper.

At the end of the sea walk he noticed some smaller, sleeker boats. These were built differently, with broad aft decks to accommodate a few fishermen, and equipped with swivel seats. The cabin and wheel were toward the pointed bow. A sign read: PRIVATE CHARTER ONLY.

For rich guys, Jake thought. The boats looked fast. Not as big as the open boats, but classier. A few salty types in blue denims wandered by. On an empty lot, kids tossed a wool sock filled with sand—a homemade football. In front of one of the charter boats a grizzled one-eyed man was cleaning whiting, tossing slimy innards to screaming gulls.

Jake came up and watched him slice and gut with a thin razor-sharp knife.

"Nice day," Jake said.

"Nice for gulls. They ain't nothin' a seagull does but eat and shit. It'll eat anything. I seen guys throw their baited hooks out offen the side of a boat and a seagull will grab the bait, hook and all. Customer catches a seagull 'stead of a bluefish. Of course, all a bluefish does is eat and shit also."

"Why should they be different from us?"

"You're right and you're wrong, mister. They got more brains than us. See my bad eye? From drinking wood alky. Some bum give me a bottle of the stuff. Claimed it was pure corn liquor. Sent me into Kings County for a week, and when I come out—well, look at that right eye. Blinder 'n a dead porgy."

Jake looked at the gray film over the old man's eye. Nobody could accuse the Chains of selling stuff that bad. Nobody had ever reported anything more than nausea, vomiting, a headache, a three-day hangover, or the enamel flaking off their teeth.

The half-blind man asked Jake if he was from Sheepshead Bay. Want a charter? Like to go after deepwater cod? Too bad bluefishing was over. His boat, right in back of him, the *Deepwater Angel,* was one of the best. Mr. Dullahan hisself and his friend Judge Younghusband chartered it once a month in the summer. And drink? The booze didn't stop all day.

"Fast?" Jake asked.

"She does fifteen knots. For fishing you don't need to do much more."

The one-eyed man sliced a whiting from gullet to tail, yanked out the guts with one hand, and tossed them into the air. Two gulls swooped down and battled for the entrails. The bigger one triumphed, batted its wings, flew off. The other squawked and buzzed the fish cutter's head as if complaining.

"You work on this boat?" asked Jake. "What's your name?"

"I'm cap'n's mate. I'm Chick Muncie. Ask anyone around Sheepshead Bay about Chick Muncie. I drove dogs in Alaska. Drove steers on the Chisholm Trail. Château-Thierry and St. Mihiel. First Marine Division. Gunnery sergeant."

"Very nice. What's the captain's name?"

"Tommy Tuttle. Don't go aboard 'nlessen you're invited. Guests ain't welcome."

"Just a friendly call. I'm interested in a charter for a few days. Some important people."

"Cap'n don't want visitors today."

"I like the way you handle that shiv," Jake said. He gave the old man a dollar bill. "Maybe someday you could teach me how to slice fish."

Chick Muncie winked his good eye and jerked a thumb over his shoulder. "Go ahead. You look big enough to git your way."

Jake descended two steps to the wooden planking, hopped from the pier to the gunwale of the rocking craft. He stepped down and looked at the wide rear deck. Plenty of space to store cases. And another storage area belowdecks.

He poked his head inside the cabin and saw a broad-beamed backside in salt-streaked blue coveralls bending into the engine of the *Deepwater Angel*. In the darkness he could discern a huge wrench. He heard a few muffled curses.

"Excuse me," Jake said. "Mr. Tuttle?"

"No business today."

The voice was high, with a lilting quality. It dawned on him. It was a woman's voice.

"Maybe I can help."

The figure in blue coveralls and boots turned around. "The pump is stuck. No charters for a week."

"I'll make a date for a week from now."

The woman stood up. She was tall, with broad shoulders. The coveralls could not hide a full bust and rounded hips that stretched the worn denim. She had an unlined throat, and a long, strong neck. Her face, although windburned, was exceptionally pretty. Jake looked her over approvingly— widely spaced dark brown eyes, eyebrows that rose from the bridge of the nose at a sharp angle, a high forehead. Her nose was a bit short, the nostrils large. Her chin was square and cleanly molded, and her chestnut hair was bound with a red bandanna.

"*You're* the captain?"

"I'm not the messboy. What are you staring at?"

"You'll excuse me. I ain't seen many boat captains of any kind in my life, and you're the first *lady* captain I seen."

She laughed and threw her head back. Jake stared at the throat—a deep hollow, skin whiter than the weather-darkened face. "You're not a fisherman, mister. You don't know Sheepshead Bay. Captain Tommy Tuttle is part of the scenery. Come back in a few days."

She turned her back and knelt. Jake saw the long curve of her buttocks, thigh, leg—a powerful woman, yet graceful. In a fancy dress, in silk stockings and jewelry, she'd be a knockout.

"The pump is barely moving. I think it caught a fifty-caliber slug. Those coast-guard kids will shoot at anything, even an honest charter boat." She grunted as she yanked at a stubborn valve.

"Gimme a try at it," Jake said. "I done a little hard work in my day."

"You? All duded up in that fancy suit and topcoat?"

"It's a disguise."

He took off his coat, making sure not to injure the bottle of Glenlivet, removed his suit jacket, and rolled up his sleeves. The lady skipper watched. She noted the oaken forearms and the enormous hands.

"About car engines I know a little," Jake said. "Just show me what has to be moved."

She spread a canvas at the edge of the oil-blackened boards and pointed to a lead elbow coupled to a threaded housing. Jake could see that bolts had been removed. But the connection and the coupling appeared to be out of true. She had doused the recalcitrant joint with oil, but the wrench could not budge it.

"Bilge water's driving me nuts," Tommy said. "This scow has more leaks than a senator's luggage after a trip to Bermuda. Go on, Dempsey, give it a whirl. Don't dirty your fancy pants."

"I been dirty before, captain."

Jake knelt, spit on his hands, and got a grip on the long wrench. He locked the head around the coupling and began to apply leverage. Muscles and veins bulged his forearms. The wrench slipped and he almost fell into the hold. His face turned scarlet. He had to admire the woman for even trying. The thing was cemented, immovable.

"What's the matter, Dempsey?"

"It's the rocking. Every time I get a grip on it, your boat moves."

"Oh, boy, some sailor. Three more tries and then out. Chickie and I will manage it."

Once more Jake locked the wrench on the coupling. He braced his body and used his back, his shoulders, and the power of his hands. Instead of trying to yank the rusted metal apart, he moved it slowly and firmly, the way he had lifted wagons when he was a kid. Never a fast, sudden move.

The coupling squeaked and rotated slightly on the worn threads. Jake gritted his teeth, applied pressure, grinned as the threads turned.

"By golly, you did it," Captain Tuttle said. "Watch out you don't get a faceful of bilge water."

Warned too late, Jake did not have a chance to escape a jet of brackish water that spurted out of the opened valve.

Laughing, the skipper dragged him back and let the water splash around until the pump emptied itself. She got down on her knees alongside him. "Too bad, big guy. That ten-dollar shirt and the silk tie look ruined. But you volunteered."

"I don't mind. I learned something. Anytime you need a pipe opened, ask Jake Chain."

"Hi there, Jake Chain. Tommy Tuttle. My real name is Henrietta Mae, can you imagine? My daddy was Mac Tuttle. He ran boats out of here and horses at Sheepshead Bay track. Tommy stuck to me 'cause I was a tomboy."

"What do I do now?" Jake asked. "I'm all *shmutzed* up so I might as well finish the job."

"Stick your hand down the pipe and see if anything's blocking it."

Jake reached into the rusted metal pipe. He probed and brought out a misshapen chunk of lead.

"What did I tell you?" She laughed. "A coast-guard souvenir. I ought to sue them. Shooting at a woman. And me with nothing but fishermen on board."

Rotating the lump of lead in his hand, Jake guessed it wasn't the first time she'd been shot at. There was a kind of knowing look that bootleggers developed—friendly, wary, a bit satisfied with themselves. Captain Tuttle had it.

"So what now?" Jake asked. "Do I get paid for all this labor? Watch it, I'm an old union official."

"Unions, huh? You don't look like a bricklayer to me."

"I was a consultant. I'm not kidding. What do I get as a reward?"

"Finish the job. What'd you say your name was?"

"Jacob Chain."

"Jew? No offense. I like anyone who plays it straight. Some of my best cust— Well, I mean, lots of my fishing clients are Jews. Doctors, lawyers, judges. A bluefish or a striper doesn't ask who catches him."

She handed Jake a shiny brass fitting. "Go on, Mr. Chain, use your muscles and get this new coupling on. I get sick of having to do heavy work myself. Old Muncie out there hasn't got the strength to bait an outrigger since wood alky almost killed him."

Jake removed the worn metal and replaced it with the new one. He whirled and pushed the giant wrench as if it were a toy. Then he wiped his hands on a rag, dusted rust from his shirt, tie, and vest, and climbed up to the cabin.

"Nice work, Jacob."

"Jake is better."

"Jake is no fake. Good job."

"My pleasure, captain."

"You look like a sport, so I won't offer you any money. But we'll sample some of my private stock."

She opened a mahogany cabinet in the cozy living quarters—two berths, gas ring, cabinets, a door to a toilet—and took out a square bottle with a label that read "Edinburgh Mist." Jake smiled. Some of Schonkeit's horse piss.

Tommy poured two half-tumblers and shoved one toward Jake across a table that was attached to the bulkhead with copper hinges. "Sit down, big man," she said. "Anyone who handles a wrench like that can be my friend."

A restrained drinker—he had firsthand knowledge of what went into what was marketed—Jake sniffed the liquid. Then he let a few drops fall on his index finger. He rubbed thumb and finger together until the "scotch" vaporized. He held his hand to his nose.

"What's that all about?" Tommy asked.

"Testing. Smell it, lady."

The skipper sniffed Jake's hand. "So?"

"Creosote and fusel oil. You know about boats, Captain Tuttle, but about whiskey, nothing. Try some of mine."

"Where'd you learn that trick?"

Jake ripped the seal from his bottle of Glenlivet and asked her for two clean glasses. She washed out the two with Schonkeit's liquor in them. Jake studied her strong figure. A different kind of woman. Inside the work clothes, a body without marks, no sagging. From all that work. Good muscles. Take the red handkerchief off her head, fix her up with a permanent, rouge, eye shadow. Pearls, a fancy black dress, silk stockings. She'd be as pretty as a movie star.

"I'm in the business, captain."

"I should have figured. Bootlegger."

"So who isn't?"

Jake raised his glass of scotch. "On the job I don't usually drink, but this is a celebration. I never fixed a pump for a lady captain before. *L'chayim.*"

"Sorry, big guy. I'm not up on my Yiddish."

"It means *life,* and it's Hebrew."

"I'll go along with it." Tommy Tuttle drained the half-glass. She moved not a muscle. Jake looked at the strong line of her throat. Something clean and alive.

"What we are now drinking isn't what my company usually sells. Too good even for rich people."

"I know. You cut it."

"Right. But any decent bootlegger should have a supply of real stuff."

"And that's why you're here. Supplies low?"

Jake nodded. They lifted glasses again. This time he only filled a quarter of the tumbler. No use getting stinko on the job. He could take or leave liquor. He never could understand what it did for people, why they fought, risked getting killed, and indeed got killed for it. They hid it in baby carriages, inner tubes, oil cans. They bought it in drugstores, paint shops, barbershops, from undertakers. Men had been caught crossing from Canada with their trousers lined with rubber hoses full of scotch. Women wore brassieres and corsets with rubber compartments next to their titties and tushies. *Goyim,* he decided, were insane. Liquor was their life. They gave up families, mistresses, homes, careers—their very lives—for it. Who was he to deny them their fun?

Captain Tuttle took Jake abovedecks. She leaned over the side and showed him a row of holes in the boat's lapstraked flank. They were bigger than any bullet holes Jake had seen.

"Coast guard," Tommy said. "That slug you took out of the pump is the last one. I need at least a week for repairs. I'm not sure I want to play ring-around-the-rosy again with them. It's a sharks' convention on Rum Row."

"I got long teeth," Jake said. "I been around. How many cases can you handle?"

"Couple of hundred."

A drop in the F & C's bucket. But if he started with the woman, he'd learn the seagoing trade, hire other boats. Better yet, with the way the money was rolling in, they could buy their own boats. Run a fleet. The ocean trade was bigger and safer than truck convoys.

"We do a big volume. What do you charge?"

"Two hundred a day for the boat. Chickie gets fifty bucks a week. You got to make good for damages, fuel, and maintenance."

It was a bargain. On two hundred cases, they could gross over ninety thousand dollars after cutting. Each bottle of real scotch or gin now yielded four bottles of Goldsturm's scorching brews.

"Tell me, Miss Tommy," Jake said. "Why don't you go into business yourself? Buy, sell, handle goods. Whaddya want to be a taxi service for? All you need is cash, connections, and guys to wrestle cases for you."

She straightened up. The sea wind whipped strands of chestnut hair peeking from the bandanna. "I couldn't get customers. The big shots didn't like a woman horning in. Bad enough getting shot at by the Coasties. I got winged by some hoodlums in a private gunboat. No, thanks. I'm a sailor. A professional captain like my daddy, not a hooch peddler. I only ran whiskey when I had bills to pay."

"But you've done it."

"A woman's got to eat. I got a daughter to feed, clothe, and send to school."

Jake smiled at her. Her motherhood pleased him. The mannishness, the coveralls, the rubber boots, hid a woman, someone who could cook, worry about a kid, sew a dress.

"Husband?" he asked.

"Ran off to Florida. He works the Keys, smuggling rum from the West Indies. I know more about boats than he ever did. My father taught me."

"Where's he?"

"Lost at sea. He had a fast fifty-footer. Fancier boat than this. Took out a party of Wall Street lawyers during the war. Nineteen sixteen. They must have hit a loose mine. The rescue parties never even found a life preserver. Just some boards. Six lawyers and Captain Mac Tuttle, gone."

Jake suggested he take her to lunch. The eighty-six-proof scotch had left him giddy, his stomach yawning for food. Lundy's? he asked. She said she'd have to change; it was a spiffy place. Why not just go to a clam bar? Jake was insistent.

He waited on the wooden pier with Chickie, who was hosing down the deck and flanks of the *Deepwater Angel*.

"Heard you talking to the skipper," the mate said. "You're in the business."

"A little bit."

"It gets scary out there. See them holes? Should have heard the noise they made when they hit. Dang near sunk us if it wasn't for Captain Tommy's nerve. She beached us off Captree. By the time the Coasties got to us we'd dumped the booze in the Atlantic or throwed it into rowboats."

"Rowboats?"

"These people are so thirsty they'll cross the ocean in a dinghy for a sniff of scotch. Quite a sight when Billy McCoy and the rest of the boats come in from the islands. Like a dang armada. All them skiffs and speedboats and cruisers coming out to load up."

"Who decides who gets the stuff?"

"Oh, contacts. Some load off to their own boats. Some got regular customers. Some hold an auction. I seen a fella fall out of a thirty-foot cruiser. Man in black suit and a derby. The skipper of the rum schooner spent two hours right under the coast guard's nose trying to fish him out of the water."

"Why was he so valuable?"

"The son of a bitch had fifty thousand dollars cash in his pockets. Can't let a buyer drown."

Tommy emerged in a blue pea coat and a light blue skirt, dark stockings, and black pumps. She'd put lipstick on, combed her long chestnut hair, and tied a royal blue band around it. Jake felt his blood jump. A different kind of woman. No whining Sarah. No preaching Eva. No fat Minnie.

They ate steamers and lobsters at the rear of the restaurant. The waiter discreetly furnished them with teacups—Captain Tommy was an old friend—from which they drank "French" wine. Jake asked to look at the bottle and laughed. It was some of Goldsturm's Château Magloire, distilled from a bit of kosher sweet Concord, grain alcohol, and bitters.

Jake's plainspoken manner appealed to her. After a few glasses of Château Magloire, Tommy became talkative.

She lived alone aboard the *Deepwater Angel*. Her daughter, a lively two-year-old named Lisa, boarded with her father's married sister in Coney Island. Tommy felt guilty. She told Jake she wanted to devote more time to the child, but the boat kept her busy—hustling charters, running booze, repairing it.

"You're not as tough as you make out," Jake said. "I like that. You're a woman. You got a right to be scared when they start shooting."

"You're not scared?"

Jake had to smile. She didn't know him. She hadn't heard the stories. "Miss Tommy, I been shot at a whole lot. You read the papers? Ever read about a guy called Crazy Jake?"

She laughed. "Yes, I make the connection. I know who you are now. You bust heads on picket lines."

"Used to. No more."

"Oh, sure. Look at those hands. I saw the way you handled the wrench."

"But I keep the palms soft for ladies." He touched the back of her tanned hand. "You are a beautiful woman. Your husband had to be a *shmendrick* to go running off to Florida."

"He was afraid of me. I had more courage than he did. Can you imagine a yellowbelly who'd hide belowdecks when he saw a coast-guard boat? Or one of the go-through boats?"

"What's a go-through?"

"Hijacker. Fast boats with machine guns and boarding hooks. They go after little guys like me. They wait until you're loaded, ram you and board you. They're worse than the Coasties. They'll kill you for a case of gin."

Jake absorbed the information. It sounded risky, but there were huge hauls of booze to be made off Long Island and Jersey. The important thing was to connect with a big operator, offer more money, get a "first" on his shipment. Even better, he thought, would be to own your own ocean-going ships, your own craft for unloading, and a fleet of trucks for the trip to New York.

Over Lundy's blueberry pie and vanilla ice cream, Jake gave her two of his cards—the F & C Cereal card and the one advertising Pacific Breeze Hair Tonic. There were phone numbers on each.

"I don't need corn flakes or hair goo, Jake."

"Let me know when your boat is ready to sail again," Jake said. "I'll pay."

"You'll pay before I go out, Dempsey. I haven't got the money to get the hull patched."

Jake pulled the roll from his pocket. "What do you need?"

"She has to go into dry dock. Four or five days' work. Fix the pump. Four hundred should do it."

"Here's five hundred. As soon as she can sail, call me. You can tell me the best time and place for buying."

"Outside the three-mile limit on a foggy day. You always carry that much cash?"

Jake paid the check, tipped liberally, and complimented the head-waiter. He held the chair back gallantly for Tommy.

"Listen, Dempsey," she said, with a mocking gleam in her eyes, "there's a horse hitched down the street. Want to see if that roll you carry will choke him?"

"It's a cash business, captain."

They parted on a windy corner on Emmons Avenue. A steel-gray sky lowered over the docks and the rocking boats. A clumsy open boat was churning the waters, nosing toward its berth. It was laden with frigid cod fishermen.

"A week maybe?" Jake asked.

"I'll call when I need corn flakes or hair tonic. You people really are a sketch. Thanks for lunch, and thanks for working the wrench."

He watched her stately figure walk off. No weakness in her. A little shy about men. A crazy life—raised on boats, no mother, her father drowning. A different kind of woman.

It was early evening when Jake got back to the plant. As soon as he had parked his car he heard screaming from within. He saw no police cars parked on the cobbled street. The double-size garage door was locked, so he entered with his key through the smaller steel door. As he crossed the threshold, he identified the shrieks as issuing from the mouth of his future daughter-in-law, Hilda.

Cautious as always, Jake waited in the brick-lined hallway that led to the office with its frosted-glass walls.

Hilda screamed again. "Mutt, Mutt! Watch the *knife!*"

Jake could hear muffled curses and angry voices. One was Mutt's, full of menace and warning. The other was a guttural snarl. Who?

He walked into the plant and glanced at the office. Hilda was wailing, pressing her hands to her face. Theresa had gone for the day, as had the third secretary, Mrs. O'Neal. Mutt was standing behind a copper mixing vat, holding a broken bottle in his hand. Opposite it, Sal Ferrante was pointing a six-inch blade at Mutt.

"Fuckin' crook, fuckin' kike," Sal was muttering. "I'll cut ya heart out."

Puzzled and wary, Jake kept a cool head. He always counted the house, figured the odds. None of the other Ferrantes was present. Buster was probably out driving a truck. Only the professor, his bulging bald pate gleaming under the overhead lights, was in the barnlike room, jigging up and down, appealing to the partners to calm down.

A good situation, Jake thought. No Baggie, no Dom, no Luigi. Even

Theresa was gone. The odds were with the Chains. Jake was unarmed. He made it a point not to carry weapons. Why give the cops an excuse? He could remember when Dopey Benny Fein, an untouchable mobster, got in big trouble in 1915 for a Sullivan Law violation.

The dispute could be handled. But he would need room to swing, arms unencumbered. He took off his topcoat and jacket and placed them on a stack of wooden crates. Then he walked stealthily into the factory.

Goldsturm saw him first. *"Mr. Chain!* Please, Mr. Chain, stop them! It's my fault! I take the blame!"

Hilda also saw Jake. "Sal says he'll kill him! Jake, do something!"

"Sure." Jake laughed. "Call a cop."

"Screw you, too," Sal said. He backed away so he could see both Jake and Mutt. Hilda danced in terror. Her breasts wobbled.

"Sal, *walyo,"* Jake said gently. "What's all this?"

"I told him to shove his home-cooked alky up his nose," Mutt said. "It's ruining the booze. We had a dozen cases sent back. The professor says we can't use it anymore. Right, Goldsturm?"

"I'm sorry I started," Goldsturm wailed. "Mr. Chain, it's true. What Mr. Ferrante brings in is *poison.* Bedbugs, mouse crap. We can't use it. Better we should buy more denatured alcohol and purify."

"No," Sal said. "My whole family's inna business. All my friends. I ain't puttin' them outta work."

Poor Sal, Jake thought. On a hot afternoon Pacific Street smelled like a garbage dump. Stinking fumes hovered over the pavement, made eyes tear, noses twitch. In each three-story building, alky cookers bubbled. The cottage industry gave income to a horde of Ferrantes, their relatives and friends.

"But, *walyo,"* Jake said sweetly, "nobody wants to take the bread from your family's mouth. It's just we can't kill our customers."

"It's awful, Mr. Chain," Goldsturm sputtered. "A disgrace. We found a sparrow in a bottle of Tennessee Morning."

"Dead, I hope," Jake said.

"Our best line," Mutt said. "Sal, put the knife down. Pop, stand back. I don't need you. I'll fight him."

Jake pondered his move. No cops, of course. Cops were people you bought, bribed, and owned. You never involved them in family disputes. But Mutt was not afraid. He was lean as a whip, leather-strong, fast on his feet. Lacking his father's size, he had inherited his strength. At Jefferson High he had won medals for the two-hundred-yard dash. Jake could remember cheering at the PSAL games when Mortimer Chain won the four-hundred-yard relay with a mighty sprint on the anchor leg. *Bright sunlight, a cool day at Boys High Field . . .*

"Okay, I'm out of it," Jake said. "Both of you drop the stuff in your hands. The knife, the bottle. You wanna fight, fight with fists."

"No!" Hilda shrieked. "No! Mr. Chain—stop them! Stop them!"

"Giddadahere," Sal said, turning to Jake. "I ain't a-scared a you."

"Sal, boychick. My little buddy who used to sell ices," Jake said. "Who wants you to be afraid?"

"Yez are after me. Your kid made me take you in. So you get two-thirds of the business and I get shit. I started it! Mutt learned it from me. Then he brings you in. Who needed you? Now it's two against one."

Jake sat on a barrel and crossed his legs. No point in using his fists on Sal. He could get the knife and beat the daylights out of him in seconds.

"You got my brothers killed," Sal said. He sounded as if he were ready to weep. "Frankie. Vinnie. You use us up like we was snot rags."

"I loved your brothers. I love you like a son. That is why you got to listen to Uncle Jake. Was I ever rotten to you? Did I ever say Salvatore Ferrante was a bum who took pennies from kids for selling lemon ice?"

Mutt winked at Hilda. She was shuddering. She had always feared Sal. Ever since the day he'd blown off the farmer's head. Mean as a snake, the eyes never looking at you.

Mutt was smiling. The old man was going to soft-soap Sal, work a con on him. He had seen his father do this before. Years ago when he was a "labor consultant" with Glauberman. Mr. Jacob Chain, playing with a gold watch on a chain, discussing a contract with a union official.

"Sal, listen to Jake. I know your poor mother is sick. I know that has upset you. Put down the knife and I'll tell you what we will do."

"No."

Mutt tried to stifle the smile. *Oi, the con game the old man was pulling.* Like the pea under the shells.

"Sal, you can keep all the rotten alky that stinks like dead fish, that your *goombahs* are making. We can't use it."

"Screw you, Chain."

"Sal, you got to listen to me. Your mother liked me. Didn't I pay for the masses in Holy Family? A whole year of candles? Be nice."

Jake thought: *If he is not nice, if he turns me down, I may have to crack his head.* But that would be a desperate move. The Ferrante muscle, manpower, and contacts were useful. A man and his son were not enough. They needed an organization. Maybe they had been unfair to Sal.

"You keep your alcohol," Jake went on. "But we'll furnish, below cost, bottles, corks, revenue stamps, and the mixers. Professor Goldsturm will be happy to hire you a cutter to make the booze. His advice will be available. Only two things we won't do."

"Whazzat?"

Sal was hooked, wiggling, Mutt saw.

"Your *own* labels. Your brands can't compete with ours. No Aberdeen Dew, no Juniper Tree, no Tennessee Morning. It's easy. Our printer will design them. So your line won't be competitive with ours."

"What's the other thing?"

"Stay away from our customers. Sure, you're still with us. But you got a

second line. You can charge less. Sell to the Polish Falcons and the
Ukrainian Social Club and the Sons of Erin. They're also thirsty. For
F & C, you're a partner. We keep the Brooklyn Democratic Club, the
speakeasies, the restaurants, the society people. You have your own business on the side. None of the alky your family makes goes to waste, right?
And who else in the home bottling business gets free bottles, corks, mixers,
and flavors?"

"It's a good deal, Sal," Mutt said. "You could clean up."

Sal blinked. He looked chastised. All breathed a sigh of relief. The
baloney slicer went into Sal's belt. "You mean it? I get bottles and stamps
and all the crap that goes into the whiskey?"

"Please," Goldsturm said. "My additives, Mr. Ferrante, are not crap.
They can do nothing but improve your vile alcohol."

"My word," Jake said. "Mutt's word. Partners, aren't we? Just don't
compete for customers. Make an inexpensive line. The Polacks and the
micks and *shwarzers* will be happy to pay. Use extract of Jamaica ginger.
Old antifreeze. The iron in it is good for the blood."

Within a week, Sal was running a cutting plant in the cellar of his father's barbershop. If the product was inferior to F & C's, it was nonetheless in
demand, even though the president of the Polish Falcons went into semi-
paralysis after a wedding at which Ferrante's Society Club Special Rye was
served and much praised by Polish *Feinschmeckers*.

Chapter 33

Each day Jake waited for a call from Tommy Tuttle. Normally a patient man—he had learned that if you waited long enough you got what you wanted—he found himself eager to see the tall woman again.

She was something refreshing to him. The women he had known (except for Eva, the unattainable) were soft, beaten, lesser beings in a man's world. The women of Brownsville—Italian, Jewish, Irish—seemed to him depressed, frustrated, and empty. He pitied his wife, was disgusted by Minnie, and found Hilda, his daughter-in-law-to-be, selfish and conceited. The Ferrante women were not much better than slaves to tyrannical brothers.

Tommy's independence and courage astonished him. Her strength intensified the sexual thrill he anticipated. She liked him. He knew it. She knew who he was. Crazy Jake. The tough guy. A man carrying a grand in cash around.

There was no telephone aboard the *Deepwater Angel*. He did not know how to reach her. But he did not ride out to Sheepshead Bay again. He preferred to wait, to delay their meeting. Then an odd thing happened. With the woman on his mind continually—*Am I in love?* Jake wondered—he approached Sarah one night, came to her bed, and made love to her. She could not believe her good fortune.

"It was like when we were young," she said. "So good."

"Because I love you, *ketzeleh.*"

A shadow of guilt hovered over his affection. Considerate of Sarah's frail body, he understood the act was a lie. He was making love to Tommy. In his mind were pictures as vivid as photographs—how he would join his body to the strong woman. What difference? he decided, as he and Sarah rested in the dark, arms around each other's body. What difference? Sarah did not know. The moments of passion had made her joyful.

"Jake, I am happy. I'm glad you came to me."

* * *

On a mild breezy day in early December, Tommy Tuttle phoned Jake at the warehouse. She was ready to sail. The *Deepwater Angel* was repaired— the holes sealed, the pump replaced, the engine reconditioned.

"You go out in winter?" Jake asked. "I don't know what kind of a sailor I am."

"What happened to the tough guy, Dempsey?"

He laughed. "I'll be there. How much money should I bring?"

"How much do you have?"

She had gotten a tip from a speakeasy owner in Coney Island. The *Grecian Venus,* under command of the legendary Captain Bob O'Hara, was due off Freeport the following morning. O'Hara always notified a few choice customers. The speak owner liked Tommy and let her in on a good thing.

Jake scrawled some notes. He was to meet Tommy at the dock in Sheepshead Bay at five the next morning. She would have Chickie and another man on board to help with the loading. She was to be paid cash in advance. As for trucks, that was his business. She told him to have the trucks wait for her boat at Rayburn's Boatyard in Clamshell Inlet east of Freeport. Tommy said she did not like to take her boat into heavy surf or land on a beach. It was asking for trouble. Mr. Rayburn was reliable. He kept numerous coast-guard employees and Prohibition agents on his payroll. If all went well, they would be able to unload cargo by six or seven that night.

"Food?" Jake asked. "Guns?"

"I'll supply the food. No guns, Dempsey. My rule is, when in trouble, run, ditch the cargo. Pay off if you have to. The Coasties have fifty-caliber machine guns and three-inch cannons."

Jake told Mutt and Sal about his plans. He'd need three trucks. Since two were out making pickups on Lake Champlain—they'd located a hotel owner who let them use his resort as a drop—they would have to rent vehicles. Buster Twine would drive the lead truck. Baggie and Stroonz Rizzo would follow.

Sal was suspicious of the seaborne operation. But he had become more subdued now that he was becoming Brownsville's chief purveyor of "nigger gin." Sullenly he consented to the new venture. When Sal left the office, Mutt asked his father if he knew what he was getting into.

"I won't know until I try. It sounds good. This lady captain knows the angles."

"A *lady* captain?"

Jake tried to be offhand. "You should see her. Tugboat Annie. Tough as nails."

"Enough drivers?" Mutt asked. "Cash?"

"Sure. Buster's got the most brains so I'll give him instructions. The *walyos* can take orders from him. I'm taking ten grand in cash. I want to see what it'll buy."

Mutt's eyebrows arched. *"Ten grand?* Did you tell Sal? Remember, he's a partner."

"You tell him."

The following morning was colder and windier. Jake got seasick a half-hour into the Atlantic. He heaved his breakfast and requested a warm mackinaw from Tommy. She laughed at him. Some tough guy. A landlubber, a baby at sea. He'd better get a pair of sea legs if he wanted to work Rum Row, she taunted.

The *Deepwater Angel* chugged noisily and left a wide churning wake, but it made good time in the choppy seas. Tommy had brought along a flat-bottomed barge. It was tied to the fishing boat with a hawser. It slowed them down, but it would be useful in case Jake planned a big purchase. She had known buyers to weep in frustration at their lack of planning. Rum boats would come in with ten or fifteen thousand cases, and buyers would have to settle for a small purchase for lack of storage space.

Chickie and Anton, a chubby Slavic-looking youth, labored about the deck, while the skipper, puffing a Fatima, handled the wheel.

"I feel useless," Jake said. "Can I help?"

"Just flash your roll when we pull alongside the *Venus*. O'Hara has sharp eyes. He can count your money from twenty feet away. What'd you bring?"

"Ten grand."

"That should get you five hundred cases, or a thousand burlocks. He'll think you're a piker. Guys come out with pokes of fifty and sixty thousand."

She explained why O'Hara had been so successful. He had a contact with the coast guard, a warrant officer who earned $153 a month. O'Hara paid him ten times that amount to look the other way. He also furnished the officer with payoffs for his crew. Unhappily, the warrant officer was not always on duty. If some other boat took up the chase or fired a shot or tried to board, O'Hara had to play it cute. Usually he presented a fake bill of lading from Bermuda or Nassau. *No need to inspect cargo, officer, we're carrying palm oil.*

Tommy, guiding the boat along the south shore and munching a liverwurst sandwich, regaled Jake with stories of Rum Row. He abstained from lunch. There was a working day ahead and his stomach was trying to crawl into his mouth.

"Getting tougher for small operators like us," she said. "Heck, I've seen customers row out four times in one afternoon to load up. Wait'll you see Rum Row. Speedboats, skiffs, fishing boats. But the big guys are closing us out. They send their buyers to the West Indies and purchase a cargo in advance. They charter schooners and meet them with speedboats off Montauk or Coney Island. Sometimes they unload under the Statue of Liberty."

Jake absorbed more information. Bootleggers were ordering rum runners built to specifications. Fast craft that could reach fifty knots, ten knots faster than a coast-guard vessel. One smuggler was experimenting with armor plate.

"People get killed doing this?" Jake asked.

"You bet they do. I've seen rum runners shot dead in New York harbor. If not by the Coasties, by some crook trying to hijack."

"I didn't bring my guns. You told me not to."

"If there's trouble, we run and dump cargo, clear?"

Jake inhaled the salt spray, the sea air. Not a bad life. Better than hanging out in the stinky plant. Goldsturm's mixtures were permeating bricks, timbers, flooring. The place smelled like the inside of an old beer barrel. Theresa, Hilda, and Mrs. O'Neal complained about the stench.

Jake stood next to Tommy at the wheel. She was perched on a high stool, eyes on the compass, guiding the boat through a choppy sea.

"You like this life?"

"What else do I know? This and my little girl are everything. I don't date much. They all think I'm one of the boys. Good old Tommy. Even the name. Sometimes I wish I were a Lydia or a Cynthia."

"You're a beautiful woman. Even in dungarees and a heavy blue sweater."

"Step down, Dempsey. The fee is the same. Two hundred for me, fifty for each of the boys."

Young Anton clambered to the bow and sighted through a pair of binoculars. "I think I see dem, cap'n. O'Hara's ship and a whole lot of others."

"Word gets around," Tommy said. "Are they loading?"

"I can't tell."

She turned the wheel to the right and headed toward open sea. "Hold on, Dempsey, it may get rough. You look gray."

"I'm okay. I'm getting excited. Listen, how does he decide who gets what?"

"Some deals are made before he leaves. We're small-timers, so we get leavings. But Bobby likes me. He gives my clients a break."

"He's a boyfriend?"

"No, he's not. He's happily married with a wife in Florida and seven kids. He just likes me. That's all."

Soon they were able to see the fleet of boats. Around the tall silhouette of the *Grecian Venus,* a score of smaller boats—cruisers, charters, outboards—circled like suckling pigs around a brood sow.

Anton hopped down from the foredeck. He gave the binoculars to Tommy. "Somethin's wrong, skipper. Nobody's unloadin'."

She left the wheel to him and ordered him to turn the boat to port. She took the binoculars.

"No wonder. Coast-guard cutter's got the *Venus* stopped. The Feds are off to starboard. If O'Hara wanted to give him a run, he could. But that would leave an awful lot of sorry customers. I guess his warrant officer isn't working."

Jake shivered and drew the plaid lumberjacket over his throat. He had overcome his queasiness. He was almost enjoying the roll and pitch of the boat, feeling himself part of the crew. But it bothered him that he was apparently on a useless errand.

"I'd guess he's outside the three-mile limit," Tommy said. "But they still won't let him unload. In fact, friends, they got the three-incher pointing at him. Look. Where the sun hits it."

Jake took the spyglasses. He could see the white government boat. A spark of gleaming metal indicated the cannon.

As they watched, some small boats started toward shore.

"Yellowbellies," Tommy said. "Well, the more leave, the better for us."

A cabin cruiser and a charter boat were turning in the choppy seas and sailing to harbor.

"What's he gonna do?" asked Jake.

"I don't know. Maybe put out to sea for another day. Then hit the island further east—Montauk, East Hampton. I sure hate to see us lose out."

"You mean I got to pay even if we strike out?"

"That's life, Dempsey. You ought to carry insurance." She winked. "Some days it doesn't pay to start up the engines."

"It's just I hate to quit. We got trucks waiting in Freeport."

The coast-guard cutter hove into full view. The craft sailed from behind the dark hull of the rum runner. Clean and white, it made O'Hara's booze ship look dingy and disreputable. Tommy said that O'Hara deliberately kept it so to fool pursuers. His engines could outrun anything the government owned. But this time he must have been surprised.

"Damn," she said. "Looks like the ball game's over."

Jake scratched the scar on his chin. Cold, damp weather. The old wounds seemed to bother him on days like this. The scars in his legs and his groin began to twitch.

"Tommy, I'm no sailor, and I never bought booze on the ocean. But I think I got an idea."

The *Deepwater Angel* lurched and righted herself. The towed barge bumped the stern, butting the rubber tires with a sucking noise. A fast cabin cruiser passed them, sending out a boiling wake that made Tommy's boat rock, rise, and settle again. A man in a captain's hat and a handsome navy blue coat was standing on the aft deck. He bellowed through a megaphone: "No use, Tommy. The Coasties won't go. O'Hara's got twenty thousand bottles of booze on board. I think they're going to board to search. It's an outrage."

Tommy thanked him through her megaphone.

"Who's he?" Jake asked.

"Van Dyke. Rich guy from Old Westbury. Polo player. He likes to buy his booze off the boat so he's sure it isn't cut."

The speedboat flew past them, churning the steel-gray waters. Gulls wheeled and squawked in its snowy wake.

Jake asked: "You got extra gasoline on board? Engine oil?"

"Sure."

"We used to do this when I was *shtarking*. To get the cops off our back when we wanted to throw a bomb or hit the scabs."

"You're ahead of me, Dempsey."

"Soak the barge with gasoline and oil to make it smoke. I know from fires. When it starts to burn, we shove it off. I'll give you five to two the coast-guard ship comes after it."

"You're crazy," she said.

"Crazy Jake."

"If we wreck the barge," Tommy said, "we'll have only half as much space for the whiskey."

Jake said, "I always take what I can get when I can get it. Tomorrow, your friend O'Hara could be arrested and the government could grab the booze."

She turned to Chickie. "Get out a gasoline can and five quarts of engine oil."

"Miss Tommy, we could all go up in smoke," the mate said. "Blown to hell."

"You'll go first, Chickie. All that alcohol in you. Turn the barge loose when it starts to burn."

"Not me, Miss Tommy. Let that big guy try it. He ain't no sailor. If we lose him, so what?"

Jake suggested they pull several hundred yards closer to shore to give the coast guard a longer run. Tommy agreed. But she didn't want the flaming wreck to run aground. It would be too easy to put out the fire. Drifting in the choppy seas, it would be harder to control.

Chickie came from belowdecks with a ten-gallon jerrican of white gasoline and two five-quart cans of motor oil. He was breathing heavily. *Scared,* Jake saw. He'd do the job himself. He'd show them how Crazy Jake got things done.

Tommy raised O'Hara on the radio. She spoke to him in code words. For all she knew, the coast guard had boarded him already. He acknowledged her as "Angel," and she called him "Venus." Had he any news of her aunt in Miami Beach? O'Hara said she was sick again. Lung trouble. She sent Tommy her love. But the doctors wouldn't let her go north.

Tommy guessed he was being detained. Maybe searched. Jake Chain's daring plan sounded better and better.

"I ain't gettin' on that barge," Chickie said. "Blow me clear to hell. One spark from the engine. A backfire and *wham.*"

Jake leaped onto the barge, trying to land lightly. The boards moaned beneath him. He could see how splintered and stained the barge was. The most he'd pay for its loss, he decided, was three hundred bucks. "Chickie, toss me the cans."

Anton, the younger man, took over from the frightened mate. He threw the jerrican to Jake, then the oil cans.

"We far enough from him?" Jake called to the skipper.

"Let me swing around once more, so when we cut loose she'll drift west. If we're lucky we can load up while they're still chasing it."

Jake sprinkled gasoline and oil on the wooden deck and sides of the barge.

"How ya gonna light it?" Chickie called.

"With a match, how else?"

From the wheel, Tommy watched him. Quite a man. Nerve, brains. Like her father, Captain Mac. Same size, same coloring, same blunt hard face. And with a streak of the gambler in him.

"Not while you're in it, Mr. Chain," Anton said. "C'mon back on board. I'll untie the hawser."

Jake shook the cans vigorously. *Every last drop.* He felt like Goldsturm emptying detoxified methyl alcohol into a vat. Anton gave him a hand and pulled him over the stern of the *Deepwater Angel.*

"Gimme a hunk of cardboard," Jake said. "Like an old box, something that'll burn slow."

Chickie found the cardboard container that had held the oil cans. Jake stuffed it with newspapers and sprinkled them with gasoline.

"Untie the rope, kid," he ordered Anton. He called to Tommy: "Skipper, when I holler *go,* give her all her power."

They worked like a trained team. Anton undid the painter. He held the loose end until the last minute. Jake threw a book of lit matches into the newspaper-crammed carton and heaved it onto the barge.

"Full steam, Tommy," Jake shouted.

The *Deepwater Angel,* free of the sluggish barge, spurted away. *And just in time,* Jake thought. He felt his eyebrows singe, his skin prickle with the burst of flame. The gasoline roared. The oil sent up clouds of boiling black smoke. The old wooden craft listed away from them, staining the clear wintry air with choking bursts of smoke.

Jake came into the wheelhouse. "Can you raise a coast-guard station? Or the harbor cops?"

"I can try."

"Tell them you saw a floating wreck. Big boat burning. People in the water. Give a different name for this boat. Say you're going to try to pick people up but you need help."

She cocked her head and smiled. The arching eyebrows that had attracted him, rising from the bridge of her nose, arched even higher. "You not only have muscles, Chain, you know how to lie."

"Nobody's getting hurt."

After a few attempts on the crackling radio, Tommy was able to contact the Freeport harbor police. She did as Jake suggested, identifying herself as the *Ocean Beauty II* out of Captree. A sergeant replied he'd get to the coast guard at once. There was a cutter just off the three-mile limit.

"If I were you," Jake said, "I'd head for your friend O'Hara."

Within a half-hour they pulled alongside the *Grecian Venus.* O'Hara and his crew were tossing oddly shaped crates to a speedboat riding alongside the rum runner.

The cutter was nowhere in sight.

"What happened to the Feds?" Tommy shouted.

O'Hara laughed. "Fire at sea. They took off like war was declared."

Tommy shouted up to him: "That was our barge, skipper. You owe us seven hundred bucks, O'Hara. My customer had the bright idea."

"Same Tommy," O'Hara called back. "Stand by. I'll load you next. Who's your client?"

"Mr. Jacob Chain."

O'Hara looked through a spyglass, sizing Jake up. New face to him. The name meant nothing, but the man's size was impressive. And if it had been his idea to fake out the Coasties with a "fire at sea," he had to be a helluva man.

O'Hara ordered a Jacob's ladder lowered. He shouted at a returning customer to get out of the way so Captain Tuttle's boat could be loaded first. There was some picturesque cursing from a gray-bearded skipper in a wide-beamed open boat.

"Prior deal, Anderton," Captain O'Hara called. "She had a date."

Tommy nudged Jake's side. "Anderton hated my father's guts. He's an old crook, smuggler, go-through man. The bum has an arsenal below-decks."

Jake looked at the name on the bow of the bearded captain's boat. *Ocean Beauty II.* The name Tommy had given the harbor cops! *By God, that was a woman for him.* If a stink was raised about the fire, the Feds would come looking for Anderton.

"He wants *you,* Dempsey," Tommy said. She shoved him toward the rope ladder.

"Come aboard, Mr. Chain," O'Hara said.

A bit uneasy, Jake dug his heel into the lowest rung, then hauled himself up and aboard the rum boat. The deck was piled six- and seven-high with wedge-shaped packages swathed in burlap.

"No wooden crates?" Jake asked O'Hara.

The two men sized each other up. Both were big and wide-shouldered, with calm unemotional faces. There was a sense of recognition in their flat stares.

"My invention," O'Hara said. He was windburned, with a shock of white hair, intelligent brown eyes.

Jake picked up one of the cloth cases. "Feels like six quarts."

"You guessed it. Pack 'em three, two, and one. Each bottle gets a straw jacket. Then the colored girls in Nassau sew them into a double burlap wrapping. They use a third less space than wooden crates with twelve bottles. Every dollar counts, Cohen."

"Chain."

"Excuse me. I ever meet you?"

"No. I run an operation in Brooklyn. Me and my son. Take a few cards."

O'Hara smiled. *A cereal company. Hair tonic.* He had met bootleggers who claimed to represent pharmaceutical houses, paint and shellac factories, industrial machinery manufacturers, antifreeze producers, insecticide makers.

"I'll buy all you can get into Captain Tommy's boat."

O'Hara nodded. "Seeing as she's a friend, and how you got the Feds off my neck, it's a deal."

Prices were going up. Two burlocks—twelve bottles, the equivalent of a full case—went for fifty dollars. Two years ago, Jake remembered Mutt telling him, they were able to buy whiskey in Montreal for *ten dollars a case.*

The *Deepwater Angel,* with the aft deck crammed, every inch of the wheelhouse filled, more burlocks stacked on the foredeck, a few jammed into the hold around the engine and the pump, would take a disappointing two hundred and eighty burlocks. The loss of the barge hurt.

Tommy complained. They'd have to limp back to shore with the gunwales dangerously deep in the water. They were looking for trouble if the seas turned rougher.

Jake counted off seven thousand dollars in hundreds from the ten grand he had locked in his money belt. O'Hara's black crew paid no attention. They had seen rolls of forty, fifty, and a hundred thousand aboard the *Grecian Venus.* And their skipper never carried a gun. His fists, his reputation, and his honor were protection enough.

The deal concluded, Jake, Anton, Chickie, and two black Bahamians began securing the wedge-shaped packets with rope and tarpaulins. The seas were heavier now. The *Deepwater Angel* bumped fretfully against the steel ship. Captain Tuttle held her steady, gave orders, supervised the stowing of cargo.

Coatless, in his candy-striped shirt, sleeves rolled up, Jake outworked every man in the crew. He lifted, tossed, stacked. And did not once breathe hard. Captain O'Hara watched him, thinking, *That is one big tough Jew.*

*   *   *

They were exhausted and freezing when, under the cover of night, the *Deepwater Angel* sailed through narrow channels, past rickety waterfront homes to Rayburn's Boatyard. Tommy had ordered the two-man crew to sit on the tarpaulins. If they were stopped, they would stall for time.

But all was quiet in the marshy channels east of Freeport. They scudded past a long jetty with a red light winking on its outermost pilings, then turned into a smaller channel.

"Good haul, Dempsey?" Tommy asked.

"Yeah. But I wanted to spend ten grand. Too bad we lost the barge."

"You owe me five hundred."

"Take three. Piece of junk, good only for what we used it for."

She smiled. Dimples dented her long cheeks. A *woman*, Jake realized again. The rough blue work clothes would have to go. There were curves, and smooth skin, and warmth under the seaman's disguise. "Make it four hundred," she said.

Jake peeled off the bills. Then he gave her an extra fifty. "Buy something for your little girl."

"I like that. I also like the way you got dirty stowing burlocks. You made O'Hara's deckhands look like weaklings."

Jake touched her hand. "I done my share of hard work. I never been ashamed of it, either."

She thought: *Like my old man.*

An anxious Buster was waiting in the parking lot of Rayburn's Boatyard. The trucks had been there since late afternoon. Colin Rayburn, the owner of the boatyard, anchorage, and "drop" for rum boats, had picked up the radio signal reporting a burning derelict. Harbor police and coast-guard vessels had responded. Rayburn, a chunky egg-bald man, chewing on a cold cigar, was concerned. The signal had come from the *Ocean Beauty II,* Ulf Anderton's boat. And Anderton was first boat out that morning to contact O'Hara.

"Don't worry about it, Colin," Tommy said. "It's under control. The coast guard came through. Any word on survivors?"

"Petty officer thinks it was a fake. By the time they'd finished looking for them, O'Hara had unloaded and sailed. Bobby's on his way back to Nassau by now."

Jake ordered Buster to start unloading. To Jake's amusement, three local policemen, in uniform and armed, were enlisted to help stack burlocks in the F & C trucks. They worked hard, stacking expertly, as if they had done it many times.

"Ten bucks a man," Tommy informed Jake. "Fifty for Rayburn."

"A bargain."

Within an hour the trucks were loaded. Jake said he would ride in front with Buster and pay off. Route 25 was known as "whiskey highway." There would be six or seven payoff points before crossing the New York City line. Since the cutting plant was in Brooklyn, they could avoid the biggest payoff, the Queensboro Bridge.

Jake shook hands with Tommy. "I think I was a pretty good customer. If you contact O'Hara, tell him I'll buy his whole cargo next time."

"Two hundred thousand dollars' worth? C'mon, Chain, that's not your league. You're no Schonkeit."

He watched her walk off to her scruffy fishing boat, and he felt sorry for her. No job for a woman. And the daughter she missed so much. The dead father she had loved. In his chest were odd flutterings. Like nothing he had felt since his young manhood and his love for Eva.

The truck convoy was shot at just after leaving Oceanside. But it was a halfhearted attempt. A few bullets whistled over the hood of the first truck. Buster and Jake ducked below the windshield, ran a red light, signaled to the rear trucks to follow as fast as they could move with the heavy loads. They bounced along the highway. On a stretch of uninhabited sandy land, a motorcycle cop, siren screaming, halted them.

"Exceeding the speed limit," the helmeted officer said. "Driving on the wrong side of the double yellow line. Let's see your driver's license, Bojangles. Let's see the registration for the trucks."

It was ten after midnight, the end of a long, wearying day. Jake had no intention of losing his booty now. The two hundred and eighty burlocks held *one thousand, six hundred and eighty* bottles of genuine scotch, brandy, and gin. These could be cut four-to-one, resulting in damn near *seven thousand bottles* of phony brands, which could then be sold at eight or ten dollars a bottle.

Gross earnings on the haul from Captain O'Hara could come to more than *sixty thousand dollars*. Not bad for an outlay of seven grand, plus a thousand bucks in miscellaneous expenses. To have all this ruined by a dumb motorcycle cop? Never, Jake thought.

"Officer," Jake said politely. "I am with the F & C Cereal company. I'm bringing in a load of grain. Someone shot at us outside of Oceanside. I feel you should look for those criminals."

A flat smile transformed the cop's face. He knew, he *knew*. The word was out. O'Hara had been offshore near Freeport. Some local hoodlums were trying to scare the drivers.

Jake gave him a card. "There it is, sir. A respectable Brooklyn firm. I think it is outrageous the way we get shot at, stopped and questioned. If we violated traffic laws, then I'm ready to pay fines. Could you arrange it for us, on account of this shipment is a day late already?"

"What's your name, wise guy?"

"Dr. Jacob Chain. Consulting chemist for our company."

Trucks roared by on Route 25, some bound for Montauk, some returning to the city. The great booze parade. The cop studied Jake's innocent,
wide face.

"You might be interested in our subsidiary company, officer," Jake said.
He gave him a Pacific Breeze Hair Tonic card. Under it were a pair of
hundred-dollar bills. It was exorbitant. A holdup. But Jake was edgy. No
use in looking for bargains. Buster's eyes opened wide.

"I'll let you off this time, doctor. But watch it. Traffic laws were meant
to be obeyed."

"Absolutely. Next time we'll be more careful. Buster, I think we can go
on. Thank you, officer."

Jake's trucks rolled off the dirt shoulder, hit the asphalt, and sped toward
the city line. He kept performing primitive arithmetic in his mind. Someday, someday not far off, he would buy an entire cargo from Captain
O'Hara. He had a little trouble calculating how much bootleg hooch, how
much *real* money could be made from a two-hundred-thousand-dollar purchase of the real stuff. The amount was so huge it eluded him.

Goldsturm was ecstatic. Mutt and Sal were impressed. The whiskey from
the sea assured that they would have more than enough for the holiday
season. Almost six hundred additional cases of fake booze. Goldsturm was
so overjoyed he decided to try a new line of gin, something with a piquant
dash of sulfuric acid. He called it Tavern Table Gin and awarded it medals
from the St. Louis Exposition and the Brighton Pier Centennial. Buster
tasted it and said his tongue curled up like a window shade.

"No more small sales," Mutt told his father and Sal in the office. "We're
getting too big. From now on, no retails, no cards in hotel rooms, no indi-
vidual deliveries. Only speaks, stores, and distributors. Minimum purchase
is twelve cases. We give a ten-percent discount on anything over twenty-
four cases."

Jake nodded. Sal flickered his eyelids. Mutt imagined it meant yes. More
and more Sal was finding himself an "outside" man—supervising deliveries,
picking up alcohol, checking inventory. He seemed to have changed, to
have grown more moody ever since the Chains refused to buy his *goombahs'* home-stewed poison. Luckily he was getting a rep in Brownsville
and East New York—The King of Nigger Gin. Fussed over and pampered
by his mother, he stayed at home, set his thick black hair in a net, and
listened to a Zenith through elephant-hide earphones.

"I think we can start charging a flat ten bucks a bottle, one hundred and
twenty a case," Mutt said. "Schonkeit's getting eleven and twelve, and I'd
love to undersell the Paymaster."

Chapter 34

"He's carrying twenty-four hundred cases, Dempsey. Damn near five thousand burlocks. Interested?"

Was John McGraw a manager? Could Bobby Jones play golf?

In the F & C office, Jake listened on the phone to Tommy's breathless account of O'Hara's imminent arrival. In two days the *Grecian Venus* would be returning to Freeport. And because O'Hara had been a seagoing mate of Old Mac Tuttle's, he was giving Jake Chain "firsts."

Her fluty voice aroused him. What was better than money, adventure, and a handsome woman? Aboard her chugging fishing boat she had seemed mannish, curt, a bit tough. On the phone her voice suggested silk gowns and soft bedroom lights.

"He'll let me buy it all?"

"That's what the man said. And O'Hara's word is good. He phoned before leaving Nassau. He's damn near loaded. Scotch, brandy, and gin. A big shipment came in from England."

She told him to bring cash. Twenty-four-hundred-odd "cases" would come to *one hundred and twenty thousand dollars.* If he only wanted part of the shipment, O'Hara might not play. There were no secrets on Rum Row. Schonkeit or some other big operators would pounce on the cargo if Jake had the shorts. Word would get out.

She outlined the plan. She would hire extra boats for the ship-to-shore run. Again they would unload at Rayburn's Boatyard. But this time they would need at least fourteen trucks.

"And we're doing it *at night,*" she said. "Captain Bob's got some deal worked out to discourage the go-through guys. Our fleet will leave Sheepshead Bay at midnight. You should be out here by eleven."

"Let's make it nine o'clock. I'll buy you dinner at Lundy's."

"Sounds good. Go to the bank and get a second mortgage. Sell the farm. This'll make you and your son rich. You can buy your wife a mink coat."

Lusting for her, he kept business foremost in his mind. Jake had learned to prepare, to anticipate. He took a ruled pad from Hilda's desk and did some calculations. Thirty thousand bottles of whiskey could be cut to one hundred and twenty thousand quarts of Goldsturm's mixtures. Sold at ten dollars a quart, the gross receipts would be in excess of a *million dollars*. They had to get bottles, crates, storage space, as soon as possible.

Mutt and Sal were in the garage arguing. Mutt wanted to buy a grocery jobber's warehouse across the street and use it for storage. They had no room to move around in, Mutt complained. So much stuff was being turned out that Goldsturm needed four new vats and an automatic pumping system for filling bottles. Crated booze would have to be stored elsewhere.

Cautious as ever, Sal objected. "Whadda we wanna spend all that dough for? Who needs a new building?"

Wait, Jake thought, *wait till he hears what I got in mind.*

"Boys," he asked politely, "we can spare maybe a hundred and twenty thousand in cash?"

"The new building, pop?" Mutt asked. "Hell, we can buy that old dump for ten grand. A few thousand more to fix the bricks, put in steel doors, bar the windows."

"Not for a building, Mutt. Sal, listen to your uncle Jake. I got a tip that is gonna make us rich like we never believed. A hundred and twenty thousand for real booze. Another five grand for boats, bribes, trucks, and helpers. I got new friends."

Tommy was waiting for him in the lobby of Lundy's. She was wearing stockings and low-heeled black shoes, a black suit, a pink blouse.

"You look better this way. I can see the lines. When you're dressed like a boat captain, it's like a good racehorse under a heavy blanket."

"Thanks a lot, Dempsey."

Her hips and thighs were full and long, melding gently into a pair of well-formed legs. Her full breasts, high and firm, poked at the silk stuff. There was a double strand of pearls around her strong throat. Her wind-darkened face, a bit lined and worn, while lovely and elegantly proportioned, seemed apart from the femininity of naked throat, high breasts, well-fleshed limbs.

"All set?" he asked. "Boats and crews?"

"If you have the money."

Jake lifted a black valise. "The money belt wouldn't handle it. I had a hell of a time convincing my partners that we should take it out of the bank."

"I bet. You belt them around?"

"No. One's my son, I told you. And the other one likes money as much as we do. He agreed. In fact, he and my boy, Morty, are going to Rayburn's."

A whiff of her perfume made him giddy. He was guiding her toward the restaurant. Suddenly he felt he would swoon if he did not make love to her.

"Table for two, sir?" the headwaiter asked.

Jake edged her away from the entrance to the dining hall. "I'm not hungry. Tommy, I'm in love with you. We'll go to the Half Moon Hotel. We got time until the boats leave."

"No. Don't ask me to, Jake."

"Please. I think—I think—I'm not good with words. I can't say it. I love you."

"Then don't ask me."

"It's not just a business deal anymore."

He was moving her toward the coat check. He told the waiter they'd changed their minds.

"What will we use for luggage? They won't let us in." She looked ashamed.

"This," Jake said. He held up the black leather valise. He had a hundred and fifty thousand dollars in it.

"Maybe you'll be sorry."

"Never with you."

They made leisurely, restrained love. Jake saw at once that she was hesitant. He was considerate and undemanding. Yet the sight of her long curved body, free of wrinkles, full of strength and grace, gave him a joy he had never experienced. Her refusal to abandon herself, the suppressed noises she made in climax, made her all the more desirable.

A wintry moon sent shafts of light into the darkened bedroom. Tommy sighed and rose from the bed. With a feathery touch, he ran his hand down her spine.

"You tickle. Soft hand for a big man."

"I'm in love with you, lady captain."

"It's late, Jake. We'd better get to the boats. I'm not a lady anymore. Just an old salt. You know they call me 'one of the boys' in the bait-and-tackle shops. Maybe it's why I'm not a good lover."

"You're the best woman I ever—"

"Oh, I bet. You mobsters get show girls and models, right?"

"Not Jake Chain. My wife, God help her, is a cripple."

"Maybe I am also."

"You? You're *perfect,* Tommy. There's no woman like you anywhere."

She put on her underwear and slip, nestled close to him, and began to cry. He tried to undress her, but she did not want to be loved again. "One of the boys," she said, sniffling. "A drunken husband who used to beat me, and a father who was too good to me. Captain Mac. Maybe I'm still looking for him."

"You found him, kiddo. I'll be any kind of man you want. Papa, boy-friend, husband. I'll be a customer for your boat. I'll protect you, I'll buy you fancy silk things, furs, pearls. Maybe I said the wrong thing, huh?"

"No, Jake. You made me happy."

But she did not look happy. Her long face was solemn as he stroked her hair and kissed her forehead.

"Alligator skin," she whispered.

"You make fun of yourself too much."

She began to talk. Tommy wasn't her real name. It was Henrietta Mae, but she had been a notorious tomboy as a kid in Sheepshead Bay. She could remember her grandfather walking horses at the racetrack. As a girl of ten she would go help him, insist on "walking off" some overage plug that her grandpa, Big Joe Tuttle, owned. Neither horses nor the tough gangs fright-ened her. *She was a Tuttle.* When the track folded, her grandfather seemed to die a little every day. The few dollars he had left went to Mac, who bought a boat and traded his way up to the *Deepwater Angel* and a steady business in charter fishing. Business was good, especially in late summer and early fall when the blues were running.

Her mother "died of the booze," Tommy said. Alone a great deal, un-educated, a handsome Irishwoman, she felt that Cap'n Mac loved his rusty tub more than he did his wife. She was a secret drinker. She gave Tommy little love.

"And your husband?"

"I hated him. I thought he'd be like daddy. He wasn't. Stupid, vain man. It's no good being stupid, Jake. I'm sorry. I know you have no education. But people who don't know anything go to hell faster. I quit after two years of high school. I've always been sorry. My daddy read a lot. He and grampa *understood.* People have minds also, they knew. I feel cheated."

"Don't be ashamed, Tommy. I learned to read and write when I was twenty-five."

"I'm sick of being a—a—fake man. Boots, sou'westers, heavy sweaters. They think I'm a roundheels or a lesbian."

"I could tell them different. Listen, you want to go to school? I'll pay. You want to sell the boat and open a business?"

She rested her head on his massive chest. "No more baiting hooks with skimmers? Skin my last bluefish? It would take a carload of cold cream, Jake, to get the calluses off my hands. And my face is a mess—an old sea horse."

"It's a beautiful face. Get rid of the boat. I'll buy it. I'll hire some guy to run booze. That ain't for a lady like you. A lousy two hundred bucks a trip? While I make a fortune? You can go to Brooklyn College. You can do anything you want."

Such words, spoken with such tenderness and sincerity, he had never used to Sarah. He felt guilty.

"Nuts," she said. "Old Dempsey." She tousled his hair, got out of bed, and finished dressing. "I hate this. I have to change again on the boat. I dressed for you. Now I have to go back to dungarees and slickers and a watch cap like a merchant seaman."

"Henrietta Mae, I love you."

"Stow it, Jake. You better get dressed too. You might as well check out and save another night's rent. No encore tomorrow, understand?"

"But maybe the day after tomorrow?"

He could not remember such pleasure. Merely watching her dress—maneuvering her long body into the sheer blouse, the skirt, the jacket, the high-heeled shoes—aroused him. The magic, the strangeness of women's clothing tantalized him, all the hooks and snaps and elastics. As she was brushing her hair, he seized her from behind and ran his lips over her neck and cheeks. He took her one last time on the bed, fully clothed.

Chapter 35

The waters were reassuringly calm. A mile off Sheepshead Bay, the *Deep-water Angel* rendezvoused with three other boats of Tommy's flotilla. Two, like hers, were open fishing boats. The third was an old seagoing tug. None of them had much speed. They would be sitting ducks for the coast guard or a hijacking craft.

"Prices went up for a night haul," she said. "They get three hundred each. I gave them half of it. You can pay the rest when we unload at Ray-burn's place."

"A bargain," Jake said. They wore heavy-weather garb—navy blue watch caps, knit sweaters, boots. Jake was enjoying the life. It got him out of the warehouse.

Distantly, through fog and spray, Jake could see searchlights flashing. It seemed to be a code—three fast flashes with intervals of about a second between them.

"Trouble?" he asked.

"Heck, no. That's O'Hara's friend."

"You mean the coast guard is leading us out to him?"

"What else are they paid for? For a mobster, you can be a boy scout sometimes. You know that Dwyer, the biggest rum runner of all, uses coast-guard boats to unload his schooners? He's got New York City cops loading his whiskey into trucks. Everybody plays."

Several hours later, as the swells increased and the fog dissipated, they were able to discern the silhouette of the *Grecian Venus*. The government cutter hove to a quarter of a mile away. She had stopped flashing her blinkers.

"It's safe to pull up," Tommy said. "There's one skipper can put in for early retirement. By next Christmas he'll be a rich man."

O'Hara's schooner looked dingier and rustier than the last time Jake had seen it. Moreover (unless his eyes deceived him), he noticed a row of huge bullet holes in her starboard side.

Lanterns glowed aboard the schooner. They could see O'Hara and a black deckhand lowering a Jacob's ladder.

"He wants you, Jake," Tommy said. "Don't forget the satchel."

Chickie and Anton gave him a shove upward. The two boats nudged each other's side tentatively. He dug his work shoes into the rope and climbed aboard with one hand, holding the valise in the other.

"Good evening, Chain," the skipper said.

"Good evening to you, captain. You done me a real favor. I'd invite you to my son's wedding, but I know you stay out of New York."

"A kind thought, Chain. I like a family man. Got seven kids of my own."

"I hope you got more cases of booze."

O'Hara showed him a manifest. The heading read:

O'HARA & BEECHAM, LTD.
IMPORTERS
PRINCE STREET, NASSAU

"Read it and weep, Chain. I've got twenty-eight hundred cases, thirty-three thousand six hundred quarts. Half are sewn into burlocks. The rest are crated. We didn't have time to sew them all. The island's overloaded with liquor. Every distiller in the United Kingdom is shipping. I can't even rent warehouse space."

"Gimme a price."

"Since you're Tommy's friend, it's the same as last time. Fifty dollars a case."

"I make that a hundred and forty grand."

"Nice round figure. Plus five thousand for the United States Coast Guard who escorted you here and is standing off my port bow."

"Tommy said you'd split the payoff for the Feds."

"Did she?" O'Hara leaned over the rail and hailed Captain Tuttle. "You giving your friend ideas? What's this half-and-half on the Coasties?"

"Be a sport, Bobby," she called back.

O'Hara laughed. "Okay. Two and a half grand. Why argue over trifles?" He shouted to his crew. "Start unloading, boys. Two of you get on board Captain Tuttle's boat and stack."

Jake decided not to work that night. He opened the valise. He and O'Hara sat on a hatch cover. The purchase and the money for the coast-guard boat left him with seven thousand five hundred dollars. The drivers and loaders and bribes would eat into that. But what did it matter? He'd landed a fortune in clean booze. It would teach his kid a few things. And wise Sal up. They would be small-timers no more.

After O'Hara had counted the green bills and stowed them in an iron safe belowdecks, he came back with a submachine gun and two .45 automatics in his arms.

"I thought you never carried hardware," Jake said.

"We got word that the go-throughs are around. They're mostly dumb micks and wops, and, excuse me, Chain, a few sheenies. They can't take a good run at sea. Start heaving their guts as soon as there's a wake. But they might give you trouble on the way in."

"So?" Jake said.

"You paid up fast and you're Tommy's friend. Take these with my compliments."

Jake thanked the skipper. He tucked a .45 in his belt and handed the submachine gun and the other .45 over the side to Anton.

"No dice," Tommy said. "Give them back. If we get hijacked, Jake, it's your neck, not mine. I have no interest in your booze. Remember? I get three hundred dollars a boat and expenses."

"Obey the lady," O'Hara called. Burlocks and crates flew past his head. Jake had never seen a crew work so fast. They unloaded a fourth of the cargo in minutes, tossing wooden boxes and burlap packages, securing them with rope.

Jake gave the machine gun and one automatic back to O'Hara. The second automatic he kept in his belt.

By four in the morning all the boats were loaded and groaning under the weight of more than thirty-three thousand quarts of rye, scotch, gin, and brandy. It was by no means a record haul, O'Hara told Jake. Some of the big operators had come ashore with loads worth seven and eight hundred thousand dollars.

"I'm getting there," Jake said.

"Good luck, Chain. I'll call Tommy when I'm ready again."

Jake descended the rope ladder. Tommy took the wheel. O'Hara was a considerate purveyor. He had arranged for the coast-guard boat to escort them beyond the three-mile limit.

"We can't make any speed," Tommy said nervously. "We're loaded like pregnant whales. Just pray that when Uncle Sam says goodbye, there won't be any pirates around."

"It would be a shame," Jake said innocently. "And not a gun on board." He put his hand on the .45. He'd never used one, but he knew the trick. Aim low, *very* low. The damn thing kicked like a mule.

The boats labored through the now choppy seas. Toward the shoreline the December fog thickened. Each boat kept running lights on. Tommy had ordered the captains to keep a short interval between boats. Once they got into the main channel, they could relax. It was unusual for go-through boats to try to intercept there.

They saw the red jetty lights of Freeport, waves breaking on the long rock pilings. The cutter turned east.

As Tommy guided the *Deepwater Angel* between rocking buoys, she let out a gasp. "Trouble," she said.

"Where?" Jake asked.

She cut their speed. The overloaded boat came to a shuddering halt a hundred yards short of the channel entrance.

"Look left. He's coming our way."

A long, sleek speedboat, white as death, was cutting the water, focusing twin searchlight beams on the *Deepwater Angel*. Jake was momentarily blinded. The damn fool piloting the white boat was headed straight at them. It had a long curved bow. He could see men standing on the foredeck, others on a narrow rail-enclosed contraption.

"Flying bridge," Tommy said. "They spear swordfish from it. Only I think someone else is getting speared. Dammit, we were almost home free."

A burly man in a wool cap and a pea jacket was standing on the narrow metal bridge. He was pointing a submachine gun at the wheelhouse of the *Deepwater Angel*.

"Remember what I said," Tommy said. "To hell with the cargo. I want to live. I'm a mother."

"I'm a father. It don't mean we quit. Not with me out a hundred and fifty grand."

"Heave to," the armed man called. "Stop the tub or I'll blow your brains out."

Jake grabbed her arm. "You're gonna give in?"

"You never saw anyone so yellow."

Chickie began to shiver. He looked dolefully at Anton. "Jesus, I wish we could just go fishin', like the old days."

The white boat had no name on its bow, no identifying numbers. Tommy had told Jake about them. Fast boats, built for the rum trade. They could run rings around a government boat. They'd steal every case they could stow, force the boats to follow them to a beach, and steal the rest.

"Ask the guy in charge to come aboard," Jake said. "Tell 'em they can have anything they want. You got no guns on board. But you need help to off-load. I'll hide behind the oil drums."

"Scared, Dempsey?"

"Just trying to figure something out. Listen to me. I know these *mamzerim*. I talk their language. Do anything you want, tell him you'll kiss him, but get the top guy on board."

The white boat came alongside the *Deepwater Angel*. Tommy told Anton to signal the other boats to stand by. Their skippers understood. They would never stand a chance making a run for it. They'd be overtaken in minutes.

"You've got us," Tommy shouted down to the speedboat. "Just don't start shooting. We don't carry guns."

"But booze, huh? From O'Hara? Move, bitch."

"I don't know any O'Hara," she said. "And please speak with respect to a lady."

Crouched behind oil drums, Jake thought he recognized a voice. A whiney high-pitched voice.

"Tell the whore to start throwin' the stuff over the side, don't go on board. . . ."

"Whaddya think, I'm scared?"

"Ya goin', boss, take a piece. Manny, give the boss a rod."

"Against a skirt I don't need a rod. Hey, she's good-lookin'. . . ."

Jake could hear Tommy ordering Anton to throw a ladder over the side.

There was a clatter of heavy heels, waves lapping, the noise of the boats bumping. Then thudding, as a man landed on deck. Then the sounds of two more men.

He peeked from behind the drums.

Shikey Frummer.

No question about it. Short, dapper in a fur-collared greatcoat and a black beaver hat pulled over his ears. The lanterns pinpointed lights on his waxed moustache. The little thug removed his hat and bowed. "A pleasure. Lady, what's your name? Whaddya got on board? It don't look like bicarbonate of soda."

Tommy lied. It was cheap booze, she said. Stuff from a floating "cutting plant." The other boats were empty. He'd waste his time unloading a lot of fake liquor.

"Good try, lady, but you're a liar," Shikey said. He smashed the butt of his gun against a burlock, reached in with a gloved hand and took out a shard. "Cut, my Yiddish ass. Look at that. Old Cumberland, eighty-six-proof. Start unloading. Anyone gets smart, this broad here'll have an extra hole to go with the ones she's got already."

"Anton. Chickie. Do what the man says."

Tommy's crew began tossing crates over the side. Two of Shikey's crew clambered aboard to help. Shikey did not pull his gun. He had two toughs with him who did no work but kept shotguns trained on the loaders. The bulky man on the flying bridge aimed the Thompson at the wheelhouse.

All my life I took chances, Jake thought. Then, stupidly, he said to himself: *Sarah will never forgive me if I miss Morty's wedding.* The old lust for violence was bursting inside him. Like sex, like the way some men craved the booze.

"I never seen a dame running a rum boat," Shikey said. He guffawed. "Jesus, look at the size of that broad. Tony, ya'd get lost in there, right?"

Tony, one of the men armed with a shotgun, said nothing. Women were not to be insulted. Even rum runners.

"What's ya name, beautiful?" Shikey asked.

"Captain Tuttle. Take what you want and go. I don't want any trouble."

Shikey patted his moustache and peered around the wheelhouse. He could see the other boats turning. "Hey, you wanna get your head blown off, captain? Tell those guys to stay where they are. They move, you're dead. Dummy, give 'em a blast."

The man on the flying bridge leveled the Thompson at the first boat. Bullets peppered the side of the turning boat, caused tiny waterspouts. The boat stopped.

"Through the horn," Shikey said to Tommy.

Tommy picked up the megaphone. "Stand to, Ole. Tell the others. No one will get hurt."

"Atta girl," Shikey said. He pinched Tommy's behind. "I seen it *all* now. A lady bootlegger. Ya must be workin' with somebody. Anyone I know?"

"Some man sent me the money. It's not my booze, you know that. I get three hundred dollars a boat, that's all."

"What else do you get, baby?"

Tommy walked toward the drums. Jake waited. She was working with him. Shikey had no weapon in his hands, but he probably was carrying one. Jake edged to the side of the drum nearest the open deck. Ten feet away, Anton and Chickie were tossing burlocks into the speedboat. Jake suspected they'd be there for hours. The armed men would keep them riding outside the channel. The white speedboat would need a dozen trips to off-load.

"Three hundred a boat?" Shikey asked. He followed her across the slippery deck. "Whaddya get without the boat? I mean, like if I wanna *shtup* you?"

A few hours ago Jake had been in bed with her. He had decided that he loved her and would marry her. To hear Frummer insulting his woman was more than he could tolerate. He yanked the .45 from his belt. It was a chance. They all might be blown to hell. But the old brute confidence, the stolid belief in the Chain luck, asserted itself.

Stealthily Jake came out of the darkness like a footpad. In one swift move he grabbed Shikey, coiled his left arm around the furry neck, and pressed the barrel of the automatic to his victim's right temple.

"Tommy!" Jake shouted as Shikey floundered. "Put the lantern on us so they can see!"

The brief struggle drew the attention of the men with shotguns. The man on the flying bridge had temporarily left his post. He was shouting orders at one of the boats.

"I got Frummer!" Jake shouted. "I got a forty-five next to his head! You want a dead man here? You want I should blow his brains out?"

"What the fuck's going on?" Tony asked. "Shikey? You there?"

"He's here, wop," Jake said. "Look at him."

Tony halted. He saw his boss locked in Jake Chain's iron embrace. Shikey's eyes bugged. His cheeks worked like pink bellows. The moustache seemed ready to crackle and fall apart.

"Kfff—kffff—kfff—Ch—Ch—Chain—"

"Take a good look, gentlemen," Jake said. "Look at where the gun is. Maybe you'll get me, but you'll have a lot of explaining to do to Mr. Schonkeit if I kill this *mamzer*."

"Shikey, whah?" Tony cried. "Who? Whah?"

"Eh, who's 'at guy?" a man shouted. He aimed the machine gun at Tommy.

Jake released his grip slightly. "Tell that son of a bitch to throw the violin in the water! Fast! You wanna choke to death?"

"D—dr—drop it," Frummer called.

The submachine gun splashed into the water.

"Now the guys with shotguns. Give them to the old guy and the kid. Anton, Chickie, get 'em."

"I want one," Tommy said. "Chickie, give it here."

Jake braced his back against the door of the wheelhouse. He dug a knee into Shikey's kidneys. The barrel of the black automatic never moved from the right temple.

"Listen to me. This is Crazy Jake Chain. You heard of me? This is my booze. These are my boats. First, you'll load back every bottle you stole. You don't move fast, this guy's brains'll be all over the place. Schonkeit'll cut your balls off."

Tommy leveled the shotgun at Tony. "You, start loading. *Move!*"

"Shike?" the hoodlum asked. "Is it okay?"

Before Frummer could nod his head, Tommy double-pumped the shotgun and fired a blast past Tony's head.

"Jesus, lady. I heard you. Jesus!"

"Move, assholes," Jake said. "Excuse the language, Miss Tommy. It's all these people understand."

Wheezing, pissing his pants, Shikey Frummer tried to squeeze words out. That bastard Chain! A gorilla! He was barely letting him breathe. There was no killing him, no stopping him.

"Listen, Jake," Shikey gasped. "Go easy. I'll choke. I'll die. I'm dead, they'll kill you."

"Your brother's dead and nobody killed me."

"Yeah, I figured. It was you blew him up."

"And you're next, if those ginzos don't work faster. Tony, move your ass. Tommy, next time take the bum's head off. Nobody'll miss him."

"Ch—Chain, gimme a break," Shikey cried.

"Never. Not to people who insult women. Me you can insult. But a lady you should never insult, Shikey. That's why I'm angry."

"Yeah, and a hundred thousand bucks' worth of booze."

"Booze I can always get. Apologize to the captain. Say, 'Miss Tommy, I am sorry I made dirty remarks to you.' Say it!"

Reduced to a lump of boneless flesh, Shikey mumbled his apologies.

In fifteen minutes the burlocks and crates had been reloaded. Jake now had to take a chance. He guessed there were still guns aboard the hijackers' speedboat. But they had three weapons of their own now. And Rayburn had surely paid off the local police to assist O'Hara's customers.

"Okay," Jake said. "All of you, back on your boat."

"Lemme go," Shikey whimpered. "Ten grand for you, Chain. Lemme go. I ain't kilt no one. I ain't even carrying a rod."

"Shut up. Who's the captain there? Show your face, sailor, or you'll have a passenger with no head."

A light went on on the bridge and a stout man appeared. "What do you want, Chain? Don't make trouble for me. I was just hired for a job."

"Get out of here fast. Don't follow us into the inlets. Just beat it."

"Understood."

Tommy added a few instructions. She thought she recognized the skipper. A man from Bayshore, a ferryboat skipper who'd graduated to whiskey speedboats.

"What about my client?" the captain called.

"He comes with me. You pull anything, you get out any hardware you haven't used, he gets it in the *kugel*. He won't be the first I had to stiff."

The crew of the white boat needed no further orders. They returned to the deck, cursing. Jake heard Tony refer to him as "a Jew ape, so crazy he's kilt ten guys already."

Tommy reversed engine and let the white boat pass. Then she led her convoy past the red jetty lights, through the bobbing buoys, and into the waterway to Rayburn's.

Mutt, Sal, and the brothers were waiting nervously. They had heard the bursts from the machine gun. Rayburn had heard that Schonkeit was determined to clean up along the south shore.

Jake tied Shikey's hands behind his back and prodded him off the boat to Rayburn's dock.

"Who's the cake-eater, pop?" Mutt asked. "Man, look at that fancy moustache. Fur-collar coat, shine on his kicks."

"An old friend. Shikey—what is your real name?—say hello to Mortimer Chain, my son and partner."

"My name is Saul. Chain, gimme a break. I'm just a guy on the make like you. I take orders."

"I don't. I give them."

The Ferrante brothers stared at the man. They wanted to burn him alive. Or perhaps weight him with cement and leave him to the crabs. Wasn't he the guy who got Vinnie killed in Plattsburgh?

Jake was glad Tommy did not hear any of this. She remained aboard the *Deepwater Angel,* giving instructions to the off-loaders. Rayburn had outdone himself. Half the local police department, two deputy sheriffs, three volunteer firemen, and a Prohibition agent were hired for the night's work. Each would get fifty dollars and a bottle.

"Nah," Jake said. "Why make more trouble? I want this bum to go to Schonkeit and tell him to leave the Chains alone. They tell me the Paymaster respects people with guts. Right, Shikey?"

"Burn the bastard," Baggie said.

Sal stroked his melting nose. "I'll do it. First ya stuff his mouth so he can't holler. Then you tie him up to a post or a tree. One can of gasoline. Burn like a Fourth of July sparkler. Right, Dom?"

The brothers nodded in solemn agreement. This man had murdered Vinnie. He had to be destroyed.

"I like cement better," Dom said thickly. "Two blocks tied to his feet. Cut his belly open so he sinks, and the crabs have a feast."

Vaguely frightened, Mutt listened, aware of the awful power his father had. As dreadful as the Ferrantes were, his father dominated them. Jake was smiling, enjoying Frummer's terror. They had shoved him, trussed, onto a stack of lobster traps. Behind them, the loading of the trucks proceeded. Buster Twine supervised.

Jake said, "We'll let Frummer walk home. With his hands tied and his mouth stuffed, he might make it by 1925."

"Chain, I'll make a deal with you."

"Shut up. You used filthy language in front of a lady."

"Lady?" Mutt asked. "What lady?"

"The captain. The woman on the deck."

Mutt squinted in the gloom. He saw a tall woman in a bulky sweater, moving among the men. A new one on him.

"I'm sorry, Chain. I apologize. Don't let these dagos kill me, please. I'll make it up with Schonkeit. You'll have your own territory."

Baggie hit him on the nose. Blood squirted, covered his mouth.

Rayburn ran to them. "Chain, no rough stuff around here. Nobody gets stomped in my boatyard. Take the guy into the woods. How dumb can these guys be? There's fifteen cops working around here."

"You're right, Mr. Rayburn," Jake said. "Dom, Baggie, lay off."

He settled the issue. Shikey would be left bound and gagged on the sandy shoulder of Sunrise Highway. It was five in the morning. At daylight, his fur-collared figure would be noticed by a motorist and he would be returned to the Paymaster.

The trucks were loaded and ready to move. Jake paid everyone off. He had enough money left to cover the police in the towns and the big payoff at the city line. The Brooklyn cops had doubled the price for passage. He'd handle them himself. They knew Jake Chain. Sergeant Pope had spread the word about the big guy with the free hand.

"Be with you in a second, kid," Jake said to Mutt.

He jumped aboard the *Deepwater Angel* and entered the wheelhouse. He took Tommy gently in his arms, kissed her, explored her mouth with his tongue, kissed her neck and throat and cheeks and ears, and said he would call her in two days.

"You're all right, Jake. But for God's sake, no more nights like this."

"On the boat or in bed?"

"You know what I mean. I value my life. I have a child. Go on. I can see your son trying to peek in. I hate breaking up marriages."

"Maybe mine needs breaking. So long, sweetheart."

Mutt could barely see into the dim cabin. What was going on? Was his father holding the big dame?

The haul from O'Hara's schooner made rich men out of the partners. They would now be able to buy a new cutting plant, own their own boats, and make deals with the biggest suppliers.

The new booze was contracted for and sold as fast as Goldsturm could mix it. The thirty-three thousand, six hundred quarts of unadulterated liquor translated into *one hundred and thirty-five thousand* bootleg quarts, labeled, corked, stamped, and crated. As an added insult, they decided to *undersell* Schonkeit by a dollar, charging nine dollars a bottle.

Gross profits from the shipload came to a little over one million dollars.

The money was a problem. They soon had fifteen bank accounts under a variety of names. Sal kept his share separate, a great deal of it stored in sealed tin cans buried in his father's tomato garden. Mutt and Jake shared some accounts, owned some independently. Others were opened in Sarah's name, in Hilda's, and under the names of Sarah's aged parents, the Klebanows.

The empire was expanding, a power that defied the lazy law, murderous rivals, and the bluenoses who feared legal alcohol.

Chapter 36

"Every time Brunstein looks at you, he looks like he's going to faint," Dr. Abe Heilig said. He glanced across the crowded beflowered tables at the Buffalo Manor. Mortimer Chain had married Hilda. The wedding feast had begun.

Eva smiled, shifted her weight. She was five months pregnant. The loose blue chiffon gown camouflaged her abdomen. She had come to the wedding without Halstead. No explanations were given. Seated with her family at a table near the dais, she tried to make herself heard over Willy Klugman's Brownsville Society Six. They were playing minor-key melodies from the old country. A drunken Heshy Otzenberger was trying to do the *kazotzky* and kept falling on his ass.

"Ike always looks as if he's going to faint," Eva said. "Poor man. I'm glad he's married."

Abe sighed. Brownsville was getting on. It was 1923. A good year loomed. *Brunstein married?* Progress of sorts. Brokenhearted by Eva (who wasn't?), he had married a radical firebrand, Yetta Maltz.

"I like the way the crowd is divided up," Abe said. "What a mixture. Only with the Otzenbergers and Chains could you find such a mob. One-fourth are carrying guns, one-fourth copies of *Das Kapital,* and the rest are respectable, hardworking people who don't know from such *chuchmas.*"

"Abe, you're being a snob," his wife said. "Isn't he, Dr. Abelman?"

"He's telling the truth," Abelman said. "For a hoo-hah wedding, there are lots of *gonovim* around."

The union of bootlegging and politics, long honored in the city and the nation, had been personified an hour earlier in the marriage of Mortimer J. Chain and Hilda Otzenberger.

That they were two young people in love, none doubted, least of all the Heiligs. As distant relatives of the groom, they knew the misery of his early life, the dreadful poverty of his parents' early years. And now *tri-*

umph! Wealth, power, a career—and the ripe daughter of Brownsville's political boss.

"Take a look, Sam," Abe Heilig said. "A whole table of Hibernians. Old Dullahan himself, O'Toole, Mulqueen, Roark. All drunk."

"Not so drunk, Abe." Abelman winked. "They hold it. It's a game with them. I was in Polachek's office in back. Jake's got a bar set up. His best booze. Those Irishmen are drinking it like it's seltzer, and look at them. Not a bleary eye. They live for it."

Eva shook her blond curls. "Dr. Abelman, you and my brother are a pair. Racial stereotypes! All Irishmen drink, all blacks are dumb, all Jews smart—"

"I never said that," Dr. Abelman said. "I just meant that some of Benny's friends are here because they like Jake's whiskey. It's their reason for living. It keeps them going. Dullahan's got to be eighty. I can remember the crook handing out cigars from the back of a Cadillac on election day. The bum once voted my father's name four times. Ten years after my old man died."

Sol Heilig rubbed thumb and forefinger together, said, "Benny knows where the power is. Someday it'll catch up with him. Maybe it'll even catch up with the Chains."

"Don't hold your breath till it happens," Abe said.

Sol's wife, Rose, a thin woman who affected a pince-nez and was studying for a Ph.D. in education, kicked her husband under the table.

"Ouch," Sol said. "Rose doesn't like me to make cracks about our cousin."

"She's right, Sol," Eva said. "Bootlegging is the government's fault. If they repealed Prohibition, the hoodlums would wither and die. People wouldn't get murdered, or die from poison liquor. Am I right, Dr. Abelman?"

"Like always, Eva."

"Anyway, the Dullahans and the rest of those bosses are through," Sol said. "They'll go the way of the dinosaur."

"Don't bet on it," Abe said. "While you and your kid investigators are interviewing witnesses, Dullahan will be a hundred and three years old and still running Brooklyn."

"Not true," Eva said. "I'm with Sol. We'll change the system."

"To what?" asked Abe. "To what *you* want? Or what Brunstein wants? Everyone's happy, kiddo. Jobs, food, booze, the stock market, Babe Ruth. This is *America Gonif,* Evitchka. I'm glad papa forced sour milk on us, so our bodies can handle it all."

Matla Heilig, the matriarch, blinked her eyes and dragged on a Sweet Caporal. She was sixty and worked seventy hours a week in her stationery store. She wore a black bombazine dress, two heavy necklaces of antique gold, and had her white hair done up in a pile of buns. The mention of her late husband's name awakened her.

"What? What about sour milk?"

Her three children roared. Memories of the house on Haven Place! The pitchers of sour milk, the old man's ledgers with his equations! Socialism must triumph! The square root of wealth divided by the square of man-hours, extrapolated as x to show productivity, and plotted on a graph to show profits . . .

Ike Brunstein's mind could not digest it. How explain the Chains? Were they part of the fabric of American life, like the flamboyant Jewish gangs of Odessa from whence his own parents had come? (Ike always felt a bit superior about his Ukrainian origins, amid the Litvaks and Galitzianers of Brownsville.)

No matter. The Chains were a force, part of the scheme of things. If not labor *shtarking* (how well Brunstein knew the value of a strong arm or a lead pipe), then bootlegging and God knows what else. He could say this for Jake and his son: The dynasty had begun with a noble heart, and was merely supplying a service now. Maybe there were worse things in the world. What he could not answer in his own mind was whether the Chains impeded or accelerated the triumph of the proletariat. *Neither,* he decided. When the workers' paradise dawned, people like Jake and Mutt would be crushed.

Other matters muddied Brunstein's mind. His own failures. He was in Glauberman's clutches. Hiring gangsters to win him contracts. Forced to sell out, compromise, pay off. A fine model to the Third International! He was glad Glauberman was not present to lord it over him. Something mysterious hovered about the Jewish Teddy Roosevelt's breakup with Jake Chain; it had come suddenly and angrily. Glauberman was now Melvin Schonkeit's man in Brooklyn. A man to be feared.

If I had Jake's courage, Brunstein thought bitterly, *I could tell the comrades—the party functionaries and theorists—what really makes America go, what the people want, what they respond to.* Not red flags and *Das Kapital.* Otzenberger, Chain, Dullahan—they understood Alexander Hamilton's great beast.

Ike watched Mort Chain, plug-hatted, in white tie and tails, getting a faceful of wedding cake. Morty returned the favor, ramming a chunk into Hilda's mouth. Flash powder popped smokily. The bride sputtered, hammered at him with soft fists. Mounds of white satin, her breasts shook in mock anger. Morty embraced her. Cake-to-cake, they kissed feverishly. He all but ran his hands over her rear end. She was lush and lavish, a woman suggesting harems. Her head would never be shaved and she would wear no *sheytl.* Hilda and Mortimer, Ike Brunstein realized gloomily, would inherit the earth. And maybe they deserved it.

And Jake Chain would get his share. Brunstein saw him—rugged, handsome, wearing his white tie and tails and shiny black topper like a society swell on his way to J. P. Morgan's.

Eva, too, was staring at Jake as he rose to toast the bridal couple. Ruddy-faced, his body straight and powerful, his gestures those of an athlete, he spoke haltingly but with authority. He knew he possessed power. Unlettered, crude, probably a killer, surely a mobster, violator of too many laws to even think about, he commanded respect.

"To my new daughter, beautiful Hilda, and my only son, my dear boy Mortimer, long life, happiness, lots of children, *l'chayim!*" Jake Chain said.

Applause. Cheers. Morty kissed Hilda again. He would not let go.

"By the way, what are we drinking?" Sol Heilig asked his brother.

"Real Concord," the doctor replied. "The rabbi gave it his blessing. It isn't cut with wood alcohol or prune juice. Jake saved a dozen cases for the wedding."

Rabbi Piltz, seated at a table with Shimen Klebanow and other elders of the synagogue, was rising to leave. He had done his work. The holy words had been uttered beneath the canopy. The glass broken. Vows made. Rings exchanged. No need to observe these goings-on. Austere, craggy-faced, a scholar of repute, he told his *shammes* to get his hat and coat.

Jake approached. "Rabbi, we haven't paid for your services."

"Mr. Otzenberger took care."

"Please, could I talk to you? In Polachek's office, if you don't mind? It'll be an honor."

Jake and Rabbi Piltz walked past the dancers, the wedding table, the remains of the giant cake ("shoulda had a bottle of gin on top," Dr. Abelman commented), and into a storage room, where the bar had been set up. A bartender dispensed the best Chain line—uncut scotch, rye, brandy, and gin. Clear-eyed, Dullahan and O'Toole and Roark were drinking purposefully and slowly, savoring the velvety goodness.

Each man bowed as the rabbi walked past. "Your Honor," Dullahan said, "a grand service."

"So it was. Grand." Roark winked at O'Toole.

And O'Toole: "An honor to all of us, rabbi."

Rabbi Piltz nodded but did not smile. Better these Irishers than the Lithuanian anti-Semites who had stoned synagogues and beaten Jews in the old country. In a sense he was grateful to men like Otzenberger, and possibly even Chain. They were Jews, they were Americans, and they understood the system. They spoke the tongue of the angry *goy*. God in his infinite wisdom sometimes put bad people on earth to perform (unwittingly perhaps) certain good deeds.

A Roman Catholic who drank whiskey with you and attended the wedding of your children (Rabbi Piltz reflected as he followed Jake into Polachek's office) was less likely to burn down your synagogue or beat your children.

In the office, Jake sat behind Polachek's desk. *Wrong,* he thought. It is the rabbi who should be there. Not me. He is the teacher, I am the pupil.

"A nice ceremony, rabbi," Jake said. "I am sorry I am not a better Jew. I never learned Hebrew. You know how I lived."

"And how do you live now?"

"I make a living.'

"Mr. Chain, I hear stories. I know about you. The Jewish community is a good one. In Brownsville we are building. Doctors, men of law, rabbis. Our children go to college. Merchants open stores. Life is rewarding. People worship God. Our faith must be part of our life. You are part of this, Mr. Chain?"

"Of the life, yes. I have no secrets. That I have no faith, I apologize. All right, I'm not a good Jew. I don't go to shul. I am not proud of it. I never learned anything. I had no parents. I learned to use these instead of my brains." Jake held up his blocklike fists.

"Joshua was a soldier. So was David. But they were good Jews."

"Maybe it was easier to be good then."

"The Jewish soldiers of our forefathers fought and died for their faith and for the Almighty. For whom do you fight, Mr. Chain?"

"For myself. I admit it."

The rabbi shook his head. "Solomon tells us to avoid those who 'lie in wait for blood,' to 'walk not with them,' and 'make not haste to shed blood.' "

"I'm sorry, rabbi. I told you I was a stupid man."

"Not so stupid that you do not understand, Mr. Chain. Solomon also says, 'So are the ways of every one that is greedy for gain, which taketh away the life of the owners thereof.' "

He spoke in Hebrew. Jake was lost; he admitted it. Rabbi Piltz translated what he had said into Yiddish.

"You make me ashamed of myself," Jake said. "I know what I am and what I'm doing. I don't hurt innocent people. The people I hurt are worse than I am. Thieves and murderers. Chain only hits back. He doesn't hit first."

"But you are part of this world of violence and blood and death, Mr. Chain. Maybe it is wrong for me to lecture you. But I performed your son's marriage and his bar mitzvah and I feel I must say this."

"I can't change, rabbi. What I do is part of the world."

"No, Mr. Chain. I knew about people getting their heads broken, thrown down stairs, factories burned, goods destroyed. Now perhaps you are doing worse things."

Jake did not smile. He reminded Rabbi Piltz how he had gotten into the labor movement. Had not the rabbi heard of the day he had rescued old Jews at Amsterdam Creek?

"Today what you do is different. But I am not a policeman. I am not the law of America." He got up. "Mr. Chain, I am pained to say this. You bring shame to the Jewish community."

"I'm sorry I'm not a doctor or a lawyer. But each of us makes his way the way he can. Mine was with my fists."

"Wrong. Especially for a Jew."

Jake escorted Piltz to the door, then stopped him. "I know Mr. Otzenberger paid for your services. But I want to help also. For the shul, rabbi."

He took a huge roll from his pocket, peeled off a thousand dollars in hundreds, and handed them to Rabbi Piltz. "Nobody has to know. For the school. The building fund. And there'll be more."

The rabbi shook his head. "Mr. Chain, tell me something."

"Yes?"

"This money you give me. It came maybe from the wine you stole from the government with my stationery? Forged papers, forged copies of my signature? Men who should know better, pretending to be rabbis? To you, it is clever. To me, it is a desecration. I have said nothing because I know you will bribe your way out of it, the way you bribed the *goyim* in the warehouse."

"I made sure you got your wine also."

"I do not want your thousand dollars. I will pray that you can be a different man. If not you, your son maybe or his children. Goodbye, Mr. Chain."

"With all respect, rabbi, I hope you are right. I'll give the money to the Brownsville Hebrew Orphan Asylum in the name of your synagogue. All right?"

"The deed is a good one. The man who does it might be a good one someday. Good night, Mr. Chain."

Rabbi Piltz left, and Jake made his way through the dancers to the Heilig table and asked Eva to dance. Just then, one of Polachek's waiters approached.

"Mr. Chain, excuse it, but there's a cop wants to see you."

"Cop?"

"Give him his ten bucks and tell him to beat it," Dr. Abelman said.

"A sergeant," the waiter said.

Everyone laughed.

"Make it twenty-five," Dr. Heilig said. "Jake, I hear prices have gone up. Some nerve, those chumps, coming around for a *shmear* during Morty's wedding!"

Jake excused himself. "Next dance is mine, Eva," he said. "And maybe a few after that." He followed the waiter.

A whiff of Eva's perfume lingered in his nostrils. The maddening desire for her would never leave him. It was useless, he realized. People regarded him as a clod, a killer with no feelings. He would go back to Tommy, his lady captain. Maybe he could love her and be good to her. And forget Eva.

Sergeant Pope was standing outside the checkroom. He looked pale and sweaty.

"Jake, bad news. Your place is burning."

"The plant?"

"Went up like a bonfire. A four-alarmer. The firemen been trying for fifteen minutes, but all that alcohol burns like gasoline. You can hear the bottles popping four blocks away."

Morty followed Jake into the lobby. Hilda, waltzing with her father, was oblivious to the crisis. She blew a kiss to her top-hatted husband.

"What happened, pop?" Morty asked.

"Fire. Our place.'

"Bad?"

Sergeant Pope nodded sadly. Oh, the income he would lose! The drop in earnings that would affect the morale of his men! The Chains had been good providers. "Total loss, the chief thinks. They can't control it. Jake, you guys must have bought up half the alky in New York."

"Let's go," Jake said. He took Pope by the elbow and started for the glass double doors, past the banks of carnations and geraniums, the displays of daisies, dahlias, and roses. No expense had been spared to make the Chain-Otzenberger nuptials the event of the Brownsville social season.

"I'm going with you," Morty said. "It's my place too."

"It's also your wedding, Mutteh. You got to stay."

"Like hell I do."

Father and son got their coats from the checkroom girl and followed the sergeant. Sal Ferrante, in a tuxedo two sizes too large, slithered after them. He had a sixth sense. He knew something bad had happened.

Hilda, gliding around the waxed floor with her father, holding the hem of her satin gown high, saw Morty leaving. She hobbled on spiked heels toward the doors. "Morty! What are you doing? What kind of way is this to treat your wife?"

"Be back soon, honey. Wait for me."

Hilda collapsed into her father's arms bawling. Benny understood them better than she did. You married a Chain, you asked for it. Who knew what those bandits were up to at eleven o'clock at night, in their cutaways, boiled white shirts, and stovepipe hats, running off with a sergeant?

"Papa, papa," Hilda wailed. "Make him come back."

"He'll come, he'll come, *ketzeleh*. It's his wedding night, right?"

Angry and vengeful, the three partners of F & C Cereal and Pacific Breeze Hair Tonic looked on as roaring flames devoured the cutting factory.

The scene had its idiotic overtones: Jake and Mutt in black toppers, soup and fish, snowy starched shirts and white satin vests stained with cinders.

Sal slunk around, his eyes unwilling to focus on the gusting flames and choking smoke that spewed from the blackened warehouse.

A half-dozen engines pumped water on the long brick building. Kolodny's old place, expanded, fortified, the garage added. Loading platforms, office, mixing room, storage rooms, all were engulfed in roaring cones of fire. The stench was overwhelming. The roof was a sea of boiling black smoke.

"It's Goldsturm's flavoring," Jake said unemotionally, sniffing the air. "He was using too much fusel oil."

"Son of a bitch," Mutt said. He wiped tears from his smudged face. "You think Schonkeit did it, pop?"

"Who else?"

"We'll cut his balls off," Sal whispered.

"Shikey Frummer," Jake said. "He gets it first."

Revenge, however, was hardly the answer now. Times were changing. They were in the big time. Like a corporation. Only they were not insured. Who would insure an illegal business?

"On my wedding night, the bastards," Mutt said. "Wasn't anybody on duty?"

"I forget," Jake said. "The wedding and all. Sal, someone was working here?"

"I don't remember. Maybe Buster."

The firemen had brought the flames belching from the doors under a semblance of control. But the smoke was undiminished, bubbling dark clouds of alcohol-fed fumes, pouring out to the street, fouling the air. Behind the brick walls they could hear bottles popping like cherry bombs.

Three firemen were prying at the oven-hot steel door with crowbars. A hose kept dousing and cooling it so they could approach it. The water sizzled and formed clouds of steam. Finally the red-hot hinges gave way. Under showers of water, the rubber-coated firemen pulled the door apart.

Two bodies were lying athwart the entrance. They seemed to have died— suffocated or scorched to death—trying to claw their way to freedom. Although the faces were blackened and peeling, Mort, Jake, and Sal saw at once who they were. Buster Twine. Professor Goldsturm.

Firemen dragged the corpses into the street. Chunks of flesh peeled from Buster's mighty black arms. Goldsturm's chickenlike body appeared to have shriveled to half his size. Crazily, the pince-nez was still on his nose. Cracked, but in place.

"Burned to death?" Jake asked. He felt a surge of emotion. The two had been loyal workers. Good men. Buster preached in the Holy United Army of God church. Goldsturm was sending a son to CCNY.

Pope and an intern from Brownsville Jewish Hospital leaned over the bodies. "Oh, boy," the doctor said. "Somebody slit their throats first."

The sergeant and the intern flipped the bodies of the chemist and the black man on their backs. Their heads lolled, unhinged. From ear to ear, each man's neck had been slashed, one long deep cut, severing arteries, ending life in a rush of blood. The blood had congealed in the furnace heat of the fire. Their faces and throats seemed smeared with raspberry jam.

"Run them hoses through the front door," a fireman said. "Bust everything standing."

Great arching jets of water splashed on the tar roof, on the ember-hot brick flanks of the building. Five firemen in rubber coats, helmets, and boots went through the broken door. Axes smashed against walls, doors, partitions.

"Bastards," Mutt said. "Buster was a good guy. And there wasn't a better mixer than Goldsturm. Pop, we oughta get those guys. Tonight."

Jake knelt next to the corpses. *You played rough, you lost sometimes.* Schonkeit, of course. Probably Shikey. But there were no witnesses. The two who had seen the arsonists were dead.

There was a chunk of scorched material in Buster Twine's right hand. Jake touched it. *Fur.* The fur collar on Shikey's fancy coat? The coat he wore the night he tried to hijack the *Deepwater Angel?*

"At least the new place didn't burn," Jake said. He looked across the cobbled street to the building they had bought for storage. Jake did some quick calculating—maybe three hundred, four hundred thousand dollars' worth of booze in there. Enough to get them started again.

Mutt was crying. Jake put an arm around him. The kid was nineteen. The Boy Wonder of Bootleggers. But a boychick, a child. And on his wedding night. Schonkeit's present.

Sal was on his knees, vomiting noisily into the murky river flowing along the curb. He had taken a look at Buster's head, at Goldsturm's slashed throat.

Jake thought: They had done a job. Killed the witnesses. A little torture, maybe. Maybe they had tried to tie them up and let them burn in the fire. Buster had probably fought back. A decent man. Jake would have to do something for his wife and his four kids. Goldsturm was widowed. They'd make sure his son finished college.

A fireman came out with a scorched case of Aberdeen Dew. "Here's one we saved." He laughed. "But there ain't much left in there. Jake, can you drink this without going blind?"

"Our top of the line," Jake said. "But look for some Glenderrie. It's the real stuff."

"We're ruined, pop, and you're kidding around?" Mutt sniffled.

"Not ruined, Mutteh. Stop with the tears. You're a Chain. You're not a dumb guinea like our partner. Look at him puking."

Sal was leaning against the red fender of a fire truck, heaving his cookies. Wedding cake, roast chicken, stuffing, the works. Polachek's kosher dinner was working its way up.

"What do we do, pop?" Mutt asked.

"What else? Go back to the wedding. I don't want your mother and Hilda to holler on us. Pope, you'll give us a lift?"

"Sure, Jake."

Jake turned to the fire chief. He was a popeyed man named Gallagher. Jake had kept him on payroll for over a year, contributed lavishly to firemen's charities, Christmas fund drives. They all knew Jake. A tough hebe who kept his promises.

"Chief Gallagher," Jake said. "Whatever's left inside and is fit to drink—"

His voice was smothered. There was a massive explosion. Flames roared through the roof. Goldsturm's vats, Jake figured. The big copper mixing kettles, detonating in the blast that drove them across the street, sent a dozen firemen flying out of the opened door behind a sheet of flame.

"—whatever's left is for you and the cops."

"Pop!" Mutt shouted. "It's all we got left!"

"Eh," Sal gagged, wiping his bleached face. "Eh, I got a say in it."

"Calm down, kids," Jake said. "It's a present for your men, chief. For Pope and all of his boys. You fellas decide how you divvy it up. Chief, for yourself, make sure you take only Mount Vernon rye and Glenderrie."

They walked toward Pope's prowl car. Coated with cinders, their formal garb wet with spray, the partners were silent a moment. Pope held the door open for Jake. He knew class when he saw it.

"Pop," Mutt moaned. "There's over a hundred thousand bucks' worth of booze left in there."

Pope gunned the engine. They splashed through the flooded street. A crowd had gathered. People knew what went on behind the brick walls of the F & C Cereal company. The curbs ran not only with water but with bootleg alky. Two stumblebum drunks were on their knees, sniffing the runoff, licking at it.

"Nah, it's almost finished," Jake said. He nudged Sergeant Pope in the ribs. He winked at Mutt and Sal. No point in being gloomy. Not on his son's wedding night. There was always the extra warehouse, where they had put away a supply. And there was Tommy and her fleet, and other friends he had made. And most of all, his undiminished strength and courage and cunning.

"It's generous of you, Jake," the cop said. "The guys will appreciate it."

"Appreciate, *fongool*," muttered Sal. "Givin' away my share. Who said you could?"

"It's goodwill for the future, Salvatore," Jake said. He tipped his plug hat to Pope. "Ask the sergeant. His pals would have taken it anyway, right? Between you and the firemen and the snoopers, there'd be nothing left. Right, Pope?"

"Right, Jake."

"So let's go back to the party. I ain't danced with my daughter-in-law yet."

Jake Chain was planning ahead. Shikey and his friends could expect a few surprises. And Schonkeit the Paymaster would someday learn about Crazy Jake, a man who enjoyed a fight.

1960

Myron Malkin's Notebook

We're sitting on a screened porch of a luxurious log-cabin lodge, Mr. Mortimer J. Chain, fifty-six (a tough and stringy fifty-six), and me, boy reporter.

The porch is on the second story of the ritzy rustic bungalow. *Bungalow?* It's like Wotan's palace—bearskins, stone fireplaces, beamed ceilings, redwood furniture. M. J. Chain's retreat in the Adirondacks. The place where his son, Martin, hides him for most of the summer. There's a twenty-room mansion in Palm Beach, I'm told, where they stow Mortimer the rest of the year. To keep him away from nosy people like me.

Below us an intercamp baseball game is in progress. Camp Spruce Grove, once owned by the Chain family, battling the visitors, Camp Holy Spirit, a Catholic charity camp further south on Lake Champlain. Distantly I see the cool blue of the mountain lake.

"What's the score?" Mortimer J. Chain asks me.

"Your kids are ahead. Bottom of the fifth. Spruce Grove five, Visitors zip."

He laughs. "I figured we'd have an undefeated season. The rich people from Great Neck pay six hundred bucks a summer to send us their *pishers* from Horace Mann and Poly Prep. But I always give a few free athletic scholarships to tough kids from Brooklyn. That pitcher we got? Blum? He's an all-city ballplayer from Tilden. His old man drives a truck. The catcher, the big kid? Brooklyn Tech. Joe Tuttle. I knew his family."

Mortimer Chain taps my knee. "Malkin, in kids' baseball, all you need is a pitcher and a catcher. You could put dummies in the other positions and win. Another winning season for Camp Spruce Grove. Four years in a row we'll be the Adirondack League champions."

He tells me he has no financial interest in the boys' camp anymore. Sold it after the war to an old NYU football star, Ed DiBiasi, who gives speeches on Americanism and sportsmanship every Sunday. But the Chain family kept the lodge overlooking the ball field, and a private beach on the lake.

"I never knew you were in the camp business," I say. "Uncle Doc never mentioned it."

"*Camp?* Who cared about a *camp?* I needed a place to drop booze from Canada. The camp was for fun."

I'm stupid. Lake Champlain. *Canada.* A gorgeous way to smuggle whiskey into the country. Mortimer J. Chain sits, lean, dark, hard-faced, long-nosed, in his wicker chair, hands clenched around his knees. He has black hair, parted in the middle, sun-browned skin. Kafka as criminal. He's smiling at my stupidity.

"I got a lot of laughs out of this place. Would you believe, Malkin, the counselors carried guns at night? That's right. When the campers were asleep, after the bugler played taps, we'd let the boats from Canada tie in at the swimming dock. You saw our waterfront? A nice cover."

I nod. A beautiful, immaculate waterfront on the pine-bordered lake— floats, docks, a huge canoe rack. And a hard dirt road.

"The trucks would be waiting. The speedboats would come in after ten o'clock. The counselors got five bucks each for helping with the loading. Before dawn the trucks were on their way to Brooklyn. That was after I took over from my father. He had good ideas, but I think I was smarter. I think I ran in almost as much hooch here at Camp Spruce Grove as he did on Long Island. And never a word from the Feds or the state troopers. To them, it was a boys' camp. Counselors from Cornell and Syracuse."

"How'd you get the idea?"

He shrugs. There is a lot of lean power in his shoulders and his arms. He's wearing a white LaCoste shirt, white duck pants. No fat on him. No signs of wear. Except for the huge dark glasses. At the edges of the smoked lenses, white scar tissue on his cheeks.

"My older kid, Martin, went to this camp. You talk to Martin?"

Yes, I tell him. No cooperation from the emperor of the Chain dynasty. But a pleasant meeting. (A lie on my part; Martin sent me packing.)

"I took one look at that lake, that coastline, the way the lake runs to Canada, and I said, Pop, we need a *camp.* DiBiasi was the perfect front man. A great running back for NYU. He beat Fordham single-handed twice. Anyway, that's how it started. Around 1928. Anyone score?"

"No. Your pitcher, Blum, struck out the side. Those kids from Holy Spirit can't touch him."

Morty Chain chuckles and shakes his head. "I hate to do it to them. Father Gurney is a good friend. But what the hell, winning is all that counts. I wish I could see a ball game again. We had a box on first base at Ebbets Field for years. I knew Max Carey and Dazzy Vance personally. Martin and his wife, they know from horses, not the Brooklyn Dodgers."

Joe Tuttle, the rawboned catcher for Camp Spruce Grove, belts a home run far into a stand of pine trees. Two men on base. The home team leads eight–nothing. Kids are screaming. Holy Spirit is taking its lumps.

Mortimer Chain hears the cheering and gets up. I tell him what's happened. His "scholarship" campers are annihilating the opposition. The former "Mutt" Chain sits on the log rail around the porch. In his excitement he whips off the smoked glasses.

He's blind. Photostats of the New York papers' reporting the attack on him are in my briefcase. God, he's been blind damn near ten years.

His eyes are two filmy gray orbs, disfigured, the eyes of a cold statue. But the face is alert, intelligent, hard.

"Your catcher is touching home plate," I say.

"Atta boy!" M. J. Chain shouts. "Give 'em good! I get a kick out of a winning ball team. I could have been a ballplayer myself but I started working when I was eighteen."

He's reminiscing. The taxi ride to Montreal with one of the Ferrantes. The details elude me. They're not in the literature on bootlegging, but there are old newspaper accounts about his start. One thing about the Chains: They laid low, gave no interviews, had a wondrous talent for evading the law. No strong-arm stuff unless necessary.

The Tuttle kid is big, rangy, and blond. The other ballplayers, rich Jewish kids from Fieldston and other fancy schools, swarm around him, lift him to their shoulders.

The name rings a bell with me. Wasn't there a Captain Tuttle? I'll have to check my files. Something about a rum-running boat skippered by a *woman,* a friend of the Chains'?

Mortimer puts on the dark glasses. "You saw my eyes, Malkin? What's left of them?"

"I'm sorry. I remember when it happened. My uncle Doc took you to a specialist on Park Avenue."

"Your uncle was right. We lived on Ocean Parkway then, but Abelman was a doctor I trusted. It was no use. They did a job on me." His voice is flat and calm. He's accepted his curse. The way he has accepted Martin's domination of the empire. "What good am I blind? I never read much even when I had eyes, so who could bother with Braille? Thank God for the radio. And I'm alive, right?"

"Right, Mr. Chain."

It's pleasant on the screened porch. Giant oaks and soaring pines cast late afternoon shadows. Cries rise from the ball field. I hear the sound of ball cracking on bat. A wonderfully nostalgic noise. Yet I can't help marveling at the lunacy of it. Mortimer Chain bought a boys' camp in 1928 so he could run booze from Canada!

"Didn't the parents complain?" I ask the sightless man. "All those rich people sending their kids to a camp that was a front for smuggling?"

"Most of them didn't know. Those snooty Central Park West *Yiddlich!* German Jews. They drank my booze. They liked the camp. They were honored to shake hands with the immortal Ed DiBiasi."

His wife is dead. Three years now. Hilda Otzenberger Chain, dead at fifty-five of a heart attack. She'd been a diabetic, overweight. I gather she was a tough one, with more than a little of her father's cunning and gall. It must have destroyed her when Morty was blinded. Schonkeit's mob had waited a long time to get him. (I've heard a story that a *woman* blinded him.) But in the end the Chains won. They survived. They made it to the top.

He asks me again: *What do I want?* A book? A magazine article? Never, he says. Plenty of stuff in the newspapers about the Chains. Why don't I talk to Lillian Halstead, who tried to prosecute them? Or talk to Eva Heilig, her mother? I tell him I have spoken to Eva. She's old. She wants no part of the story. It's history. Jake is dead. Morty is blind. Martin is a young tycoon, a prince of money and power, running his corporations from a tower on Park Avenue.

"Martin married one of our campers. My daughter-in-law Dorothy. A real German Jewish aristocrat." Pride in his high voice.

"DeeDee? The former Dorothy Grau?"

"Her parents were so ritzy they looked down on Sephardim. Old money from Nashville, Malkin. Can you imagine a German Jew from Nashville and my cocker of a Marty marries her? Her parents hollered, until they figured out I was richer than the whole Grau family together. By then we were in legitimate distilling, proprietary drugs, war surplus. You know something, Malkin? I once controlled every pound of calcium carbonate in the country. I never saw a barrel of it. I never stored it anywhere. But I owned it. I could sell it for my own price."

"Calcium carbonate?"

"That's right. And four or five other basic chemicals. Prussic acid. Sodium oxalate. I had five congressmen on my payroll and two federal judges. A director of the War Surplus Commission took orders from me. I set the *vontz* up for life."

"And he set you up in chemicals?"

"Up to my ass. I showed Marty a few things. We cleared over twenty million on chemicals. I figured it was time to get out. Real estate looked better." His pointed ears seem to twitch. I see Kafka again. Kafka as hoodlum, with his sharp nose, low-growing inky hair, blade of a nose, taut mouth. Cocking an ear, he listens to my ballpoint pen scratching on a copybook.

"Taking notes, kid?"

"If you don't mind."

"Do me a favor and don't write about us. Martin's got a few little problems with the SEC. Who needs this?" He cranes his corded neck and muscular throat, listens to the cheers of the campers. Uncle Ed DiBiasi is leading a sportsmanlike cheer for the losing visitors.

Two, four, six, eight,
Who do we appreciate?

Holy Spirit, Holy Spirit, Holy Spirit!

"We win big?" he asks.

"Eleven–nothing. That big kid, the catcher, hit a double with the bases loaded."

"Joey. Great kid. Don't tell anyone, Malkin, but he's eighteen. The age limit in this league is sixteen."

"But that's cheating."

"So? A few years? All the camps do it. If Father Gurney had a good eighteen-year-old pitcher, he'd use him. Who checks birth certificates?"

I watch a downcast Holy Spirit team pile into a yellow bus. They have natty maroon uniforms. I comment on them. Morty Chain tells me he bought them for the charity camp. He remembers when he was poor—as he puts it, "on the balls of my ass."

I explain my notion. A history of the Chain empire, from Crazy Jake, the *shtarker,* to Martin, the young captain of industry, breeder of prize-winning horses.

"No. Sorry you had to shlep all the way to Lake Champlain to get a turndown. What do you want from me anyway? I'm out of the rackets for years. So I was a bootlegger. So what? Yeah, I made a fortune. I made even more after 1934, I made even more during the war, and my son is still making it. You know why?"

"No, Mr. Chain."

"We don't quit. We don't take crap from anyone. Most of all, we're never afraid. *Never.* It's in the Chain blood from Crazy Jake down."

He wants to know about Cousin Eva. Is she happy in Long Beach? Does she need anything? She was always loyal to the Chains, even when she hated what they did. It goes back a long way, he says. Back to sweatshop days in Brownsville. . . . Did she talk about her brothers? Who could guess the Heiligs were related to the no-good Chains! Mortimer J. Chain chuckles. Dr. Abe, a surgeon. Sol, who ran for Congress twice, a special prosecutor, an aide to a governor.

A woman appears in the high-beamed living room. She's about thirty, very pale, and with soft yellow hair and a bovine face.

"My nurse," Morty says. "Miss Hanratty."

Some nurse. Hilda is dead, a victim of overeating and a bad heart. Of course he needs a companion. No eyes. But everything else is in working order. Young Martin keeps him out of harm's way, away from board-rooms, exclusive clubs, the corporate offices, comforted by a nurse-mistress.

"Go talk to my other kids," Morty says. "I'm as proud of them as I am of Martin. They didn't want the business. Okay by me. Davey's on a kib-butz in Israel. He makes jokes about our money, but I financed their hy-droelectric project."

"And Iris? Your daughter?"

"A famous Hollywood writer. You saw her last movie?"

I confess that I haven't. A crappy love story. It's apparent to me that his two youngest children have opted to break away from the empire. Martin carries on.

A file of younger campers, in swim trunks, slapping at each other with towels and herded by a weedy counselor wearing a T-shirt that reads DARTMOUTH A.A., parades under the porch.

Hi, Uncle Morty!

We won, Uncle Morty!

The nurse helps Mortimer Chain to his feet. "Hi, kids," he shouts back. The elder statesman of Camp Spruce Grove. Unbelievable. He now spends summers here like an old sage. Later Miss Hanratty tells me that he is widely loved in the area, endowing local hospitals and fire departments.

I shake hands with Mr. Chain. A grip like a clamp. Crazy Jake's strength. But he looks like his mother. I've seen photos of the late Sarah Chain—dark, pretty, with birdlike features. On his face the sharpness suggests a fox.

"Forget the whole thing, Myron," he says warmly. "So I was a bootlegger. The Chains provided a service. People needed us. Today, look what we do. Nothing but good. Maybe my two ringers beat Camp Holy Spirit this afternoon, but I buy Father Gurney uniforms, bats, balls. I painted his mess hall. The Chains go first-class and don't forget it. Give my regards to Mrs. Abelman. I never had a doctor as good as your uncle."

Miss Hanratty escorts me down the wooden stairs and into a clearing in a grove of pines, where a taxicab waits to take me to the Trailways Bus Company depot.

"He was glad to see you," she says. "He talks a lot about the old days in Brooklyn. People think he's so hard and tough, but he isn't."

There's more than professional care going on here, I speculate. I imagine Mort remains something of a sexual athlete. High-rumped and thick-thighed, Miss Hanratty is more than your everyday R.N.

"Thank you, Miss Hanratty. If he changes his mind about discussing the family, will you let me know?"

"He won't. Goodbye, Mr. Malkin."

The cab drives along a dirt road, past the neat green-and-white bungalows, the empty ball field, a mess hall glittering white in the afternoon sun, past a vista of Lake Champlain, where, years ago, the Chains smuggled oceans of booze.

PART III

1931

Chapter 37

Mort parked his white Pierce-Arrow, locked the doors, and squinted through thin January sunlight and banks of gray-black snow at the breadline.

It was twice as long as last week. A muddy river of shabbily dressed men. Ragged caps, lumpy coats, beat-up shoes. They hunched in the chill morning air, blew on callused hands, waited for the sluggish file to move into the Salvation Army soup kitchen that had been set up in an abandoned laundry.

Suckers, Morty thought. Bowl of soup, a margarine sandwich. That would be their day. When things went bad, you went out and scratched and screamed, made noises, made the guys in charge uncomfortable. And you trusted no one.

He and Jake had agreed years ago. Not a penny of their bootleg profits was to go into the stock market. Jake didn't understand it. He didn't believe in it. Mort, a shrewd twenty-two at the time, turned down brokers and salesmen with a smile and a handshake. He sold them his best booze even as he rejected their offers to make him even richer than he was. "Screw General Motors," Mort would tell them. "I don't trust any of them. I trust what I can see."

The breadline snaked past the empty lot where the old F & C warehouse had once stood. All that remained were piles of scorched bricks. Schonkeit's revenge. They had salvaged nothing. But Mutt's foresight in buying the auxiliary building had saved them. It was now three times as large; an adjacent "taxpayer" joined to it via sliding doors. It was no longer F & C Cereals. The phony grain company, along with its hair-tonic affiliate, had been liquidated. A discreet shingle outside the metal door read:

BROOKLYN GENERAL SUPPLY COMPANY

Mort paused and looked at the shuffling file of hungry men. He shook his head. They were blocking the garage. Deliveries would be a problem.

Worse, they would be pestered all day by men wanting jobs. It was no secret what went on inside the blind walls of Brooklyn General Supply. Even as Mort crossed the street, dapper in black cashmere coat and dove-gray hat, he could see Baggie Ferrante talking with three men. Italian words dropped into the conversation now and then. They were *goombahs,* begging for a day's labor. Italians, like Jews, detested handouts, the "re-lief." They wanted work.

"We ain't got nothin'," Baggie was saying. *"Niente, amici.* Full up. Every guy in Brownsville wants we should hire him. It's full up." His one-inch brow furrowed in commiseration.

Two trucks were turning the corner. The morning shipment from Free-port, from Jake's operation. On oiled hinges the steel doors opened. A whiff from Harris Weltfish's vats wafted out to the cold street. A few un-employed men sniffed the illegal air. The cops grinned. Steady income. Sergeant Pope had retired with sixty grand in his poke before Christmas of 1930. The Chains had made him a rich man.

Morty followed the trucks into the garage and nodded at Luigi and Stroonz as they locked the doors. The new cutting plant was twice the size of the place that Shikey Frummer had burned to the ground. The office, enclosed in frosted glass, was separate from the mixing and bottling area and the storage bins. It was a handsome office, well lit, spacious, furnished with heavy oak pieces. There was a wide oak desk for Mort and a smaller one for Sal. On the stuccoed rose walls were reproductions of "The End of the Trail" and "The Last Post." There were also framed photographs of Mort Chain with Mayor James J. Walker, Francis Fagan Dullahan, Ben-jamin Otzenberger, and other noted political figures. There were auto-graphed photos of ballplayers, boxers, and entertainers.

Mort was well liked in all areas—politics, sports, show business. Hand-some, dark, soft-spoken, a man of his word, a supplier of decent whiskey, always on time, he was ever willing to give a hard-pressed speak owner (now that the Great Depression was beginning to hurt) an extra week or two to pay. M. J. Chain had developed a reputation as the "Gentleman Bootlegger." Often he was called upon to supply beverages for society weddings on Long Island or in Westchester. He got to know polo players, men who played court tennis, traveled first-class to Europe, bred horses, sailed yachts, and screwed each other's wives. They all liked the sharp-featured young Jew. He had excellent manners, never raised his voice, and, for all his polite demeanor, carried with him a whiff of sulfur, of a murky underworld of mutilation and murder.

Theresa Ferrante helped Mort off with his cashmere coat, took the dove-gray Borsalino with the slanted brim, lingered long enough at his desk for him to finger her breasts. She shuddered. "Stop. Not in the office, Mort."

"Why do you think there's frosted glass on the partitions? To keep your brothers from peeking in."

"They suspect us, Mort."

"They're too dumb."

She was forty. He was twenty-seven. Unmarried, enslaved for years by her slightly daft mother, she had accepted a spinster's life. Yet she was a darkly attractive woman, slender, long-legged, with small assertive breasts and enough of a rise and swell in hip and buttocks to make men stare.

Mort had been making love to her in a room in the St. George Hotel for five years. She was a compliant and passionate mistress. Miraculously, her grim brothers had not the faintest idea that she was bedding down twice a week with their boss. Mort Chain would always have a remarkable talent of telling little, hiding things, giving nothing away. In that respect he was his father's superior. Blunt and iron-headed, the old man had used fists and courage to make his way. Mortimer was a different breed of cat—cautious, a planner, a man with a capacity to see ahead, to organize, to out-guess.

"Anything important from yesterday?" Mort asked. He sat behind his desk. In the office, he rarely took off his pin-striped blue jacket. Beneath it, he wore a sedate matching vest, a gold watch chain. His white collars were starched by a Chinese laundryman, and he favored dark blue or maroon ties. He rarely smoked or drank and he worked out four times a week at the Brooklyn Jewish Center, playing furious handball.

"Your father called. They're giving the new boat a trial run."

Theresa lingered. She looked twenty-five, not forty. Morty was intrigued with her. The age difference excited him. He could not explain why. And she was slender, mysterious. She always smelled of musty perfumes and wore a gold cross on her dusky throat.

"The big one? The seventy-five-footer?"

"Who knows? He said the new boat."

Mort nodded. Jake spent most of his time at the waterfront warehouse and dock. Five years ago they had bought Rayburn's Boatyard and converted it into a vast efficient operation for the delivery of seaborne booze. Radio operators worked with their fleet. Local cops helped guard it. Tommy Tuttle no longer went to sea but supervised a dozen boats under the Chain flag.

"Theresa," Mort said softly. "Five o'clock today. The St. George."

"No. I told you, my brothers are suspicious."

"Tell them it's school. You're taking bookkeeping at Brooklyn College, right?"

"I've been taking that course four years, Morty. They know I'm lying."

"Five o'clock." She placed his mail on his desk. He ran a strong hand under her skirt, stroked her naked thigh.

"Stop." She sighed. "Stop. I can't say no to you."

When she left, he stared a bit guiltily (or as guiltily as a Chain could) at the photographs on his desk. There was a new one of his wife, Hilda. She was getting fat. But a beautiful soft woman, with chubby red lips, a snub nose, staring dark brown eyes. She wore her hair bobbed and spit-curled. Diamond earrings dangled from pink ears. A five-thousand-dollar brooch decorated her proud bosom. Yet she did not look joyful. The red brick mansion on Ocean Parkway, surrounded by clipped privet hedges and a brick wall, the summer home on Lake Champlain, the vacations in Florida —none of these eased her moroseness.

The truth was, Mort reflected, Hilda was a spoiled, lazy, conceited woman. She did not golf. She rarely read. She ate too much. She refused to do any charity work. He wondered how she got through a day. There were three in help at the Chain house to look after the three children, to cook, clean, sew, wash, and drive.

But Mort was not a man to moon over a somewhat soured marriage. Theresa, thirteen years his senior, a moaning bed partner, supplied what Hilda no longer could. Dutifully, he made love to his wife, lavished gifts on her, and tried to keep her reasonably happy. Benny looked after the Chain interests, and Mort knew a happy daughter would keep Benny on his side. The Irishmen who ran Brooklyn politics—the judges and commissioners, Jimmy Walker's buddies—listened to Benny and did him favors. The next year, 1932, would be a Democratic year, Benny said. Hoover was a dead duck. The micks would want every Jewish vote they could get in Brooklyn. Thus Mort Chain and his hoodlum father remained favored men among the bootlegging fraternity. These high political connections, Mort understood, had often saved them from Schonkeit's wrath.

He checked his mail—bank statements, orders from customers, a complaint about the quality of the booze. One of the chief Prohibition agents in New York had "an interesting proposition" for Mr. Chain. Why not set the snooper up in a speakeasy of his own? He would take the heat off the Chain organization, and operate as a *customer* instead of a prosecutor. At a reduced price for booze, of course. He would expect to be supplied at half the going rate. It was not a bad idea, Morty thought, not bad at all. Corrupt them at their own request and keep them on the string.

Bored, Morty yawned. He looked forward to his five-o'clock rendezvous with Theresa. Forty years old and she often came nine and ten times in an hour. By contrast, Hilda had become lazy in bed, sluggish. She gave lavish bridge parties, entertained a growing crowd of "girls"—wealthy young matrons, wives of physicians and lawyers and "allrightniks."

Gloomy thoughts about Hilda were sweetened by the photographs of his children on his desk. In gold frames they smiled at him. The oldest boy, Martin, was seven. He was a Klebanow. Like his grandmother Sarah Chain and her deceased father, he was sharp-featured and slender, with intense deep brown eyes. There was a feverish energy in him. But the younger children were throwbacks to Jake, their paternal grandfather. They were large-boned and fair-skinned, with clear blue eyes and thatches of yellow hair. The younger boy, David, was five. He grinned good-naturedly at Papa Morty and the world. His chunky legs were astride a kiddy car. The baby, Iris, a year old, was fat and fair and resembled Davey.

Mort spoiled them all. He tried to make up for Hilda's finicky attitude, her disdain for the grubbier aspects of motherhood. She was affectionate but standoffish. Since the Chains were rich and help was cheap, there had always been a nurse or a maid to change diapers, wipe up after accidents, clean pools of vomit. On the maid's day off, Mort changed diapers. Often he fed and burped Iris. Hilda sniffled when he grew angry at her inadequacy.

"I can't help it," Hilda cried. "I'm sensitive. I'm afraid of *drek*. But I love them. I do."

"You're lazy."

"I want to go back to work. Why can't I work at the place? You could use me. I helped you get it started."

"Stay home and be a mother and a housewife like everyone else."

And, he wanted to add, don't come to the warehouse, because you'll get in the way of my happy hours with Theresa.

Chapter 38

"Sixty miles an hour," Tommy Tuttle said breathlessly to Jake, "and not even breathing hard."

"And with a thousand cases." He laughed.

The newest boat of the Chain fleet ripped through the Atlantic, cutting a creamy wake, roiling the choppy waters. They were well inside the three-mile limit, after a wave-lashed night unloading from a boat from the St. Pierre and Miquelon islands. As usual Jake paid in cash. He was a "priority" customer along Rum Row.

The new boat was seventy-five feet long, streamlined, powered by three Liberty engines. They had taken her out for laughs and she had run rings around a coast-guard cutter. Jake had two more like it on order. Soon the fleet would number twelve boats, all built with ample deck and hold areas for stacking burlocks and cases.

Long Island boatbuilders vied for the Chain business. The Depression had hit them hard. But rumrunners were flourishing. The demand was for even bigger and faster boats. Tommy had designed the new boat herself. A craft, she said, unfit for anything but carrying booze on short runs.

Anton was at the wheel. He was the best of Tommy's skippers, cool, bright, as skillful at navigating the channels around the coastal villages as he was at evading a Coastie or pulling alongside a rum boat. Now he was guiding the craft into the safe harbor of what was still called Rayburn's Boatyard, but which was, in fact, the Chain maritime branch.

Jake had long ago conquered an early disposition to seasickness. Tommy had taught him to be a sailor, helpful on deck, knowledgeable about lines, rigging, engines. She was in her late thirties now, a statuesque woman with the same open gaze, the broad pretty face, the thick chestnut hair. The woman who had attracted Jake nine years ago in Sheepshead Bay.

The new boat nudged the dock gently. A light snow was falling, dusting the pilings, the pier, the cream-colored stucco house Jake had had built over the foundation of Rayburn's place. It was a thick-walled Tudor mansion with fifteen rooms, a double basement, and living and working quarters. In the third-floor attic, Jake had installed a shortwave radio transmitter, with which he communicated with his own boats and, via code, with the rumrunners. A retired navy petty officer, a gray-haired man named French, ran the radio and kept track of seagoing trade.

Alongside the house was a three-car garage for storage purposes. It was rarely used. Jake had deliveries down to a tight schedule. As soon as a boat arrived, the work gangs, recruited from local police, firemen, and other civil servants, got to work stacking the whiskey into waiting trucks. No time was lost in trucking the cargo to Brooklyn.

Years past, Jake had taken care of every cop along the route. New policemen were broken in by old-timers. The last truck was the payoff vehicle. One of Jake's loaders was always there with a leather briefcase to *shmear* the bagman.

In the swirl of January snow, Jake and Tommy paused a moment to watch the crates being manhandled from the boat to the trucks. Jake had set up a portable conveyor—oiled rollers bolted between steel rods—to speed the process. Tommy shivered, squeezed his hand, and walked to the Tudor house. The only part of the business that interested her was the work at sea. They might just as well have been carrying sacks of turnips.

A northern wind whipped across the inland canals, piling snow against the high fencing around the Chain piers, around the edges of the great house. Jake could see a light in the attic. French, the radio operator, was on duty. He was widowed and lonely and never left his transmitter when a boat was out. A reliable man.

Patsy Camilli, a Ferrante relative, came by for the payoff money. Jake took him into the ground-floor office. From a Mosler safe he took out a black leather briefcase. It contained a thousand dollars in cash, more than enough to fix every cop along the way, and extra money for emergencies.

"The usual road," Jake said. "I'll call the plant and tell them you're on your way."

Patsy nodded. He seemed brighter than the other Ferrantes. He had attended Boys High School for two years.

"Give me an accounting," Jake said. "Pay the drivers and the guards the usual, and you get fifty, Patsy."

"Thanks, boss."

Jake took a .45 from his belt and gave it to the young man. "Only in an emergency, Patsy. And never on a cop. Them you *buy*."

Jake waited until the trucks were almost loaded. Grizzled old Rayburn, on the Chain payroll as a caretaker, opened the fence. He batted his arms, dusted snow from his beard.

Snow bit at Jake's face. He was pleased with the night's work. The haul was worth more than a million dollars after cutting, mixing, bottling, and sales. And they handled shipments like this two, three times a week. The

Depression might not have existed as far as the Chains were concerned. As poor as people were, they were always thirsty. The rich especially seemed thirstier than ever. They joked about booze, sought it out, compared brands, and looked upon their bootleggers as romantic heroes. The government's agents were the real criminals.

Jake returned to the house, after checking the trucks, wondering if perhaps he owed Sarah more than the two-story yellow brick house on Haven Place. It was by no means a bad house. Jake had bought it from Rimkoff three years ago and they now used both floors. But by comparison to his home in Freeport, it was a dump. Sarah never came to Freeport. The rule was firm.

It bothered him. He had a second wife, a second home. By all that made sense, he should divorce Sarah, marry Tommy, and cut his ties to Haven Place. But it was unheard of. One did not desert a crippled woman who had stood by you when you were a bum driving a wagon. A woman who had worked long hours, lived in a basement, raised a son. So the existing situation seemed to him the easiest: two wives, two lives, two homes . . . and two sons.

He dusted the snow from his boots on the veranda, removed them, and set them in the rack outside the door. Everything about the Freeport house was solid and durable. Oak, plaster, and cement had gone into it. "Strong enough to stop bullets," Jake told the contractor and winked. "Maybe strong enough to stop a cannon."

The builder understood; he appreciated his client.

In a bright yellow kitchen, Tommy, who had changed to an aqua velvet robe, was making an omelet with American cheese and green peppers. She was a talented "fry cook," able to turn out superb dishes using only a skillet and the stovetop. From years of going to sea, she told Jake. She could make do with a bare minimum of utensils and ingredients.

He kissed her cheek and hugged her. One hand stroked the firm buttocks beneath the robe.

"As your mother would have said, Jake, eat first." She pushed him away.

"I never knew my mother. Maybe I don't want to remember her or my old man."

"I bet he's sorry for what he did to you."

Jake wondered. He had no idea what had happened to Yussel Chain, the ne'er-do-well farmer from Lithuania. Maybe they could have been a happy father and son. Worked together. The way he and Morty got along. Two against the world. They had handled Sal Ferrante, made peace with Schonkeit, kept the cops and the judges happy, and now had an empire worth fifteen million dollars and growing.

They sat at the kitchen table, enjoying the tangy omelet, sipping hot English tea, munching on buttered muffins. It had been bitter cold at sea. Returning, they had been covered with icy spray.

Tommy laughed. She wanted to take the speedboat out and race the *Ile de France* or the *Normandie* just to see how fast she could push it.

"Kid stuff," Jake said. "Don't take it out unless it's for money."

"Oh, my smart Jewish lover."

"It's not the Jew in me, kid, it's the businessman. Never forget it, Tommy: There's more *goyim* bootlegging than there are Jews. Dwyer, Duffy, Higgins, Madden, all that crowd."

"They're Irish. They aren't *my* people."

"Close enough. I tell you something else I'm proud of. Morty and me haven't killed anyone in eight years."

Tommy shuddered. She did not want to hear about killing anymore. A tolerant woman, betrayed by a drunken husband, she had looked for security, someone to give her strength. The tall booted woman in the sou'-wester, her hair tied in a blue kerchief, suggested a seagoing Amazon, a distaff pirate. But the image was a fake. As Jake had learned in their eight-year liaison, she was unsure of herself and lonely until they began their life together.

"Don't tell me any more," Tommy said. She stroked his hand.

"I won't. I was never that kind of guy when I was a kid. I didn't start fights. It started with the union business. But I only hit back when I was hit."

Jake wondered: *Am I going soft?* Forty-six, and ashamed of his violent past. He thought of Moishe Nigger drowning in chicken blood. Of what he had done to Futka Frummer and his mob in the woods. And others he had *klopped,* leaned on. Most of them deserved it. But he had little stomach for violence now. He loved Tommy Tuttle. Someday he would figure out a way to get rid of Sarah. Guilt, a strange dependence, an old loyalty born in poverty, sent him back to the house on Haven Place.

A seven-year-old boy, rubbing his eyes, wearing a green wool bathrobe, walked into the kitchen. He was barefoot.

"Ma, I couldn't sleep. The trucks woke me up."

Outside they could hear the last of the convoy gunning its engine, leaving.

"Come here, precious," Tommy said.

The boy was towheaded. He had Jake's Slavic face and the rangy long-limbed body of both parents. His name was Mackenzie Tuttle, after his grandfather. To Jake and Tommy he was Little Mac. Jake was his father. Jake sometimes referred to him as "the Half Moon Kid"—the product of their affair in the Sheepshead Bay hotel. After Tommy became pregnant, Jake was more careful. They adored the blond handsome youngster but they wanted no more children. Her daughter, Lisa, was in a boarding school in Connecticut.

A story had been concocted for Little Mac's benefit. His father had died in Florida. The big man who gave him presents and came to his birthday parties and took him fishing was "Uncle Jake." Relationships were left vague. Little Mac was a happy child. He attended public school in Freeport, and was fast becoming a water rat, wise in the ways of the channels, streams, and beaches in the area, a powerful swimmer, a cunning fisherman. Summers, he went crabbing and clam-digging. His skin turned brown-gold.

"Uncle Jake, you gonna get me a two-wheeler?"

"Sure, Little Mac. Wait till the weather's better. The snow is no good to ride in."

Little Mac stretched. *My God,* Jake thought. *My son.* My little *shagitz.* He had lied to Morty about the boy, said he was Tommy's, son of a vanished boyfriend. Morty saw through Jake's clumsy subterfuges. He knew at once that the blond kid was his half brother. *The same age as his son Martin!* Mac, meet Martin, your nephew. How do you like being an uncle at age seven, Mac Chain? Mort wanted to ask. No matter. He did not hold the *mamzer* against Jake. He knew that his parents had no life in bed. Let the old man have his *shiksa* mistress, with the wide hips and the legs like a two-miler.

Jake asked the boy to come to him. He lifted him to his lap and stroked the yellow hair. A small version of Jacob Chain. Broad face, blunt nose, fair skin, big feet, strong hands. More of him in the kid than in Morty, or Morty's eldest, Martin. It was funny the way things worked out. He wondered what kind of life Little Mac would have. Jake resolved he would take care of him the same way he would take care of his three grandchildren.

"Kiss Uncle Jake."

"Nope. That's for sissies."

A true *goy,* Jake thought. No caressing and fussing for him.

"Go ahead, Little Mac," Tommy said. "Kiss Uncle Jake."

"He ain't my father."

"He's almost a father," she said. "And he loves you."

"Maybe the two-wheeler could come tomorrow or the next day," Jake said. "So there's snow, so what? When the streets are clean, you can ride. Right, mama?"

"If he's careful."

The boy bounced off Jake's lap and clapped his hands. "Oh, boy! Uncle Jake, I want an Ivar-Johnson! With a Troxell saddle!"

"You'll come with me to the store, Little Mac. Only one thing I got to ask you. You'll give the bike a name?"

"Sure. All the kids do. Racing Queen. Speedy."

"This bike I want you to call Half Moon."

Covering her mouth, Tommy laughed. Her crude lover was a romantic at heart.

"Half Moon? That's a dopey name."

"A favor for Uncle Jake."

"What's a half moon?"

"Something beautiful," Jake said. "Someday you'll know."

Tommy took her son's hand. She reminded him to kiss Uncle Jake, then led him to his upstairs bedroom. It was twice as large as Mutt's old room on Haven Place. But Jake felt no guilt. Mort lived lavishly now. He owed his first son nothing; he owed his wife nothing.

French, the radio operator, knocked on the kitchen door and walked in. "All under control, Jake. Patsy called in from Queens. They'll be at the plant in fifteen minutes. The cops took a little over five hundred this time."

"A bargain," Jake said. "I guess it's the Depression. They'll settle for less."

He yawned, stretched, looked forward to losing himself in Tommy's warm body, unwinding, restoring his manhood. In winter, on wet days, the old wounds ached and gnawed at him. His jaw became taut. The white scar seemed to expand, as if the jaw had been glued together ineptly. He rubbed it. He wished he were through with violence, shooting, killing, all the rotten stuff he had endured and inflicted. Maybe he was. They were secure, vastly wealthy, respected. Morty deserved a great deal of the credit. Smooth, secretive, a step ahead of everyone, he had built the business. With guile and planning, he had kept the most vicious killers, the Italians and the Irish gangs, away from Chain trucks and boats and warehouses.

We are good combination, Jake decided. A father who could not be killed. The man with iron fists. And a son who used his brains and his nerve and let nobody get the jump on him.

Chapter 39

Eva stopped at the apple vendor's crate alongside the newsstand in front of Bryant Park. She bought six apples for thirty cents, more than she could possibly eat. A gesture, she thought as she paid the vendor, a pointless one.

"Thanks, lady," the unshaven man said. His gray coat was held together at the waist with a rope, and there were streaks of dirt on his neck.

"It's shameful," Eva said. In her mid-forties, she had not lost her urge to lecture, improve the unfortunate, spread understanding. "The way you're forced to do this. Can't you find work?"

"You kidding, lady? I'm a machinist. They closed down my place in Joisey. The boss took the gas pipe. Every cent he made on the business was in the stock market. Hunnert and forty of us out of work."

"It's a crime."

"Don't tell me. *Apples, hey, apples, fi' cents!*"

Eva shook her head in anger. Nineteen twenty-nine had come. The prophets of Marxism were proven right. The built-in contradictions. The inevitable collapse. Nobody was in charge. Nobody cared. What next for the country? She cursed herself for not having answers. She saw nothing hopeful in the future. President Hoover and his dull-headed advisers (several of whom were friends of her father-in-law) kept assuring the people that prosperity was just around the corner.

The truth was, the labor movement depressed her. Between the Communists, the gangsters, and the stricken bosses—many of them ruined—the movement was in disarray. Her heart still went out to the underpaid, exploited, weary people at the machines. How they remained so honorable and hardworking, how they raised children who struggled to go to CCNY, to improve their lives, continued to astonish and delight her. Garrison agreed. It was what had fascinated him about Jews. The life force in these ghetto people amazed him. And there were good, honest, overworked union officials—bedeviled, underpaid, hounded by criminals.

Perhaps, Eva thought ruefully, I was never anything more than a symbol of Garrison's admiration for working Jews. Less of a wife, hardly a mistress, a late-in-life mother, but always a symbol. Not the soundest basis for a good marriage.

Sol, in a brown tweed topcoat and a vested green suit (as befitted a newly appointed state official), was motioning her toward a bench. He had picked one in the sunlight. A few bums in various states of alcoholic decomposition surrounded the bench.

A chunky man with frizzy brown hair and a wry smile on his gentle face, Sol Heilig fooled people. Beneath the paunchy exterior there was a core of steel. A scholarship boy at NYU Law School, he possessed a keen mind. A "reform" Republican, a freak in Brooklyn, he had decided to devote his life to public service. Let the Leo Glaubermans make the big bucks. Let others struggle to worm their way into fancy New York firms. Sol liked politics. He enjoyed being an underdog. Old friends in Brownsville had never understood why he had become a Republican. The party of the rich, the bosses, the oppressors, the party of Harding, Coolidge, and Hoover?

Sol would wink and laugh his noiseless laugh. "Democrats and Socialists we got by the barrel in Brooklyn," he would say. "Some Jews should be Republicans. Besides, how else do I get to be county chairman, get on committees, get my name in the paper?"

Benny Otzenberger, Democrat to the marrow of his mammoth bones, scorned Solomon Heilig for this defection. A Socialist he could understand, even a Communist. Like that shmuck Brunstein, who had to beg Melvin Schonkeit to save his *tuchas*. But Eva Heilig's brother?

Sol kissed Eva's cheek and hugged her. A ragged bum tipped his frazzled fedora and rolled off the bench to make room for her.

"Oh, I'm sorry," Eva said. "We could move . . ."

" 'S all right, lady."

The man walked away, his feet slithering, his legs dancing to a diseased rhythm in his muddled head.

"Jake leg," Sol said. "From bad alcohol."

"Named for our esteemed cousin?"

"Hardly. Although it might be appropriate. They get it from drinking alcohol distilled from Jamaica ginger."

"How do you know so much about whiskey, my abstemious brother?"

"We prosecutors get to know these things. Eva, I'm becoming an authority on loan sharks, goons, bootleggers, *shtarkers,* and other assorted villains. It's fascinating. Things Marx and Engels never dreamed about."

"Coming from Brownsville must be an asset."

"And how. I'm regarded as the office tough guy."

"You, Solly? You're a cream puff, a charlotte russe."

"Don't be so sure, Evitchka. I was a great punchball player in my day. I could hit two sewers. I didn't like to fight, and mama said I had weak ankles, but I was a champ at Chinese handball."

Sol's wife and kids were fine—healthy, vigorous, showing all of the

Heilig enterprise and cheerfulness, plunging into schoolwork and neighborhood activities. His older boy had won six merit badges with the Boy
Scouts and was on his way to becoming a Life Scout.

"A whiff of fascism just passed my nose, Sol."

"Eva, for God's sake. That stale radicalism of yours."

"Not so stale. Look at Europe. Mussolini, Hitler. Every country has
some kind of reactionary demagogue. And here, Coughlin and all kinds of
right-wingers surfacing. Your Republicans are better?"

"We are. So are the Boy Scouts. And so are the Democrats. I don't sell
the system short."

He opened a *New York Times* he had under his arm. Governor Franklin Roosevelt was cracking down on the rackets. He'd asked his special
commissioner, Mr. Seabury, for minutes of the hearings on rackets. A
district attorney was about to be removed for inefficiency. The man had
complained to Seabury that "racketeers are virtually immune from punishment." The D.A., an elderly man, had protested that he was helpless against
gangsters who infested the business structure of the city.

"Don't tell *me*," Eva said. "My old enemies in the needle trades."

"Not just there. Trucking, building trades, food. From both ends. And
not only in the unions. The bosses also. In fact, these rats *are* the bosses
today. They were sneaked in, they did their dirty work, and they took
over."

Eva was solemn: memories of Jake as her first enlistee.

Sol explained that the belief was that Franklin D. Roosevelt would make
a run for the presidency. He had to come in clean in his own state, a crusader who had knocked the political-underworld alliance out. Mayor
Walker was sure to get hit. Most of the crooked politicians were in Roosevelt's own party and most of them were in New York City. But the governor was shrewd and tough. The wheelchair and the aristocratic manner
hid a man of vision and strength. He'd picked the Republican Seabury,
thorough and intelligent, to investigate rackets. The D.A.'s were scared
stiff of the new prober, a circumstance that delighted Sol.

"I'm a small fish in a big pond," Sol said happily. "But, boy, will I enjoy
nailing some of these rats."

"Sheriff Sol Heilig to the rescue," she giggled. "Two-gun Heilig."

"Luckily I got a famous surgeon for a brother. I get shot up, the way
our cousin Jake used to, Abe can stitch me up. Anyway, these bums don't
go after people like me. They kill their own kind. Every time Jake got shot
at, it was some other gangster. Police, D.A.'s they leave alone."

With new respect, Eva studied his round, good-natured face and remembered him as a boy, with his eyes riveted on a textbook, furiously making
notes on a yellow pad, making *extracts* of his notes, getting the pith and
substance of his courses. His mind could summon up a word or a phrase—
separation of powers—and a whole paragraph would flow from his pen,
accurate, precise, worthy of a teacher's "A" and a "well written." He'd

graduated Phi Beta Kappa from CCNY and at the top of his class from law school. Withal, he wore his intelligence lightly. People liked Sol Heilig. Even the hoodlums he interrogated found they enjoyed talking to this rumpled pudgy man from Brownsville.

Sol told Eva that Schonkeit had emerged as the First Lord of Crime. It had begun in the mid-twenties, when union leaders had come to him for help. The Paymaster, a respected figure, soon became a mediator between employers and workingmen. For these services (and for fixing police and judges) he was paid vast sums, by *both* sides. Fees as high as half a million dollars to settle a strike were not unusual.

"Ike?" Eva asked.

"He's been to him. Ike's in trouble up to his neck. He paid Schonkeit to back the Communists and now he's sorry. Ike is not an immoral man, Eva. He's got a good heart. But when he saw that the Red flag wasn't going anywhere, he hired guns. Schonkeit couldn't care less about politics. Money interests him. What's soured Ike is that, at the last furriers' strike, Schonkeit worked for the bosses. His goons, Frummer and Wesselberg, were beating up strikers."

"He is a fascist," Eva said. Rage splotched her cheeks.

A panhandler shuffled by. Eva gave him an apple and a quarter. He tipped his hat.

Sol shook his head sorrowfully. A city, a nation of beggars. "Melvin Schonkeit is no fascist. He's a moneyman. They all come to him—real estateniks, gamblers, garment-industry people, bookmakers." Sol frowned. "It's crazy. He's a middle-class boy from a good family. He has the golden touch. Know how he got it?"

"With guns."

"Wrong. By betting on sure things. Schonkeit is a gambler. But only when the odds are big and he knows he has to win. He started past-posting when he was a teen-ager."

"Past—?"

"Getting the results of races from a tipster at the track. Then placing a bet *after* he knew the winner. They've never found out how he did it. He's fixed fights, ball games. He's run fifty stock swindles. He pulled out of the market with ten million dollars from his bucket shops a week before the crash. He's a wizard."

"A disgrace."

Eva sighed and crossed her silk-clad legs. Two bums stared and staggered away. Bryant Park. Memories of gracious old New York. And the library, full of books that could save the world. But the world hardly seemed ready for salvation. The foundations were shaking. Nothing was simple anymore. Old answers were immaterial. Melvin Schonkeit seemed to run half of New York.

"He's taken over several firms in the garment industry. You see, they depend on trucks. He controls trucking through his gangsters. All he has to do is pull a drivers' strike, and goodbye to the fall line. Frummer and Wesselberg took over factories in the garment district. They forced them to close, then moved in. Ike was in a rage. The father and son who owned one factory committed suicide. Now the workers are forced to accept a wage cut and have to kick back a buck and a half a week to Schonkeit."

"This is outrageous." *Wesselberg*—who tried to rape her.

"Eva, being married to Garry and making hoo-hoo speeches on birth control and interviewing Mr. Gandhi aren't the same as getting your hands dirty in the labor movement. Anyway, we're going to nail Frummer and Wesselberg. Ike is getting ready to cooperate with us. He knows enough to send Schonkeit to jail. And maybe send Shikey and Herman to the electric chair."

"Good God. Will Ike be protected?"

"Of course."

Eva blinked in the morning sunlight. A rush of pity for Ike overwhelmed her. Poor adoring Ike with his mooning eyes and ratty moustache. Chained now to Yetta, a firebrand writer for the *New Masses* and *The Daily Worker*. He was in double jeopardy. The Communists would disown and denounce Ike for revealing that the party had hired gangsters. The hoodlums would seek vengeance.

"Ike wants to do this?"

"I convinced him on the basis of old Brownsville loyalties. He asked me a funny thing. He said, 'Sol, I've known you a long time, and I know you know how I admire your sister Eva.' I said I knew. So he asked me did I think you would approve of his talking and would I ask you."

"You never did."

"So what? I told him you approved. You do, don't you? The labor movement is changing. There are good men gaining power. Real leaders, men concerned with hours, wages, conditions, education, medical help. People like Potofsky, Dubinsky, Hillman. They want the movement cleaned up. Ike can help us get rid of parasites like Frummer."

"You used my name without my permission?"

Sol tucked the *Times* into his bulging briefcase. "The magic words. Eva Heilig Halstead. He's in love with you, the shnook. I mentioned your name and he looked like a bloodhound with a bad stomach. Sorry, but that's how a special investigator gets things done."

"I don't admire you for duping Ike that way."

"He'll recover."

Sol got up. They munched on apples and walked toward the subway station at Sixth Avenue. "Listen, Eva. There's racketeering in twenty-six industries in New York. The poor guys on the machines, at the cutting tables, with paintbrushes in their hands, they're getting a screwing. It's got to stop. The bosses get away with it because Schonkeit is the connection between gangsters and politicians. Roosevelt can't allow that if he wants to be president. We're helping workingmen get rid of murderers like Frummer. Ike's doing the right thing."

"But his safety—"

"Forget it, will you, Eva?"

He asked her about Garrison, about her seven-year-old daughter, Lillian. Eva seemed tentative in her responses. Garrison was traveling a great deal. He was in California at the moment, reporting on Upton Sinclair's EPIC movement, doing articles for the *Nation*. Lillian (whom Sol could not have seen more than a dozen times) was attending the Little Red Schoolhouse. She was a bright, moody child, already competing with her mother by writing compositions.

"Got a picture of her?"

"I'm afraid not, Sol."

He said nothing. Eva seemed cold and detached. Something compassionate and warm was lacking in her. All her heart, her emotion, had gone into political movements, social reform. The marriage had to be a bit sour. He invited her to a Passover seder the following week. Garrison always enjoyed those he had attended. He remained a sincere philo-Semite. Little Lillian, Sol recalled, had loved the singing and the rituals. Matla would be there. And Abe and his family.

"I'm not much on religion, Sol. I never have been."

"So what? We're your family, kiddo. The Heiligs of Haven Place. It's a short ride to Brooklyn."

She shook her head. Sunlight gleamed on the edges of the tight curls. How beautiful, Sol thought. Brainy, courageous. Maybe she'd been loved too much. All that worship—from the laboring girls, from Jake, from Ike, from her rich husband.

"I'm going out of town next week. Speech in Chicago for the birth-control movement."

"As usual."

They stopped at the subway entrance. Sol looked at an afternoon headline. The king of Spain was out on his royal *tuchas*. They were declaring a republic. Progress, progress. "You and Garry are away a lot. Who looks after Lillian?"

"Sol, we're rich. There's always three in help. Lillian likes it better that way. At least that's what she tells mommy."

When he had descended the IND steps, leaving her to hail a cab—she was off to a meeting at the League for Industrial Democracy—he worried about her.

Curious, Sol thought. She had not asked about Jake and Mort Chain, their underworld relatives. But what was there to ask? Sol had seen the file on the Chains. It was three inches thick. Under the protection of Otzenberger and Dullahan, they had prospered beyond anyone's imagination. Phone taps, stolen records, interrogation of disaffected hoodlums who had

worked for the "Brooklyn General Supply Company" indicated that the
Chain bootleg empire was now worth in excess of twenty-five million dollars.

Hoo boy, thought Sol as he put his nickel in the slot, will they be in for
a surprise when Prohibition ends! They could retire on their millions, of
course. But it was no secret that Roosevelt would run. And Roosevelt
would win. And that would be the end of the Volstead Act and fortunes
made from illegal booze. He shed no tears for the Chains.

A week later Ike Brunstein began to talk. Once his lips opened, the flood
of words drowned Sol's office. Two stenographers were needed to get the
story down. Ike had made his mind up. For once in his life he would do
something courageous.

For a week Brunstein sat in a guarded hotel room, while Solomon Heilig
got him to spill his guts.

Shikey Frummer, under Schonkeit's patronage, had formed a "truck-
men's association," Ike revealed. Delivery prices for the garment industry
were hiked. Frummer got the biggest share. His *shtarkers* divided another
huge chunk, leaving the drivers with less than they had earned before.

For Shikey, the sleek brother of Futka, this was a mere start. Along
with Herman Wesselberg, the elephantine Meal Ticket, he founded "part-
nerships" with terrified manufacturers. They began to ship unfinished
garments out of New York for completion in nonunion shops. Honest
union officials of the Amalgamated Clothing Workers and the International
Garment Workers Union battled Shikey and the Meal Ticket. These honorable men demanded better wages, hours, and conditions for their people,
and no more out-of-city work. In defiance, Shikey increased the scab work.
A protesting shop steward had his throat slit.

Cutters, most of them aged Jews who were wary of a fight with the
gangsters (Ike told Sol), tried to keep tabs on garments being trucked out
of New York for "finishing." It was useless. Garments kept leaving New
York to be completed by low-salaried workers in New Jersey and Connecticut.

Acting on Brunstein's information, an attempt to strike back at the gangsters was launched. Sol demanded—and, surprisingly, got—the cooperation of the police commissioner. FDR's cleanup was having good effects.
For once Schonkeit's power was frustrated. Public officials feared the Seabury Commission. They saw that Roosevelt meant business and that his
appointees could not be bought off. A corrupt local run by stooges of
Frummer and Wesselberg was raided and the books impounded. It took no
mathematical genius to see that the crooked officials, besides indulging in

illegal trucking, had misappropriated eighty-five thousand dollars of the unemployment relief fund.

The morning after the raid, younger union officials, elected by the workers, took over the local. For the moment Frummer and Wesselberg were stopped. They were forbidden to use their trucks to remove unfinished garments. The new leaders had won a temporary victory on the basis of Ike's testimony.

Ike, under police guard twenty-four hours a day, whether in the investigator's office or at home in Flatbush with pouting Yetta, or in the secret hotel room, sang and sang and sang. Frummer and Wesselberg raged. *That punk! That dirty yellowbelly of a Red!*

Three weeks after Ike began to talk, subpoenas were served on Saul "Shikey" Frummer and Herman "Meal Ticket" Wesselberg, together with six union officials they had illegally installed.

The investigator who took the depositions from the new union officials, and the outraged cutters, furriers, pressers, and deliverymen in the needle trades, was Solomon Heilig. The source of his information—the former Socialist, former Communist, full-time idealist Isaac Brunstein—was now locked into a suite of rooms in the Whitman Manor Apartments in Dyker Heights, Brooklyn. Ike had a view of the Narrows, of April's greening trees, and two city detectives who lived with him around the clock while he sang.

"A bird in a gilded cage," Ike said humorlessly to his guardians.

Out on bail and in defiance of a court order, Frummer and Wesselberg came to see Schonkeit at the Polo Pony Club.

"We got to lean on that canary Brunstein," the Saratoga Avenue Meal Ticket said. "We shut his mouth, we'll be okay."

Shikey sipped celery tonic. "Heilig got no case without him."

Schonkeit counseled caution—at the right time he would fix a judge. His subordinates looked glum and frightened. It wasn't working too good anymore. The industry wasn't totally in their control now that Roosevelt demanded action. The crippled *shmuck!* He wanted to be president. Seabury would not stop until they caught a few big fish.

"I don't like being a pike or a carp, Mr. Schonkeit," Wesselberg said. "I been loyal to you. Me and Shikey. What are you gonna do to help us?"

"When you need help, you'll get it," the Paymaster said. He sipped milk.

"We got to kill Brunstein," Shikey whispered. "Before he kills us."

"No," the Paymaster said. "You do, you'll be sorry."

"How about that *putz* Heilig?" the Meal Ticket asked. "He started this."

"Herman, you never kill a cop or a D.A. or an investigator. You kill them only if they take and then double-cross you."

They didn't like it. Shikey and his friends feared indictment. Heilig was getting tons of information from old union stiffs—the frightened, pasty-faced shlemiels who worked in the lofts. Brunstein, opening his yap, had given them courage. There were rumors that the Wallowitz case was being reopened. Shikey shuddered.

"I'll get Leo Glauberman to defend you," Schonkeit said airily. Through the smoky haze, he signaled a waiter by tapping a diamond solitaire against his glass. He wanted another tumbler of Borden's Grade-A. It was good for his ulcer.

Shikey's manicured hands brushed his sleek ebony hair. "Mr. Schonkeit, from what I hear, Glauberman is next. Heilig ain't stopping with us. If Leo sings, what happens? Maybe even you—"

"Please, Shikey," Schonkeit said. "You're giving me a headache. Glauberman will plead lawyer-client privilege. When the time comes, we'll handle Brunstein, Heilig, all of them. Anyone can be bought."

Chapter 40

Morty, refreshed after his hour in the St. George Hotel with Theresa, came home to a late supper. He always approached the three-story sprawling house slowly, his eyes alert for movement, signals. If there was trouble, Hilda and the servants knew, the tall exterior lamp, standing amid the privet and hawthorn, was to be lit. Real trouble: the carriage lamps on either side of the massive front door were to be turned on.

It was dusk. Only the interior lights, behind pale yellow chiffon curtains, illuminated the high mullioned windows. He always stopped the Pierce-Arrow outside the garage, unlocked the door, and turned on the interior light before parking it. His father had taught him caution. Ever since the ambush at Haven Place, when Jake had absorbed twelve bullets, the old man had told him: *Go slow, look, see what's behind you.*

The garage was immaculate. Harry Twine, Buster's twenty-two-year-old son, employed as a man-of-all-work at the Chain household, opened the door from the garage to the house. "Evening, Mr. Mortimer." He was carbon black, tall and broad-shouldered. Harry served as a butler, in white coat and white gloves. He could also rake, seed, and fertilize the lawns and backyard garden. And he was a whiz at repairs, from carpentry to wiring. His younger brother, Eddie, was a foreman at the Chain warehouse. Jake and Mort were supporting six members of Buster's family. If a man got his throat sliced for them and was burned to a charred chunk by monsters like Frummer, then his family deserved a break.

"Hi, Harry. Quiet?"

"Your in-laws here."

Mort groaned to himself. *Benny and Jessie.* All he needed.

After a strained dinner—Hilda full of complaints, Mort engaged in reading box scores to Martin—they retired to the living room. Hilda and her mother sat near the arched stone window and listened to Rudy Vallee on the floor-model Zenith. Soupy music issued from its mahogany hull.

Mort and his father-in-law settled into easy chairs apart from the women.

"You better look ahead, son," Benny said. He lit a dark brown Partagas. "When Roosevelt lets everyone buy real booze, the game is over. You and Jake should start looking for another business. But not unions. That'll be even worse. They'll be honest."

Mort nodded. He'd see to it that the next generation of Chains would never suffer the stain of the preceding two. No strong-arm stuff, no guns, no bribing of cops. It would all be legit. And far more lucrative than selling rotten whiskey.

"I think I'll give Hilda a birthday present," Mort said suddenly.

Hilda's ears perked. She looked across the parlor. *"Huh?* What kind of present? That sunburst brooch I wanted from Tiffany's?"

"No, sweetie. A trip to England. Maybe France also."

"Ooooh, Morty!"

"You'll need a whole new wardrobe, *tsatske.* The works. The Chains go first-class."

She heaved herself out of the overstuffed chair, jiggled toward her husband, embraced him, and covered him with soggy kisses. He liked it. She was beautiful, *zaftig,* smartly dressed, aromatic of expensive perfumes. He patted her bountiful butt. "When, *when,* Morty?"

"Soon, Hilda. Just you and me. No kids."

"Like another honeymoon! You hear that, ma? Papa?"

"My son-in-law, God bless him."

Mort, locking lips with his wife, thought ahead. *Contacts, contacts.* And lots of cash. Money would have to be transferred to English and French banks. A lot more money than they would need for a deluxe trip. And for more important reasons.

"Mussolini can't be all bad," Garrison Halstead said, "if he's cracking down on the Vatican."

Eva looked quickly around the candlelit dining-room table. The only Catholics present, she quickly decided, were Mr. and Mrs. O'Loughlin, Long Island aristocrats. They did not take umbrage—at least they did not manifest any—at Garry's blunt remark.

"Remarkable fellow," Garrison went on, as a white-gloved butler passed the cheese tray. "Mussolini suspended Catholic Action, closed down the Knights of Columbus, and has thrown guards around the Vatican."

"Well, he did start as a Socialist," Eva said uneasily.

"What makes you think that's admirable?" asked Mrs. O'Loughlin.

Eva, radiant in a bare-shouldered pearl-gray gown, a necklace of lapis lazuli and onyx on her alabaster neck, said nothing. *Let goyim fight goyim,* Dr. Abelman used to say.

"Oh, they'll work it out," Mr. O'Loughlin said. "After all, the church and the fascists have the same goal—stopping communism in its tracks."

Someone laughed. The host, Mr. Van Dorn, tried to change the subject. He was a Yale classmate of Garrison's, a polo player and banker. (He spent very little time at the bank.) His wife, Dorinda, was six feet tall, with an elongated tanned face and muscular arms. Eva suspected Garry had had an affair with her before their marriage. Perhaps they still enjoyed an occasional "return engagement." Garry and Dorinda Van Dorn seemed to share small secrets, arch glances. They laughed at the same jokes. Eva was uneasy.

"Mind you, I'm not exactly a friend of Mussolini's—"

"Garry," Eva said tautly. "He jailed *five* intellectuals this week. Professors, economists, bankers, lawyers. Hardly Reds. Everyone at this table should be concerned about him. He is a menace. And Hitler is worse. I wonder why people never take these monsters at their word."

"Hear, hear," Dwight Enos said. He was a fat, unraveled, perpetually boozed "world traveler." Secretly he envied Halstead his career as a "journalist," lusted for his exotic "Jew wife." *And how is the fair Deborah, the temptress of West Tenth Street?* Enos would ask. He had a drunk's shrewd eye. Eva's white shoulders, her blazing green eyes, the bobbed yellow hair were too much for one man to contend with. Enos had known Halstead in college. A rake, a lecher. He could not have changed. *Oh, the mythical Jewish woman!* Enos had read about the heroine of the picket lines. And he divined that she and Halstead were in trouble. Their daughter was said to be the problem. Too smart for her own good. Jews, Enos decided, suffered from a surfeit of brains.

"All I'm saying is that Mussolini, like him or not, seems to have some kind of plan, some vision of the future," Halstead said.

"His plan is murder, torture, lies, and exploitation," Eva said.

The women listened with bovine expressions. None of them trusted Eva Halstead. It was a good thing that she was (a) beautiful; (b) famous; and (c) married to a Halstead. Otherwise this slum-bred woman would never be allowed to sit at a table on East Sixty-first Street.

"Now, Eva, no soapbox," O'Loughlin said, winking. Corpulent and walleyed, he was a Knight of Columbus, a Knight of Malta, a Knight of Saint Gregory, a rather genial man. He entertained warm feelings for the fair-skinned girl Halstead had married. In fact, grudgingly he admired her. Dullahan was an old friend of his, and Francis Fagan had more than once paid tribute to her as a tough cookie. Moreover, Dullahan informed O'Loughlin, Eva Heilig came from tough stock. Know the Chains, O'Loughlin? the boss asked. The bootleggers? *Her family.* Crazy Jake and his tough kid. The Irishmen winked. Nothing generated respect as did violence, power, wealth, and illegal hooch.

"I've graduated from soapboxes," Eva said. "Those lunatics in Europe are heading for a war."

"Maybe a good idea," Van Dorn said. "Get rid of the Bolsheviks. I'd support that war."

"Would you fight in it?" Eva asked.

"Too old, Eva, my dear. Too old for war, sex, or politics."

Later, Garrison backed Dorinda Van Dorn into a corner of the living room. They sipped brandy and appeared to be laughing a bit too loudly.

Eva sat, a lone missionary amid the Zulus, with a sozzled Dwight Enos. He had turned a shade of pale violet, but he made more sense than the others. Writers missed an essential about the very rich. They were dull, dull, *dull*. Not necessarily bad people, but of a dullness that parched the throat and glazed the eyes.

"Eva, I agree with you," Enos said. He had once entertained radical notions. Daringly he had ridden into Mexico to observe the peasant revolution, been shot at, written an article for *Scribner's*.

"About what?"

"Europe. A mess. Fascisti all over the place. We asked for it. It's obvious our class—not yours—ruined everything. No one in charge. No one making rules—or if there were rules, no one obeyed them. Good for you for popping off."

Cigar smoke, the aroma of brandy, filled the room. Eva felt vaguely nauseated. She had been to too many such parties. The guests had learned to check their anti-Semitism with their coats when she was present. But a lifetime of such inane blabber appalled her. Garrison did it because he had no choice. He could not offend his father's friends, the class in which he had been raised.

"Roosevelt is a Red," O'Loughlin was saying. "If the Democrats nominate him and he's elected, he'll wreck the country. Pauperize the people. Giveaways, socialistic notions. Someone should assassinate that crippled madman. Besides, the Depression's over."

Eva was tempted to respond. Dwight Enos was stroking her hand. A well-meaning idiot. Tempted by a soapbox Venus. Oh, the utter *shmuckiness* (as Sol would have said) of these people.

She saw Garrison in his odd tippy-toed way walk into the Van Dorns' library, one hand on Dorinda Van Dorn's naked shoulder blades.

At Eva's insistence they now slept in separate rooms. Sex had never been a success with them. Less and less Garrison came to her at night. She did not mind. She was trying to give more of herself to their daughter, Lillian, a difficult and distant child. It was likely that Halstead, jealous of the girl— he had claimed he wanted a child, but paid little attention to her—was having affairs. Mrs. Van Dorn, surely. Like getting into bed with a race-horse, Eva thought. Good breeding, potent legs, an elongated face.

My fault, she thought. I was never responsive enough. Something in my repressed Jewish background. All those taboos that I scorned, all those *don'ts* that I claimed to have mocked, have left their mark. Stir a crowd, get an audience to its feet, confront a politician, present a challenge to the mayor, talk back to a policeman . . . all these she had done. There was no shortage of passion in her. The *Eagle* called her "Fighting Eva," the workingman's Joan of Arc.

But her emotional life had suffered. She and Halstead led discrete lives. His magazine assignments (which rarely paid the cost of the trip) often sent him to Europe, around the country. He wrote for radical or eccentric periodicals. The Halstead fortune, untarnished by the stock-market crash, supported his travels and their comfortable style of living.

"I don't need all this," Eva told him one day, over their morning grapefruit. "I came out of poverty, and I can manage with a great deal less."

"I know you can," he said kindly. "But I need *you*. You are important to me."

"Your conscience? Your sweatshop protégé?"

When you are pumping away at Dorinda Van Dorn's body? she wanted to ask. When you are meeting your Yale friends' wives for an afternoon of semiclad sex? And do they gossip about your Brownsville Salome?

Eva was too strong to let these matters deter her. She lectured continually. Radicalism was on the rise. As a sometime Socialist she stood her ground—no bolshevism, no fascism. A middle way. The country would be saved by a peculiarly American red-white-and-blue radicalism. In small stages, reforms would be enacted.

She rearranged the pillows on the four-poster. After almost twenty years of marriage, she felt an intruder in the ancestral bed. *Does my Hebraic flesh recoil from these boards and springs and comforters fashioned by the purest of Americans?* she wondered. Maybe if she and Garrison had made love in hotel rooms she would have responded more ardently. Whenever their bodies were conjoined (less and less the past few years), she sensed that platoons of fierce Halsteads glowered down on them, venerable Puritans, nonplussed, if not horrified, by the Jezebel opening her legs to the thrusts of their fine-boned heir.

"*That,* Eva Heilig," she said in a loud whisper, "is a plate of yesterday's *tsimmes.*"

She could hear Garrison in the bathroom. His bedroom was across from hers. He gargled, spit, worked at his morning ablutions with military snap. Her husband was one of the most orderly of men. He wrote flat declarative sentences, searched Webster's unabridged for the precise word, edited galleys with a needle-pointed pencil.

Lillian had left her homework for her mother to check. A gesture, Eva knew, one that made her sad. She should have been more attentive to the child, a precocious third-grader. Lillian wrote brilliant original compositions. She was far ahead of her class in everything. Garrison and his parents hated the school. They wanted her enrolled at Emma Willard or the Madeira School. Halsteads did not attend these free-form progressive schools. And of course, Mount Holyoke, which four generations of Halstead women had attended, was inevitable.

Eva looked at the photo of Lillian on her night table. Not a pretty child, possessing Garrison's extended jaw, his narrow face, the high color that hinted at hypertension. Eva's fair hair and green eyes were evident, to be sure, but the effect was diminished on the elongated face. A lonely child, Eva realized. She had come to them late, and they were both a bit selfish, too much involved with causes.

I *will* pay more attention to her, Eva thought. I owe it to her.

The child seemed to enjoy her visits to Brooklyn, an afternoon of romping along Eastern Parkway with Abe's children, or playing in Sol's garden at his modest East Flatbush house. Grandma Heilig, the cigarette-puffing old lady in the high-buttoned black dress, amused her. (And Grandma Heilig always loaded her with pencils, pens, paper, pads, scissors, glue, colored paper—a rich haul from the stationery store.)

After breakfast, when Halstead had left for an appointment with his stockbroker and Lillian had gone off to school, Eva took a call from Ike Brunstein.

"Can't tell you where I am, Eva," he said huskily. "You've been reading about me, I suppose."

"Yes. Is Sol being rough on you?" She was overcome with pity for Ike.

"He is the essence of kindness."

"Can I help?"

"Isaac Brunstein is past help. I dined with the devil and he had a long spoon. Eva, as I'm talking to you, Sergeant Cooney and Sergeant DeVitale are standing on either side of me listening to every word."

"Yetta is all right? Can I bring her anything? Is the Trades Council looking after her?"

"Hah! Trades Council! I'm a pariah, Eva, a diseased dog. You would think people would be grateful that I'm telling everything. There'll be fifty indictments by the time I'm through. Gangsters, crooks, union chiselers. But Brunstein will be branded a traitor. The Communists hate me. The Socialists hate me. The regulars hate me. And the *shtarkers*—" His voice became a convulsed sob.

Oh, dear, Eva thought. *The old days.* When she, Ike, and old Flugelman had talked Jake Chain into protecting their girls. How had it come to this? It was no one's fault. It was inevitable in *America Gonif*. You played tough. You struck back. You won respect. Ike had gotten caught in the middle.

"Why did you call me, Ike?"

"I don't know," he sobbed. "It was so wonderful years ago. Our plans. We were sure of ourselves. Now look at me. I'm a prisoner. Talking, talking, talking."

She lowered her voice. It would be foolish of her to mention the Chains.

Surely, one of Sol's young lawyers was monitoring Ike's calls. "Have you talked about . . . the early days? . . . I mean . . . you know. The man who saved the people at *tashlik?*"

He caught on. The battle at the creek. "No. I haven't. Your brother knows everything. He'll get around to it. Eva, I'm sorry I bothered you."

Distraught, she worried about him. Maybe she should have married Ike. She could have put starch in his spine, made him a leader, not a weakling playing at revolution. But then she would not have had a townhouse in New York, an estate in Sag Harbor, a grand career.

A few days later, two husky men in police uniforms entered the Whitman Manor Apartments. It was four in the afternoon, the time at which the detectives guarding Brunstein changed shifts. Detectives Flannery and Cane had been delayed at the station house by a malfunctioning squad car. Someone had poured granulated sugar into the tank. While the detectives tried vainly to get the engine to turn over, the two uniformed men rode the elevator to the penthouse.

Sol, having concluded his interviewing in the morning, had left for a meeting with his boss, one of Seabury's aides. The men on duty, Cooney and DeVitale, liked to leave early and were glad to see the uniformed men. They asked why their usual relief men were not on hand. "Car busted at the precinct," one of the men said. "I'm Carretta and this is Wahlstrom. We'll watch Mr. Brunstein until they show. How'd the Dodgers do?"

Cooney glanced at Ike. Their ward was stretched on the couch shoeless, smoking his fortieth cigarette of the day. The former radical, the man who confessed he had hired criminals to win local elections, looked like an Egyptian mummy. Yellow-brown skin, shrunken cheeks, lips like leather shoelaces, ears like dried apricots. The graying moustache drooped below his chin. *Poor dumb bastard,* Cooney thought. *And hebes were supposed to be smart.*

"Why uniformed men?" Ike asked.

"Until the detectives get here," Wahlstrom said. "Don't worry, Mr. Brunstein. The captain said we should order dinner for you. Care for me to call the deli? Something to drink?"

"It's too early," Ike said. He slumped deeper on the sofa, turned his back, drew his scrawny legs up into a fetal position. "I'm not hungry."

"Never eats," Cooney said on his way out. "The Dodgers got beat again. Braves knocked 'em off, ten to eight. Berger hit two."

"As Berger goes, so go the Braves," Carretta said.

His partner listened to the elevator rising, the clank of the door closing, the rattle of cables as it descended.

Ike never had a chance to shout. The two "policemen" leaped upon him and bludgeoned him into silence with one blow of a blackjack across his temple. They dragged him to the eleventh-story window. It was a clear drop, unimpeded by landings or setbacks.

For a terrified moment Ike regained consciousness. He flailed about and grabbed at a radiator. He tried to scream. The men stuffed a rag soaked with gasoline into his mouth, jammed it deep into his throat. One of them smashed his clutching hand with a lead sap. Tormented eyes pleaded. He wept gouts of tears. All for nothing—Marx, sacrifice, his love of the workingman.

"Fa chrissake, throw him," Wahlstrom said. "Grab an arm."

They each took an arm and leg. They waved Ike's frail body back and forth three times. On the fourth airborne sally, they hurled him out of the window. Ike sailed down eleven flights to an enclosed courtyard. They heard the heavy *splat*. One man grinned and said: "The bum could sing but he couldn't fly."

Swiftly they left by the fire stairs. A stolen car and a driver awaited them on the street. Inside, the men discarded their police uniforms. Beneath, they wore dark business suits. An hour later the driver and the "cops" were on a Greyhound bus for Cleveland, sitting separately, never speaking to each other. In Buffalo a fourth man came aboard and gave each voyager five hundred dollars. None of them would ever know that their employer had been Melvin Schonkeit.

Although a professed atheist and a former Stalinist, Brunstein was buried in the faith of his fathers. Yetta objected. It was sheer hypocrisy, she said. But Ike's aged mother insisted. The workers for whom he had toiled so long, suffered so much, taken beatings, humiliations, insults, turned out en masse. Political differences were temporarily laid aside.

"Isaac Brunstein, whatever his failings, and for these we forgive him," said Rabbi Piltz, "was one of us, of our blood, and of our faith, and had the Almighty permitted him to live longer, and not to have fallen victim to the jackals who stalk our city, would surely have returned to the Jewish faith. Let the King of the Universe accept him now, and let us join in prayer for Isaac Brunstein."

The procession extended for two blocks, behind a stark pine coffin on the bed of a laundry delivery truck. In his later years Ike had done the wet-wash workers much service. He had tried to unseat the gangsters he had helped bring in. Perhaps Wallowitz's memory stirred him.

Yetta rode in the cab of the truck. Behind the "hearse," limousines from Eckowitz's Funeral Parlor bore Ike's relatives. In one car sat Eva Halstead, her brother Sol, his wife Rose, and Dr. and Mrs. Abe Heilig.

"I'll never get over a feeling of guilt," Sol said. "Those dumb cops. The way they let those killers in. If I find out those detectives were in on it . . ."

"Any idea who they were?" Abe asked.

"Not a trace. They import them."

Eva wiped her eyes. Ike was gone. A part of her life. For a moment she regretted having spurned him. Had he ever kissed her? Once, twice, three times? A few pecks. Panting, worshipful Ike. He would have died for her. In a sense, he had died for her younger brother. The Heiligs had been no help to him.

"Yetta?" Eva asked. "Is she taken care of?"

"She won't take a cent from us," Sol said. "She says her political allies will pay the funeral expenses and give her a job."

"The Trotskyites," Eva said hopelessly. "Ah, the way they kill each other off. The Nazis will take over Germany, the fascists will run Europe, and the left will be denouncing each other."

It was an unnaturally cold rainy day in late May. The procession rolled at a measured pace through Brownsville, down Pitkin Avenue, past Leo Glauberman's law office (the mob's attorney watched from his window), past Otzenberger's Democratic Club (Benny was sorry Ike was dead but he felt that the man was a *shmuck*), toward East New York and thence to the cemetery.

The routing of the procession, because of a Consolidated Edison blockade on Liberty Avenue, took the wet-wash hearse and the limousines past the four-story fortress of the Brooklyn General Supply Company, the heart of the Chain empire.

Dr. Abe Heilig shook his head. "The Chains go on and on, and poor Ike is dead."

"Yeah," Sol said. "With a rag stuffed in his mouth. We found traces of his skin on the radiator. They had to pry his hands off."

Eva shuddered. "I don't want to hear any more." She cried again. "Ike was part of our growing up. That he should have to die this way— It's wicked."

"He tried to use rotten people," Sol said. "And they used him. Cruel world, Eva."

Two buildings down from the Chains' whiskey warehouse was a large machine shop with high opened windows and smoky gray walls. The hideous building housed the Unruh Tool and Die Works.

As the truck bearing Ike's coffin passed by, a hail of stones cascaded from the opened windows. Bricks bounced off the wooden lid. One smashed the truck's windshield. The limousines stopped. Behind them, people ran for cover. Chauffeurs were not going to undergo that hail of dornicks and debris.

"Red!"

"Commie!"

Stones and bricks clattered and skipped. The truck proceeded alone. Yetta had been cut on the forehead.

"Your beloved working class," Abe said to Eva. "Behold, the noble proletariat, paying tribute to one of their fallen. Those bricks are being thrown by machinists and mechanics."

"Ignoramuses, galoots," Eva said. "What do they know about Ike?"

The limousines were still halted. *"Move!"* Eva shouted. "Follow the truck!"

"Not me, lady." The driver signaled to the drivers behind him to back up to the corner and take another route.

None of them saw Jake Chain standing in the doorway of Brooklyn General Supply. Two of his workers were with him, Stroonz Rizzo and Baggie. Jake had a gutter awareness of violence.

As Eva and her brothers watched in amazement, Jake and his friends raced to the front entrance of the tool-and-die factory. They hurled a watchman into the street and vanished inside the building.

In minutes the brick-throwing ended. Eva and her brothers, peering from the window of the Cadillac, saw Jake Chain holding a gangly youth by the ankles, dangling him outside a second-story window. Every now and then Jake shook him a little to let him know that he could be dropped. He was educating a brick-thrower.

Wild shouts, sounds of objects being thrown, issued from the factory. Baggie and Rizzo were keeping order. Amid the hubbub, Jake Chain stood his ground, gripping the white ankles of the writhing boy, shouting at the drivers to proceed. All was secure now.

Not another brick was thrown.

"Holy jeez," Eva's chauffeur said. "Get a loada that big guy up there. Now he's holdin' him by *one hand.*"

He was indeed. One of Jake's fists gripped the brick-thrower's leg. The other, waving a crowbar, was fending off the youth's co-workers.

"So much for the united front, dear sister," Abe said. "Behold the enlightened worker. Jake has the right idea. All those men inside Unruh's? They believe every word in the Hearst papers. Ike was a Communist. Ike deserved what he got."

Sol laughed. "A Jake Chain they'll always understand."

Eva lit a cigarette. She crossed her legs and pulled down her too-short black silk skirt. She'd bought an elegant Saks dress for the funeral. "Both of you are disgusting cynics. We can't spend the rest of our lives depending on the Jake Chains to effect reform. They're as bad as Schonkeit."

"Not quite, Eva, not quite," Sol said.

An idea was germinating in his mind. Jake had always had a bit of the knight-errant in him. Maybe he could help where Ike had failed. An unlikely reformer, that *bulvan,* that smuggler of booze. But who knew what went on inside that iron skull? And was it worth finding out?

Chapter 41

In June of 1931 Mort and Hilda, with twenty-one pieces of luggage, sailed for England on the *Queen Mary*. Mort carried fifty thousand dollars in a money belt. He also bore letters of introduction to three London banks and letters of credit which would allow him to open accounts in the United Kingdom totaling five million dollars, a fifth of the family fortune.

Mort had developed a cool, low-keyed manner. He had spent a great deal of time (as a supplier of goods and services) with North Shore society people and wealthy residents of Manhattan mansions. He had learned to wear dark well-tailored suits, white shirts, dark blue ties. His conservative shoes gleamed. His nails were manicured. He wore no jewelry except for a gold watch and a simple gold wedding band. A gifted mimic, he soon picked up the locutions of the rich, lost his Brooklyn cadences. They regarded him as a curiosity—a refined hoodlum, a mannerly gangster, a fellow whose word was his bond, and whose best whiskey was bottled in bond. Darkly handsome, sharp-featured, graceful, he impressed the rich and influential.

Hilda had not kept pace with him. But cruelly corseted in boned elastic, she made a decent appearance. Her clothes—Mort insisted on this—were always sedate and demure and her jewelry was expensive but never showy. When in doubt, he ordered her, keep your mouth shut and smile. She managed to do both quite decently. Her hair was her glory—naturally curly, lustrous, the color of Coca-Cola, and usually piled high over her round face. Fashionably clothed, always in low-heeled shoes (Mort insisted that spikes had a whorish look), she held her own in snooty company. Often, suffocating her Brownsville accent, she used her Brooklyn origins to tell funny stories about her roguish father, a man who knew Governor Roosevelt, senators, corporate presidents.

Of all the documents that Mortimer J. Chain, dapper in black homburg and black chesterfield, carried to London in his Mark Cross attaché case, none was of more value than a letter that his cousin, Eva H. Halstead, had secured for him. It was from her father-in-law, Garrison Halstead, Sr., chairman of the board of two New York banks and a member of the presidential commission to reform the stock exchange.

Eva had always gotten along well with Garry's white-haired father. The old man admired "Hebrews." They worked. They produced. They did not commit crimes. They were good at business. Their sons became excellent physicians. His daughter-in-law's radicalism (like his son's) could be overlooked. Besides, she was quite a beauty. Old Halstead, a bit of a goat, had more than once stroked Eva's knee, pinched her behind.

Knowing the value of an ally, Eva had not discouraged the lusty gentleman. She did not tell Garry. An accomplished flirt, she winked at her father-in-law, a Byzantine temptress teasing a Crusader knight. At dinner parties old Halstead demanded that Eva be seated next to him. At the opera or the theater, the patriarch insisted on sitting next to his son's "Deborah" and occasionally sneaking a mottled hand up her skirt. *Let him,* Eva thought. *Some day he'll be of use.* To her radical friends she said that when the revolution came, they'd spare old Halstead a violent death. He would ride to the gallows with dignity, reading the *Wall Street Journal* and the *Yale Alumni News.*

"Cousin Eva," Mort had asked, in his sincerest manner, "can I get a character reference from your father-in-law? The old cocker?"

"He is no old cocker, Morty, and your character is unknown to him."

"Ah, come on, Eva. I'm Crazy Jake's son. Just a letter. That he knows me, he knows my company, and I'm a terrific guy."

"I'd phrase it more felicitously, Mort. Let me compose it. I'll talk to Mr. Halstead."

All that was needed was an open-mouthed kiss on Daddy Halstead's shriveled lips. Eva did not mind. The Chains continued to intrigue her. She'd had the feeling, ever since Ike's murder, she might be needing Jake. Odd, how she kept returning to him for help. The brutish flat-faced man. She shuddered remembering her last view of him. An angry giant, holding the brick-thrower out of the window.

On his bank letterhead, a name recognizable in any financial office in the world, Halstead, Sr., wrote:

This letter will introduce Mr. Mortimer J. Chain, president of the Brooklyn General Supply Company of New York City.

Mr. Chain and his associates are known to me personally. They are men of the highest caliber, both professionally and in their private lives. This young executive is active in charitable organizations, and conducts his affairs with probity and respectability.

Any services you can give him will be appreciated by the undersigned.

On reading the letter at her father-in-law's Wall Street office, she gave him a second kiss and let him squeeze her left breast. She left him gasping and gaping.

A month later Morty was seated in the gloomy offices of the Caledonian and Northern Distilleries, Ltd., of the United Kingdom. He produced his references, his letters, his bank accounts, and talked business with a bloodless man named Colin McVey. (*Oi vay*, Morty called him later, when he and Hilda celebrated with champagne in their suite at the Savoy.)

"But you chaps can only do this—ah—illegally," Mr. McVey said. He had a glass eye. It had more life in it than the real eye, Morty thought. Both were snot green in color. His smooth flesh was the color of borsht before the sour cream was added. The Scotsman's nose, round as a tennis ball, was a road map of burst blood vessels. Senior partner of one of the hugest distillers of scotch whisky in the world, Colin McVey often sampled his product.

"It's going to change," Morty said. "And we're willing to gamble."

"We are not so sure. We are told Mr. Hoover has made no commitment on repeal. The Methodists and Baptists who support him will carry the election. He needs their vote."

Mort let him talk. *Shmuck. Putz. Farfel-head.* The British knew about America the way Americans knew about the monarchy. Mort let him believe that Hoover was a sure thing; that Roosevelt, or whoever the Democrats ran, would be pictured as a "drunken bum." What they had done to poor Al Smith in 1928! Why, then, was Mr. Chain willing to make an investment in whiskey he could not sell, or only sell illegally?

"Mr. McVey," Mort said again, "we're gamblers. I am told you British understand that. You are sporting people. Horses, cards. We're willing to take a chance. We want to be your exclusive representative in the United States. You have read the letters."

"My dear Mr. Chain. You are a bootlegger."

"So? I'm the first one you ever saw?"

"You break the laws of your country with impunity. I am not sure . . ."

Morty was not sure what "impunity" meant, but he was not a man to be discouraged by what Hilda called a "ten-dollar word." He offered McVey a Havana cigar, lit one for himself, crossed knife-creased dark blue trouser legs. "Ask anyone who has done business with us. We don't cheat. We don't haggle. We pay on time. I assure you, Mr. McVey, we never kill anyone. Unless *they* make trouble first."

It took five seconds for the last part of Mort's sales pitch to register. *"Trouble first! Trouble first!* Oh, that is jolly good! *Jolly good!"*

Mr. McVey laughed so hard his throat clogged with phlegm. He coughed for thirty seconds. When he was composed, Mort handed him an envelope containing fifteen thousand dollars in cash.

"Mr. McVey, count this. It has nothing to do with any business arrangement we might come to. It is for *you*. I am told you are a racing fan and you own horses. What's in that envelope will buy you a prize yearling. The Chains are grateful people. You give us the concession, you'll have a racing stable as good as the king's."

McVey lost no time in counting the money. Before Mort left they agreed to a second meeting, which their solicitors would also attend, to draw up a contract between the Brooklyn General Supply Company and Caledonian and Northern Distilleries, Ltd., for the purchase, importation, and distribution of whiskey and gin.

"I don't get it," Hilda said nervously, as they dined at the Savoy before leaving to see a Noel Coward play. Hilda looked lush and Oriental in a flowing black gown, strands of pearls. "I don't get it. Suppose there's still Prohibition?"

"So what?" Mort asked. "We'll stash the booze in the Bahamas and run it in on boats. Pop is buying a big ship like a fishing schooner. We can cut, mix, and bottle on board so we don't lose any time. We win either way."

Mort sipped a dark claret. Not much. The English went nuts over it. Wine was not a big money item. Years ago, after Rabbi Piltz's tirade at Jake, they'd given up the business with fake rabbis. *Wine, shmine.*

The money was in booze. Americans were the thirstiest people in the world. It was not just drinking, getting drunk, but the ceremony, the religion they made about it. Jokes, talk, teasing, as if to take a slug of gin were the greatest sin since the first guy screwed another guy in the ass. Jake, in his primitive way, had understood this love-hate relationship with alcohol. Mort understood it even better. He saw the shining light in their eyes when you mentioned the real stuff, listened to their dumb jokes about "hollow legs" and "human sponges," their college boys bragging, "Boy was I pissed last night," businessmen laughing their heads off over a colleague's ability to "put it away."

"So long as there are Christians who have to have alcohol, even if it's the piss we sell now, or the good whiskey we will get from McVey," Mort told his wife as he toasted her, "the Chains will do all right."

The play bored them, but they enjoyed sex in the hotel suite later. Almost as good as with Theresa, Mort thought with surprise. He would have to make more trips abroad with Hilda. New business contacts would demand it, anyway.

Dispensing large cash bribes in fresh hundred-dollar bills, presenting his letters of recommendation and bank accounts as evidence of his reliability, Mortimer J. Chain won distribution rights from two more distilleries. He signed contracts. He hired a graduate of Oxford, who wore a double-breasted vest and glasses on a black string, to run the London branch of the Brooklyn General Supply Company.

Mort took the wavy-haired blond man to lunch at a private club—Mort's banker was a member and accompanied them—and told funny stories about his father's career as union organizer, enforcer, bootlegger, and now captain of a seagoing rum fleet.

The new employee, Horace Bain-Foxx, found it jolly amusing. So did the banker. Both were intrigued by the sharp-faced, gentle-voiced young man who informed them that he was a graduate of Dartmouth and had already registered his sons (in the English tradition) for that fine college.

"But that's a lie," Hilda said, as they made afternoon love, half-clothed. "You never finished Thomas Jefferson High School."

"They'll believe anything I tell them so long as the money keeps coming."

Chapter 42

Soon after Mort and Hilda left for England, Sol had Wesselberg picked up for questioning. After several hours of interrogation, Sol stepped outside his office and signaled to his assistant, a young lawyer named Bertram Dunphy. Dunphy was an ex-cop, unshakably honest. A married man with five children, he had attended law school at night while walking a beat in Brooklyn Heights. He was fair-skinned, dark-eyed, with the characteristic shock of thick dark brown hair of many Irish. He and Sol worked well together. Dunphy was tough and unsubtle. Sol could be gentle and conciliatory.

"How's your shorthand, Bert?" Sol asked.

"Good enough."

"I don't want the secretaries to hear this. Can you sit by the tube and make notes? Wesselberg is beginning to sweat. Maybe he's ready to pop."

"Good luck. The fat bum. I wish I were on the force again. Fifteen minutes with the slob."

"Be nice, Bert."

Dunphy seated himself at a camouflaged aperture in the plaster wall through which Sol Heilig's interrogation could be heard. Sol winked at him and reentered his office.

What a monster was Herman Wesselberg, thought Sol. Now in his late fifties, the Meal Ticket sagged and drooped. His gut was a great ball of flesh encased in specially tailored gray trousers. His cannonball head was mottled with red-brown warts, and the pouches under his eyes looked like uncooked gray blintzes. His hair grew long and unkempt, in ratty strands that covered his ears and his creased neck. Wesselberg had asked for a hard-backed chair, complaining that once he sank into a stuffed chair he fell asleep.

Sol studied the fat man's hands: delicate, dainty, manicured. How many people had he killed with them? Sol could guess. Ten, twelve, more. He was a merciless, useless son of a bitch, with nothing to redeem him. For a moment, Sol, who tried to make excuses occasionally for Schonkeit, found himself detesting the Paymaster for elevating this monster to be his lieutenant. And Wesselberg was rich now; he and Shikey had made fortunes.

"Why do they call you the Saratoga Avenue Meal Ticket, Herman?" Sol asked genially. He sat behind his desk. One neighborhood kid to the other.

"In Brownsville, when I was a kid. I always was good for a free meal. Y'know, Mr. Heilig? Before I moved to the East Side, I had a good heart. I still got one."

Sol laughed, as if appreciating the man's high estimate of himself. "But what about Wallowitz? You remember a steward in the wet-wash union named Wallowitz?"

"Nope."

Sol read a clipping from the *Times*. It was ten years old. Hyman Wallowitz, 42, a shop steward for the laundry workers, shot to death as he lay recovering from a beating in Brownsville Jewish Hospital . . .

"I never heard a him. What do I know from wet wash?"

"Herman," Sol said, "you're in trouble up to your big *tuchas*. We have witnesses. They were afraid to talk ten years ago. No more. They saw you and Frummer in the hospital that day."

"Which Frummer?"

"Futka."

"He's dead. If he did it, good riddance. I never touched Walkowich, whatever the *putz's* name was."

"Suppose I told you we've subpoenaed records from the office of Leo Glauberman and that there are some interesting letters between Glauberman and Schonkeit." He got up.

Wesselberg placed his soft hands on his paunch, as if trying to keep it from falling to the floor. An old killer, he had undergone his share of interrogations. He did not scare easily. He had always been bailed out by political connections, sharp lawyers. But this *vontz* Heilig was bothering him.

"Name somebody who might have shot Wallowitz," Sol said.

"Jake Chain."

Sol halted halfway across the room. "Good try, Wesselberg, but Jake was clean."

"He's your relative also, right?"

Sol did not smile. "Distant cousin. He's been checked out. He has an alibi. Besides, he liked Wallowitz. Chain was getting religion. That's why he got out of *shtarking* and into booze. He worked you over once, right?"

"Screw Jake Chain. I got no idea what happened to Halavich."

Sol ignored him a moment. What he was really after was the Brunstein case. Wallowitz was a red herring. He began to ask the Meal Ticket about kickbacks from union members, the beating of elected officials, sweetheart contracts that sold out the union to the employers. Sol asked about the control of trucking, something Shikey and Wesselberg had organized into a fine art. Then he got around to Ike.

"Why was Brunstein killed, Herman?"

The fat man did not flinch. "Don't ask me. I hardly ever saw the bum." "You knew him."

"So did you, Mr. Heilig. Could be lots of reasons. Maybe he welshed on a bet."

Sol sat on his desk. The Cleveland police, on a tip from an informer, had arrested a man named Santo, a killer-for-hire. Santo wasn't talking, but they had found the stub of a Greyhound bus ticket to New York in his coat.

"You got friends in Cleveland?" asked Sol.

Outside, Bert Dunphy, taking notes, whistled softly to himself. Heilig was playing his best card early.

"Cleveland? I never been in Pennsylvania."

"Know a man named Santo?"

Wesselberg shifted his butt, lowered his head. *Oi, that bastard Schonkeit. The things he did for him.* It did not trouble Wesselberg or Frummer to kill a stool pigeon like Brunstein. But Heilig was a tough bastard. *Thirty indictments in the works.* Who knew if he and Shikey would be included? As much as Wesselberg detested the Paymaster, he needed him. He needed the smooth, quiet man who paid off judges, assemblymen, aldermen, and political leaders.

"Thinking it over, Herman?"

"I got nothing to think. I never been in Cleveland."

"Schonkeit'll do the same to you someday. But it'll take more than two men to heave you out of a window. They'll need a platoon of marines to throw you."

The Meal Ticket gargled a laugh. "You just lost your case, counselor. Why should I talk to you, if that's what's gonna happen? Brunstein was a Red who shouldna played with tough guys. I run a trucking business. I pay taxes. I'm a well-known person in the garment industry."

Outside, Sol's secretary gave Bert Dunphy a memo. An anonymous caller from Cleveland. Mr. Heilig was advised to use the name Calabrese in his interrogation regarding the Brunstein murder. Dunphy recognized the name at once. A mob boss, an underworld power. Santo's employer.

Dunphy knocked on the door, summoned Sol, whispered to him, and gave him the slip of paper.

In the chair, Wesselberg yawned and scratched his balls. He drank a tumbler of water. *Boy Scout Heilig.* He should know that he almost screwed his sister once. In a hallway in Brownsville. That blonde with the round ass and neat boobies who married the rich *goy.* Oh, he remembered Eva Heilig with the big voice. The rainy day they'd boiled his pal Moishe Nigger. It was that bastard Jake Chain.

"Who is Mr. Calabrese?" Sol asked.

Wesselberg tugged at his collar. "Never heard a him."

"Mr. Calabrese in Cleveland."

"Ya wastin' ya time, Mr. Heilig." But he was turning grayish, the fat on his face like softened tallow, the bags under the eyes darkening. "I been here long enough. Ya can't keep me here all day. Next time I'm coming with Mr. Glauberman."

"Mr. Calabrese and his employee Santo are getting cooperative. They think they know you. How about it, Meal Ticket?"

"I wanna lawyer. I ain't talking no more."

"Okay. You can go."

Driving back to New York, Herman Wesselberg thought it over. He wouldn't talk. Never. Schonkeit would protect him. Anything could be fixed. But that scumbag Heilig! How had he found Calabrese? The man he had met in Cleveland, the man to whom he had given ten grand to finish Brunstein. If those Cleveland wops talked, H. Wesselberg would be in trouble.

"They'll have to build a special electric chair for you, Herman," Melvin Schonkeit said jovially. "Louise dear, would you leave us?"

They were in the Paymaster's penthouse apartment on Central Park West. Schonkeit's wife smiled and departed. Usually the more disgusting of Melvin's associates—like this fat man—were not received at home.

"It ain't funny, Mr. Schonkeit."

"Just deny everything. Our friends in Cleveland are protected."

A phone was off the hook, near enough to Schonkeit so that he could hear a voice. Someone was shouting into it. Wesselberg watched. He knew what was going on. He was amazed that the Paymaster would let him see his dirty work. Schonkeit picked up the phone and nodded. He listened for a fraction of a second, hung up. Then he asked the operator for a number. Into the phone he said softly, "Four."

Oh, the sly bastard, Wesselberg thought. Always on sure things. Somehow he was getting race results from Jamaica. The number-four horse had won. A "beard" had just been given the word and was placing a bet with some sucker of a bookie. The bookie would be paying through the nose when the results came through on the wire.

"This punk Heilig," Wesselberg said. "You got to buy him off, Mr. Schonkeit."

"He can't be bought. You and I are crooks in our hearts. There aren't many Jews like us. We're the exceptions, freaks. We—"

"I ain't no freak, Mr. Schonkeit."

"I was not referring to your weight, Herman. I know about the Heiligs. His brother is a surgeon. His sister, the one who writes and lectures. They're better than we are. A lot better. And they don't frighten. So I'm afraid we will have to let Solomon Heilig proceed and let the chips fall where they may." Schonkeit believed every word he said; he admired achievement, respectability.

"I think, Mr. Schonkeit, you want me to be the fall guy."

"Don't be concerned. If Heilig gets an indictment, it won't stick. I'll see to that."

Wesselberg got to his feet. "Mr. Schonkeit, I don't like the way this is going. I may have to lean on Heilig."

"I forbid it."

"Scare the guy. Maybe threaten his wife or his kids."

Schonkeit got up. His manner was calm, but there were scarlet splotches on his shiny cheeks. "I warn you, Herman. You are not to touch the prosecutor. We have rules. That's why I was put in charge. People like you and Shikey, left to your own devices, would ruin everything. An honest lawman like Solomon Heilig cannot be touched. We'll move around him. We'll handle him in court."

The Paymaster escorted Wesselberg to the private elevator. "Remember, I'll be annoyed if you try any rough stuff on Heilig. Let nature take its course. We'll all survive and prosper."

The meeting enraged Wesselberg. He had lived with violence since he was a fat boy of eleven. A *psychopath,* a doctor had once called him in court. Heilig and Schonkeit were two of a kind—one on the side of the law, one working against it. Brains. Nice clothes. Rich friends. And he was fat, hideous, hated and feared. He would not only get Heilig but arrange to have it pinned on Schonkeit. Let the Paymaster work on that one.

Not long after Wesselberg's audience with Schonkeit, Eva was typing furiously in her cluttered study. She took a morning telephone call from her brother Abe. "Busy, busy, Abe. I can't talk."

"Rest easy, kid," Dr. Heilig said. "Bad news, but not that bad. Solly's been shot."

"Good God. Is he—"

"He's all right. In front of his house. He was getting into his car. Two wounds, one in the arm, one high in the chest. No vital organs. He's going to be all right. He's conscious, he's fine, he'll make it."

She began to cry, forced herself to stop. The Heiligs handled themselves with courage and self-discipline. "Where is he, Abe?"

"Crown Hill Hospital. I operated on him myself."

"Operated?"

"Just to remove the bullets. One of them shattered his collarbone. We called in an orthopedic surgeon. He says it'll be okay, maybe with a bump in it."

"Rose and the kids?"

"They're all right. Rose had a bad time at first, but she's gutsy. A car pulled alongside when Sol was getting into his and they opened up. He must have been suspicious, because he hit the ground at once. The rest of the shots bounced off his Buick."

"Are you at the hospital now?"

"With Rose and mama. Mama's in bad shape. I didn't want her to come. Grab a cab and get out here."

Crossing the Brooklyn Bridge in a taxi, Eva cried again. They had tried once. They would try again. Sol was too courageous for his own good. She knew about the underworld. For a moment she wondered why the secret rulers had permitted the attack. The unspoken law was never to go after D.A.'s, investigators, or cops. It served no purpose but to arouse public fury. Anger replaced fear. She knew at once where she would go for advice to protect Sol.

Bertram Dunphy, Sol's young assistant, met Eva outside the hospital room. There were three uniformed cops standing guard. Eva could hear her mother weeping in the room. But Sol's voice was comforting and un-afraid.

"He could have used the police this morning, Bert," Eva said.

"He refused. He didn't want to scare Rose and the children. The judge just issued an order. He's to have twenty-four-hour guards, at the house, the office, everywhere." Dunphy looked pale, controlling his fury.

"It's outrageous. Do you have any suspects?"

"Just suspects. No evidence. No one saw the car. No one got a license number. Your brother leaves early, even before his children go to school."

In the room Eva gingerly embraced Sol. He was sitting up in bed, left arm and shoulder in an elevated plaster cast. An IV dripped plasma into his right arm.

Abe was talking to the orthopedic surgeon. They were not concerned. He'd be out of commission only a few weeks.

"But the gangsters will come again," Matla Heilig wailed. She was old and feathery. "Once they try, they'll try again. Solly, Solly, why *you?* Why you with this gangster business? Let someone else go after them."

Eva watched Sol's eyes. As ever they were bright and merry. He was putting on a good act. "Eva, explain it to mama. It was an accident. They had me mixed up with someone else."

Rose Heilig entered. She had done her crying already. It served no purpose now. She was an elementary-school principal, an ambitious woman. She and Eva embraced.

"Room's too crowded," Dr. Heilig said. "This isn't a family reunion, it's a hospital room."

Eva found a pay phone. A talk with Jake Chain was in order.

Sarah answered the phone. She had been sitting in the kitchen, fanning herself, watching Jake eat a late breakfast—orange juice, corn flakes with cream, three fried eggs, rye toast, and coffee. It was one of his twice-a-week visits to the house on Haven Place. She overfed him, looked after his laundry, hovered over him. She knew about the woman in Freeport.

"Eva," Sarah said, "you're lucky you caught him. He came in last night. More and more he's at the place on the island. Business, business."

Eva's voice was shaky. Hearing that Jake was in the house, she sounded calmer. "Please, Sarah, could you put him on?"

Just like her, Sarah thought. Nothing to ask about me, my health, the house, Morty, the grandchildren. Only Jake interested her. Bitterly Sarah thought, She's rich and famous and pretty, so what does she want with my husband? Sarah blamed Jake's alienation on Eva. Jake's ideal. His dream. No wonder he had run off to other beds, to that *shiksa* tramp, that lady pirate.

Irene Twine, widow of the murdered Buster, who worked as Sarah's maid (the only maid on Haven Place), came in. She complained about the awful heat, switched on a fan, and began clearing the kitchen table.

The clatter of dishes, the hum of the metal fan, the chattering of his wife and the black woman unnerved Jake. He told Sarah he would take the call in the living room.

"You hang up, Sarah," he said, "after I get on."

"So what's to listen? She only calls when she needs a favor."

Nagger, Jake thought. And yet he pitied her, hating himself for the way he neglected her. He could not help it. He loved Tommy. He loved their bastard son, Little Mac. The sprawling stucco-and-timber house was his real home.

The living room was shaded against the hot morning sun. The thick leaves on the Lombardy poplars Doc Abelman had planted formed checkered patterns on the drawn blinds. Jake sat at his desk and heard Eva's voice. It never failed to make his blood jump.

"Jake, someone shot my brother Sol."

"He's all right?"

She filled him in. A car had paused in front of Sol's house on Eastern Parkway. Someone—the police guessed there were at least two men—had emptied guns at him. Luckily Sol had taken only two bullets. He would live.

"What do you want me to do, Eva?"

"Find out. Tell them not to hurt him. You know all those people."

He was thinking: Always me when there is dirty work. Always Crazy Jake. Loving her, he was resentful. Never a kiss. Never embracing her, never seeing her naked. But full of desire for the small woman. So smart, so brave, so much a part of his life. She did not go running to her rich husband Halstead, or to his millionaire father, or to her brother, the surgeon. But she appealed to Crazy Jake, the bad one, the violent one, the *verdamte blut.*

"Sol must have more Chain blood in him than I thought," Jake said. "He learned how to duck. Not like Brunstein."

"Don't make fun of us, Jake."

"Who is making fun? I'm glad Sol is okay."

She asked him who he thought had tried to kill her brother. Dunphy, Sol's assistant, was certain it was Wesselberg and Frummer or their hired killers. The same monsters who hurled Ike out of a window.

Jake sighed. He saw Sarah standing sullenly in the doorway, seething over the way her husband was being dragged into the Heiligs' affairs. Jake Chain was wealthy, feared, respected, a businessman like any other. Why did Eva Halstead have to bother him? Why didn't she mind her own business, that ritzy one?

A mischievous notion seized Jake. Yes, he would talk to Eva. He would discuss what they could do. But only at the place in Freeport. He'd pick her up at the hospital in an hour. She argued a bit at first. Why all the way out there? She had appointments, lunch with the women's reform movement, a dozen things to do.

"Cancel everything, Eva. You make enough speeches," Jake insisted. He wanted her to see Tommy. To let her know she was not the only woman he could love.

"Freeport, *Freeport,*" Sarah mocked. "Getting all your *nafkas* in one place? Is that it? Look at me, Jake. Look at your wife. I am a pretty woman. I am young. Is this my life? Card games and shopping, and a *shwarzer* to do my work?"

No anger generated in him. He pitied her. He longed for her to be happier. "I'm sorry, Sarah. This summer maybe we could take a place in Long Beach. Near the ocean. It'll be nice. I have this customer who runs a hotel a block from the boardwalk."

She slammed the door.

Chapter 43

"I'm ashamed to ask for lemonade here," Eva said. She smiled her most charming smile, smoothed her white linen skirt.

"It's all right, Mrs. Halstead," Tommy said. "I hardly ever drink myself."

"Eva, please. I'm family."

Jake watched the two women warily. His pale eyes were amused and gratified. A little lesson for Eva. A bit of showing off to Tommy. A high-class lady, his cousin. A society lady. A well-known writer. But in a crisis, her brother wounded, she had come to him, the mobster.

"Lemonade is easy," Tommy said. "Jake?"

"Same all around. It's funny how, working with booze all my life, I lost the taste for it."

Tommy laughed and threw her head back. "Jake, really. Who wouldn't lose their taste, considering the poison you sell to people!"

"I dunno," said Jake. "Whoever pays the right price gets the good stuff. You pay less, you get rotgut."

A breeze from the Sound ruffled strands of Eva's curling blond hair. Jake stared at her a moment. Forty-five. Almost his age. And she looked twelve years younger. Unlined skin, clear green eyes.

Tommy noticed the way her man was looking at the visitor. He had told her often about Eva. She went inside the house and left them on the second-floor veranda with its view of the winding canals and the distant white-capped ocean. A Chain boat was chugging slowly into dock. In broad daylight it would unload a cargo of English gin.

"Just like that?" Eva asked.

"Why not? The guys unloading and stacking are the local cops. The Feds, Morty and I took care of long ago. We set them up in their own speakeasy. How can they turn us in if they're customers?"

"Same Jake. Same Morty. Same Chains."

"Yeah, we manage."

Eva could see the woman inside the house preparing lemonade for them. A fine-looking woman. Tall, big-boned, with a strong throat and somewhat coarse skin, but stunning features—a high brow; a fall of chestnut hair, luminous in the afternoon sun; arched eyebrows; sharply defined features. She was a different kind of woman.

"You love her," Eva said.

"Yes. We have a son."

She smiled and took his hand. "I'm glad. A good boy?"

"Sure. Little Mac. After her father. Mackenzie Tuttle. That's a name for a half-Jew?" He laughed. "There he is, by the truck."

Eva got up and leaned over the wooden railing. She saw a muscular blond boy of about seven or eight. He had the same shock of thick blond hair that Jake had had as a boy. He was barefoot, in ragged pants, his skin a golden brown. He carried a bamboo fishing pole with a red-and-white bobber.

"Good God, Jake. He's so—so—*American*. Huckleberry Chain."

"What? Oh, I get it. I never read the book, but I get it."

He told her about Tommy's daughter, who was in the boarding school in Connecticut. Money was no problem. Jake supported two households and what amounted to two wives.

Tommy came out with a tray, pitcher, and three glasses filled with ice. Eva had to smile. Surrounded by oceans of booze, warehouses and boatloads and trucks, they drank lemonade.

It was balmy and sun-warm on the broad veranda. Wicker chairs, chintz pillows, a sense of peace and isolation. No wonder Jake loved it, Eva thought. And the woman had a certain strong quality. No great beauty, but graceful, despite her large body. There was honesty and independence on her sun-lined face.

Eva had to keep reminding herself. Jake Chain was a mobster, a man who made his living outside the law, a violent man. He had killed people. She had lost track of the Chains the past few years. Sol said that father and son had become enormously rich and powerful. So powerful that the secret rulers of the underworld let them go their way. Schonkeit, arbiter, decision maker, was content to let the Chains run their operation untouched.

"It's lovely here," Eva said.

A second Chain boat was moving slowly through the inland canal, cutting a gentle swath in the shallow waters. Eva could see that it was loaded with wooden crates and wedge-shaped burlap packages.

"Ours," Jake said. He was smiling. "We buy whole cargoes. No more *shnurring* around, picking up a load here, a load there."

"The wonders of modern capitalism."

Tommy Tuttle laughed. "Jake told me you were a radical, Mrs. Halstead. We're sort of outside the economy. You know, not part of the system."

"I realize that." She wanted to say, Economic systems come and go, but crime and the Chains go on forever. A Communist friend had told her that in the Soviet Union the black market flourished.

Jake was as rugged and handsome as ever. The flattened face, broad cheekbones, calm blue eyes. The blond hair, a bit graying, was still thick, falling over his forehead. His body had not run to fat. Strong, lithe, broad-shouldered, he looked indestructible.

Below, Sal Ferrante was shouting instructions to the drivers. A convoy assembled on the driveway. So it goes in big business, Eva reflected. Organization was everything. Ike had predicted that the Chains were doomed. They were *lumpenproletariat,* criminals who would die when the perfect society evolved. But the perfect society, to a disillusioned Eva, seemed light-years away. Everything was going downhill. In 1929 all belief had been shattered. What if the Chains inherited the earth?

"Let's go for a boat ride," Jake said. "Come on, Eva. I'll show you how fast we can go. It'll be safe. There won't be a drop of booze on board. You, me, and Tommy. We'll let Anton skipper."

"I'm not dressed for an outing at sea, Jake."

"The boat is like a hotel. Tommy?"

She shook her dark hair. She knew of Jake's lost love. "I'll stay here. You two go."

Anton guided the speedboat through winding canals, past bulkheads and piers, into the "rip" where the deep blue ocean broke against the stone jetties in foaming bursts. It was a hot July day, but refreshingly cool on the water. Gulls and terns dipped about the flashing boat.

Eva sat on a canvas chair, laughing, tucking her flapping white skirt under her legs. Very good legs, Jake thought. Slender, tiny ankles. She wore smart little flapper's shoes. White and brown straps.

"Cut the speed, Anton," he said. "Let her drift."

"Right, Jake."

Jake took her hand. "So? Always to me when there's trouble."

"I'm frightened for Sol. They almost killed him. I want you to help."

"Shoot somebody?" He smiled. "I never do those things. Not anymore."

"But you know those people. You know Schonkeit. Sol's been questioning Wesselberg. He's that garment-industry gangster."

Jake rubbed his knuckles. He thought: *I should have killed him.* Outside Frummer's political club, a long time ago. After what they tried to do to Eva . . .

"I don't want you to get hurt or to hurt anyone," Eva said. "But Mr. Dunphy says that Wesselberg is insane. They think he has syphilis and it's affected his brain. He has a notion he must get rid of Sol."

"So let Schonkeit take care of him."

He wondered how much weight he could swing with Schonkeit. The Paymaster had made his peace with the Chains long ago. They were too tough, too smart. Brooklyn was far enough away so that he could surrender the territory. Jake wondered how much control Schonkeit exercised over Wesselberg and Frummer.

"I'll try. But, Eva, it's a long time since I used my fists on anyone. I don't take chances like I used to. You saw why."

"I did. She's a beautiful woman. And the boy. I'm glad for you."

Aimlessly, he hated Halstead. In her. Joined. His *shagitz* body, pale and knock-kneed. How white she was, unlined, graceful. A small woman, all courage, passion, devotion. But something was wrong with the marriage. He'd heard gossip. From Rose Heilig, via Matla, Eva's mother. Separate bedrooms. Traveling without each other . . .

Anton turned the speedboat. It rocked gently in its own wake. Distantly they could see two large boats riding at anchor.

"More booze," Jake said. "Everyone's stocking up. We're buying ship-loads." He was glad to change the subject. Self-pity was a waste. Her silken legs, exposed by the insistent wind, were driving him wild. That fancy Halstead. Too good for him. She was too good for anyone.

"You'll talk to Schonkeit?"

"Could I ever say no to you?"

She kissed his cheek, ran fingers through his hair. "Jake, I know you'll get them to stop. People listen to you."

Everyone except you, he thought. "I love you," he whispered.

"No. You love Tommy. Remember that."

Eva called him three days later. Rose Heilig had been threatened on the phone by a muffled voice. Rose and Sol's daughter, Celia, had been stopped in the street by a dark man in a black suit and handed a note. It read: YOU AND YOUR WHOLE FAMILY GONNA GET IT. Terrified, Celia had run home. Dunphy took her to police headquarters and had her look at mug shots. Celia could not identify the man.

A reinforced police guard was ordered for Sol's home and family. Two men were assigned to Sol's house on Eastern Parkway—one monitoring phone calls, another watching the door. Sol never traveled anywhere without a detective escort.

Again Wesselberg was called in for questioning. This time he threw a tantrum in Sol's office, cursed him and threatened to "get" everyone connected with it.

"He's off his nut," Bert Dunphy said.

"Or it's an act," Sol said.

Leo Glauberman, the aging Teddy Roosevelt of Pitkin Avenue, showed up to complain that his client was being unjustly persecuted. From now on he would not cooperate.

"How about Shikey Frummer?" Sol asked. "You represent him also?"

"I do."

"He's next. If you want, you can sit in on the meetings. Glauberman, maybe *you* want to answer some questions. About Wallowitz. About Brunstein."

Glauberman did not rise to the bait.

"Warn Wesselberg to lay off Mr. Heilig," Bert Dunphy said. "He should know better."

The following day, Rose Heilig took her children and moved for the summer to a boardinghouse in Liberty, New York. Again, two police officers were assigned to the family. She complained to Sol that she felt that she was in jail. She wept a great deal, begged Sol to resign from the investigator's office. The hoodlums got her phone number in the Catskills. Threatening calls continued.

Just back from Europe, Mort heard about Eva's appeal to his father, the attacks on Sol and his family. On learning of Jake's intention to meet with Schonkeit, he was upset.

"It's not our business, pop," he said. In a vested blue suit, newly barbered, getting his nails manicured, Morty sat in his private office in the Brooklyn General Supply Company. He had relegated Sal Ferrante and his brothers to an outside "workroom." They shared space with file cabinets, desks, telephones, three secretaries. Sal was spending less time at the place. He was learning the ropes in narcotics, investing time and money with an old mobster named Mafalda.

"For Eva," Jake said. "Schonkeit I can talk to. Wesselberg is a lunatic. Nobody knocks off cops and D.A.'s. I should have killed him ten years ago, when I—"

"It's okay, pop. I won't try to stop you. Just be careful."

"I owe the Heiligs." His father appeared to Mort strangely innocent and trusting. "They taught me to read. I respect people like the Heiligs. It's like Rabbi Piltz told me when you and Hilda got married. There's all kinds of Jews. I ain't the best kind and I know it."

"You're good enough."

"Eva, Sol, the doctor—they're the kind of people the rabbi meant. I done rotten things."

"So have I. But if we stopped to worry about it, we'd go out of business."

London was calling Mr. Mortimer Chain. Urgent. Something about the wording of a contract. Morty winked at his father, as if to say, *Don't worry, pop, we're going legit soon.*

"You're smarter than I am," Jake said. "You got class, brains. You look ahead. Maybe I can retire in a year. We won't need the place in Freeport if repeal comes in. We can unload right on the New York docks, right?"

"Right, pop. Give my best to Schonkeit. You want to carry something?"

"I ain't carried a gun in years. Except on the boat, and only when Tommy is along. Nobody'll start in with a Chain. It's like starting in with a Rockefeller."

Mort laughed, talked into the phone. Funny, Jake thought, he's got a different voice, a different accent when he talks legitimate business. Almost like an Englishman, or one of those Long Island society people.

"Ah, Mr. McVey," Morty was saying. "How are you, sir? Yes, the contracts look fine. . . ."

Jesus, Jake thought, Thomas Jefferson High School! And fighting in the gutter twenty years ago with Bernie Feigenbaum! For a moment he recalled the day Sarah was crippled when the K & R factory collapsed. Driving the wagon to the tenement, having to tell Mutteh that his mother had been injured. And Eva. A vision in her shirtwaist and skirt, her hair undone, more beautiful than he could ever remember her, walking toward him with a bowl of soup.

Schonkeit was convinced that Wesselberg was going insane. The fat man's physician had warned him. The Meal Ticket had paresis. Latent syphilis. Wesselberg had become violent in the doctor's office, threatened a nurse, smashed equipment. He was obsessed with Solomon Heilig.

The Paymaster decided Wesselberg would have to be killed. Moreover, something besides the demise of the Meal Ticket loomed. Some brilliant scheme that could wound the Chain dynasty. The Paymaster had long ago made a shaky peace with them. But he had been getting disturbing reports from England. That young entrepreneur, Mort Chain, had been signing contracts in the British Isles, grabbing liquor-distributing rights. When Prohibition ended, the Chains would be ready.

Schonkeit was jealous of this kind of foresight. Melvin Schonkeit should have been doing it *first*. Who knew how far the Chains could rise? And while they were not bred-in-the-bone killers, not bloody bastards like Frummer, they would be an impediment. Too big to control. A future source of friction, of rivalry for the big dollar.

And so he looked forward to seeing Jake Chain. They met at Schonkeit's private table in the rear of the Home Stretch Club on East Fifty-sixth Street off Park Avenue. It was another of Schonkeit's own speakeasies, an elegant one, frequented by the kind of people to whom Mort sold his most expensive brands.

"Jake, you look good. You never get old."

"I stay in shape."

Schonkeit signaled a waiter. Jake wanted a glass of ginger ale.

"Wesselberg has to smarten up," Jake said.

"You understand, Jake, I can't control him anymore."

"Why not? He's yours. You set him and Frummer up in business. Trucking, extortion, kickbacks. This was your way of getting union contracts, Melvin?"

Schonkeit detested his given name. Jake enjoyed calling him by it. The Paymaster did not smile. He smoothed back his gleaming black hair.

Patent-leather Kid, they once called him. Jake knew he disdained violence, ran from fights, never packed heat. He was a thinker, a brain, a schemer.

How much was real and how much was crap? Jake wondered. You get a reputation, and it grows and grows, and people believe it. He admitted that it was also true of the Chains. They were unbeatable, the other mobs and the police had begun to think. Too tough, too smart. It wasn't true. And he wondered for a moment why he had let Eva sweet-talk him into this errand.

"The guy has got to lay off Sol Heilig and his family," Jake said. "It's bad for everyone. He hurts anyone in Heilig's family, Melvin, it's the end for you also. They know you financed Wesselberg. You use him. You're the one should be stopping him, not me."

Schonkeit smiled. "Why don't we both try? He's here."

"I figured. The Paymaster knew when I called what I wanted."

"No rough stuff. I'll take you to him and you can talk. But keep your hands to yourself. He's under orders to do the same. He's afraid of you. You beat him up once, didn't you?"

"I should have killed him."

Schonkeit got up. "Wrong. If I did anything for the mobs, I taught them not to be violent, and especially to lay off cops. We can do anything we want with a fix. Come on."

Jake followed the Paymaster's dapper figure through the speakeasy. Society people ogled him. A famous reporter waved to him. He was a celebrity. He never missed a World Series, a championship fight, a theater opening. But there were rumors he was losing his grip. If the Democratic bosses went under, if Seabury nailed some crooks, Schonkeit would not possess the same power.

He led Jake down steep stairs and into a room where a poker game was in progress. Five men, unknown to Jake, were deeply engaged in reading their hands. They did not even nod at the two passersby. Down a corridor to a metal door the Paymaster led Jake. He knocked twice and the door opened.

"Go ahead, Jake. It's all right."

Jake stepped into a storage room. High shelves full of booze. The room had a cement floor and high cement walls. It smelled musty, winy, the way Goldsturm's old mixing vats used to smell after a busy day. There was a drain in the floor, a gutter running around the walls. For broken bottles.

Wesselberg was the only one in the room. There were two chairs and a small desk.

"Hello, Chain."

"Hiya, Meal Ticket."

"If it's all right with you, Jake," the Paymaster said softly, "Hymie would like to frisk you. You do the same to him. Then I'll beat it."

"Okay."

Jake held his arms up. If they tried anything, he was confident that he could move fast enough. Strangle Wesselberg and throw the fear of God into the coward Schonkeit.

Wesselberg felt Jake's pockets and trousers, nodded his head. When it was Jake's turn, he felt disgust and revulsion as he fingered the gross body of the old killer. No, he did not have a gun. So far so good.

"Both of you listen to me," Schonkeit said. "I want an agreement. I made peace with the Chains a long time ago, Herman. And you owe me plenty. So work something out. I'm going back upstairs."

Schonkeit motioned to them to sit. Nobody would listen in. Two businessmen, two men who had been around and could talk to one another. He left.

Bulging his elephant-gray suit, unshaven, Wesselberg gave off a stink like a swamp.

"So. You want I should lay off Sol Heilig."

"That's it, Meal Ticket."

"It ain't me. I didn't shoot at him. But I'd be happy if the slugs took his head off."

"Meal Ticket, you and Shikey are bringing in hit men from out of town. Dagos. You don't pull a trigger, but you got people who do. Schonkeit feels the way I do. It's lousy."

Wesselberg's face contorted with rage. The fat cheeks inflated, the eyes retreated in fleshy pouches. "He's trying to burn me. I never done what he said I done."

"So why are you worried? You come to trial, you'll beat it."

"Schonkeit says I got to take the fall. I'm the stand-up guy."

"Get any fatter, you won't be able to stand up."

"You Polack bum. You been on my back a long time. I remember when I seen you shoveling crap in Kolodny's stable."

"That's right. Remember what I did to Bunchik and Mendel with a shovel?" Jake leaned forward and cracked his knuckles under Wesselberg's nose. "I won't need a shovel. Big as you are, I could tear you apart. There's so much fat on you it might take a little longer to choke you, but, believe me, it'll be a pleasure."

Wesselberg said nothing. He gulped, mopped his brow.

Jake crossed his legs and smiled. "Get smart, Meal Ticket. Leave Sol Heilig alone. You'll have *tsuris.*"

Wesselberg folded his hands on the table. "What do you know? I got a legitimate business. I'm well known in the garment industry. People respect me."

"Not for long. Labor rackets are finished. There's new guys in the needle trades. They'll get rid of you and Frummer. They'll cooperate."

"Not for long."

"Do me a favor. Lay off Sol Heilig."

"Screw you, Chain. You tell Heilig to lay off *me.* I'll get him the way I got his sister—"

Jake lunged from his chair. He yanked Wesselberg's flabby arms apart and went for his throat. The man was enormous, a dead weight of three hundred pounds. Lard, garbage. His odor infuriated Jake. He cracked the Meal Ticket across the face, tried to yank him from the chair. Wesselberg did not fight back; he bent his gray, long-haired head, ducking blows, whimpered, fell to the floor. Jake yanked him to his feet and hit him once in the gut.

"Bastard!" the Meal Ticket wailed. "I screwed your broad."

Jake punched him again, his fist swallowed by the gluttonous gut.

"Hit, hit, Polack. I'll kill Heilig. I'll kill his wife, all of them."

Jake stopped hitting him. What good would it do? He had *shtarked,* hit, beaten, gotten hit, for a long time. Violence was not for him any longer. Morty was smarter. Do it with contracts, papers, lawyers. What was he trying to do, beating this useless son of a bitch? There had to be another way. Let the cops protect Sol and his family. That was their job. He had his own life to live. Tommy, Little Mac, the boats . . .

The metal door opened. Both men were heaving and gasping. Wesselberg was wiping blood from his face. He looked at the doorway, goggling.

Sal Ferrante walked in. He looked sheepish and apologetic, as if he had interfered in something important. He stood in the doorway, hunched, his head drooping, his melting brown eyes full of self-pity.

"Sal?" Jake asked. "Morty sent you? I don't need help."

"No fair," Wesselberg growled. He blotted blood from his nose. "No fair. Beat it, wop."

"Mr. Schonkeit said I could help."

The suspicion formed too late in Jake's mind. He was vaulting across the cement-floored room. But Sal was twenty feet away. Too late. Jake could duck, hit the floor. But the chances were bad.

He was figuring the odds, reaching for the nearest chair as a weapon, when Sal opened fire with a .45 automatic.

Jake, who had taken twelve bullets and lived, took one this time and died.

Sal's first shot struck him in the forehead, made his face a crimson mask. Jake staggered forward. The body responded blindly. But there was no brain left. He clutched at the racks of bottles, dragged a few with him to the floor.

They clattered, broke, spilled liquor. Odors of fake scotch and adulterated bourbon clotted Jake's nose. He went slowly to his knees. His hands tried to wipe the blood from his eyes.

Sal shot him again at close range. The side of Jake's head blew away. Bits of brain and bone splattered the racks.

"Dead, ya bastid," Sal said.

Wesselberg wiped his face and stumbled away. He gagged and vomited into a grate-covered drain. "Leave it to the Paymaster. Using Chain's guinea."

His back was turned to Sal. Sal fired four times into Wesselberg's padded, hunched-over body. As the fat man, clutching at bottles, collapsed, Sal walked up to him and fired a final shot into the base of his brain.

When the five poker players entered the room, Ferrante was leaning against the racks, weeping discreetly.

One of the men shook him. "The gun, asshole. Gimme the gun."

Sal gave him the .45. He turned his head away as the men carried the bodies out of the storeroom and into the corridor.

One of the men came back and threw a wet sponge and a towel at Sal. "Clean up, jerk-off. We tol' you to keep it clean."

Three men dragged Jake's body along the floor, lifted it over the threshold, and bore it down a flight of stairs. The others followed with the Meal Ticket. The corpses went into separate cars to separate destinations.

Chapter 44

"He isn't at home," Sarah said shakily to her son. "Is he at Freeport?"

"No, ma. Don't worry. Pop is probably calling on a customer."

Morty stayed late in the office. Slow day, hot July weather. He turned on the Zenith behind his desk. Post and Gatty were due to end their record flight. Around the world in eight days! A record heat wave was under way. The estate of Baron Astor had just won a sixteen-million-dollar tax case. That's the way it goes, Mort thought. You had it, you kept it.

He wondered about Jake. He'd probably finished his meeting with Schonkeit and was on his way out to Freeport. Tommy had not seen him all day.

Mort had Schonkeit's private number. He called it. A secretary said that Mr. Schonkeit had left town. But she would leave a message that Mr. Chain had called.

It was now past six. Mort had forgone his evening session with Theresa. Too hot, too clammy. He had sent her home early. He called Long Beach, where Hilda and the kids were spending the summer in a palatial house a block from the beach. The kids were fine, she told him. Spent the whole day at the Lafayette Pool. But they missed him. Would he promise, for sure, little Marty asked, that he would come out for the weekend? And bring him a great big beach ball?

"Promise, Marty. Kiss mama for me. Be nice to Davey and Iris. Learn to swim."

He began to worry about the old man. Crazy Jake. The wild man. Believing in his own power to survive, to wade into guns.

Over the years, Mort realized, his father had changed. Tommy had been the difference. Calmed him down, made him less prone to violence, rid him of that wild fearlessness. But Jake would do anything for Eva. Anything. Sol was in danger, and Jake had ridden into combat again. Like an old western movie Mort had seen: Jesse James taking his guns out of a trunk to avenge someone.

Hell, life was not a cowboy movie. Schonkeit would surely have more sense than to lean on a Chain. But Wesselberg, that maniac . . .

To ease his mind, he called in Harris Weltfish and they talked about future plans—their line of legitimate brand names, how they would run their own distilleries for blending whiskey. It was bound to come about. If not after Hoover lost, soon enough. The country could not tolerate any more gang killings, deaths from poison whiskey, corruption. Wealthy people, politicians, university presidents, even ministers were against Prohibition. It would go. And the Chains would be ready.

Dr. Weltfish agreed. The key would be "blending." A less expensive process, turning out a cheaper line with a gentler taste, a light color, something easy on the mouth and digestive system. After years of throat-scorching poisons, vile and sickening concoctions, the public would appreciate soothing "blends." Weltfish wanted money for experiments. He wanted to hire distillers from England or Scotland.

Mort agreed and dismissed the young man. He liked him. A Ph.D. in chemistry from City College was nothing to sneeze at. Mort respected learning, dedication, intelligence, loyalty. Sometimes he regretted he had not finished high school. Or taken courses at night. Still, a man could read, improve himself, learn about the world. Maybe this fall he and Hilda would not only visit England and France (he was arranging contracts to import French Cognac) but go to Germany, Austria, Switzerland. The world didn't end in Brooklyn. Of one thing he was certain: His children would go to the best colleges.

At six-forty-five he called Tommy again. No word from Jake. She was concerned also. He was usually in Freeport by midafternoon. He would take a swim, stretch his powerful body in the sun, look over the purchases.

A little past seven, as Mort was wondering whether a call to the police would be in order, his phone rang.

It was Sergeant McHenry, the new bagman.

"Mr. Chain, I got bad news. You better come out here before we move the car."

"Car?"

"Your father's dead. We found him in the trunk of a stolen Buick. In an empty lot down from the hardware store."

"You're sure? You're positive, McHenry?"

"Mr. Chain, I knew your father real good. I'm sorry as hell. You want us to take him to the morgue or you want to come out here? I could send a car for you."

"I'll drive myself."

It was a few minutes to the sooty garbage-strewn street. Police ropes had been set up. An ambulance was on hand with its flasher blinking.

A mob of beanie-hatted kids were standing behind the restraining ropes. One kid had a wooden gun made of the end of an orange crate and a rubber band and was miming shots into the opened trunk of the old car.

"The guy is dead."

"Hey, he got no face. Ya seen it, Mikey, no face?"

"Jeez, what a mess."

Heat, dust, stink. Mort braced himself as he walked through a gathering crowd of the curious. Mothers in cotton dresses yanked their children away. *Don't look, don't look, it's a disgrace.*

The words bounced against Morty's ear. His Brownsville. He was part of the streets, the gutter. He and his father.

"A dead guy. Someone got shot."

"Morris! Come upstairs! Geddada there!"

Sergeant McHenry shoved people away. He yelled at the police to make room. Two interns were removing a stretcher from the back of a Brownsville Jewish Hospital ambulance.

"It ain't pretty, Mr. Chain," the sergeant said. Mort was *Mr.* Chain. Jake was always Jake to the cops.

"How long . . . when was it . . . ?"

"They left the trunk slightly open. Wanted to make sure it was found. Some kids opened it. About fifteen minutes ago. He ain't been dead long."

Dusk settled over the steamy street. Hot, hot, as only asphalt and cement could be in July. Mort swallowed. He tried to calm himself. Not just a dead father. An empire was under threat. To kill a Chain was no small matter. Whoever did it had connections. For years the Chains had avoided violence. Mort had taught his father a better way—pay off, make it profitable for everyone, give service, organize.

He stared at his father's ruined head. Half of it blown away. A hole in the forehead, small, neat. A dark red gouge. But the side of his head . . .

"At close range, we figure," McHenry said. "If I know Jake, he wasn't ready for it. Someone pulled a fast one on him."

"Pop was getting careless, I guess." His voice was hoarse, distant. "Oh, my God. Oh, pop . . ."

They wrapped the corpse in a rubber sheet. It wasn't long enough. Jake's polished brown-and-white shoes, expensive summer kicks, protruded from the stretcher.

Mort made his mind up. Closed coffin. Short service. And he would get the murderers.

Sarah collapsed. She had to go back to the wheelchair. She rarely left it after Jake's murder. At the cemetery she wailed uncontrollably. Mort and Hilda stood behind her and tried to comfort her.

In the funeral home on Pitkin Avenue, Rabbi Piltz had been brief and casual, a little too much so for Mort's comfort. But the son did not take issue with the rabbi's stingy words. You lived hard, you died hard. The rabbi had no use for people like Jake Chain, or even Morty, he had made clear on many occasions.

It was a surprisingly small turnout. The Ferrantes came, Sal unable to look anyone in the eye. Baggie, Dom, and Theresa, she in appropriate black.

The Otzenbergers were there, and Eva and her daughter. Halstead was not present. Nor was Sol, who was still recuperating. Old Yussel Kuflik showed up, and Kalotkin the roofer and a wheezing Flugelman.

The last prayers were said. Stones were tossed on the burnished walnut coffin. Mort had selected a giant stone to be unveiled in a year's time. Sorrow was eating at him internally, but his vulpine face showed nothing. *Control. Confidence.* Courage in the face of disaster, he told himself. Somewhere, people were celebrating Jake Chain's death at age forty-six. A hard man, a troublemaker who couldn't be stopped, finally dead.

In the limousine on the way back to Haven Place, where they would sit in mourning for five days, Hilda took his hand. "Cry, Morty, cry."

"I cry inside."

"I really liked your father. I really did. He was a great guy. Who would want to do such a thing?"

Sarah's mouth was hard. "He lived bad, he died bad. Oh, my Jake."

Love had gone out of the marriage years ago, Mort understood. He was sorry for his mother, but he sensed a bitter sound of fulfillment in her mourning. Jake had provided well, comforted her, helped her to walk again. But there had been no love. Mort flinched inwardly. Was his own marriage going the same way? Were the Chains incapable of love?

"Some guy, your old man," Benny was saying. "Strong? I never seen a guy like him. Afraid of nothing. Right, Eva?"

"Right, Benny." Eva had sat down with Sarah in the parlor on Haven Place after they arrived and was holding her palsied hand. In the backyard, her daughter, Lillian, a shy, solemn girl, was climbing a sour-cherry tree. Marty Chain, seven, was trying to look up her skirt.

"What a man," Benny said. "No more like him. Afraid of nothing."

Dr. Abelman and his wife dropped by to pay their condolences. "A damn shame," Doc said. "I liked Jake. He was the only man on Haven Place could lick me at arm wrestling. You all right, Sarah?"

"Yes, yes, I'll manage, doctor. I'm going to live with my son."

Hilda looked horrified. She opened her red mouth. Her eyes popped slightly. News to her.

Abelman asked Mort how his children were. He had delivered all of them—Martin, Davey, Iris. Hilda and Mort bragged about them. They apologized for not calling Dr. Abelman more often, but it was a long trip from Ocean Parkway to Brownsville. He would understand. . . .

Abelman looked into the backyard. Weeds and stunted trees. Only the cherry tree, in which a leggy girl was climbing, was worth anything. His own yard was magnificent—peonies, roses, pepper bushes, magnolia. But the Chains were not people of the soil; they were people of violence.

Eva took Mort aside in the yard. They sat on a slatted bench and watched their children playing. Lillian had come down from the tree. Martin was showing her his marbles. He took out a "realie" and a "purie" and two "immies" and marked off a square in the packed dirt. "Ya ever play marbles?" he asked.

"No."

"I'll learn ya."

"Teach you, *teach* you," Mort shouted to his son. "Go on, Lillian, it's fun."

Eva laughed. "Very good, Mort. Lillian is a bit protected. It would do her good to learn some of the games we played. Hide-and-seek. Boxball. Potsy."

Mort smiled. No wonder his father had loved his cousin. What a face. What a woman! But today she was subdued, something gone out of her.

Lillian hiked her skirt, knelt, knuckled an "immie," and tried to hit one of the stationary marbles. Martin shook his head and showed her how.

" 'My mother, your mother live across the way,' " Eva said. " 'Every night they have a fight, this is what they say.' I forget the rest. Mort, do you remember it?"

"No. I never had much time for games. I wanted to work with pop as long as I can remember."

Through an opened rear window they could hear Dr. Heilig and Dr. Abelman discussing Jake's death.

The coroner says the first one killed him. . . .

Second to make sure, took his head apart. . . .

Funny, Sam, I had the feeling no one could ever kill Jake. . . .

"Eva, you asked pop to help you, didn't you?" Mort asked. "About Sol?"

She nodded and put a handkerchief to her mouth.

"You wanted him to see Schonkeit."

"I—I—was sure Jake could help. Mort, I'm sorry. I don't know what he did, who he talked to. He said maybe he could stop them. Everyone said that fat man, Wesselberg, was part of Schonkeit's mob. I thought . . . Oh, my God, if I had anything to do with Jake's death . . ."

"Jake could take care of himself. Schonkeit didn't want any more killing. But the Meal Ticket . . ."

She looked at him. Tears filmed her eyes. Hard to believe Jake was dead. That powerful presence. Protector of the pickets. His primitive mind was never quite sure what it was all about—hours, wages, working conditions. Only that if you got hit, you hit back. She had induced him, with her smile, her face, the charms that made him dizzy and desirous, to go back into violence. And now he was dead.

"I can't apologize to you enough, Mort. You, Sarah, your children. Jake wasn't even fifty years old."

"It's all right, Eva. They won't get away with it."

Their children ran to them. Lillian liked her cousin Martin. He was so smart! He was giving her a "realie" and a "purie." He had taught her how to shoot marbles.

Mort stared a moment at Eva's daughter. Long, thin, pale, like her father. Not pretty, the way Eva was. Too much jaw and a narrow head. Suddenly he felt competitive. The need to match Eva's child with his own. She had found an easy way, marrying a rich *goy*. Nothing had been easy for the Chains. Everything had been dangerous. But for his children, it would be pie and ice cream all the way.

Hilda was summoning him from the window. Mr. Dunphy, Sol's assistant, was on the phone. Mort entered the house and took the call, pausing to kiss his weeping mother, accepting condolences from Dr. Heilig.

Dunphy had interesting information. On the same day that Jake had gone to meet Schonkeit, Wesselberg had vanished. Nobody knew where he had been that afternoon. His girlfriend said he had been checking his trucks in the morning, had lunch at his office, and then had gone to an afternoon meeting. Nobody knew where. It was not unusual for the Meal Ticket to make the rounds, intimidating customers, picking up bribes.

"What do you think, Mr. Dunphy?" Mort asked. "You think it's connected with what happened to my father?"

"I don't know, Mr. Chain. It could be. You said you think your father saw Schonkeit that afternoon?"

"He said he was."

"We'll have to have a chat with Schonkeit. And Wesselberg."

As Dunphy spoke, Herman Wesselberg was lying in six feet of lime in a grove of swamp maples and pin oaks ten miles from Route 17, the Catskills highway. The nearest habitation was a farm seven miles away. The grave had been well covered, and the Saratoga Avenue Meal Ticket was doomed to remain buried there forever, mourned by few.

Chapter 45

"You can stay here," Mort said to Tommy Tuttle. "You and the children. My father would have wanted it that way."

They sat on the upper veranda of the stucco house. It was a quiet afternoon. The Chain fleet rode quietly at the moorings. Bobbing gently, water slapping their sleek sides, they rested like domesticated dolphins.

"I loved him," she said. "I'm sorry. It's not the right thing to say to you. Your mother must hate me. And hate my children."

Mort looked over the railing and saw his half brother, Mackenzie (*Mackenzie? What kind of a name for a Chain?*), fishing for snapper blues from the pier. The boy was rugged, towheaded. Mort felt no kinship with him, but no enmity. A stranger. He was glad his father had known the good-looking woman, had the kid. They were nothing to Mort, less than nothing. But in deference to his father, he owed her favors.

"There's no will," Mort said.

"I guess that leaves me broke. I'm not worried. I managed for a long time on my own."

Mort knew about the lady captain running open boats out of Sheepshead Bay. Some reporter had called her "Madame Pirate," printed a lurid account of how she carried guns in her skirt, cursed like a petty officer. All lies. Tommy had dignity and style.

"We'll take care of you," Mort said. "And your children. You can stay in the house as long as you want. Pick out any of the boats. It's yours. Take two for yourself."

She shaded her eyes. She did not want to discuss property or money. She had loved the big man. "Stop," she said. Weeping, she turned her head. "Don't talk about those things. He's dead. He was the best man I ever knew. He wasn't afraid of anything. And he was kind. If he'd been educated or treated decently when he was little . . ."

"I know. But you'll be looked after. The company will keep you on as manager. In a few years we'll close this down, but you can have the boats, I'll see to it your kids go to school."

Tommy wiped her eyes and got up. Below, Sal Ferrante, in white-on-white shirt and brown silk trousers, appeared from the warehouse. He watched Little Mac fishing. Sal spit into the water, squinted up at the veranda, but did not wave to Tommy or Mort. He slithered into the garage. He liked dark, damp places, Mort thought. Always in the shadows. He belonged in warehouses, underground garages, storage rooms. A goddamn lizard or a spider.

"Why was he killed?" she asked Mort.

"I'm not sure. Maybe he was killed by mistake. I can't figure it out." He would tell her no more. She was not of the Chain blood. His plans for revenge were of no concern to her.

There was in Mort Chain a gutter instinct, street wisdom, cunning. Like his father, he could often anticipate connivance, treachery. He had not liked the way Sal had stared at them silently. Usually Sal came to him. He whined, complained, moaned. Another odd circumstance: Since Jake's death, Sal, a perpetual *kvetcher,* had not come pleading for a bigger chunk of the profits. *The little bastard,* Mort thought. You'd think he'd be breaking my chops, demanding part of Jake's profits. But not a word. The same shuffling creep, the same cockroach eyes. Why?

"The day my father said he was going to New York," Mort said. "Remember? The day they found the body?"

"What? Six days ago?"

"Yeah. Thursday. Was Sal around here?"

"Let me see. He's usually here afternoons, four or five days a week. Thursday . . . I don't think so. Wait. I'm sure he wasn't. Baggie came in with Anton. He was upset because Sal wasn't here to check the cargo. Baggie thought the skipper had shortchanged them. In fact he tried to call Sal in Brooklyn."

Mort dropped the subject. It was a tough one to figure. Schonkeit didn't usually resort to violence. And why be suspicious of Sal? Ferrante had gotten rich with the Chains. Stubborn as he was, he understood that he was a cheap hoodlum, a *cafon',* without the Chain brains and muscle. Mort and Jake had built the business, come up with the big-money ideas. When they went legit, Mort decided, he'd buy Sal out. Maybe he'd keep Theresa on the payroll.

He was leaving Tommy, kissing her dutifully on the cheek, assuring her again she'd be taken care of, when an overseas call came through for him. London wanted Mr. Chain.

Mort took it in the radio operator's shack. Slow day, French, the old navy man, said, greeting Mort. No calls from the big boats.

It was McVey, the British executive. He was a bit upset. A New York attorney with important bank references had come to see him. Poking

about, telling McVey of the unfortunate death of Mortimer Chain's father
—"Awfully sorry, Mr. Chain, terrible tragedy"—and that McVey's firm
might be making a dreadful mistake getting involved with people like the
Chains. Odd thing was, this very lawyer showed up in Edinburgh two days
later and gave the same story to the North Border Distillers, Ltd., another
of the firms Mr. Chain had a contract with.

"It sounds as if he wants me out and his people in," Mort said. "What
was his name?"

"A Mr. Bunthorne. Rather elegant young man. Wall Street firm."

"Who did he say he represented?"

"It was in confidence, Mr. Chain. Ah, well, you and I are partners, so
to speak." (Mort had a secret deal with McVey and the other British distillers he had lined up. They were getting huge kickbacks, more money
than they earned in three years' salary from their pinchpenny firms.) "He
said he represented a Mr. Melvin Schonkeit."

Mort thanked the Englishman. It didn't take the Paymaster long to
move. Whether he had anything to do with Jake's death or not, he sure as
hell was going to use it. *Only sure things* was Schonkeit's creed. Mort felt
confined, threatened. He had to move fast. He remembered the name:
Bunthorne.

In early September, after Jake had been buried, and Wesselberg listed
among missing persons, Mort relaxed in the Ocean Parkway mansion, eating a lonely dinner and listening to the radio.

*. . . a canvass by supporters of Governor Franklin D. Roosevelt re-
vealed that he will have enough delegate support for nomination on the
first ballot, an Albany citizens' group announced today. Governor Roosevelt's friends say he can muster eight hundred and six first-ballot votes,
more than enough to secure the Democratic nomination for the presidency. . . .*

Goodbye bootlegging. Mort made notes on a lined pad as he ate his
chicken salad and sipped ice tea. Harry Twine, the Chains' man-of-all-
work, served him. The black youth sat opposite Mort, waiting his employer's word. Hilda would never have permitted the help to sit at the
table. But Hilda was in Long Beach with the children, the nursemaid, and
the cook, cool in a ten-room house. Buster's son stayed in Brooklyn to
help Mort.

"That Roosevelt, he good?" Harry asked.

"Yeah, I guess so. Don't interrupt, Harry."

Mort continued making notes. They had more capital, more cash, than
they needed. What they would need was plant space, a delivery system, and,
above all, unlimited supplies of neutral grain spirits. They would have to
start distilling alcohol in advance of the inevitable repeal of the Volstead

Act. There were millions of gallons of pure alcohol remaining in government warehouses. The Chains had tapped much of it. But not nearly enough.

Mort decided that was his next order of business. Sharp operators like Remus, in the Middle West, had made a fortune working scams with government alky. Mort needed the same kind of access until such time as Harris Weltfish could start manufacturing pure grain alcohol on a mass scale. It would no longer be possible to make a living selling rotgut, detoxified alky, fake scotch, phony gin.

"Mist' Chain," Harry said as he served Mort a dish of chocolate ice cream, "can I get an advance on my salary?"

"Why? You lose a big one to the bookie?"

Harry cleaned the table as the radio concluded the newscast. FDR was asking for twenty million dollars to help the unemployed; Hoover was warning that this would lead to communism; the French and the United States were lending the English four hundred million dollars to keep them from going broke.

"No, sir. I'm busted 'cause I *won* my bet."

Mort nailed Harry with a steely eye. He had always liked the kid, loved old Buster. Burned to a chunk of charcoal in the old place. He and Jake had promised Mrs. Twine the boys would always have jobs.

"You *won* on a horse and you're broke?"

"Rocco tapped out. He tell his customers someone hit him for a hundred grand on a horse and he is broke. All of us small bettors got to wait to get paid."

Rocco Lentini was the local bookmaker. He worked out of a speakeasy in Coney Island, one of Mort's customers. Mort knew the bookie, even though he and Jake had never played the horses.

"Someone took Rocco?" Mort asked. "I can't believe it."

"Yeah. He suspicious. Some hard guys make him pay off. So he broke. He think someone past-posting him."

Something stirred in Mort's mind. Something he had heard from Baggie about a racket, a way of screwing bookmakers. Getting race results *before* the bookies got them.

Mort had Harry call Rocco. Yeah, he'd be at the Golden Surf Social Club late. For the time being he was paying off with markers. He was sure Mr. Chain would understand. Harry Twine, that nice coon, would get paid as soon as Rocco got healthy.

An hour later, Mort sat in the damp cellar of the wire room, chatting with Rocco. The bookie was a neckless ex-pug who had fought under the name of Mickey Haggerty. Pinkie ring, a squashed left ear, a few gold teeth. At one time he had been a very hard guy. Two murder raps and countless arrests. But he had gone as straight as he could.

"I catch the punk he'll be floating in the river," Rocco said hoarsely.

"There ain't nothing worster in the world than a creep cheats a bookie with a sure bet."

"Tell me what you think is happening."

"Some guy is getting results faster'n we do. He's smart as a snake, because he uses a different beard every time. And he never hits a bookie more than oncet a week. How can we tell when he's gonna hit?"

"How bad was the last one?"

Rocco studied a stack of betting slips. Behind him, his brother, Jimmy Guts, posted results from Santa Anita. A few bettors groaned. Losers again. Mort wondered where all the money came from. Guys selling apples, guys out of work, breadlines, relief, but the wire rooms had no shortage of suckers.

"The prick hit me for near a hundred grand, Mr. Chain. We got a twenty-to-one limit, and he bets five grand on Rosemary Kay at Jamaica. An allowance race. Horse pays eighteen-to-one. Guy's name was O'Toole, a fat mick. Says he's from Gerritsen Beach. If we don't pay, he's got a brother in City Hall. So I pay. I can't shit in my own kitchen."

"Rocco, how do you think they do it?"

"Beats me. A semaphore maybe, like in the navy. From the roof. Or a telegraph hidden somewhere on the track. Phones are out—they're illegal at the track. The Pinkertons patrol the tracks pretty good."

"Any suspicions?"

Rocco scratched his neck. "Every book I know thinks Schonkeit has something to do with it. I can't believe it. With all his dough, picking on bookies? The Paymaster set up half the bookies. It can't be him."

"Suppose I found out."

Rocco's eyes turned the color of raw calf's liver. The lids drooped and his voice was a growl. "Big as he is, he'll end up part of the Belt Parkway."

The following day, Mort visited one of the Pinkerton supervisors at Jamaica racetrack. He gave the man two thousand dollars in cash and promised to deliver a case of scotch to his home in Valley Stream that night. In return, the Pink was to "sweep" the track with a special squad, looking for hidden phones, a signaling system, or a Morse telegraph that might be sneaking out race results.

Two days later the Pinkerton assured Mort Chain (a pleasure to do business with one of the Chains, and sorry about your father, sir) that the track was clean. His men could find nothing.

Sol Heilig, recovered from his wounds, was back on the job, a bit stiff in the arm and shoulder but ready to pursue his probe of the rackets. Jake's death had added a new element; but Sol and Dunphy were still mainly concerned with the Brunstein murder. They were convinced that Wesselberg and Frummer were behind it. But the fat man had evaporated without a trace. Shikey remained untouchable, secure in his offices in the garment district.

Sol regretted Jake's murder. He knew all about Crazy Jake's past. But he had a Brownsville loyalty to the tough man. After all, he and his brother Abe had taught Jake to read and write. Not a truly bad man, Sol reflected. There were a lot worse. He told Mort he would keep him informed if he learned anything.

One morning he telephoned Mort at the new Brooklyn Supply plant in Long Island City. Mort operated out of a fancy suite of rooms. Dr. Weltfish occupied an adjoining office when he wasn't in the laboratory.

"There's no question, Mort," Sol said. "Your father was with Schonkeit the day he was shot. He says Jake came to talk business. He denies anything to do with Jake's death. They talked, and then Jake said he had to see Wesselberg."

"Where?"

"Schonkeit says he has no idea."

Mort mulled the notion. Logic there. The Meal Ticket could have killed his father, then skipped town. He would lie low until the heat was off.

"We're also working on some old hoodlum who gambles in Schonkeit's game. The guy says he saw your father."

"What's the bum's name?"

"Joe Kuflik."

Mort paused. "He's an old *gonif* who used to work for my father. There's something fishy, Sol."

Chapter 46

"That got to be it, boss," Harry Twine said. "I been round and round the neighborhood. Lookin' for a place with a clear shot at the finish line. Three stories high. Big window."

Mort and the young black man were in the cab of a Brooklyn General Supply truck on a tree-lined street in Queens. Behind them and to their right was the Jamaica racetrack. In the back of the truck was Harry's brother Eddie, a huge muscular man. He worked as foreman for Mort.

"You sure?" Mort asked.

"I cased every house, every street. I climbed on roofs and over fences. Good thing you got me this phone-company suit and the tools."

Lithe and leathery, Harry was dressed in the olive-green uniform of a phone-company repairman. A leather belt laden with tools dangled from his lean waist. He also carried a .22 pistol. Mort had a .38 in his inner coat pocket. It was mid-September. A hot, hazed, nose-choking day, heavy with pollen and grit.

"On the third floor?" Mort asked.

"I figure. Hey, look."

A glint of sunlight bounced off something in the window. A glassy brilliant object was poking between the blue curtains.

"Okay," Mort said. "What can we lose? Park the truck opposite the place. You go first. You mind?"

"For Jake, I do damn near anything."

"Me and Eddie will be behind you. You get any lip, pull the gun."

The three men paused at the house. "Third floor, back stairs," Harry said. "Front door for the ground floor only. Landlord lives there."

They followed Harry up the narrow wooden stairs at the rear. No one seemed to be at home in the other two apartments. In fact, it almost seemed to Mort that they were deserted. Dust, old newspapers, silence.

Harry knocked at the third-floor door.

"A moment, sir, just a moment." The voice was frail and dignified. Mort motioned Eddie to stand behind him.

"Phone company," Harry Twine said.

"Ah, the inevitable phone company. AT and T, avaunt."

The door was opened by a slender, hollow-faced man of about sixty. He wore an eye patch and was smoking a cigarette in an ivory holder. His nose was invalid-thin and his Adam's apple bobbed. Long pepper-and-salt hair was parted in the middle. His tongue flicked at a hairline moustache as he studied Eddie's innocent black face.

"Ah, an Ethiopian. I sent for no phone company."

"There been a complaint," Harry said. "Got it here." He consulted a pink pad and read off the address.

"Cops," Mort said. He moved Harry aside. Eddie, towering, followed him into the room. Mort shoved his gun into the man's kidney. "Turn around. Frisk him, Eddie."

The man was unarmed.

"I daresay," he said. "I daresay, this is irregular."

"Here it is, boss," Harry said.

A pair of enormous binoculars were mounted on a tripod at the window. Harry looked into them. *"Sheee-it.* Got him a clean look at the finish line. Ain't you smart?"

"A hobby, gentlemen," the man said. "My name is Colonel Elwood Craig, former owner of a large stable in Landona, Maryland. Undone by the events of 1929. This is my only mode of relaxation."

Mort shoved him into a sagging easy chair adjacent to the window. In front of it was a bridge table with four telephones, several pads, pencils, and a stack of *Morning Telegraph*s and *Daily Racing Form*s.

"Schonkeit want action today?" Mort asked.

"I don't believe I know the name."

Mort crashed the .38 against his jaw. Trembling, Colonel Craig wiped blood from his lip. "Dear me. I cannot abide pain. You're wrong, sir. What was the name?"

Mort pulled up a folding chair and sat down, leveling the gun at the man's head. Eddie and Harry wandered around the apartment. Unmade bed, kitchen sink filled with dirty dishes, an old white cat lapping milk from a cracked plate. There were large photos of Man o' War and Regret pinned to the wall. Old racing and horse-breeding journals littered the shabby furniture and the unswept floor.

"Tell us how it works, Craig. I'll blow your head off if you don't. But first I'll let these two guys work you over so you'll hurt like you never hurt in your life."

"He mean it," Harry said. "Eddie, look at this."

Eddie squinted through the binoculars. "Man, he got him the whole homestretch and the finish line. A race finishin' right now. Can see the number on the horse. Number five win."

Mort pointed the revolver at Colonel Craig's nose. "Schonkeit waiting?"

"Ah, no. No, sir. He usually gives me instructions between one and two o'clock. He can't be tied to a phone, so he usually restricts himself to the sixth and seventh races."

"You expect a call?"

"Yes." His filmy eyes pleaded for mercy. "I shouldn't be revealing this. I'm paid rather well, and betraying Mr. Schonkeit . . ."

Eddie and Harry were taking turns looking through the binoculars, shifting the focus.

"Mr. Chain," Harry said, "you ain't gonna believe this. I can see the tote board. Payoffs and all. This a maiden race. Pay five-to-two. Eddie, how come we ain't this smart?"

Mort picked up a telephone and dialed Rocco Lentini in Brooklyn. He told the bookmaker to drive out to the house near the Jamaica track. It might be a good idea, Mort suggested, to bring some other bookie who'd been caught with a big late bet recently.

It took a few more slaps, cuffs, and kicks to open Craig's mouth. It was pretty much as Mort figured. Schonkeit was using an army of beards. Not just in New York, but in Buffalo, Detroit, Cleveland, as far west as St. Louis. He'd get a confirmed winner from the "colonel," and while the bookies were accepting bets before the results came in, the beards would be given a number, bet the horse heavily, collect, and lie low for a few weeks.

"What does he pay you, colonel?" Mort asked.

"A hundred dollars a week."

"Cheap bum."

Rocco arrived an hour later with a bookie named Calloway, a choleric Irishman from Hell's Kitchen. He had tufted orange eyebrows and raging yellow eyes. Mort knew about him. Newsstand Calloway, an eccentric who wore Salvation Army suits, slept on a cot in back of his bookie establishment, and was worth four million dollars. He rarely spoke, but did a great deal of spitting on Colonel Craig's cracked linoleum floor.

They waited in the hot musty room. Eddie Twine went out for sandwiches and beer. It became chokingly warm; too many sweaty bodies lolling about on Craig's ramshackle furniture. Mort sent Eddie out again, this time to buy an electric fan and a cake of ice.

At three in the afternoon, Schonkeit called. Mort warned Craig not to give anything away.

"Yes, sir," Craig whispered. "The sixth race. Allowances for three-year-olds and up."

Rocco rubbed his chin. His bagging eyes were full of hate and sorrow. Any man who would cheat his bookmaker would eat shit, would make a whore of his sister. Schonkeit may have been the Paymaster, King Fixer, but from now on he was a target as far as Rocco Lentini was concerned. Newsstand Calloway agreed.

Post time for the race approached. Mort shoved Craig into the folding chair. The colonel held his head and whimpered.

"You be ready to phone him. Understand, colonel?"

"I do, Mr. Chain."

"You pull a smart one, the colored boys will tear your arms off. They'll pull your eyes out so you can't spot horses."

"Be my pleasure," Eddie Twine said.

"Race started," Mort said. He sat in Craig's chair and watched the race through the magnifying lenses. It was a mile and one-sixteenth. The finish line was in direct line of sight with the Zeiss-Ikon lenses. The number-two horse, Sandycove Boy, won by a length. Not a bad price either. Seven-to-two.

Mort turned to the colonel. "You getting him?"

Craig nodded. He was gray. The operator was buzzing Mr. Schonkeit.

"Tell him number six won," Mort said.

"I can't . . . I can't, really, Mr. Chain."

"Tell him number six or you're a dead colonel." He put the barrel into Craig's ear.

In a hoarse voice Craig said, "Number six." He hung up.

Rocco picked up a phone. "Let's see if the prick picks on me or you this time, Newsstand."

Calloway went to another phone. In a few minutes they had determined that neither of their establishments had been hit with a bet on the six horse in the sixth race. Rocco called a half-dozen more bookies. He hit pay dirt in Queens. Somebody named Lifton had placed a bet for five thousand dollars on the six horse, Andiron Dog, with a Maspeth betting parlor. Lifton had looked like he'd swallowed a live bluefish when the results came in with Sandycove Boy the winner. The Queens bookie told Rocco that Lifton had almost fainted, then raced to a phone when he learned the result.

Rocco grinned and slammed the phone down. "Thanks, Mr. Chain. You're okay. This clinches it. We'll learn Schonkeit a lesson."

Mort nodded. "Give him five minutes to eat his heart out. If he's placing bets around the country, he might have how much bet, Craig?"

"Forty thousand dollars, sir."

"It's forty thousand he can flush down the toilet, not to mention what he won't win." Mort looked at Rocco and Newsstand Calloway. "You guys are gonna have to do something. What's he taken you for over the last few years? Two hundred? Four? Five? The bookies' association is going to have to teach him a lesson."

They waited another five minutes. Mort ordered Craig to call Schonkeit again. The Paymaster was in his duplex penthouse on Central Park West.

Mort seized the phone. "Schonkeit? Mort Chain. I'm here with your spotter, Colonel Craig. We just screwed you on that race. The number-two horse won."

"Chain? What . . . ?" It was a rare moment of panic for the gambler.

"You heard it. A couple of bookies are with me and they watched the procedure. Rocco Lentini and Newsstand Calloway. There is going to be a meeting of the Greater New York Bookmakers Association tonight. A decision will be reached on how to handle people who indulge in past-posting."

Rocco ripped the phone from Mort's hand. "This is Lentini, Schonkeit. Tell your beard O'Toole he'd better run and hide. I'll blow his head off when I find him."

Mort offered the phone to Calloway. Newsstand waved his hand. No need to waste words. The code had been broken.

"Chain, what do you want?" Schonkeit asked. "This is a mistake. I don't know anyone named Craig. I wouldn't dream of past-posting. Something can be worked out. Tell me what you want."

"Who killed my father?"

"Wesselberg."

"Not good enough, Schonkeit. How? Where? He was with you that day. You better have some more ideas or I won't be able to influence Mr. Lentini."

Negotiations with Schonkeit for the repayment of the four hundred thousand dollars he had bilked from bookies went on for several weeks. Where money was concerned, the Paymaster stood firm: a misunderstanding; Chain had framed him. Craig had vanished. Schonkeit tried to divide the delegation of bookies that called on him—Rocco and Newsstand against the others. He threatened, cajoled, promised to pay off in installments. And he refused to tell Mort Chain anything about the death of Crazy Jake.

The first installment was ten thousand dollars in treasury notes, paid to Rocco Lentini. On attempting to deposit them, Lentini discovered that they were stolen. The bookie spent an uncomfortable day with federal agents.

Schonkeit tried to pay off a lesser bookie from Queens. The money, five thousand in hundreds, was counterfeit. Later, people wondered why he had panicked. They did not understand Schonkeit; cheating someone was more important than cash value.

On Saturday, October 17, 1931, Schonkeit was returning to his apartment on Central Park West in his chauffeured limousine. He had just attended the NYU-Rutgers football game at Yankee Stadium and had won ten thousand dollars betting on NYU, a 27–7 victor.

As he leaned into the window of his car to give the driver instructions, a man in a tan overcoat and a brown cap walked out of the lobby of the building and shot the Paymaster four times in the head and neck. He was dead before he hit the pavement.

The bookmakers' association professed no knowledge of the killing, arguing that, with Schonkeit dead, they now stood no chance whatever of regaining their stolen dollars.

The death of Schonkeit got Mort no closer to solving the riddle of his father's murder. But he was patient. He could wait.

His son Marty, an intelligent seven-year-old, had been enrolled in September in the Polytechnical Preparatory Country Day School (Poly Prep), the fanciest private school in Brooklyn. Davey was in kindergarten. Iris was at home.

Hilda became active in charitable affairs. Mort spent long hours at his new offices with Dr. Weltfish, laying the groundwork for repeal. They were working to beat the clock—a year away, they figured—and get into heavy production of legal whiskey.

Schonkeit's death had left a vacuum in the underworld, and into the void stepped meaner, more brutal men. They were largely Sicilians, once used by Schonkeit as enforcers, but now taking over as executives of the crime empire the Paymaster had put together.

An intelligent and imaginative man of twenty-seven, Mort Chain knew that he could not function in their world, and that in time they would seek him out. It was therefore obligatory that as soon as the Volstead Act was repealed, the Chains shed their underworld connections.

Cerrone, Razzini, Nudo, Notaro—they were names Mort had seen in the papers. Hoarse, dark-eyed men he had met in the past, as customers, suppliers, or as people who had to be paid off. Now they were rising like scum to the surface of a dank pool. Schonkeit may have been a liar and a cheater, but he had, Mort reflected (as he sat with Dr. Weltfish in his office), a kind of shiny class. The new criminal lords would have to be by-passed. Early on they would have to be impressed with the independence and legitimacy of the Chain operation.

Weltfish advised Mort to form a new corporation—a pharmaceutical house legitimately engaged in manufacturing cough medicines, tonics, and the like. Thus they could make new claims for government grain alcohol. Once they impressed the right combination of public functionaries, they would arrange it so that the moment repeal came, Chain interests would purchase entire warehouses and distilleries.

"We need them, Mr. Chain," Weltfish said. He was arrow-thin, with a beaked nose, black eyebrows that met over the bridge of his nose, a pointed chin, piercing black eyes. At City College he had been a champion high hurdler.

Mort and Dr. Weltfish worked long hours planning the takeover of warehouses. The bribes would be staggering. Government employees already paid off would have to be paid off again. Higher-ups and supervisors would have to be reached. Bonded warehouses could then supply them with pure alcohol until such time as Weltfish's distilleries went into operation. As importers of English gin and scotch, they would have a head start in the marketplace. But the big money, Weltfish explained, would be in "blended" whiskey.

"I'm sorry the old man didn't live to see this," Mort said sadly. "He would have appreciated it."

"Quite a guy, your dad," Weltfish said. The chemist did not go beyond that. Like Mort, he had a vision of the future. In it, there would be no place for a thug like Jake.

Mort buzzed Theresa and asked for the name of the firm that employed Bunthorne, the Wall Street lawyer, who had been cruising around England representing Schonkeit and trying to steal the Chains' distillers.

Theresa called back in a few minutes. "Horace Bunthorne is with Weed, Belanger, Ballison, Dean, and Bunthorne. They're at Ten Wall Street."

"Call him, Theresa."

They would need not only supplies, government contacts, customers, and a pharmaceutical company, they also would need the best legal counsel available. Mort studied the books, reviewed their profits and anticipated income, and realized they could afford the best. *Horace Bunthorne.* The name alone, Mort decided, would make him worth his fee.

He thumbed through the *Times.* Al Capone had gotten eleven years for income-tax evasion. Two misdemeanors and three felonies. The Chains would strive for respectability, operate within the law, say farewell to *shtarking,* violence, thuggery.

Except, of course, in the matter of his murdered father. He would pursue the truth until he learned it, and he would exact vengeance in the Chain tradition.

Chapter 47

The week before Christmas, Mort and Hilda shopped on Pitkin Avenue, their old neighborhood, buying Chanukah-Christmas presents for their three children. Prices were much lower in Brownsville, Hilda argued. She was an Otzenberger at heart, part of the old tradition. Her father, Benny, was getting old and lazy, anchored to the padded swivel chair in his office. But he still carried clout. Five times he had been summoned upstate for meetings with Democratic leaders, once by Louis Howe, Roosevelt's right-hand man. Would Brooklyn back FDR? they asked Benny. Was Carl Hubbell a pitcher? he responded.

Mort and Hilda, lugging games, dolls, a kiddy-car for Iris, a paint set for Davey, boxing gloves for Marty, came out of the toy store. Harry Twine jumped from the driver's seat of the Pierce-Arrow to help them carry the presents. He had been reading the morning edition of the *Daily News*. "Legs" Diamond was dead. The clay pigeon had taken a fatal slug in an Albany hotel.

Mort shrugged when Harry showed him the headline. One more dumb hoodlum dead. The Chains were putting all that behind them. Soon the new company, backed by the Chain fortune, would lead them into corporate America.

"Beat it, bum," Harry Twine said. He was pushing a ragged panhandler, a shuffling vagrant. The man was trying to get to Mort.

"Mr. Chain, please, you got a buck for me? A little Chanukah gelt?" the man asked.

"Morty, get in the car," Hilda said. "Bums I don't need. Harry, get rid of him. Give him a dime."

"You and Rockefeller." Mort laughed.

"Mr. Chain, please?" He was a mass of rags, scraps of patched clothing. An unraveling woolen cap was pulled over his ears.

"How come you know my name?"

"I'm Joe Kuflik. I used to *shtark* for your father, God bless him. I'm sorry he died. They called me Yussel the Bear. I won't sell apples or go on relief. You got a job for an old man? Anything. Because I got something you should know."

"No promises. What do you know?"

"Could I have a dollar?"

Mort peeled off a ten and gave it to him. The hand that reached for it was like a hairy paw.

"Morty, come on!" Hilda called from the car. Harry tucked the raccoon blanket around her legs, stacked the packages in the trunk.

"When your father was killed, Mr. Chain . . ."

Mort grabbed the man's frayed lapels. "What about it?"

"I was working for Shikey Frummer. Shikey sent a bunch of us to the speakeasy where your father came. Later I carried out Wesselberg's body. Someone else got rid of it."

"What about my father?"

"Some—somebody—got both of them. I don't know how it happened. A fight—who knows? Downstairs, like a second basement. So they buried the Meal Ticket. Some other guys took away your father."

"Who killed him?"

"Please don't tell no one, Mr. Chain. That skinny guy who works for you. He was hanging around. I had to take a leak. I went outside and I seen him in the hall."

"Who? *Who?*"

"The kid who sold hokey-pokey. The one with the crazy eyes."

"Sal."

"I swear I seen him there. Maybe he came to protect your old man."

Mort gave him another ten dollars.

"Thanks, Mr. Chain. A Happy Chanukah to you and the missus. A good year, also."

"Same to you, Kuflik. Buy yourself a warm coat."

In the car, Hilda nestled close to him, locked arms, kissed his neck. "What was that all about?"

"An old friend of pop's."

"Such a long talk?"

"He wanted a job."

Careful, careful, Mort thought. Sal would have to be dealt with. With the Chain enterprises ready to turn respectable, there would be no need for Sal Ferrante anyway.

He might, he thought, keep Theresa on payroll for a while, then retire her when her age began to tell and she no longer satisfied him.

1960

Myron Malkin's Notebook

It's a plain office and he's a plain man, Sol Heilig. Mid-sixties. Stocky, rumpled, gray hair needing cutting. He's got tired gentle eyes, a snub nose, and a slightly ornate way of speaking. I can picture him in a courtroom. Polite, patient. *If it please the court, Your Honor, my client, Mr. Chain, has not been given an opportunity* . . .

"So you're out of politics, Mr. Heilig?" I ask.

"More or less. I don't like the way the Republicans are going. My heart was with the Fusion movement. Good government, no party labels. After LaGuardia died, I lost interest."

"How does the election look to you?"

"Kennedy. Close, but Kennedy. The fact that he's an Irish Catholic won't hurt him. It'll elect him. The Democrats are losing their grip on the blue-collars. The workers would run to Nixon in a second, but Kennedy will be one of theirs, so they'll vote for him. The only better candidate would be an Irish Catholic southerner."

"You're for Nixon?" I ask, amazed.

"I may sit this one out. I've always been my own man. I wish Norman Thomas was around."

"You're a Republican-Fusion-Socialist, Mr. Heilig?"

"Why not? I like General MacArthur. Myron, read about what he did in Japan after the war. The man was a liberal reformer. But the right-wing idiots who worshiped MacArthur didn't understand him. Politics is more complicated and subtle than you think."

A good man. Still at 60 Court Street, Brooklyn, the lawyers' building. He handles civil rights, criminal cases, class actions.

He's never gotten rich, like his brother, the noted surgeon, Abraham M. Heilig. He reminds me of my late uncle, Dr. Sam Abelman. A moral, honest man. But he isn't cramped by Uncle Doc's perpetual outrage. There's gentleness in Sol Heilig, a remarkable tolerance for human frailty.

A book on the Chains? He laughs. He anticipates my problems. Mort and Martin will never cooperate. When the time comes, they'll hire a historian and tell the story the way they want it told.

"And leave out all the rich stuff. You know a great deal of it, Mr. Heilig."

"Yeees," he drags the word out and stretches. His air-conditioning isn't working too well. There are cracks in the yellow plaster on the walls. Framed photos of Darrow, Debs, LaGuardia. A photograph of Eva Halstead taken sometime in the twenties. Out of doors, her hair flying, standing on a ladder, addressing a rally in Union Square. About what? Sacco and Vanzetti? She's beautiful in the darkened picture. I stare at it.

"You saw my sister?"

"Yes. She's fine. Too peppy for that old folks' home."

He shakes his head. "What a woman. She influenced Abe and me, let me tell you. Made us stay in college while she worked. I guess not many people remember her. Nineteen ten, nineteen twelve, the big strikes. People are more likely to recall the famous wedding. Jewish radical girl, rich Protestant fella."

"I have the clippings. It made big news."

"All us *shnorrers* from Brownsville, elbow-to-elbow with WASP society. Garrison wasn't a bad guy. But the marriage had to break up. It didn't matter that they were from different backgrounds. They were independent souls, big egos. Garry always felt she upstaged him, and I guess she did."

"And their daughter?"

"Lillian? Takes after me, ha-ha. She went into government work. Youngest deputy attorney general in the state. One of the first women to head the special prosecutor's office. She's in Washington now."

Sol Heilig shrugs. His successors came close to nailing Mort. I want to ask about the Ferrante murder, the blinding of Mort.

I tell him about the sightless man sitting on the screened porch overlooking a baseball field. And how he's rigged the game by recruiting overage high-school stars for Camp Spruce Grove and how he loves a winning team. *That's Mort,* Sol agrees. And does he know the story of the counselors hefting guns during Prohibition, while the Chains smuggled whiskey across Lake Champlain?

He knows, he knows. What about Martin? Have I seen him?

I tell Sol that Martin was polite, firm, emphatic, and unemotional. Too busy with his horses, his estates, his corporations. In fact, there was almost a threat from him when I said I wanted to do a book on the Chain family.

"Marty's all right. Got a lot on his mind. Hell, he isn't even forty and he's the head of America's rising conglomerate. Liquor, pharmaceuticals, real estate, vending machines. Martin's so smart he scares me. Not that I see him much. I hear the other boy, Davey, the one in Israel, is a sweetheart. Big, tough, blond kid. Looks like Jake."

"Do you handle any legal work for the Chains?"

"Me? You kidding, Myron?" He laughs noiselessly. No, he's just a Brooklyn lawyer, shlepping along. Do I know the name Horace Bunthorne? he asks. Of Weed, Belanger, Ballison, Dean, and Bunthorne? One of those unpublicized multimillion-dollar Wall Street outfits. Not a Jew in the place, Sol says. But their biggest client is Chain Enterprises. A funny story, he says. Bunthorne, a young hotshot lawyer in the thirties, representing Melvin Schonkeit, went to Europe to try to steal Mort Chain's distilleries.

"Mort not only kept the distilleries but he hired Horace Bunthorne."

His mention of the legendary Schonkeit prompts me to ask him about the Paymaster's death in 1931. Unsolved. Wasn't Sol Heilig a rackets investigator then? Did they look into Schonkeit's murder?

"The story was that he outsmarted himself. Cheating bookies. They tried to get their money back, he refused, and pretty soon he was dead. Right in front of his apartment house on Central Park West. Nobody cried except his wife."

"But—the Chains—were they . . . ?"

"Nobody ever proved anything. Mort and Jake were never in gambling. I might be a prejudiced witness, being related to them. But we never could figure out a connection. There were rumors. Jake was probably murdered by one of Schonkeit's thugs. And it might seem logical that Mort would want to avenge his father. But it wasn't Mort's style to hire gunsels. We also felt Schonkeit was too sharp to be involved in Jake's death. But he did use those monsters, the Meal Ticket and Shikey."

"You sent a Frummer to the electric chair. Which one?"

"Shikey."

"That's right. In 1936, for the murder of a union official named Isaac Brunstein."

"Poor Ike."

"Eva said he was in love with her years ago."

"Who wasn't? I've become an anti–capital punishment man but I didn't mind nailing Shikey. He was no good. A heartless bastard. A disgrace to the unions. Bert Dunphy and I found the Italians in Cleveland who pitched Ike out of the window. Shikey and Wesselberg had put out the contract."

"And out of that kind of—of—horror, the Chain empire grew?"

"Hold it, Myron. The Chains were bootleggers. Culture heroes. Morty was invited to society parties in Great Neck. Mr. Chain, the importer. Jake had a wild streak in him, but his rule was to hit you only if you hit first. Mort was never a real mean guy. He didn't carry a gun, can you believe it? And Martin? He's so respectable he makes me dizzy. If I see his photograph at one more worthy charity event, raising money for orphans, medical research, scholarships, and the Clean Up New York Campaign, I'll puke. Morty and Jake were more fun."

I remark that it's odd how many loose ends there are in the Chain saga. Nobody knows who killed Schonkeit. Nobody knows who killed Jake. And what about a thug named Salvatore Ferrante? Found floating in a Catskill lake with a dozen bullets in him? Was that ever solved?

370   GERALD GREEN

"I'm afraid not, Myron. These people have a tendency to knock each other off. Sal was a spooky little creep. Big family. They were kind of expendable. The Chains used them up. Couple of them got killed in the early days. There was this good-looking sister who never married. Terrific body, long hair, skin like porcelain. She was an old friend of my sister Eva's. A sewing-machine heroine."

"And a friend of Mort's."

"Could be." He shrugs. "She was beautiful for a long time. Dropped out of sight during the war, sometime after Mort was blinded."

Another mystery. Two assailants. One a woman. Hurling acid into Mort's face as he came out of Loew's Flatbush in 1935. They couldn't save his eyes. One was destroyed, the other slowly deteriorated. The man and the woman escaped. Hilda went a little batty after that, Sol says. I make a quick connection: Sal Ferrante's corpse showed up for roll call around that time.

He's hiding something. Playing dumb. Weren't the Chains suspects in the Ferrante murder? I ask.

"But why kill Ferrante? Guys like that you can buy. And nobody ever beat the Chains at that. They bought half a congressional committee in 1946 when they wanted war-surplus chemicals."

"What's your guess?"

Sol says, "When people like Sal, or even a Schonkeit, get killed, it's not easy finding a suspect. Not that there's a shortage. The opposite. Too many people. In Brunstein's case, we narrowed it down pretty fast and were able to pin it on Frummer."

"It's funny, Mr. Heilig . . ."

"What is?"

"You and your family. And the Chains. Not the blood relationships, but the way you both came out of Brownsville. And it's like you and your brother and sister are one side of the coin, and the Chains are the other."

"I'm flattered. Look at me, a lawyer with two suits. I had to take loans to get my sons through college."

"It's not the money that counts. You've done a hell of a lot of admirable things. You still do. Your sister helped build the trade-union movement for women. And your brother—"

"Professor of surgery at Mount Sinai. Inventor of the Heilig procedure in thoracic surgery. We're what you might call achievers. Martin Chain can buy and sell all of us in one afternoon."

"But look how he got it. You can't kid me. There may have been a lot of bootleg whiskey in their rise, but there had to be a lot of blood also."

"Some. Some."

He won't be of much more help than the Chains themselves, than his sister Eva. It's not exactly a conspiracy of silence. It's a kind of grudging admiration for those skirters of the law, survivors, hard guys. A willingness to overlook their faults?

"What do you think of them? Make believe I'm not a reporter, just Dr. Abelman's nephew. What made them tick? What made them go?"

Sol Heilig brushes back his mussed gray hair. His eyes are misted with memories of Haven Place. "I don't know. Jake was a good egg. Not very bright. Good instincts. Morty was different. Smarter, meaner. My God, eighteen years old and he was running booze in a taxi. Ran the whole bootleg business when he was twenty. And Martin? Mort with a Dartmouth education, Harvard Business School, horses, a fancy wife."

"But they all must have had something in common, Mr. Heilig."

"Guts. Sheer guts. One thing about the Chains, kid. They were never afraid of anything or anybody."

PART IV

1950

Chapter 48

On the flagstone patio of the Roaring Brook Country Club (of which he was past president and founder), Mortimer J. Chain, with his one good eye—the left—watched the women's foursome, dragging a bit, walk off the eighteenth green and trudge up the vivid green incline.

Hilda had been dieting. She looked marvelous, although the iron girdle she wore, a tough contraption covering waist, butt, thighs, and the tops of her knees, gave her the appearance of a woman made of poured cement. But her lush hair gleamed black. Red lights winked in the wavelets. When she took off her white visor and shook her head, men stared. A big, well-formed behind and a smooth white face is much admired, Mort thought. Forty-eight. Two years older than he was and turning heads.

"Morty?" she called. "The gals and I are going to play a rubber of bridge before lunch."

He nodded. A happy family Sunday at Roaring Brook. The average annual income of members at this glossy new club, Mort estimated, was a quarter of a million dollars. There were (he had access to records) not less than twenty-six millionaires, and twelve men with net worths in excess of ten million.

Mortimer J. Chain, one-eyed, handsome, tanned, polite, helpful, was the richest member of Roaring Brook. He could not estimate his worth. Nor could the Internal Revenue Service. But he guessed that Chain Industries, Inc., the parent corporation, had to be worth over three hundred million dollars in inventories, plant, sales, cash, investments.

The club was elegant but not showy. Mort, planning it with a dozen other millionaires, had consulted the Chain lawyer, Horace Bunthorne, and asked for a tour of *his* club, the restricted, all-Christian Heather Cliff Country Club in Greenwich, Connecticut. Mort wanted to see how they did it.

As a result, the food at Roaring Brook was far better, the liquor was as good (the Chains' top lines), and both clubs manifested the same subdued elegance. Platoons of gardeners, maintenance men, and private police worked ceaselessly to keep Roaring Brook the showplace of the North Shore of Long Island. When problems arose, the helpful "Mr. Morty" was always available to solve them. He was a man, the members learned, who could talk to police, garbage collectors, town officials, golf pros, and his fellow oligarchs with equal ease. A few knew his background and understood why.

The women's bridge game included Mort's daughter-in-law, DeeDee Grau Chain, married to his son Martin; Martin's sister, Iris, recently graduated from Smith; and Horace Bunthorne's crosshatched, ash-blond, assless wife, Tucky. Mort hoped that Tucky Bunthorne, a reckless drunk, would stay sober long enough to finish the bridge game. She'd forgo lunch, of course. Christians, Mort knew (and was grateful), *drank* at country clubs. Eating was considered a sin against their religion. Roaring Brook, on the other hand, set a buffet table of such lavishness that the desserts alone were said to have caused more coronaries among the clientele than the crash of 1929.

"That's a nice bridge game," Martin said. "Mom's the best, by far. She can beat the other three with one hand. They ought to play three against one."

He and his father were seated, after a relaxed eighteen holes, at a mosaic table. They sat in the sun, away from the green-and-white-striped awning (Mort had ordered it from the English firm that made the Wimbledon awnings), soaking up warmth and heat.

Father and son could have been brothers. Both were dark, thin men with foxlike faces. Handsome, with thick hair rising in a black mane, growing somewhat low on the broad forehead. Long straight noses, rather harsh mouths, small ears flat to the narrow heads. The black patch on Mort's right eye, anchored with two bits of Scotch tape (a trick he'd learned from an advertising salesman who'd lost an eye in the Battle of the Bulge), seemed a device for telling the two apart. They wore white LaCoste shirts, identical Patek watches. Speaking, they made identical small emphatic gestures.

There was one outstanding difference, of course. Horace Bunthorne had noticed this as soon as he became aware of young Martin, then a student at Poly Prep (before transferring to Choate). Mort retained the cadences and dentalized *T*'s of Brownsville. The hint of gutter would never fully leave the patriarch of Chain Industries. Martin, while not speaking Eastern Seaboard Lockjaw (Bunthorne, an Iowa man, noticed these things), had adopted constricted vowels, a slurring of consonants. Poly Prep, Choate, Dartmouth (where he'd played varsity lacrosse), and Harvard Business School. All of these overlays, the observant Bunthorne understood, had minimized the Brooklynese in Martin Chain and created a strange-sounding, Christian-appearing young man, mysterious and candid at the same time. Martin, now twenty-six, would be more than a worthy successor to his father, Bunthorne felt.

"Mrs. Bunthorne's off," Martin said quietly. "Second martini, dad."

"Don't worry, Marty. She has her keeper with her."

A table away, in the cool shade, a large young black woman in a white uniform sat reading the *Daily News*. She looked powerful, slightly angry, and unimpressed by the surroundings. She sipped a Pepsi.

"I only hope she grabs Tucky Bunthorne before she hits the flagstone," Marty said. "All those fine bones. *Cr-ack.*"

Mort rubbed his nose and sipped his club soda. "Margaret's got fast moves. Reflexes. Harry trained her. Bunthorne says she's the best nurse Tucky's ever had. And between us, she ain't afraid to belt Tucky on her chops when she needs it."

Margaret Twine was Harry's oldest daughter. The Chains took care of those who were loyal. Harry and Eddie Twine and their children would always have jobs in the empire. Fidelity and honesty were rewarded. Betrayers were destroyed. Of the multitudinous Ferrantes, none remained in the distilling corporation or its subsidiaries.

Although none knew the details (the secret had been buried with the death of old Kuflik), the police had long suspected that someone acting for Mort Chain had sent a perforated Sal Ferrante to the bottom of a pond in the Catskills. And the acid attack on Mort's eyes, years later, had been the obligatory act of vengeance from Sal's family.

Behind the Chains, hidden by a green canvas windscreen anchored to a Cyclone fence, Mort and Martin could hear the popping sounds of a tennis ball struck by good players. David, Mort's younger son, bursting with energy, was playing the club pro, Paco Guerrero. Paco had been a Davis Cup player for Venezuela. He could beat Davey any day of the week, but Davey would never stop trying. His tennis was rusty, but his strength and his desire were limitless.

"If only he had that kind of interest in the business." Mort sighed. He caught a glimpse of Davey's flashing figure. Tan, white, a shock of yellow hair. Jake's hair. Davey reached up, smashed, laughed as the ball sailed yards out.

"He's happy, pop," Martin said. "Let him alone."

"Happy. Yeah, I guess so."

Through the green screen, Mort watched the outlines of his son's leaping body. Yes, he was Jake. The strength, the long limbs, the huge hands and feet, the need to use the big body. This, as much as ideals, Mort sensed, was what had sent Davey to Israel in 1948. Mort remembered Hilda's ear-shattering hysterics, her buckets of tears, her threats to kill herself. Marty was away at Harvard, Iris at Smith. Davey was deserting them. Why not stay, now that he was out of the marine corps, and help pop in the business? My God, it was a miracle he had lived through the marines! Pop needed someone from the family at the corporate headquarters on Park

Avenue. Mr. Bunthorne was fine, and so was Dr. Harris Weltfish, and the lawyer Sol Heilig had sent to Mort, Bertram Dunphy. But a Chain needed a Chain to work alongside him—Hilda sobbed her misery—especially now that his father was blind, *blind, do you hear, Davey?*

"In one eye, mom," Davey had said. "Pop's one eye is better than three on most people."

More shrieks. Sobbing in the bathroom. Fainting in the bedroom.

"You want to go, kid, *go,*" Mort had said.

Former Marine Lieutenant Al Seligman, Davey's platoon commander on Okinawa and Iwo, embraced Davey and hugged Mort. They'd leave that night and join a Palmach unit, special attack forces, at a camp outside Haifa.

"Mr. Chain," Al Seligman had said, "I hate to do this. It's not fair. I've been a guest here three days, brainwashing your son, and I've made your wife hysterical. But those people need everything. Medicine, guns, signal equipment. I took a son. Can I take something else?"

Mort took the chunky young man and Davey into his study. "What did you have in mind?"

"Money."

Mort gave Seligman a business card. "Come to my office with Davey tomorrow at noon. You'll get a check for a hundred thousand dollars. Tell me how to make it out, the best way to convert the funds."

"No problem. We've got banks all over Europe. The guns come from everywhere."

"Seligman, one more thing. Bring Davey back alive and there's another hundred thousand. Win the war against those *mamzerim* and there's another hundred thousand. Maybe more."

Davey shook his thick blond hair. Embarrassed. Humiliated. "Holy smoke, pop. If you think this means I'm going to be Al's stooge, a cook, or a clerk, you're nuts. They need soldiers. I'm qualified with twelve weapons. Al, don't listen to him."

Seligman winked at Mort. "No favors for you, Dave. You weren't that kind of marine, and you won't be that kind of *Palmachnik.*"

Mort understood. He'd suddenly cried, risen from his desk, and embraced his younger son. The wild one, the lousy student, the college dropout, the taker of chances, the fighter.

Jake, Jake again. Hit me, I'll hit you back.

Davey and Seligman left three days later, with the international money transfer to be deposited in the Athens branch of a London bank. A month later they were smuggling M-1 rifles onto deserted beaches. In late May their unit helped capture Safat and liberate the northern Galilee.

Now what for Davey? Mort wondered. He decided not to worry. The kid would always have something to do. But the business, no. That was Martin's. Martin had brains, tact, education. He enjoyed handling money, lunching with bankers and investors, buying French wine, selecting fine horses.

The waiter brought club soda for father and son. They rarely drank. Mort knew too much about booze. Martin, a bit of a health nut, found it did nothing but parch his throat. He never understood why people who craved alcohol said they were "thirsty." Or writers about Prohibition who spoke of the "thirst" of the people.

"Thanks, Juan," Mort said. He handed him five dollars.

"Thank you, sir. Note from the gentleman at that table."

Mort's left eye looked across the sun-splashed patio, the bright green plantings of ilex, yews, and privet, the burnished flagstone, the tables at which animated, handsomely dressed golfers drank and ate. He located the sender of the note. It was old Leo Glauberman, waving feebly, pointing to a dark thickish man seated with him.

Glauberman! Good God, he went back to Jake's era—1910, 1912. The "labor consultant," the Teddy Roosevelt of Brownsville. He had to be in his eighties. But fixing, *hondling,* arranging. He'd outlived his old rival for power, Benny Otzenberger, and was an enormously rich man, sleek and fat on profits from labor rackets, fees for defending hoodlums. After the death of Schonkeit, the Sicilians had moved in. Glauberman had survived among those snakes, advising, consulting, trying to make them appear respectable.

"Old bastard," Mort said. "My father hated his guts. I think he tried to finger Jake once."

With cold shaded eyes, Martin glanced at Glauberman's beaming face. The hair was roached, white, stiff. The skin was the color of an oiled bicycle saddle. "What does he want, pop?"

"The guy with him wants to shake my hand."

Mort showed the card to his son. Four tables away, Mort could hear Hilda saying to Mrs. Bunthorne, "Tucky, never play trump on my honor."

"Sorry, Hilda."

"Mother, stop being so *technical,*" Iris said. She was bored by bridge. But her father had asked that she be nice to Mrs. Bunthorne.

Martin read:

Dear Morty,

My friend and client Mr. Ruggiero Pisano wants to say hello and shake your hand. He's a sweet guy. I'll stay here and sip my tea. I'm old and I don't move too good.

Leo

"Important?" Martin asked.

"As important as horse shit in the street."

"Why does Glauberman do this?" Marty asked. "He knows you hate him." He twisted his Dartmouth ring, winced inwardly. The scum that surfaced from time to time! Memories of his grandfather's bloody past. He yearned for the day when no one would remind him.

"Leo's soft in the head. But who knows when people will be useful?"

"You know this ape?"

"No. But I can guess."

Mr. Pisano, potbellied, in crimson shirt and rose Daks, exuding Habit Rouge and patting his artfully barbered hair, silver-gray on coal-black, approached the Chains' table. He wore, Martin noticed, black alligator shoes that sold for a hundred and fifty dollars.

Thwack. *Thwack*.

Mort heard the sounds of Davey's racket, of Paco's hard strokes. He envied them. Someone said Davey could have been tournament caliber if he hadn't screwed around so much with contact sports. He'd broken a knee, sprained a shoulder, sustained a concussion. Enlisted in the marines in time for two of the bloodiest invasions of the war. Then Israel, and getting wounded again, and enduring God knows what with Al Seligman.

The cleanness of Davey's life and character filled Mort with a murky hatred for the likes of Ruggiero Pisano. He could not explain it. It was as if he would like to kill Pisano, throttle him then and there, to preserve Davey, to let Davey live forever.

"A pleasure, Mr. Chain," Pisano croaked. "I think we met after the war. When you was in the chemical business."

"I still am."

"Oh, I din't know. I think we done some hauling for ya."

Mort made no move to introduce Martin. His children did not have to be exposed to such vermin. Marty, more tolerant, extended a tanned hand. "Mr. Pisano, I'm Martin Chain, Mr. Chain's son."

"Pleasure, pleasure. Hey, ya look like your father. I wish I could buy a drink, but it's your club. Mr. Glauberman, he won't let me pay for nothin', and, gennulmen, I'm the kind of guy who picks up tabs." He stopped talking as the Chains regarded him with stony eyes. "What am I sayin'? Since when do the Chains need anybody should buy a drink for them?"

"That's right," Martin said.

Mort had gone rigid, silent. Martin, a more polished man, feared these moments. The old Chain capacity to hate. To draw back. To calculate. Yet Pisano seemed harmless enough. A hoodlum looking to meet "high-class" people.

Martin glanced away from the uninvited guest's swarthy face. He'd seen many such faces working for his father—drivers, warehousemen, sweepers. But there was more in Mr. Pisano's morose features. A sense of command.

Martin could see Davey toweling off, shaking hands with Paco, who was a head shorter. They were laughing, teasing. Jock talk. "That's all she wrote," Davey said. "You beat me like a gong, *amigo*."

Across the patio, his mother, his sister, his wife, and the blond woman with a face like a road map of drunken disasters were bidding.
Three hearts.
Pass.
Three spades?
Four diamonds.
Oh, is it my turn? Sorry. Three hearts. I guess.

"Tucky," Hilda said with great patience, "you bid three hearts *last* time. Iris just bid four diamonds. It's got to be four hearts, if you want to stay in hearts."

DeeDee turned her head and blew a kiss to Martin. He winked at her. German-Jewish by way of Central Park West. And he was Russian-Jewish by way of the Brownsville gutter. And they'd ended up on Fifth Avenue. A fun couple. A couple everyone wanted at their parties. *Bullshit,* Martin thought. DeeDee's beautiful and I'm rich.

"My idea is this, Mr. Chain," Pisano was gargling. "I got services to offer. Maybe cost you less than what you're paying. Cartage. Pickups on chemical waste. A contract for the distillery workers, the clerks, to your advantage. I got connections."

"What else do you have?" Mort asked.

Bulky white sweater thrown over his shoulders, Davey walked up the stone steps. He sat on the brickwork balustrade some distance from his father and brother, and listened. Around his neck was a gold chain. The Hebrew letter *Ch'ai* on a gold amulet.

"Like I said, Mr. Chain, connections. You would never have a day's labor trouble—"

The sons watched attentively. Davey was puzzled. Martin (who spent much of each day with his father and knew him well) was smiling. Mort interrupted Pisano. "Hold it, Pisano. Hold it."

"Whatever you say, Mr. Chain."

"Two years ago I had labor troubles. Some bastards tried to organize my drivers. We already had a contract. We pay more than scale. We got better pensions. Some tough guys come to see me. Mr. Chain, we'll give you a better contract so you can fuck the drivers—"

The word "fuck" hung in the hot clear air like a fart, and DeeDee's alert pearly ears caught it. She glanced archly at her husband, as if to say: *Oh, your elegant family.*

"—and I said, if you dagos think you're gonna get my drivers to strike or organize them in a union they don't want, think again. I'm a Chain. My old man was Jake Chain, and he was the toughest bastard ever walked the streets of Brownsville. So I—"

"Please, Mr. Chain," Pisano said. "I'm only trying to help. Mr. Glauberman said—"

"I said to this *walyone,* you throw a picket line around my distillery, I'll be the first one to drive a truck through. And there'll be a shotgun on the seat next to me and a forty-five in my lap. The first picket, whether he's a coon, a wop, a hebe, or a mick, who tries to stop a Chain truck gets a head full of lead. *Capisce,* Pisano?"

"Yeah, sure, Mr. Chain." His jaw dropped. The silver-on-black head looked debrained. "But look—take cartage, for example—"

"No cartage. No hauling. Go home and kiss your godfather's hand. You don't scare a Chain. Pisano, the worst thing you could have going for you is that Glauberman recommended you. Beat it. I'm having lunch."

Chastised, Pisano walked back to Glauberman.

"Easy, pop," Martin said. He locked his hands, watched the hood closely. Pisano looked as if he'd been pistol-whipped.

An innocent, Davey was astonished by his father's vehemence. He pulled the sweater around his shoulders. In the shade of the awning he was chilled. So little contact had he had with his father, and his father's way of life, that the savage encounter had shaken him.

"Pop," Davey said, "you really let him have it. You turned him down and you insulted him."

"That's what he understands. To a bank president I talk different." Mort patted the black patch. He made sure the Scotch tape was anchored. People used to whisper that he could see out of the right eye, that there was an invisible pinhole in the patch through which he clearly saw his rivals, associates, government officials. More than they wanted him to see. Mort's *camera oscura,* Horace Bunthorne called the patch.

Martin was shaking his head in appreciation of his father's performance. He got up. The bridge game was over. There'd be seven for lunch. Tucky Bunthorne would join them, eat nothing, swill martinis. Margaret Twine would be seated out of view, watching for the first signs of collapse.

Davey lifted his rackets and followed his father and brother toward the bridge table. "Pop, who was the guy tried to muscle you a few years ago? The one you mentioned to him?"

"It was *him.* Ruggiero Pisano. The dumb bastard called himself Rocky O'Brien then. They always want to be Irishmen."

Mort kissed Hilda's cheek. Even with Tucky as a partner, she'd thrashed her daughter and daughter-in-law.

"Mom's too good," Iris said. "She should play with a handicap, like in golf."

They were given a prize table overlooking the golf course. Halfway through the meal, Tucky Bunthorne began sliding toward the floor. Margaret Twine, gliding on rubber-soled white space shoes, was there to prop her up and walk her to the car. She would drive her home and put her to bed.

"I wish Horace were here," Hilda said. "Why he lets his wife run around getting boozed like that . . ."

"He's doing his own weekend boozing on his boat," Mort said coldly. "It keeps them alive. That's why I hired him. In my *ganze leben* I never saw a man drink so much, stay so clearheaded, and get so much work done. Right, Martin?"

"He's a damned good executive. Great lawyer, too."

As they ate—tangy seafood, satiny avocados, crisp salads, hot rolls, iced drinks—Martin studied his wife. She was disdainful of Roaring Brook. It was a "new money" place, DeeDee complained. A bit excessive. Martin would have to learn the advantages of the worn look, casual understatement.

Mortimer J. Chain, her father-in-law, did nothing that was not distressingly in excess. He had supervised the kitchen, found the best lobster pound, ordered vegetables directly from Chinese growers on Long Island.

This Central Park West snootiness had not deterred DeeDee's father from permitting his ivory-skinned daughter to marry the grandson of a gangster. The truth was that the rarefied Graus were broke. Mr. Grau had lost it all in 1929 and was supported largely by his second wife, an aristocrat with a small inheritance.

"Money is not everything," DeeDee's stepmother, Grace Korn Grau, told father and daughter when DeeDee announced she would marry Marty Chain.

"Yeah," Mr. Grau said moodily. "Confederate money. Czarist rubles. What the Chains have is real money. We should not complain, Grace dearest. DeeDee can take off their rough edges."

The in-laws had nothing to do with one another. Both Martin and DeeDee liked it that way. DeeDee was talking about taking a master's degree in business. The Chain empire intrigued her. She wondered if she could work somewhere in it. Martin had no objection. Hilda and Mort thought it a dreadful idea. DeeDee was much too refined, too exquisite, for the rough-and-tumble of the Chain businesses.

Sulking, DeeDee secretly met with Mr. Bunthorne, Mort's operating officer and chief counsel. Horace Bunthorne thought it was a sensational idea. So DeeDee registered for business courses at NYU, dropped them in a week, and was now trying her hand at ceramics.

Squeezing her knee under the table, Martin decided she could do anything, be anything, so long as she remained his wife, let him possess her long body, share the fineness, the good breeding, the indefinable superiority that coursed in her veins. Through the magic of sexual union she would make him a better person. It was no small thing to be a Grau. They were Jews who had come to the United States in 1849, and at times seemed to Martin more Christian than the midwestern likes of Horace Bunthorne and his sodden Tucky.

"My children are all together for a change," Hilda sighed. "I'm so happy today. Just as well that drunken lady went home. Our dear family, seated at one table. If only my father, your father, Morty, were here to see us. Look at Davey, how big, handsome! And Marty, handsome also. And what a head for business! And DeeDee, our new daughter. And—"

Iris held up a hand. "Stop. *Stop,* mother. I don't want to hear about your dollink daughter Iris. The black sheep. Or ewe, or something."

"Never mind, Iris. It's very few people got a daughter who graduated from Smith's."

"Smith, Mother. No apostrophe *s.*"

"So I'm proud of you," Hilda said. "No matter how much you knock it. Tell me, Martin and DeeDee, you have heads on your shoulders. Why do young people knock everything? All Iris does is poke fun at her achievements."

"She's kidding, mother," DeeDee said. "Aren't you, Iris?"

"Like hell I am."

Iris planned a future as a screenwriter. She had not told her parents. They would not have understood. Writers? What were they? But she had confided in Davey, with whom she had been close since childhood. She was physically similar to Davey. Both were throwbacks to Jake. Broad-shouldered, heavy-breasted, she had long strong limbs, a superb throat, fair skin that freckled easily, and thick brown-gold hair. She was not a beauty—a wide Slavic nose, narrow slanted eyes—but she carried herself well and her flippant manner attracted men.

"Language, Iris," Hilda said.

Iris marveled at her mother's gentility. Out of a steamy slum, daughter of one of New York's more flamboyant political fixers, Benjamin Otzen-berger. Hilda never read a book, merely glanced at newspaper headlines, owned a head full of bridge games, Mah-Jongg, beauty parlor appointments, benefits. And yet so genteel, so grand. Iris preferred her father's coarse-ness. Martin? A bit too slick. Eldest son, beneficiary of primogeniture, plunging into the family millions, the supercorporation that had exploded after the war.

Davey was her favorite. A little empty-headed, wonderfully naïve. He would not have lasted a day making the rounds of bars peddling Chain brands, bribing owners, buying drinks for the boys—the usual appren-ticeship for a Chain executive. Davey was a man you could never nail to a desk and a swivel chair, with an adding machine, a date calendar, *In* and *Out* baskets. Indeed, Iris thought as she looked at Davey's unsubtle face, he was a man you could hardly force to wear a tie and a suit. She had seen pictures of him as a marine corporal in battle fatigues, as a *Palmachnik* dynamiter in desert tans and jump boots. Dusty, sweaty, full of courage.

"I'm so proud of my children," Hilda sobbed.

Mort cautioned Iris, who was tossing her hair angrily, not to interrupt. Let Hilda have her *nachas,* her pleasure. It was rare that all of them were together. Mort, too, was glad that Mrs. Bunthorne had gotten herself sod-den and been carted home to Greenwich. Let six-foot-eight Horace, with his praying-mantis face and arms, have his Sunday ruined. When he got back from his "drinking boat," they'd battle all night.

"Marty, my oldest, the executive. DeeDee, God bless her, from Wellesley's. Iris, a graduate of Smith's."

"It's plain Wellesley, mom," Iris said sharply. "It's Smith, not Smith's."

"Let me enjoy," Hilda said. She sniffled into a handkerchief. In her mind she was recalling the day she'd taken the taxi ride to Montreal with Morty and the repulsive Salvatore. And how Sal had blown the Canadian's head off. The mad chase across the border. Hilda sobbing and puking all the way to Plattsburgh. It was as if her relationship to Mort had been sealed in blood.

"And Davey, who'll finish college now that he fought two wars, my hero," Hilda went on.

Davey smiled tolerantly. Not a conniving or ambitious bone in him, Iris knew. The best of the three. No plans, no commitments, not even a steady girl.

"I'll finish college in Israel, mom," he said.

"Come on," his father taunted. "You told me your Hebrew stinks. If all the guys in your outfit weren't mostly Americans, you'd be dead by now. You couldn't holler 'duck' in Hebrew."

"I'll learn."

"No!" Hilda said. "Enough being a hero! You'll stay here! You'll go to college. You'll work for your father!"

"Do what you want, Davey," Iris said.

"He will without you telling him," Martin said. "He always has."

Mort sipped iced tea, accepted obeisances from club members who wanted to exchange stock-market talk or political chatter.

Christ, Iris thought, they do everything but get on their knees and kiss the old man's ring. She loved her father, but she was rendered uncomfortable by his power. It was not just the massive wealth, the millions that poured in endlessly, but a kind of mystical power that he possessed. She knew the old stories. The origins of the fortune in blood, violence, and crookedness. She did not fear it. But she could not fathom it, nor did she wish to be part of it.

Paco, the tennis pro, came by. He was doll-size and muscular, with forearms of a man twice his size. Browner than a Polynesian, he spoke softly to Davey. "I got no lessons, *amigo*. You wanna try to beat me again?"

"Why not? If I get three games from you it's a moral victory."

Davey was on his feet. A big man with an agile body. "Sorry, folks. Paco's not happy unless he gets in three hours with me."

When they had left, Mort laughed. "He thinks the pro lets him play for free. Wait, it'll be on my monthly bill. Tennis lessons at twenty bucks an hour."

"You can afford it," Iris said. "You can afford a pro, a court, and your own tennis team. Daddy, what can't you afford?"

"Iris, stop at *once,*" Hilda said. "Don't ruin what has been a lovely day."

Mort pinched his daughter's tanned cheek. A big blond woman, twenty years old, a bit unformed. *"Ketzeleh,* you're right. I can afford anything. As a matter of fact you got an appointment with United Artists on Wednesday. They heard my daughter was interested in writing for the movies and they loved the idea."

Hilda beamed.

Martin nudged DeeDee under the table, as if to say: What we want, we get.

Iris overcame her humiliation. She gritted her teeth.

Chapter 49

"I thought you might have chosen Luchow's out of sentiment," Eva said. "Good God, wasn't that a long time ago . . . ?"

"Our first date," said Halstead. "No, my dear, the memories are hazy and a bit painful. Our very first date was at Gage and Tollner's. Luchow's was later. The German barbarousness didn't faze you in the least. Not even the enormous schnitzel. But then nothing ever did."

They were in the Sixty-Eight restaurant on lower Fifth Avenue, not far from the brownstone Eva had been awarded in their divorce settlement. Halstead had not remarried. He lived with a woman thirty years younger, an abstract artist of ancient Boston lineage, a gaunt woman with a face like white granite. They shared an apartment in the West Village. He and Eva had been divorced in 1941. Prior to that, they had not slept together for many years. The breaking point (insanely, Eva recalled) was Halstead's refusal to accept lend-lease.

Garrison Halstead, once a devotee of Eugene Debs and Norman Thomas, a man of moderation, a believer in democratic reform, had nestled closer and closer to the Stalinists. Ultimately he had become, to Eva's distress, an avowed Communist. True to her Social Democratic principles, she backed Roosevelt on aid to Britain and France. She had seen what had happened in prewar Germany—Communists letting the Nazis take over, rubbing their hands, convinced they'd pick up the pieces. *After Hitler, us.* Outsmarted, beaten into submission by the SS, they ended up in the same concentration camps with the Socialists they'd attacked as "Social Fascists."

It's strange, Eva thought, how two of the men who loved me drank of the Red cup. Ike Brunstein, who ended up sailing out of a window. And now Halstead, a millionaire's son, one of the walking wounded, a brand from the burning. When the anti-Red probes had started in Congress after the war—the House Un-American Activities Committee, McCarthy, others—Halstead had proved a voluble, cooperative, blabbing witness. He named everyone he could think of, including his ex-wife, the writer and lecturer, Eva Heilig. His communism, overnight, became anticommunism. His wife's socialism, for the benefit of congressional probers, became communism.

"I'm glad you're not angry with me," Halstead said now.

"But I am. I think you're dreadful. How do you sleep at night?"

"Not too well. But I did the right thing. The Hiss case bears me out. Guilty. A traitor."

"As usual, you haven't got it right. Hiss was convicted on two counts of perjury. Not treason."

Halstead stroked his iron-gray hair and lifted his prognathous jaw. "Precise as always, Eva. Good God, you're the most beautiful sixty-four-year-old woman in New York City. Snowy hair, not a lock out of place. I like it piled high like that. And the carnelian earrings I bought you in India. Oxford-gray suit, elegant legs, smart pumps. You look ravishing. How do you manage?"

"Garry, you are a bore."

They ordered mussels, veal piccata, tossed green salads, a pale dry Chablis. Indifferent to food, Eva had always let him order. She listened to his slightly cracked voice and marveled at his staying power. Liberal, radical, Socialist, Communist, anti-Communist, reactionary. When would he agitate for a corporate state with pink-cheeked prep-school storm troopers?

. . . The chairman, and the rest of the committee, Mr. Halstead, is most appreciative of your cooperation. Mr. Halstead, it puzzled many of us that a man of your background and education could involve himself with such subversive and un-American elements, that you should give them funds and advance their causes, and the committee wants to thank you for so frankly revealing . . .

"I'm sorry I named you, Eva," Halstead said, as he extracted a hot *moule* from its silvery-black shell. "Why did I do it? You were never a party member. You fought us. You denounced us in little magazines."

"Revenge."

"Oh, no. Don't think that."

"Of course. I was better known than you for many years. I think that I had twice as many articles published as you."

"That's not so. I was traveling a great deal."

"Fellow-traveling?"

"I guess I didn't hurt you too much, did I? I mean, your income, and so on?"

Like most of his class, he was conveniently deaf, dumb, and blind when it suited him. The committees hadn't called her. They had the files. She had anticommunist credentials. And besides, she was not a name that would make a headline. A forgotten white-haired woman who had once had something to do with the labor movement. They craved big names. Actors, writers, professors, state department officials. Eva Heilig was not a headline-making name. She wasn't worth a subpoena.

"I like to think," Halstead said, "that I didn't hurt anyone. They already had all the names I gave them. Except yours, of course. I called up some of our old radical friends and asked their permission to give their names. They didn't care. I even offered a *quid pro quo:* You can give my name if you let me give yours."

"Garrison, you continue to astonish me. That conviction that you can do anything you want, anything in the world. The Chains have more honor than your kind."

He blinked behind rimless eyeglasses. More and more, Eva thought, her ex-husband looked like FDR. He prided himself on the resemblance, although he had never had much use for Roosevelt. During Roosevelt's first two terms he regarded him as a fascist. Now that Halstead had made a sharp right turn, he looked back upon Roosevelt as a crypto-Red, a conniver with the international communist movement. Eleanor was even worse, more treacherous.

These political meanderings, these excesses, Eva understood, were games for Garry, the way his Yale classmates became absorbed in squash, yachting, or horses. Yet she could not eradicate the memory of the man who had stood bail for her many years ago. And the good years in the house on West Tenth Street.

"Are you all right financially?" he asked her.

"I manage. I've rented the two upstairs floors of the house."

His cheeks splotched scarlet, an old Halstead habit. The house had been all that Eva had asked for. And some minimal payments until she got a job. She had been fifty-five at the time, with a daughter in college. (Halstead agreed to pay for Lillian's education.) But she wanted no money from him. Her pride, self-wounding, was as lofty as it was when she battled policemen and strikebreakers. No money, just a place to live. She'd managed all these years writing for the *New Republic,* the *New Leader,* union publications, birth-control magazines, tenants' groups. But her income was meager. She was not in much demand anymore as a lecturer. For a period during the war she had sold books in Brentano's. Miserable pay, but nice surroundings. The manager had remembered her. He confessed to having heard her lecture at the Community Church during the Depression.

"I'm sorry," Halstead said. "I'll have my lawyers look over the alimony agreement. I'm a cad, Eva. I should have insisted . . . tenants, good God." Giving up the townhouse had embittered him.

"Your ancestors would be horrified. A marvelous young Japanese sculptor has the top floor and we've put in huge skylights—"

"Oh, God. All that plaster and marble dust."

"Worse. He's a welder. We've had two fire alarms since Sunichi moved in." She laughed. "And below him, two homosexuals, polite, sweet, middle-aged men who are gourmet cooks."

"Poets? Set designers? What?"

"One's a stockbroker and the other is a claims adjuster. And they both went to the University of Alabama."

"You have this tolerant view of the world and its people. Why doesn't it include me? Would you feel triumphant if I told you I miss you terribly? That I love you? I've never been happy since we broke up. And why in God's name *did* we break up?"

"Garrison, this is a lunatic conversation for two old people suffering from arthritis and hypertension. We should be comparing medications, not trying to revive a dead love."

He seized her hand and kissed it. "I mean it. Why don't we . . . ? Damn, what did I do wrong to get you so angry? *You* asked for the divorce. I know there was no other man."

"I wasn't passionate enough for you. Admit it. You strayed. So what? My slum-bred body didn't respond. Nothing as proper as a working girl. Maybe I nursed guilt over getting so much wealth, such fame, such power, for no other reason than my face. Your intoxication with an exotic Jewess. Hildah the prophetess, whom some biblical scholars contend was a sacred prostitute. Sorry I didn't fill the bill."

"Wrong. I enjoyed our—our—sex."

"No you didn't. You probably are very good in bed even now, very satisfying to handsome ladies and artistic girls. How is the incumbent?"

"Not as beautiful as you."

Halstead poured Chablis for Eva. "You overestimate my powers. I saw a lot of women. Not one of them diminished my respect for you. I remember that day in court. Your battered face and torn shirtwaist. And those weeping girls. Brunstein flapping his arms like a wounded crow."

"You were gallant. I appreciated it."

"Then . . . let's try again. We'll get the homosexuals to move out so I can have my study back."

"No, Garry. Never. Do you remember the last screaming fight we had? The night after you debated a Columbia professor on American aid to the Allies? There you stood. The voice of the pigheaded self-destroying left. The voice of the idiots in the Communist party. 'This is an imperialist war,' you brayed. 'Aid to England and France is aid to encourage imperialist expansion.' As if Hitler were the same thing. As if the Jews were being arrested and killed in England the way they were in Germany. How stupid could you have been? How much Stalinist nonsense could you swallow and still respect yourself?"

"The Russians were buying time. After all, the western Allies had been their enemies as much as the Nazis."

"You still believe that?"

"To an extent. You know how I've changed. I'm unshakably anticommunist. What I'm saying is the Russians and Germans were two sides of the same coin. We should have let them destroy each other. Rid the world of both."

"Stop *funfering*, Mr. H. How a man could equate England and France with the Nazis! And my relatives were soon to be gassed and burned in the Vilna ghetto. I could have strangled you. And how you changed once Hitler invaded Russia? Oh, what a different tune you sang!"

"You shame me with these recollections. That's why I've changed again. I now believe—"

Eva clapped her tiny hands and guffawed. The waiter turned his head. "Coffee, folks?"

"Yes, black," Eva said. "Strong. And brandy. We're celebrating Operation Barbarossa."

Crazy lady, he thought.

"Eva, less exuberance," Halstead said.

" 'This is no longer an imperialist war!' " she cried. "Remember that one? After June 1941? What a thrilling line! *'This is no longer an imperialist war!'* So long as the English and the French and the Low Countries— and the Jews—were dying and suffering, but the Soviet Union had a pact, you were neutral. But when the panzers moved east, the party gave you a new speech, right, Garry? That's when I decided we'd gone far enough. Your trouble was you followed too many banners and too many women."

"You're the only woman that's ever mattered to me. Eva, I do wish you'd call a moratorium on these hurtful reminiscences. Nothing is gained by them. Give me credit at least for a certain broadness of mind. A willingness to change."

"It was party-line poison you were spouting. And look at you now. Running off to committees, blabbing your old friends' names, editing a magazine that considers Eleanor Roosevelt as bad as Stalin, denouncing the New Deal as a plot to socialize America, telling your readers that Joe McCarthy is a great patriot and the savior of the republic. Disgusting."

"I believe deeply in everything that's printed in *Manifest Destiny.*"

At the mention of the monthly magazine that Halstead financed and edited, a rallying ground for ex-Stalinists, disaffected Trotskyites, right-wing Brahmins, fringe fascists, and witty anti-Semites, Eva pounded the table. "Believe that garbage if you will, Garry. Maybe it's where you belonged all the time. Why is it that former party members are the worst of the lot? Is it because you hate yourself so much?"

"Unfair, my dear—"

"Unfair, my foot. I hope you take pride in that snotty fascist rag you publish. Death to the Rosenbergs. Hang Hiss. Democrats and liberals are worse than Communists because there are so many of them. *Preventive war!* Drop atom bombs on Russia and China before they catch up! Cut spending, cut taxes, no welfare! Do you really believe you have a constituency with such wicked nonsense? As Dr. Abelman would have said, you and your new colleagues are a bunch of galoots."

"We will soon have a much larger following than you can imagine. Your musty liberal convictions will fall of their own weight soon enough."

"I love you ex-Communists. Anyone who favors child-labor laws is suspect. *You* were deceived by Stalin, so anybody who *wasn't* is a traitor. Go on, throw out the humanist baby with the communist bath water. That's what you'd like to do. Maybe put a few of us in concentration camps while you are at it."

"That is unkind."

"You sicken me. Tell me how you're going to get this vast constituency."

"Quite simply. Spies and traitors being exposed by Senator McCarthy and others will convince people of the Red plot. A *liberal* plot, I might add. There is no difference. Beyond that, we have a much stronger card to play."

"The Jews?"

"Oh, goodness, no. They're by-and-large business and professional types. If they had any sense they'd support us. People like your multi-millionaire relatives the Chains should be casting their lot with us."

"The Chains are too smart for you, and too tough. They have no politics. They understand what makes the country go. Much better than you do. But enlighten me. What is your secret plan to take over Washington?"

Halstead set a fresh cigarette in his ivory holder, lit up, cocked his head. *Damn,* Eva thought, *he still thinks he's Roosevelt.* Some curious aberration was at work in his mind. Admiring FDR years ago (one of his own class who rebelled), he now hated him, but could not shake the identification. Self-hatred, Eva concluded. Detesting and defaming Roosevelt, Eleanor, the New Deal, liberals, was a way of despising himself. And he probably hates me, she thought, for never having gone as far left as he had, for refusing to dance to Stalin's tunes, for refusing to defend the Soviets no matter what bloody excesses they committed. That was the secret. He, like other former Communists, could not exorcise their own demons without convincing themselves that reformers, humanists, liberals, and socialists *were worse than they ever were.*

"Negroes will be our salvation. And the nation's."

Eva cocked her head. "Negroes?"

"They will soon be demanding rights, as they call them, upsetting the natural order, trying to replace whites in the social and economic order. They will become violent and angry, commit crimes, destroy cities. Liberals will encourage them. We old-fashioned patriots will seize on this ravaging of America to create a new social conservatism. The criminality and brutality of coloreds will be the anvil on which we smash the spine of the left-liberal conspiracy."

He exhaled a thick cloud of smoke, rested back in his seat, and waited for her explosion. A bit of the old Heilig temper seemed in order. The angry voice of the picket captain. It was what had drawn him to her: that undiluted courage, pristine anger, moral outrage.

"I am so repelled by you, Garry, that I can't even respond. You'll use Negroes the way Hitler used Jews. Is that it?"

"Not at all. The Jews were innocent. They did not mug or steal or rape or ruin neighborhoods. I've said many times I sympathized with their plight. You and I signed petitions for them and tried to increase the immigration quotas. But Negroes are a different matter. I have no grudge against them, but their fate is inevitable. They'll give us the excuse to form an honorable, virtuous, moral society."

"You are insane. I'm leaving."

He followed her to the door, pausing to sign the check, scrambling after her on birdlike legs. Furious, Eva walked south on Fifth Avenue. Halstead caught up with her. He took her arm. She yanked it away.

"Don't be wroth with me, Eva. A lot of what I say is intellectual doodling. But I see the future. I see an opportunity to move this country away from gnosticism, creeping socialism, all the liberal-left dogma that have failed, that have betrayed—"

She cracked him across the face with her tiny hand. "Get away from me. I don't want to see you. I despise you."

"Pity," Halstead said, rubbing his inflamed cheek. "I was going to offer you a monthly column in *Manifest Destiny*. That was the reason for the lunch. Let you give us the view from the left for balance. I'll overlook what happened. Are you interested?"

"Go to hell."

He watched her walk off, a slender and vigorous woman, looking fifteen years younger than her age. He realized he had failed to ask about their daughter, Lillian. Lillian was quite close to Eva. Halstead rarely saw her.

Chapter 50

Lillian Halstead, twenty-seven, graduate of Columbia Law School, was one of the few women in the office of the New York State attorney general. She was a tall, solemn young woman, with her father's gangly limbs and rather awkward physical appearance. But she had clear green eyes like her mother, fair skin, and curling tawny hair. She might have been beautiful were it not for the prolonged Halstead chin and her disregard for hairdressers, cosmetics, artifice of any kind. "Plain" was the word used to describe her—an honest face, an interesting face. The young lawyers who worked with her decided she was a rather sexless woman. Talked little about herself. Very private. No coasting on the Halstead name. She had gotten the job on merit after outstanding volunteer work in the office of the Brooklyn district attorney during summer vacations. From both parents she had inherited a talent for expressing herself effectively—verbally and in her written briefs.

In the New York office of the attorney general, Miss Halstead, a rather odd sort to her co-workers, studied a long report on illegal practices in the liquor industry. Her superior wanted a review.

Distillers were complaining about the unfair practices of Chain Industries and Chain Distillers. It was an old file. To Lillian's surprise, no action had ever been taken to investigate the charges. Revealingly, several distillers of much greater size, and vaster income than the Chains, were the complainants.

Lillian crossed her legs, let a low-heeled shoe dangle on one foot, and smiled. Mr. O'Neal, her boss, would be shocked out of his shoes if he knew that Mortimer J. Chain and his son Martin Chain, accused in the file of bribery, kickbacks, and payoffs, were her distant cousins.

She knew little about the Chains. Her mother had sometimes spoken of them. Jacob Chain, a violent hoodlum, dead some nineteen or twenty years, was the progenitor of the line. Quite a man, Eva used to tell her. A third cousin on her mother's side, related to old Grandma Matla, herself long dead. A man who had been shot at with depressing regularity and survived, until a fatal ambush.

The son, chief target of the accusers, was Mortimer J. Chain, a reclusive man of uncountable wealth. She vaguely remembered visiting his home once with her mother—climbing a tree with his son Martin. A newspaper clipping in the file showed Mr. M. J. Chain, darkly handsome, nattily dressed, a piratical black patch over his right eye. He was coming down the steps of the Federal Courthouse with his attorney, Mr. Horace Bunthorne, and other lawyers. The appellate court of the second district had reversed a lower court's findings against the Chains for unfair labor practices. She looked at the date—1948. Only two years ago.

Strange, Lillian thought. Her mother had always depicted Jake Chain, for all his crudeness and violence, as a friend to workingmen. What a difference, Lillian thought, a generation makes.

Mortimer Chain was quoted in the article. "We feel vindicated. This was not a labor-employer matter," he told reporters, "it was a fight between two unions, one that we recognize, and one run by a bunch of gangsters who want to take over. Our wage scale and our pension benefits are the best in the distilling industry and we don't need hoodlum-run outfits in our corporation."

That took courage, Lillian knew. Gangster-dominated unions did not take kindly to such accusations. There seemed to be a fearless, outspoken strain in the Chains. Old Jake (she could recall her mother telling her) had been a hero to beaten pickets. The essence of courage. A huge and enormously strong man. Lillian mused: Can courage, boldness, and daring be inherited? She wished she knew more about the son she dimly remembered as a boy, Martin. His name appeared only once in the file, as executive vice-president of the corporation.

One of her predecessors had summed up the complaints:

Although the Chain organization is not among the top half-dozen distillers and importers of alcoholic beverages, it is the most aggressive in selling and distributing its products.

Much of this has to do with imaginative advertising and the exploitation of trends in the liquor business, which is subject to fads and fashions. Moreover, they seem to have established an effective, if somewhat involved, method of maintaining inventories of neutral grain spirits and the straight whiskeys needed for the best-selling blends.

None of the above practices are *per se* illegal. Complaints from competitors stem rather from the Chain corporation's illegal payments to retailers, bars, and restaurants to push their lines. There are three complaints on record to the effect that the Chain salesmen resorted to veiled, and not-so-veiled, threats when meeting resistance from retailers. These, of course, are accusations by their competitors and must be carefully weighed. Van Alst and Rimmelberger, the giants in the liquor trade, are not themselves angels of mercy.

The bulging file amused Lillian. A perceptive woman, with her mother's tolerant view of people, she almost had to laugh at the complaints. They had the ring of the whinings of bullies, the mean boys in the schoolyard, who had been shown up by a tough upstart kid.

There were letters and affidavits from haughty law firms, from the rival distiller Van Alst, making accusations. One irate corporate president accused the Chains of theft, of "stealing" neutral grain spirits from a government warehouse to launch their business in the thirties. The businessman charged that the Chains were still, in 1950, not above such chicanery—paying off government storekeeper-gaugers and bribing suppliers as well as retailers. In short, bringing their bootlegging habits into a gentlemen's industry.

One line caught her eye. It seemed to her to sum up the argument, or indeed the lack of any. She scanned the paragraph.

Distillers admit they fail to understand why some brands catch on and some do not. They concede that, in terms of the market, each corporation enters the field with more or less identical products, all priced within a given range. Labels differ, content is the same. Success or failure is the result of a mystical affair called "brand loyalty," a capricious matter. The Chains have apparently been very apt at developing this "brand loyalty." A great deal of money and energy is devoted to advertising, promotion, public relations, contacts with retailers, packaging, display, and distribution.

Good for the Chains, she thought. A disreputable, crude, ambitious, hard-handed branch of the family. Richer than any Heilig, light-years removed from her respectable uncles, Sol the idealistic lawyer and Dr. Abe. Mortimer Chain, she had heard, had never finished high school. Martin? She was not sure. He looked shrewd and knowing in his photographs.

Lillian decided to make a few calls, to see if any new evidence was available on the alleged improprieties of the Chain liquor interests, and then write a report for her superior. She was about to close the file, having jotted down names and phone numbers of informants, when she noticed a few yellowing clippings. The first was from the *Times* of July 1931.

JACOB CHAIN, MOB FIGURE, SLAIN
BODY FOUND IN BROOKLYN

Jacob Chain, 46, a bootlegger and labor racketeer, was found shot to death in the trunk of a stolen automobile in the Brownsville section of Brooklyn yesterday.

Chain, known to police and the underworld as "Crazy Jake," had been shot twice in the head. Police said the murder had taken place that day. The body had been driven to Sutter Avenue, four blocks from Mr. Chain's place of business, Brooklyn General Supply.

Chief of Detectives William Kane said there were no suspects, or any motive, as of yesterday evening. Chain had a long record of arrests for assault in connection with labor disputes. At one time he ruled a mob that specialized in wrecking factories and beating up nonunion laborers. He was, a source said, no longer involved in union activities.

Chain and his son, Mortimer, 27, were said to be Brooklyn's major bootleggers, operating behind the facade of a chemical supply business, a cereal company, and a hair-tonic factory.

Lillian Halstead was her mother's daughter. She could smile at life's absurdities, the ironies of the world. *Hair tonic! Cereals! Chemicals!* She laughed, then read on.

There have been several attempts on Mr. Chain's life in the past twenty years. In 1911 he survived twelve bullets, and about ten years later he survived a second barrage from underworld rivals, earning him a reputation as Brownsville's foremost "clay pigeon."

This time, police theorized, Mr. Chain was shot and killed by people he knew, and whom he had no reason to fear. . . .

Lillian paused, listened to the hum of the electric fan in her cubicle. She heard the voices of her fellow prosecutors outside the frosted glass partition.

"Something about Korea on the radio . . ."
"What? A communist invasion? Jesus, and I'm in the reserve. . . ."
"It can't be for real. . . . Who needs another war so soon?"

The Chain past preoccupied her. The invasion, or whatever it was— probably a border incident; the radio newscasts had a way of magnifying these things—could wait.

She wondered about Jake Chain, ignominiously murdered; a young man. Her mother had often spoken of him with grudging affection. Yes, he was a terrible man in many ways. But at heart a gentle hulk, simple, with decent instincts. "I got him into his business, Lil," Eva would say. "Maybe it was a mistake, but I can tell you, we would not have won those strikes without him. And he wasn't crazy, not at all. . . ."

A second clipping reported the discovery of a hoodlum's corpse in a lake in the Catskills.

BODY SURFACES IN CATSKILL LAKE
BELIEVED TO BE MOBSTER FERRANTE

Local police today discovered the bullet-riddled, decomposed body of a man believed to be Salvatore Ferrante, a Brooklyn gangster, who vanished three years ago.

James Collins, a farmer, discovered the body floating on Carrington Lake yesterday afternoon, while looking for lost cows. The body had apparently been weighted down with cinder blocks, but the wires attaching them to the corpse's limbs had rusted and come loose. Tentative identification was made from dental work and fingerprints.

Ferrante, member of a Brownsville family of mobsters, union strong-arm men, and bootleggers, vanished in February of 1932 without a trace. A coroner's report was awaited to determine the cause of death.

Lillian decided she would have to talk to Dugan, the man who drew up the file. Why the clippings? She knew the name Ferrante. Her mother had spoken of a family of thugs who had worked for Jake and Mort. The connection had been broken in 1934 after the repeal of Prohibition. She looked at the date on the clipping: *1935.* For three years, Salvatore Ferrante had rested amid the sunfish and perch of Carrington Lake.

The third clipping was about an attack on Mortimer J. Chain by unknown persons. It was from the *Daily News.*

ALKY EXEC VICTIM OF ACID ATTACK
M. J. CHAIN BLINDED OUTSIDE THEATER

Lillian saw the date: 1935. The report stated that Mortimer J. Chain and his wife, Hilda, of Ocean Parkway, Brooklyn, were coming out of Loew's Flatbush theater at 10:00 P.M. when an unidentified woman threw sulfuric acid in his face. The woman, clad in a dark coat and black hat, escaped in a car. Some observers said she was accompanied by a man. In the confusion that followed the attack, no one got a clear look at her or noted the car's license number. Preliminary medical examinations, the *News* said, indicated that Mr. Chain, president of Chain Industries, would lose the sight in his right eye, but that the left, though suffering damage, would heal.

She called the office of George X. Dugan, the man who had collected the file some years ago and was now in private practice.

"Lil," Dugan said, "that Chain thing is a bat's nest. Why the boss wants to reopen it—"

"I'm curious about the clippings. Jacob Chain's murder, the Ferrante case. Why are they in there?"

"Ferrante was a two-bit bootlegger who worked with the Chains."

"Who were the suspects?"

"Half of Brooklyn."

"And who were the suspects in the Chain murder?"

"The other half."

Lillian laughed. "Thanks, George. I won't even ask you about the acid attack on Mortimer Chain."

"Another spin-off from their bootlegging, we figured."

"Nothing like private enterprise, right, George?"

"Who am I to argue? Excuse me, Lil. I got to turn the radio on. All hell's breaking loose in Korea. Truman's sending in troops."

Chapter 51

The weekly executive meeting took place in Mort's boardroom on the twentieth floor of their Park Avenue headquarters. Around the table sat his high command. Son Martin, executive vice-president. Horace Bunthorne, vice-president, chief operating officer, and counsel. Bertram Dunphy, vice-president for the Imports Division and assistant counsel. Dr. Harris Weltfish, vice-president for quality control and production. Mr. Mackenzie Tuttle, storekeeper-gauger at the major Chain distillery in Wisdom, New Jersey. There were three others, all respectable, bright, aggressive men, all under forty, all skilled in the savagely competitive liquor business.

"This damn Korea thing," Bunthorne was saying. "We have no idea how long it'll last. If it runs on, we may have a problem with inventories. The Big Four may not want to sell to us."

"Horace, I'll be counting on you to convince them it's in their own interest," Mort said softly.

Bunthorne's goggling eyes wandered to the buildings on Park Avenue. "Mort, I'll try like the devil. But they're trying to crowd us now for using leverage with retailers."

"Look who's talking," Martin said. "Monopolists, price fixers."

"They want it all, Van Alst and Rimmelberger." Bunthorne stroked his purplish cheek. "Of course, our inventories are high, aren't they, Harris?"

Dr. Weltfish, with his stone-gray hair parted in the middle, a curved pipe drooping from his ragged moustache, hid in a fog of smoke. Rum and maple? Martin wondered. Walnut? Weltfish's pipe always made him think of the dormitories at Dartmouth.

"Horace, I'd say we have a three-year lead. A long war could hurt us. The problem will be straight whiskey, the four-year-old stuff. Neutral spirits may also be a problem until our own distilleries make us self-sufficient."

Mort listened and made notes. They had pioneered blended whiskeys in the late thirties. They had set the pace for other distillers. And he had to admit that lanky noodle Bunthorne had showed him the way. Whiskey was Horace Bunthorne's only religion, his reason for living, his guiding light.

Listening to the discussion—big Mackenzie Tuttle, Mort's half brother, was talking about neutral spirits available in government warehouses— Mort smiled, and recalled his first meeting with Bunthorne.

Nineteen years ago. Bunthorne had returned from his fruitless errand for Schonkeit—fruitless because Mort had already bought off the British distillers. Still, Mort had to hand it to the Paymaster for picking so refined and well-spoken a front man. Bunthorne was invited to lunch with Mr. M. J. Chain at the Chambord.

The two men had studied each other warily. Mort, in his late twenties, dapper in a vested blue suit, starched white collar, his foxlike face and thick ebony hair suggesting something of the gypsy to the Iowa-bred Bunthorne. The youthful lawyer, in turn, intrigued Mort with his dead-center, on-the-nose, middle-of-the-road *goyishness*. At once Mort realized this was the kind of man he wanted to help him run the business after repeal. An absolute American Baptist who could drink forever and never fall down.

"What are you earning now?" Mort asked. "You're with one of those old-time Wall Street outfits, right? Harvard and Yale fellas?"

"I'm a very junior member, Mr. Chain. I went to the University of Iowa and its law school."

Even better, Mort thought. "That isn't what I asked. What do they pay you?"

"Thirty thousand a year."

"I'll give you sixty."

"But, Mr. Chain . . ." The six-foot-eight-inch man, with his beet-red cheeks, a capillary-bursting boozer at age thirty-one, an all-day, nonstop drinker with impeccable taste and a rich farmboy's voice, opened his eyes wide. Horace had huge staring eyes. The pupils were the color of burned sugar. Already the whites were yellowing, the sure sign of an orthodox alcoholic. What impressed Mort was that Bunthorne never behaved drunkenly, never slurred a word, never staggered, never became noisy, or goosed women, or threw up, or showed physical damage. He golfed, sailed, and played bad tennis, worked fourteen hours a day, looked lovingly after his sozzled wife, and was active in community affairs in his hometown of Greenwich.

"I know very little about the liquor business, Mr. Chain," the lawyer said cautiously.

"Like hell you don't. You ran around England trying to steal my suppliers. You ran errands for Schonkeit. You're worth sixty grand. Whaddya say, Mr. Bunthorne?"

"Let me be candid, sir. You ask me to leave one of New York's most prestigious law firms to be counsel for a bootlegger? I know a little of your history, Mr. Chain."

"Those guys you work for on Wall Street? They're bigger crooks than any Chain ever was. In a couple of years we'll go legitimate. I want you to be with us. If you took a job for Schonkeit, you can't be that fancy. All money is the same color. Besides, we haven't killed anyone in years, and the few we killed deserved it. Deal?"

Bunthorne opened his mouth, as if the mantis were ready to eat a horsefly. He laughed soggily and shook Mort's hand. "Deal, Mr. Chain."

"Mort."

"Mort. My goodness, I've never called any of our senior partners by their first names. And I've been with the firm four years."

They would be a great combination. Bunthorne knew secrets about the vast American heart, the people who hated New York and distrusted Jews but wanted their liquor served well and abundantly, in nice bottles and at a decent price. Horace possessed that wondrous faith in booze that had made rich men of bootleggers, that half-jesting, worshipful, dear-to-the-heart love of drunkenness, of wobbly feet and dulled minds, that characterized a basically puritanical people. As they drank, they joked, teased, lost their inhibitions. To drink was to be a patriot above reproach.

"Every time I look at that *langhe luksh*," Mort later told Hilda and the children, as they sat around the dinner table in the Ocean Parkway mansion, "I see all of America out there, making their cockamamie jokes about whiskey, hollow legs, human sponges, all that kidding around. Men falling down, women puking on expensive dresses, college boys boasting how potted they were, the marines Davey was with making hooch out of raw alcohol and grapefruit juice, the little *shiksas* in Iris's class at Smith sneaking bourbon from daddy's bottle—I see all of them combined in this one skinny man who never eats, but who gets healthy and smart and nicer, the drunker he gets. God gave me Horace Bunthorne."

"Daddy, you have to be teasing," Iris said. "Jews also drink."

"I have no idea what your father is talking about," Hilda said.

"I do," Martin said. "But it's more complicated than that. Pop likes to kid about Bunthorne, but he's a hell of a lawyer."

Davey listened a bit opaquely, never quite sure what his father meant, faintly jealous of Martin's quickness, of Iris's sharp tongue. He was more comfortable in battle fatigues. He knew he could never work for Chain Distilleries. What could he possibly do around sharpies like his father, his brother, Bunthorne, Weltfish, Bert Dunphy? Even the thick-bodied quiet man, Mackenzie Tuttle, the storekeeper-gauger, who (officially at least) was a United States government employee, was smarter than he was. Funny kind of guy, Tuttle. With that flat face and soft blue eyes, and the slow movements of a man laden with more weight and strength than he knew what to do with. Davey liked him.

"God bless Bunthorne," Mort said. He patted his black patch. "He gave me a peek into people's minds. Legitimate booze was different from bootlegging. I needed him."

As the men around the conference table talked about advertising campaigns, better distribution, competition from cheap brands, marketing experiments with gin and vodka, the need to covertly establish their own banks to meet enormous prepaid taxes for the removal of bonded whiskey, Mort let his mind wander back again to those early years, the bursting thirties, when he had expanded, gambled, battled competition, paid off the right people, and gotten into liquor production in a big way.

He could recall Bunthorne gently agitating the bourbon in his glass, sipping it, rolling it over his tongue, and rendering his verdict to Mort. It was the spring of 1934, Mort recalled, a few months after repeal. The Chains had started slowly. Their one small distillery was lagging. They could not produce enough neutral grain spirits. The law required that straight whiskey had to be aged in charred oak barrels, which were hard to come by. The big boys—Canadians, English, Van Alst—came in with a head start. Undaunted, Mort had set the Chain company up as mere "rectifiers," purchasers and mixers of whiskeys, putting their own labels on blended brands created from a combination of products.

"Too strong, too hot for the mouth," Bunthorne was saying. "And it costs too much." He was sipping straight bourbon whiskey, distilled from corn and aged in charred oak barrels for a minimum of four years to give it the designation "bottled in bond." There was lots of it, along with bonded straight rye and straight wheat whiskey, being distilled. To Bunthorne it was a waste of time and money. A small market, high costs, a four-year wait.

"Blends, *blends,*" Bunthorne told Mort, whose indifference to hard liquor applied to expensive whiskey as much as it had to rotgut.

They were on the verge of concluding the purchase of a large distilling plant in upstate New York. They would soon be ready to threaten the "big four" of the whiskey business. They would be operating from a solid base, their own supply of neutral grain spirits, which formed forty-nine percent of a typical Chain blend. Mac Tuttle, nominally a government man, was explaining how he would see to it that a sympathetic "storekeeper-gauger" —the man who supervised whiskey production—was appointed.

The job was an odd one, little known to the general public. Although distilleries had been privately owned and operated since 1934, "control" was under the eagle eye of the "storekeeper-gauger," a man required to possess absolute integrity and knowledge of the business. (Gone were the good old corrupt days, Mort mused, when they bought and sold shmucks like O'Connor and Curtis, the jerks who were supposed to control alcohol warehouses. Mort smiled as he recalled Jake's squad of fake "rabbis" who regularly procured government-sequestered wine from venal government men with forged letters from Rabbi Piltz.)

Mackenzie Tuttle held the keys to the distilling rooms, the cisterns, the grain bins, all functioning parts of the distillery. Not a single employee, not Mort Chain or Martin or Bunthorne or Dr. Weltfish, could go from one part of the plant to another until the federal employee gave his permission and unlocked the area. In theory, the distilling process was carried out under Tuttle's bland blue eye. Tuttle and two assistants examined grains, extracts, and sampled all spirits. Even the affixing of the green federal revenue stamp was part of Tuttle's job.

Through an intricate process of influence, visits to key congressmen, a sympathetic assistant secretary of the Treasury, M. J. Chain had arranged for Mac Tuttle to get the job at the Chains' main distillery. No one knew that Tuttle was Mort's half brother. Indeed, Mort suspected, possibly Mackenzie himself did not know. They never discussed the matter. From time to time Mort visited the statuesque gray-haired woman who lived alone in the stucco house in Freeport and ran a fleet of charter boats. *Mrs. Tuttle.* Old Jake's mistress, the woman who'd made him happy and given him another son.

Sometimes Mackenzie would look at Mort with his flat eyes as if summoning up the courage to ask something. *Are you . . . ? Are we . . . ?* But the words never came. Just as well, Mort thought. I've taken care of my own blood. Jake probably loved the boy as much as he loved Mort. And Tuttle was a good man, intelligent, reliable, extremely knowing about the business.

I do better with my associates than my father did, Mort thought. Jake had been stuck with the Ferrantes most of his life, and one of them, that bastard Sal, had surely been involved in his death. Kuflik, the old *shtarker,* had said as much that snowy night on Pitkin Avenue. Schonkeit had used Sal to get rid of the insane Wesselberg and Jake in one cunning stroke. . . .

"*. . . the nerve of those people using prune juice and sherry in their blends,*" Bunthorne was saying. He was talking about a leading competitor. *"Love to tell the newspapers about it, catch them red-handed. . . ."*

Mort Chain had had his revenge. It had been sweet. Honey to the lips. The way he'd trapped Schonkeit, framed him with his own dirty game, gotten the bookmakers to take care of him. It had taken a couple of months to arrange Sal Ferrante's disappearance. The job saddened him a little. After all, Sal with his farting taxi had gotten Mort started back in 1922. But the violent and treacherous streak in the youngest Ferrante was bound to do him in. Mort had wept a little the night he got word that Sal was dead, resting at the bottom of a pond in the Catskills.

Mort thought of the turbulent thirties, the rise of the Chain corporation from rectifiers—people who merely mixed and bottled a "blend"—into major distillers, innovators in the field, satisfiers of the great American thirst.

Bunthorne, backed by Weltfish's skills, put them into blends with vigor and imagination. *Mildness, a uniform taste, something easy on the palate and throat, but with the same gently fuzzing and forgetful effect.* Render the limbs loose, the tongue active, the sex glands aroused, let the world glow rosily. Bunthorne had pointed out that while straight whiskeys required at least two years of aging and bottled-in-bond liquor straight needed four years—an expensive lengthy process—blends could be sold damned near *green.*

To the astonishment of the corporate giants, the Chains' milder product, beautifully bottled, smartly labeled, advertised as smooth, mellow, and satisfying, a drink that left the imbiber clearheaded and bright-eyed, caught on. Straight rye and straight bourbon became regional tastes. Especially among the young, the cry was for "whiskey"—and whiskey meant a lighter, younger product.

When grain alcohol was in short supply during the war, the big boys had vast inventories of it and did not suffer badly. Production of whiskey and grain spirits was shut off for a time. Industrial alcohol took precedence. Daringly Bunthorne and Weltfish flew to Cuba and started buying up vast quantities of sugarcane for alcohol. They also bought up entire crops of potatoes, excess cereal grains, and fruit orchards, to provide them with the clear liquid, distilled at 190 proof, which formed the basis of their popular brands. Chain's Old Oak Tree was soon proving a runaway favorite at officers' clubs, night spots, defense plants.

Some experts complained that Weltfish's cane-based alcohol gave the Chain products a rummy aftertaste, not what they expected in an honest blend. The defect was soon corrected by the use of a neutralizing agent. The public continued to like Chain brands.

Sullen and greedy, the big four, led by the octopus Van Alst, watched angrily. Who the hell was M. J. Chain and his nervy gang of newcomers? *Sugarcane? Potatoes?* The word was spread to bar owners, restaurants, hotels, and retailers: Chain whiskey was rotten whiskey. It was made from anything that would ferment, including garbage. What else could people expect from people who had gotten their start as bootleggers?

But the Chains fought back. Scrambling for grain alcohol, buying up small distilleries, working overtime to make sure they would never be at the mercy of the big operators, they survived. The richest of all the whiskey families, the Van Alsts, had accumulated huge stores of grain alcohol. Quietly, under Bunthorne's shrewd guidance, Mort set up a "cover company," presumably in the cough-medicine business. Hundreds of thousands of gallons were bought from Van Alst, until he found out and threatened to sue. But it developed that he himself was vulnerable to the law on a variety of counts. Bunthorne arranged a truce, and the Chains soon got a share of grain alcohol to tide them over.

Glancing around the boardroom now, Mort felt proud of his organization, pleased with his choices. Bunthorne, Dunphy, Weltfish, Tuttle, and now young Martin, a graduate of Harvard Business School and smarter than the old man. Immediately Martin had understood the value of their subsidiaries—Chain Chemicals, founded on brokering postwar surpluses; Chain Pharmaceuticals, a flourishing line of proprietary drugs; and now the Patriots and Citizens Bank and Trust Company, a means of easing tax payments.

"Any other business?" Mort asked.

"The foundation, pop," Martin said.

"That's a whole other meeting, Martin. Talk to Horace and Bert about it."

For some months Martin had been advising his father to establish the Chain Foundation, a tax-free charitable institution, directing resources toward medical research and education. It not only made sense from a financial standpoint but it was sound public relations. It would also take away the lingering stigma, the snide references in the press, the whispers at conventions, the buzzing about the origins of the Chains, the trail of violence and blood, shadowy memories of a murdered father.

"One other thing," Martin said. "When I made the last European trip, pop? With the trade group?"

"Yes?"

Martin had been active in a campaign to get Jewish survivors of the Holocaust out of Eastern Europe and into Israel. His intelligence, his access to funds, his Washington contacts were invaluable. The trip to Europe had been one of several he had made in the company of affluent businessmen, bankers, and educators. The distinguished group had rejected him at first. But Martin, with his Ivy League charm, his discreet manner, his ability to listen and then add constructive ideas, won them over. DeeDee had been a great asset, too. She was, after all, a Grau.

"Quite a trip, as I recall," Bunthorne said. "Maybe we can tie some rescue and rehab work into the foundation."

"I didn't mean that," Martin said. "I did some shopping in Poland. Look at this."

He put a bottle on the table. Colorless liquid, clumsily corked and without a label.

"Vodka, gentlemen," Martin said. "One hundred proof, distilled in Krakow, Poland. No taste, no smell, no congeners, less headaches, no whiskey breath. Mixes with anything."

"Hell, it isn't even booze," one of the men said.

"Martin, we know about vodka," Harris Weltfish said politely. "A fraction of the market. Our blends are for the masses. Who wants a whiskey you can't see, smell, or taste? No one buys vodka."

"Horace, do me a favor," Martin said. "Take this home and try it out.

With orange juice, tomato juice, any way you want. With quinine water, vermouth, with Rose's lime juice. You and Tucky have a ball."

"I have never been known to refuse a free bottle of the disturbance," Bunthorne said solemnly.

"It's got to succeed," Martin said. "With college kids. With women. Less headaches, less hangovers, less puking, no bad breath. And you can flavor it any way you want. Mix it with vitamin-rich juices."

Mort adjourned the meeting. He was pleased with Martin's enterprise. But a colorless booze that looked like water? . . .

His musings were interrupted by his secretary. Mrs. Chain was on the phone and was having hysterics. "Again?" Mort asked. He took the phone. David had just tried to reenlist in the marines, Hilda sobbed. He had been rejected because of wounds he'd gotten in Israel, but he was calling a senator to use his influence. The boy was crazy. Only his father could stop him. *Korea! Who needed Korea?*

Martin followed his father to his office. "Something wrong at home, pop?"

"Your brother wants to fight a war again."

The older son volunteered to ride out to Brooklyn with Mort and talk Davey out of it. Mort dissuaded him. Davey'd been rejected already, and Mort would see that the rejection stuck, if it involved calling the secretary of defense. No military unit would ever accept former sergeant David Chain.

Martin was relieved. DeeDee was jumping that weekend in a horse show in Armonk, and they had invited guests over for a Friday night "bird and bottle."

Chapter 52

When Mort got home, he found the house on Ocean Parkway cluttered with trunks, valises, and packing cases. In two days Hilda would be moving to Lake Champlain for two months at the lodge at Camp Spruce Grove. Mort owned a minor interest in the prosperous summer camp, but was little concerned with it apart from ensuring a winning baseball team by giving "scholarships" to New York City high-school stars. Spruce Grove had a twenty-seven-game winning streak. Looking at the luggage, Mort had a wistful reminder of Davey, as a counselor, making an incredible running catch in center field against an army team from Plattsburgh. The tall, suntanned figure racing into the woods to turn a home run into the final out . . .

"Thank God you're here," Hilda wept. "He's driving me crazy. I listen to the radio. Americans are getting killed, and your son wants to reenlist. Already they told him his leg is no good. He called two congressmen."

In a Dior robe, Hilda rested on a white velvet sofa. A year ago Iris had demanded that the house be redone by a fashionable decorator. Mort hated the new furniture, the cockeyed paintings and screwy statues. Mostly blacks, whites, and grays. It looked like an old movie. No color, no life. But Iris loved it. The house had been featured in the *New York Times Magazine* section. *Bauhaus in Brooklyn,* whatever the hell that meant, Mort thought gloomily.

"Is this true, Dave?" he asked.

"It's true."

Iris tossed her golden mane. They were so much alike, the younger Chain children. Jake's big body, strong limbs, fair skin, blond-brown hair. Even the hands. Long, thick, corded with veins and muscle. Mort always thought of his father when he saw them.

"Let Davey do what he wants, pop. The world doesn't begin or end with neutral grain spirits." Iris winked at her brother.

"No, but that's what pays the bills," Mort said. He sighed, sat down, summoned Harry Twine to bring him a glass of seltzer.

"I don't want to be paid off," Davey said. "I never have. I'm no hero. I just want to go."

Hilda hefted her weary body into a sitting position. The gold-and-black dressing gown dazzled against the white sofa. Her thighs stretched the gossamer fabric of the seven-hundred-dollar robe. Mort looked at her hips approvingly. Still round and unmarked. Forty-eight years old and men stared at her soft, seamless face, the staring dark eyes, the crimson mouth. He loved her. They had been through a great deal. He did not like to see her hurt.

"You fought two wars, David," she sobbed. "You were lucky the first time. I know how you were wounded in Israel, how you almost lost your leg and lied to us. You and your father tried to keep it from me. But your friend Al Seligman—who needs that *nudnik?*—he let the cat out of the bag. Now you have a knee with a brace, and thank God you won't have to go to Korea or anywhere else. . . ."

"Your mother's right," Mort said wearily. Jesus, how did kids contrive to make their parents so miserable? He'd never been a burden to Jake. He'd begun smuggling booze when he was eighteen, taken the old man into the business. They'd been partners and friends.

Davey ducked his head, sat hunched over on the famous Otzenberger ottoman that was shaped like a hideous frog. Iris and her decorator detested it. Mort insisted it stay. When they entertained, Iris hid it in a closet.

Mort smiled. "Dave, take that job I offered you. You'll run the chemical division—"

Iris got up, frowned, paced the wall-to-wall steel-gray carpet. "Daddy, forget it. Davey can do anything he wants."

"Iris, sweetheart," Mort said, "this isn't your argument. It's Davey, mama, and me. Dave, the chemical end is a piece of cake. We don't have a single warehouse, a truck, no manufacturing. It's all done on the phone. We broker government surpluses. We find the customers and take the commission—"

"We've heard it, daddy," Iris snapped. "Whatever the traffic will bear."

"Don't make fun of it. It sent you to Smith. It paid for your Jaguar. It set Martin up to be a millionaire with a horse farm in Armonk and a society wife. And I won't apologize to anyone. I support every charity around. When the cardinal wants help, he comes to me. The UJA got a problem, it's Mort Chain they call on. The NAACP, the Protestant charities. They don't care that your grandfather was a *shtarker*. He was more of an American than a lot of people who went to Smith and Harvard."

"What in God's name does that have to do with the subject under discussion?" Iris asked.

"A lot, a lot," Mort said.

He felt his younger children slipping away. What the hell, they'd never go hungry. The Chain fortune would make it easy for them. Good kids, both of them. But what did they understand about his struggles, the death threats, the shootings, the bombs, snakes like Schonkeit and Wesselberg and Sal Ferrante? How little they knew—even Martin—about the battles, the bloodshed, the dangers.

"All right, forget this Korea business," Mort said firmly. "You did your share. Iwo Jima, Okinawa. Navy Cross, Bronze Star. We're proud of you. So why do you have to go back?"

"To show them Jews aren't afraid."

"Oh, God, Davey," Hilda cried. "Some reason! We don't owe anyone any apologies. After what they did to us in Europe?"

"That's exactly why," Davey said.

"Don't try to change his mind," Iris said. "Davey, remember when we spent summers in Long Beach? And those redheaded kids would come out of Mass on Sunday and shout 'Go back to Hitler' at us?"

"I never forgot," Davey said. "I fought five of those kids one day under the boardwalk. Iris was there. Tell them, Iris."

"He won every fight. My brudda." She jabbed at her nose, tossed a right at Davey's towhead. "I stopped his bloody nose. We never told you. So there."

"Listen, mom, pop," he said earnestly.

No guile in him, nothing hidden, Mort saw. He loved David for his openness. No, he could never run the chemical division, or sell Chain brands.

"The Korea business is probably a punk idea," Davey said. "My leg might give out, I know that. I'm leaving anyway. Seligman called me last week from Tel Aviv."

"Oh, another fine offer!" Hilda cried. "Who needs him, that lunatic with machine guns and grenades? He almost got you killed! He left you with a broken knee! You had to fight the whole Syrian army!"

"I've made my mind up," Davey said. "I'm going back. Maybe for good."

"*No!*" his mother shouted. "No! Since when are you a Zionist? You had trouble reading for your bar mitzvah!"

"Hilda, sweetheart, please." Mort took her hand.

"Terrible, what I have to live with," she said. "All the blood I had to look at in my time. Never mind, you kids don't know the half of it. Better you shouldn't. Never knowing if your father would be all right."

"Oh, mom," Iris said. "What are we, morons? We know about grampa. And the old days. The boats. The gangsters. Who cares anymore? We're so respectable it's disgusting. Martin belongs to fancy horse clubs. Pop is best friends with the cardinal. The president of NYU calls him on the phone. Money talks."

"That's why I want my children *here!*" Hilda nestled under Mort's protective arm. "I grew up with all that rottenness, people getting beaten up, and worse. Now, at least let me enjoy my children in peace."

"Davey, what do you want?" Iris asked.

"You're no help!" Hilda cried. "Mort, talk to him. I want him here, in the business, not getting shot at by Arabs. I read how they torture Jewish boys, cut off their hands. I read—"

"Dave, give it some thought," Mort said. He sounded exhausted.

"I have, pop. Seligman says they need trained soldiers to work with the kids on the border *kibbutzim*. They call these places *Nahals*. It's a farming community, but they have to stand guard, do military jobs. Most of them are kids who've never fired a gun. So they need instructors. I'd travel from one place to another and give lessons."

"Some lessons," Hilda said. "To blow people up. To shoot people. To get your head blown off. Let your crazy friend Seligman do it. For this lunacy you have to volunteer? Davey, think of us!"

Harry Twine knocked and entered. He asked if the children would be staying for dinner. He and his wife would be happy to make fried chicken for four. No problem.

"I'm in," Davey said.

"I'm not," Iris said sharply.

"You're finished with college, you have no job, no steady fella, and we never see you," Hilda said. "Once maybe you could have a meal with us and tell us a little about yourself?"

"Why? So you can jump all over me the way you're jumping on Davey now?"

Mort waved a hand, pleading with her to abandon the argument. A tough, shrewd man, he was gentle, considerate, and accommodating with his children. Especially Iris. His golden-haired baby. A woman now. A bit heavy-bodied and slightly mannish but a beauty nevertheless. She'd have the finest wedding ever. The Plaza, the works. He'd connive for her to fall in love with the proper man. Maybe an inheritor of vast wealth, who could merge businesses with the Chains.

Iris got up and started for the stairs.

"So where are you going?" Hilda asked petulantly.

"New York, if you must know."

"It's a big city. Where exactly?"

Iris turned dramatically on the curving marble staircase. Was there another stairway like it in Brooklyn? Mort wondered. Sometimes he longed for the narrow house on Haven Place. Doc Abelman still lived on Haven Place. Eva's mother, Matla Heilig, had died in such a house a few years ago. If it weren't for the invasion of wild *shwarzers*, it was a pretty decent place. But of course corporate giants did not live in Brownsville. Damned few, as a matter of fact, lived anywhere in Brooklyn.

"I might as well give you a double dose," Iris said imperiously. "Steady, mama. Hold her, pop. I'm leaving town also. I'm meeting with a producer tonight, a very important producer. Mr. Ernest Parvus. He's interested in a script idea I have. He says they'll pay me four hundred dollars a week at the studio to develop the screenplay. We'll make the final arrangements tonight and then I'm leaving in two or three days."

"*What? What is this?*" Hilda shrieked. "Mort, stop them! We're losing our children, God help us. This one off to the desert to shoot guns. That one off to be a movie writer. I know what women do to get jobs there. Even Martin we hardly ever see. He likes his horses better than he likes us."

Iris ran up the stairs.

Eager to avoid further recrimination, Davey went after her. They would talk, arrange strategies, examine their satisfaction in throwing off the Chain stranglehold. They loved their parents. But they had made their minds up long ago. The empire was not for them. Let Martin, the sharp one, the favorite, the dynamo, inherit it.

"What did I do so terrible to them?" Hilda cried. "Why? Why? Are they ashamed of us?"

Mort stroked her uncreased neck. White, white, his true love. He regretted his hours of passion with Theresa Ferrante. Unquestionably the woman who had blinded him, sought her revenge for the death of her brother Salvatore. Mort kissed Hilda's cheek, wiped the salty tears.

"Think of it this way, *ketzeleh*," Mort said. "You always wanted to travel. Now we have excuses. To California to see Iris. To Israel to see Davey. I'm thinking of buying up wine in a big way. Maybe whole vineyards. Weltfish says it's a coming thing. I'm looking forward to the trips already."

"I'm not happy."

Mort patted her shoulder and kissed her. She smelled of Joy. Hilda Chain went first-class. So did Iris and Martin. All except Davey, who would never need the Chain money. The kid would make his own way, training Jews to fire guns, string barbed wire, handle explosives. It was what he wanted, and Mort would not stop him.

David knocked softly on Iris's door. She told him to come in. The room looked like Beverly Hills, not Brooklyn—nubby fabrics, raw silks, Japanese grass cloths. Everything in beige, brown, and cream. The colors made Davey think of the desert.

"We rocked them a little," he said.

She turned her back, hooking stockings to her girdle. A big woman, she had to work on her figure. They had joked about her at Smith: the Hebrew Amazon, the Brooklyn Bomber. It didn't bother her. A poor student, she had been popular, generous, unashamed of her Brooklyn accent (somewhat diminished by her years away at school) and her reputation as a "hot neck."

"They'll get over it, Dave. We have to shake this Chain crap sooner or later or it'll smother us. Martin can bottle gin the rest of his life."

"They love us, Iris. But I don't want it. I liked the easy money and the cars and the expensive clothes. Summer camps. Ski vacations. But I don't belong here. In this house or on Park Avenue or in the corporation. I'm dumb to begin with. I never understood the Dow-Jones."

"If *you* don't, what about me?" She dabbed at her face with cleansing cream. Her skin tended to dry in the warm months. She saw faint wrinkles from too much golf, tennis, and riding. Mature, yet youthfully strong, Parvus had said. If Parvus tried to lay her, Iris thought, he was in for a shock. She had Jake's strength. She had inflicted bodily pain on more than one amorous swain.

"You think you can write movies?" he asked. "That would be a switch for a Chain. Oh, I forgot about Cousin Eva. She was a writer. A pretty famous one, once."

"Keep a secret, Davey?" She constricted her mouth and applied vermilion lipstick.

"Who would I tell? I'm no snitcher."

"Parvus wants to marry me. Imagine. A Hollywood producer. He says we'd make a great husband-and-wife team. He hates his wife and kids."

An uncomplicated young man, Davey Chain rubbed his chin. He could not think of anything appropriate to say. "How old is he?"

"Forty-six."

"Holy smoke. The same age as pop. Are you serious? I mean, would you . . . ?"

Iris brushed her hair with fierce strokes. "Hell no. But he'd leave his wife and kids and the fifteen-room house in Beverly Hills in a second if I said I'd marry him."

"Did you—I mean . . ."

"No. Would you believe I'm a virgin?"

"If you say so, sis."

She strode toward the door in a hurry to escape the Chain house. "We can do anything we want, Dave. Or we don't have to do a damn thing. Don't forget it."

After dinner, in the soft dusk of a late June day, Mort sat with his son in the large garden. Phlox, forsythia, iris bloomed about them. Hilda had retired to an air-conditioned bedroom. Too much emotion all day. She claimed her heart was missing beats. Father and son listened to the radio. Truman was sending the works into Korea—army, navy, air force. MacArthur was on his way. The stock market had rallied after a big drop.

Mort talked about business. Chemicals, drugs, liquor. The war would give a tremendous boost to Chain products. He was sorry, of course, that the fighting had broken out. It all sounded like a stupid mistake, a screw-up, something that could have been avoided. But now that it was here, the Chains would try to make the best of it.

"A tricky business, Dave," Mort said. The radio droned on. Harry Twine moved amid lilacs and azaleas, cutting flowers for the house. His workday never seemed to end, but he didn't mind. He and his brother Eddie had an iron loyalty to Mort. They remembered their father's murder. Both men knew that the Chains had evened the score with the people who had slit old Buster's throat.

"What is, pop?" Dave thought his father was talking about Korea.

"Whether we should buy more straight whiskey. The price is too damned high. We'll take a loss on every bottle."

Davey looked blank. "Pop, I don't understand the business. That's Marty's department."

Mort laughed. "I know, kid. It bores the hell out of you. Too bad. You'd have made a hell of a salesman. A vice-president in no time."

Davey barely heard him. His mind was on the sun-bright desert country of prefab homes, tractors, apricot and orange trees, suntanned young people. He would leave as soon as he settled his affairs. A girl named Aviva whose parents had been murdered in Treblinka was on his mind.

"You're not listening. So why am I talking business? What do you care whether I buy or sell or whether the booze is four years old or a day old?"

"Sorry, pop. I never was good at paying attention."

Mort said huskily, "But you were one hell of a linebacker. Your coach at Poly Prep used to say he never saw a kid hit so hard or take so much punishment. Maybe you should have played in college."

Dave leaned forward on the green plastic chair. He locked his huge hands between his knees. "I let you down, I guess. Every way. No interest in the business. Never even stayed with football. Lousy marks. Getting myself wounded. Making mom cry all the time."

The sorrow clotted in Mort Chain's throat, and he realized how painfully he loved the hulking youth. His son, his blood. Martin was like a brother, a crisp colleague around a polished conference table. Iris was his baby, precious and spoiled. But the innocence and the generosity in Davey made him want to weep. He got up from the chaise and put his arm around Davey's shoulders.

"Listen, kid, I love you. Don't be embarrassed. I don't care if Harry hears. Harry knows. And *my* father loved *me,* poor Jake. Davey, do what you want. Go to Israel. Don't worry about mama or me or what anyone thinks. And, Davey, you're not dumb." He was crying. "You're the best of the lot. You're what—what—my old man could have been if things had been different."

*　*　*

Some days later, Mr. Ernest Parvus called on Mortimer Chain. He proved to be a diet-slender tanned man with a creased face, a moustache thinner and nattier than the late Shikey Frummer's (which made him suspect to Mort at once), and a button of a nose. He wore a honey-colored Italian silk suit, and his eyeglass frames were shiny black and a half-inch wide.

"My daughter has writing talent?" Mort asked.

"Unquestionably, Mr. Chain."

"You're not just giving her a fast shuffle because she's rich and pretty?"

"Ernest Parvus is in business to make films. There are lots of rich pretty women around. I respect Iris. Our relationship is nothing more than professional."

It developed that Parvus was not, as Iris had said, with a studio, but was an "independent," who put together "packages" and then tried to get financing and induce a "major" to make the film. Mort knew nothing about motion pictures. He much preferred a baseball game or a prizefight to any movie, since the outcome was unknown; whereas in any film or play or TV show, *somebody* knew how it was going to end.

It did not take Mr. Parvus long to plead his case. Mort was a leap ahead of him. The slender man in the silk suit, with the airy manner and death's-head smile, wanted *money*.

"I'm not in the movie business," Mort said. "I don't know what my daughter told you, but we don't go into those fancy things. Not that we aren't gamblers. What my son Martin would call innovators. Nice word, huh, Mr. Parvus?"

"The Chains have a way with words. I'd like to meet your sons. Iris has spoken a great deal about them. The young business tycoon and the war hero."

"The war hero is in Israel. He's got a notion Jews should stop apologizing and should hit back when somebody hits them."

"I admire that. I'm something of a fighter myself."

Mort suppressed a sneer. Some fighter, this Hollywood *shmeichler*. But he was reasonably cordial. He'd discuss the matter with his son Martin. But Martin was at a meeting of the distillers' association.

"Fascinating," Parvus said. "You're almost like a—a—separate nation. I mean, you and your competitors."

"Yeah." Nation, my ass, Mort thought. "Mr. Parvus, what kind of money do you have in mind?"

"A million, a million and a half. We call it *front* money. To get the project started. Some of it would go to pay your daughter's weekly stipend and the agreed-upon price for the screenplay."

A hustler, Mort thought, a scam artist. The moustache was the giveaway. If he was such a big wheel in Hollywood, why was he working a con on a twenty-year-old girl who had never written anything but poems for her college magazine? But he wanted his baby to be happy. And he was certain she could handle this dapper *vontz* if he ever made a pass at her.

"I need more information," Mort said. "A financial statement. Points, risks, guarantees, tax angles. I can't make the decision myself. It'll go to our board. They're cold-eyed business people, Mr. Parvus."

Parvus understood. He bragged a moment about his own business expertise.

"By the way," Mort said, as the nifty man got up, "what is this movie about?"

"I thought Iris told you. It's a period piece. Nineteen ten, nineteen twelve. About a wonderful woman, a relative of yours, Mrs. Halstead. A marvelous story."

So that was Iris's big idea. A movie about Eva?

"Mr. Parvus, I don't know anything about movies, but that sounds to me like a lousy idea. People want to laugh, to forget their troubles in the movies."

"I agree. But from what Iris says, Mrs. Halstead led a dramatic and romantic life—"

"She was a radical in the labor movement. Sweatshops, strikes, boycotts. So she married a rich man and it was a sensation in the newspapers. But this isn't my idea of a movie."

"Iris says her grandfather was close to Eva Heilig. He must have been a colorful fellow, your late father, from what she says."

"What does she say?"

"Heart of gold. But a very tough man."

And anything else, Mort thought, is none of your damn business. Iris was getting on his nerves, as only a beloved, indulged daughter could.

"One other thing, Parvus," Mort said. "No fooling around with my daughter. By you or anyone else."

"I wouldn't dream—"

"The Chains have long memories and a long reach. I'm sure you've heard talk about us. Don't hurt her. Don't make trouble for her. I can't stop her from this nonsense, but I'll see to it that our people in Los Angeles keep an eye on her. And on you."

Ernest Parvus swallowed, and thanked Mr. Chain for his time. He left with a queasy stomach. He'd heard stories of the Chain mob, the labor racketeers and bootleggers. He would have to be extremely careful with their daughter. She was a princess whose touch could kill. Luckily, Parvus was impotent, and married to a stern older woman who watched him constantly.

Chapter 53

"Daddy's flipped," Lillian said to her mother. "Can he take this garbage he prints seriously?"

Lillian Halstead was having lunch with Eva in the kitchen of the townhouse on West Tenth Street. Once a month the unwed daughter came to visit. She knew that her mother was lonely, had few friends, rarely traveled. A faded red rose of the twenties and thirties, Eva called herself. The New Deal had preempted a great deal of socialism's programs. Norman Thomas said so. Minimum wages, plant safety, child-labor laws, social security, labor negotiations. Who needed the old organizers and pamphleteers of yesteryear? Disdaining Garrison Halstead's money, Eva lived on the rentals from the upper floors, wrote a bit, lectured at the New School, thought about writing her memoirs.

Lillian made herself a tongue-and-cheese sandwich (cooking had never been Eva's strong suit) and looked at the blue-and-gold cover of her father's magazine, *Manifest Destiny*. The articles advertised on the cover astonished her.

> "Why Not Nuclear Bombs on Korea?"
> "There Are More Alger Hisses!"
> "FDR: Hero or Traitor?"
> "The Plot to Communize Harvard"

"What's gotten into him?" Lillian asked.

"He's following new banners. Lillian, your father always lusted after strange gods. And maybe strange women. I never could figure out why he wanted me."

"Exotica. The Oriental beauty."

"Me? I looked more Polish or Russian when I was a girl. Dr. Abelman used to say the Heiligs and the Chains had cossacks in the family tree. More coffee?"

"Thanks, mother. I really enjoy these visits. Do you have everything you need?"

Her needs were minimal, Eva said.

Lillian marveled at the strong sound of her voice. She looked well, had kept her figure slim, her white hair bouffant, always dressed in a simple black or gray suit. They had never been too close during Lillian's childhood and adolescence. Both parents had careers and spent long hours at meetings, parties, fund raising. They traveled a great deal, left Lillian with governesses. They had battled for sharecroppers, Tom Mooney, Sacco and Vanzetti, the Scottsboro boys, Angelo Herndon, the Jews in Germany, migrant workers, anarchists in Spain.

Such dedication took its toll on personal relationships. After the Little Red School House, Lillian had attended boarding schools, college, law school—a shy plain girl, incapable of flirtation, jealous of her mother's beauty. Even now, in her sixties, Eva had grace and flair. Lillian was uneasily aware that her new tweed suit did not flatter her angular figure. Her mother's old tailored jacket and pleated skirt were damned near seductive.

"I manage, Lil. The rentals are good. I get some interest on bonds Garrison gave me."

"I'll never understand why you refused alimony. With all his money? Why such pride?"

"Oh, we old Socialists. When all else fails us, we retain our pride. Most of us, anyway. Do you know—I hate to sound like this rag your father publishes—that there are editors who won't print my articles because I never was a Red? Because I was wise to them from the time they corrupted Ike? Those noble Stalinists! They used gangsters the way everyone else did. And they ruined good unions, sold out to Hitler, and looked the other way when the Jews were persecuted in the Soviet Union."

She mentioned two left-wing editors. Powers, major names in the literary world. And oddly, they were "reformed" Communists. But they had no interest in the memoirs of Eva Heilig. Only the *chosen,* those who had been through the fiery furnace, yes, even Communists-turned-reactionary, were welcome.

"It's like McCarthy said to the witness who protested he was anti-Communist," Lillian said. " 'I don't care *what* kind of Communist you are.' Your editor friends *do* care."

Eva sipped her black coffee. "It's senseless, this political *Sturm und Drang.* One thing Marx was right about, maybe the only thing. Economics is at the root of everything. Just about everything, anyway. The Korean business will end when someone decides it's bad for business."

"It won't end with nuclear bombs? The way father seems to want it?"

Eva flicked the pages of Halstead's magazine. "Be tolerant, Lil. I predict that, within a year, your father converts to Roman Catholicism. It's the logical end for him—socialism, communism, right-wing reaction, the mother church. I hope he'll be happy."

"So do I. I don't have any mean thoughts about him. He was sort of—well, a presence. The long face, the pince-nez, that upper-crust accent. I liked him even if I never loved him."

"And me? The mama who was never home?"

"I love you, mother. Really. Everyone does."

"Lillian, stop. Who remembers the Golden Voice of the pickets? The last time anyone wrote about me was that book from the WPA Writers' Project. I was embarrassed. They got everything wrong."

Lillian took her mother's hand. It felt like a bird's wing.

"Old Social Democrats never die," Eva said. "They just write for Hearst."

Her daughter laughed. "That's funny! Who said that?"

"Dr. Abelman. I went to see him last week. We have all sorts of fancy doctors around here. Beth Israel, University Hospital. But I like him. He and his wife, that lovely woman, they're still in Brownsville."

"And you're all right?"

Eva cocked her head, as if to say, More or less. "You notice how I limp? Dr. Abelman took X rays. I'm going to see an orthopedist next week. There's some kind of bone deterioration in my left knee. Nothing serious. Part of getting old."

She talked mistily about Brownsville. It was half black now. The old-time Jewish families had by and large departed, except for the Abelmans, Kalotkin the roofer, a few others. Sarah Chain was long dead, surviving Jake by less than five years. Rabbi Piltz, in his eighties, carried on a lonely struggle in the moldering synagogue, aided by a young rabbi from Poland, a scholar who had been mugged twice by blacks.

"It's sad," Eva said. "I'll never go back. I went to where the old K and R factory was, the one that collapsed. You know the story. . . ."

"My mother the heroine. The strikes, the battles. Mama, you're part of history."

"A relic. There's a school there now. Mostly black and Puerto Rican kids. Half the windows were broken. It made me want to cry."

Lillian moved the chair closer and put an arm around the white-haired woman. "Mama, I do love you. And I admire you. We sometimes get union cases at the office, and I want to say to people—my mother, a little woman with a big voice, made this law possible. She's the reason you get raises, pensions, and benefits."

"Stop, Lil. I didn't do that much. You exaggerate."

They talked about Eva's brothers. Uncle Sol, with his law practice in Brooklyn, working as a public defender, devoting spare time to Israel, the resettlement of concentration-camp survivors, improving black slums, organizing good-government groups, battling for tenants' rights. Sol would never be rich. At one time he could have had a lucrative job with Mort Chain. But he had sent Bert Dunphy instead to make his fortune as a Chain lawyer. Candidly, Sol told Mort he would never feel comfortable arguing cases involving shipments of grain alcohol, truth-in-advertising, brand labeling.

And Abe? A rich man, an eminent surgeon. Performing specialized thoracic surgery, conducting experiments for a new kind of operation, teaching, lecturing, traveling, revising medical-school curricula. Like Sol, he and his wife were *involved*. Fund raising was one of Abe's specialties. Find a good cause and Abe and his wife were on the letterhead. Right now they were concerned with training black doctors and nurses, integrating hospital staffs, and supplying better medical services to Harlem, Bedford-Stuyvesant, and the South Bronx.

"The Heilig syndrome," Lillian said. "I guess I have a little of it also."

"I'm glad you do."

Lillian mentioned the request from the major distillers for an investigation of the Chains. The state liquor authority had asked her office to look through their files. It was no secret that Mortimer J. Chain and his late father had been among the East's most successful bootleggers.

Eva snorted. "Hmph. They should talk about illegal operations? My cousins were small-timers compared to them. Van Alst, the others."

"Not so small, mother. Give the Chains another ten years, they'll be in the *Fortune* Five Hundred."

"What's that? It sounds like a track meet or an auto race."

Laughing, Lillian explained the magazine's ratings of corporations. The Chain empire was growing, diversifying. Besides chemicals and drugs, they were now into nutrient additives for cattle and poultry, soft drinks. Mortimer Chain was rumored to be investing in motion pictures and television.

"I don't doubt it," Eva said. "Where there's money to be made, Mortimer will be there. God, I remember him with snot dribbling out of his nose, no shoes, dirt on his face. Fighting with Bernie Feigenbaum. They lived in a cellar. Jake and Sarah and the boy. No wonder he was always such a shrimp."

"Your shrimp is now a captain of industry. His son Martin may end up a general."

Hesitantly, Lillian got around to the clippings about the murder of Jake Chain, the discovery of Sal Ferrante's body some years later, and the blinding of Mort. Did her mother recall anything? Did she know Sal Ferrante?

"Of course. I didn't know him well, but his sister Theresa was one of my picket captains. Let's see, later she went to work for the Chains. She went to secretarial school. An interesting girl."

By the twenties, Eva said, she had lost track of the Chains. She rarely saw them. She recalled attending Mort's wedding to Hilda, the politician's daughter. But Sal Ferrante? He had been around for years, she remembered, he and his brothers. They seemed to get picked off by attrition, used up like spare parts. A connection between Jake's death, Sal's death, and the attack on Mort? Eva had no idea. She had become respectable, a rich man's wife, a writer and lecturer. Part of another world. Odd, she told Lillian, how the people in this world—the rich, the brainy, the elite—had so little knowledge of that other world. She conceded that the Chains were hardly subjects for veneration. But they existed. They served a purpose. Yet they remained imperfectly understood, ignored. And it seemed to Eva that, in some perverse way, they were closer to something in the national ethos, in the structure of society, than all the hoo-hoo intellectuals and snobs she had known.

Lillian said if that was so, it was terrifying.

Eva agreed. The question was, she said, why had the Chains risen to eminence? Why were they tolerated and encouraged? Was there something in the nation's soul that hungered for this stew of violence?

"One thing I've learned, Lil," Eva said, cleaning the table and walking to the sink with a distinct limp. "In this great country, the right things get done for the wrong reasons."

Lillian wasn't sure what her mother meant. But she had an inkling. She told her mother she had spoken to the Brooklyn district attorney. He had looked up the old file on Jake's murder and the killing of Sal Ferrante. Nothing. Closed cases. No one had any information.

"What do you intend to do?" asked Eva.

She wasn't certain. Some old loyalty stirred in her. The Brownsville strain was getting the best of the Halstead genes. Jake Chain and his son were names to her, poorly limned memories. But she had heard the old tales from her mother. Would it not be worth a few inquiries? There was no statute of limitations on murder.

It all seemed far away to Eva. Lost in the mists of two wars, a depression, union battles, Red scares, bootlegging, the Roaring Twenties. She had been a part of it. So had Jake and his precocious son. For a moment she wanted to warn her daughter: *Let it rest, ignore it. They're dead, and they lived the kind of lives that courted death.* There was blood on Jake's hands.

As Lillian was leaving, Eva said, "There was a woman Jake lived with for a long time. A Mrs. Tuttle."

"What do you know about her?"

"She helped Jake and Mort run the ships that transported the liquor. She's still alive. In Freeport. She even had a son with Jake. There was once a write-up about her in the paper a long time ago. A lot of nonsense about a pirate queen who carried guns. None of it true. I met her once. She was quite nice."

"And I thought you were his only love."

"Who ever told you that, Lil?"

"Father. He said Jake worshiped you."

"Your father was inclined to exaggerate, dear. It's only since he's become a right-wing publisher and a professional informer that he's become an out-and-out liar."

Mother and daughter embraced affectionately. They kissed, wondered why they did not see each other more often. They made a date to meet again for dinner.

"Don't worry about me, dear. I'm a tough old hen, on one leg or two. I promised you I'd never be a Jewish mother to my half-Jewish daughter. But aren't there any eligible men around the office? Someone who won't be frightened by all that money your father will settle on you someday? Think of it! *An heiress!* And a magazine into the bargain!"

"Mama, I won't spurn father's money, but the magazine he can will to the Liberty League, if it's still in business. I'll let you know if someone proposes."

When she had left, it occurred to Eva that she had been less than honest. Perhaps intentionally forgetful, perhaps hypocritical. She had not mentioned to Lillian that it was Eva Halstead who had come to Jake with a last appeal. In my old age, Eva thought, perhaps I have the right to protect myself.

Chapter 54

"How did you find me?" Tommy Tuttle asked.

"Not hard. Our office can find people." Lillian smiled, and was relieved that her smile was accepted by the woman.

Mrs. Tuttle had iron-gray hair, swept back off a serene forehead and gathered in a bun at the nape of a strong neck. She wore a blue denim shirt, revealing a suntanned throat. Her body, seated in a wicker chair, looked fatless and well formed. She wore a darker blue denim skirt, no stockings, leather sandals.

Beyond the old stucco house, over the dock and the pilings, was a large green-and-white sign:

TUTTLE'S BOATYARD
CHARTER AND OPEN BOATS
MARINE REPAIRS AND SUPPLIES

A breeze from the Sound undid a strand of gray hair. The older woman tucked it in. She had an unwavering gaze. Lillian understood how Jake could have loved her. There was a palpable strength and honesty in the face. An outdoor woman, an independent one, someone who earned her own way.

"I met your mother once," Tommy said. "But I never knew there was a daughter."

"And here I am."

"What do you want to know? You say you're a lawyer?"

Lillian explained her job—the inquiries about Chain business practices. Then she mentioned the old newspaper articles. Jake's murder, Sal's. Mort blinded.

The woman shook her head slowly. "I don't know anything. Jake kept his business to himself. I was part of the Chain organization. Just the boats. Nothing else. I've become a local character in my old age. They know I used to be a lady bootlegger. It helps to have a reputation, even a bad one. The truth is, Jake and Mort did all the buying and selling."

"He loved you," Lillian said.

The gray-haired woman did not respond. She looked out to the white-capped steel-blue Sound. A Tuttle boat, a charter flying sassy pennants, with long whiplike outriggers shivering in the wind, was easing into a berth.

Tommy squinted at it. "Two blue shark," she said. "They'll be angry they didn't catch stripers. I can't guarantee the catch. It's a little different from rum-running. In the old days we knew exactly what we'd bring in, down to the last bottle."

A self-contained, honest woman, Lillian could see. No wonder Jake had been attracted to her. A look of the sea about her. The skin was lined, healthy, wind-reddened.

"I don't know what I can tell you," she said. "I have a son who works for the Chains. Actually for the government, but he supervises one of their distilleries. He's married and has a son."

Why does she tell me this? Lillian wondered. Perhaps because she knows I have Chain blood in me. The woman talked easily. No, she did not see Mortimer or Martin. They were very rich, very important men. They wanted to blot out the old lawless days.

"About this man Salvatore Ferrante . . ."

"I never trusted him. The other brothers weren't too bad, and Jake was loyal to them. Sal was the worst. He'd killed several men. They say Jake went to see Schonkeit. I remember some terrible man named Frummer whom Jake almost tore apart when they tried to hijack our first boat. Jake was afraid of nothing."

"I got curious when I saw these newspaper articles. All those unsolved deaths. Some connection, perhaps."

"May I give you some advice?"

"Of course."

"Don't keep asking questions. Of me or anyone else." She got up. "It won't bring Jake back. But if you insist on trying to find out, at this late date, you might ask your mother."

"My mother?"

Tommy sat on the heavy wooden balustrade and exchanged a few words with Anton. He was making the painters fast, securing the boat bearing the blue sharks. She turned back to Lillian.

"Miss Halstead, Jake was more honest with me than with anyone in the world. He told me that Eva Heilig was the one person in the world he couldn't refuse. He'd worshiped her when he was young. She was an ideal to him."

"I'm aware of my mother's past."

"Ask the people who lived there. Her brothers, the old doctor on Haven

Place, the girls who worked in the factory with your mother. They all knew that Jacob Chain worshiped his cousin."

Lillian zipped up her briefcase. What was she searching for? What answers did she want? Perhaps some explanation of the relation between the Chains' violent world and her mother's altruism?

"Your mother sent Jake to see Schonkeit. To ask him to stop some men from trying to kill your uncle. I'm convinced it led to Jake's death."

Horrified, Lillian covered her lips with a hand. "Oh, I am sorry, Mrs. Tuttle. I never heard anything about that."

"Mort might be able to tell you about it. He didn't want to cooperate with the police. The Chains did things their own way."

She thanked Tommy Tuttle, lifted her briefcase, and descended the stairs. Gulls and terns wheeled over the inland waters, snatching at garbage, chasing baitfish.

A boy of about seven or eight, waving a large crayon drawing, walked down the gravel path leading from the blacktop road into the boatyard. He had Jake's flat face. He was towheaded and strong-limbed.

"Hey, grandma," he called. "Last day of school. I made a pitcha for you of the big boat."

"That's nice. Come up for your milk."

Lillian turned on the steps. "Your—"

"Grandson," Tommy said.

Jake Chain's grandson, Lillian thought.

Chapter 55

"Your father looks like an old pirate up there on the porch," DeeDee said. "Captain Kidd on the foredeck. All he needs is a spyglass."

"Lay off, DeeDee," Martin said irritably.

"But he does. He *is* a pirate. God, why doesn't he get a glass eye instead of that hideous patch?"

"I said lay off." He pinched her thigh: firm, muscular, well nourished.

Martin and his wife were returning to the lodge after a morning of golf. The Chains had built the nearby country club and sold it at a profit. Martin parked the Olds convertible under a soaring hemlock adjacent to the lodge, his father's "headquarters" at Camp Spruce Grove. Beyond stretched the immaculate green campus, the white-and-green bungalows, the ball field and grandstand.

"Good God," DeeDee said. "I thought I'd seen my last sleep-away camp when I was fifteen. Schoolgirl crushes and masturbating. So I marry a man whose father insists we spend a week here to help root for a baseball team."

"There are worse eccentricities, DeeDee. I'll do anything you want for the rest of the summer. East Hampton? Europe?"

"No you won't," she said. "I heard you talking to Mort. The Chain empire is in some kind of gloves-off fight."

Dazzled by her ineffably beautiful face—high forehead, long assertive nose, wide red mouth, intense brown eyes, arched eyebrows—Martin hugged her as they walked toward the lodge. "Don't pout, Dee. You had fun this morning, didn't you? We can drive to the summer theater tonight. We'll have dinner away from the family. We can screw in the back seat of the car. You always liked that."

"Vulgar."

"That's why you fell in love with me. A Brooklyn gutter rat with a veneer of Dartmouth and Harvard. You know I won you in a crap game?"

She laughed and put an arm around his waist. Martin was handsome and lean, a pantherish man. A cleaned-up Mort, with black hair growing low into a widow's peak, lush sideburns, piercing dark eyes. All the features were sharply hewn, alert.

"I don't believe anything a Chain says."

"It's true. I used to run the big crap game at Harvard Business. There was that rich little shit you used to date—"

"Martin, for God's sake—"

"An Oppenheim, or a Loeb, or a Lehman. Fine old money. I cleaned him for seven hundred dollars one night, and then I said I'd roll him once, high point, for you. First time a Wellesley girl was the stake. The punk rolled an eight. I fingered the dice the way Harry Twine taught me when I was a kid. Then I rolled a nine. A five and a four. He almost fainted."

From the porch, Mort waved at them. He had a letter in his hand. Hilda was sitting nearby crocheting. A reporter from the *Wall Street Journal* had once remarked that Mortimer J. Chain and his wife remained "plain Brooklyn folks," for all their power and wealth, and had to be admired for their simple pleasures.

"You lie, Martin Chain," DeeDee said. She kissed his ear. Their sex was vibrant, quivering. It sometimes seemed to pass electric shocks, waves, between their young bodies.

"I rolled the dice and I shouted something I'd learned from a South Philadelphia guinea in army ordnance: *'What killed Jesse James? A forty-five!'* "

"Oh, God."

"Up came a four and a five. I said to Oppenheim, or whatever his name was, never shoot craps with a Brownsville poolroom bum."

"Another lie. You were raised in a twenty-room house on Ocean Parkway."

"The doctor who delivered me was from Brownsville. I told your fella, from now on *I* date DeeDee Grau, not you. You just lost her. If I catch you with her, I'll break your arm. A week later, you and I were in a motel in Boston finding out how much we loved each other."

"You're a horrid man. Like all of your family. Nothing stops you. Any way, you're handsome, and a pretty good golfer."

Martin took her hand and squeezed it as they walked on to the lodge. "You left out rich, cocky, mean, and a great lover, husband, and father. Hi, pop. Mom, still on that afghan? In midsummer?"

"It keeps me from getting bored. I could use a nice bridge game. Mah-Jongg I'd never find up here."

It was odd, DeeDee reflected: Nobody except Mort enjoyed these vacations at a noisy boys' camp, yet to please the one-eyed *capo di casa,* they migrated north.

"Letter from Davey," Mort said. "Some kid. They put him in charge of ten of those settlements. He's got a girl, a small house, four soldiers, and some old machine guns and rifles that don't work. Martin, we have to help Davey."

Gunrunners, DeeDee Chain thought. Smugglers, evaders of the law, undercover men.

Martin agreed with his father. Davey, the simple idealist, the blond kid with the innocent face and the heavyweight boxer's body—Jake's body—would be helped. Through normal channels the Chains had contributed lavishly and often anonymously to Israel. Guns were a special matter.

"Get in touch with that guy in Italy," Mort said. He held the flimsy airmail letter in his lap, as if reluctant to let go of the remainder of his younger son. "What was his name?"

"Levin."

Martin made a note in a memo book and tucked it into his back pocket. The mysterious Levin, who had once looked into the purchase of European vineyards for the Chains. Levin floated in and out of Rome, smuggling camp survivors, orphans, the lost and scarred and bereaved, into Palestine. Later he purchased and transported arms, darting in and out of France, Sweden, Cyprus.

"Make sure Davey gets whatever he needs, Davey *personally,*" Mort said.

"Mort, really," DeeDee said. "You can't have everything your way."

"Will you please call me pop, or daddy, or whatever German Jews call their fathers?"

"Mort!" Hilda snapped. "Your manners!"

"It's all right, Hilda," DeeDee said. "Daddy, pop, papa, we understand one another." Delicate as a ballerina, she walked up to her father-in-law and kissed his cheek. Mort patted her backside. Ah, the flesh of good inbreeding, fresh air, country homes, the right food.

"What else does Davey say?" Martin asked.

"That he's happy," Mort said. "Here, read it."

Martin sat on the log railing and read. It was rest hour at the camp. The vast lawn, the neat houses, the towering pines and spruce were silent, save for a lulling hum of summer insects. A squadron of angry jays chased two invader crows.

Not much in Davey's letter. A few misspellings (why couldn't he learn? Martin wondered), words crossed out, fumbling attempts at expressing his love for his family, his decision to make a new life without the benefits of being a rich man's son. He and Aviva were thinking of getting married. It was dry, hot, and dusty in the border settlements. But they loved it. Davey was not only training the settlers in the arts of self-defense but running a sports program.

Martin gave the letter back to his father. Hilda began to sniffle and excused herself. She wanted all her children together, the way it was when they were little. Iris? She rarely phoned. She had been gone a month, rooming in a garden apartment in Westwood with a Smith classmate. Mort and Hilda were relieved. They didn't want her living with "producer" Ernest Parvus.

As for the great project, the movie based on the career of Eva Heilig, it had gone nowhere. Mort had made a decision. He would support Iris, give her a chance to try her hand at writing. But the dude with the moustache, who reminded him of Shikey Frummer, would get not one penny of Chain money. Iris sulked and accepted the judgment. Like all Chains, she took rebuffs in stride and proceeded to the next business at hand. But she appeared to have cut the ties to Hilda and Mort.

Whistles blew on the green campus. Ed DiBiasi, director and head counselor, was coming out of his cabin. NYU baseball cap, T-shirt, lanyard with whistle around his size-seventeen neck, clipboard.

Mort stood up and overlooked his former domain. He could hear Dee-Dee and Martin ordering soft drinks from Harry Twine, kidding about the golf game. He watched Uncle Ed DiBiasi gathering his staff, bellowing through a megaphone to get the campers out for afternoon activities.

Sophomores, softball . . . juniors, volleyball . . . seniors, boating and canoeing . . .

Slowly, in a manner that terrified him, Mort was seeing Ed DiBiasi and the group of T-shirted boys and men in blurred, shaky outlines. Ed's thick body was losing its hard edges. The arms and legs were going soft and melting into the green background. The boys looked wobbly, formless. As if seen underwater.

Damage to the corneas, Mr. Chain. One eye is gone, but the other appears to be all right. Of course, we'll have to watch it, and you'll need periodic checkups. . . .

Jesus Christ, Mort thought, *I'm going blind.*

He dug his hands into the log railing and braced his feet. The figures shifted in focus. Blurred, muddled, watery. He waited, hearing his daughter-in-law and his wife discussing lunch with Harry. A door slammed behind him. A phone rang. *Goddammit,* he thought, *Chains do not accept punishment.* For a moment the old Chain urge to avenge, to refuse to be hurt, caused the blood to rush to his head, to roar in his ears.

In a minute or so his vision seemed to clear. Ed DiBiasi was waving at him, making some joke about the nature counselor's snakes. Mort saw the brawny figure more clearly and waved back.

A curious sense of rightness steadied him. He breathed deeply and stared into the cloudless summer sky, the soaring stands of evergreens, not hearing Hilda's plaintive voice. There seemed to Mort a rude justice in all that had happened. He remembered Theresa's wild sexual encounters with him, her demonic cries. Forty, she had been nurturing erotic fires inside her belly for a long time. In bed, her black hair tumbled over his chest, her mouth devoured his lips. She had bit him, dug nails and heels into his young back. And had surely hated him for years, even before Sal vanished.

Score's even, Mort thought grimly. Jake dead, Sal dead, Theresa in a mental institution on Long Island. And I'll be blind soon, rid of the violence, but ravaged by memories. Once he had overheard Iris and a girlfriend talking in that funny way those rich girls had. It was about love, sex, dying. Sex, one of them was saying, was like death. It killed you a little. Especially if it was wild enough. Mort was not quite sure what they meant. Now he thought he was beginning to understand. A flashing memory of Theresa, dark, lithe, her black curly mound confronting him like a magical symbol. Oh, once more, once more. . . .

Bunthorne was on the phone. Pop, something urgent, Martin called from inside the house. The lawyer was taking the private seaplane up that evening.

"They're after us," Horace Bunthorne said when he arrived.

His flight had been delayed by a thunderstorm. Now, with summer thunder and lightning crashing in the Adirondack woodlands around the lodge, the lawyer sat, nursing a straight vodka, with Mort and Martin in the den.

Hilda and DeeDee had gone to the movies in Crown Point. Bunthorne had brought his wife along. Tucky had promptly drunk herself into a snoring stupor. It did not seem to bother Bunthorne.

"Who, *who*, Horace?" Mort asked angrily.

In the dimly lit pine den, with logs flickering in the stone fireplace, Harry Twine refilled glasses, emptied ashtrays. Mort, Martin, and Bunthorne talked in low voices. On the campgrounds outside, a bugler blew a woeful taps.

Fortified by Chain vodka, Bunthorne relaxed. He admired the tapered bottle with its white-and-gold label. It was giving the Big Four fits. White Prince. No one knew exactly who the white prince was. The assumption was that it was a drink of nobility. The whiteness conveyed purity. The prince himself appeared in gold chain mail, bearing a lance with black pennant, resembling Tyrone Power. Actually the beverage was one hundred percent neutral grain spirits, distilled from "choice American grains," in case any purchaser got the notion he was supporting Red Russian communism by drinking it.

"Go, Horace," Mort said. "Your tank is full."

"Right you are, Mort. It's been a hell of a day. Van Alst and Rimmelberger have made a deal. They're going to put us out of business."

John Van Alst's Global Distillers and A. M. Rimmelberger's American Beverage Corporation were the giants of the field. They permitted lesser liquor companies to exist at their sufferance. Now, Van Alst and Rimmelberger wanted it all. Mort had met the two men. Van Alst was old Long Island money, deeply rooted in a bootlegging operation that made the Chains look like a "ma and pa" store. He was gray, cold, retiring, and hated Jews. Rimmelberger, of Alsatian-Jewish ancestry, was another variety of business glutton. He was showy, loud, a backer of Broadway shows, and, in his seventieth year, an escort of young actresses. He and Van Alst detested each other.

"So, Van Alst and Rimmelberger have got together finally?" Mort asked.

Bunthorne gargled vodka. "It started with their own problems with each *other*. A Mexican standoff. They figured one way to settle their differences was to put *us* out of business."

"What's the fight about? Why do they want to put the shiv in *us?*" Mort asked.

Bunthorne explained. Rimmelberger had accumulated the largest stock of whiskey and neutral spirits in the country. Van Alst, more conservative, had concentrated on well-promoted brand names and higher-priced blends, for which he required considerable outside buying. Van Alst was faced with a dilemma. He could pay Rimmelberger's high price for whiskey and make less profit on his brand names, or he could switch to cheaper brands and make less money.

As for Rimmelberger, his position was the reverse. He could make an immediate profit by selling to Van Alst, and suffer reduced sales of his own cheaper products, or he could sit on his stores and use them to blend more costly brands in competition with Van Alst.

"If Van Alst sustains his name-brand sales," Bunthorne said, "Rimmelberger gets most of the profit. It's *his* straight whiskey that's being sold. If Rimmelberger starts emphasizing brand sales, he makes less money in the retail end. Van Alst can stay ahead of him just by waiting. But they don't like that idea."

"Sounds like a draw," Martin said. "Which way will they jump, Horace?"

"On us," Bunthorne said.

"Why us?" Martin asked.

Bunthorne covered his face. "I hate to say this, Mort, but they think we're vulnerable. Old stuff. About Mr. Chain, Senior, the founding father."

Mort betrayed no emotion. It could touch him. The whole Schonkeit-Ferrante-Wesselberg mess. Blood and more blood. Christ, why couldn't people stay in their graves?

"To hell with that," Mort said. "Ancient history. What's their plan?"

The lawyer had spies inside the rival distilleries. What he did not learn from them, he learned from Mackenzie Tuttle.

"Rimmelberger will take over light whiskeys, white stuff, vodka and gin. Van Alst will grab all the straight whiskey we own."

"How can they do that?" Martin asked. "We don't issue stock. We're a privately held corporation."

"With the help of Uncle Sam," Bunthorne said. "They're going to have the Feds and the state people crack down on us. We'll be nailed for violations that the big guys have been pulling for years. They'll accuse us of unfair advertising, harassment of their salesmen, and goodness knows what else. Dunphy got word from the Brooklyn district attorney that people have been asking questions about your grandfather's death. And other murders connected with it."

Mort was immobile. A dark brooding figure. The eye patch seemed to have grown, in the half-light, covering half his shadowy face. "What else, Horace?"

"They'll refuse to sell us neutral spirits. They'll force the third, fourth, and fifth distillers to go along with them. A boycott of the Chains. In a few months we'll be desperate to sell at bargain prices. That's the plot."

Mort rubbed his hands. "Sounds like the old days. We could use Crazy Jake."

"Now, now, Mort," Bunthorne said. "That doesn't work anymore. But I'm not finished. They've hired that thug Pisano. He's going to hit us with a wildcat strike."

Scribbling on a pad, Martin reviewed what Bunthorne had told them. First, the leaders in the field were going to unearth what they believed to be old scandals involving the Chains. Second, they would complain to government agencies of illegal practices. Third, they would refuse to sell the Chains whiskey for blending—a standard practice among distillers. Fourth, they would pay Pisano to hit the Chains with a strike.

"Great," Martin said. "How do we start?"

"Counterpunch," Mort said. "If they're cutting off our supplies, it's restraint of trade. We can win that one, Horace, can't we?"

"I would think so."

Mort nodded. "The illegal practices, so-called. Worse comes to worst we sign a consent decree. We promise to be nice boys. The labor crap I'll handle myself. One thing I learned long ago is how to deal with filth like Pisano."

"And the old stuff?" Bunthorne asked warily. "The unexplained deaths, your father's problems?"

"Nobody ever learned anything," Mort said.

Among his many virtues, Bunthorne knew when to be silent. As a young lawyer he had worked briefly for Schonkeit. Although he had no precise knowledge of what had set off the chain—apt word!—of murders, he had his suspicions.

Mort got up. The Olds was pulling into the parking space behind the lodge. His wife and daughter-in-law were home from the movies. "It won't be the first time people have tried to knock off the Chains. Marty, we'll go back to the city tomorrow and go to work."

In bed with her husband later, Hilda asked for, and got, vigorous love. His virility was that of a man of thirty. She was soft and pliant. He was like metal. They made love like teen-agers.

Afterward, caressing his thick hair, kissing his chest, Hilda said: "I can't sleep. Tucky is snoring."

In the guest room, Bunthorne and wife, pickled in booze, slept as if under anesthesia.

Mort did not answer. Awake, his good eye stared at the beamed ceiling. Were the brown logs melting into the white plaster? The way DiBiasi and his counselors had turned mushy on the campus under the summer sun?

"You're worried about something," she said.

"Me? Never. A few business adjustments."

"I never saw you upset like this," Hilda said. "Hold me, I'm cold."

So am I, Mort thought. And scared. A terrifying recollection of Jake's ravaged head, sticky with blood and brains, the huge figure doubled up, crammed into the trunk of a car, made him shudder. He turned to Hilda. Old love, old partner.

"I ever tell you I really liked your father?" Mort asked. He stroked her smooth back, the ample rise of rump, thigh, unblemished, seamless.

"Why shouldn't you have liked him?" She grasped his member with soft hands, kissed his throat. "He bailed you and your father out often enough."

"And I love his daughter."

"Even if I'm two years older. I'll kill you if you ever tell anyone. I've been lying about my age since Martin was born."

He allowed himself to be drawn into her again. Cursing to himself, he regretted, in dull middle-class fashion, his affairs with chorus girls, high-priced hookers (not too often, and not with much pleasure), and especially his tempestuous sex with Theresa. Cracking her body like a whip. And blinding him.

DeeDee, lithe and lean, her white ass tantalizingly rounded, walked around their bedroom, shivering as she got into her nightclothes.

"Jesus, you'd think your old man could afford a fireplace in here. A gas heater. My boobies are like a pair of refrigerated muffins."

"Get in the sack, I'll warm them."

Martin, sitting up in bed, reading the *Wall Street Journal,* watched her trotting around the rustic room. Their baby daughter was in Armonk with a Scottish nanny. Sarah Babette Chain, they'd named the child. Sarah for Martin's dead grandmother, memorialized by the family as a heroine of the K & R disaster. Babette was a Grau name. For generations, going back to the late eighteenth century in Frankfurt, Germany, Graus had named daughters Babette. A dumb name, Martin thought, but if it indicated class, he'd accept it.

In a polka-dotted flannel nightgown, bright with pink ribbons at the collar, DeeDee got into bed and cuddled next to her husband.

"Why does a bride have fur on the bottom of her nightgown?" she asked Martin.

"Give up." He'd gone back to checking big-board listings. Chemical companies, distillers, drugs.

"To keep her neck warm, stupid."

"You learn that in college? Or at Dalton?"

"My first date told it to me. I was fourteen. It took me a week to figure it out. His name was Arnold Hoffenberg and he is an abstract painter today. I hated him. He had yellow teeth."

DeeDee always seemed to know artists, writers, theatrical people. *Interesting people.* It frosted Martin's ass. What was wrong with selling liquor and making a fortune at it? She sneered: *business.* What did intrigue her, she told him, as they wrestled for position, rearranged each other's nightclothes, made the lubricious connection, was his family's bloody past.

She enjoyed taunting her well-married former classmates with tales of terror in her husband's background. Poly Prep, Choate, Dartmouth, Harvard Business, none of this cut any ice with her Wellesley friends and their husbands. Nor, indeed, did Martin's eminence as a young executive. But the old stories of battles royal, gunfire and stabbings (DeeDee invented a great deal), were always good for laughs.

"You're not yourself tonight," she said. "Is it the mountain air?"

"Business problems."

"Ah, that's better. Now you're with me."

She made love the way she played tennis or golf, Martin concluded. It could have been a lot worse. In fact, he rather enjoyed the atmosphere of teamwork and competition. It was as if, in an adjoining bed, another young executive and his wife were humping away, keeping score with the Chains. We'd win two out of three, Martin thought.

"I'm glad, Dee."

"But—*ah, ah, good*—what's it all about? Why did the praying mantis fly up here on gossamer wings?"

"Not for you to worry about, angel."

Chapter 56

Lillian Halstead sifted through the stack of information she had accumulated on the Chain case. State and federal liquor authorities were pestering her again for the data. Everything her office could put together via interviews, searches of old newspapers, reviews of business deals, sales figures, mergers, acquisitions, court proceedings.

It did not take Lillian long to realize that an orchestrated assault against the Chains was under way. Queries came from local, state, and federal authorities. Could a request be made for records, tax returns? Had anyone interviewed salesmen for Chain products? What about that war-surplus business? Which congressmen had been friends of Mortimer and Martin Chain? Did they not often entertain government officials at expensive restaurants, furnish them with theater tickets, vacations, and perhaps women?

How much was true and how much was the work of partisans of Van Alst and Rimmelberger she could not tell. But she could see a convergence of tactics aimed at destroying the Chains.

An old loyalty stirred in her. Perhaps memories of stories her mother had told her about Crazy Jake. Eva had hinted at other acts of generosity and courage on the part of the hardfisted founder of the dynasty. Her knight, she had joked, her champion in a checked cap and a celluloid collar.

What her mother had *not* told her was even more disturbing. The Tuttle woman had spoken of an errand Eva had asked Jake to perform. An appeal, a visit to the potent Schonkeit.

One day a batch of material, what Lillian assumed to be old investigations and court proceedings, was left on her desk. She lit a cigarette, sipped her morning coffee, got out her pad and pencil, and started to read.

The first papers were copies of an interrogation of a bookmaker named Rocco Lentini, seventy-six, retired, living in Central Islip, Long Island. The more she read, the more unnerved she became.

Q.: Mr. Lentini, did you know Melvin Schonkeit?

A.: Sure, I knew him.

Q.: In what capacity?

A.: The way I knew most people. He made bets with me.

Q.: Big ones?

A.: Big enough. The bum took me for plenty. He was past-posting. He cheated plenty of bookies.

Q.: So you weren't sorry when he was killed?

A.: You kidding? If ever a guy deserved to get his head blowed off, it was Schonkeit.

Q.: Can you tell us anything about his murder?

A.: No.

Q.: You ever hear any rumors about why he was killed?

A.: There got to be a hundred reasons when a bastard like Schonkeit gets knocked off.

Q.: Do you know Mr. Mortimer Chain?

A.: Who?

Q.: Mort Chain.

A.: Oh, the bootlegger.

Q.: Did he have any dealings with Schonkeit?

A.: What are you asking *me* for? I'm a bookie. Ask Chain.

Q.: Did you know his father, Jake Chain?

A.: Yeah, yeah. I heard of him. He was a bootlegger also. Very tough guy.

Q.: Did you have business dealings with the Chains?

A.: Nah. They weren't horseplayers. They sold booze. Then they went legit.

Q.: You know that Jacob Chain was murdered? A few months before Schonkeit was killed?

A.: Yeah. Well, he was a stand-up guy. His kid, Morty, he was tough also, but he never used his fists. Brains. He had every cop in Brooklyn on the payroll.

The interrogation meandered on. Rocco Lentini was a closemouthed fellow, typical of his breed. He revealed nothing. But the questioner, an assistant D.A., was clearly trying to connect the Chain and Schonkeit murders.

Lillian lit another cigarette—dreadful habit, her mother said—and reread the bookie's responses. Old stuff. Nothing that could be acted on. Then she noticed, for the first time, the date of the interview. *August 15, 1950.*

Martin and Bunthorne were going over a list of Rimmelberger's major stockholders. The Chain heir, at age twenty-six, was proving as cunning as his father. Perhaps more so.

"What fascinates you about Bernard J. O'Toole?" asked Bunthorne. At ten in the morning, he was sipping an apple juice and vodka.

"He's the son of an old speakeasy owner my family used to supply. Made a fortune in contracting. Political clout also."

"And he is now the second biggest stockholder in the Rimmelberger corporation."

"If we can get his ear, maybe talk to a few more big stockholders, we may be able to educate them," Martin said.

"I think I see where you're going."

"They might like the idea of quick profits. Who knows how long this Korean business will drag on?"

Bunthorne shut his eyes. "See if I read you. You work the Chain charm on Mr. Bernard O'Toole, others. You convince them that Mr. Rimmelberger should sell off an ocean of his whiskey to Mr. Van Alst. Huge profits are realized at once. Rimmelberger stock rises. O'Toole can then reap great rewards by selling out or banking the dividends."

"Right," Martin says. "It takes the heat off us. Van Alst may decide it's advisable. Avoid tangling with us, avoid getting other distillers sore at him. Horace, we can shout conspiracy in restraint of trade. We put pressure on Rimmelberger through his stockholders to sell to Van Alst. Van Alst keeps bottling brand names in volume. We let them fight over brown whiskey. We keep shifting into whites."

"My palate tells me you may be right."

"How do we reach O'Toole?" Martin asked. "How do we convince him to rally his fellow stockholders and prevail upon Mr. R to sell?"

Bunthorne cleared his throat as the buzzer on Mort's desk sounded. "Oh, a hundred thousand dollars might get him started," the company lawyer said. "With the promise of another hundred if he can deliver for us. I hear he enjoys a glass. I could have a few with him."

Martin nodded his approval. It was worth a try. He was even more certain that this back-door approach was obligatory when he heard Dr. Harris Weltfish's shaking voice on the phone.

"Martin, we've got troubles. A wildcat strike. They've burned a delivery truck and thrown up picket lines. There were fights all morning. We've got the police out, but the men are walking off the job."

"Who called the strike?"

"Pisano's goons. The police captain told me that half the guys picketing have records a mile long. Martin, it's bad. They slashed tires and broke windshields, including mine."

"Why didn't the cops stop them?"

Harris stuttered. "Th-they got here too late. Nobody'll identify the men who did it."

"I'll be right out."

Weltfish felt his confidence surge. There was something about the Chains that made you feel better when things went sour. Perhaps it was their absolute faith in themselves; the hard way they looked at the world, refused to quit, showed no fear.

He told Martin that Mackenzie Tuttle, the government man at the New Jersey plant, was on the phone with Washington. Mac knew people who could help. If the strike and the violence did not stop, they would seek injunctions.

Martin called for his car. Without chauffeur, he told his secretary. He'd drive it himself. Meanwhile Bunthorne was to get in touch with union leaders with whom they had contracts. The Chains had always paid generously, both in contractual agreements and in gifts to union officials.

On Martin's way out of the office, his father met him in the anteroom. Mort looked grayish under the tanned skin. He was wearing a thick lens over his good eye. It distorted the pupil.

"Trouble in Jersey, pop," Martin said. "You all right?"

"Yeah, yeah. The doctor put drops in. Nerve fatigue. I got to rest it a few days. What kind of trouble?"

Martin told him about the wildcat strike by their drivers. Weltfish had sounded worried. Bert Dunphy was bargaining with Ruggiero Pisano and his hoodlums. Martin did not tell Mort that a truck had been wrecked, fires set, that the plant was in danger of shutting down.

"So where are you going?" Mort asked.

"To settle it. Pisano is part of the competition's scheme."

"I'm going along."

Martin tried to stop him as they waited for the private elevator. The receptionist and the uniformed guard watched as father and son argued.

"You have a bad eye, pop. Dr. Shapiro said to rest it. Do me a favor. Go home. Relax. Since when does a hood like Pisano worry the Chains?"

"And since when does a Chain back down? Move, kid. I'm going with you."

They could see the ruined hulk of the van, lying on its side, scorched and twisted. A large area of the macadam entrance to the distillery was littered with smashed bottles, pools of whiskey, cardboard cases. Three trucks, loaded and ready to leave, were halted inside the parking area behind the Cyclone fence with its barbed-wire crown. Fifty feet away on the grassy shoulder of the state road, a Chain tank truck, loaded with neutral grain spirits, waited. The windshield was cracked. No driver was in evidence.

"Go through the gate," Mort said to his son.

"Maybe we should park here and walk in," Martin said. "Those animals may throw a brick. If we walk, at least the cops can protect us."

About thirty men in work clothes had formed a picket line at the gates to the distillery. The Chains saw Ruggiero Pisano at once. A golf-playing strong-arm man. He carried no sign, but wore a white cap with the name and number of his local on it.

"I only see about nine or ten of our men on the line," Martin said. "There's a couple of hundred inside the plant, still on the job."

Strike Chain!

New contract! New contract!

Twenty more a week!

The pickets charged and waved their signs but kept their distance from the fence. Ten local cops and a dozen state police in dark blue breeches and jackboots lolled about, resting against prowl cars.

"Can't you clear them out?" Mort asked one of the troopers on the highway.

"Oh, hi, Mr. Chain. We're waiting on a court order. Mr. Pisano claims he's got a permit."

"You see it?"

"Yessir."

Four men in work clothes, newer employees, came out of the gate and joined the pickets. Behind the gate, Eddie Twine, wearing his union button, in peaked cap and green coveralls, watched with solemn black eyes. If there was going to be action, he wanted part of it.

In one of the casement windows Dr. Weltfish and Bert Dunphy looked out gloomily at the scene.

"This plant is *struck!*" Pisano was shouting. He was standing on the bed of a red pickup truck. His voice was a croak, as if he had been hit too often in the throat.

"Cheap bum," Mort said. "In the old days, we'd give a bum like that a cement overcoat."

"It's not the old days, pop," Martin said.

Mort, seeing dimly, figures vague and blurred, lights flashing where they should not flash, corners of his field of vision turning muddy, told his son to drive through the gate.

"We'll escort you," the trooper said. Two motorcycle cops preceded the blue Cadillac.

The big car was halfway through the gates when the pickets surged around it, trying to strong-arm their way through the police cordon.

"That's them!"

"Get the Chains!"

"Tear his fucking eye patch off!"

"Crooks! Bloodsuckers!"

"Bastards! Robbers!"

From the truck bed, Pisano egged his goons on. "Police brutality! Lay off my guys! We got a right to a living wage!"

A rock bounced off the roof of the car. Another struck a side window, shattering it. Bits of glass stung Martin's neck, cut Mort's cheek.

Unwilling to run over their tormentors, Martin inched the big car forward. He could see Weltfish and Dunphy pleading with two men, obviously asking them not to leave the plant. Hell, he thought as a third rock bounced off the trunk, it doesn't matter. If they won't take trucks out with deliveries, or bring in spirits for blending, we'll have to close anyway.

"Stop the car," Mort said.

"Why?"

"I'm getting out. No dago bastard is going to get the best of us. I told him at the golf club I'd be the first one to drive a truck through if he pulled a strike, and I never back off a threat."

Martin did not try to stop him. A trooper shoved a burly man in a windbreaker away and leaned in the window. "I wouldn't if I were you, Mr. Chain."

"You aren't me. Let me out."

Once his father was out, feet planted on the tar parking lot, Martin inched the car forward again, stopped, and also got out. Strangely, the shouting pickets, quick to throw rocks at the car, now retreated a few steps.

Mort stood his ground. A slender dark man in a tan suit. The black patch suggested a pirate clothed by J. Press. Martin looked at him. It was in the blood, in the nervous system, this appetite for combat.

"Pisano," Mort said. "You want to talk? Come up to my office. I don't talk with a gun to my head."

Shuffling his feet, the union boss did not descend from his perch on the red pickup.

"Come on, Pisano. You a man or a coward? I won't hurt you. You want to be a man, you'll sit down with me in my office and we'll talk. The way my father used to talk to union guys. Want an election? NLRB? A mediator? Or you want a funeral with lots of flowers?"

Eddie Twine and two other black employees, muscle-heavy men, came out of the area behind the opened gates. They watched with understanding eyes. One thing they knew about Mr. Mort Chain and young Mr. Martin Chain—they had more black people on payroll than any factory in the county. Your color never counted with them. Your work did. Your loyalty.

"Wise guy, huh, Chain?" Pisano yelled. "Think you can sweet-talk me? We're gonna unionize your goddamn plant all over. Close you down. You see that delivery truck?" Pisano pointed to the tank truck on the grassy roadside outside the gate, like an abandoned space ship. "That's the last one gets as far as any distillery of yours. Try *sucking* the alky out of it."

Mort pounded a fist into his palm. "You won't come in like a gent and talk? What kind of *walyo* are you, Pisano?"

The state trooper whispered in Mort's ear: "Let us handle it, Mr. Chain. They aren't distillery workers. They're Pisano's hoods."

Mort smiled at the officer. "Captain, you think the Chains don't know about wrongos? I guess you're too young to remember Prohibition. We've been on that side of the fence."

From the line of pickets two more rocks were thrown by the hooting, cursing men. One glanced off Mort's arm. The other sailed toward the gate and hit Eddie Twine in the chest.

Mort understood Pisano's strategy. He could not possibly strike the plant. He would never get enough men to walk off. Dunphy had taken care of the shop steward and the business agent. But if they could put a crimp in deliveries, they'd be serving the purposes of the men who wanted to destroy the Chains—Van Alst and Rimmelberger.

"All right, Pisano. Have it your way. You see that tank truck? I am going into that truck and I'm driving it through the gate. Me, Mortimer Chain. I promised you I'd do it. Every time you stop a truck, I'll be here to drive it through. Anyone tries to stop me gets his head ventilated. Understand, *paisan?*"

"Scab!" Pisano shouted. "Try it!"

Martin pulled the Cadillac to one side and swung it into a parking area. He wanted the entrance to the distillery clear. More rocks were hurled. Three state troopers unhooked their clubs and started to shove Pisano's people away. The mob churned, struggled, cursed. Two of Pisano's gang unfurled an American flag.

Martin got out of the Cadillac and surveyed the scene. He seemed an unlikely participant in the confrontation—a handsome, whippy-looking man in a khaki-colored Ivy League suit, white button-down shirt, green and white Dartmouth tie. His cordovan loafers gleamed.

Eddie Twine and friends came toward him. "You need us, Martin?"

"No. Maybe later, Ed."

Martin walked across the tarry pavement and looked at his father, as if assuring him that he, son and heir, was a true Chain. Something worried Martin. His father looked hesitant. It was the eye, Martin knew; it had been a long time since Mort had indulged in rough stuff.

"Pop, I'll drive it," Martin said.

To Martin's surprise, his father did not dissuade him. "Okay, kid. It's part of our life, right?"

Pisano shouted, "Anyone goes near that truck gets a pair of broken chops. Augie, Angie, Mike, stop them."

Four men ran from the picket line to the truck. The terrified driver, who had been sitting on the shoulder of the highway, got up and ran. As Pisano's men neared the cab, Eddie Twine and his friends converged on them.

"Nigger assholes," one snarled.

"You get near that truck," Eddie said, "you be suckin' nigger assholes. Devoe, Morland, git on either side of me."

Pisano's men stopped short. Sneaks, experts at the low blow, the shot in the back, they did not like the look of these huge coons. The Chains always had a few big dinges hanging around. Besides, Augie, Angie, and the others were hired help. Their contract did not require them to get beaten or arrested.

Father to son, Martin thought as he walked to the truck. *We have to prove it in every generation.* He recalled his grandfather, the stories of his battles. And his father, daring when he had to be. *Now me,* Martin thought. His heart pounded as if wanting to tear itself loose and burst through the sternum. *Thank God I'm in shape,* he thought. He was tireless, leathery, a boxer in college and the army.

"You know how to drive that big mother, Martin?" Eddie asked.

"You kidding? I drove semis in army ordnance. I'll double-clutch her all the way to the loading dock."

Pisano's apes picked up stones. They tossed a few, then retreated as Eddie lumbered toward them.

An incongruous driver, Martin thought. *In my narrow lapels and green argyle socks. I smell of Habit Rouge, my hair was styled by Dmitri of Fifth Avenue, and I'm wearing a one-thousand-dollar Philippe Patek watch.*

He gunned the motor. Double-clutching the giant tractor, Martin eased it off the slope and swung it wide.

"You got no union card!" one of the men shouted. "You ain't allowed to drive!"

"Scab bastard!"

A brick sailed at the windshield. The glass blasted itself into a crystalline fretwork but did not shatter. Martin eased himself toward the door and looked out the side window. He completed his turn at five miles an hour and moved through the open gates.

"Get the guy who threw the brick!" Mort shouted at the troopers.

Pisano's mob had moved off, willing to concede a temporary victory to the Chains. They'd get their ten bucks for the day and go home. Pisano would call his contact later for new orders.

Mort saw the truck dimly, the long gray metallic body, the giant double tires, as it passed through the chain-link gate and rolled toward the loading platform.

The pavement shimmered in the sunlight, the beige flanks of the four-story distillery wavered and shook. Light was vanishing, clouds hemming in the enormous building, the storage areas, the parking lot.

Outside the gate, Eddie and his friends had been attacked by Pisano's thugs. The state troopers and the local cops were trying to separate them. There were curses and shouts.

Get the big nigger!

Cut his balls off!

'Ey, Angie, look out, he got a knife!

The police separated the brawling men, thwacked heads and backs with their clubs. Eddie floored Pisano with a left hook; swung at two clawing men.

Mort tottered, covered his eye. Bert Dunphy came running out of the building to take his arm.

"You okay, Mort?"

"My eye. Everything's turning gray. Cloudy, Bert?"

"No, Mort. It's sunny."

Outside, Pisano's men were hurling rocks and bricks again. Eddie, his head a bloody mass, was trying to choke Angie. The hoodlum spit, slavered, struggled. Eddie's friends Devoe and Morland were retreating to the gate, warding off blows and bricks. Two state policemen pulled Eddie away and dragged him into the factory area. His shirt was a mass of dark blood. He did not mind. He would give blood for the Chains.

A rusted four-inch bolt, thrown as if from a crossbow, whistled through the closing gates and struck Mort's forehead. Blood spurted and flooded his eyes. Dunphy caught him.

"Son of a bitch," Mort said. "You see the guy who threw it?"

"No, Mort. It's a mob scene. You hurt?"

"Nah, nah. But I can't see. Wipe the blood away, Bert."

A local policeman came running to Mort's side. "Want an ambulance, Mr. Chain? A doctor?"

Dunphy took his handkerchief and stemmed the flow of blood from a long gash over Mort's right eye. "Better?"

"A little."

The blood was gone from his eye. But everything looked darker than it should. He saw Dunphy's face turning slate, the sharp edges going furry. He barely discerned Martin—a blackish smudge—getting out of the tractor and talking to someone. Weltfish? Tuttle?

Christ, he thought, it's all cloudy, everything covered with a curtain of soot.

"Send for a doctor," Dunphy said to the policeman.

Chapter 57

Mr. Bernard J. O'Toole had mauve dewlaps, a burnished pink pate, a nose like a crimson mushroom cap, and popping gray eyes. He was chunky and solid, and although well into his fifties, he looked mean and tough. In fact, he informed Horace Bunthorne as they sat down for lunch at the University Club, he had just played two hours of strenuous four-wall handball.

Earlier, in the bar, Mr. O'Toole, tightly suited in navy blue, a stiff white shirt collar constricting his neck so that a purplish coloration infused jowls, jaw, and cheeks, had gulped three scotches. He had ordered Rimmelberger's top name brand, Highland Drum, and downed the amber booze without taint of water or ice.

"Loyalty to the firm, Mr. O'Toole?" Bunthorne asked.

"I believe in brand names and brand sales. Mr. R does too. Except for that bastard Van Alst, we'd own the market."

Bunthorne measured his man. Rich, very rich. Son of a speakeasy owner. The son, like Mort Chain, had risen higher. Bootlegger, nightclub owner, patron of the turf. Mr. O'Toole had kept his nose clean, muted the rough stuff, gone legit about the time the Chains had; then found it expedient, profitable, and conducive to his leisure to sell his considerable interests to the voracious Rimmelberger.

At once Bunthorne realized the key to Bernie O'Toole's character. He would have to match him drink for drink. If necessary Bunthorne would have to outdrink him. Perhaps drink him into unconsciousness. There was, Bunthorne knew in his midwestern heart, a variety of rich and powerful person who is awed, and can be ultimately won over, by someone who can demonstrate a superior thirst.

At the preliminary session in the bar, Bunthorne had downed three White Prince vodkas, unblemished except for freshly ground black pepper. The condiment intrigued O'Toole and he asked about it.

"The Russians like it that way. Claim it gives a bead."

"A *bead*. I haven't heard that since Prohibition. When we poured fusel oil or sulfuric acid into the piss for the suckers. I didn't know you worked for the Chains then, Bunthorne."

"I didn't. But you pick up a lot of interesting folklore around Mort."

"How is the one-eyed wonder?"

Bunthorne gauged O'Toole. A bit of Irish sentiment in him, probably. Sheds a tear when he hears sad songs about Galway and Cork. Heavy infusions of alcohol would undoubtedly increase his sympathy quotient.

"I thought you might have heard," the lawyer said. "He's lost the sight in his other eye. He was injured when Pisano tried to strike the Jersey plant. It was always a chancy business, ever since he lost the right eye. Mort's blind, I'm afraid. Sees a little light and shadows, but the doctors say it's hopeless. They've decided against an operation."

O'Toole drained his scotch. He shook his head. "Jesus, Mary, and Joseph, I'm sorry to hear that. I never was a close friend of the Chains, but I knew Mort when he ran trucks up to Canada. Well, anyway, they didn't turn yellow at a few dagos. There never was any ki-yi in the Chains."

Stroking his pink scalp, Bernie O'Toole, over bluepoints and double lamb chops and three more scotches (Bunthorne matched him, White Prince to Highland Drum), reminisced about the rough old days. He and his father, the departed speak owner who had made the first ride north with Ferrante, had always respected the Chains.

"Y'see, Mr. Bunthorne," the Irishman said candidly, "hebes are usually soft. White hands, yellow in a fight, full of schemes. The old guys with long whiskers and faces the color of dry dog shit, the young ones with them little round hats, burying their noses in books to be doctors or lawyers. Like those Heilig kids." Not that Bernie O'Toole didn't admire learning. It was just that mockies went at it too avidly and closed other people out. They were a race who would rather study than drink. It was unnatural.

"Their privilege, sir," Bunthorne said. "America is wide open for everyone. I was a dirt farmer's son."

"That ain't what I mean. The Chains were smart even if they never went to college. But, besides brains, they weren't afraid. My father told me about the old man, Jake. Lift a wagon by the rear axle. Unload an ice truck faster than a gang of spades. And fight? Eat bullets? You had to admire a son of a bitch like Crazy Jake."

"I'm sorry I never knew the man. He died before I joined the firm."

"Died? Schonkeit had him killed."

"A shame."

"Yeah. He never learned to duck, Crazy Jake. I am sorry about Mort losing his vision. In the old days we never got in each other's way. Territorial rights, respect for each other. In fact my later interests were largely in improving the breed."

"An American success story," Bunthorne said. He ordered another round. His quarry's face was turning scarlet, inflating, cheeks puffing out like a blowfish's belly, the tracery of burst blood vessels on the nose fiery hot. Scotch seemed to issue in droplets from O'Toole's fuchsia forehead, as if bypassing the digestive system and oozing from gullet to skin.

As for Horace Bunthorne, who had consumed as much one-hundred-proof vodka as O'Toole had imbibed ninety-proof scotch, he showed no sign of wear. He was clear-eyed and clear-skinned. His loud midwestern voice was warmer and more sincere than ever.

Skillfully the lawyer soft-soaped Bernard O'Toole. Terrible, all that bloodshed. Did Mr. O'Toole know that the Chains were reputed to have had something to do with the departure of Melvin Schonkeit? And was that not a blow for liberty, for honest horse breeders, turf enthusiasts, bookmakers?

O'Toole agreed. It was a boon to mankind, an act of kindness that the Paymaster had been removed.

Disdaining dessert or coffee—it left less room for alcohol—the men retired to a quiet corner of the bar. Bunthorne calculated that O'Toole had drunk the equivalent of a fifth of scotch.

The Irishman comprehended he was in a battle of heroic proportions. Finn McCool against Brian Borrhu. If there was one other thing Bernie O'Toole respected beyond raw courage, it was a capacity for the disturbance. He looked at Bunthorne's sloped face, the enormous eyes, the imprinted American smile. Sweatless, steady. No wonder Mort Chain and his kid had such confidence in this tall bag of bones.

"Brandy," Bunthorne commanded. "It helps the digestive process."

O'Toole nodded dreamily. He would go to the mat with this sponge, match him shot for shot.

On the third round from the decanter—it was Courvoisier—Bunthorne began his appeal to the second biggest stockholder in A. M. Rimmelberger's American Beverage Corporation. Yes indeed, Mr. O'Toole, Mr. R would do well to start selling his whiskey to Van Alst. Profits, enormous profits beckoned. A rise in American Beverage stock, dividends, benefits for all . . .

O'Toole's eyes turned to jellied yellow lumps. Sweat drenched the rim of his shirt collar. Bunthorne assured him that the Chains' government contacts hinted that there would be no curtailment of whiskey production because of the Korean War.

After the fourth brandy, Mr. O'Toole excused himself and went to the men's room. He returned fifteen minutes later, looking bleached and wet-eyed. Bunthorne greeted him with a poisonous-looking green drink, a grasshopper. Vodka and green crème de menthe.

"Jesus God," the Irishman said. "What's that green piss you're drinking?"

Bunthorne revealed the ingredients. His voice was loud and cheery. It settled the stomach, the lawyer said. It would do wonders for Mr. O'Toole's tormented gut.

The poor fellow had just heaved his cookies. And met his match. But he could not let a WASP skeleton drink him into blind paralysis. "I'll try one," O'Toole said shakily. "You long-legged prick." He drained the goblet, spit ice cubes, and fainted, sliding from the leather club chair to the mahogany parquet floor.

Bunthorne smiled. He had his man.

"Our proposal was accepted," Bunthorne told Mort and Martin briskly. "Mr. O'Toole said he understood the validity of our arguments re the sale of Rimmelberger's whiskey to Van Alst. He agrees that we must not be made the victims of their unseemly greed."

Mort's face was hidden by dark eyeglasses. The black lenses were connected to black plastic sidepieces that rested against his temple and locked out light. He nodded. "You're a genius, Horace. You can talk to these people better than me. They know you have an edge on them."

They were seated on the sun porch of the house in Brooklyn, amid slants of sunlight passing through louvered windows. In the living room, DeeDee and Hilda's voices drifted out. There was some strain evident. Hilda was complaining that DeeDee never came to visit, that she kept their granddaughter, Sally, from her grandma. There was an unspoken accusation: We aren't fancy enough for you.

Martin wished they would shut the door. He loved his mother, but he had come to regard her as a spoiled and selfish woman. Uneducated, uninterested in books, theater, or politics, she had grown increasingly lazy, sullen, and humorless. Men stared at the busty figure, the high crown of gray-streaked black hair, the immaculate white skin and dark red lips. Her eyes burned with what seemed feverish passion, but her mind was constricted. Martin pitied her. But he was learning a valuable lesson. You needed resources beyond money to survive. Education helped. So did an active mind, interests beyond family, money, acquisitions. His brother Davey knew this.

"You'll come for dinner next weekend?" his mother was asking.

Jesus, Martin wanted to scream, *food, family, home, possessions, prices! Open your mind!*

"We can't, Hilda," DeeDee said. "We have horses entered in the Carillon Show." No invitation was extended to Hilda and Mort.

Martin tried to close out their conversation as he listened to his father and Bunthorne.

"Rimmelberger will come around," Bunthorne said. "Dunphy tells me the old guy is having marital problems with his twenty-eight-year-old wife. He's getting monkey-gland injections. Nothing gets a man on edge as much as woman troubles. He may lack the kidney for a knockdown fight."

Removing the dark glasses, Mort blinked. "Good work, Horace."

Martin felt a draining sorrow. His father's sightless eyes were unfocused, recessed.

"See anything, pop?" Martin asked. He held up his manicured tanned hands. "See my hands?"

"Just some light from the window. The rest is dark."

Nursing his fourth vodka, Bunthorne thought sorrowfully: He can't see the hands of his heir. Or the beige twill hacking coat, the polished brown boots. Young Martin Chain, horseman. A shame the father couldn't perceive the glory. Bunthorne never ceased to admire the awesome leap these intense Jews had made. Three generations. Horses to horses. But no taking of anyone's horse shit. Not even from giants like Van Alst.

"When do you see Dr. Shapiro again?" Martin asked.

"Next week. He says that, for now, all I should do is rest. The cornea may heal. If it doesn't, what the hell, I'll get a dog."

Bunthorne and Martin saw his jaw go taut. The teeth flashed in the old Chain anger. But his voice did not crack. His big hands remained clenched in his lap.

Compassion gnawed at Martin's heart. The old man—*he was only forty-six!*—was doomed. He had talked to the doctors. The cornea was shot, the old trauma worsened by the new injury. Darkness for the rest of his life. We Chains, Martin thought, are hard and mean and smart, but we don't wear too well. Jake blasted into a bloody ruin at age forty-six. His own father blinded at the same age! Martin struggled with the cold fears and gray doubts in his heart, sensed shudderings in his soul. He looked into the sun-bright living room where Hilda was now weeping gently as she held DeeDee's hands.

"I think the cops know the guy who threw the bolt," Bunthorne said. "Some small-time bum." He helped himself to another shot. "Bert and I had a meeting with the local D.A. Pisano was questioned. He isn't the tough cookie he thinks he is. We may be able to hang a few old raps on him unless he talks about who paid him."

"I'd like to see long enough to meet him," Mort said softly. "Blow his head off."

"Easy, pop," Martin said. "It's different today."

"Not much. We do it in boardrooms, courtrooms, government agencies. We kill each other nicely."

Things were looking better for the Chains, Mort agreed. It was not like them to roll over and die, to surrender, to let competitors and hoods walk all over them. Jake knew this when he was upsetting wagons carrying scabs in pickle barrels. Young Martin, full of Dartmouth and Harvard wisdom, understood it also.

There remains, Mort thought, the old bloody business. Ferrante, Schonkeit, Jake, Wesselberg. He'd gotten a call from the old bookie Lentini. Interrogated again. Who knew when some surviving Ferrantes, those unlucky bastards they'd used up like spark plugs, might decide to break the code of *omertà?*

DeeDee and Hilda came out on the porch. Hilda had pulled herself together.

Martin got up. "Horace, anything you need to make the Jersey cops more helpful and keep Pisano on ice, you'll get. Just ask. What about the government? All that nonsense about us restraining trade?"

"Not to worry. Once Van Alst and Rimmelberger start trading booze, they'll lay off. You know who tells government agencies what to do. If the big guys can dominate the market without killing us, the government will go away."

"I got something else in mind," Mort said. He patted Hilda's soft hand. The ride to Montreal kept forming images in his mind. Hilda; Lamotte, the garage owner and whiskey supplier; the wild ride back; Sal blowing out the brains of the Canuck who tried to hijack them . . .

"I'll tell Horace, pop. You relax."

Bunthorne, assembling his stalklike limbs, his face the color of a Burpee tomato, got up. He could guess. He knew his employers. One did not threaten them with impunity. Not even a Van Alst.

"We intend to file that countersuit we talked about," Martin said. "You and Bert will talk to some congressmen. There's one guy who owes his election to us, another whose brother is a federal judge, thanks to the Chains. We're going to ask the Feds to turn the thing around. Van Alst and Rimmelberger are about to be investigated for restraint of trade and unfair competition."

"Fighting, fighting, always *fighting,*" Hilda said. She rested her head against Mort's dark thick hair. "Retire, Mort. Let Martin run it."

"As soon as I have my innings, Hilda."

DeeDee, in riding habit, her ass a perfect tan peach, her waist constricted and muscular, watched these alien presences. Jews unlike any she had been raised with. Not like the people who sent daughters to Dalton or Emma Willard or Madeira. Nor did you meet such as the Chains at the Winding Ridge Hunt Club.

"I'll drink to that," Bunthorne said.

"Since when do you need an excuse?" DeeDee laughed. In a way she understood Bunthorne better than she did her in-laws. He was shrewd, energetic, manipulative, but he seemed less concentrated, less ready for combat, less the coiled spring. The Chains were another species. Struggle, violence if necessary, was in their genetic code.

"To what?" Hilda asked.

"The Chains going on the offensive," Bunthorne said.

"Take a look at the *Wall Street Journal,* page two," Garrison Halstead said to Eva on the phone.

"I never read it, Garry."

"Your cousins the Chains are about to pull off one of the great corporate coups of the year. Listen." He read the headline: " 'Justice Department to Probe Major Distillers: Chain Organization Brings Suit Against Others.' "

"So?" Eva asked.

"It's unbelievable. I've talked to banking friends and people in government."

He reviewed the astonishing turn of events. Two giant distilleries had been trying to destroy Mortimer and Martin Chain. Suddenly roles were reversed. Someone in Washington had seen the light. Certain powers had decided that the real offenders were not the Chains but the very people trying to wipe them out.

"I'm not surprised," Eva said. "How does it concern me?"

She'd been feeling ill all morning. A hot Indian-summer day. Her legs aching. Short of breath after climbing stairs to collect overdue rent from the artist. She had listened to radio newscasts. The Americans landing at Inchon. MacArthur trying to trap the North Koreans and liberate Seoul. She no longer had strong political interests. Her radicalism was subdued, tolerant.

"I want you to do a piece for *Manifest Destiny* about the Chains," Halstead said. "Eva, you know them. You can recall that gamy stuff you used to tell me about. The old days in Brownsville. Darling, remember when I put up bail for you?"

"I do, Garry. But don't hold me in debt forever. I married you. That was enough."

"But you said you wanted to start writing again. We don't pay much, but we're widely read."

"By the John Birch Society, the Committee Against Taxation, and every right-wing, crypto-fascist group in the country. I would no more have my name in your rag than in the *Daily Worker*. People like me will end up in the same concentration camp with the Reds when your friends come to power."

"Take a little insurance, Eva. Join us. Really, you could do a marvelous article. We believe in free enterprise. Who could be freer than the Chains? I admire them. I really do. You never gave them enough credit."

"More than you think. The answer is no."

"Did you know that Lillian is looking into them? She's had requests for investigations from the state liquor authority and the Treasury Department."

Lillian, Eva thought, you should never tell your father a damned thing. Garrison, in his groping way, would be bound to misuse it. He was the ultimate political dilettante and nincompoop.

"Lillian says it's of no importance," Eva said. "I'd advise you not to print anything in your magazine."

"I would print nothing to hurt the Chains. I wanted a sympathetic piece from you. As believers in the laissez-faire system, I feel that the Chains are paradigms of the system."

Gagging, Eva bid him goodbye. There would be no article from her on any subject. She cautioned him not to call their daughter for information about the Chains.

Before hanging up—Halstead always seemed reluctant to leave off—he asked, like an embarrassed boy, if he could call Martin Chain about a contribution to the magazine. For all of Halstead's wealth, he was losing money keeping *Manifest Destiny* afloat. Would not a beneficiary of the private-enterprise system, a man harassed by government regulation, be happy to give a hundred thousand dollars toward the furtherance of the free market?

"Don't waste your breath, Garry," she said. "Martin Chain is ten times as smart as you. He won't sleep any sounder at night knowing you're in his corner." She hung up.

"I miss Davey." Mort wept that night. "I miss the kid. Why doesn't Iris call? Why do we always have to call her?"

Hilda embraced the blind man in the canopied double bed. "Please, Mort. We can't hold them here. I should be the one crying. Jewish mothers, that's our business. We'll make a trip to California to see—"

"See? Me? Who can I see?"

"You will see again."

The doctors lied to you, or you are lying to me, he thought. Waste no tears, he told himself as he embraced Hilda's pillowy roundness, stroked her back.

Davey kept haunting him. He'd neglected the youngest son, ignored him for the favorites—Martin, the brainy one; Iris, the flashy daughter. Davey had always gone his own way, quiet, uncomplicated, making his own decisions.

What was it he missed with the boy away? A simpleness, a goodness that he knew had always been lacking in himself. He cried again. Never to see Davey's trusting flat-nosed face again, the shock of dark blond hair, the half-smiling eyes, a little cautious, as if ill at ease in the complex world in which his father and brother moved so easily.

"Make love to me, Mort."

"Sure, baby. I'll try."

"You're the only man I ever had sex with, and no one could have been better."

He wanted to say: We are some lovers—wife forty-eight, husband forty-six and blind as an earthworm.

Mort decided to call Davey in the morning. "That Davey," Mort said.

"He has the right idea. He doesn't own two pairs of shoes, but he's happy. Maybe we should try it."

"Mort, don't be crazy. We're used to this life. Servants, cars, homes. I admire what Davey is doing. But he'll wake up someday. What sort of existence is that for a boy with his advantages? Marching around the desert, getting shot at by Arabs, training boys and girls to throw grenades?"

Dear wife, Mort thought. Truly, Otzenberger's daughter. But he forgave her. She had shared a great deal with him; he could be tolerant. Sightless now, he would need her more than ever. A practical, humorless, efficient woman, and still—he gagged as the thought surfaced—beautiful.

Chapter 58

"Signals are switched," Bunthorne said on the interoffice phone. "Game plan is changed." Two weeks had passed; the Chain counterattack was under way.

Mort, with his therapist Miss Hanratty at his side, took the phone. She gently guided his hand to the receiver.

"What's up, Horace?"

The lawyer had good news. Van Alst and Rimmelberger were asking for a truce. They'd lay off if the Chains would withdraw their counter-complaint to the Justice Department. Bunthorne was letting them sweat. Their lawyers had decided that the game wasn't worth the candle. But they both now realized they had stuck their hands into a snake pit.

"Pisano started to sing," Bunthorne said. "I think that's what got them to come around. That and Mr. Bernard O'Toole's complaints. Bernie felt he owed me one since I outdrank him in a fair fight."

Mort chuckled. Bunthorne related new developments. Another mob of thugs masquerading as pickets had gathered outside the New Jersey distillery. There had been acts of sabotage against Chain trucks. An over-turning, tires slashed. Martin had given firm orders. An armed man was to ride with each driver. Eddie Twine and friends, armed with shotguns, manned the trucks. The attacks stopped.

The enemy, Bunthorne said, was in retreat. However, it would be wise to spare them humiliation, to accept a truce. At the appropriate moment, Horace would withdraw the brief filed with the Justice Department.

Good news and a good future, Mort thought. Yet he was restless.

He put in a call to Iris. She was working on another "screen treatment" for Parvus. It was on "spec," she said. No money until a studio accepted the outline and authorized a script. It sounded like a scam to Mort. A pity she wasn't raised in Brownsville, he told her, so she could spot bucket-shop operators.

Iris's voice grew cold. Before she hung up, she asked for an additional ten thousand dollars from her trust. Without a moment's hesitation, Mort agreed. Let her learn. Who could tell? She might turn out to be Brooklyn's gift to Hollywood.

Displeased with his daughter, he felt the need for Davey's voice. The kid who was never good with words, but knew how to tackle, forecheck, block home plate. The operator could not get through to the frontier out-post. Communications were down.

"Miss Hanratty, I can't hang around the house. Tell Dr. Shapiro I want to work in the office. I feel like a baby. Tell Mrs. Chain I want to talk to her."

"She's shopping, Mr. Chain."

He suspected his nurse was pretty. She used pungent perfume, rustled her starched uniform, brushed soft hair against his face when she waited on him or led him from one part of the house to the other.

When she brought his lunch tray, he stroked her behind, thrust his hand under the skirt, let it linger over her full thigh.

"Please, Mr. Chain. That isn't part of the training."

"Why not? I bet you're beautiful."

"I'm plain and rather fat."

"You smell delicious. Your hair is like silk."

She removed his hand. "Really, Mr. Chain. This won't do."

No, it wouldn't, he decided. One mistress had taken out an eye and left him with a damaged cornea. It would be pointless, humiliating. A blind man stumbling around the house, clawing at his nurse.

"Nothing serious, Miss Hanratty. Just let me touch you now and then."

"Just a touch, that's all. I wasn't hired for that."

Once more he slipped a hand under her skirt, probed, stroked, listened to her sigh. As efficiently as if she were about to give him an intravenous, she disengaged his fingers. "Time's up, Mr. Chain. I'll get your coffee."

A hell of a thing, he thought. Grab-ass with a middle-aged nurse. No point in wasting tears or feeling sorry for himself. The Chains took chances, ran risks, hit, got hit, adapted. Someday, when Hilda was away for a long spell, Miss Hanratty would oblige him. He wasn't dead yet. Not by a long shot. Sightless, he would crush self-pity, go to work, oversee the expanding business, donate to charities, maintain his friendships. He would reward those who were friends to the Chains, and punish enemies.

Miss Hanratty bent over him to take away the luncheon tray and he nuzzled her starched breasts. "Thirty-six B?" he asked.

"C."

"You seem to be a nice person, Miss Hanratty. I think I'll learn braille in no time."

Lillian Halstead enjoyed the drive through the rolling hills, past the white-fenced pastures of northern Westchester County. Her father had cousins in the area—Cross River, Lewisboro. They were members of a world he had forsworn when he chose to be a radical. Perhaps, now that he had moved to the right, extolling Chiang Kai-shek, finding virtue in Calvin Coolidge, raging at the Securities and Exchange Commission in his magazine, Garrison Halstead would return to these places.

Odd, she thought, as the car radio spun out the day's dread events, how Martin Chain, two generations removed from Brownsville, now owned the most lavish estate in the area. He and his wife bred prizewinning hunters, ran the local horse shows, dominated politics. She, who could have moved easily into that world, had rejected it without a second thought.

Bert Dunphy, her uncle Sol's old lieutenant, laughed when he telephoned Lillian to invite her to the Winding Ridge Horse Show.

"Martin is the local laird up here, Lil," Dunphy said. "Didn't take him long. The old guard learned he was brighter than any of them and that he had the touch."

"The Chains are noted for that, Bert."

"Underneath that Harvard veneer, there's a very hard and very smart guy. Martin can talk to the fire department and the sheriff and get things done. The Episcopalians love him. They adore DeeDee. How many of their wives own three Monets and four Renoirs? And once visited Picasso in his studio?"

"They sound formidable."

"Just folks."

"But why am I invited to the annual show?" Lillian asked. "I don't ride."

"Martin thought it was a good idea. You're family."

"Could it be because I'm reviewing the file on the Chains? Bert, don't gasp. You know it. I've been collecting interviews, court records, police papers. Does the name Rocco Lentini mean anything? An awful lot of people were getting themselves killed in those days."

"Don't tell me, Lillian. It was the way things were. Thank God they only killed each other."

So she agreed to the trip to Armonk. Now she was glorying in the fall foliage, the air, the chance to have a look at the world of Martin Chain and wife. There was grand irony to all of it, Lillian realized. The setting could have been her natural habitat, had she so chosen. Instead, Crazy Jake's grandson had saddled up and become an Honorary Gentile.

She had been her mother's daughter. Concepts of work and justice had been bred into her. Eva had been a less than attentive mother. But the gawky, long-faced girl, boarded in private schools, left to herself, had learned to respect her mother's life and ideals. She read old newspaper clippings, the yellowing magazine articles. In a course in labor history at Mount Holyoke she had come across a reference to Eva in a book on the early days of the labor movement.

Among the most eloquent and colorful of the needle-trade organizers was a young girl, Eva Heilig, a sewing-machine operator, self-educated, the daughter of immigrant Jews. In her twenties, Miss Heilig single-handedly called a strike of workers in the bathrobe industry. It became a landmark, one of the unions' first victories. Articulate, forceful, and courageous, she was a legend among working girls. Because of her stirring powers of oratory, Eva Heilig was known as "The Golden Voice." . . .

Quite an act to follow, Lillian thought. She turned at a rustic sign reading WINDING RIDGE HORSE SHOW and drove down a dirt road lined with red oaks. The upper branches had been pleached to form a shimmery green and yellow bower.

She parked on a golf-green lawn, directed to a space by a golden-haired boy wearing a T-shirt reading GROTON. The car door was opened for her by a matching golden-haired girl in jeans.

People in riding habits and sports clothes were eating tailgate lunches around folding tables. Aromas of potent martinis and char-broiled steaks endowed the nippy air with an appropriately aristocratic edge. Faces were ruddy and healthy. Bodies were lean and strong. Lillian noticed that the guests spoke in unnecessarily loud and uninhibited tones. They laughed a great deal. They made bold jokes, shouting across tailgates. Is it, she wondered, because the foundations are shaking underneath them? Will they have to be saved by a Martin Chain?

"Grandstand's that way, ma'am," the Groton T-shirt said to Lillian.

Bert Dunphy spotted her as she entered the grandstand area. In front of the green wooden seats, on the sunlit lawn, riders and horses, to polite applause, were taking the jumps. Judges wearing ribboned badges sat at a long table.

"Lillian. Welcome to horse country. Don't laugh when you see your cousin. Squire Chain himself."

"Hi, Bert. Nobody laughs at the Chains. Not for long, anyway."

The lawyer complimented her on her outfit—tan suede and tweed, with low-heeled brown suede shoes, a matching bag slung over her shoulder. "Miss Abercrombie and Fitch," Dunphy said. "You've got more of a right to that rig than half the people here. And you handle it better."

"Flattery, flattery, Dunphy. Sol always said you were an Irish *shmeichler.*"

"Oh, I've become very Protestant since I started working for Mort and Marty Chain. Nothing like a pair of Jews to teach you how to act like an Episcopalian. What's a *shmeichler?*"

Laughing, Lillian shook her hair and took his hand. "It means you're a soft-soaper, Bert. A flatterer."

Mr. Martin Chain, seated in the president's box, was watching intensely as DeeDee, high in the saddle on Field of Rye, spurred the roan gelding gently, eased him into a canter, and took the first fence effortlessly.

Martin saw Dunphy with a young woman. He gestured to her to join him. "You're Lillian. Come in."

Lillian shifted her shoulder bag and entered the enclosed area. "Hi, Martin. It's sweet of you to ask me up."

"My pleasure. We shouldn't neglect our cousins."

A woman in her eighties, built like a Patton tank, layered in leathers and nubby clothes, her powdery face dotted with freckles, her hair rising in an orange duplicate of Mrs. Katzenjammer's coiffure, glared balefully at Lillian.

Seated next to the huge woman was a starveling man in a riding habit. His scarlet face was crosshatched like a cartoon by Hype Igoe; he sported a guards' moustache and a monocle. On his undersized head was a wicker riding helmet. *He has to be kidding,* Lillian thought. Human beings do not dress like that. The skinny man kept slapping a riding crop against the sides of his blood-red Kauffman boots.

She studied Martin. He was handsome as sin, dark and lean, with his foxy face and low-growing tarry hair. A scent of Habit Rouge rose from his corded throat. Pale gray jodhpurs and black boots emphasized his muscular figure. No fat, no sloth.

Martin kissed her cheek. "What a nice reunion."

"I think so, Martin."

She looked at the gold badge pinned to his Brooks Brothers shirt, windward of the lambkin. It read: CHAIRMAN, WINDING RIDGE HORSE SHOW. "I'm impressed," she said.

"Hold it, Lil. DeeDee's ready for the jump-off."

All necks were craned—the dowager, the man in the wicker basket helmet, Martin, Bert.

Grimly authoritative on the horse's broad back, DeeDee turned the gelding, picked up speed, and cleared the wooden fence with room to spare.

Lillian had ridden for a few years and found it tiresome.

"Nice jump, Dee," Martin called. He motioned Lillian to sit next to him. "Oh, excuse me," he said. "This is Miss Halstead, my cousin. Mrs. Redfern, our vice-president. This is Colonel Dodge Buchanan, master of the Abingdon Hunt."

They shook hands. The old woman did so warily, the man with a lecherous vigor. Lillian wanted to say, *And I am the grand duchess of Luxembourg.* She felt proud of her alienated father for having deserted such as Mrs. Redfern and Colonel Buchanan for Eva Heilig.

DeeDee finished her round of jumps to much applause. There were murmurs that she was a certain winner. Her "seat" was superb and her control of the mount perfection.

Mrs. Redfern leaned forward and tapped Lillian firmly on the shoulder. "Did I hear Mr. Chain say your name was *Halstead?*"

"Yes, that's right." Lillian smiled. Her long face was tolerant and patient.

"Your husband is a Halstead?"

"I am. I have no husband."

The woman kept staring at Lillian. "I knew the Halsteads quite well. Which branch are you? Are you—*the* Halsteads? The Garrison Halsteads?"

Lillian marveled (as Martin called everyone's attention to the dressage) at the utter lack of grace and manners among these people. No wonder they kept losing elections to FDR, to Harry Truman. They could not be polite.

"I'm Garrison Halstead's daughter."

"Oh, I see. I knew his father. Your grandfather. He had a superb collection of hand-wound clocks."

"I guess he did."

"Yes," Mrs. Redfern went on. "Your father was an odd sort. As a matter of fact I may have attended his wedding in Sag Harbor. If I remember correctly, the bride was a Jewish girl, quite a beauty—"

"She was my mother."

Colonel Buchanan was squinting through his monocle at Lillian as if she were some species of undersea life. "Halstead. *Halstead.* They were quite a family. Knew the daughter. Became some kind of Florence Nightingale. Died."

"My Aunt Mildred."

Martin asked her if she wanted a drink. He had a Thermos filled with martinis. Chain's best. White Prince vodka and Treviso vermouth. He didn't touch it himself, but his guests took a nip now and then.

"No, thanks, Martin. Have to keep a clear head. It's the Heilig in me."

"We'll have a bite later on the terrace," Martin said.

"I can't wait to meet your wife. I'm envious of the way she handles horses. It's wonderful the way life reverses roles. If my father hadn't married your cousin, *I'd* be out there. Tall in the saddle, winning medals."

"You're where you should be," Martin said. He took her hand. He told her he remembered climbing a cherry tree with her after his grandfather's funeral. And hadn't they crossed backyard fences on Haven Place that day and visited Dr. Abelman, who had given them peonies from his garden? "I can still smell them. You smelled wonderful, too."

Lillian said, "I remember the street. The house where my grandmother lived. And Dr. Abelman's. And your grandfather's house. Yellow brick, two stories. And poplars on the street."

"I like *this,*" Dunphy said. "We're at the world's snootiest horse show and my friends are talking *Brooklyn.* I'm a Williamsburg boy myself. Boys High School. Ask me about Indian Yablock."

DeeDee, alarmingly beautiful with her alabaster face, high brow, and proud nose, dark hair tied in a jigging bun, commanded the gelding through a series of mincing steps.

"Your wife is beautiful," Lillian said. "You deserve her."

"Thanks, Lil. Eva okay? Your father?"

Eva managed. Independent, living with memories, collecting marginal rents in an old townhouse. Her father? She found it hard to talk to him. He would spend the rest of his life proving that Roosevelt was a traitor and that Communists in the State Department lost China.

"And you?" Martin asked. He took her hand.

"Investigating the Chains."

"We know."

"Is that why I was asked here? No dice, Martin. Not for a free lunch and a few lecherous winks from the master of the Abba-Dabba Hunt."

They were silent for a while. Bumpy gray clouds appeared suddenly; a fall chill hovered over the sunny arena and the grandstand. Decorous, restrained applause was swallowed in the rising autumn winds.

"Why are you staring at me?" Martin asked.

"You're a wonder."

"You're like Eva. You talk in circles when it suits you. Come on, Lil. I'm Crazy Jake's grandson. Level with me."

"I'm marveling at the leap across the Grand Canyon. From horse and wagon to this. The ultimate glory."

"Don't knock it, Lil."

Martin waved to DeeDee. He indicated he'd meet her in the clubhouse. She doffed her helmet and glanced at Lillian.

"It's easy, Lil," Martin said. "Money makes the difference. The blood has run thin in a lot of these people. They need a Chain to get them cranked up. I bought a hundred more acres for the club. I rebuilt the grandstand. I get us better coverage in the *Times*. I do it all."

"I'll bet you've figured out a way for the club to make a profit on manure."

"That's next. A little bit of Brooklyn goes a long way."

Dunphy excused himself. He had to leave early. A long drive back to Jersey. The lawyer liked living within fifteen minutes of the distillery. He shook Lillian's hand and kissed her cheek. "My best to Sol, to Abe, all the Heiligs. God bless them. They hang in. And most of all your mother. Tell her that Bert asked about her. I'm a sentimental harp, I guess."

Martin got up and greeted several couples. People with the assured, secure glow of winners. He escorted Lillian past groups of noisy people with scrubbed tanned faces, women with high cheekbones and lank blond hair held in place with a gold clip, snowy-mantled men with patrician features and flesh tones suggesting cold borsht, children of such physical perfection that Lillian wanted to cry for them.

Very much the monarch of the club, Martin pointed out a senator, a man who advised the governor, an undersecretary of the treasury, three corporate presidents, the board chairman of a bank, the board chairman of a coal company, a heart surgeon, an owner of racetracks in Maryland, and a deputy director of the CIA.

Martin turned down (Lillian noted) five invitations to have drinks.

"Bend the elbow, Marty?"

"Have an El Belto with the old man."

"Try some of your own poison, Mart?"

"They love you," Lillian said. "It is love, isn't it?"

"More or less."

Martin guided her toward a table on the flagstone terrace. It was unbearably beautiful. A lake, lush willows, lawns of preternatural greenness, rustic buildings. Beyond, horses grazed in a corral behind the obligatory white fencing. They nuzzled, broke into spirited gallops.

"They love the way I got them on their feet," he said. "That's the secret of their love."

"How many Jews are members?" asked Lillian.

"Three couples. I decide. We can't let too many in at once, but I'm working on it. Nobody says no to me. Anyway, Jews aren't interested in joining until I improve the food. The kitchen stinks. The people at pop's club would revolt. There's DeeDee."

Sweating delicately, DeeDee Chain was removing her helmet, setting it carefully on a mosaic table. She looked flushed and radiant.

The women conversed cautiously. DeeDee, who knew of Lillian's odd parentage, was less her acerb self. With fools and *arrivistes* she could be knifingly sarcastic, uttering insults with a bland innocence that set Martin's teeth on edge. With Lillian, she was on her best behavior.

"So you're up in Albany saving us from stock manipulators or whatever your office does?"

"The New York office, DeeDee."

"How wonderful. Martin tells me how smart you are. I admire you. I wish I had a career."

"Dee, you know how you hate to let the servants run the apartment and the house."

The apartment. The house. Cocking her head, smiling as if to let them know she understood them too well, Lillian thought of the apartment. A fifteen-room duplex on Fifth Avenue. The house was a twenty-room 1775 clapboard set on a hundred acres of undulant meadows and forests.

Amused, Lillian wondered about DeeDee's desire for a career. The woman was as finely crafted and assembled as a Fabergé, or one of those mechanical marvels that Da Vinci designed for royal festivals. The serene pale face was more than beautiful; it was harmonious. Modulated voice, precise gestures. Yet there seemed to be a great deal of passion in DeeDee Grau Chain. No fragile shepherdess she, who, at a sparrow's death, would dissolve in tears.

DeeDee excused herself. She wanted to change. It was getting cool; she felt sweaty, a bit weary.

"You have a lovely, lovely wife," Lillian said.

"Thanks, Lil. I adore her."

"The baby?"

"Sally's a dream. Looks like—you won't believe this—Davey and Iris. Not the dark look, Mort's face or my face. She's a big blond girl who laughs all the time. We're going to have three kids. Or keep trying till we have a son."

"To keep the dynasty going."

"Why not? The Chains built it. It should stay in the family. We hope to go public in a year or so. Interested in a ground-floor investment? At an insider's price?"

"Martin, that could be interpreted as attempting to bribe a public servant."

"I'm kidding. I know better. Maybe your mother would like some Chain stock. She deserves a break."

"Mother manages."

Martin studied his cousin's long earnest face. Something strong and able and decent there. Probably hadn't married because she couldn't find a man to measure up to her. Moreover, she might have had personal problems— the weakling father, the heroic mother. Is Lillian ever sure who she is? he wondered. Or where she belongs? It was easier when you were a Chain. You understood money, power, politics, and force.

"I could open an account for her," Martin said. "She wouldn't have to know about it until it was done. We could say it's for research, tie it into the foundation."

"Foundation?"

"The Chain Foundation."

Martin clicked his fingers for a waiter. He ordered Heinekens, draped a tan cashmere sweater over his broad shoulders. Colonel Buchanan came by. He looked elated.

"Great news," the man in the wicker helmet said. "A couple of Puerto Ricans tried to assassinate Truman."

"That was on Wednesday," Lillian said. "Not again?"

The colonel winked at her. "It's a joke, Miss Halstead. Two more just tried. They went to Washington to shoot the shit."

Martin did not smile. Nor did Lillian. The colonel sashayed off in his jodhpurs.

"My apologies," Martin said. "He's drunk."

"Tell me something, Martin. Why did it mean so much to you not only to get into this mob of horse lovers but to run the place?"

"To prove that a Chain can do it."

She shook her head. "The old sidewalk toughness. I'd have thought you'd outgrown it."

"Maybe my kids will. Me, never. With pop out of commission, it's my ball game."

With pride, Martin talked about Davey, training kibbutz youngsters to fire weapons, to track in the desert, to string barbed wire and lay mines. Iris's movie was temporarily held up. But her first television play, a half-hour murder story, would be aired in a month. Mort had promised to find a sponsor.

"I'm glad," Lillian said. "Mother will be happy to hear about them. She always felt a close tie to the Chains. She was fond of your grand-father."

"A lot of people liked Crazy Jake." Martin sipped his beer. "Tough old bastard. He took a lot of killing."

"The Chains are a hardy breed," Lillian said. "I suppose I should say 'more power to them.' But, as you know, I'm on the opposite side of the street these days. Martin, I know why you asked me here. You have the virtue of frankness. You want to know about the investigation into the Chain corporation."

"Only whatever you want to tell me."

She hesitated. It would be breaking every tenet of law enforcement. But it was sometimes done. Enforcers had friends. And their friends got special treatment. She thought she could never act in that way, giving away in-formation, playing favorites. But Martin's dark face was profoundly appealing. It was a face that was part of her past.

"Much of the investigation has come to a halt. Your competitors are pulling back. I don't know the details."

With a tolerant smile, he summed up events of the last few months. Van Alst and Rimmelberger had agreed to help one another, take their chances on quick profits, and let the Chains fend for themselves.

"So you're in the clear," she said cautiously. "Government, unions, competitors, all rendered impotent."

"You could say so." He rapped his riding crop softly against his boots. The breeze stiffened. People left the terrace for the clubhouse. A piano was playing "This Love of Mine."

A husky black man in a chauffeur's uniform approached. "When will you want the car, Martin?"

"Half-hour, Harry."

The man left. He walked with an athlete's tread. He had sorrowing dark eyes, a mass of graying kinky hair.

"A chauffeur who calls you by your first name?"

"Harry Twine's been with the family since he was a kid, Lil. He and his brother Eddie helped raise us. Before I was born, our old place in Brooklyn was burned to the ground by Schonkeit's mob. Harry's father, Buster, worked for us. They slit his throat before they torched the factory. We lost one hell of a man and a lot of booze."

"I'm glad you put the man first."

"Friends, business, same thing. Harry and Eddie have been with us ever since. He wouldn't think of calling me anything but Martin. He taught me to box, shoot fouls, and roll dice."

"Better than Dartmouth or Harvard, Mr. Twine's training."

"It helped. Everything does."

Lillian wondered: *How much does he know? How much should I tell him?* She decided she would tell him a great deal. Eva had told her about Crazy Jake. Not just the courage on the picket lines. But hints at how he had protected her from monsters. There was also the mission to Schonkeit to save Sol's life.

"Martin, the investigation into the bootleg murders has been reopened. They've been interviewing witnesses. No one can tie anything together yet, but it might make things embarrassing for you."

He did not seem concerned. The old Chain bravado, the cocky air, the walk down dark streets, unarmed and defiant.

"Lil, all that stuff was investigated years ago. When my father was killed, when they shot the Paymaster, and after they found Ferrante's body."

"I do wish some of your fellow club members could hear this conversation. It's too rich."

"Tell you what, Lil," Martin said, bending over the green table. "I'm not afraid of this investigation. I just wouldn't want it to harm the foundation. Newspapers can hang you even when you're in the clear."

"The foundation . . ."

"Funded at seventy million dollars for medical research. Grants for research in every branch of medical science. Because of my father's blindness, the first grant is going to an eye hospital in Brooklyn. Some young genius is rebuilding corneas and retinas."

She nodded. It was logical. The wealth went to work.

"Get some of the money out where it can do good. We should be furnishing people with something besides hangovers and cirrhosis of the liver."

"Martin, what do you think was the story behind those killings? The police tell me Ferrante was murdered by imported hoodlums."

"Maybe."

"Weren't you curious? Mort must have been. What did he say?"

"Crazy Jake lived a dangerous life."

"I've had the feeling for some time this shouldn't be my job, poking into the Chain past. After all, I'm family."

"A distinguished branch, Lillian," Martin said with evident sincerity. "I don't fear anything. But it might hurt us enough to put a crimp in the foundation. Whiskey we can always sell. Competitors we can handle. Labor thugs? We eat them alive."

"You seem to have it all wrapped up, don't you, Martin?"

"We understand what the country is all about. Buying and selling. Getting to the top. I admit it. We're not an eleemosynary institution."

"Splendid word. Good for all that money Mort spent on your education. You've almost convinced me that those killings twenty years ago are none of my business. Maybe nobody's business."

"I won't stand in your way." Martin stretched—leathery, strong. "There's an important opening in Bunthorne's department. Bert Dunphy brought your name up. Maybe a job in Bunthorne's old Wall Street outfit. They're looking for a woman. Interested?"

Lillian shook her head. "Martin, please. I'm Eva Heilig's daughter. We can't be bought."

"The Chains aren't subtle. We never were."

Showered, glistening, DeeDee, wearing an olive corduroy suit, came out of the clubhouse. She stopped to talk to a couple whom Lillian recognized from the society pages—a financial boy wonder and a wife who endowed museums.

The utter perfection of the moment made Lillian smile and emboldened her. Bluntly she asked Martin: "Who killed your grandfather?"

"Ferrante. On Schonkeit's orders. Jake was trapped."

"I thought as much. And who killed Ferrante?"

"It wasn't who you think. No professional hoods from Cleveland or Detroit."

"Martin, I've made my mind up. I'm dropping the whole thing. Whatever you tell me is in confidence. I won't leave a memo for a successor. My mother owes your grandfather too much."

"I can't tell you. But you can guess."

Martin let his eyes move significantly to the white rail fence around the pasture. His black-suited chauffeur, Harry Twine, was resting there, one foot on the lower rail, thick arms folded on the upper rail. He seemed lost in a reverie.

"Lil, Harry Twine is a deacon of the African Baptist church. I'm sending his sons to Cornell. Harry and his brother Eddie are two of the finest men I've ever known. So I know you won't say a word, right?"

She nodded. "Right." Old loyalties. The Chains demanded it from her. Just as they had from the sons of Buster Twine.

Clanking gold bracelets, DeeDee strode toward them. She appeared to Lillian Halstead to be the distillation (apt word), the essence, the personification of all the power, beauty, style, status, and high standards that a certain heaven demanded. Martin Chain's heaven.

The week before Christmas, on the Monday after President Truman had proclaimed a national emergency, rolled back auto prices, and terminated the railroad strike, a memo was passed to Lillian by a staff investigator.

An old loan shark named Biagio (Baggie) Ferrante had died in Brownsville Jewish Hospital. It was, the memo said, a natural death, from kidney malfunction. This in itself was odd, in that Ferrante's brothers had a propensity for getting themselves fatally shot.

A detective had questioned the mobster at his bedside about the murder of his brother Salvatore. The dying Baggie professed no knowledge of the death. He implicated no one. He gasped that he barely knew the Chain family. It was, the investigator said, the underworld code at work—silence, *omertà,* to the end.

And I, too, will be silent, Lillian thought. She included the memo in her report to her superior. Then she added:

It would appear that the murders in the early thirties involving the Chain family and other underworld figures have been thoroughly investigated. Nothing in the files implicates Mortimer Chain or any of his associates. It is recommended that the investigation be terminated, since it is our feeling that it will produce nothing new. Moreover the request to reopen the Schonkeit, Ferrante, and Jacob Chain murders seems to be part of an orchestrated campaign by business competitors who could benefit from defaming the Chain heirs.

That evening, over supper at her mother's house, Lillian told Eva what she had done.

"Just as well," Eva said. She wiped a trickle of tears. "As the poet said, let the dead be dead."

1960

Myron Malkin's Notebook

I'm here by mistake, I'm certain. Mr. Martin Chain's secretary, who helped usher me out of his office a few months ago, probably found my name in her Rolodex and sent me a fancy embossed invitation.

As usual the Chains have gone first-class.

Would you believe Nixon *and* Kennedy are seated on the bunting-bright platform with Mr. Mortimer J. Chain, Mr. Martin Chain, wives, colleagues, and medical big shots?

But why not? It's an election year. Senator John F. Kennedy is running like Eulace Peacock in the hundred-yard dash. Our vice president has made no bones about it. He hungers to succeed Ike.

And believe me, the Chains are worth knowing. I did a little digging. They're backing *both* sides generously. They give to anyone they think has a chance. Why not? It's a free country, isn't it?

Mild October morning. I cross my legs, lean back in the folding camp chair, and glance at the front page of the *Times*. Life goes on, more or less. Korea. The AMA is denouncing Eisenhower's health plan. Trouble in Laos. U.N. debate on the Congo . . .

Plus ça change, plus c'est la même chose. Or, as Mr. Dooley once said, he saw great changes in the country every week, but no changes at all every fifty years.

So I'm back in Brooklyn, about ten miles from Brownsville. On a pass, so to speak.

Behind the speaker's platform rise the sixteen stories of the spanking new Chain Medical Center, a forty-million-dollar addition to Central Brooklyn Hospital. Granite, stainless steel, modular design. The last word in medical construction.

A journalist on my left, a kid from the *News,* whispers to me: "Give the coons two years they'll turn it into a slum. They'll be peddling scag in the clinics and mugging nurses in the parking lot."

I say nothing. I hope he's wrong.

I know the neighborhood. East Flatbush. It used to be largely Jewish, with enclaves of Irish and Italians. Now it's becoming *verschwarz'd* as my late uncle Doc would have said. But at least it stands a chance of surviving. Houses are clean and neat. The blacks who buy them are people with jobs—civil servants, blue-collar workers.

The Chain Medical Center will be a research facility for metabolic diseases of children, and a children's hospital. It's a good idea. Someone in that tower on Park Avenue, the money-filled Chain Building, is thinking constructively. Who am I to be critical? When did I ever fork over forty million for a hospital?

A fellow from United Press is sitting on my right. He's dozing. The uniformed band from the Department of Sanitation wakes him up with a stirring rendition of "America the Beautiful." He's an older reporter, beery, heavy-jowled. "Who the hell are the Chains?" he asks. "You know anything about them?"

"Anonymous wealth."

Handouts enlighten us about the medical center. Ten years in the planning. The personal project of Mr. Mortimer J. Chain and his son Martin Chain. The foundation has funded many worthy projects in the past ten years, the brochure states, but this is the first major institution to bear their name. Up to now they preferred to keep their benefactions quiet.

Safe enough to go public now, I guess.

I scan the platform. Senator Kennedy, ruddy, too handsome, is talking to Mrs. Martin Chain. She is by far the most exquisite person on the platform. Her beauty is like a reproach, a warning. No one should be that gorgeous, that poised. Clear skin, large features, wide brown eyes, arched brows. Her children are just as magnificent. How do some people get so lucky? There is a blond girl of about eleven, in a blue fairy-princess dress and long braids; two dark bright-eyed little boys.

And blind Mort. My uncle remembered him when he lived in a basement hole and was known as Mutt. A wild street brat, good with his fists, sharp as a scalpel. Running booze from Canada in a taxicab when he was eighteen years old. The last time I saw him was at the camp on Lake Champlain. Now he looks hunched, uncertain, shrunken behind his dead eyes, talking to no one. His starched nurse is by his side.

Martin Chain is seated next to the vice president of the United States. They are in earnest conversation. Hell, a vote's a vote. And a fat campaign contribution is even better than a vote. Nixon looks pretty good—young, trim, his suits fitting better. He gestures a great deal.

The speeches aren't much. Both candidates pay tribute to the generous donation the Chain Foundation has made to maintaining the health of Brooklyn citizens. More such bountiful acts from the private sector are needed, the rivals agree.

Others speak. The mayor, the hospital commissioner, and finally Martin Chain himself, as he hands over the deed to the Chain Medical Center to Hizzoner and says a few pleasant words about his own boyhood not far from here, on Ocean Parkway. He recalls the family's roots in Brownsville, how much they owe the great city and its wonderful people. . . .

Corny? Sure. I wonder if his gratitude includes all the cops, federal agents, coast guardsmen, and politicians who benefited from the Chains' largesse back in the glorious years of bootlegging. In a way, the family has always been philanthropically inclined. And it all goes back to Jacob Chain. I think of the poor union guys and the exploited girls who got better contracts, increases in salary, because a hardhanded mobster named Crazy Jake was courageous and reckless and hungry enough to take on company-paid bullies.

It's not my business to remind anyone. Besides, DeeDee Chain has just crossed her legs and I'm frantically trying to sneak a look. She should wear longer skirts. Who can listen to speeches about the future of our city when what may be the sexiest legs in New York are on display? How do some people (Martin Chain, for example) win so many good things? I almost cried when I learned he was welterweight boxing champion at Dartmouth and that he finished in the top ten percent of his class at Harvard Business School. He's even a pretty good public speaker.

"With the dedication of the Chain Medical Center," Martin is saying, "we of the Chain Foundation launch our first major effort in improving medical care in the city in which our family was raised. . . ."

The UP man mutters, "How about a center for kidney and liver diseases, considering all the poison hooch they've sold?"

"Cynic," I say.

". . . research in thoracic diseases of children under the direction of Dr. Abraham Heilig and his outstanding staff."

Abe Heilig is giving up his career as a surgeon—he's a bit long in the tooth and maybe the OR is too demanding—to administer the Chain Medical Center. He'll be bringing in teams of hot shots, kids from Mount Sinai, Einstein. He's told his associates he wants them to come up with a Nobel in three years. Don't bet they won't.

I notice lawyer Sol Heilig on the platform. Sol looks weary and gray. Last time his name was in the paper was when he represented tenants being chased out of their brownstones by a landlord who employed thugs. He hasn't lost his ideals. He's a Heilig. They hang on. They don't turn sour or mean or greedy.

Martin Chain finishes to loud applause. The Department of Sanitation band strikes up "Stars and Stripes Forever." DeeDee Chain uncrosses her legs. Insanely jealous, I watch her every move. Covering her edible mouth, she is chatting with Senator Kennedy.

Oh, 'tis a grand day, as Mulqueen, the old speakeasy owner, would have said.

The crowd rises. People begin to leave. Lots of white-coated doctors, nurses, technicians, and employees of Central Brooklyn. They're moving up a notch now that the Chain Medical Center has attached itself to their crumbling red brick building. But they look happy. Blacks, Puerto Ricans, Jews, Italians—a nice Brooklyn mix. And who can fault the Chains for what they're doing with their money? It beats buying modern art.

The presidential candidates leave hurriedly. Shave-headed men in gray suits usher them out, although the senator from Massachusetts acts as if he'd like a few more words with DeeDee.

Late-afternoon shadows fall. It's cool. I spot Sol Heilig and his wife Rose—they were Uncle Doc's patients until he died—talking to one of the skinniest, weirdest-looking men I've ever seen. A flunky tells me this is Horace Bunthorne, the top Chain lawyer—boozer, brain, fixer.

Sol Heilig, walking gimpily, his suit rumpled, notices me. "Hey, Myron," he says. "Doc Abelman's nephew?"

"The same, counselor. How are you, Mr. Heilig? Mrs. Heilig?"

"Rose, remember this guy? He used to drive his uncle crazy shooting fouls in the backyard while Doc was taking my blood pressure."

We agree that it has been a beautiful day for Brooklyn. And for the Chain family.

"The speeches were a little stiff," Sol says. "Martin's so buttoned-up he could be an archbishop."

"Sol," his wife scolds. "Not nice. Not nice at all."

"Is your sister here?" I ask. "Mrs. Halstead?"

No, he says, Eva's not in good shape. Confined to a wheelchair. It's hard for her to get around. Paget's disease.

"Know something?" Sol asks. His eyes are bright and laughing. "That's what this clambake needed. A speech from Eva. A little of the old radical fire."

"From what I've heard, it would have been a rouser."

He slaps his thigh. "Eva would have turned them on. She'd have had them standing up and cheering. She was good at that."

We walk to the parking lot in back of the new hospital. Sol is reminiscing about his late mother, the old chatelaine of the stationery store, about his ne'er-do-well Socialist father, raising children on sour milk. And Crazy Jake, the Brownsville Hercules.

"Eva would have given them good," Sol Heilig says to me. "She'd have had the interns and nurses calling a strike the first day the hospital opened."

"I'm sorry I never heard her in action. Is her daughter here today? That girl with the attorney general?"

"Lillian. She's in Washington. New job. Federal Trade Commission."

I'm wondering: Did the Chains have anything to do with it? I recall Mort Chain mentioning the senators and congressmen he knew personally. People who had helped him—and vice versa—when he was buying chemicals, building a fortune with a phone, an office, and an account book.

We pause in the lot. Two motorcycle cops shoo us away with wailing sirens.

"Nixon or Kennedy?" I ask Sol. "Which one gets the first escort?"

"Neither," Sol says.

A black limousine is threading its way through knots of guests, police officials, hospital personnel. Martin Chain sits in the limo with wife and children. A huge black man is at the wheel.

"It figures," Sol says. "Chains go first-class."

"Leave it to them." Rose sniffs.

"No, it's the way it should be," her husband says. "There'll be a Chain Medical Center here long after both those guys are out of office."

A nice thought. But I wish old Eva, the white-haired heroine, the captain of the pickets and the orator of the union halls, had been there.

In some way (I'm not sure how) she has a lot to do with the Chain gift. Someday I'll find out. Someday when the dust has settled and people are willing to talk.